PENGUIN TWENTIETH-CENTURY CLASSICS

THE RAINBOW

David Herbert Lawrence was born into a miner's family in Eastwood, Nottinghamshire, in 1885, the fourth of five children. He attended Beauvale Board School and Nottingham High School, and trained as an elementary schoolteacher at Nottingham University College. He taught in Croydon from 1908. His first novel, *The White Peacock*, was published in 1911, just a few weeks after the death of his mother, to whom he had been extraordinarily close. His career as a schoolteacher was ended by serious illness at the end of 1911.

In 1912 Lawrence went to Germany with Frieda Weekley, the German wife of the Professor of Modern Languages at the University College of Nottingham. They were married on their return to England in 1914. Lawrence had published *Sons and Lovers* in 1913; but *The Rainbow*, completed in 1915, was suppressed, and for three years he could not find a publisher for *Women in Love*, completed in 1917.

After the war Lawrence lived abroad, and sought a more fulfilling mode of life than he had so far experienced. With Frieda, he lived in Sicily, Sri Lanka, Australia, New Mexico and Mexico. They returned to Europe in 1925. His last novel, *Lady Chatterley's Lover*, was published in 1928 but was banned in England and America. In 1930 he died in Vence, in the south of France, at the age of forty-four.

Lawrence's life may have been short, but he lived it intensely. He also produced an amazing body of work: novels, stories, poems, plays, essays, travel books, translations, paintings and letters (over five thousand of which survive). After his death Frieda wrote, 'What he had seen and felt and known he gave in his writing to his fellow men, the splendour of living, the hope of more and more life . . . a heroic and immeasurable gift.'

Anne Fernihough is Fellow and Lecturer in English at Girton College, Cambridge where she has taught since 1989. She was educated at St Hilda's College, Oxford and Sidney Sussex College, Cambridge, where she studied for her Ph.D. on D. H. Lawrence; in 1988 she returned to

St Hilda's as Randall McIver Junior Research Fellow. She is the author of *D. H. Lawrence: Aesthetics and Ideology* (1993) and of articles on nineteenth- and twentieth-century literature.

John Worthen is advisory editor for the works of D. H. Lawrence in Penguin Twentieth-Century Classics. Currently Professor of D. H. Lawrence Studies at the University of Nottingham, he has published widely on Lawrence; his acclaimed biography, *D. H. Lawrence: The Early Years 1885–1912*, was published in 1991. He has also edited a number of volumes in the authoritative Cambridge Lawrence Edition whose texts Penguin Twentieth-Century Classics are reproducing.

D. H. LAWRENCE

THE RAINBOW

EDITED BY MARK KINKEAD-WEEKES
WITH AN INTRODUCTION AND NOTES BY
ANNE FERNIHOUGH

PENGUIN BOOKS

PENGUIN BOOKS

Published by the Penguin Group
Penguin Books Ltd, 27 Wrights Lane, London w8 5tz, England
Penguin Books USA Inc., 375 Hudson Street, New York, New York 10014, USA
Penguin Books Australia Ltd, Ringwood, Victoria, Australia
Penguin Books Canada Ltd, 10 Alcorn Avenue, Toronto, Ontario, Canada m4v 3b2
Penguin Books (NZ) Ltd, 182–190 Wairau Road, Auckland 10, New Zealand

Penguin Books Ltd, Registered Offices: Harmondsworth, Middlesex, England

First published 1915
Cambridge University Press edition published 1989
Published with new editorial matter in Penguin Books 1995
1 3 5 7 9 10 8 6 4 2

Printed in England by Clays Ltd, St Ives plc

Contents

Note on the Penguin Lawrence Edition

D. H. Lawrence stands in the very front rank of English writers this century; unlike some other famous writers, however, he has always appealed to a large popular audience as well as to students of literature, and his work still arouses passionate loyalties and fervent disagreements. The available texts of his books have, nevertheless, been notoriously inaccurate. The Penguin Lawrence Edition uses the authoritative texts of Lawrence's work established by an international team of scholars engaged on the *Cambridge Edition of the Works of D. H. Lawrence* under its General Editors, Professor James T. Boulton and Professor Warren Roberts. Through rigorous study of surviving manuscripts, typescripts, proofs and early printings the Cambridge editors have provided texts as close as possible to those which Lawrence himself would have expected to see printed. Deletions deliberately made by printers, publishers or their editors, accidentally by typists and printers – at times removing whole pages of text – have been restored, while house-styling introduced by printers is removed as far as is possible. The Penguin Lawrence Edition thus offers both general readers and students the only texts of Lawrence which have any claim to be the authentic productions of his genius.

Chronology

1885   David Herbert Richards Lawrence (hereafter DHL) born
        in Eastwood, Nottinghamshire, the fourth child of Arthur
        John Lawrence, collier, and Lydia, née Beardsall, daughter
        of a pensioned-off engine fitter.

1891–8 Attends Beauvale Board School.

1898–   Becomes first boy from Eastwood to win a County Council
  1901 scholarship to Nottingham High School, which he attends
        until July 1901.

1901   Works three months as a clerk at Haywood's surgical
        appliances factory in Nottingham; severe attack of
        pneumonia.

1902   Begins frequent visits to the Chambers family at Haggs
        Farm, Underwood, and starts his friendship with Jessie
        Chambers.

1902–5 Pupil-teacher at the British School, Eastwood; sits the
        King's Scholarship exam in December 1904 and is placed
        in the first division of the first class.

1905–6 Works as uncertificated teacher at the British School;
        writes his first poems and starts his first novel 'Laetitia'
        (later *The White Peacock*, 1911).

1906–8 Student at Nottingham University College following the
        normal course leading to a teacher's certificate; qualifies in
        July 1908. Wins *Nottinghamshire Guardian* Christmas 1907
        short-story competition with 'A Prelude' (submitted under
        name of Jessie Chambers); writes second version of
        'Laetitia'.

1908–11 Elementary teacher at Davidson Road School, Croydon.

1909   Meets Ford Madox Hueffer (later Ford), who begins to
        publish his poems and stories in the *English Review* and
        recommends rewritten versions of *The White Peacock*
        (1911) to William Heinemann; DHL writes *A Collier's
        Friday Night* (1934) and first version of 'Odour of Chrysan-
        themums' (1911); friendship with Agnes Holt.

1910   Writes 'The Saga of Siegmund' (first version of *The Trespasser*, 1912), based on the experiences of his friend, the Croydon teacher Helen Corke; starts affair with Jessie Chambers; writes first version of *The Widowing of Mrs. Holroyd* (1914); ends affair with Jessie Chambers but continues friendship; starts to write 'Paul Morel' (later *Sons and Lovers*, 1913); death of Lydia Lawrence in December; gets engaged to his old friend Louie Burrows.

1911   Fails to finish 'Paul Morel'; strongly attracted to Helen Corke; starts affair with Alice Dax, wife of an Eastwood chemist; meets Edward Garnett, publisher's reader for Duckworth, who advises him on writing and publication. In November falls seriously ill with pneumonia and has to give up schoolteaching; 'The Saga' accepted by Duckworth; DHL commences its revision as *The Trespasser*.

1912   Convalesces in Bournemouth; breaks off engagement to Louie; returns to Eastwood; works on 'Paul Morel'; in March meets Frieda Weekley, wife of Ernest, Professor at the University College of Nottingham; ends affair with Alice Dax; goes to Germany on a visit to his relations on 3 May; travels however with Frieda to Metz. After many vicissitudes, some memorialized in *Look! We Have Come Through!* (1917), Frieda gives up her marriage and her children for DHL; in August they journey over the Alps to Italy and settle at Gargnano, where DHL writes the final version of *Sons and Lovers*.

1913   *Love Poems* published; writes *The Daughter-in-Law* (1965) and 200 pp. of 'The Insurrection of Miss Houghton' (abandoned); begins 'The Sisters', eventually to be split into *The Rainbow* (1915) and *Women in Love* (1920). DHL and Frieda spend some days at San Gaudenzio, then stay at Irschenhausen in Bavaria; DHL writes first versions of 'The Prussian Officer' and 'The Thorn in the Flesh' (1914); *Sons and Lovers* published in May. DHL and Frieda return to England in June, meet John Middleton Murry and Katherine Mansfield. They return to Italy (Fiascherino, near Spezia) in September; DHL revises *The Widowing of Mrs. Holroyd*; resumes work on 'The Sisters'.

1914   Rewrites 'The Sisters' (now called 'The Wedding Ring') again; agrees for Methuen to publish it; takes J. B. Pinker as agent. DHL and Frieda return to England in June, marry on 13 July. DHL meets Catherine Carswell and S. S. Koteliansky; compiles short-story collection *The Prussian Officer* (1914). Outbreak of war prevents DHL and Frieda returning to Italy; at Chesham he first writes 'Study of Thomas Hardy' (1936) and then begins *The Rainbow*; starts important friendship with Ottoline Morrell, Cynthia Asquith, Bertrand Russell and E. M. Forster; grows increasingly desperate and angry about the war.

1915   Finishes *The Rainbow* in Greatham in March; plans lecture course with Russell; they quarrel in June. DHL and Frieda move to Hampstead in August; he and Murry bring out *The Signature* (magazine, three issues only) to which he contributed 'The Crown'. *The Rainbow* published by Methuen in September, suppressed at the end of October, prosecuted and banned in November. DHL meets painters Dorothy Brett and Mark Gertler; he and Frieda plan to leave England for Florida; decide to move to Cornwall instead.

1916   Writes *Women in Love* between April and October; publishes *Twilight in Italy* and *Amores.*

1917   *Women in Love* rejected by publishers; DHL continues to revise it. Makes unsuccessful attempts to go to America. Begins *Studies in Classic American Literature* (1923); publishes *Look! We Have Come Through!* In October he and Frieda evicted from Cornwall on suspicion of spying; in London he begins *Aaron's Rod* (1922).

1918   DHL and Frieda move to Hermitage, Berkshire, then to Middleton-by-Wirksworth; publishes *New Poems*; writes *Movements in European History* (1921), *Touch and Go* (1920) and the first version of 'The Fox' (1920).

1919   Seriously ill with influenza; moves back to Hermitage; publishes *Bay*. In the autumn, Frieda goes to Germany and then joins DHL in Florence; they visit Picinisco and settle in Capri.

1920   Writes *Psychoanalysis and the Unconscious* (1921). He and Frieda move to Taormina, Sicily; DHL writes *The Lost Girl* (1920), *Mr Noon* (1984), continues with *Aaron's Rod*; on summer visit to Florence has affair with Rosalind

Baynes; writes many poems from *Birds, Beasts and Flowers* (1923). *Women in Love* published.

1921   DHL and Frieda visit Sardinia and he writes *Sea and Sardinia* (1921); meets Earl and Achsah Brewster; finishes *Aaron's Rod* in the summer and writes *Fantasia of the Unconscious* (1922) and 'The Captain's Doll' (1923); plans to leave Europe and visit USA; puts together collection of stories *England, My England* (1922) and group of short novels *The Ladybird, The Fox* and *The Captain's Doll* (1923).

1922   DHL and Frieda leave for Ceylon, stay with Brewsters, then travel to Australia; he translates Verga. In Western Australia meets Mollie Skinner; in Thirroul, near Sydney, he writes *Kangaroo* (1923) in six weeks. Between August and September, he and Frieda travel to California via South Sea Islands, and meet Witter Bynner and Willard Johnson; settle in Taos, New Mexico, at invitation of Mabel Dodge (later Luhan). In December, move up to Del Monte Ranch, near Taos; DHL rewrites *Studies in Classic American Literature.*

1923   Finishes *Birds, Beasts and Flowers.* He and Frieda spend summer at Chapala in Mexico where he writes 'Quetzal-coatl' (first version of *The Plumed Serpent*, 1926). Frieda returns to Europe in August after serious quarrel with DHL; he journeys in USA and Mexico, rewrites Mollie Skinner's *The House of Ellis* as *The Boy in the Bush* (1924); arrives back in England in December.

1924   At dinner in Café Royal, DHL invites his friends to come to New Mexico; Dorothy Brett accepts and accompanies him and Frieda in March. Mabel Luhan gives Lobo (later renamed Kiowa) Ranch to Frieda; DHL gives her *Sons and Lovers* manuscript in return. During summer on ranch he writes *St. Mawr* (1925), 'The Woman Who Rode Away' (1925) and 'The Princess' (1925); in August, suffers his first bronchial haemorrhage. His father dies in September; in October, he, Frieda and Brett move to Oaxaca, Mexico, where he starts *The Plumed Serpent* and writes most of *Mornings in Mexico* (1927).

1925   Finishes *The Plumed Serpent*, falls ill and almost dies of typhoid and pneumonia in February; in March diagnosed as suffering from tuberculosis. Recuperates at Kiowa Ranch, writes *David* (1926) and compiles *Reflections on the Death of a Porcupine* (1925). He and Frieda return to Europe in September, spend a month in England and settle at Spotorno, Italy; DHL writes first version of *Sun* (1926); Frieda meets Angelo Ravagli.

1926   Writes *The Virgin and the Gypsy* (1930); serious quarrel with Frieda during visit from DHL's sister Ada. DHL visits Brewsters and Brett; has affair with Brett. Reconciled, DHL and Frieda move to Villa Mirenda, near Florence, in May and visit England (his last visit) in late summer. On return to Italy in October he writes first version of *Lady Chatterley's Lover* (1944); starts second version in November. Friendship with Aldous and Maria Huxley; DHL starts to paint.

1927   Finishes second version of *Lady Chatterley's Lover* (1972); visits Etruscan sites with Earl Brewster; writes *Sketches of Etruscan Places* (1932) and the first part of *The Escaped Cock* (1928). In November, after meetings with Michael Arlen and Norman Douglas, works out scheme for private publication with Pino Orioli, and starts final version of *Lady Chatterley's Lover* (1928).

1928   Finishes *Lady Chatterley's Lover* and arranges for its printing and publication in Florence; fights many battles to ensure its despatch to subscribers in Britain and USA. In June writes second part of *The Escaped Cock* (1929). He and Frieda travel to Switzerland (Gsteig) and the island of Port Cros, then settle in Bandol, in the south of France. He writes many of the poems in *Pansies* (1929); *Lady Chatterley's Lover* pirated in Europe and USA.

1929   Visits Paris to arrange for cheap edition of *Lady Chatterley's Lover* (1929); unexpurgated typescripts of *Pansies* seized by police; exhibition of his paintings in London raided by police. He and Frieda visit Majorca, France and Bavaria, returning to Bandol for the winter. He writes *Nettles* (1930), *Apocalypse* (1931) and *Last Poems* (1932); sees much of Brewsters and Huxleys.

1930   Goes into Ad Astra Sanatorium in Vence at start of February; discharges himself on 1 March; dies at Villa

Robermond, Vence, on Sunday 2 March; buried on 4 March.

1935   Frieda sends Angelo Ravagli (now living with her at Kiowa Ranch – they marry in 1950) to Vence to have DHL exhumed, cremated, and his ashes brought back to the ranch.

1956   Frieda dies and is buried at Kiowa Ranch.

John Worthen, 1994

Introduction

> The past material conditions of life have gone forever; no will of man
> can recall them; but *this* is our demand: We demand that, in that
> strange new world that is arising alike upon the man and the woman,
> where nothing is as it was, and all things are assuming new shapes
> and relations, that in this new world we also shall have our share of
> honoured and socially useful human toil, our full half of the labour of
> the Children of Woman.[1]

Thus pleads Olive Schreiner on behalf of womankind in *Woman and
Labour* (1911), the book that Ursula Brangwen reads with her friend
Maggie Schofield when both young women are teaching at Brinsley
Street school, struggling to make their mark in 'the man's world' of
work (379:28). Like *The Rainbow*, Schreiner's study inhabits two
different levels of reality, two different time-scales, simultaneously:
it is apocalyptic, quasi-biblical in its cadences, prophesying the dawn
of a new age and the passing away of the old; but it is also a work of
social realism, rooted in the rapidly changing social and material
conditions of its time, demanding new forms of work for women to
suit those changing conditions. Schreiner recognizes, as Lawrence
does, that the advancement of science and technology implies a sea-
change in the relations between the sexes. In 1913, while working
on the novel that would later split into *The Rainbow* and *Women in
Love*, Lawrence found in the relations between man and woman '*the*
problem of today'; what was needed, he felt, was 'the establishment
of a new relation, or the readjustment of the old one'.[2] *The Rainbow*
pins its hopes for such a new relation on the figure of Ursula, who is
described in the novel's original jacket blurb as 'waiting at the
advance post of our time to blaze a path into the future'.[3]

   If *The Rainbow*'s apocalyptic rhetoric is appropriate to Lawrence's
intense yearning for a new order of things, it also, ironically, harks
back to the early-nineteenth-century millenarian tradition, out of
which the feminist and socialist movements grew. Millenarians believed that Christ would return to earth to reign for a thousand years,
as prophesied in the Book of Revelation, but early socialists appropri-

ated the visionary language of millenarianism for more secular purposes, to express a sense of radical change for which there was no other vocabulary available. The socialist future was frequently described as the New Jerusalem or the Promised Land. Female emancipation was often a part of this utopian vision, and some believed in a female Messiah whose appearance would prefigure the transition from old to new.[4] Schreiner's *Woman and Labour* belongs, in a sense, to this millenarian tradition, albeit as a very late example. It would, moreover, be possible to see Ursula Brangwen as a latter-day female Messiah, proffering redemption from a world characterized, as Lawrence saw it, by a masculinism run riot, a masculinism nourished to such a point that it had turned to destroy the very society that had made it what it was. Such was Lawrence's interpretation of the First World War, during the early months of which the final versions of *The Rainbow* were written. Lawrence believed that the way out of this cultural quagmire lay in a feminization of culture at large: 'Our souls', he wrote, must be 'fertilised by the *female*'.[5] But if Ursula signifies the possibility of redemption from 'the man's world', the future she articulates verbally is far from the feminist-socialist future heralded by Schreiner. Symbolically, Lawrence's novel embarks on the same path as *Woman and Labour*; discursively, it arrives at a completely different destination.

The Rainbow charts the lives of three generations of the Brangwen family across the second half of the nineteenth century and into the first few years of the twentieth. The main story opens in 'About 1840' (13:20) with the construction of a canal across the Brangwens' farmland, recalling the opening of *Sons and Lovers* (1913), which had also registered 'a sudden change' in the landscape, with the appearance of 'six mines like black studs on the countryside, linked by a loop of fine chain, the railway'.[6] In each case, an apparently localized, physical change carries meanings which reach far beyond the merely local and physical. From *The Rainbow*'s start, we find ourselves entangled in that curious mesh of myth and history that critics of the novel have always found so baffling. *The Rainbow* is neither a piece of social realism in the conventional sense nor the complete refutation of history that some critics have seen it to be; it is a work into which history obtrudes obliquely and in complex ways not easy to unravel. The date '1840' nominally marks the inception of industrial capitalism, a moment in history to which Lawrence insistently returns throughout his career. But *The Rain-*

bow's prologue, in its rich evocation of 'the teeming life of creation' (11:14), is also a reworking of the Genesis myth, signifying nothing less than the coming into consciousness of the human race, the eating of the apple of knowledge. The prologue's pulsing, incantatory prose draws us into the ceaseless cycle of the seasons, a cycle in which man and nature are virtually indistinguishable, existing in perfect symbiosis: 'They took the udder of the cows, the cows yielded milk and pulse against the hands of the men, the pulse of the blood of the teats of the cows beat into the pulse of the hands of the men' (10:11–13). But the closed circuit is broken by the Brangwen women's craving for knowledge, for something beyond the simple life of the land, and the cycle of the seasons gives way to the linearity of history, to the construction of the canal, 'About 1840'. In a grand myth-making gesture, Lawrence connects the defacement of the earth's surface implemented by industrial capitalism (the appearance of the canal, the mines, the railway) with what he, along with numerous other modernist writers, sees to be a severance, in Western cultures, of mind and body, and a subsequent privileging of the mind. He sees a complicity between the mind/body split (what T. S. Eliot later called the 'dissociation of sensibility')[7] and the violence or coercion he associates both with industrial capitalism and with relationships conducted in an industrialized, technological culture. Lawrence's version of the myth of a 'fall' into self-consciousness and idealism (a myth he inherited in the first instance from Nietzsche) replaces the more orthodox biblical account of a fall into 'carnal' knowledge. The connection between industrial capitalism and a certain mode of consciousness is one which is examined with greater or lesser explicitness throughout Lawrence's work.

If *The Rainbow* is a complex tangle of myth and history, we find that women play a central role in both the myth and the history. It is the Brangwen *women's* desire for knowledge (they 'looked out from the heated, blind intercourse of farm-life, to the spoken world beyond' (10:28–9)) that simultaneously marks the coming into consciousness of the human race, the more historically specific onset of industrialization, and, more specifically still, a consequence of that industrialization: women's demand for entry into 'the man's world' of work. In a letter to Edward Garnett in 1914, Lawrence describes the germ of his novel as 'Woman becoming individual, self-responsible, taking her own initiative'.[8] It is seemingly women in their craving for 'higher being' (11:37) who bring to fullness the process of individuation charted by *The Rainbow*; they clamour for 'entry into the finer, more vivid circle of life' (12:21). At the outset the Brangwens are undifferentiated except in gender terms, starkly typologized as 'the men' and 'the women'; into their midst comes Lydia Lensky, whose foreignness and 'detachment' are repeatedly stressed; later on we are told that Lydia 'caused the separateness and individuality of all the Marsh inmates' (225:25–6). But by the same token, it is *women* who bring about the fallen 'man's world' of industrialization and technology, in which the balance between human beings and their environment is destroyed, their relationship with the world becoming one of confrontation, where previously they had been an integral part of nature, 'feeling the pulse and the body of the soil' (10:5–6) as they worked in the fields, their blue eyes charting 'all the irresolute stages of the sky when the weather is changing' (9:20–21). Now the idyll is ruptured, and the Brangwens become 'strangers in their own place' (14:20). This apparent paradox, whereby women signify both development and decline, is responsible for many of the interpretative difficulties posed by *The Rainbow*, a text riven with contradictions. To some extent, these contradictions emerge from the way in which the novel was composed; it was written, rewritten and reworked over a number of years, starting out as 'The Sisters' in 1913, mutating into 'The Wedding Ring' in 1914, then in 1915 splitting into *The Rainbow* and what would become *Women in Love*. During this period, Lawrence's opinions, especially on questions of feminism, fluctuated dramatically. At the same time, though, the ambiguities surrounding the idea of woman, far from being specific to this novel, or even to Lawrence's work as a whole, were written into the culture out of which *The Rainbow* grew.

Ruskin had remarked as early as 1860 that 'progress and decline' were 'strangely mingled in the modern mind'.[9] Schreiner's argument in *Woman and Labour* is that the future of the race, its regeneration, lies with women; it is the condition of women, as bearers of future generations, that determines the fate of the race as a whole. Hence it is crucial, for Schreiner, that women be given the opportunity to realize themselves through challenging and fulfilling labour. But if Schreiner believed that educated, economically self-supporting women were necessary for regeneration, there was another view commonly held at this period: that the educated 'New Woman' was in fact a symptom of degeneration. Such a view was put forward, for example, by the early translator of Nietzsche, A. M. Ludovici, in works like *Woman: A Vindication* (1923) and *Lysistrata, or Woman's Future and Future Woman* (1925). If, for Schreiner, woman's entry into male spheres of endeavour heralded a new dawn, for Ludovici, feminism signalled the Apocalypse in the negative sense: the end of civilization. *The Rainbow* inherits this cultural contradiction.

Right-wingers like Ludovici routinely drew on evolutionary theory to give scientific credence to their views. Evolutionists had been claiming since Darwin's *The Descent of Man* (1871) that the human male had struggled out of a condition of sexual indeterminacy, of bisexuality or hermaphroditism, and that it was only on reaching a higher form that he had emerged into a pure masculine state. This evolutionary discovery was then used to argue that the roles of men and women were meant to be clearly separate and that woman's evolutionary course was towards a more and more clearly differentiated femininity. For a woman to take on 'masculine' qualities, therefore, by seeking access to higher education and the professions, was taken to be a sign of reversion or degeneracy, just as the male who showed signs of 'effeminacy' was seen to be regressive.[10] This kind of rhetoric surfaces unmistakably in *The Rainbow* in the Wiggiston scenes involving Winifred Inger and Ursula's Uncle Tom, the industrialist.[11] Winifred, as a New Woman 'interested in the Women's Movement' (318:15), is described in androgynous terms as 'proud and free as a man, yet exquisite as a woman' (312:35–6), just as there are hints of effeminacy surrounding Uncle Tom, who is 'something of a woman' (223:18). Both characters are strongly associated with devolution, putting Ursula in mind of reptiles in a primeval swamp: 'She saw gross, ugly movements in her mistress, she saw a clayey, inert, unquickened flesh, that reminded her of the great prehistoric lizards'; Uncle Tom 'had something marshy about him – the succulent moistness and turgidity, and the same brackish, nauseating effects of a marsh, where life and decaying are one' (325:24–6, 29–31). This passage bears comparison to Lawrence's blatantly homophobic letters on visiting the 'marsh-stagnancy' of Cambridge in March 1915, where the imagery again connects to the blurring of gender boundaries.[12]

As soon as Ursula's lesbian flirtation with Winifred is over, it is viciously exorcized from her consciousness as an episode in her life that she 'could not think of without feeling blasted' (405:5–6). It is as though Ursula were being restored to 'true' femininity along Ludovician lines, yet equally, she rejects what Olive Schreiner calls the 'parasitism' of economic dependence on the men around her. Her momentary rejection of her teaching career in favour of marriage and motherhood is made heavily ironic: 'For what had a woman but to submit? What was her flesh but for childbearing, her strength for her children and her husband, the giver of life? At last she was a woman' (450:1–3). These sentiments are shortly followed by miscarriage and news of the impossibility of marrying Skrebensky, freeing Ursula for the 'undiscovered land' that lies ahead (457:17–18). Through Ursula's painful quest for something other than the conventional paths allotted to women at the beginning of the century, the novel rejects any straightforward reactionary stance towards the social and cultural upheaval that engendered it.

The coming into consciousness of woman is, then, paradoxically, both evolutionary and devolutionary in *The Rainbow*, as the very first reviewer of the novel seemed obscurely to grasp when he or she ventured that 'Something comes into [the Brangwens] which may be called degeneracy, but is more likely a painful and tortuous development.'[13] But feminism in the specific sense of suffragism and the Women's Movement is seen to be unequivocally devolutionary. All the female friends that Ursula makes during the course of the novel are involved in suffragism: Winifred is 'interested in the Women's Movement'; Maggie Schofield is 'a great suffragette, trusting in the vote'; Dorothy Russell spends her spare time 'slaving for the Women's Social and Political Union' (318:15, 377:18–19, 400:33–4). Ursula turns her back on these women one by one, paradoxically associating their feminism with the patriarchy, with 'the man's world' of industrial capitalism, with 'the husk of an old fruition' which must be burst if 'new germination' is to take place (457:40–458:2). It is indeed the case that historically, organized feminism, like socialism, grew out of industrial capitalism and out of the tangled, confused responses of men and women to that capitalism. The years spanned by the novel, 1840–1905, which register the insidious spread of industrialization from the appearance of the canal at the Marsh to the vast sprawl of Wiggiston or Beldover, were also crucial to the Women's Movement. An increasingly industrialized, urbanized society needed a more and more elaborate bureaucracy to run it, and this ever-expanding bureaucracy needed in its turn an ever-larger educated work-force, fuelling educational reforms on behalf of both women and working men. In 1841, a year after the novel's opening, the first campaign for female suffrage was mounted, and in 1904, a year before the novel's close, Parliament rejected the Women's Enfranchisement Bill, precipitating the most violent phase of suffragette history. For Lawrence, problematically, feminism remained contaminated by the industrial capitalism that had produced it. Hence we are told at the end of the 'Man's World' chapter that 'Ursula broke from that form of life wherein Maggie must remain enclosed' (382:36–7). Feminism *per se* is rejected in favour of a more mystical and abstract understanding of what 'women becoming individual' entails.

This mystical emphasis on individuality stems in part from Lawrence's strong connections with German philosophy and culture during the years prior to the writing of *The Rainbow*. Several critics of the novel have read it as a work of German Expressionism, and there is much to support such a reading: *The Rainbow* shares the German Expressionists' sense of a clash between aspiration and actuality (Kandinsky laments 'the collision of spiritual and material'),[14] as well as their hatred of capitalism, patriotism and war; and it shares the apocalyptic spirit of Expressionism: the editors of the *Blaue Reiter Almanac* (1912), probably the best-known anthology of Expressionist works, announce that 'We are standing at the threshold of one of the greatest epochs that mankind has ever experienced, the epoch of great spirituality.'[15] Above all, *The Rainbow* shares with German Expressionism a debt to the philosophy of Stirner and Nietzsche. As a young man, Lawrence was a keen reader of the influential periodical *The New Age*, the title of which suggests obvious connections with *The Rainbow*.[16] From 1907, it was edited by the Nietzsche enthusiast A. R. Orage, and German philosophy, especially that of Stirner and Nietzsche, figured prominently in its pages. Moreover, on taking up a teaching post in Croydon in the autumn of 1908, Lawrence gained access to English translations of Nietzsche's work.[17] Then in 1912, Lawrence met Frieda Weekley (née von Richthofen), the German woman he would subsequently marry. Through Frieda and her older sister Else Jaffe, Lawrence was exposed to the ideas of a number of prominent German intellectuals in a variety of fields (psychology, sociology, economics).[18] It is worth recalling that 'The Sisters' was the title of an earlier version of *The Rainbow*, and that if Lawrence married one of the sisters (Frieda), he dedicated *The Rainbow* to the other (Else). He had, moreover, originally wanted the dedication to be in German, in Gothic script, as if thereby declaring the cultural provenance of the text, though the publishers, not surprisingly in 1915, had refused this.

Else Jaffe had, like Ursula in *The Rainbow*, become a schoolteacher at a very young age; she had made enough money to pay for her studies at university, going on to take a doctorate in economics and then in 1900 to become 'the first woman ever to be appointed by the state of Badenia to protect the rights of women factory workers'.[19] Through the distinguished economist Max Weber, she would come into contact with the leaders of the Women's Movement in Germany. Her sister Frieda, on the other hand, was far less interested in this 'man's world' of work, and it is perhaps in the differences between Else and Frieda that we find a clue to some of *The Rainbow*'s ambiguities. While Else had achieved success in worldly terms, Frieda seemed to identify more closely with the ideas of psychological and sexual liberation put forward by the Freudian disciple Otto Gross (with whom both sisters had affairs). Gross was closely associated with the *Lebensphilosophie* movement, and with a group called *die kosmische Runde* (the Cosmic Circle), which stood for 'life-values, for eroticism, for the value of myth and primitive cultures, for the superiority of instinct and intuition to the values of science, for the primacy of the female mode of being'.[20]

Although Gross has gone down in history as a 'Freudian disciple', he was if anything more interested in Nietzsche than in Freud, as well as in the ideas of the less well-known philosopher Max Stirner who was undergoing something of a revival at this period, and whose ideas seemed in many ways to anticipate those of Nietzsche. Stirner had written a work entitled *Der Einzige und sein Eigentum* (1844), which had recently been translated into English as *The Ego and His Own* (it was reviewed in *The New Age* in 1907). As this title would suggest, Stirner insisted on a personal code of 'egoism', by which he meant the forceful assertion of the individual in opposition to the state. He dismissed abstractions like 'equality', 'unity', 'humanity' and 'law' as spurious intellectual constructions, and denounced all political programmes, especially those depending on 'humanitarian' or progressive opinions. Given that many intellectuals, Lawrence included, felt threatened by the steady process of democratization that was under way in the decade preceding the War, they quickly latched on to Stirner's argument (an argument which Nietzsche also used) to the effect that democracy was based on abstractions, and not on the realities of individual lives. To define concepts like 'equality' as abstractions was a way of spiriting them into thin air, of denying them any reality or validity. In an article in *The New Age*, Ezra Pound cites a remark made by Allen Upward which could just as easily have been made by Lawrence: 'When, instead of thinking of men one by one you think of them all at once and call your thought humanity, you have merely added a new word to the dictionary and not a new thing to the universe.'[21] Compare the following comment on Skrebensky in *The Rainbow*: 'it was not born in him to see, that the highest good of the community as it stands is no longer the highest good of even the average individual. He thought that, because the community represents millions of people, therefore it must be millions of times more important than any individual, forgetting that the community is the abstraction from the many, and is not the many themselves' (305:9–15). Similarly, Winifred's feminism is implicitly associated with her worship of the machine and 'the impure abstraction' (325:7–8); we are told of her interest in the Women's Movement very shortly before being subjected to an image of 'human bodies and lives subjected in slavery to that symmetric monster of the colliery' (324:24–6). Feminism is equated with technology on the grounds that it supposedly subordinates individual lives to some larger purpose.

Intellectuals tended, then, during the years immediately preceding the First World War, to react to an increasingly feminist and socialist political climate by retreating from politics and public life into the consciousness of the individual. The history of *The Freewoman*, the periodical founded in 1911 which eventually became *The Egoist*, perfectly exemplifies this move: its subtitle changed from 'A Weekly Feminist Review' to 'A Weekly Humanist Review' in 1912, and again to 'An Individualist Review' in 1913. Finally, late in 1913, Pound and others addressed a letter to its editor, complaining that the title of the journal, which was by now *The New Freewoman*, was misleading, and suggesting that it be changed to one 'which will mark the character of your paper as an organ of individualists of both sexes, and the individualist principle in every department of life'.[22] In January 1914, *The New Freewoman* became *The Egoist*, a name suggesting homage to Max Stirner. This name change was highly symbolic of something happening in modernism at large – a suppression not just of political movements in general but specifically of the Women's Movement.

Ursula's development in *The Rainbow* follows exactly the same course. If Lawrence had set out to show '*woman* becoming individual' (my emphasis), the novel seems to renege on itself by insisting that Ursula is first and foremost an *individual*, not a woman. In his study of Hardy, written while working on *The Rainbow*, Lawrence states his view that while the work of the suffragists is 'worthy and admirable' it is by no means radical enough, since it is 'content to fight the old battles on the old ground', and 'Law can only modify the conditions, for better or worse, of that which already exists.' He goes on, in Max Stirner fashion, to condemn all laws as inadequate to deal with the complexities of individual human beings, arguing that 'law is a very, very clumsy and mechanical instrument, and we people are very, very delicate and subtle beings'. 'Could you make any law in any land', he asks, 'empowering the poppy to flower?'[23] It is this 'flowering' of what Lawrence calls the 'soul' which ultimately takes precedence over social and economic questions. The paradox is that such notions of the 'soul' are, if anything, even more abstract and intangible than the so-called abstractions of socialism and feminism.

The ethic that Ursula more and more explicitly embraces as the novel goes on is a Nietzschean ethic of the 'aristocracy of the soul'. Indeed, it would be difficult to overestimate Nietzsche's presence in *The Rainbow*. Towards the end of the novel, Ursula ponders the words of the Indian Rig-Veda. 'There are so many dawns that have not yet risen,' words that Nietzsche had cited on the title-page of *Morgenröte* ('The Dawn') (in April 1915, Lawrence contemplated the title *Morgenrot* for a philosophical work he was writing).[24] For Nietzsche, as for many of the New Age contributors, this new dawn was understood largely in the terms of evolutionary theory: 'The *goal of humanity* cannot lie in its end, but only *in its highest exemplars*.'[25] It was on such evolutionary grounds that Nietzsche was opposed to socialism and democracy, always rejecting generality as inauthentic, as appealing to the lowest common denominator. 'Your true nature', he proclaimed, 'lies . . . immeasurably high above you, or at least above that which you usually take yourself to be.'[26] Nietzsche believed that only if gifted souls stretched themselves to full capacity, showing self-reliance and self-assertion, could the race as a whole make progress.

For Lawrence, the process of individuation was also understood in evolutionary terms, as he made clear in the Hardy study, a text which has often been treated, justifiably, as *The Rainbow*'s companion text, making more explicit what is only implicit in the novel. Tellingly, Lawrence had considered the title *Le Gai Savaire* for his study, a title clearly modelled on Nietzsche's *The Gay Science*. It is here in the Hardy study that Lawrence defines aristocracy as the antithesis in every way to bourgeois conformity: 'the aristocrat alone has occupied a position where he could afford to *be*, to be himself, to create himself, to live as himself'.[27] Similarly in *The Rainbow*, Ursula thinks she can sense in Skrebensky 'the nature of an aristocrat': 'He was in possession of himself . . . Other people could not really give him anything nor take anything from him. His soul stood alone' (217:21–3). A sense of selves restlessly striving to reach their full potential, of ever-widening horizons, pervades not only Ursula's life but the lives of all three generations of Brangwens, men as well as women. Tom Brangwen, on comparing his life with that of the mysterious foreigner he meets in Matlock, feels like 'a little creature caught in bird-lime' (26:32); or, after visiting his brother Alfred's mistress, like 'a prisoner, sitting safe and easy and unadventurous' (86:34–5). Anna in her turn 'felt always belittled, as if never, never could she stretch her length and stride her stride' (99:29–30), while Will 'was aware of some limit to himself . . . of some buds which were not ripe in him, some folded centres of darkness which would never develop and unfold' (195:5–8). Strikingly the chapter-title 'The Widening Circle' is used twice within the same novel.

Indeed, it would be possible to read *The Rainbow* in Nietzschean terms of the birth and subsequent overcoming of subjectivity. For Nietzsche, the Judaeo-Christian era marked the birth of subjectivity, in that it brought to an end a barbaric era of compulsion, and initiated a period of voluntary submission to moral codes or laws; the Judaeo-Christian emphasis on the notion of 'virtue' represented for Nietzsche an internalization, on the part of individuals, of the authority that had previously been externally imposed upon them. For Nietzsche, this was to give way in its turn to a new era in which we could overcome our subjectivity and systems of morality (this is the capacity of the *Übermensch*) and give the law unto ourselves, become the artists of ourselves.[28] *The Rainbow*'s prologue stresses the way in which the church-tower dominates the Brangwens' mental and physical horizons, and *The Rainbow* as a whole is saturated with biblical imagery; yet it is also a novel about the shedding of our Christian heritage, and by the end the church-tower has become a symbol of 'hideous obsoleteness' (458:22). Anna

Brangwen finds herself resenting the Sunday sermons on the grounds that 'Everything seemed to be merely a matter of social duty, and never of her *self*' (146:24–5) and as Ursula passes from girlhood to womanhood, 'The religion which had been another world for her, a glorious sort of play-world ... now fell away from reality, and became a tale, a myth, an illusion' (263:14–19). She comes to recognize that the burning question is 'How to become oneself, how to know the question and the answer of oneself' (264:14–15). What Lawrence repeatedly calls the 'utterance' of self is what each generation of Brangwens struggles for in turn.[29]

If ideas of selfhood ultimately take precedence over any concern with the female sex in *The Rainbow*, it is none the less impossible to overlook the fact that Lawrence chooses to make a *woman* into a Nietzschean figure of sorts, where Nietzsche's vision of individuation was a decidedly male-centred one (the *Übermensch* was distinctly male). Nietzsche often used the metaphor of femaleness to describe the decadence that he thought was setting in, whereas Lawrence makes decadence into a specifically 'masculine' phenomenon (his chapter-title 'The Man's World' makes this explicit). Here, perhaps most clearly, we see the influence of Frieda Weekley and Otto Gross. If Nietzsche was the most important philosopher for Gross and the *kosmische Runde*, they gave Nietzsche's ideas a distinctly 'female' twist. In fact, the *kosmische Runde* was uncompromisingly hostile to patriarchal culture in its entirety, turning instead to the prehistorical, matriarchal cultures that had been described by the anthropologist J. J. Bachofen in his book *Mutterrecht* ('Mother Right') (1861). Gross in fact rewrote the Genesis myth in matriarchal terms,[30] just as Anna does in *The Rainbow* when contemplating Will's wood-carving of Adam and Eve: 'She jeered at the Eve, saying: "She is like a little marionette. Why is she so small? ... It is impudence to say that Woman was made out of Man's body," she continued, "when every man is born of woman. What impudence men have, what arrogance!"' (162:6–11). Anna herself, moreover, is living proof of the inadequacy of the patriarchal Genesis myth. Will is forced to acknowledge that his wife 'was everything to him, she was his life and his derivation. He depended on her. If she were taken away, he would collapse as a house from which the central pillar is removed' (173:1–3). One of the most powerful images in the novel is that of Anna, big with child, dancing naked in the firelight, in perfect self-sufficiency 'like a full ear of corn', as Will watches in dismay (169:38–171:31). The passage as a whole is an unflinching analysis of the male fear of female generative power; Will is left conceding, 'And upon what could he stand, save upon a woman? Was he then like the old man of the seas, impotent to move save upon the back of another life? Was he impotent, or a cripple, or a defective, or a fragment?' (174:3–6).

One of the most extraordinary aspects of *The Rainbow* is that a novel so intensely preoccupied with the process of individuation also repeatedly asserts the power of the unindividuated maternal-feminine from which all identity springs. This is in spite of the fact that it is a novel which at one level charts the ever-tightening grip of the values of 'the man's world'. The novel is replete with images, both literal and metaphorical, of gestation and birth, so much so that, as Tony Pinkney points out, the novel's overarching symbol, the rainbow, can be seen to represent 'the legs of a woman opening in childbirth, ejecting the new life into the world'.[31] It is in the 'Cathedral' chapter that the imagery of gestation is at its most insistent: on entering Lincoln Cathedral, Will Brangwen's soul 'quivered in the womb, in the hush and the gloom of fecundity, like seed of procreation in ecstasy' (187:3–5). In fact, all the churches and cathedrals in the novel seem to share Anna's fertility: while Lincoln Cathedral is 'the perfect womb' (186:38), in Cossethay church at Christmas 'the stone broke out into dark, rich leaf, the arches put forth their buds' (260:3–4). The double impulse of *The Rainbow*, forwards towards ever-finer individuation, and backwards towards the womb, is interesting in the light of the post-Lacanian feminist theories that have become so central to cultural studies. For theorists like Julia Kristeva and Luce Irigaray, the drive towards individual identity entails a repression of the mother, a denial of the mother's generative power: in order to become a subject, the child must separate from the mother's body and repress all connection with it, though he or she will subsequently fear being sucked back into it. Irigaray argues in her monumental *Speculum of the Other Woman* that the maternal-feminine is the 'origin' which threatens subject-formation, especially masculine subject-formation; the male child constructs a self which is then fiercely defended against the threat of dissolution and the 'abyss', a threat associated with female sexuality and fecundity.[32] That the search for perfect, detached selfhood as the goal of evolution is based on an implicit erasure of the female body was also obscurely recognized by the evolutionary theorists of the late nineteenth and early twentieth centuries, many of whom fantasized about being able to leave the female body behind. One eccentric evolutionary theorist, Joseph Le Conte, had actually argued that if evolutionary progression took its course unhindered, men might be able to transcend this material realm altogether, moving from an 'outer lower life' to an 'inner higher life', the life-force distilling itself into a kind of embodied spirit. In order to facilitate this process, man would have to divorce himself from nature: 'Spirit must break away from physical and material connection with the forces of Nature', he wrote, just as 'the embryo must break away from physical umbilical connection with the mother'.[33] But to leave the female body and the 'womb of Nature' behind in this way is not something that *The Rainbow* is prepared to do.

This insistent emphasis on the maternal in the novel suggests a preoccupation with what Lacanian psychoanalysts call the 'pre-Oedipal' stage of development. In the very early stages of the child's life, according to Lacan, the child cannot distinguish between itself and its environment; it has no awareness of its corporeal boundaries, perceiving itself to be in a state of seamless unity with the mother. At this stage, the child has not yet entered what Lacan calls the 'Symbolic Order' of language and culture, a realm of law and separation and categorization, in which the speaking 'subject' differentiates itself sharply from the world as 'object'. In order to enter the Symbolic, in order to say 'I am', the child must also say 'I am *not* the mother, *not* the other, *not* the rest of the world.'[34] Until that entry into the Symbolic is effected, however, and the child enters into the dominant language and culture, mother and child inhabit a pre-linguistic realm of communication. Julia Kristeva identifies the survival of this prelinguistic babble into adulthood via 'poetic' language, which 'posits its own process as an undecidable process between sense and nonsense, between *language* and *rhythm*', and 'introduces wandering . . . into language'.[35]

This linguistic 'wandering' seems to correspond to Lawrence's practice in *The Rainbow*. In the more experimental passages, the unorthodox syntax and the insistent repetition with variation, which so bewildered the earliest reviewers, seek to undo the rigid division between subject and object, evoking a pre-Symbolic experience in which subject and object have not yet separated. In a novel that concerns itself with the individual and with immediacy of experience, the logic of immediacy does not stop at the boundaries of the coherent individual, but goes beyond to reach the sensations and emotions that exist prior to any sense of individuated subjectivity. As Lawrence famously wrote to Garnett while working on *The Rainbow*, 'You mustn't look in my novel for the old stable ego of character. There is another ego, according to whose action the individual is unrecognisable, and passes through, as it were, allotropic states which it needs a deeper sense than any we've been used to exercise, to discover are states of the same single radically-unchanged element.'[36] This emphasis on what might be called the preconscious can be read as a challenge to the law of patriarchy: Kristeva claims that 'in a culture where the speaking subjects are conceived of as masters of their speech, they have what is called a "phallic" position. The fragmentation of language in a text calls into question the very posture of this mastery.'[37] *The Rainbow* likewise challenges the 'phallic' position, not only through its imagery of labour and birth, but through the strenuous labour of the language itself, where the thick, almost tangible linguistic textures are often in excess of any discursive content, reminding the 'Symbolic' of that which it has had to repress. The horizontal axis of evolutionary 'progress' in the conventional sense (figured in *The Rainbow* as the march of industrialization and as increased individuation from one generation to the next) is challenged by a vertical axis, making us aware of the presence of the preconscious *within* the conscious.

As *The Rainbow* proceeds, however, the horizontal axis threatens to triumph over the vertical one: images of the life-giving 'labour' of childbirth or artistic creation, images of a self in fruitful connection with its context, seem to give way to those of the alienated 'labour' of industrialism. Unlike the stone arches of Cossethay, the colliers are unable to germinate ('It was as if a hard, horny shell enclosed them all' (321:18–19)), and the 'perfect womb' of the cathedral (186:38) which nurtured Will's artistic impulses has been replaced by a travesty of nurturing maternity, that 'great mistress' the pit (324:19). Midway through the novel, Anna seems to intuit the direction it will take: 'She was in touch so intimately. All things about her had become intimate, she had known them near and lovely, like presences hovering upon her. What if they should all go hard and separate again, standing back from her terrible and distinct, and she, having known them, should be at their mercy' (157:19–23). Increasingly in *The Rainbow*, people seem to take on the characteristics of the technologized world around them, asserting that link between technology and a certain mode of consciousness made in the prologue. Ursula becomes 'fierce, corrosive, seething . . . like some cruel, corrosive salt around the last substance of his [Skrebensky's] being' (229:7–9). She finds herself locked in an internecine struggle with Skrebensky: 'The same iron rigidity, as if the world were made of steel, possessed her again. It was no use turning with flesh and blood to this arrangement of forged metal' (411:2–4). The violent episode by the moonlit cornstacks casts us back to the earlier scene in which Will and Anna had gathered the sheaves by moonlight in a kind of prenuptial ritual: 'They worked together, coming and going, in a rhythm, which carried their feet and their bodies in tune' (114:25–6). There the dance-like rhythm of the prose and the anthropomorphic imagery ('the wet, soft hair of the corn' (114:11)) had suggested that harmonious interfusion with nature evoked by the prologue. With Ursula and Skrebensky, on the other hand, the cornstacks have become metallic and threatening: 'All was intangible, a burning of cold, glimmering, whitish-steely fires,' and the relationship with nature inimical: 'The stack stung him [Skrebensky] keenly with a thousand cold, sharp flames' (298:8–9, 25–6).

In choosing individualism as his theme, then, Lawrence finds himself caught in a double bind. On the one hand, he seems to welcome the conditions in which the growth of the individual might be possible to a degree that it had never been possible before. Ursula sees in her parents, Anna and Will, an abnegation of the self that repels her: 'They were neither of them quite personal, quite defined as individuals, so much were they pervaded by the physical heat of breeding and rearing their young. How Ursula resented it, how she fought against the close, physical, limited life of herded domesticity' (329:4–8). Yet on the other hand, Lawrence shows how the coming into definition of the individual is achieved at great cost; there is always a danger that the overweening 'I' will set out to devour the 'not-I', that its own expansion will turn into appropriation, becoming the will-to-power in a negative sense, and wrenching the world into conformity with its own shape, as Gerald, the arch-technologist, does in *Women in Love*. The relationship between Ursula and Skrebensky becomes 'a magnificent self-assertion on the part of both of them . . . And after all, what could either of them get from such a passion but a sense of his or her own maximum self, in contradistinction to all the rest of life?' (281:17–23). Lawrence recognizes that this kind of mastery has nothing to do with freedom; on the contrary, when the whole world is ingested by the subject in its own urge to develop, freedom no longer exists because there is nothing outside the subject to guarantee that freedom: 'otherness' has been eliminated. This is what seems to happen in Ursula's relationship with Skrebensky: 'She knew him all round, not on any side did he lead into the unknown.' Skrebensky in his turn finds that the people he meets are 'mere permutations of known quantities' (438:40–439:1, 424:21).

The Rainbow's quest for an uncompromised selfhood goes hand in hand with a diagnosis of the breakdown of communal ties in favour of the competitive, self-seeking ethos of capitalism, the disintegration of *Gemeinschaft* (community) into *Gesellschaft* (society), though it is left to *The Rainbow*'s sequel, *Women in Love*, to explore the full implications of this. We are given a foretaste of *Women in Love* when Winifred introduces Ursula to 'various women and men, educated, unsatisfied people' (318:27–8); if phenomena are made into objective entities, separate and distinct from the perceiving subject, then human beings are, as it were, severed from the environment, uprooted, and consigned to an errant, purposeless existence. The philosopher Martin Heidegger, who shares so many of Lawrence's concerns, points to *The Rainbow*'s central predicament when he states that 'The higher its consciousness, the more the conscious being is excluded from the world.'[38]

In a sense, *The Rainbow* sets itself an impossible task, seeking out a social structure in which the full expansion of the individual might be possible without causing that social fabric to fall apart. The novel yearns to incorporate *both* individualism *and* the security of the close-knit community, *both* development *and* stasis at once. Yet it is unable to articulate such a social structure, except in terms of the microcosm of marriage, or in aesthetic terms, specifically those of architecture. Will Brangwen dreams of 'the establishment of a whole mystical, architectural conception which used the human figure as a unit' (259:6–8), a conception resembling the marriage of Alfred Brangwen and the 'woman from Heanor' at the start of the novel: 'They were two very separate beings, vitally connected, knowing nothing of each other, yet living in their separate ways from one root' (15:12–13). Often marriage is described in terms of architecture and vice versa: cathedrals and churches experience 'consummation' and 'pregnancy', while Tom and Lydia's marriage is evoked in the imagery of buildings, archways, gateways and doorways (90:37–91:3, 91:23–4, 29, 38–40, 187:2–5, 188:3–10).

But it is above all in the terms of Gothic architecture that the novel articulates its aspirations; Gothic seems to be able to incorporate individuality within a larger structure. In his 'Study of Thomas Hardy', Lawrence sees the details of Gothic cathedrals as a subversion of the 'monism' of the architectural whole: 'All the little figures, the gargoyles, the imps, the human faces, whilst subordinated within the Great Conclusion of the Whole, still, from their obscurity, jeered their mockery of the Absolute, and declared for multiplicity, polygeny.'[39] Lawrence elaborates on this in the 'Cathedral' chapter of *The Rainbow*:

> They knew quite well, these little imps that retorted on man's own illusion, that the cathedral was not absolute. They winked and leered, giving suggestion of the many things that had been left out of the great concept of the church. 'However much there is inside here, there's a good deal they haven't got in,' the little faces mocked.
>   Apart from the lift and spring of the great impulse towards the altar, these little faces had separate wills, separate motions, separate knowledge, which rippled back in defiance of the tide, and laughed in triumph of their own very littleness. (189:20–29)

John Ruskin had also seen in Gothic a valuable undercutting of a dangerously homogenizing instrumentalism, an antidote to the wrenching of the multifarious human spirit into the standardized shapes of the machine (we are told of Will Brangwen that 'The influence of Ruskin had stimulated him to a pleasure in the mediaeval forms' (105:38–40)). Skrebensky is savagely ironized in *The Rainbow* for assuming that 'The Whole mattered – but the unit, the person, had no importance, except as he represented the Whole' (304:29–31). And, as we have already seen, when Ursula visits Wiggiston she is confronted with a horrific picture of 'human bodies and lives subjected in slavery to that symmetric monster of the colliery' (324:24–6). Werner Sombart, the economist and friend of Else Jaffe, had used the term *Teilmensch* ('half-person') to describe the way in which capitalist society reduced people to their anonymous social functions, though Ruskin in his famous essay 'The Nature of Gothic' had already made the point that 'it is not, truly speaking, the labour that is divided; but the men: – Divided into mere segments of men.'[40] Gothic is both a creaturely and, in this novel, a specifically 'feminine' architecture which none the less, with its soaring, pointed arches, reaches upwards as if towards a perfect, detached selfhood and a transcendence of the material; in this way, it embodies the double gesture of *The Rainbow* as a whole.

Lawrence thought that the war would end in 1915 and that the appearance of his novel, with its fragile glimmerings of hope, would be timely. But as he was forced to realize, 'I set my rainbow in the sky too soon, before, instead of after, the deluge.'[41] In November 1915, *The Rainbow* was seized by the police and its publishers, Methuen, prosecuted for obscenity and forced to withdraw the book. Ursula's oscillation between utopianism and disillusionment – 'Always the shining doorway ahead: and then, upon approach, always the shining doorway was a gate into another ugly yard . . .' (404:35–7) – seems grimly prophetic both in view of *The Rainbow*'s barbaric reception and in view of the novel's sequel (*Women in Love*), whose title was at various points going to be *The Latter Days*, *Love Among the Ruins* and *Dies Irae*. Jacques Derrida has argued that it is in the nature of apocalyptic writing that it promises, yet fails, to bring to an end a process of deferral; with its constant opening of doors and breaking of seals, it promises revelation, a sight of the signified, but leaves us instead with the shape of the signifier.[42] There is a sense in which this is true of *The Rainbow* too; the image of the arc in the sky over Beldover stays in the mind long after the book has closed, but we are left guessing about the reality that the rainbow can only foreshadow.

As his career progresses, Lawrence turns more and more towards art as the only locus in which individuality and connectedness can coexist, and in particular he turns towards the novel form. If *The Rainbow* cannot point outside itself to the utopian reality it so passionately strives for, it is perhaps to the novel's own delineaments that we should turn, to the richly laboured craftsmanship of the work itself. *The Rainbow* is a novel which, like Gothic architecture, allows for the coexistence of conflicting ideological impulses (the imps and gargoyles) within a single work, whether these impulses be towards feminism or anti-feminism, Ruskinite socialism or Nietzschean aristocracy. But it is also a novel in which the narrative drive towards perfect selfhood is countered, both imagistically and rhythmically, by the 'otherness' of the maternal-feminine, creating what Lawrence elsewhere calls 'the living conjunction or communion between the self and its context'.[43]

Introduction

NOTES ON THE INTRODUCTION

1. Olive Schreiner, *Woman and Labour* (T. Fisher Unwin, 1911), p. 68.
2. James T. Boulton, ed., *The Letters of D. H. Lawrence*, volume I (Cambridge University Press, 1979), 546. (Hereafter referred to as *Letters*, i.)
3. *The Rainbow* was first published by Methuen on 30 September 1915.
4. See Barbara Taylor, *Eve and the New Jerusalem: Socialism and Feminism in the Nineteenth Century* (Virago, 1983).
5. George J. Zytaruk and James T. Boulton, eds., *The Letters of D. H. Lawrence*, volume II (Cambridge University Press, 1981). (Hereafter referred to as *Letters*, ii.)
6. D. H. Lawrence, *Sons and Lovers*, ed. Helen and Carl Baron (Penguin Books, 1994), 9:14, 10:1–3.
7. T. S. Eliot, 'The Metaphysical Poets' (1921), in *Selected Essays* (Faber and Faber, 1932), pp. 281–91 (p. 288).
8. *Letters*, ii. 165.
9. *Modern Painters*, in *The Works of John Ruskin*, ed. E. T. Cook and Alexander Wedderburn, 39 vols (Allen, 1903–12), v, 327.
10. A typical view was that expressed in a 1912 issue of *The Freewoman*, on the subject of 'Uranians': 'If the tendency of evolution is to segregate the sexes, as it appears to be, since the lower we go in the scale of living organism the greater the tendency towards hermaphroditism and a protoplasmic condition of self-impregnation, then these types [i.e. homosexuals] must be recessives' (vol. i, no. 7 (4 Jan. 1912), 127–8).
11. These scenes, and the distinctive strand of vocabulary that accompanies them, centring on marshes and corruption, were a late addition to the novel, appearing between March and August 1915 and seemingly triggered both by a bitterness at the course the war was taking and by Lawrence's visit to Cambridge (see note 12).
12. *Letters*, ii. 309; see also *Letters*, ii. 311, 319, 320–21.
13. *The Standard*, 1 October 1915, p. 3 (unsigned).
14. Quoted in Wolf-Dieter Dube, *The Expressionists* (Thames and Hudson, 1972), p. 96.
15. *The Blaue Reiter Almanac*, ed. Klaus Lankheit (Thames and Hudson, 1974), p. 250.
16. Jessie Chambers notes that Lawrence took *The New Age* regularly for a time, in about 1909, though 1908 seems a more likely year. Lawrence quotes *The New Age* in 'Art and the Individual', a paper delivered to the Eastwood 'Debating Society' in March 1908. See *Study of Thomas Hardy and Other Essays*, ed. Bruce Steele (Cambridge University Press, 1985), pp. 133–42 and Jessie Chambers, *D. H. Lawrence: A Personal Record* (1935; Cambridge University Press, 1980), p. 120.

17. *A Personal Record*, p. 120.
18. See Martin Green, *The von Richthofen Sisters: The Triumphant and the Tragic Modes of Love* (Weidenfeld and Nicolson, 1974), for the fullest account of the von Richthofen circle. In Frieda, Lawrence found a fellow Nietzsche enthusiast. In 1901, for example, Frieda wrote to Else telling her of a 'Nietzsche calendar' she had been given by a friend, and asking for a copy of Nietzsche's *Zarathustra*. See *Frieda Lawrence: The Memoirs and Correspondence*, ed. E. W. Tedlock (Heinemann, 1961), p. 169.
19. *The von Richthofen Sisters*, p. 16.
20. *The von Richthofen Sisters*, p. 73.
21. Ezra Pound, 'Allen Upward serious', in *Selected Prose 1909–1965*, ed. William Cookson (New Directions, 1973), p. 409.
22. Pound and others, *The New Freewoman*, vol. i, no. 13 (15 December 1913), 244.
23. *Study of Thomas Hardy*, 14:21–2, 23–4, 18–19.
24. *Letters*, ii. 315.
25. Nietzsche, *Untimely Meditations*, trans. R. J. Hollingdale (Cambridge University Press, 1983), p. 111.
26. *Untimely Meditations*, p. 129.
27. *Study of Thomas Hardy*, 46:32–3.
28. Nietzsche, *Beyond Good and Evil: Prelude to a Philosophy of the Future*, trans. R. J. Hollingdale, revised edition (Penguin Books, 1990), section 262 (pp. 199–202).
29. See for example 192:1, 330:15.
30. Otto Gross, 'Die Kommunistische Grundidee in der Paradiessymbolik', *Sowjet* (1920), cited in *The von Richthofen Sisters*, p. 44.
31. Tony Pinkney, *D. H. Lawrence* (Harvester Wheatsheaf, 1990), p. 68.
32. Luce Irigaray, *Speculum of the Other Woman* (1974), trans. Gillian C. Gill (Cornell University Press, 1985).
33. Joseph Le Conte, *Evolution: Its Nature, Its Evidences, and Its Relation to Religious Thought* (1888–91), cited in Bram Dijkstra, *Idols of Perversity: Fantasies of Feminine Evil in Fin de Siècle Culture* (Oxford University Press, 1986), pp. 216–17. An extraordinary article in *The New Age* in 1911 entitled 'Nietzsche and Woman' also announces that woman will be left behind in the course of evolution (vol. viii, no. 19, 9 March 1911).
34. Compare Ursula at 456:10–19.
35. Julia Kristeva, *Desire in Language: A Semiotic Approach to Literature and Art*, trans. Thomas Gora, Alice Jardine, and Leon S. Roudiez (Basil Blackwell, 1981), pp. 135, 136.
36. *Letters*, ii. 183.
37. Julia Kristeva, 'Oscillation Between Power and Denial', in *New French Feminisms*, ed. Elaine Marks and Isabelle de Courtivron (1980), p. 165.

38. Martin Heidegger, 'What Are Poets For?' (1926), in *Poetry, Language, Thought*, trans. Albert Hofstadter (Harper and Row, 1971), pp. 89–142 (p. 108).

39. *Study of Thomas Hardy*, 66:2–5.

40. See Jeffrey Herf, *Reactionary Modernism: Technology, Culture and Politics in Weimar and the Third Reich* (Cambridge University Press, 1984), p. 134; John Ruskin, 'The Nature of Gothic', in *Unto this Last and Other Writings*, ed. Clive Wilmer (Penguin Books, 1985), pp. 77–109 (p. 87).

41. 'Introduction to *A Bibliography of D. H. Lawrence*, by Edward D. McDonald', in *Phoenix: The Posthumous Papers of D. H. Lawrence*, ed. Edward D. McDonald (Heinemann, 1936), p. 234.

42. Jacques Derrida, *D'un ton apocalyptique adopté naguère en philosophie* (Galilée, 1983).

43. *The Symbolic Meaning: The Uncollected Versions of Studies in Classic American Literature*, ed. Armin Arnold (Centaur Press, 1962), p. 117.

Note on the Text

The manuscript of *The Rainbow*, which is in the possession of the Harry Ransom Humanities Research Center of the University of Texas at Austin, dates from November 1914 to 2 March 1915. It was DHL's fourth attempt at the novel, though the first to bear the title 'The Rainbow'. The text had been written, rewritten and reworked over a number of years, starting out as 'The Sisters' in 1913, mutating into 'The Wedding Ring' in 1914, then in 1915 splitting into *The Rainbow* and what would become *Women in Love*. The third version of the novel, 'The Wedding Ring', had been rejected by Methuen in August 1914, though to what extent this was on grounds of obscenity, as was later alleged during the Court Proceedings against *The Rainbow*, is not clear.[1] Two portions of 'The Wedding Ring' survive in revised form in the manuscript of *The Rainbow* (corresponding to 343:23–390:9 and 391:38–396:4 of the present text). They run from Ella's (later Ursula's) first day at Brinsley Street school to the Brangwen family's removal to their new house.

The typescript of *The Rainbow*, also in the possession of the Harry Ransom Humanities Research Center, dates from February 1915 to 31 May 1915, and was produced in batches by at least three, possibly four, typists, including Viola Meynell and Eleanor Farjeon. The typists themselves made numerous errors, some of a purely mechanical nature and some arising from mistaken attempts to 'correct' what they saw as DHL's errors. Because he did not check the typescript against the original manuscript, DHL often failed to notice these. He tended instead, as he received each batch of typescript, to recast and revise extensively, sometimes even inserting new sections, as in Chapter Seven, 'The Cathedral' (118:11–192:24) and the Nottingham episode of Chapter Eight 'The Child' (210:22–222:7). His wife Frieda also made occasional revisions to the typescript. Methuen's first edition of *The Rainbow* was set from this revised version of the typescript, though the proofs of the novel, to which DHL made still further changes, have not survived.

Note on the Text

After the prosecution of Methuen in November 1915 under the Obscene Publications Act of 1857 for publishing the novel, DHL's agent J. B. Pinker continued to seek the American publication of *The Rainbow* which he had put in motion in March 1914. The proposed publisher, George H. Doran, withdrew on hearing of the scandal surrounding the novel, but a more open-minded publisher, Benjamin W. Huebsch, agreed to proceed. The Huebsch text followed the Methuen closely, except that Huebsch expurgated the novel in thirteen places; in addition, some of the errors of the Methuen text were corrected, sometimes mistakenly.

The Huebsch text was used by Seltzer in his American edition of the novel in 1924 and indeed was used for almost all subsequent editions of *The Rainbow* in both England and America, including the 1926 Secker edition which claimed, falsely, to be 'new and revised'. The only exceptions to this were two Penguin editions: the 1949 edition, which reverted to the Methuen text but also 'corrected' it without reference to either the manuscript or the typescript of the novel, and the 1981 English Library edition, which was a direct reprint of the Methuen text.

The text of this Penguin edition is that of the Cambridge edition of *The Rainbow* edited by Mark Kinkead-Weekes. The aim of this text is to take into account all the changes made in the process of transmission from the manuscript to the first Methuen edition, via the typescript, its extensive revisions, and the missing proofs. The editor has distinguished carefully between errors made by the typists and compositors, and changes made by DHL himself. In practice, this means that the manuscript version has been accepted in the case of 'accidentals' – punctuation, styling and so on – except where changes can be proven to be, or argued to be, authorial. In cases of doubt, the manuscript version has been preferred. The exception to this is that DHL's idiosyncratic paragraphing has been standardized. When determining substantives, on the other hand, the general rule has been to incorporate all the revisions at each stage of transmission, with the exception of typing errors and obvious mistranscriptions in typesetting. In other words, an attempt has been made to confine the novel's successive changes to those made by DHL himself. In the absence of proofs, it is sometimes difficult to establish whether certain final changes were made by DHL or the compositors; in such cases, the changes have been accepted.

A particular problem is posed by the fact that the final revisions made by DHL at proof-stage may have been due to pressure from publishers, entailing compromise on the author's part. In a letter to Pinker of July 1915, DHL is seen conceding to such pressure by agreeing to change particular phrases, though he refuses to change whole passages and paragraphs.[2] In almost all cases, the present text follows these final changes, which often relate to the sexually or religiously 'improper', on the grounds that DHL's motives for making changes cannot finally be recovered. An example is the passage in which the pregnant Anna dances naked before the Lord, where a number of changes occur at proof-stage. The almost blasphemous overtones of the revised typescript (we see Anna 'lifting her hands and her body to the Lord, to the unseen Lover whose name was unutterable') become, in the Methuen first edition, the less overtly sexual 'lifting . . . to the Unseen, to the unseen Creator who had chosen her, to Whom she belonged'.[3] Whether the reference to the 'unseen Lover' was found specifically offensive by the publishers it is impossible to say; but given DHL's tendency to re-create afresh at every stage of revision, the change has been preserved. A similar toning down of the erotic can be seen in the betrothal scene of Tom and Lydia. In the manuscript version, DHL refers unmistakably if delicately to Tom's erection ('the liveliness of the front of his body where she had reclined on him'), a reference which is subsequently cut.[4] Here there would be a case for arguing that the cut must have been a response to the demands of the publishers, yet equally DHL may have wished to shift the emphasis from the sexual to the psychological, and to the man's feelings of resentment at the woman's sudden self-sufficiency after a moment of intimacy ('He sat up, unable to bear a contradiction in her' (46:33–4)), an emotional pattern that will recur in the relationship between Will and Anna, and again between Ursula and Skrebensky. It is impossible to ascertain to what extent DHL desired the cut regardless of outside pressure: consequently the cut has been preserved.

On the other hand, the four occasions on which DHL deleted the word 'belly' were, as Mark Kinkead-Weekes argues, almost certainly forced upon him, so the word has been restored (see 175:4, 296:22, 316:8, 335:3). It would seem that the term was considered objectionable in itself in 1915, however innocuous the context in which it was used.[5] In short, the underlying aim of the present edition is to present a state of the text which, though never actually seen by DHL, is closer to what he actually wrote than any previous text.

Note on the Text

NOTES

1. See Mark Kinkead-Weekes's scholarly Introduction to the Cambridge edition of *The Rainbow* (Cambridge University Press, 1989), pp. xxx–xxxi.
2. *Letters*, ii. 369–70.
3. See Textual apparatus for 170:1 in the Cambridge edition, p. 585.
4. See Textual apparatus for 46:33 in the Cambridge edition, p. 556.
5. See Introduction to the Cambridge edition, p. lxvi.

Advisory Editor's Note

I would like to thank Professor James T. Boulton and Professor Warren Roberts, General Editors of the *Cambridge Edition of the Works of D. H. Lawrence*, and Andrew Brown, of Cambridge University Press, for their work in the preparation of this edition; Anne Fernihough and I would also like to thank Mark Kinkead-Weekes for his help, scholarship and expertise, and Lindeth Vasey of Cambridge University Press for her advice and assistance.

John Worthen, 1995

Facsimile of the title page of the first English edition

THE RAINBOW

BY

D. H. LAWRENCE

AUTHOR OF "SONS AND LOVERS"

METHUEN & CO. LTD.
36 ESSEX STREET W.C.
LONDON

CHAPTER I

How Tom Brangwen Married a Polish Lady

I

The Brangwens had lived for generations on the Marsh Farm, in the meadows where the Erewash twisted sluggishly through alder trees, separating Derbyshire from Nottinghamshire. Two miles away, a church-tower stood on a hill, the houses of the little country town climbing assiduously up to it. Whenever one of the Brangwens in the fields lifted his head from his work, he saw the church-tower at Ilkeston in the empty sky. So that as he turned again to the horizontal land, he was aware of something standing above him and beyond him in the distance.

There was a look in the eyes of the Brangwens as if they were expecting something unknown, about which they were eager. They had that air of readiness for what would come to them, a kind of surety, an expectancy, the look of an inheritor.

They were fresh, blond, slow-speaking people, revealing themselves plainly, but slowly, so that one could watch the change in their eyes from laughter to anger, blue, lit-up laughter, to a hard, blue-staring anger; through all the irresolute stages of the sky when the weather is changing.

Living on rich land, on their own land, near to a growing town, they had forgotten what it was to be in straitened circumstances. They had never become rich, because there were always children, and the patrimony was divided every time. But always, at the Marsh, there was ample.

So the Brangwens came and went without fear of necessity, working hard because of the life that was in them, not for want of the money. Neither were they thriftless. They were aware of the last halfpenny, and instinct made them not waste the peeling of their apple, for it would help to feed the cattle. But heaven and earth was teeming around them, and how should this cease? They felt the rush of the sap in spring, they knew the wave which cannot halt, but every year throws forward the seed to begetting, and falling back, leaves the young-born on the earth. They knew the intercourse between heaven and earth, sunshine drawn into the breast and bowels, the rain sucked up in the daytime, nakedness that comes under the wind in autumn, showing the birds' nests no longer worth hiding. Their life and inter-relations were such; feeling the pulse and body of the soil, that opened to their furrow for the grain, and became smooth and supple after their ploughing, and clung to their feet with a weight that pulled like desire, lying hard and unresponsive when the crops were to be shorn away. The young corn waved and was silken, and the lustre slid along the limbs of the men who saw it. They took the udder of the cows, the cows yielded milk and pulse against the hands of the men, the pulse of the blood of the teats of the cows beat into the pulse of the hands of the men. They mounted their horses, and held life between the grip of their knees, they harnessed their horses at the wagon, and, with hand on the bridle-rings, drew the heaving of the horses after their will.

In autumn the partridges whirred up, birds in flocks blew like spray across the fallow, rooks appeared on the grey, watery heavens, and flew cawing into the winter. Then the men sat by the fire in the house where the women moved about with surety, and the limbs and the body of the men were impregnated with the day, cattle and earth and vegetation and the sky, the men sat by the fire and their brains were inert, as their blood flowed heavy with the accumulation from the living day.

The women were different. On them too was the drowse of blood-intimacy, calves sucking and hens running together in droves, and young geese palpitating in the hand whilst food was pushed down their throttle. But the women looked out from the heated, blind intercourse of farm-life, to the spoken world beyond. They were aware of the lips and the mind of the world speaking and giving utterance, they heard the sound in the distance, and they strained to listen.

It was enough for the men, that the earth heaved and opened its furrow to them, that the wind blew to dry the wet wheat, and set the young ears of corn wheeling freshly round about; it was enough that they helped the cow in labour, or ferreted the rats from under the barn, or broke the back of a rabbit with a sharp knock of the hand. So much warmth and generating and pain and death did they know in their blood, earth and sky and beast and green plants, so much exchange and interchange they had with these, that they lived full and surcharged, their senses full fed, their faces always turned to the heat of the blood, staring into the sun, dazed with looking towards the source of generation, unable to turn round.

But the woman wanted another form of life than this, something that was not blood-intimacy. Her house faced out from the farm-buildings and fields, looked out to the road and the village with church and Hall and the world beyond. She stood to see the far-off world of cities and governments and the active scope of man, the magic land to her, where secrets were made known and desires fulfilled. She faced outwards to where men moved dominant and creative, having turned their back on the pulsing heat of creation, and with this behind them, were set out to discover what was beyond, to enlarge their own scope and range and freedom; whereas the Brangwen men faced inwards to the teeming life of creation, which poured unresolved into their veins.

Looking out, as she must, from the front of her house towards the activity of man in the world at large, whilst her husband looked out to the back at sky and harvest and beast and land, she strained her eyes to see what man had done in fighting outwards to knowledge, she strained to hear how he uttered himself in his conquest, her deepest desire hung on the battle that she heard, far off, being waged on the edge of the unknown. She also wanted to know, and to be of the fighting host.

At home, even so near as Cossethay, was the vicar, who spoke the other, magic language, and had the other, finer bearing, both of which she could perceive, but could never attain to. The vicar moved in worlds beyond where her own menfolk existed. Did she not know her own menfolk: fresh, slow, full-built men, masterful enough, but easy, native to the earth, lacking outwardness and range of motion. Whereas the vicar, dark and dry and small beside her husband, had yet a quickness and a range of being that made Brangwen, in his large geniality, seem dull and local. She knew her husband. But in the vicar's nature was that which passed beyond her knowledge. As Brangwen had power over the cattle so the vicar had power over her husband. What was it in the vicar, that raised him above the common men as man is raised above the beast? She craved to know. She craved to achieve this higher being, if not in herself, then in her children. That which makes a man strong even if he be little and frail in body, just as any man is little and frail beside a bull, and yet stronger than the bull, what was it? It was not money nor power nor position. What power had the vicar over Tom Brangwen—none. Yet strip them and set them on a desert island, and the vicar was the master. His soul was master of the other man's. And why—why? She decided it was a question of knowledge.

The curate was poor enough, and not very efficacious as a man, either, yet he took rank with those others, the superior. She watched his children being born, she saw them running as tiny things beside their mother. And already they were separate from her own children, distinct. Why were her own children marked below those others? Why should the curate's children inevitably take precedence over her children, why should dominance be given them from the start? It was not money, nor even class. It was education and experience, she decided.

It was this, this education, this higher form of being, that the mother wished to give to her children, so that they too could live the supreme life on earth. For her children, at least the children of her heart, had the complete nature that should take place in equality with the living, vital people in the land, not be left behind obscure among the laborers. Why must they remain obscured and stifled all their lives, why should they suffer from lack of freedom to move? How should they learn the entry into the finer, more vivid circle of life?

Her imagination was fired by the squire's lady at Shelly Hall, who came to church at Cossethay with her little children, girls in tidy capes of beaver fur, and smart little hats, herself like a winter rose, so fair and delicate. So fair, so fine in mould, so luminous, what was it that Mrs Hardy felt which she, Mrs Brangwen did not feel? How was Mrs Hardy's nature different from that of the common women of Cossethay, in what was it beyond them? All the women of Cossethay talked eagerly about Mrs Hardy, of her husband, her children, her guests, her dress, of her servants and her housekeeping. The lady of the Hall was the living dream of their lives, her life was the epic that inspired their lives. In her they lived imaginatively, and in gossiping of her husband who drank, of her scandalous brother, of Lord William Bentley her friend, member of Parliament for the division, they had their own Odyssey enacting itself, Penelope and Ulysses before them, and Circe and the swine and the endless web.

So the women of the village were fortunate. They saw themselves in the lady of the manor, each of them lived her own fulfilment in the life of Mrs Hardy. And the Brangwen wife at the Marsh aspired beyond herself, towards the further life of the finer woman, towards the extended being she revealed, as a traveller in his self-contained manner reveals far-off countries present in himself. But why should a knowledge of far-off countries make a man's life a different thing, finer, bigger? And why is a man more than the beast and the cattle that serve him? It is the same thing.

The male part of the poem was filled in by such men as the vicar and Lord William, lean, eager men with strange movements, men who had command of the further fields, whose lives ranged over a great extent. Ah, it was something very desirable to know, this touch of the wonderful men who had the power of thought and comprehension. The women of the village might be much fonder of Tom Brangwen, and more at their ease with him, yet if their lives had been robbed of the vicar, and of Lord William, the leading shoot would have been cut away from them, they would have been heavy and uninspired and inclined to hate. So long as the wonder of the beyond was before them, they could get along, whatever their lot. And Mrs Hardy, and the vicar, and Lord William, these moved in the wonder of the beyond, and were visible to the eyes of Cossethay in their motion.

II

About 1840, a canal was constructed across the meadows of the Marsh Farm, connecting the newly opened collieries of the Erewash Valley. A high embankment travelled along the fields to carry the canal, which passed close to the homestead, and, reaching the road, went over in a heavy bridge.

So the Marsh was shut off from Ilkeston, and enclosed in the small valley bed, which ended in a busy hill and the village spire of Cossethay.

The Brangwens received a fair sum of money from this trespass across their land. Then, a short time afterwards, a colliery was sunk on the other side of the canal, and in a while the Midland Railway came down the valley at the foot of the Ilkeston hill, and the invasion was complete. The town grew rapidly, the Brangwens were kept busy producing supplies, they became richer, they were almost tradesmen.

Still the Marsh remained remote and original, on the old, quiet side of the canal embankment, in the sunny valley where slow water wound along in company of stiff alders, and the road went under ash-trees past the Brangwens' garden gate.

But, looking from the garden gate down the road to the right, there, through the dark archway of the canal's square aqueduct, was a colliery spinning away in the near distance, and further, red, crude houses plastered on the valley in masses, and beyond all, the dim smoking hill of the town.

The homestead was just on the safe side of civilisation, outside the gate. The house stood bare from the road, approached by a straight garden path, along which at spring the daffodils were thick in green and yellow. At the sides of the house were bushes of lilac and guelder-rose and privet, entirely hiding the farm-buildings behind.

At the back a confusion of sheds spread into the home-close from out of two or three indistinct yards. The duckpond lay beyond the furthest wall, littering its white feathers on the padded earthen banks, blowing its stray, soiled feathers into the grass and the gorse bushes below the canal embankment, which rose like a high rampart near at hand, so that occasionally a man's figure passed in silhouette, or a man and a towing horse traversed the sky.

At first the Brangwens were astonished by all this commotion around them. The building of a canal across their land made them strangers in their own place, this raw bank of earth shutting them off disconcerted them. As they worked in the fields, from beyond the now familiar embankment came the rhythmic run of the winding engines, startling at first, but afterwards a narcotic to the brain. Then the shrill whistle of the trains re-echoed through the heart, with fearsome pleasure, announcing the far-off come near and imminent.

As they drove home from town, the farmers of the land met the blackened colliers trooping from the pit-mouth. As they gathered the harvest, the west wind brought a faint, sulphurous smell of pit-refuse burning. As they pulled the turnips in November, the sharp clink-clink-clink-clink-clink of empty trucks shunting on the line, vibrated in their hearts with the fact of other activity going on beyond them.

The Alfred Brangwen of this period had married a woman from Heanor, daughter of the "Black Horse." She was a slim, pretty, dark woman, quaint in her speech, whimsical, so that the sharp things she said did not hurt. She was oddly a thing to herself, rather querulous in her manner, but intrinsically separate and indifferent, so that her long lamentable complaints, when she raised her voice against her husband in particular and against everybody else after him, only made those who heard her, wonder and feel affectionately towards her, even whilst they were irritated and impatient with her. She railed long and loud about her husband, but always with a balanced, easy-flying voice and a quaint manner of speech that warmed his belly with pride and male triumph whilst he scowled with mortification at the things she said.

Consequently Brangwen himself had a humorous puckering at the eyes, a sort of fat laugh, very quiet and full, and he was spoilt like a lord of creation. He calmly did as he liked, laughed at her railing, excused himself in a teasing tone that she loved, followed his natural inclinations, and sometimes, pricked too near the quick, frightened and broke her by a deep, tense fury which seemed to fix on him and hold him for days, and which she would give anything to placate in him. They were two very separate beings, vitally connected, knowing nothing of each other, yet living in their separate ways from one root.

There were four sons and two daughters. The eldest boy ran away early to sea, and did not come back. After this the mother was more the node and centre of attraction in the home. The second boy, Alfred, whom the mother admired most, was the most reserved. He was sent to school in Ilkeston and made some progress. But in spite of his dogged, yearning effort, he could not get beyond the rudiments of anything, save of drawing. At this, in which he had some power, he worked, as if it were his hope. After much grumbling and savage rebellion against everything, after much trying and shifting about, when his father was incensed against him and his mother almost despairing, he became a draughtsman in a lace-factory in Nottingham.

He remained heavy and somewhat uncouth, speaking with broad Derbyshire accent, adhering with all his tenacity to his work and to his town position, making good designs, and becoming fairly well-off. But at drawing, his hand swung naturally in big, bold lines, rather lax, so that it was cruel for him to pedgill away at the lace designing, working from the tiny squares of his paper, counting and plotting and niggling. He did it stubbornly, with anguish, crushing the bowels within him, adhering to his chosen lot whatever it should cost. And he came back into life set and rigid, a rare-spoken, almost surly man.

He married the daughter of a chemist, who affected some social superiority, and he became something of a snob, in his dogged fashion, with a passion for outward refinement in the household, mad when anything clumsy or gross occurred. Later, when his three children were growing up, and he seemed a staid, almost middle-aged man, he turned after strange women, and became a silent, inscrutable follower of forbidden pleasure, neglecting his indignant bourgeois wife without a qualm.

Frank, the third son, refused from the first to have anything to do with learning. From the first he hung round the slaughter-house which stood away in the third yard at the back of the farm. The Brangwens had always killed their own meat, and supplied the neighbourhood. Out of this grew a regular butcher's business in connection with the farm.

As a child Frank had been drawn by the trickle of dark blood that ran across the pavement from the slaughter-house to the crew-yard, by the sight of the man carrying across to the meat-shed a huge side of beef, with the kidneys showing, embedded in their heavy laps of fat.

He was a handsome lad with soft brown hair and regular features something like a later Roman youth. He was more easily excitable, more readily carried away than the rest, weaker in character. At eighteen he married a little factory girl, a pale, plump, quiet thing with sly eyes and a wheedling voice, who insinuated herself into him and bore him a child every year and made a fool of him. When he had taken over the butchery business, already a growing callousness to it, and a sort of contempt made him neglectful of it. He drank, and was often to be found in his public-house blathering away as if he knew everything, when in reality he was a noisy fool.

Of the daughters, Alice, the elder, married a collier and lived for a time stormily in Ilkeston, before moving away to Yorkshire with her numerous young family. Effie, the younger, remained at home.

The last child, Tom, was considerably younger than his brothers, so had belonged rather to the company of his sisters. He was his mother's favorite. She roused herself to determination, and sent him forcibly away to a Grammar School in Derby when he was twelve years old. He did not want to go, and his father would have given way, but Mrs Brangwen had set her heart on it. Her slender, pretty, tightly covered body, with full skirts, was now the centre of resolution in the house, and when she had once set upon anything, which was not often, the family failed before her.

So Tom went to school, an unwilling failure from the first. He believed his mother was right in decreeing school for him, but he knew she was only right because she would not acknowledge his constitution. He knew, with a child's deep, instinctive foreknowledge of what is going to happen to him, that he would cut a sorry figure at school. But he took the infliction as inevitable, as if he were guilty of his own nature, as if his being were wrong, and his mother's conception right. If he could have been what he liked, he would have been that which his mother fondly but deludedly hoped he was. He would have been clever, and capable of becoming a gentleman. It was her aspiration for him, therefore he knew it as the true aspiration for any boy. But you can't make a silk purse out of a sow's ear, as he told his mother very early, with regard to himself; much to her mortification and chagrin.

When he got to school, he made a violent struggle against his physical inability to study. He sat gripped, making himself pale and ghastly in his effort to concentrate on the book, to take in what he had to learn. But it was no good. If he beat down his first repulsion, and got like a suicide to the stuff, he went very little further. He could not learn deliberately. His mind simply did not work.

In feeling he was developed, sensitive to the atmosphere around him, brutal perhaps, but at the same time delicate, very delicate. So he had a low opinion of himself. He knew his own limitation. He knew that his brain was a slow hopeless good-for-nothing. So he was humble.

But at the same time his feelings were more discriminating than those of most of the boys, and he was confused. He was more sensuously developed, more refined in instinct than they. For their mechanical stupidity he hated them, and suffered cruel contempt for them. But when it came to mental things, then he was at a disadvantage. He was at their mercy. He was a fool. He had not the power to controvert even the most stupid argument, so that he was forced to admit things he did not in the least believe. And having admitted them, he did not know whether he believed them or not; he rather thought he did.

But he loved anyone who could convey enlightenment to him through feeling. He sat betrayed with emotion when the teacher of literature read, in a moving fashion, Tennyson's "Ulysses" or Shelley's "Ode to the West Wind." His lips parted, his eyes filled with a strained, almost suffering light. And the teacher read on, fired by his power over the boy. Tom Brangwen was moved by this experience beyond all calculation, he almost dreaded it, it was so deep. But when, almost secretly and shamefully, he came to take the book himself, and began the words "Oh wild west wind, thou breath of autumn's being," the very fact of the print caused a prickly sensation of repulsion to go over his skin, the blood came to his face, his heart filled with a bursting passion of rage and incompetence. He threw the book down and walked over it and went out to the cricket field. And he hated books as if they were his enemies. He hated them worse than ever he hated any person.

He could not voluntarily control his attention. His mind had no fixed habits to go by, he had nothing to get hold of, nowhere to start from. For him there was nothing palpable, nothing known in himself, that he could apply to learning. He did not know how to begin. Therefore he was helpless when it came to deliberate understanding or deliberate learning.

He had an instinct for mathematics, but if this failed him, he was helpless as an idiot. So that he felt that the ground was never sure under his feet, he was nowhere. His final downfall was his complete inability to attend to a question put without suggestion. If he had to write a formal composition on the Army, he did at last learn to repeat the few facts he knew: "You can join the army at eighteen. You have to be over five foot eight." But he had all the time a living conviction that this was a dodge and that his commonplaces were beneath contempt. Then he reddened furiously, felt his bowels sink with shame, scratched out what he had written, made an agonised effort to think of something in the real composition style, failed, became sullen with rage and humiliation, put the pen down and would have been torn to pieces rather than attempt to write another word.

He soon got used to the Grammar School, and the Grammar School got used to him, setting him down as a hopeless duffer at learning, but respecting him for a generous, honest nature. Only one narrow, domineering fellow, the Latin master, bullied him and made the blue eyes mad with shame and rage. There was a horrid scene, when the boy laid open the master's head with a slate, and then things went on as before. The teacher got little sympathy. But Brangwen winced and could not bear to think of the deed, not even long after, when he was a grown man.

He was glad to leave school. It had not been unpleasant, he had enjoyed the companionship of the other youths, or had thought he enjoyed it, the time had passed very quickly, in endless activity. But he knew all the time that he was in an ignominious position, in this place of learning. He was aware of failure all the while, of incapacity. But he was too healthy and sanguine to be wretched, he was too much alive. Yet his soul was wretched almost to hopelessness.

He had loved one warm, clever boy who was frail in body, a consumptive type. The two had had an almost classic friendship, David and Jonathan, wherein Brangwen was the Jonathan, the server. But he had never felt equal with his friend, because the other's mind outpaced his, and left him ashamed, far in the rear. So the two boys went at once apart on leaving school. But Brangwen always remembered his friend that had been, kept him as a sort of light, a fine experience to remember.

Tom Brangwen was glad to get back to the farm, where he was in his own again. "I've got a turnip on my shoulders, let me stick to th' fallow," he said to his exasperated mother. He had too low an opinion of himself. But he went about at his work on the farm gladly enough, glad of the active labour and the smell of the land again, having youth and vigour and humour, and a comic wit, having the will and the power to forget his own shortcomings, finding himself violent with occasional rages, but usually on good terms with everybody and everything.

When he was seventeen, his father fell from a stack and broke his neck. Then the mother and son and daughter lived on at the farm, interrupted by occasional loud-mouthed, lamenting, jealous-spirited visitations from the butcher Frank, who had a grievance against the world, which he felt was always giving him less than his dues. Frank was particularly against the young Tom, whom he called a mardy baby, and Tom returned the hatred violently, his face growing red and his blue eyes staring. Effie sided with Tom against Frank. But when Alfred came, from Nottingham, heavy jowled and lowering, speaking very little, but treating those at home with some contempt, Effie and the mother sided with him and put Tom into the shade. It irritated the youth that his elder brother should be made something of a hero by the women, just because he didn't live at home and was a lace-designer and almost a gentleman. But Alfred was something of a Prometheus Bound, so the women loved him. Tom came later to understand his brother better.

As youngest son, Tom felt some importance when the care of the farm devolved on to him. He was only eighteen, but he was quite capable of doing everything his father had done. And of course, his mother remained as centre to the house.

The young man grew up very fresh and alert, with zest for every moment of life. He worked and rode and drove to market, he went out with companions and got tipsy occasionally and played skittles and went to the little travelling theatres. Once, when he was drunk at a public-house, he went upstairs with a prostitute who seduced him. He was then nineteen.

The thing was something of a shock to him. In the close intimacy of the farm kitchen, the woman occupied the supreme position. The men deferred to her in the house, on all household points, on all points of morality and behaviour. The woman was the symbol for that further life which comprised religion and love and morality. The men placed in her hands their own conscience, they said to her "Be my conscience-keeper, be the angel at the doorway guarding my outgoing and my incoming." And the woman fulfilled her trust, the men rested implicitly in her, receiving her praise or her blame with pleasure or with anger, rebelling and storming, but never for a moment really escaping in their own souls from her prerogative. They depended on her for their stability. Without her, they would have felt like straws in the wind, to be blown hither and thither at random. She was the anchor and the security, she was the restraining hand of God, at times highly to be execrated.

Now when Tom Brangwen, at nineteen, a youth fresh like a plant, rooted in his mother and his sister, found that he had lain with a prostitute woman in a common public-house, he was very much startled. For him, there was until that time only one kind of woman—his mother and sister.

But now? He did not know what to feel. There was a slight wonder, a pang of anger, of disappointment, a first taste of ash and of cold fear lest this was all that would happen, lest his relations with woman were going to be no more than this nothingness; there was a slight sense of shame before the prostitute, fear that she would despise him for his inefficiency; there was a cold distaste for her, and a fear of her; there was a moment of paralysed horror when he felt he might have taken a disease from her; and upon all this startled tumult of emotion, was laid the steadying hand of common sense, which said it did not matter very much, so long as he had no disease. He soon recovered balance, and really it did not matter so very much.

But it had shocked him, and put a mistrust into his heart, and emphasized his fear of what was within himself. He was, however, in a few days going about again in his own careless, happy-go-lucky fashion, his blue eyes just as clear and honest as ever, his face just as fresh, his appetite just as keen.

Or apparently so. He had, in fact, lost some of his buoyant confidence, and doubt hindered his outgoing.

For some time after this, he was quieter, more conscious when he drank, more backward from companionship. The disillusion of his first carnal contact with woman, strengthened by his innate desire to find in a woman the embodiment of all his inarticulate, powerful religious impulses, put a bit in his mouth. He had something to lose which he was afraid of losing, which he was not sure even of possessing. This first affair did not matter much: but the business of love was, at the bottom of his soul, the most serious and terrifying of all to him.

He was tormented now with sex desire, his imagination reverted always to lustful scenes. But what really prevented his returning to a loose woman, over and above the natural squeamishness, was the recollection of the paucity of the last experience. It had been so nothing, so dribbling and functional, that he was ashamed to expose himself to the risk of a repetition of it.

He made a strong, instinctive fight to retain his native cheerfulness unimpaired. He had naturally a plentiful stream of life and humour, a sense of sufficiency and exuberance, giving ease. But now it tended to cause tension. A strained light came into his eyes, he had a slight knitting of the brows. His boisterous humour gave place to lowering silences, and days passed by in a sort of suspense.

He did not know there was any difference in him, exactly; for the most part he was filled with slow anger and resentment. But he knew he was always thinking of women, or a woman, day in, day out, and that infuriated him. He could not get free: and he was ashamed. He had one or two sweethearts, starting with them in the hope of speedy development. But when he had a nice girl, he found that he was incapable of pushing the desired development. The very presence of the girl beside him made it impossible. He could not think of her like that, he could not think of her *actual* nakedness. She was a girl and he liked her, and dreaded violently even the thought of uncovering her. He knew that, in these last issues of nakedness, he did not exist to her nor she to him. Again, if he had a loose girl, and things began to develop, she offended him so deeply all the time, that he never knew whether he were going to get away from her as quickly as possible, or whether he were going to take her out of inflamed necessity. Again he learnt his lesson: if he took her it was a paucity which he was forced to despise. He did not despise himself nor the girl. But he despised the net result in him of the experience—he despised it deeply and bitterly.

Then, when he was twenty three, his mother died, and he was left at home with Effie. His mother's death was another blow out of the dark. He could not understand it, he knew it was no good his trying. One had to submit to these unforeseen blows that come unawares, and leave a bruise that remains and hurts whenever it is touched. He began to be afraid of all that which was up against him. He had loved his mother.

After this, Effie and he quarrelled fiercely. They meant a very great deal to each other, but they were both under a strange, unnatural tension. He stayed out of the house as much as possible. He got a special corner for himself at the "Red Lion" at Cossethay, and became a usual figure by the fire, a fresh, fair young fellow with heavy limbs and head held back, mostly silent, though alert and attentive, very hearty in his greeting of everybody he knew, shy of strangers. He teased all the women, who liked him extremely, and he was very attentive to the talk of the men, very respectful.

To drink made him quickly flush very red in the face, and brought out the look of self-consciousness and unsureness, almost bewilderment, in his blue eyes. When he came home in this state of tipsy confusion his sister hated him and abused him, and he went off his head, like a mad bull with rage.

He had still another turn with a light-o'love. One Whitsuntide he went a jaunt with two other young fellows, on horseback, to Matlock and thence to Bakewell. Matlock was at that time just becoming a famous beauty-spot, visited from Manchester and from the Staffordshire towns. In the hôtel where the young men took lunch, were two girls, and the parties struck up a friendship.

The Miss who made up to Tom Brangwen, then twenty four years old, was a handsome, reckless girl neglected for an afternoon by the man who had brought her out. She saw Brangwen, and liked him, as all women did, for his warmth and his generous nature, and for the innate delicacy in him. But she saw he was one who would have to be brought to the scratch. However, she was roused and unsatisfied and made mischievous, so she dared anything. It would be an easy interlude, restoring her pride.

She was a handsome girl with a bosom, and dark hair, and blue eyes, a girl full of easy laughter, flushed from the sun, inclined to wipe her laughing face in a very natural and taking manner.

Brangwen was in a state of wonder. He treated her with his chaffing deference, roused, but very unsure of himself, afraid to death of being too forward, ashamed lest he might be thought backward, mad with desire yet restrained by instinctive regard for women from making any definite approach, feeling all the while that his attitude was ridiculous, and flushing deep with confusion. She, however, became hard and daring as he become confused, it amused her to see him come on.

"When must you get back?" she asked.

"I'm not particular," he said.

There the conversation again broke down.

Brangwen's companions were ready to go on.

"Art commin' Tom," they called, "or art for stoppin'?"

"Ay, I'm commin'," he replied, rising reluctantly, an angry sense of futility and disappointment spreading over him.

He met the full, almost taunting look of the girl, and he trembled with unusedness.

"Shall you come an' have a look at my mare," he said to her, with his hearty kindliness that was now shaken with trepidation.

"Oh, I should like to," she said, rising.

And she followed him, his rather sloping shoulders and his cloth riding gaiters, out of the room. The young men got their own horses out of the stable.

"Can you ride?" Brangwen asked her.

"I should like to if I could—I've never tried," she said.

"Come then, an' have a try," he said.

And he lifted her, he blushing, she laughing, into the saddle.

"I s'll slip off—it's not a lady's saddle," she cried.

"Hold yer tight," he said, and he led her out of the hôtel gate.

The girl sat very insecurely, clinging fast. He put a hand on her waist, to support her. And he held her closely, he clasped her as an embrace, he was weak with desire as he strode beside her.

The horse walked by the river.

"You want to sit straddle-leg," he said to her.

"I know I do," she said.

It was the time of very full skirts. She managed to get astride the horse, quite decently, showing an intent concern for covering her pretty leg.

"It's a lot better this road," she said, looking down at him.

"Ay, it is," he said, feeling the marrow melt in his bones from the look in her eyes. "I dunno why they have that side-saddle business, twistin' a woman in two."

"Should us leave you then—you seem to be fixed up there?" called Brangwen's companions from the road.

He went red with anger.

"Ay—don't worry," he called back.

"How long are yer stoppin'?" they asked.

"Not after Christmas," he said.

And the girl gave a tinkling peal of laughter.

"All right—by-bye!" called his friends.

And they cantered off, leaving him very flushed, trying to be quite normal with the girl. But presently he had gone back to the hôtel and given his horse into the charge of an ostler and had gone off with the girl, into the woods, not quite knowing where he was or what he was doing. His heart thumped and he thought it the most glorious adventure, and was mad with desire for the girl.

Afterwards he glowed with pleasure. By Jove, but that was something like! He stayed the afternoon with the girl, and wanted to stay the night. She, however, told him this was impossible: her own man would be back by dark, and she must be with him. He, Brangwen, must not let on that there had been anything between them.

She gave him an intimate smile, which made him feel confused and gratified.

He could not tear himself away, though he had promised not to interfere with the girl. He stayed on at the hôtel over-night. He saw the other fellow at the evening meal; a small, middle-aged man with iron-grey hair and a curious face, like a monkey's, but interesting, in its way almost beautiful. Brangwen guessed that he was a foreigner. He was in company with another, an Englishman, dry and hard. The four sat at table, two men and two women. Brangwen watched with all his eyes.

He saw how the foreigner treated the women with courteous contempt, as if they were pleasing animals. Brangwen's girl had put on a ladylike manner, but her voice betrayed her. She wanted to win back her man. When dessert came on, however, the little foreigner turned round from his table and calmly surveyed the room, like one unoccupied. Brangwen marvelled over the cold, animal intelligence of the face. The brown eyes were round, showing all the brown pupil, like a monkey's, and just calmly looking, perceiving the other person without referring to him at all. They rested on Brangwen. The latter marvelled at the old face turned round on him, looking at him without considering it necessary to know him at all. The eyebrows of the round, perceiving, but unconcerned eyes were rather high up, with slight wrinkles above them, just as a monkey's had. It was an old, ageless face.

The man was most amazingly a gentleman all the time, an aristocrat. Brangwen stared fascinated. The girl was pushing her crumbs about on the cloth, uneasily, flushed and angry.

As Brangwen sat motionless in the hall afterwards, too much moved and lost to know what to do, the little stranger came up to him with a beautiful smile and manner, offering a cigarette and saying:

"Will you smoke?"

Brangwen never smoked cigarettes, yet he took the one offered, fumbling painfully with thick fingers, blushing to the roots of his hair. Then he looked with his warm blue eyes at the almost sardonic, lidded eyes of the foreigner. The latter sat down beside him, and they began to talk, chiefly of horses.

Brangwen loved the other man for his exquisite graciousness, for his tact and reserve, and for his ageless, monkey-like self-surety. They talked of horses, and of Derbyshire, and of farming. The stranger warmed to the young fellow with real warmth, and Brangwen was excited. He was transported at meeting this odd, middle-aged, dry-skinned man, personally. The talk was pleasant, but that did not matter so much. It was the gracious manner, the fine contact that was all.

They talked a long while together, Brangwen flushing like a girl when the other did not understand his idiom. Then they said goodnight, and shook hands. Again the foreigner bowed and repeated his goodnight.

"Goodnight, and *bon voyage*."

Then he turned to the stairs.

Brangwen went up to his room and lay staring out at the stars of the summer night, his whole being in a whirl. What was it all? There was a life so different from what he knew it. What was there outside his knowledge, how much? What was this that he had touched? What was he in this new influence? What did everything mean? Where was life, in that which he knew or all outside him?

He fell asleep, and in the morning had ridden away before any other visitors were awake. He shrank from seeing any of them again, in the morning.

His mind was one big excitement. The girl and the foreigner: he knew neither of their names. Yet they had set fire to the homestead of his nature, and he would be burned out of cover. Of the two experiences, perhaps the meeting with the foreigner was the more significant. But the girl—he had not settled about the girl.

He did not know. He had to leave it there, as it was. He could not sum up his experiences.

The result of these encounters was, that he dreamed day and night, absorbedly, of a voluptuous woman and of the meeting with a small, withered foreigner of ancient breeding. No sooner was his mind free, no sooner had he left his own companions, than he began to imagine an intimacy with fine-textured, subtle-mannered people such as the foreigner at Matlock, and amidst this subtle intimacy was always the satisfaction of a voluptuous woman.

He went about absorbed in the interest and the actuality of this dream. His eyes glowed, he walked with his head up, full of the exquisite pleasure of aristocratic subtlety and grace, tormented with the desire for the girl.

Then gradually the glow began to fade, and the cold material of his customary life to show through. He resented it. Was he cheated in his illusion? He balked the mean enclosure of reality, stood stubbornly like a bull at a gate, refusing to re-enter the well-known pound of his own life.

He drank more than usual to keep up the glow. But it faded more and more for all that. He set his teeth at the commonplace, to which he would not submit. It resolved itself starkly before him, for all that.

He wanted to marry, to get settled somehow, to get out of the quandary he found himself in. But how? He felt unable to move his limbs. He had seen a little creature caught in bird-lime, and the sight was a nightmare to him. He began to feel mad with the rage of impotency.

He wanted something to get hold of, to pull himself out. But there was nothing. Steadfastly he looked at the young women, to find a one he could marry. But not one of them did he want. And he knew that the idea of a life among such people as the foreigner was ridiculous.

Yet he dreamed of it, and stuck to his dreams, and would not have the reality of Cossethay and Ilkeston. There he sat stubbornly in his corner at the "Red Lion," smoking and musing and occasionally lifting his beer-pot, and saying nothing, for all the world like a gorping farm-laborer, as he said himself.

Then a fever of restless anger came upon him. He wanted to go away—right away. He dreamed of foreign parts. But somehow he had no contact with them. And it was a very strong root which held him to the Marsh, to his own house and land.

Then Effie got married, and he was left in the house with only Tilly, the cross-eyed woman-servant who had been with them for fifteen years. He felt things coming to a close. All the time, he had held himself stubbornly resistant to the action of the commonplace unreality which wanted to absorb him. But now he had to do something.

He was by nature temperate. Being sensitive and emotional, his nausea prevented him from drinking too much.

But, in futile anger, with the greatest of determination and apparent good-humour, he began to drink in order to get drunk. "Damn it," he said to himself, "you must have it one road or another—you can't hitch your horse to the shadow of a gate-post—if you've got legs you've got to rise off your backside some time or other."

So he rose and went down to Ilkeston, rather awkwardly took his place amongst a gang of young bloods, stood drinks to the company, and discovered he could carry it off quite well. He had an idea that everybody in the room was a man after his own heart, that everything was glorious, everything was perfect. When somebody in alarm told him his coat pocket was on fire, he could only beam from a red, blissful face and say "Iss-all-ri-ight—iss-a'-ri-ight—it's a' right ——let it be, let it be——" and he laughed with pleasure, and was rather indignant that the others should think it unnatural for his coat pocket to burn:—it was the happiest and most natural thing in the world—what?

He went home talking to himself and to the moon, that was very high and small, stumbling at the flashes of moonlight from the puddles at his feet, wondering What the Hanover!, then laughing confidently to the moon, assuring her this was first class, this was.

In the morning he woke up and thought about it, and for the first time in his life, knew what it was to feel really acutely irritable, in a misery of real bad temper. After bawling and snarling at Tilly, he took himself off for very shame, to be alone. And looking at the ashen fields and the putty roads, he wondered what in the name of Hell he could do to get out of this prickly sense of disgust and physical repulsion. And he knew that this was the result of his glorious evening.

And his stomach did not want any more brandy. He went doggedly across the fields with his terrier, and looked at everything with a jaundiced eye.

The next evening found him back again in his place at the "Red Lion," moderate and decent. There he sat and stubbornly waited for what would happen next.

Did he, or did he not believe that he belonged to this world of Cossethay and Ilkeston? There was nothing in it he wanted. Yet could he ever get out of it? Was there anything in himself that would carry him out of it? Or was he a dunderheaded baby, not man enough to be like the other young fellows who drank a good deal and wenched a little without any question, and were satisfied.

He went on stubbornly for a time. Then the strain became too great for him. A hot, accumulated consciousness was always awake in his chest, his wrists felt swelled and quivering, his mind became full of lustful images, his eyes seemed blood-flushed. He fought with himself furiously, to remain normal. He did not seek any woman. He just went on as if he were normal. Till he must either take some action or beat his head against the wall.

Then he went deliberately to Ilkeston, in silence, intent and beaten. He drank to get drunk. He gulped down the brandy, and more brandy, till his face became pale, his eyes burning. And still he could not get free. He went to sleep in drunken unconsciousness, woke up at four o'clock in the morning and continued drinking. He *would* get free. Gradually the tension in him began to relax. He began to feel happy. His riveted silence was unfastened, he began to talk and babble. He was happy and at one with all the world, he was united with all flesh in a hot blood-relationship. So, after three days of incessant brandy-drinking, he had burned out the youth from his blood, he had achieved this kindled state of oneness with all the world, which is the end of youth's most passionate desire. But he had achieved his satisfaction by obliterating his own individuality, that which it depended on his manhood to preserve and develop.

So he became a bout-drinker, having at intervals these bouts of three or four days of brandy-drinking, when he was drunk for the whole time. He did not think about it. A deep resentment burned in him. He kept aloof from any women, antagonistic.

When he was twenty eight, a thick-limbed, stiff, fair man with fresh complexion, and blue eyes staring very straight ahead, he was coming one day from Cossethay with a load of seed out of Nottingham. It was a time when he was getting ready for another bout of drinking, so he stared fixedly before him, watchful yet absorbed, seeing everything and aware of nothing, coiled in himself. It was early in the year.

He walked steadily beside the horse, the load clanked behind as the hill descended steeper. The road curved downhill before him, under banks and hedges, seen only for a few yards ahead.

Slowly turning the curve at the steepest part of the slope, his horse britching between the shafts, he saw a woman approaching. But he was thinking for the moment of the horse.

Then he turned to look at her. She was dressed in black, was apparently rather small and slight, beneath her long black cloak, and she wore a black bonnet. She walked hastily, as if unseeing, her head rather forward. It was her curious, absorbed, flitting motion, as if she were passing unseen by everybody, that first arrested him.

She had heard the cart, and looked up. Her face was pale and clear, she had thick dark eyebrows and a wide mouth, curiously held. He saw her face clearly, as if by a light in the air. He saw her face so distinctly, that he ceased to coil on himself, and was suspended.

"That's her," he said involuntarily. As the cart passed by, splashing through the thin mud, she stood back against the bank. Then, as he walked still beside his britching horse, his eyes met hers. He looked quickly away, pressing back his head, a pain of joy running through him. He could not bear to think of anything.

He turned round at the last moment. He saw her bonnet, her shape in the black cloak, the movement as she walked. Then she was gone round the bend.

She had passed by. He felt as if he were walking again in a far world, not Cossethay, a far world, the fragile reality. He went on, quiet, suspended, rarified. He could not bear to think or to speak, nor make any sound or sign, nor change his fixed motion. He could scarcely bear to think of her face. He moved within the knowledge of her, in the world that was beyond reality.

The feeling that they had exchanged recognition possessed him like a madness, like a torment. How could he be sure, what confirmation had he? The doubt was like a sense of infinite space, a nothingness, annihilating. He kept within his breast the will to surety. They had exchanged recognition.

He walked about in this state for the next few days. And then again like a mist it began to break to let through the common, barren world. He was very gentle with man and beast, but he dreaded the starkness of disillusion cropping through again.

As he was standing with his back to the fire after dinner a few days later, he saw the woman passing. He wanted to know that she knew him, that she was aware. He wanted it said that there was something between them. So he stood anxiously watching, looking at her as she went down the road. He called to Tilly.

"Who might that be?" he asked.

Tilly, the cross-eyed woman of forty, who adored him, ran gladly to the window to look. She was glad when he asked her for anything. She craned her head over the short curtain, the little tight knob of her black hair sticking out pathetically as she bobbed about.

"Oh why—" she lifted her head and peered with her twisted, keen brown eyes—"why, you know who it is—it's her from th' vicarage— you know—"

"*How* do I know, you hen-bird," he shouted.

Tilly blushed and drew her neck in and looked at him with her squinting, sharp, almost reproachful look.

"Why you do—it's the new housekeeper."

"Ay—an' what by that?"

"Well, an' *what* by that?" rejoined the indignant Tilly.

"She's a woman, isn't she, housekeeper or no housekeeper? She's got more to her than that! Who is she—she's got a name?"

"Well, if she has, *I* don't know," retorted Tilly, not to be badgered by this lad who had grown up into a man.

"What's her name?" he asked, more gently.

"I'm sure I couldn't tell you," replied Tilly, on her dignity.

"An' is that all as you've gathered, as she's housekeeping at the vicarage?"

"I've 'eered mention of 'er name, but I couldn't remember it for my life."

"Why yer riddle-skulled woman o' nonsense, what have you got a head for?"

"For what other folks 'as got theirs for," retorted Tilly, who loved nothing more than these tilts when he would call her names.

There was a lull.

"I don't believe as anybody could keep it in their head," the woman-servant continued, tentatively.

"What?" he asked.

"Why, 'er name."

"How's that?"

"She's fra some foreign parts or other."

"Who told you that?"

"That's all I do know, as she is."

"An' wheer do you reckon she's from, then?"

"I don't know. They do say as she hails fra th' Pole. *I* don't know," Tilly hastened to add, knowing he would attack her.

"Fra th' Pole, why do *you* hail fra th' Pole? Who's set up that menagerie confabulation?"

"That's what they say—*I* don't know—"

"Who says?"

"Mrs Bentley—says as she's fra th' Pole—else she *is* a Pole, or summat."

Tilly was only afraid she was landing herself deeper now.

"Who says she's a Pole?"

"They all say so."

"Then what's brought her to these parts?"

"I couldn't tell you. She's got a little girl with her."

"Got a little girl with her?"

"Of three or four, with a head like a fuzz-ball."

"Black?"

"White—fair as can be, an' all of a fuzz."

"Is there a father, then?"

"Not to my knowledge. I don't know."

"What brought her here?"

"I couldn't say, without th' vicar axed her."

"Is the child her child?"

"I s'd think so—they say so."

"Who told you about her?"

"Why Lizzie—a-Monday—we seed her goin' past."

"You'd have to be rattling your tongues if anything went past."

Brangwen stood musing. That evening he went up to Cossethay to the "Red Lion," half with the intention of hearing more.

She was the widow of a Polish doctor, he gathered. Her husband had died, a refugee, in London. She spoke a bit foreign like, but you could easily make out what she said. She had one little girl, named Anna. Lensky was the woman's name, Mrs Lensky.

Brangwen felt that here was the unreality established at last. He felt also a curious certainty about her, as if she were destined to him. It was to him a profound satisfaction that she was a foreigner.

A swift change had taken place on the earth for him, as if a new creation were fulfilled, in which he had real existence. Things had all been stark, unreal, barren, mere nullities before. Now they were actualities that he could handle.

He dared scarcely think of the woman. He was afraid. Only all the time he was aware of her presence not far off, he lived in her. But he dared not know her, even acquaint himself with her by thinking of her.

One day he met her walking along the road with her little girl. It was a child with a face like a bud of apple-blossom, and glistening fair hair like thistle-down sticking out in straight, wild, flamy pieces, and very dark eyes. The child clung jealously to her mother's side when he looked at her, staring with resentful black eyes. But the mother glanced at him again, almost vacantly. And the very vacancy of her look inflamed him. She had wide grey-brown eyes with very dark, fathomless pupils. He felt the fine flame running under his skin, as if all his veins had caught fire on the surface. And he went on walking without knowledge.

It was coming, he knew, his fate. The world was submitting to its transformation. He made no move: it would come, what would come.

When his sister Effie came to the Marsh for a week, he went with her for once to church. In the tiny place, with its mere dozen pews, he sat not far from the stranger. There was a fineness about her, a poignancy about the way she sat and held her head lifted. She was strange, from far off, yet so intimate. She was from far away, a presence, so close to his soul. She was not really there, sitting in Cossethay church beside her little girl. She was not living the apparent life of her days. She belonged to somewhere else. He felt it poignantly, as something real and natural. But a pang of fear for his own concrete life, that was only Cossethay, hurt him, and gave him misgiving.

Her thick dark brows almost met above her irregular nose, she had a wide, rather thick mouth. But her face was lifted to another world of life: not to heaven or death: but to some place where she still lived, in spite of her body's absence.

The child beside her watched everything with wide, black eyes. She had an odd little defiant look, her little red mouth was pinched shut. She seemed to be jealously guarding something, to be always on the alert for defense. She met Brangwen's near, vacant, intimate gaze, and a palpitating hostility, almost like a flame of pain, came into the wide, over-conscious dark eyes.

The old clergyman droned on, Cossethay sat unmoved as usual. And there was the foreign woman with a foreign land vivid about her, inviolate, and the strange child, also foreign, jealously guarding something.

When the service was over, he walked in the daze of another existence out of the church. As he went down the church-path with his sister, behind the woman and child, the little girl suddenly broke from her mother's hand, and slipped back with quick, almost invisible movement, and was picking at something almost under Brangwen's feet. Her tiny fingers were fine and quick, but they missed the red button.

"Have you found something?" said Brangwen to her.

And he also stooped for the button. But she had got it, and she stood back with it pressed against her little coat, her black eyes flaring at him, as if to forbid him to notice her. Then, having silenced him, she turned with a swift

"Mother—," and was gone down the path.

The mother had stood watching impassive, looking not at the child, but at Brangwen. He became aware of the woman looking at him, standing there isolated yet for him dominant in her foreign existence.

He did not know what to do, and turned to his sister. But the wide grey eyes, almost vacant yet so moving, held him beyond himself.

"Mother, I may have it, mayn't I?" came the child's proud, silvery tones. "Mother"—she seemed always to be calling her mother to remember her—"Mother—" and she had nothing to continue, now her mother had replied "Yes my child." But, with ready invention, the child stumbled and ran on "What are those people's names?"

Brangwen heard the abstract:

"I don't know dear."

He went on down the road as if he were not living inside himself, but somewhere outside.

"Who *was* that person?" his sister Effie asked.

"I couldn't tell you," he answered unknowing.

"She's *somebody* very funny," said Effie, almost in condemnation. "That child's like one bewitched."

"Bewitched—how bewitched?" he repeated.

"You can see for yourself. The mother's plain, I must say—but the child is like a changeling. She'd be about thirty five."

But he took no notice. His sister talked on.

"There's your woman for you," she continued. "You'd better marry *her*." But still he took no notice. Things were as they were.

Another day, at tea-time, as he sat alone at table, there came a knock at the front door. It startled him like a portent. No-one ever knocked at the front door. He rose and began slotting back the bolts, turning the big key. When he had opened the door, the strange woman stood on the threshold.

"Can you give me a pound of butter?" she asked, in the curious detached way of one speaking a foreign language.

He tried to attend to her question. She was looking at him questioningly. But underneath the question, what was there, in her very standing motionless, which affected him?

He stepped aside and she at once entered the house, as if the door had been opened to admit her. That startled him. It was the custom for everybody to wait on the doorstep till asked inside. He went into the kitchen and she followed.

His tea-things were spread on the scrubbed deal table, a big fire was burning, a dog rose from the hearth and went to her. She stood motionless just inside the kitchen.

"Tilly," he called loudly, "have we got any butter?"

The stranger stood there like a silence in her black cloak.

"Eh?" came the shrill cry from the distance.

He shouted his question again.

"We've got what's on t' table," answered Tilly's shrill voice out of the dairy.

Brangwen looked at the table. There was a large pat of butter on a plate, almost a pound. It was round, and stamped with acorns and oak-leaves.

"Can't you come when you're wanted?" he shouted.

"Why what d'you want?" Tilly protested, as she came peeking inquisitively through the other door.

She saw the strange woman, stared at her with cross eyes, but said nothing.

"*Haven't* we any butter?" asked Brangwen again, impatiently, as if he could command some by his question.

"I tell you there's what's on t' table," said Tilly, impatient that she was unable to create any to his demand. "We haven't a morsel besides."

There was a moment's silence.

Then the stranger spoke, in her curiously distinct, detached manner of one who must think her speech first.

"Oh, then thank you very much. I am sorry that I have come to trouble you."

She could not understand the entire lack of manners, was slightly puzzled. Any politeness would have made the situation quite impersonal. But here it was a case of wills in confusion. Brangwen flushed at her polite speech. Still he did not let her go.

"Get summat an' wrap *that* up for her," he said to Tilly, looking at the butter on the table.

And taking a clean knife, he cut off that side of the butter where it was touched.

His speech, the "for her," penetrated slowly into the foreign woman, and angered Tilly.

"Vicar has his butter fra Brown's by rights," said the insuppressible servant-woman. "We s'll be churnin' tomorrow mornin' first thing."

"Yes"—the long-drawn foreign yes—"Yes," said the Polish woman, "I went to Mrs Brown's. She hasn't any more."

Tilly bridled her head, bursting to say that, according to the etiquette of people who bought butter, it was no sort of manners whatever coming to a place as cool as you like and knocking at the front door asking for a pound as a stop-gap while your other people were short. If you go to Brown's you go to Brown's, an' my butter isn't just to make shift when Brown's has got none.

Brangwen understood perfectly this unspoken speech of Tilly's. The Polish lady did not. And as she wanted butter for the vicar, and as Tilly was churning in the morning, she waited.

"Sluther up now," said Brangwen loudly after this silence had resolved itself out; and Tilly disappeared through the inner door.

"I am afraid that I should not come, so," said the stranger, looking at him inquiringly, as if referring to him for what it was usual to do.

He felt confused.

"How's that?" he said, trying to be genial and being only protective.

"Do you—?" she began deliberately. But she was not sure of her ground, and the conversation came to an end. Her eyes looked at him all the while, because she could not speak the language.

They stood facing each other. The dog walked away from her to him. He bent down to it.

"And how's your little girl?" he asked.

"Yes, thank you, she is very well," was the reply, a phrase of polite speech in a foreign language, merely.

"Sit you down," he said.

And she sat in a chair, her slim arms, coming through the slits of her cloak, resting on her lap.

"You're not used to these parts," he said, still standing on the hearthrug with his back to the fire, coatless, looking with curious directness at the woman. Her self-possession pleased him and inspired him, set him curiously free. It seemed to him almost brutal to feel so master of himself and of the situation.

Her eyes rested on him for a moment, questioning, as she thought of the meaning of his speech.

"No," she said, understanding. "No—it is strange."

"You find it middlin' rough?" he said.

"—a— —" Her eyes waited on him, so that he should say it again.

"Our ways are rough to you," he repeated.

"Yes—yes, I understand. Yes, it is different, it is strange. But I was in Yorkshire—"

"Oh well then," he said, "it's no worse here than what they are up there."

She did not quite understand. His protective manner, and his sureness, and his intimacy, puzzled her. What did he mean? If he was her equal, why did he behave so without formality?

"No—" she said, vaguely, her eyes resting on him.

She saw him fresh and naïve, uncouth, almost entirely beyond relationship with her. Yet he was good-looking, with his fair hair and blue eyes full of energy, and with his healthy body that seemed to take equality with her. She watched him steadily. He was difficult for her to understand, warm, uncouth, and confident as he was, sure on his feet as if he did not know what it was to be unsure. What then was it that gave him this curious stability?

She did not know. She wondered. She looked round the room he lived in. It had a close intimacy that fascinated and almost frightened her. The furniture was old and familiar as old people, the whole place seemed so kin to him, as if it partook of his being, that she was uneasy.

"It is already a long time that you have lived in this house—yes?" she asked.

"I've always lived here," he said.

"Yes—but your people—your family?"

"We've been here above *two* hundred years," he said.

Her eyes were on him all the time, wide-open and trying to grasp him. He felt that he was there for her.

"It is your own place, the house, the farm—?"

"Yes," he said.

He looked down at her and met her look. It disturbed her. She did not know him. He was a foreigner, they had nothing to do with each other. Yet his look disturbed her to knowledge of him. He was so strangely confident and direct.

"You live quite alone?"

"Yes—if you call it alone."

She did not understand. It seemed unusual to her. What was the meaning of it?

And whenever her eyes, after watching him for some time, inevitably met his, she was aware of a heat beating up over her consciousness. She sat motionless and in conflict. Who was this strange man who was at once so near to her? What was happening to her? Something in his young, warm-twinkling eyes seemed to assume a right to her, to speak to her, to extend her his protection. But how? Why did he speak to her! Why were his eyes so certain, so full of light and confident, waiting for no permission nor signal.

Tilly returned with a large leaf and found the two silent. At once he felt it incumbent on him to speak, now the serving-woman had come back.

"How old is your little girl?" he asked.

"Four years," she replied.

"Her father hasn't been dead long, then?" he asked.

"She was one year when he died."

"Three years?"

"Yes, three years that he is dead—yes."

Curiously quiet she was, almost abstracted, answering these questions. She looked at him again, with some maidenhood opening in her eyes. He felt he could not move, neither towards her nor away from her. Something about her presence hurt him, till he was almost rigid before her. He saw the girl's wondering look rise in her eyes.

Tilly handed her the butter, and she rose.

"Thank you very much," she said. "How much is it?"

"We'll make th' vicar a present of it," he said. "It'll do for me goin' to church."

"It 'ud look better of you if you went to church and took th' money for your butter," said Tilly, persistent in her claim to him.

"You'd have to put in, shouldn't you?" he said.

"How much, please?" said the Polish woman to Tilly.

Brangwen stood by and let be.

"Then, thank you very much," she said.

"Bring your little girl down sometime to look at th' fowls and horses," he said; "—if she'd like it."

"Yes, she would like it," said the stranger.

And she went. Brangwen stood dimmed by her departure. He could not notice Tilly, who was looking at him uneasily, wanting to be reassured. He could not think of anything. He felt that he had made some invisible connection with the strange woman.

A daze had come over his mind, he had another centre of consciousness. In his breast, or in his bowels, somewhere in his body, there had started another activity. It was as if a strong light were burning there, and he was blind within it, unable to know anything, except that this transfiguration burned between him and her, connecting them, like a secret power.

Since she had come to the house he went about in a daze, scarcely seeing even the things he handled, drifting, quiescent, in a state of metamorphosis. He submitted to that which was happening to him, letting go of his will, suffering the loss of himself, dormant always on the brink of ecstasy, like a creature evolving to a new birth.

She came twice with her child to the farm, but there was this lull between them, an intense calm and passivity like a torpor upon them, so that no active change took place. He was almost unaware of the child, yet by his native good-humour he gained her confidence, even her affection, setting her on the horse to ride, giving her corn for the fowls.

Once he drove the mother and child from Ilkeston, picking them up on the road. The child huddled close to him as if for love, the mother sat very still. There was a vagueness, like a soft mist over all of them, and a silence as if their wills were suspended. Only he saw her hands, ungloved, folded in her lap, and he noticed the wedding-ring on her finger. It excluded him: it was a closed circle. It bound her life, the wedding-ring, it stood for her life in which he could have no part. Nevertheless, beyond all this, there was herself and himself which should meet.

As he helped her down from the trap, almost lifting her, he felt he had some right to take her thus between his hands. She belonged as yet to that other, to that which was behind. But he must care for her also. She was too living to be neglected.

Sometimes her vagueness, in which he was lost, made him angry, made him rage. But he held himself still as yet. She had no response, no being towards him. It puzzled and enraged him, but he submitted for a long time. Then, from the accumulated troubling of her ignoring him, gradually a fury broke out, destructive, and he wanted to go away, to escape her.

It happened she came down to the Marsh with the child whilst he was in this state. Then he stood over against her, strong and heavy in his revolt, and though he said nothing, still she felt his anger and heavy impatience grip hold of her, she was shaken again as out of a torpor. Again her heart stirred with a quick, out-running impulse, she looked at him, at the stranger who was not a gentleman yet who insisted on coming into her life, and the pain of a new birth in herself strung all her veins to a new form. She would have to begin again, to find a new being, a new form, to respond to that blind, insistent figure standing over against her.

A shiver, a sickness of new birth passed over her, the flame leaped up him, under his skin. She wanted it, this new life from him, with him, yet she must defend herself against it, for it was a destruction.

As he worked alone on the land, or sat up with his ewes at lambing time, the facts and material of his daily life fell away, leaving the kernel of his purpose clean. And then it came upon him that he would marry her and she would be his life.

Gradually, even without seeing her, he came to know her. He would have liked to think of her as of something given into his protection, like a child without parents. But it was forbidden him. He had to come down from this pleasant view of the case. She might refuse him. And besides, he was afraid of her.

But during the long February nights with the ewes in labour, looking out from the shelter into the flashing stars, he knew he did not belong to himself. He must admit that he was only fragmentary, something incomplete and subject. There were the stars in the dark heaven travelling, the whole host passing by on some eternal voyage. So he sat small and submissive to the greater ordering.

Unless she would come to him, he must remain as a nothingness. It was a hard experience. But, after her repeated obliviousness to him, after he had seen so often that he did not exist for her, after he had raged and tried to escape, and said he was good enough by himself, he was a man, and could stand alone, he must, in the starry multiplicity of the night humble himself, and admit and know that without her he was nothing.

He was nothing. But with her, he would be real. If she were now walking across the frosty grass near the sheep-shelter, through the fretful bleating of the ewes and lambs, she would bring him completeness and perfection. And if it should be so, that she should come to him! It should be so—it was ordained so.

He was a long time resolving definitely to ask her to marry him. And he knew, if he asked her, she must really acquiesce. She must, it could not be otherwise.

He had learned a little of her. She was poor, quite alone, and had had a hard time in London, both before and after her husband died. But in Poland she was a lady well born, a landowner's daughter.

All these things were only words to him, the fact of her superior birth, the fact that her husband had been a brilliant doctor, the fact that he himself was her inferior in almost every way of distinction. There was an inner reality, a logic of the soul, which connected her with him.

One evening in March, when the wind was roaring outside, came the moment to ask her. He had sat with his hands before him leaning to the fire. And as he watched the fire, he knew almost without thinking that he was going this evening.

"Have you got a clean shirt?" he asked Tilly.

"You know you've got clean shirts," she said.

"Ay,—bring me a white one."

Tilly brought down one of the linen shirts he had inherited from his father, putting it before him to air at the fire. She loved him with a dumb, aching love as he sat leaning with his arms on his knees, still and absorbed, unaware of her. Lately, a quivering inclination to cry had come over her, when she did anything for him in his presence. Now her hands trembled as she spread the shirt. He was never shouting and teasing now. The deep stillness there was in the house made her tremble.

He went to wash himself. Queer little breaks of consciousness seemed to rise and burst like bubbles out of the depths of his stillness.

"It's got to be done," he said as he stooped to take the shirt out of the fender, "it's got to be done, so why balk it?" And as he combed his hair before the mirror on the wall, he retorted to himself, superficially: "The woman's not speechless dumb. She's not clutterin' at the nipple. She's got the right to please herself, and displease whosoever she likes."

This streak of commonsense carried him a little further.

"Did you want anythink?" asked Tilly, suddenly appearing, having heard him speak. She stood watching him comb his fair beard. His eyes were calm and uninterrupted.

"Ay," he said, "where have you put the scissors."

She brought them to him, and stood watching as, chin forward, he trimmed his beard.

"Don't go an' crop yourself as if you was at a shearin' contest," she said, anxiously. He blew the fine-curled hair quickly off his lips.

He put on all clean clothes, folded his stock carefully, and donned his best coat. Then, being ready, as grey twilight was falling, he went across to the orchard to gather the daffodils. The wind was roaring in the apple-trees, the yellow flowers swayed violently up and down, he heard even the fine whisper of their spears as he stooped to break the flattened, brittle stems of the flowers.

"What's to-do?" shouted a friend who met him as he left the garden gate.

"Bit of courtin', like," said Brangwen.

And Tilly, in a great state of trepidation and excitement, let the wind whisk her over the field to the big gate, whence she could watch him go.

He went up the hill and on towards the vicarage, the wind roaring through the hedges, whilst he tried to shelter his bunch of daffodils by his side. He did not think of anything, only knew that the wind was blowing.

Night was falling, the bare trees drummed and whistled. The vicar, he knew, would be in his study, the Polish woman in the kitchen, a comfortable room, with her child. In the darkest of twilight, he went through the gate and down the path where a few daffodils stooped in the wind, and shattered crocuses made a pale, colourless ravel.

There was a light streaming on to the bushes at the back from the kitchen window. He began to hesitate. How could he do this? Looking through the window, he saw her seated in the rocking chair with the child, already in its nightdress, sitting on her knee. The fair head with its wild, fierce hair was drooping towards the fire-warmth, which reflected on the bright cheeks and clear skin of the child, who seemed to be musing, almost like a grown-up person. The mother's face was dark and still, and he saw, with a pang, that she was away back in the life that had been. The child's hair gleamed like spun glass, her face was illuminated till it seemed like wax lit up from the inside. The wind boomed strongly. Mother and child sat motionless, silent, the child staring with vacant dark eyes into the fire, the mother looking into space. The little girl was almost asleep. It was her will which kept her eyes so wide.

Suddenly she looked round, troubled, as the wind shook the house, and Brangwen saw the small lips move. The mother began to rock, he heard the slight crunch of the rockers of the chair. Then he heard the low, monotonous murmur of a song in a foreign language. Then a great burst of wind, the mother seemed to have drifted away, the child's eyes were black and dilated. Brangwen looked up at the clouds which packed in great, alarming haste across the dark sky.

Then there came the child's high, complaining, yet imperative voice:

"Don't sing that stuff, mother, I don't want to hear it."

The singing died away.

"You will go to bed," said the mother.

He saw the clinging protest of the child, the unmoved far-awayness of the mother, the clinging, grasping effort of the child. Then suddenly the clear childish challenge:

"I want you to tell me a story."

The wind blew, the story began, the child nestled against the mother, Brangwen waited outside, suspended, looking at the wild waving of the trees in the wind and the gathering darkness. He had his fate to follow, he lingered here at the threshold.

The child crouched distinct and motionless, curled in against her mother, the eyes dark and unblinking among the keen fleece of hair, like a curled up animal asleep but for the eyes. The mother sat as if in shadow, the story went on as if by itself. Brangwen stood outside seeing the night fall. He did not notice the passage of time. The hand that held the daffodils was fixed and cold.

The story came to an end, the mother rose at last, with the child clinging round her neck. She must be strong, to carry so large a child so easily. The little Anna clung round her mother's neck. The fair, strange face of the child looked over the shoulder of the mother, all asleep but the eyes, and these, wide and dark, kept up the resistance and the fight with something unseen.

When they were gone, Brangwen stirred for the first time from the place where he stood, and looked round at the night. He wished it were really as beautiful and familiar as it seemed in these few moments of release. Along with the child, he felt a curious strain on him, a suffering, like a fate.

The mother came down again, and began folding the child's clothes. He knocked. She opened wondering, a little bit at bay, like a foreigner, uneasy.

"Good-evening," he said. "I'll just come in a minute."

A change went quickly over her face; she was unprepared. She looked down at him as he stood in the light from the window, holding the daffodils, the darkness behind. In his black clothes she again did not know him, she was almost afraid.

But he was already stepping on to the threshold, and closing the door behind him. She turned into the kitchen, startled out of herself by this invasion from the night. He took off his hat, and came towards her. Then he stood in the light, in his black clothes and his black stock, hat in one hand and yellow flowers in the other. She stood away, at his mercy, snatched out of herself. She did not know him, only she knew he was a man come for her. She could only see the dark-clad man's figure standing there upon her, and the gripped fist of flowers. She could not see the face and the living eyes.

He was watching her, without knowing her, only aware underneath of her presence.

"I come to have a word with you," he said, striding forward to the table, laying down his hat and the flowers, which tumbled apart and lay in a loose heap. She had flinched from his advance. She had no will, no being. The wind boomed in the chimney, and he waited. He had disembarrassed his hands. Now he shut his fists.

He was aware of her standing there unknown, dread, yet related to him.

"I came up," he said, speaking curiously matter-of-fact and level, "to ask if you'd marry me. You are free, aren't you?"

There was a long silence, whilst his blue eyes, strangely impersonal, looked into her eyes to seek an answer to the truth. He was looking for the truth out of her. And she, as if hypnotised, must answer at length:

"Yes. I am free to marry."

The expression of his eyes changed, became less impersonal, as if he were looking almost at her, for the truth of her. Steady and intent and eternal they were, as if they would never change. They seemed to fix and to resolve her. She quivered, feeling herself created, will-less, lapsing into him, into a common will with him.

"You want me?" she said.

A pallor came over his face.

"Yes," he said.

Still there was suspense and silence.

"No," she said, not of herself. "No, I don't know."

He felt the tension breaking up in him, his fists slackened, he was unable to move. He stood looking at her, helpless in his vague collapse. For the moment she had become unreal to him. Then he saw her come to him, curiously direct and as if without movement, in a sudden flow. She put her hand to his coat.

"Yes I want to," she said, impersonally, looking at him with wide, candid, newly-opened eyes, opened now with supreme truth. He went very white as he stood, and did not move, only his eyes were held by hers, and he suffered. She seemed to see him with her newly-opened, wide eyes, almost of a child, and with a strange movement, that was agony to him, she reached slowly forward her dark face and her breast to him, with a slow insinuation of a kiss that made something break in his brain, and it was darkness over him for a few moments.

He had her in his arms, and, obliterated, was kissing her. And it was sheer, blenched agony to him, to break away from himself. She was there so small and light and accepting in his arms, like a child, and yet with such an insinuation of embrace, of infinite embrace, that he could not bear it, he could not stand.

44

He turned and looked for a chair, and keeping her still in his arms, sat down with her close to him, to his breast. Then, for a few seconds, he went utterly to sleep, asleep and sealed in the darkest sleep, utter, extreme oblivion.

From which he came to gradually, always holding her warm and close upon him, and she as utterly silent as he, involved in the same oblivion, the fecund darkness.

He returned gradually, but newly created, as after a gestation, a new birth, in the womb of darkness. Aërial and light everything was, new as a morning, fresh and newly begun. Like a dawn the newness and the bliss filled in. And she sat utterly still with him, as if in the same.

Then she looked up at him, the wide, young eyes blazing with light. And he bent down and kissed her on the lips. And the dawn blazed in them, their new life came to pass, it was beyond all conceiving good, it was so good, that it was almost like a passing-away, a trespass. He drew her suddenly close to him.

For soon the light began to fade in her, gradually, and as she was in his arms, her head sank, she leaned it against him, and lay still, with sunk head, a little tired, effaced because she was tired. And in her tiredness was a certain negation of him.

"There is the child," she said, out of the long silence.

He did not understand. It was a long time since he had heard a voice. Now also he heard the wind roaring, as if it had just begun again.

"Yes," he said, not understanding. There was a slight contraction of pain at his heart, a slight tension on his brows. Something he wanted to grasp and could not.

"You will love her?" she said.

The quick contraction, like pain, went over him again.

"I love her now," he said.

She lay still against him, taking his physical warmth without heed. It was great confirmation for him to feel her there, absorbing the warmth from him, giving him back her weight and her strange confidence. But where was she, that she seemed so absent? His mind was open with wonder. He did not know her.

"But I am much older than you," she said.

"How old?" he asked.

"I am thirty four," she said.

"I am twenty eight," he said.

45

"Six years."

She was oddly concerned, even as if it pleased her a little. He sat and listened and wondered. It was rather splendid, to be so ignored by her, whilst she lay against him, and he lifted her with his breathing, and felt her weight upon his living, so he had a completeness and an inviolable power. He did not interfere with her. He did not even know her. It was so strange that she lay there with her weight abandoned upon him. He was silent with delight. He felt strong, physically, carrying her on his breathing. The strange, inviolable completeness of the two of them made him feel as sure and as stable as God. Amused, he wondered what the vicar would say if he knew.

"You needn't stop here much longer, housekeeping," he said.

"I like it also, here," she said. "When one has been in many places, it is very nice here."

He was silent again at this. So close on him she lay, and yet she answered him from so far away. But he did not mind.

"What was your own home like, when you were little?" he asked.

"My father was a landowner," she replied. "It was near a river."

This did not convey much to him. All was as vague as before. But he did not care, whilst she was so close.

"I am a landowner—a little one," he said.

"Yes," she said.

He had not dared to move. He sat there with his arms round her, her lying motionless on his breathing, and for a long time he did not stir. Then softly, timidly, his hand settled on the roundness of her arm, on the unknown. She seemed to lie a little closer. A hot flame licked up from his belly to his chest.

But it was too soon. She rose, and went across the room to a drawer, taking out a little tray-cloth. There was something quiet and professional about her. She had been a nurse beside her husband, both in Warsaw and in the rebellion afterwards. She proceeded to set a tray. It was as if she ignored Brangwen. He sat up, unable to bear a contradiction in her. She moved about inscrutably.

Then, as he sat there, all unused and wondering, she came near to him, looking at him with wide, grey eyes that almost smiled with a low light. But her ugly-beautiful mouth was still unmoved and sad. He was afraid.

His eyes, strained and roused with unusedness, quailed a little before her, he felt himself quailing and yet he rose, as if obedient, and as if obedient to her, he bent and kissed her heavy, sad, wide mouth, that was kissed, and did not alter. Fear was too strong in him. Again he had not got her.

She turned away. The vicarage kitchen was untidy, and yet to him beautiful with the untidiness of her and her child. Such a wonderful remoteness there was about her, and then something in touch with him, that made his heart knock in his chest. He stood there and waited, suspended.

Again she came to him, as he stood in his black clothes, with blue eyes very bright and puzzled for her, his face tensely alive, his hair dishevelled. She came close up to him, to his intent, black-clothed body, and laid her hand on his arm. He remained unmoved. Her eyes, with a blackness of memory struggling with passion, primitive and electric away at the back of them, rejected him and absorbed him at once. But he remained himself. He breathed with difficulty, and sweat came out at the roots of his hair, on his forehead.

"Do you want to marry me?" she asked slowly, always uncertain.

He was afraid lest he could not speak. He drew breath hard, saying:

"I do."

Then again, what was agony to him, with one hand lightly resting on his arm, she leaned forward a little, and with a strange, primeval suggestion of embrace, held him her mouth. It was ugly-beautiful, and he could not bear it. He put his mouth on hers, and slowly, slowly the response came, gathering force and passion, till it seemed to him she was thundering at him till he could bear no more. He drew away, white, unbreathing. Only, in his blue eyes, was something of himself concentrated. And in her eyes was a little smile upon a black void.

She was drifting away from him again. And he wanted to go away. It was intolerable. He could bear no more. He must go. Yet he was irresolute. But she turned away from him.

With a little pang of anguish, of denial, it was decided.

"I'll come an' speak to the vicar tomorrow," he said, taking his hat.

She looked at him, her eyes expressionless and full of darkness. He could see no answer.

"That'll do, won't it?" he said.

"Yes," she answered, mere echo without body or meaning.

"Goodnight," he said.

"Goodnight."

He left her standing there, expressionless and void as she was. Then she went on laying the tray for the vicar. Needing the table, she put the daffodils aside on the dresser without noticing them. Only their coolness, touching her hand, remained echoing there a long while.

They were such strangers, they must forever be such strangers, that his passion was a clanging torment to him. Such intimacy of embrace, and such utter foreignness of contact! It was unbearable. He could not bear to be near her, and know the utter foreignness between them, know how entirely they were strangers to each other. He went out into the wind. Big holes were blown into the sky, the moonlight blew about. Sometimes a high moon, liquid-brilliant, scudded across a hollow space and took cover under electric, brown-iridescent cloud-edges. Then there was a blot of cloud, and shadow. Then somewhere in the night a radiance again, like a vapour. And all the sky was teeming and tearing along, a vast disorder of flying shapes and darknesses and ragged fumes of light and a great brown circling halo, then the terror of a moon running liquid-brilliant into the open for a moment, hurting the eyes before she plunged under cover of cloud again.

CHAPTER II

They Live at the Marsh

She was the daughter of a Polish landowner who, deeply in debt to the Jews, had married a German wife with money, and who had died just before the rebellion. Quite young, she had married Paul Lensky, an intellectual who had studied at Berlin, and had returned to Warsaw a patriot. Her mother had married a German merchant and gone away.

Lydia Lensky, married to the young doctor, became with him a patriot and an émancipée. They were poor, but they were very conceited. She learned nursing as a mark of her emancipation. They represented in Poland the new movement just begun in Russia. But they were very patriotic: and, at the same time, very "European."

They had two children. Then came the great rebellion. Lensky, very ardent and full of words, went about inciting his countrymen. Little Poles flamed down the streets of Warsaw, on the way to shoot every Muscovite. So they crossed into the south of Russia, and it was common for six little insurgents to ride into a Jewish village, brandishing swords and words, emphasising the fact that they were going to shoot every living Muscovite.

Lensky was something of a fire-eater also. Lydia, tempered by her German blood, coming of a different family, was obliterated, carried along in her husband's emphasis of declaration, and his whirl of patriotism. He was indeed a brave man, but no bravery could quite have equalled the vividness of his talk. He worked very hard, till nothing lived in him but his eyes. And Lydia, as if drugged, followed him like a shadow, serving, echoing. Sometimes she had her two children, sometimes they were left behind.

She returned once to find them both dead of diphtheria. Her husband wept aloud, unaware of everybody. But the war went on, and soon he was back at his work. A darkness had come over Lydia's mind. She walked always in a shadow, silenced, with a strange, deep terror having hold of her, her desire was to seek satisfaction in dread, to enter a nunnery, to satisfy the instincts of dread in her through service of a dark religion. But she could not.

Then came the flight to London. Lensky, the little, thin man, had got all his life locked into a resistance and could not relax again. He lived in a sort of insane irritability, touchy, haughty to the last degree, fractious, so that as assistant doctor in one of the hospitals he soon became impossible. They were almost beggars. But he kept still his great ideas of himself, he seemed to live in a complete hallucination, where he himself figured vivid and lordly. He guarded his wife jealously against the ignominy of her position, rushed round her like a brandished weapon, an amazing sight to the English eye, had her in his power, as if he hypnotised her. She was passive, dark, always in shadow.

He was wasting away. Already when the child was born he seemed nothing but skin and bone and fixed idea. She watched him dying, nursed him, nursed the baby, but really took no notice of anything. A darkness was on her, like remorse, or like a remembering of the dark, savage, mystic ride of dread, of death, of the shadow of revenge. When her husband died, she was relieved. He would no longer dart about her.

England fitted her mood, its aloofness and foreignness. She had known a little of the language before coming, and a sort of parrot-mind made her pick it up fairly easily. But she knew nothing of the English, nor of English life. Indeed, these did not exist for her. She was like one walking in the Underworld, where the shades throng intelligibly but have no connection with one. She felt the English people as a potent, cold, slightly hostile host amongst whom she walked isolated.

The English people themselves were most deferential to her, the Church saw that she did not want. She walked without passion, like a shade, tormented into moments of love by the child. Her dying husband with his tortured eyes and the skin drawn tight over his face, he was as a vision to her, not a reality. In a vision he was buried and put away. Then the vision ceased, she was untroubled, time went on grey, uncoloured, like a long journey where she sat unconscious as the landscape unrolled beside her. When she rocked her baby at evening, maybe she fell into a Polish slumber song, or she talked sometimes to herself in Polish. Otherwise she did not think of Poland, nor of that life to which she had belonged. It was a great blot looming blank in its darkness. In the superficial activity of her life, she was all English. She even thought in English. But her long blanks and darknesses of abstraction were Polish.

So she lived for some time. Then, with slight uneasiness, she used half to awake to the streets of London. She realised that there was something around her, very foreign, she realised she was in a strange place. And then, she was sent away into the country. There came into her mind now the memory of her home where she had been a child, the big house among the land, the peasants of the village.

She was sent to Yorkshire, to nurse an old rector in his rectory by the sea. This was the first shake of the kaleidoscope that brought in front of her eyes something she must see. It hurt her brain, the open country and the moors. It hurt her and hurt her. Yet it forced itself upon her as something living, it roused some potency of her childhood in her, it had some relation to her.

There was green and silver and blue in the air about her now. And there was a strange insistence of light from the sea, to which she must attend. Primroses glimmered around, many of them, and she stooped to the disturbing influence near her feet, she even picked one or two flowers, faintly remembering in the new colour of life, what had been. All the day long, as she sat at the upper window, the light came off the sea, constantly, constantly, without refusal, till it seemed to bear her away, and the noise of the sea created a drowsiness in her, a relaxation like sleep. Her automatic consciousness gave way a little, she stumbled sometimes, she had a poignant, momentary vision of her living child, that hurt her unspeakably. Her soul roused to attention.

Very strange was the constant glitter of the sea unsheathed in heaven, very warm and sweet the graveyard, in a nook of the hill catching the sunshine and holding it as one holds a bee between the palms of the hands, when it is benumbed. Grey grass and lichens and a little church, and snowdrops among coarse grass, and a cupful of incredibly warm sunshine.

She was troubled in spirit. Hearing the rushing of the beck away down under the trees, she was startled, and wondered what it was. Walking down, she found the bluebells around her glowing like a presence, among the trees.

Summer came, the moors were tangled with harebells like water in the ruts of the roads, the heather came rosy under the skies, setting the whole world awake. And she was uneasy. She went past the gorse bushes shrinking from their presence, she stepped into the heather as into a quickening bath that almost hurt. Her fingers moved over the clasped fingers of the child, she heard the anxious voice of the baby, as it tried to make her talk, distraught.

And she shrank away again, back into her darkness, and for a long while remained blotted safely away from living. But autumn came with the faint red glimmer of robins singing, winter darkened the moors, and almost savagely she turned again to life, demanding her life back again, demanding that it should be as it had been when she was a girl, on the land at home, under the sky. Snow lay in great expanses, the telegraph posts strode over the white earth, away under the gloom of the sky. And savagely her desire rose in her again, demanding that this was Poland, her youth, that all was her own again.

But there were no sledges nor bells, she did not see the peasants coming out like new people, in their sheepskins and their fresh, ruddy, bright faces, that seemed to become new and vivid when the snow lit up the ground. It did not come to her, the life of her youth, it did not come back. There was a little agony of struggle, then a relapse into the darkness of the convent, where Satan and the devils raged round the walls, and Christ was white on the cross of victory.

She watched from the sick-room the snow whirl past, like flocks of shadows in haste, flying on some final mission out to a leaden, inalterable sea, beyond the final whiteness of the curving shore, and the snow-speckled blackness of the rocks half-submerged. But near at hand on the trees the snow was soft in bloom. Only the voice of the dying vicar spoke grey and querulous from behind.

By the time the snowdrops were out, however, he was dead. He was dead. But with curious equanimity the returning woman watched the snowdrops on the edge of the grass below, blown white in the wind, but not to be blown away. She watched them fluttering and bobbing, the white, shut flowers, anchored by a thread to the grey-green grass, yet never blown away, not drifting with the wind.

As she rose in the morning, the dawn was beating up white, gusts of light blown like a thin snowstorm from the east, blown stronger and fiercer, till the rose appeared, and the gold, and the sea lit up below. She was impassive and indifferent. Yet she was outside the enclosure of darkness.

There passed a space of shadow again, the familiarity of dread-worship, during which she was moved oblivious to Cossethay. There, at first, there was nothing—just grey nothing. But then one morning there was a light from the yellow jasmine caught her, and after that, morning and evening, the persistent ringing of thrushes from the shrubbery, till her heart, beaten upon, was forced to lift up its voice in rivalry and answer. Little tunes came into her mind. She was full of trouble almost like anguish. Resistant, she knew she was beaten, and from fear of darkness turned to fear of light. She would have hidden herself indoors, if she could. Above all, she craved for the peace and heavy oblivion of her old state. She could not bear to come to, to realise. The first pangs of this new parturition were so acute, she knew she could not bear it. She would rather remain out of life, than be torn, mutilated into this birth, which she could not survive. She had not the strength to come to life now, in England, so foreign, skies so hostile. She knew she would die like an early, colourless, scentless flower that the end of the winter puts forth mercilessly. And she wanted to harbour her modicum of twinkling life.

But a sunshiny day came full of the scent of a mezereon tree, when bees were tumbling into the yellow crocuses, and she forgot, she felt like somebody else, not herself, a new person, quite glad. But she knew it was fragile, and she dreaded it. The vicar put pea-flour into the crocuses, for his bees to roll in, and she laughed. Then night came, with brilliant stars that she knew of old, from her girlhood. And they flashed so bright, she knew they were victors.

She could neither wake nor sleep. As if crushed between the past and the future, like a flower that comes above-ground to find a great stone lying above it, she was helpless.

The bewilderment and helplessness continued, she felt surrounded by great moving masses that must crush her. And there was no escape. Save in the old obliviousness, the cold darkness she strove to retain. But the vicar showed her eggs in the thrush's nest near the back door. She saw herself the mother-thrush upon the nest, and the way her wings were spread, so eager down upon her secret. The tense, eager, nesting wings moved her beyond endurance. She thought of them in the morning, when she heard the thrush whistling as he got up, and she thought "Why didn't I die out there, why am I brought here?"

She was aware of people who passed around her, not as persons, but as looming presences. It was very difficult for her to adjust herself. In Poland, the peasantry, the people, had been cattle to her, they had been her cattle that she owned and used. What were these people? Now she was coming awake, she was lost.

53

But she had felt Brangwen go by almost as if he had brushed her. She had tingled in body as she had gone on up the road. After she had been with him in the Marsh kitchen, the voice of her body had risen strong and insistent. Soon, she wanted him. He was the man who had come nearest to her for her awakening.

Always, however, between-whiles she lapsed into the old unconsciousness, indifference, and there was a will in her, to save herself from living any more. But she would wake in the morning one day and feel her blood running, feel herself lying open like a flower unsheathed in the sun, insistent and potent with demand.

She got to know him better, and her instinct fixed on him—just on him. Her impulse was strong against him, because he was not of her own sort. But one blind instinct led her, to take him, to have him, and then to relinquish herself to him. It would be safety. She felt the rooted safety of him, and the life in him. Also he was young and very fresh. The blue, steady livingness of his eyes she enjoyed like morning. He was very young.

Then she lapsed again to stupor and indifference. This, however, was bound to pass. The warmth flowed through her, she felt herself opening, unfolding, asking, as a flower opens in full request under the sun, as the beaks of tiny birds open flat to receive, to receive. And unfolded she turned to him, straight to him. And he came, slowly, afraid, held back by uncouth fear, and driven by a desire bigger than himself.

When she opened and turned to him, then all that had been and all that was, was gone from her, she was as new as a flower that unsheathes itself and stands always ready, waiting, receptive. He could not understand this. He forced himself, through lack of understanding, to an adherence to the line of honorable courtship and sanctioned, licensed marriage. Thereafter, after he had gone to the vicarage and asked for her, she remained for some days held in this one spell, open, receptive to him, before him. He was roused to chaos. He spoke to the vicar and gave in the banns. Then he stood to wait.

She remained attentive and instinctively expectant before him, unfolded, ready to receive him. He could not act, because of self-fear and because of his conception of honor towards her. So he remained in a state of chaos.

And after a few days, gradually she closed again, away from him, was sheathed over, impervious to him, oblivious. Then a black, bottomless despair became real to him, he knew what he had lost. He felt he had lost it for good, he knew what it was to have been in communication with her, and to be cast off again. In misery, his heart like a heavy stone, he went about unliving.

Till gradually he became desperate, lost his understanding, was plunged in a revolt that knew no bounds. Inarticulate, he moved with her at the Marsh in violent, gloomy, wordless passion, almost in hatred of her. Till gradually, she became aware of him, aware of herself with regard to him, her blood stirred to life, she began to open towards him, to flow towards him again. He waited, till the spell was between them again, till they were together within one rushing, hastening flame. And then again he was bewildered, he was tied up as with cords, and could not move to her. So she came to him, and unfastened the breast of his waistcoat and his shirt, and put her hand on him, needing to know him. For it was cruel to her, to be open and offered to him, yet not to know what he was, not even that he was there. She gave herself to the hour, but he could not, and he bungled in taking her.

So that he lived in suspense, as if only half his faculties worked, until the wedding. She did not understand. But the vagueness came over her again, and the days lapsed by. He could not get definitely into touch with her. For the time being, she let him go again.

He suffered very much from the thought of actual marriage, the intimacy and nakedness of marriage. He knew her so little. They were so foreign to each other, they were such strangers. And they could not talk to each other. When she talked, of Poland or of what had been, it was all so foreign, she scarcely communicated anything to him. And when he looked at her, an over-much reverence and fear of the unknown changed the nature of his desire into a sort of worship, holding her aloof from his physical desire, self-thwarting.

She did not know this, she did not understand. They had looked at each other, and had accepted each other. It was so, then there was nothing to balk at, it was complete between them.

At the wedding, his face was stiff and expressionless. He wanted to drink, to get rid of his forethought and afterthought, to set the moment free. But he could not. The suspense only tightened at his heart. The jesting and joviality and jolly, broad insinuation of the guests only coiled him more. He could not hear. That which was impending obsessed him, he could not get free.

She sat quiet, with a strange, still smile. She was not afraid.

Having accepted him, she wanted to take him, she belonged altogether to the hour, now. No future, no past, only this, her hour. She
did not even notice him, as she sat beside him at the head of the
table. He was very near, their coming together was close at hand.
What more!

As the time came for all the guests to go, her dark face was softly
lighted, the bend of her head was proud, her grey eyes clear and
dilated, so that the men could not look at her, and the women were
elated by her, they served her. Very wonderful she was, as she bade
farewell, her ugly wide mouth smiling with pride and recognition,
her voice speaking softly and richly in the foreign accent, her dilated
eyes ignoring one and all the departing guests. Her manner was
gracious and fascinating, but she ignored the being of him or her to
whom she gave her hand.

And Brangwen stood beside her, giving his hearty handshake to
his friends, receiving their regard gratefully, glad of their attention.
His heart was tormented within him, he did not try to smile. The
time of his trial and his admittance, his Gethsemane and his
Triumphal Entry in one, had come now.

Behind her, there was so much unknown to him. When he
approached her, he came to such a terrible painful unknown. How
could he embrace it and fathom it? How could he close his arms
round all this darkness and hold it to his breast and give himself to
it? What might not happen to him? If he stretched and strained for
ever he would never be able to grasp it all. And to yield himself
naked out of his own hands into an unknown power! How could a
man be strong enough to take her, put his arms round her and
have her, and be sure he could conquer this awful unknown next
his heart? What was it then that she was, to which he must also
deliver himself up, and which at the same time he must embrace,
contain?

He was to be her husband. It was established so. And he wanted it
more than he wanted life, or anything. She stood beside him in her
silk dress, looking at him, strangely, so that a certain terror, horror
took possession of him, because she was strange and impending and
he had no choice. He could not bear to meet her look from under her
strange, thick brows.

"Is it late?" she said.

He looked at his watch.

"No—half past eleven," he said. And he made an excuse to go

into the kitchen, leaving her standing in the room among the disorder and the drinking-glasses.

Tilly was seated beside the fire in the kitchen, her head in her hands. She started up when he entered.

"Why haven't you gone to bed?" he said.

"I thought I'd better stop an' lock up an' do," she said.

Her agitation quieted him. He gave her some little order, then returned, steadied now, almost ashamed, to his wife. She stood a moment watching him, as he moved with averted face. Then she said:

"You will be good to me, won't you?"

She was small and girlish and terrible, with a queer, wide look in her eyes. His heart leaped in him, in anguish of love and desire, he went blindly to her and took her in his arms.

"I want to," he said, as he drew her closer and closer in. She was soothed by the stress of his embrace, and remained quite still, relaxed against him, mingling in to him. And he let himself go from past and future, was reduced to the moment with her. In which he took her and was with her and there was nothing beyond, they were together in an elemental embrace beyond their superficial foreignness. But in the morning he was uneasy again. She was still foreign and unknown to him. Only, within the fear was pride, belief in himself as mate for her. And she, everything forgotten in her new hour of coming to life, radiated vigour and joy, so that he quivered to touch her.

It made a great difference to him, marriage. Things became so remote and of so little significance, as he knew the powerful source of his life, his eyes opened on a new universe, and he wondered in thinking of his triviality before. A new, calm relationship showed to him in the things he saw, in the cattle he used, the young wheat as it eddied in a wind.

And each time he returned home, he went steadily, expectantly, like a man who goes to a profound, unknown satisfaction. At dinner-time, he appeared in the doorway, hanging back a moment from entering, to see if she was there. He saw her setting the plates on the white-scrubbed table. Her arms were slim, she had a slim body and full skirts, she had a dark, shapely head with close-banded hair. Somehow, it was her head, so shapely and poignant, that revealed her his woman to him. As she moved about clothed closely, full-skirted and wearing her little silk apron, her dark hair smoothly parted, her head revealed itself to him in all its subtle, intrinsic beauty, and he knew she was his woman, he knew her essence, that it was his to possess. And he seemed to live thus in contact with her, in contact with the unknown, the unaccountable and incalculable.

They did not take much notice of each other, consciously.

"I'm betimes," he said.

"Yes," she answered.

He turned to the dogs, or to the child if she were there. The little Anna played about the farm, flitting constantly in to call something to her mother, to fling her arms round her mother's skirts, to be noticed, perhaps caressed, then, forgetting, to slip out again.

Then Brangwen, talking to the child, or to the dog between his knees, would be aware of his wife, as, in her tight, dark bodice and her lace fichu, she was reaching up to the corner cupboard. He realised with a sharp pang that she belonged to him, and he to her. He realised that he lived by her. Did he own her? Was she here for ever? Or might she go away? She was not really his, it was not a real marriage, this marriage between them. She might go away. He did not feel like a master, husband, father of her children. She belonged elsewhere. Any moment, she might be gone. And he was ever drawn to her, drawn after her, with ever-raging, ever-unsatisfied desire. He must always turn home, wherever his steps were taking him, always to her, and he could never quite reach her, he could never quite be satisfied, never be at peace, because she might go away.

At evening, he was glad. Then, when he had finished in the yard, and come in and washed himself, when the child was put to bed, he could sit on the other side of the fire with his beer on the hob and his long white pipe in his fingers, conscious of her there opposite him, as she worked at her embroidery, or as she talked to him, and he was safe with her now, till morning. She was curiously self-sufficient, and did not say very much. Occasionally she lifted her head, her grey eyes shining with a strange light, that had nothing to do with him or with this place, and would tell him about herself. She seemed to be back again in the past, chiefly in her childhood or her girlhood, with her father. She very rarely talked of her first husband. But sometimes, all shining-eyed, she was back at her own home, telling him about the riotous times, the trip to Paris with her father, tales of the mad acts of the peasants when a burst of religious, self-hurting fervour had passed over the country.

She would lift her head and say:

"When they brought the railway across the country, they made afterwards smaller railways, of shorter width, to come down to our town—a hundred miles. When I was a girl, Gisla, my German gouvernante, was very shocked and she would not tell me. But I heard the servants talking. I remember, it was Pierre, the coachman. And my father, and some of his friends, landowners, they had taken a wagon, a whole railway wagon—that you travel in—"

"A railway-carriage," said Brangwen.

She laughed to herself.

"I know it was a great scandal: yes—a whole wagon, and they had girls, you know, *filles*, naked, all the wagon full, and so they came down to our village. They came through villages of the Jews, and it was a great scandal. Can you imagine? All the countryside! And my mother, she did not like it. Gisla said to me, 'Madame, she must not know that you have heard such things'————

"My mother, she used to cry, and she wished to beat my father, plainly beat him. He would say, when she cried because he sold the forest, the wood, to jingle money in his pocket, and go to Warsaw or Paris or Kiev, when she said, he must take back his word, he must not sell the forest, he would stand and say 'I know, I know, I have heard it all, I have heard it all before. Tell me some new thing. I know, I know, I know——' Oh, but can you understand, I loved him when he stood there under the door, saying only 'I know, I know, I know it all already.' She could not change him, no, not if she killed herself for it. And she could change everybody else, but him, she could not change him——"

Brangwen could not understand. He had pictures of a cattle-truck full of naked girls riding from nowhere to nowhere, of Lydia laughing because her father made great debts and said "I know, I know"; of Jews running down the street shouting in Yiddish "Don't do it, don't do it," and being cut down by demented peasants—she called them "cattle"—whilst she looked on interested and even amused; of tutors and governesses and Paris and a convent—. It was too much for him. And there she sat, telling the tales to the open space, not to him, arrogating a curious superiority to him, a distance between them, something strange and foreign and outside his life, talking, rattling, without rhyme or reason, laughing when he was shocked or astounded, condemning nothing, confounding his mind and making the whole world a chaos, without order or stability of any kind. Then, when they went to bed, he knew that he had nothing to do with her. She was back in her childhood, he was a peasant, a serf, a servant, a lover, a paramour, a shadow, a nothing. He lay still in amazement, staring at the room he knew so well, and wondering whether it was really there, the window, the chest of drawers, or whether it was merely a figment in the atmosphere. And gradually he grew into a raging fury against her. But because he was so much amazed, and there was as yet such a distance between them, and she was such an amazing thing to him, with all wonder opening out behind her, he made no retaliation on her. Only he lay still and wide-eyed with rage, inarticulate, not understanding, but solid with hostility.

And he remained wrathful and distinct from her, unchanged outwardly to her, but underneath a solid power of antagonism to her. Of which she became gradually aware. And it irritated her to be made aware of him as a separate power. She lapsed into a sort of sombre exclusion, a curious communion with mysterious powers, a sort of mystic, dark state which drove him and the child nearly mad. He walked about for days stiffened with resistance to her, stiff with a will to destroy her as she was. Then suddenly, out of nowhere, there was connection between them again. It came on him as he was working in the fields. The tension, the bond, burst, and the passionate flood broke forward into a tremendous, magnificent rush, so that he felt he could snap off the trees as he passed, and create the world afresh.

And when he arrived home, there was no sign between them. He waited and waited till she came. And as he waited, his limbs seemed strong and splendid to him, his hands seemed like passionate servants to him, goodly, he felt a stupendous power in himself, of life, and of urgent, strong blood.

She was sure to come at last, and touch him. Then he burst into flame for her, and lost himself. They looked at each other, a deep laugh at the bottom of their eyes, and he went to take of her again, wholesale, mad to revel in the inexhaustible wealth of her, to bury himself in the depths of her in an inexhaustible exploration, she all the while revelling in that he revelled in her, tossed all her secrets aside and plunged to that which was secret to her as well, whilst she quivered with fear and the last anguish of delight.

What did it matter who they were, whether they knew each other or not?

The hour passed away again, there was severance between them, and rage and misery and bereavement for her, and deposition and toiling at the mill with slaves for him. But no matter. They had had their hour, and should it chime again, they were ready for it, ready to renew the game at the point where it was left off, on the edge of the outer darkness, when the secrets within the woman are game for the man, hunted doggedly, when the secrets of the woman are the man's adventure, and they both give themselves to the adventure.

She was with child, and there was again the silence and distance between them. She did not want him nor his secrets nor his game, he was deposed, he was cast out. He seethed with fury at the small, ugly-mouthed woman who had nothing to do with him. Sometimes his anger broke on her, but she did not cry. She turned on him like a tiger, and there was battle.

He had to learn to contain himself again, and he hated it. He hated her that she was not there for him. And he took himself off, anywhere.

But an instinct of gratitude and a knowledge that she would receive him back again, that later on she would be there for him again, prevented his straying very far. He cautiously did not go too far. He knew she might lapse into ignorance of him, lapse away from him, farther, farther, farther, till she was lost to him. He had sense enough, premonition enough in himself, to be aware of this and to measure himself accordingly. For he did not want to lose her: he did not want her to lapse away.

Cold, he called her, selfish, only caring about herself, a foreigner with a bad nature, caring really about nothing, having no proper feelings at the bottom of her, and no proper niceness. He raged, and piled up accusations that had some measure of truth in them all. But a certain grace in him forbade him from going too far. He knew, and he quivered with rage and hatred, that she was all these vile things, that she was everything vile and detestable. But he had grace at the bottom of him, which told him, that above all things, he did not want to lose her, he was not going to lose her.

So he kept some consideration for her, he preserved some relationship. He went out more often, to the "Red Lion" again, to escape the madness of sitting next to her when she did not belong to him, when she was as absent as any woman in indifference could be. He could not stay at home. So he went to the "Red Lion." And sometimes he got drunk. But he preserved his measure, some things between them he never forfeited.

A tormented look came into his eyes, as if something were always dogging him. He glanced sharp and quick, he could not bear to sit still doing nothing. He had to go out, to find company, to give himself away there. For he had no other outlet, he could not work to give himself out, he had not the knowledge.

As the months of her pregnancy went on, she left him more and more alone, she was more and more unaware of him, his existence was annulled. And he felt bound down, bound, unable to stir, beginning to go mad, ready to rave. For she was quiet and polite, as if he did not exist, as one is quiet and polite to a servant.

Nevertheless she was great with his child, it was his turn to submit. She sat opposite him, sewing, her foreign face inscrutable and indifferent. He felt he wanted to break her into acknowledgment of him, into awareness of him. It was insufferable that she had so obliterated him. He would smash her into regarding him. He had a raging agony of desire to do so.

But something bigger in him withheld him, kept him motionless. So he went out of the house for relief. Or he turned to the little girl for her sympathy and her love, he appealed with all his power to the small Anna. So soon they were like lovers, father and child.

For he was afraid of his wife. As she sat there with bent head, silent, working or reading, but so unutterably silent that his heart seemed under the millstone of it, she became herself like the upper millstone lying on him, crushing him, as sometimes a heavy sky lies on the earth.

Yet he knew he could not tear her away from the heavy obscurity into which she was merged. He must not try to tear her into recognition of himself, and agreement with himself. It were disastrous, impious. So, let him rage as he might, he must withhold himself. But his wrists trembled and seemed mad, and seemed as if they would burst.

When, in November, the leaves came beating against the window shutters, with a lashing sound, he started, and his eyes flickered with flame. The dog looked up at him, he sunk his head to the fire. But his wife was startled. He was aware of her listening.

"They blow up with a rattle," he said.

"What?" she asked.

"The leaves."

She sank away again. The strange leaves beating in the wind on the wood had come nearer than she. The tension in the room was overpowering, it was difficult for him to move his head. He sat with every nerve, every vein, every fibre of muscle in his body stretched on a tension. He felt like a broken arch thrust sickeningly out from support. For her response was gone, he thrust at nothing. And he remained himself, he saved himself from crashing down into nothingness, from being squandered into fragments, by sheer tension, sheer backward resistance.

During the last months of her pregnancy, he went about in a surcharged, imminent state that did not exhaust itself. She was also depressed, and sometimes she cried. It needed so much life to begin afresh, after she had lost so lavishly. Sometimes she cried. Then he stood stiff, feeling his heart would burst. For she did not want him, she did not want even to be made aware of him. By the very puckering of her face he knew that he must stand back, leave her intact, alone. For it was the old grief come back in her, the old loss, the pain of the old life, the dead husband, the dead children. This was sacred to her, and he must not violate her with his comfort. For what she wanted she would come to him. He stood aloof with turgid heart.

He had to see her tears come, fall over her scarcely moving face, that only puckered sometimes, down on to her breast, that was so still, scarcely moving. And there was no noise, save now and again, when, with a strange, somnambule movement, she took her handkerchief and wiped her face and blew her nose, and went on with the noiseless weeping. He knew that any offer of comfort from himself would be worse than useless, hateful to her, jangling her. She must cry. But it drove him insane. His heart was scalded, his brain hurt in his head, he went away, out of the house.

His great and chiefest source of solace was the child. She had been at first aloof from him, reserved. However friendly she might seem one day, the next she would have lapsed to her original disregard of him, cold, detached, at her distance.

The first morning after his marriage he had discovered it would not be so easy with the child. At the break of dawn he had started awake hearing a small voice outside the door saying plaintively:

"Mother!"

He rose and opened the door. She stood on the threshold in her nightdress, as she had climbed out of bed, black eyes staring round and hostile, her fair hair sticking out in a wild fleece. The man and child confronted each other.

"I want my mother," she said, jealously accenting the "my."

"Come on then," he said gently.

"Where's my mother?"

"She's here—come on."

The child's eyes, staring at the man with ruffled hair and beard, did not change. The mother's voice called softly. The little bare feet entered the room with trepidation.

"Mother!"

"Come, my dear."

The small bare feet approached swiftly.

"I wondered where you were," came the plaintive voice.

The mother stretched out her arms. The child stood beside the high bed. Brangwen lightly lifted the tiny girl, with an "up-a-daisy," then took his own place in the bed again.

"Mother!" cried the child sharply, as in anguish.

"What, my pet?"

Anna wriggled close into her mother's arms, clinging tight, hiding from the fact of the man. Brangwen lay still, and waited. There was a long stillness.

Then suddenly, Anna looked round, as if she thought he would be gone. She saw the face of the man lying upturned to the ceiling. Her black eyes stared antagonistic from her exquisite face, her arms clung tightly to her mother, afraid. He did not move for some time, not knowing what to say. His face was smooth and soft-skinned with love, his eyes full of soft light. He looked at her, scarcely moving his head, his eyes smiling.

"Have you just wakened up?" he said.

"Go away," she retorted, with a little darting forward of the head, something like a viper.

"Nay," he answered, "*I'm* not going. You can go."

"Go away," came the sharp little command.

"There's room for you," he said.

"You can't send your father from his own bed, my little bird," said her mother, pleasantly.

The child glowered at him, miserable in her impotence.

"There's room for you as well," he said. "It's a big bed, enough."

She glowered without answering, then turned and clung to her mother. She would not allow it.

During the day, she asked her mother several times:

"When are we going home, mother?"

"We are at home, darling, we live here now. This is our house, we live here with your father."

The child was forced to accept it. But she remained against the man. As night came on, she asked:

"Where are you going to sleep, mother?"

"I sleep with the father now."

And when Brangwen came in, the child asked fiercely:

"*Why* do you sleep with *my* mother? My mother sleeps with me," her voice quivering.

"You come as well, an' sleep with both of us," he coaxed.

"Mother!" she cried, turning, appealing against him.

"But I must have a husband, darling. All women must have a husband."

"And you like to have a father with your mother, don't you?" said Brangwen.

Anna glowered at him. She seemed to cogitate.

"No," she cried fiercely at length, "no, I don't *want*."

And slowly her face puckered, she sobbed bitterly. He stood and watched her, sorry. But there could be no altering it.

Which, when she knew, she became quiet. He was easy with her, talking to her, taking her to see the live creatures, bringing her the first chickens in his cap, taking her to gather the eggs, letting her throw crusts to the horse. She would easily accompany him, and take all he had to give, but she remained neutral still.

She was curiously, incomprehensibly jealous of her mother, always anxiously concerned about her. If Brangwen drove with his wife to Nottingham, Anna ran about happily enough, or unconcerned, for a long time. Then, as afternoon came on, there was only one cry—"I want my mother, I want my mother—" and a bitter, pathetic sobbing that soon had the soft-hearted Tilly sobbing too. The child's anguish was that her mother was gone, gone.

Yet as a rule, Anna seemed cold, resenting her mother, critical of her. It was:

"I don't like you to do that, mother," or, "I don't like you to say that." She was a sore problem to Brangwen and to all the people at the Marsh. As a rule, however, she was active, lightly flitting about the farmyard, only appearing now and again to assure herself of her mother. Happy she never seemed, but quick, sharp, absorbed, full of imagination and changeability. Tilly said she was bewitched. But it did not matter so long as she did not cry. There was something heartrending about Anna's crying, her childish anguish seemed so utter and so timeless, as if it were a thing of all the ages.

She made playmates of the creatures of the farmyard, talking to them, telling them the stories she had from her mother, counselling them and correcting them.

Brangwen found her at the gate leading to the paddock and to the duckpond. She was peering through the bars and shouting to the stately white geese, that stood in a curving line:

"You're *not* to call at people when they want to come. You must not do it."

The heavy, balanced birds looked at the fierce little face and the fleece of keen hair thrust between the bars, and they raised their heads and swayed off, producing the long, can-canking, protesting noise of geese, rocking their ship-like, beautiful white bodies in a line beyond the gate.

"You're naughty, you're naughty," cried Anna, tears of dismay and vexation in her eyes. And she stamped her slipper.

"Why, what are they doing?" said Brangwen.

"They won't let me come in," she said, turning her flushed little face to him.

"Yi, they will. You can go in if you want to," and he pushed open the gate for her.

She stood irresolute, looking at the group of bluey-white geese standing monumental under the grey, cold day.

"Go on," he said.

She marched valiantly a few steps in. Her little body started convulsively at the sudden, derisive Can-cank-ank of the geese. A blankness spread over her. The geese trailed away with uplifted heads under the low grey sky.

"They don't know you," said Brangwen. "You should tell 'em what your name is."

"They're *naughty* to shout at me," she flashed.

"They think you don't live here," he said.

Later he found her at the gate calling shrilly and imperiously:

"My name is Anna, Anna Lensky, and I live here, because Mr Brangwen's my father now. He *is*—yes he *is*. And I live here."

This pleased Brangwen very much. And gradually, without knowing it herself, she clung to him, in her lost, childish, desolate moments, when it was good to creep up to something big and warm, and bury her little self in his big, unlimited being. Instinctively he was careful of her, careful to recognise her and to give himself to her disposal.

She was difficult of her affections. For Tilly, she had a childish, essential contempt, almost dislike, because the poor woman was such a servant. The child would not let the serving-woman attend to her, do intimate things for her, not for a long time. She treated her as one of an inferior race. Brangwen did not like it.

"Why aren't you fond of Tilly?" he asked.

"Because—because—because she looks at me with her eyes bent."

Then gradually she accepted Tilly as belonging to the household, never as a person.

For the first weeks, the black eyes of the child were forever on the watch. Brangwen, good-humoured but impatient, spoiled by Tilly, was an easy blusterer. If for a few minutes he upset the household with his noisy impatience, he found at the end the child glowering at him with intense black eyes, and she was sure to dart forward her little head, like a serpent, with her biting:

"Go away."

"I'm *not* going away," he shouted, irritated at last. "Go yourself—hustle—stir thysen—hop." And he pointed to the door.

The child backed away from him, pale with fear. Then she gathered her courage, seeing him become patient.

"We don't live with *you*," she said, thrusting forward her little head at him: "You—you're—you're a bomakle."

"A what?" he shouted.

Her voice wavered—but it came—

"A bomakle."

"Ay, an' you're a comakle."

She meditated. Then she hissed forward her head.

"I'm not."

"Not what?"

"A comakle."

"No more am I a bomakle."

He was really cross.

Other times she would say:

"My mother *doesn't* live here."

"Oh ay?"

"I want her to go away."

"Then want's your portion," he replied, laconically.

So they drew nearer together. He would take her with him when he went out in the trap. The horse ready at the gate, he came noisily into the house, which seemed quiet and peaceful till he appeared to set everything awake.

"Now then, Topsy, pop into thy bonnet."

The child drew herself up, resenting the indignity of the address.

"I can't fasten my bonnet myself," she said haughtily.

"Not man enough yet," he said, tying the ribbons under her chin with clumsy fingers.

She held up her face to him. Her little, bright-red lips moved as he fumbled under her chin.

"You talk—nonsents," she said, re-echoing one of his phrases.

"*That* face shouts for th' pump," he said, and taking out a big red handkerchief, that smelled of strong tobacco, began wiping round her mouth.

"Is Kitty waiting for me?" she asked.

"Ay," he said. "Let's finish wiping your face—it'll pass wi' a cat-lick."

She submitted prettily. Then, when he let her go, she began to skip, with a curious flicking up of one leg behind her.

"Now my young buck-rabbit," he said. "Slippy!"

She came and was shaken into her coat, and the two set off. She sat very close beside him in the gig, tucked tightly, feeling his big body sway against her, very splendid. She loved the rocking of the gig, when his big, live body swayed upon her, against her. She laughed, a poignant little shrill, and her black eyes glowed.

She was curiously hard, and then passionately tender-hearted. Her mother was ill, the child stole about on tip-toe in the bedroom for hours, being nurse, and doing the thing thoughtfully and diligently. Another day, her mother was unhappy, Anna would stand with legs apart, glowering, balancing on the sides of her slippers. She laughed when the goslings wriggled in Tilly's hand, as the pellets of food were rammed down their throats with a skewer, she laughed nervously. She was hard and imperious with the animals, squandering no love, running about amongst them like a cruel mistress.

Summer came, and hay-harvest, Anna was a brown elvish mite dancing about. Tilly always marvelled over her, more than she loved her.

But always in the child was some anxious connection with the mother. So long as Mrs Brangwen was all right, the little girl played about and took very little notice of her. But corn-harvest went by, the autumn drew on, and the mother, the later months of her pregnancy beginning, was strange and detached, Brangwen began to knit his brows, the old, unhealthy uneasiness, the unskinned susceptibility came on the child again. If she went to the fields with her father, then, instead of playing about carelessly, it was:

"I want to go home."

"Home, why tha's nobbut this minute come."

"I want to go home."

"What for? What ails thee?"

"I want my mother."

"Thy mother! Thy mother none wants thee."

"I want to go home."

There would be tears in a moment.

"Can ter find t'road, then?"

And he watched her scudding, silent and intent along the hedge-bottom, at a steady, anxious pace, till she turned and was gone through the gateway. Then he saw her two fields off, still pressing forward, small and urgent. His face was clouded as he turned to plough up the stubble.

The year drew on, in the hedges the berries shone red and twinkling above bare twigs, robins were seen, great droves of birds dashed like spray from the fallow, rooks appeared, black and flapping down to earth, the ground was cold as he pulled the turnips, the roads were churned deep in mud. Then the turnips were pitted and work was slack.

Inside the house it was dark, and quiet. The child flitted uneasily round, and now and again came her plaintive, startled cry:

"Mother!"

Mrs Brangwen was heavy and unresponsive, tired, lapsed back. Brangwen went on working out of doors.

At evening, when he came in to milk, the child would run behind him. Then, in the cosy cowsheds, with the doors shut and the air looking warm by the light of the hanging lantern, above the branching horns of the cows, she would stand watching his hands squeezing rhythmically the teats of the placid beast, watch the froth and the leaping squirt of milk, watch his hand sometimes rubbing slowly, understandingly, upon a hanging udder. So they kept each other company, but at a distance, rarely speaking.

The darkest days of the year came on, the child was fretful, sighing as if some oppression were on her, running hither and thither without relief. And Brangwen went about at his work, heavy, his heart heavy as the sodden earth.

The winter nights fell early, the lamp was lighted before tea-time, the shutters were closed, they were all shut into the room with the tension and stress. Mrs Brangwen went early to bed, Anna playing on the floor beside her. Brangwen sat in the emptiness of the downstairs room, smoking, scarcely conscious even of his own misery. And very often he went out to escape it.

Christmas passed, the wet, drenched, cold days of January recurred monotonously, with now and then a brilliance of blue flashing in, when Brangwen went out into a morning like crystal, when every sound rang again, and the birds were many and sudden and brusque in the hedges. Then an elation came over him in spite of everything, whether his wife were strange or sad, or whether he craved for her to be with him, it did not matter, the air rang with clear noises, the sky was like crystal, like a bell, and the earth was hard. Then he worked and was happy, his eyes shining, his cheeks flushed. And the zest of life was strong in him.

The birds pecked busily round him, the horses were fresh and ready, the bare branches of the trees flung themselves up like a man yawning, taut with energy, the twigs radiated off into the clear light. He was alive and full of zest for it all. And if his wife were heavy, separated from him, extinguished, then let her be, let him remain himself. Things would be as they would be. Meanwhile he heard the ringing crow of a cockerel in the distance, he saw the pale shell of the moon effaced on a blue sky.

So he shouted to the horses, and was happy. If, driving into Ilkeston, a fresh young woman were going in to do her shopping, he hailed her, and reined in his horse, and picked her up. Then he was glad to have her near him, his eyes shone, his voice, laughing, teasing in a warm fashion, made the poise of her head more beautiful, her blood ran quicker. They were both stimulated, the morning was fine.

What did it matter that, at the bottom of his heart, was care and pain? It was at the bottom, let it stop at the bottom. His wife, her suffering, her coming pain—well, it must be so. She suffered, but he was out of doors, full in life, and it would be ridiculous, indecent, to pull a long face and to insist on being miserable. He was happy, this morning, driving to town, with the hoofs of the horse spanking the hard earth. Well, he was happy, if half the world were weeping at the funeral of the other half. And it was a jolly girl sitting beside him. And Woman was immortal, whatever happened, whoever turned towards death. Let the misery come when it could not be resisted.

The evening arrived later very beautiful, with a rosy flush hovering above the sunset, and passing away into violet and lavender with turquoise green north and south in the sky, and in the east, a great, yellow moon hanging heavy and radiant. It was magnificent to walk between the sunset and the moon, on a road where little holly trees thrust black into the rose and lavender, and starlings flickered in droves across the light. But what was the end of the journey.

The pain came right enough, later on, when his heart and his feet were heavy, his brain dead, his life stopped.

One afternoon, the pains began, Mrs Brangwen was put to bed, the midwife came. Night fell, the shutters were closed, Brangwen came in to tea, to the loaf and the pewter tea-pot, the child, silent and quivering, playing with glass beads, the house, empty, it seemed, or exposed to the winter night, as if it had no walls.

Sometimes there sounded, long and remote in the house, vibrating through everything, the moaning cry of a woman in labour. Brangwen, sitting downstairs, was divided. His lower, deeper self was with her, bound to her, suffering. But the big shell of his body remembered the sound of owls that used to fly round the farmstead when he was a boy. He was back in his youth, a boy, haunted by the sound of the owls, waking up his brother to speak to him. And his mind drifted away to the birds, their solemn, dignified faces, their flight so soft and broad-winged. And then to the birds his brother had shot, fluffy, dust-coloured, dead heaps of softness with faces absurdly asleep. It was a queer thing, a dead owl.

He lifted his cup to his lips, he watched the child with the beads. But his mind was occupied with owls, and the atmosphere of his boyhood, with his brothers and sisters. Elsewhere, fundamental, he was with his wife in labour, the child was being brought forth out of their one flesh. He and she, one flesh, out of which life must be put forth. The rent was not in his body, but it was of his body. On her the blows fell, but the quiver ran through to him, to his last fibre. She must be torn asunder for life to come forth, yet still they were one flesh, and still, from further back, the life came out of him to her, and still he was the unbroken that has the broken rock in its arms, their flesh was one rock from which the life gushed, out of her who was smitten and rent, from him who quivered and yielded.

He went upstairs to her. As he came to the bedside she spoke to him in Polish.

"Is it very bad?" he asked.

She looked at him, and oh, the weariness to her, of the effort to understand another language, the weariness of hearing him, attending to him, making out who he was, as he stood there fair-bearded and alien, looking at her. She knew something of him, of his eyes. But she could not grasp him. She closed her eyes.

He turned away, white to the gills.

"It's not so very bad," said the midwife.

He knew he was a strain on his wife. He went downstairs.

The child glanced up at him, frightened.

"I want my mother," she quavered.

"Ay, but she's badly," he said mildly, unheeding.

She looked at him with lost, frightened eyes.

"Has she got a headache?"

"No—she's going to have a baby."

The child looked round. He was unaware of her. She was alone again in terror.

"I want my mother," came the cry of panic.

"Let Tilly undress you," he said. "You're tired."

There was another silence. Again came the cry of labour.

"I want my mother," rang automatically from the wincing, panic-stricken child, that felt cut off and lost in a horror of desolation.

Tilly came forward, her heart wrung.

"Come an' let me undress her then, pet-lamb," she crooned. "You s'll have your mother in th' mornin', don't you fret, my duckie; never mind, angel."

But Anna stood upon the sofa, her back to the wall.

"I want my mother," she cried, her little face quivering, and the great tears of childish, utter anguish falling.

"She's poorly, my lamb, she's poorly tonight, but she'll be better by mornin'. Oh don't cry, don't cry, love, she doesn't want you to cry, precious little heart, no, she doesn't."

Tilly took gently hold of the child's skirts. Anna snatched back her dress, and cried, in a little hysteria:

"No, you're not to undress me.—I want my mother—", and her child's face was running with grief and tears, her body shaken.

"Oh, but let Tilly undress you. Let Tilly undress you, who loves

72

you, don't be wilful tonight. Mother's poorly, she doesn't want you to cry."

The child sobbed distractedly, she could not hear.

"I want my mother," she wept.

"When you're undressed you s'll go up to see your mother—when you're undressed, pet, when you've let Tilly undress you, when you're a little jewel in your nightie, love. Oh don't you cry, don't you—"

Brangwen sat stiff in his chair. He felt his brain going tighter. He crossed over the room, aware only of the maddening sobbing.

"Don't make a noise," he said.

And a new fear shook the child from the sound of his voice. She cried mechanically, her eyes looking watchful through her tears, in terror, alert to what might happen.

"I want—my—mother," quavered the sobbing, blind voice.

A shiver of irritation went over the man's limbs. It was the utter, persistent unreason, the maddening blindness of the voice and the crying.

"You must come and be undressed," he said, in a quiet voice that was thin with anger.

And he reached his hand and grasped her. He felt her body catch in a convulsive sob. But he too was blind, and intent, irritated into mechanical action. He began to unfasten her little apron. She would have shrunk from him, but could not. So her small body remained in his grasp, while he fumbled at the little buttons and tapes, unthinking, intent, unaware of anything but the irritation of her. Her body was held taut and resistant, he pushed off the little dress and the petticoats, revealing the white arms. She kept stiff, overpowered, violated, he went on with his task. And all the while, she sobbed, choking:

"I want my mother."

He was unheedingly silent, his face stiff. The child was now incapable of understanding, she had become a little, mechanical thing of fixed will. She wept, her body convulsed, her voice repeating the same cry.

"Eh dear o' me!" cried Tilly, becoming distracted herself.

Brangwen, slow, clumsy, blind, intent, got off all the little garments, and stood the child naked in its shift upon the sofa.

"Wheer's her nightie?" he asked.

Tilly brought it, and he put it on her. Anna did not move her limbs to his desire. He had to push them into place. She stood, with fixed, blind will, resistant, a small, convulsed, unchangeable thing weeping ever and repeating the same phrase. He lifted one foot after the other, pulled off slippers and socks. She was ready.

"Do you want a drink?" he asked.

She did not change. Unheeding, uncaring, she stood on the sofa, standing back, alone, her hands shut and half lifted, her face, all tears, raised and blind. And through the sobbing and choking came the broken:

"I—want—my—mother."

"Do you want a drink?" he said again.

There was no answer. He lifted the stiff, denying body between his hands. Its stiff blindness made a flash of rage go through him. He would like to break it.

He set the child on his knee, and sat again in his chair beside the fire, the wet, sobbing, inarticulate noise going on near his ear, the child sitting stiff, not yielding to him or anything, not aware.

A new degree of anger came over him. What did it all matter? What did it matter if the mother talked Polish and cried in labour, if this child were stiff with resistance, and crying? Why take it to heart? Let the mother cry in labour, let the child cry in resistance, since they would do so. Why should he fight against it, why resist? Let it be, if it were so. Let them be as they were, if they insisted.

And in a daze he sat, offering no fight. The child cried on, the minutes ticked away, a sort of torpor was on him.

It was some little time before he came to, and turned to attend to the child. He was shocked by her little, wet, blinded face. A bit dazed, he pushed back the wet hair. Like a living statue of grief, her blind face cried on.

"Nay," he said, "not as bad as that. It's not as bad as that, Anna, my child. Come, what are you crying for so much? Come, stop now, it'll make you sick. I wipe you dry, don't wet your face any more. Don't cry any more wet tears, don't, it's better not to. Don't cry—it's not so bad as all that. Hush now, hush—let it be enough."

His voice was queer and distant and calm. He looked at the child. She was beside herself now. He wanted her to stop, he wanted it all to stop, to become natural.

"Come," he said, rising to turn away, "We'll go an' supper-up the beast."

He took a big shawl, folded her round, and went out into the kitchen for the lantern.

"You're never taking the child out, of a night like this," said Tilly.

"Ay, it'll quieten her," he answered.

It was raining. The child was suddenly still, shocked, finding the rain on its face, the darkness.

"We'll just give the cows their something-to-eat, afore they go to bed," Brangwen was saying to her, holding her close and sure.

There was a trickling of water into the butt, a burst of rain-drops sputtering on to her shawl, and the light of the lantern swinging, flashing on a wet pavement and the base of a wet wall. Otherwise it was black darkness: one breathed darkness.

He opened the doors, upper and lower, and they entered into the high, dry barn, that smelled warm even if it were not warm. He hung the lantern on the nail, and shut the door. They were in another world now. The light shed softly on the timbered barn, on the white-washed walls, and the great heap of hay; instruments cast their shadows largely, a ladder rose to the dark arch of a loft. Outside there was the driving rain, inside, the softly-illuminated stillness and calmness of the barn.

Holding the child on one arm, he set about preparing the food for the cows, filling a pan with chopped hay and brewer's grains and a little meal. The child, all wonder, watched what he did. A new being was created in her for the new conditions. Sometimes, a little spasm, eddying from the bygone storm of sobbing, shook her small body. Her eyes were wide and wondering, pathetic. She was silent, quite still.

In a sort of dream, his heart sunk to the bottom, leaving the surface of him still, quite still, he rose with the panful of food, carefully balancing the child on one arm, the pan in the other hand. The silky fringe of the shawl swayed softly, grains and hay trickled to the floor; he went along a dimly-lit passage behind the mangers, where the horns of the cows pricked out of the obscurity. The child shrank, he balanced stiffly, rested the pan on the manger wall, and tipped out the food, half to this cow, half to the next. There was a noise of chains running, as the cows lifted or dropped their heads sharply; then a contented, soothing sound, a long snuffing as the beast ate in silence.

The journey had to be performed several times. There was the rhythmic sound of the shovel in the barn, then the man returned, walking stiffly between the two weights, the face of the child peering out from the shawl. Then the next time, as he stooped, she freed her arm and put it round his neck, clinging soft and warm, making all easier.

The beast fed, he dropped the pan and sat down on a box, to arrange the child.

"Will the cows go to sleep now?" she said, catching her breath as she spoke.

"Yes."

"Will they eat all their stuff up first?"

"Yes. Hark at them."

And the two sat still, listening to the snuffing and breathing of cows feeding in the sheds communicating with this small barn. The lantern shed a soft, steady light from one wall. All outside was still in the rain. He looked down at the silky folds of the paisley shawl. It reminded him of his mother. She used to go to church in it. He was back again in the old irresponsibility and security, a boy at home.

The two sat very quiet. His mind, in a sort of trance, seemed to become more and more vague. He held the child close to him. A quivering little shudder, re-echoing from her sobbing, went down her limbs. He held her closer. Gradually she relaxed, the eyelids began to sink over her dark, watchful eyes. As she sank to sleep, his mind became blank.

When he came to, as if from sleep, he seemed to be sitting in a timeless stillness. What was he listening for? He seemed to be listening for some sound a long way off, from beyond life. He remembered his wife. He must go back to her. The child was asleep, the eyelids not quite shut, showing a slight film of black pupil between. Why did she not shut her eyes? Her mouth was also a little open.

He rose quietly and went back to the house.

"Is she asleep?" whispered Tilly.

He nodded. The servant-woman came to look at the child who slept in the shawl, with cheeks flushed hot and red, and a whiteness, a wanness round the eyes.

"God-a-mercy!" whispered Tilly, shaking her head.

He pushed off his boots and went upstairs with the child. He became aware of the anxiety grasped tight at his heart, because of his wife. But he remained still. The house was silent save for the wind outside, and the noisy trickling and splattering of water in the water-butts. There was a slit of light under his wife's door.

He put the child into bed wrapped as she was in the shawl, for the sheets would be cold. Then he was afraid that she might not be able to move her arms, so he loosened her. The black eyes opened, rested on him vacantly, sank shut again. He covered her up. The last little quiver from the sobbing shook her breathing.

This was his room, the room he had had before he married. It was familiar. He remembered what it was to be a young man, untouched.

He remained suspended. The child slept, pushing her small fists from the shawl. He could tell the woman her child was asleep. But he must go to the other landing. He started. There was the sound of the owls—the moaning of the woman. What an uncanny sound! It was not human—at least to a man.

He went down to her room, entering softly. She was lying still, with eyes shut, pale, tired. His heart leapt, fearing she was dead. Yet he knew perfectly well she was not. He saw the way her hair went loose over her temples, her mouth was shut with suffering in a sort of grin. She was beautiful to him—but it was not human. He had a dread of her as she lay there. What had she to do with him? She was other than himself.

Something made him go and touch her fingers that were still grasped on the sheet. Her brown-grey eyes opened and looked at him. She did not know him as himself. But she knew him as the man. She looked at him as a woman in childbirth looks at the man who begot the child in her; an impersonal look, in the extreme hour, female to male. Her eyes closed again. A great, scalding peace went over him, burning his heart and his entrails, passing off into the infinite.

When her pains began afresh, tearing her, he turned aside, and could not look. But his heart in torture was at peace, his bowels were glad. He went downstairs, and to the door, outside, lifted his face to the rain, and felt the darkness striking unseen and steadily upon him.

The swift, unseen threshing of the night upon him silenced him and he was overcome. He turned away indoors, humbly. There was the infinite world, eternal, unchanging, as well as the world of life.

CHAPTER III

Childhood of Anna Lensky

Tom Brangwen never loved his own son as he loved his step-child Anna. When they told him it was a boy, he had a thrill of pleasure. He liked the confirmation of fatherhood. It gave him satisfaction to know he had a son. But he felt not very much outgoing to the baby itself. He was its father, that was enough.

He was glad that his wife was mother of his child. She was serene, a little bit shadowy, as if she were transplanted. In the birth of the child she seemed to lose connection with her former self. She became now really English, really Mrs Brangwen. Her vitality, however, seemed lowered.

She was still, to Brangwen, immeasurably beautiful. She was still passionate, with a flame of being. But the flame was not robust and present. Her eyes shone, her face glowed for him, but like some flower opened in the shade, that could not bear the full light. She loved the baby. But even this, with a sort of dimness, a faint absence about her, a shadowiness even in her mother-love. When Brangwen saw her nursing his child, happy, absorbed in it, a pain went over him like a thin flame. For he perceived how he must subdue himself in his approach to her. And he wanted again the robust, mortal exchange of love and passion such as he had had at first with her, at one time and another, when they were matched at their highest intensity. This was the one experience for him now. And he wanted it, always, with remorseless craving.

She came to him again, with the same lifting her mouth as had driven him almost mad with trammelled passion at first. She came to him again, and, his heart delirious in delight and readiness, he took her. And it was almost as before.

Perhaps it was quite as before. At any rate, it made him know perfection, it established in him a constant, eternal knowledge.

But it died down before he wanted it to die down. She was finished, she could take no more. And he was not exhausted, he wanted to go on. But it could not be.

So he had to begin the bitter lesson, to abate himself, to take less than he wanted. For she was Woman to him, all other women were her shadows. For she had satisfied him. And he wanted it to go on. And it could not. However he raged, and, filled with suppression that became hot and bitter, hated her in his soul that she did not want him, however he had mad outbursts, and drank and made ugly scenes, still he knew, he was only kicking against the pricks. It was not, he had to learn, that she *would* not want him enough, as much as he demanded that she should want him. It was, that she could not. She could only want him in her own way, and to her own measure. And she had spent much life before he found her as she was, the woman who could take him and give him fulfilment. She had taken him and given him fulfilment. She still would do so, in her own times and ways. But he must control himself, measure himself to her.

He wanted to give her all his love, all his passion, all his essential energy. But it could not be. He must find other things than her, other centres of living. She sat close and impregnable with the child. And he was jealous of the child.

But he loved her, and time came to give some sort of course to his troublesome current of life, so that it did not foam and flood and make misery. He formed another centre of love in her child, Anna. Gradually a part of his stream of life was diverted to the child, relieving the main flood to his wife. Also he sought the company of men, he drank heavily now and again.

The child ceased to have so much anxiety for her mother after the baby came. Seeing the mother with the baby boy, delighted and serene and secure, Anna was at first puzzled, then gradually she became indignant, and at last her little life settled on its own swivel, she was no more strained and distorted to support her mother. She became more childish, not so abnormal, not charged with cares she could not understand. The charge of the mother, the satisfying of the mother, had devolved elsewhere than on her. Gradually the child was freed, she became an independent, forgetful little soul, loving from her own centre.

Of her own choice, she then loved Brangwen most, or most obviously. For these two made a little life together, they had a joint activity. It amused him, at evening, to teach her to count, or to say her letters. He remembered for her all the little nursery rhymes and childish songs that lay forgotten at the bottom of his brain.

At first she thought them rubbish. But he laughed, and she laughed. They became to her a huge joke. Old King Cole she thought was Brangwen, Mother Hubbard was Tilly, her mother was the old woman who lived in a shoe. It was a huge, it was a frantic delight to the child, this nonsense, after her years with her mother, after the poignant folk-tales she had had from her mother, which always troubled and mystified her soul.

She shared a sort of recklessness with her father, a complete, chosen carelessness that had the laugh of ridicule in it. He loved to make her voice go high and shouting and defiant with laughter. The baby was dark-skinned and dark-haired, like the mother, and had hazel eyes. Brangwen called him the black-bird.

"Hallo," Brangwen would cry, starting as he heard the wail of the child announcing it wanted to be taken out of the cradle, "there's the black-bird tuning-up."

"The black-bird's singing," Anna would shout with delight, "the black-bird's singing."

"When the pie was opened," Brangwen shouted in his bawling bass voice, going over to the cradle, "the bird began to sing."

"Wasn't it a dainty dish to set before a king?" cried Anna, her eyes flashing with joy as she uttered the cryptic words, looking at Brangwen for confirmation. He sat down with the baby, saying loudly:

"Sing up, my lad, sing up."

And the baby cried loudly, and Anna shouted lustily, dancing in wild bliss:

> "'Sing a song of sixpence
> Pocketful of posies,
> Ascha! Ascha!'—"

Then she stopped suddenly in silence and looked at Brangwen again, her eyes flashing, as she shouted loudly and delightedly:

"I've got it wrong, I've got it wrong."

"Oh my sirs!" said Tilly entering, "What a racket!"

Brangwen hushed the child and Anna flipped and danced on. She loved her wild bursts of rowdiness with her father. Tilly hated it, Mrs Brangwen did not mind.

Anna did not care much for other children. She domineered them, she treated them as if they were extremely young and incapable, to her they were little people, they were not her equals. So she was mostly alone, flying round the farm, entertaining the farmhands and Tilly and the servant-girl, whirling on and never ceasing.

She loved driving with Brangwen in the trap. Then, sitting high up and bowling along, her passion for eminence and dominance was satisfied. She was like a little savage in her arrogance. She thought her father important, she was installed beside him on high. And they spanked along, beside the high, flourishing hedge-tops, surveying the activity of the countryside. When people shouted a greeting to them from the road below, and Brangwen shouted jovially back, her little voice was soon heard shrilling along with his, followed by her chuckling laugh, when she looked up at her father with bright eyes, and they laughed at each other. And soon it was the custom for the passer-by to sing out: "How are ter, Tom? Well, my lady!" or else "Mornin' Tom, mornin' my Lass!" or else "You're off together then?" or else "You're lookin' rarely, you two."

Anna would respond, with her father: "How are you, John! *Good* mornin', William! Ay, makin' for Derby," shrilling as loudly as she could. Though often, in response to "You're off out a bit then," she would reply, "Yes, we are," to the great joy of all. She did not like the people who saluted him and did not salute her.

She went into the public-house with him, if he had to call, and often sat beside him in the bar-parlour as he drank his beer or brandy. The landladies paid court to her, in the obsequious way landladies have.

"Well, little lady, an' what's your name?"

"Anna Brangwin," came the immediate, haughty answer.

"Indeed it is! An' do you like driving in a trap with your father?"

"Yes," said Anna, shy, but bored by these inanities.

She had a touch-me-not way of blighting the inane inquiries of grown-up people.

"My word, she's a fawce little thing," the landlady would say to Brangwen.

"Ay," he answered, not encouraging comment on the child.

Then there followed the present of a biscuit, or of cake, which Anna accepted as her dues.

"What does she say, that I'm a fawce little thing?" the small girl asked afterwards.

"She means you're a sharp-shins."

Anna hesitated. She did not understand. Then she laughed at some absurdity she found.

Soon he took her every week to market with him.

"I can come, can't I?' she asked every Saturday, or Thursday morning, when he made himself look fine in his dress of a gentleman-farmer. And his face clouded at having to refuse her.

So at last, he overcame his own shyness, and tucked her beside him. They drove in to Nottingham and put up at the "Black Swan." So far all right. Then he wanted to leave her at the inn. But he saw her face, and knew it was impossible. So he mustered his courage, and set off with her, holding her hand, to the cattle-market.

She stared in bewilderment, flitting silent at his side. But in the cattle-market she shrank from the press of men, all men, all in heavy, filthy boots, and leathern leggings. And the road underfoot was all nasty with cow-muck. And it frightened her to see the cattle in the square pens, so many horns, and so little enclosure, and such a madness of men and a yelling of drovers. Also she felt her father was embarrassed by her, and ill-at-ease.

He bought her a cake at the refreshment booth, and set her on a seat. A man hailed him.

"*Good* morning, Tom. That thine, then?"—and the bearded farmer jerked his head at Anna.

"Ay," said Brangwen, deprecating.

"I didna know tha'd one that old."

"No, it's my Missis's."

"Oh, that's it!" And the man looked at Anna as if she were some odd little cattle. She glowered with black eyes.

Brangwen left her there, in charge of the bar-man, whilst he went to see about the selling of some young stirks. Farmers, butchers, drovers, dirty, uncouth men from whom she shrank instinctively stared down at her as she sat on her seat, then went to get their drink, talking in unabated tones. All was big and violent about her.

"Whose child met that be?" they asked of the barman.

"It belongs to Tom Brangwen."

The child sat on in neglect, watching the door for her father. He never came; many, many men came, but not he, and she sat like a shadow. She knew one did not cry in such a place. And every man looked at her inquisitively, she shut herself away from them. A deep, gathering coldness of isolation took hold on her. He was never coming back. She sat on, frozen, unmoving.

When she had become blank and timeless, he came, and she slipped off her seat to him, like one come back from the dead. He had sold his beast as quickly as he could. But all the business was not finished. He took her again through the hurtling welter of the cattle-market.

Then at last they turned and went out through the gate. He was always hailing one man or another, always stopping to gossip about land and cattle and horses and other things she did not understand, standing in the filth and the smell, among the legs and great boots of men. And always she heard the question:

"What lass is that, then? I didn't know tha'd one o' that age."

"It belongs to my Missis."

Anna was very conscious of her derivation from her mother, in the end, and of her alienation.

But at last they were away, and Brangwen went with her into a little, dark, ancient eating-house in the Bridlesmith-Gate. They had cow's-tail soup, and meat and cabbage and potatoes. Other men, other people came into the dark, vaulted place, to eat. Anna was wide-eyed and silent with wonder.

Then they went into the big market, into the corn exchange, then to shops. He bought her a little book off a stall. He loved buying things, odd things that he thought would be useful. Then they went to the "Black Swan," and she drank milk and he brandy, and they harnessed the horse and drove off, up the Derby Road.

She was tired out with wonder and marvelling. But the next day, when she thought of it, she skipped, flipping her leg in the odd dance she did, and talked the whole time of what had happened to her, of what she had seen. It lasted her all the week. And the next Saturday she was eager to go again.

She became a familiar figure in the cattle-market, sitting waiting in the little booth. But she liked best to go to Derby. There her father had more friends. And she liked the familiarity of the smaller town, the nearness of the river, the strangeness that did not frighten her, it was so much smaller. She liked the covered-in market, and the old women. She liked the "George Inn," where her father put up. The landlord was Brangwen's old friend, and Anna was made much of. She sat many a day in the cosy parlour talking to Mr Wigginton, a fat man with red hair, the landlord. And when the farmers all gathered at twelve o'clock, for dinner, she was a little heroine.

At first she would only glower or hiss at these strange men with their uncouth accent. But they were good-humoured. She was a little oddity, with her fierce fair hair like spun glass sticking out in a flamy halo round her apple-blossom face and her black eyes, and the men liked an oddity. She kindled their attention.

She was very angry because Marriott, a gentleman-farmer from Ambergate, called her the little pole-cat.

"Why you're a pole-cat," he said to her.

"I'm not," she flashed.

"You are. That's just how a pole-cat goes."

She thought about it.

"Well you're—you're—" she began.

"I'm what?"

She looked him up and down.

"You're a bow-leg man."

Which he was. There was a roar of laughter. They loved her that she was indomitable.

"Ah," said Marriott. "Only a pole-cat says that."

"Well I *am* a pole-cat," she flamed.

There was another roar of laughter from the men.

They loved to tease her.

"Well ma little maid," Braithwaite would say to her, "an' how's th' lamb's wool?"

He gave a tug at a glistening, pale piece of her hair.

"It's not lamb's wool," said Anna, indignantly putting back her offended lock.

"Why, what'st ca' it then?"

"It's hair."

"Hair! Wheriver dun they rear that sort?"

"Wheriver dun they?" she asked, in dialect, her curiosity overcoming her.

Instead of answering he shouted with joy. It was the triumph, to make her speak dialect.

She had one enemy, the man they called Nut-Nat, or Nat-Nut, a crétin, with inturned feet, who came flap-lapping along, shoulder jerking up at every step. This poor creature sold nuts in the public-houses where he was known. He had no roof to his mouth, and the men used to mock his speech.

The first time he came into the "George" when Anna was there, she asked, after he had gone, her eyes very round:

"Why does he do that when he walks?"

"'E canna 'elp 'isself, Duckie, it's tha' make o' th' fellow."

She thought about it, then she laughed nervously. And then she bethought herself, her cheeks flushed, and she cried:

"He's a *horrid* man."

"Nay, he's non horrid; he canna help it if he wor struck that road."

But when poor Nat came wambling in again, she slid away. And she would not eat his nuts, if the men bought them for her. And when the farmers gambled at dominoes for them, she was angry.

"They are dirty-man's nuts," she cried.

So a revulsion started against Nat, who had not long after to go to the workhouse.

There grew in Brangwen's heart now a secret desire to make her a lady. His brother Alfred, in Nottingham, had caused a great scandal by becoming the lover of an educated woman, a lady, widow of a doctor. Very often, Alfred Brangwen went down as a friend to her cottage, which was in Derbyshire, leaving his wife and family for a day or two, then returning to them. And no-one dared gainsay him, for he was a strong-willed, direct man, and he said he was a friend of this widow.

One day Brangwen met his brother on the station.

"Where are *you* going to, then?" asked the younger brother.

"I'm going down to Wirksworth."

"You've got friends down there, I'm told."

"Yes."

"I s'll have to be lookin' in when I'm down that road."

"You please yourself."

Tom Brangwen was so curious about the woman, that the next time he was in Wirksworth he asked for her house.

He found a beautiful cottage on the steep side of a hill, looking clean over the town, that lay in the bottom of the basin, and away at the old quarries on the opposite side of the space. Mrs Forbes was in the garden. She was a tall woman with white hair. She came up the path taking off her thick gloves, laying down her shears. It was autumn. She wore a wide-brimmed hat.

Brangwen blushed to the roots of his hair, and did not know what to say.

"I thought I might look in," he said, "knowing you were friends of my brother's. I had to come to Wirksworth."

She saw at once he was a Brangwen.

"Will you come in," she said. "My father is lying down."

She took him into a drawing room, full of books, with a piano and a violin-stand. And they talked, she simply and easily. She was full of dignity. The room was of a kind Brangwen had never known; the atmosphere seemed open and spacious, like a mountain-top to him.

"Does my brother like reading?" he asked.

"Some things. He has been reading Herbert Spencer—and we read Browning sometimes."

Brangwen was full of admiration, deep, thrilling, almost reverential admiration. He looked at her with lit-up eyes when she said "we read." At last he burst out, looking round the room:

"I didn't know our Alfred was this way inclined."

"He is quite an unusual man."

He looked at her in amazement. She evidently had a new idea of his brother: she evidently appreciated him. He looked again at the woman. She was about forty, straight, rather hard, a curious, separate creature. Himself, he was not in love with her. There was something chilling about her. But he was filled with boundless admiration.

At tea-time, he was introduced to her father, an invalid who had to be helped about, but who was ruddy and well-favoured, with snowy hair and watery blue eyes, and a courtly, naïve manner that again was new and strange to Brangwen, so suave, so merry, so innocent.

His brother was this woman's lover! It was too amazing. Brangwen went home despising himself for his own poor way of life. He was a clod-hopper and a boor, dull, stuck in the mud. More than ever he wanted to clamber out, to this visionary polite world.

He was well-off. He was as well-off as Alfred, who could not have above six hundred a year, all told. He himself made about four hundred, and could make more. His investments got better every day. Why did he not do something? His wife was a lady also.

But when he got to the Marsh, he realised how fixed everything was, how the other form of life was beyond him, and he regretted, for the first time, that he had succeeded to the farm. He felt a prisoner, sitting safe and easy and unadventurous. He might, with risk, have done more with himself. He could neither read Browning nor Herbert Spencer, nor have access to such a room as Mrs Forbes'. All that form of life was outside him.

But then, he said he did not want it. The excitement of the visit began to pass off. The next day he was himself, and if he thought of the other woman, there was something about her and her place that he did not like, something cold, something alien, as if she were not a woman, but an inhuman being who used up human life for cold, unliving purposes.

The evening came on, he played with Anna, and then sat alone with his own wife. She was sewing. He sat very still, smoking, perturbed. He was aware of his wife's quiet figure and quiet, dark head bent over her needle. It was too quiet for him. It was too peaceful. He wanted to smash the walls down, and let the night in, so that his wife should not be so secure and quiet, sitting there. He wished the air were not so close and narrow. His wife was obliterated from him, she was in her own world, quiet, secure, unnoticed, unnoticing. He was shut down by her.

He rose to go out. He could not sit still any longer. He must get out of this oppressive, shut-down, woman-haunt.

His wife lifted her head and looked at him.

"Are you going out?" she asked.

He looked down and met her eyes. They were darker than darkness, and gave deeper space. He felt himself retreating before her, defensive, whilst her eyes followed and tracked him down.

"I was just going up to Cossethay," he said.

She remained watching him.

"Why do you go?" she said.

His heart beat fast, and he sat down, slowly.

"No reason particular," he said, beginning to fill his pipe again, mechanically.

"Why do you go away so often?" she said.

"But you don't want me," he replied.

She was silent for a while.

"You do not want to be with me any more," she said.

It startled him. How did she know this truth? He thought it was his secret.

"Yi," he said.

"You want to find something else," she said.

He did not answer. Did he?, he asked himself.

"You should not want so much attention," she said. "You are not a baby."

"I'm not grumbling," he said. Yet he knew he was.

"You think you have not enough," she said.

"How enough?"

"You think you have not enough in me. But how do you know me? What do you do to make me love you?"

He was flabbergasted.

"I never said I hadn't enough in you," he replied. "I didn't know you wanted making to love me. What do you want?"

"You don't make it good between us any more, you are not interested. You do not make me want you."

"And you don't make me want *you*—do you now?"

There was a silence. They were such strangers.

"Would you like to have another woman?" she asked.

His eyes grew round, he did not know where he was. How could she, his own wife, say such a thing? But she sat there small and foreign and separate. It dawned upon him she did not consider herself his wife, except in so far as they agreed. She did not feel she had married him. At any rate, she was willing to allow he might want another woman. A gap, a space opened before him.

"No," he said, slowly. "What other woman should I want?"

"Like your brother," she said.

He was silent for some time, ashamed also.

"What of her?" he said "I didn't like the woman."

"Yes, you liked her," she answered persistently.

He stared in wonder at his wife as she told him his own heart so callously. And he was indignant. What right had she to sit there telling him these things. She was his wife, what right had she to speak to him like this, as if she were a stranger.

"I didn't," he said. "I want no woman."

"Yes, you would like to be like Alfred."

His silence was one of angry frustration. He was astonished. He had told her of his visit to Wirksworth, but briefly, without interest, he thought.

As she sat with her strange dark face turned towards him, her eyes watched him, inscrutable, casting him up. He began to oppose her. She was again the active unknown facing him. Must he admit her? He resisted involuntarily.

"Why should you want to find a woman who is more to you than me?" she said.

The turbulence raged in his breast.

"I don't," he said.

"Why do you?" she repeated. "Why do you want to deny me?"

Suddenly, in a flash, he saw she might be lonely, isolated, unsure.

She had seemed to him the utterly certain, satisfied, absolute, excluding him. Could she need anything?

"Why aren't you satisfied with me?—I'm not satisfied with you. Paul used to come to me and take me like a man does. You only leave me alone, or come to me like your cattle, quickly, to forget me again—so that you can forget me again."

"What am I to remember about you?" said Brangwen.

"I want you to know there is somebody there besides yourself."

"Well don't I know it?"

"You come to me as if it was for nothing, as if I was nothing there. When Paul came to me, I *was* something to him—a woman, I was. To you I am nothing—it is like cattle—or nothing—"

"You make me feel as if *I* was nothing," he said.

They were silent. She sat watching him. He could not move, his soul was seething and chaotic. She turned to her sewing again. But the sight of her bent before him held him and would not let him be. She was a strange, hostile, dominant thing. Yet not quite hostile. As he sat he felt his limbs were strong and hard, he sat in strength.

She was silent for a long time, stitching. He was aware, poignantly, of the round shape of her head, very intimate, compelling. She lifted her head and sighed. The blood burned in him, her voice ran to him like fire.

"Come here," she said, unsure.

For some moments he did not move. Then he rose slowly and went across the hearth. It required an almost deathly effort of volition, or of acquiescence. He stood before her and looked down at her. Her face was shining again, her eyes were shining again like terrible laughter. It was to him terrible, how she could be transfigured. He could not look at her, it burnt his heart.

"My love!" she said.

And she put her arms round him as he stood before her, round his thighs, pressing him against her breast. And her hands on him seemed to reveal to him the mould of his own nakedness, he was passionately lovely to himself. He could not bear to look at her.

"My dear!" she said. He knew she spoke a foreign language. The fear was like bliss in his heart. He looked down. Her face was shining, her eyes were full of light, she was awful. He suffered from the compulsion to her. She was the awful unknown. He bent down to her, suffering, unable to let go, unable to let himself go, yet drawn, driven. She was now the transfigured, she was wonderful, beyond him. He wanted to go. But he could not as yet kiss her. He was himself, apart. Easiest he could kiss her feet. But he was ashamed for the actual deed, which were like an affront. She waited for him to meet her, not to bow before her, and serve her. She wanted his active participation, not his submission.

She put her fingers on him. And it was torture to him, that he must give himself to her actively, participate in her, that he must meet and embrace and know her, who was other than himself. There was that in him which shrank from yielding to her, resisted the relaxing towards her, opposed the mingling with her, even whilst he most desired it. He was afraid, he wanted to save himself.

There were a few moments of stillness. Then gradually, the tension, the withholding relaxed in him, and he began to flow towards her. She was beyond him, the unattainable. But he let go his hold on himself, he relinquished himself, and knew the subterranean force of his desire to come to her, to be with her, to mingle with her, losing himself to find her, to find himself in her. He began to approach her, to draw near.

His blood beat up in waves of desire. He wanted to come to her, to meet her. She was there, if he could reach her. The reality of her who was just beyond him absorbed him. Blind and destroyed, he pressed forward, nearer, nearer, to receive the consummation of himself, be received within the darkness which should swallow him and yield him up to himself. If he could come really within the blazing kernel of darkness, if really he could be destroyed, burnt away till he lit with her in one consummation, that were supreme, supreme.

Their coming together now, after two years of married life, was much more wonderful to them than it had been before. It was the entry into another circle of existence, it was the baptism to another life, it was the complete confirmation. Their feet trod strange ground of knowledge, their footsteps were lit-up with discovery. Wherever they walked, it was well, the world re-echoed round them in discovery. They went gladly and forgetful. Everything was lost, and everything was found. The new world was discovered, it remained only to be explored.

They had passed through the doorway into the further space, where movement was so big, that it contained bonds and constraints and labours, and still was complete liberty. She was the doorway to him, he to her. At last they had thrown open the doors, each to the other, and had stood in the doorways facing each other, whilst the light flooded out from behind on to each of their faces, it was the transfiguration, the glorification, the admission.

And always the light of the transfiguration burned on in their hearts. He went his way, as before, she went her way, to the rest of the world, there seemed no change. But to the two of them, there was the perpetual wonder of the transfiguration.

He did not know her any better, any more precisely, now that he knew her altogether. Poland, her husband, the war—he understood no more of this in her. He did not understand her foreign nature, half German, half Polish, nor her foreign speech. But he knew her, he knew her meaning, without understanding. What she said, what she spoke, this was a blind gesture on her part. In herself she walked strong and clear, he knew her, he saluted her, was with her. What was memory after all, but the recording of a number of possibilities which had never been fulfilled? What was Paul Lensky to her, but an unfulfilled possibility of which he, Brangwen, was the reality and the fulfilment. What did it matter, that Anna Lensky was born of Lydia and Paul? God was her father and her mother, He had passed through the married pair without fully making Himself known to them.

Now He was declared to Brangwen and to Lydia Brangwen, as they stood together. When at last they had joined hands, the house was finished, and the Lord took up His abode. And they were glad.

The days went on as before, Brangwen went out to his work, his wife nursed her child and attended in some measure to the farm. They did not think of each other—why should they? Only when she touched him, he knew her instantly, that she was with him, near him, that she was the gateway and the way out, that she was beyond, and that he was travelling in her through the beyond. Whither?—What does it matter? He responded always. When she called, he answered, when he asked, her response came at once, or at length.

Anna's soul was put at peace between them. She looked from one to the other, and she saw them established to her safety, and she was free. She played between the pillar of fire and the pillar of cloud in confidence, having the assurance on her right hand and the assurance on her left. She was no more called upon to uphold with her childish might the broken end of the arch. Her father and her mother now met to the span of the heavens, and she, the child, was free to play in the space beneath, between.

CHAPTER IV

Girlhood of Anna Brangwen

When Anna was nine years old, Brangwen sent her to the dame's school in Cossethay. There she went, flipping and dancing in her inconsequential fashion, doing very much as she liked, disconcerting old Miss Coates by her indifference to respectability and by her lack of reverence. Anna only laughed at Miss Coates, liked her, and patronised her in superb, childish fashion.

The girl was at once shy and wild. She had a curious contempt for ordinary people, a benevolent superiority. She was very shy, and tortured with misery when people did not like her. On the other hand, she cared very little for anybody save her mother, whom she still rather resentfully worshipped, and her father, whom she loved and patronised, but upon whom she depended. These two, her mother and father, held her still in fee. But she was free of other people, towards whom, on the whole, she took the benevolent attitude. She deeply hated ugliness or intrusion or arrogance, however. As a child, she was as proud and shadowy as a tiger, and as aloof. She could confer favours, but, save from her mother and father, she could receive none. She hated people who came too near to her. Like a wild thing, she wanted her distance. She mistrusted intimacy.

In Cossethay and Ilkeston she was always an alien. She had plenty of acquaintances, but no friends. Very few people whom she met were significant to her. They seemed parts of a herd, undistinguished. She did not take people very seriously.

She had two brothers, Tom, dark-haired, small, volatile, whom she was intimately related to but whom she never mingled with, and Fred, fair and responsive, whom she adored but did not consider as a real, separate being. She was too much the centre of her own universe, too little aware of anything outside.

The first *person* she met, who affected her as a real living person, whom she regarded as having definite existence, was Baron Skrebensky, her mother's friend. He also was a Polish exile, who had taken orders, and had received from Mr Gladstone a small country living in Yorkshire.

When Anna was about ten years old, she went with her mother to spend a few days with the Baron Skrebensky. He was very unhappy in his red-brick vicarage. He was vicar of a country church, a living worth a little over two hundred pounds a year, but he had a large parish containing several collieries, with a new, raw, heathen population. He went to the north of England expecting homage from the common people, for he was an aristocrat. He was roughly, even cruelly received. But he never understood it. He remained a fiery aristocrat. Only he had to learn to avoid his parishioners.

Anna was very much impressed by him. He was a smallish man with a rugged, rather crumpled face and blue eyes set very deep and glowing. His wife was a tall thin woman, of noble Polish family, mad with pride. He still spoke broken English, for he had kept very close to his wife, both of them forlorn in this strange, inhospitable country, and they always spoke in Polish together. He was disappointed with Mrs Brangwen's soft, natural English, very disappointed that her child spoke no Polish.

Anna loved to watch him. She liked the big, new, rambling vicarage, desolate and stark on its hill. It was so exposed, so bleak and bold after the Marsh. The Baron talked endlessly in Polish to Mrs Brangwen; he made furious gestures with his hands, his blue eyes were full of fire. And to Anna, there was a significance about his sharp, flinging movements. Something in her responded, to his extravagance and his exuberant manner. She thought him a very wonderful person. She was shy of him, she liked him to talk to her. She felt a sense of freedom near him.

She never could tell how she knew it, but she did know that he was a knight of Malta. She could never remember whether she had seen his star, or cross, or his order or not, but it flashed in her mind, like a symbol. He at any rate represented to the child the real world, where kings and lords and princes moved and fulfilled their shining lives, whilst queens and ladies and princesses upheld the noble order.

She had recognised the Baron Skrebensky as a real person, he had had some regard for her. But when she did not see him any more, he faded and became a memory. But as a memory he was always alive to her.

Anna became a tall, awkward girl. Her eyes were still very dark and quick, but they had grown careless, they had lost their watchful, hostile look. Her fierce, spun hair turned brown, it grew heavier and was tied back. She was sent to a young ladies' school in Nottingham.

And at this period she was absorbed in becoming a young lady. She was intelligent enough, but not interested in learning. At first, she thought all the girls at school very ladylike and wonderful, and she wanted to be like them. She came to a speedy disillusion: they galled and maddened her, they were petty and mean. After the loose, generous atmosphere of her home, where little things did not count, she was always uneasy in the world, that would snap and bite at every trifle.

A quick change came over her. She mistrusted herself, she mistrusted the outer world. She did not want to go on, she did not want to go out into it, she wanted to go no further.

"What do *I* care about that lot of girls?" she would say to her father, contemptuously, "they are nobody."

The trouble was that the girls could not accept Anna at her measure. They would have her according to themselves or not at all. So she was confused, seduced, she became as they were for a time, and then, in revulsion, she hated them furiously.

"Why don't you ask some of your girls here?" her father would say.

"They're not coming here," she cried.

"And why not."

"They're bagatelle," she said, using one of her mother's rare phrases.

"Bagatelles or billiards, it makes no matter, they're nice young lasses enough."

But Anna was not to be won over. She had a curious shrinking from commonplace people, and particularly from the young lady of her day. She would not go into company because of the ill-at-ease feeling other people brought upon her. And she never could decide whether it were her fault or theirs. She half respected these other people, and continuous disillusion maddened her. She wanted to respect them. Still she thought the people she did not *know* were wonderful. Those she knew seemed always to be limiting her, tying her up in little falsities that irritated her beyond bearing. She would rather stay at home, and avoid the rest of the world, leave it illusory.

For at the Marsh life had indeed a certain freedom and largeness. There was no fret about money, no mean little precedence, nor care for what other people thought, because neither Mrs Brangwen nor Brangwen could be sensible of any judgment passed on them from outside. Their lives were too separate.

So Anna was only easy at home, where the common sense and the supreme relation between her parents produced a freer standard of being than she could find outside. Where, outside the Marsh, could she find the tolerant dignity she had been brought up in? Her parents stood undiminished and unaware of criticism. The people she met outside seemed to begrudge her her very existence. They seemed to want to belittle her also. She was exceedingly reluctant to go amongst them. She depended upon her mother and her father. And yet she wanted to go out.

At school, or in the world, she was usually at fault, she felt usually that she ought to be slinking in disgrace. She was never quite sure, in herself, whether she were wrong, or whether the others were wrong. She had not done her lessons: well, she did not see any reason why she *should* do her lessons, if she did not want to. Was there some occult reason why she should? Were these people, school-mistresses, representatives of some mystic Right, some Higher Good? They seemed to think so themselves. But she could not for her life see why a woman should bully and insult her because she did not know thirty lines of "As You Like It." After all, *what* did it matter if she knew them or not? Nothing could persuade her that it was of the slightest importance. Because she despised inwardly the coarsely working nature of the mistress. Therefore she was always at outs with authority. From constant telling, she came almost to believe in her own badness, her own intrinsic inferiority. She felt that she ought to be always in a state of slinking disgrace, if she fulfilled what was expected of her. But she rebelled. She never really believed in her own badness. At the bottom of her heart she despised the other people, who carped and were loud over trifles. She despised them, and wanted revenge on them. She hated them whilst they had power over her.

Still she kept an ideal: a free, proud lady absolved from the petty ties, existing beyond petty considerations. She would see such ladies in pictures: Alexandra, Princess of Wales, was one of her models. This lady was proud and royal, and stepped indifferently over all small, mean desires: so thought Anna, in her heart. And the girl did up her hair high under a little slanting hat, her skirts were fashion-ably bunched up, she wore an elegant, skin-fitting coat.

Her father was delighted. Anna was very proud in her bearing, too naturally indifferent to smaller bonds to satisfy Ilkeston, which would have liked to put her down. But Brangwen was having no such thing. If she chose to be royal, royal she should be. He stood like a rock between her and the world.

After the fashion of his family, he grew stout and handsome. His blue eyes were full of light, twinkling and sensitive, his manner was deliberate, but hearty, warm. His capacity for living his own life without attention from his neighbours made them respect him. They would run to do anything for him. He did not consider them, but was open-handed towards them, so they made profit of their willingness. He liked people, so long as they remained in the background.

Mrs Brangwen went on in her own way, following her own devices. She had her husband, her two sons, and Anna. These staked out and marked her horizon. The other people were out-siders. Inside her own world, her life passed along like a dream for her, it lapsed, and she lived within its lapse, active and always pleased, intent. She scarcely noticed the outer things at all. What was outside was outside, non-existent. She did not mind if the boys fought, so long as it was out of her presence. But if they fought when she was by, she was angry, and they were afraid of her. She did not care if they broke a window of a railway carriage or sold their watches to have a revel at the Goose Fair. Brangwen was perhaps angry over these things. To the mother they were insignificant.

It was odd little things that offended her. She was furious if the boys hung round the slaughter-house, she was displeased when the school reports were bad. It did not matter how many sins her boys were accused of, so long as they were not stupid, or inferior. If they seemed to brook insult, she hated them. And it was only a certain *gaucherie*, a gawkiness on Anna's part that irritated her against the girl. Certain forms of clumsiness, grossness, made the mother's eyes glow with curious rage. Otherwise she was pleased, indifferent.

Pursuing her splendid-lady ideal, Anna became a lofty demoiselle of sixteen, plagued by family shortcomings. She was very sensitive to her father. She knew if he had been drinking, were he ever so little affected, and she could not bear it. He flushed when he drank, the veins stood out on his temples, there was a twinkling, cavalier boisterousness in his eyes, his manner was jovially overbearing and mocking. And it angered her. When she heard his loud, roaring, boisterous mockery, an anger of resentment filled her. She was quick to forestall him, the moment he came in.

"You look a sight, you do, red in the face," she cried.

"I might look worse if I was green," he answered.

"Boozing in Ilkeston."

"And what's wrong wi' Il'son?"

She flounced away. He watched her with amused, twinkling eyes, yet in spite of himself sad that she flouted him.

They were a curious family, a law to themselves, separate from the world, isolated, a small republic set in invisible bounds. The mother was quite indifferent to Ilkeston and Cossethay, to any claims made on her from outside, she was very shy of any outsider, exceedingly courteous, winning even. But the moment a visitor had gone, she laughed and dismissed him, he did not exist. It had been all a game to her. She was still a foreigner, unsure of her ground. But alone with her own children and husband at the Marsh, she was mistress of a little native land that lacked nothing.

She had some beliefs somewhere, never defined. She had been brought up a Roman Catholic. She had gone to the Church of England for protection. The outward form was a matter of indifference to her. Yet she had some fundamental religion. It was as if she worshipped God as a Mystery, never seeking in the least to define what He was.

And inside her, the subtle sense of the Great Absolute wherein she had her being was very strong. The English dogma never reached her: the language was too foreign. Through it all she felt the great Separator who held life in His hands, gleaming, imminent, terrible, the Great Mystery, immediate beyond all telling.

She shone and gleamed to the Mystery, Whom she knew through all her senses, she glanced with strange, mystic superstitions that never found expression in the English language, never mounted to thought in English. But so she lived, within a potent, sensuous belief that included her family and contained her destiny.

To this she had reduced her husband. He existed with her entirely indifferent to the general values of the world. Her very ways, the very mark of her eyebrows were symbols and indication to him. There, on the farm with her, he lived through a mystery of life and death and creation, strange, profound ecstasies and incommunicable satisfactions, of which the rest of the world knew nothing; which made the pair of them apart and respected in the English village, for they were also well-to-do.

But Anna was only half safe within her mother's unthinking knowledge. She had a mother-of-pearl rosary that had been her own father's. What it meant to her she could never say. But the string of moonlight and silver, when she had it between her fingers, filled her with strange passion. She learned at school a little Latin, she learned an Ave Maria and a Pater Noster, she learned how to say her rosary. But that was no good. "Ave Maria, gratia plena, Dominus tecum, benedicta tu in mulieribus et benedictus fructus ventris tui Jesus. Ave Maria, Sancta Maria, ora pro nobis peccatoribus, nunc et in hora mortis nostrae, Amen."

It was not right, somehow. What these words meant when translated was not the same as the pale rosary meant. There was a discrepancy, a falsehood. It irritated her to say "Dominus tecum," or "benedicta tu in mulieribus." She loved the mystic words "Ave Maria, Sancta Maria": she was moved by "benedictus fructus ventris tui Jesus," and by "nunc et in hora mortis nostrae." But none of it was quite real. It was not satisfactory, somehow.

She avoided her rosary, because, moving her with curious passion as it did, it *meant* only these not very significant things. She put it away. It was her instinct to put all these things away. It was her instinct to avoid thinking, to avoid it, to save herself.

She was seventeen, touchy, full of spirits, and very moody: quick to flush, and always uneasy, uncertain. For some reason or other, she turned more to her father, she felt almost flashes of hatred for her mother. Her mother's dark muzzle and curiously insidious ways, her mother's utter surety and confidence, her strange satisfaction, even triumph, her mother's way of laughing at things, and her mother's silent overriding of vexatious propositions, most of all her mother's triumphant power maddened the girl.

She became sudden and incalculable. Often she stood at the window, looking out, as if she wanted to go. Sometimes she went, she mixed with people. But always she came home in anger, as if she were diminished, belittled, almost degraded.

There was over the house a kind of dark silence and intensity, in which passion worked its inevitable conclusions. There was in the house a sort of richness, a deep, inarticulate interchange which made other places seem thin and unsatisfying. Brangwen could sit silent, smoking in his chair, the mother could move about in her quiet, insidious way, and the sense of the two presences was powerful, sustaining. The whole intercourse was wordless, intense and close.

But Anna was uneasy. She wanted to get away. Yet wherever she went, there came upon her that feeling of thinness, as if she were made smaller, belittled. She hastened home.

There she raged and interrupted the strong, settled interchange. Sometimes her mother turned on her with a fierce, destructive anger, in which was no pity nor consideration. And Anna shrank, afraid. She went to her father.

He would still listen to the spoken word, which fell sterile on the unheeding mother. Sometimes Anna talked to her father. She tried to discuss people, she wanted to know what was meant. But her father became uneasy. He did not want to have things dragged into consciousness. Only out of consideration for her he listened. And there was a kind of bristling rousedness in the room. The cat got up and stretched itself, went uneasily to the door. Mrs Brangwen was silent, she seemed ominous. Anna could not go on with her fault-finding, her criticism, her expression of dissatisfactions. She felt even her father against her. He had a strong, dark bond with her mother, a potent intimacy that existed inarticulate and wild, following its own course, and savage if interrupted, uncovered.

Nevertheless Brangwen was uneasy about the girl, the whole house continued to be disturbed. She had a pathetic, baffled appeal. She was hostile to her parents, even whilst she lived entirely within them, within their spell.

Many ways she tried, of escape. She became an assiduous church-goer. But the *language* meant nothing to her: it seemed false. She hated to hear things expressed, put into words. Whilst the religious feelings were inside her, they were passionately moving. In the mouth of the clergyman, they were false, indecent. She tried to read. But again the tedium and the sense of the falsity of the spoken word put her off. She went to stay with girl friends. At first she thought it splendid. But then the inner boredom came on, it seemed to her all nothingness. And she felt always belittled, as if never, never could she stretch her length and stride her stride.

Her mind reverted often to the torture cell of a certain Bishop of France, in which the victim could neither stand nor lie stretched out, never. Not that she thought of herself in any connection with this. But often there came into her mind the wonder, how the cell was built, and she could feel the horror of the crampedness, as something very real.

She was, however, only eighteen when a letter came from Mrs Alfred Brangwen, in Nottingham, saying that her son William was coming to Ilkeston to take a place as junior draughtsman, scarcely more than apprentice, in a lace-factory. He was twenty years old, and would the Marsh Brangwens be friendly with him.

Tom Brangwen at once wrote offering the young man a home at the Marsh. This was not accepted, but the Nottingham Brangwens expressed gratitude.

There had never been much love lost between the Nottingham Brangwens and the Marsh. Indeed, Mrs Alfred, having inherited three thousand pounds, and having occasion to be dissatisfied with her husband, held aloof from all the Brangwens whatsoever. She affected, however, some esteem of Mrs Tom, as she called the Polish woman, saying that at any rate she was a lady.

Anna Brangwen was faintly excited at the news of her cousin Will's coming to Ilkeston. She knew plenty of young men, but they had never become real to her. She had seen in this young gallant a nose she liked, in that a pleasant moustache, in the other a nice way of wearing clothes, in one a ridiculous fringe of hair, in another a comical way of talking. They were objects of amusement and faint wonder to her, rather than real beings, the young men.

The only man she knew was her father; and, as he was something large, looming, a kind of Godhead, he embraced all manhood for her, and other men were just incidental.

She remembered her cousin Will. He had town clothes and was thin, with a very curious head, black as jet, with hair like sleek, thin fur. It was a curious head: it reminded her she knew not of what: of some animal, some mysterious animal that lived in the darkness under the leaves and never came out, but which lived vividly, swift and intense. She always thought of him with that black, keen, blind head. And she considered him odd.

He appeared at the Marsh one Sunday morning: a rather long, thin youth with a bright face and a curious self-possession among his shyness, a native unawareness of what other people might be, since he was himself.

When Anna came downstairs in her Sunday clothes, ready for church, he rose and greeted her conventionally, shaking hands. His manners were better than hers. She flushed. She noticed that he now had a black fledge on his upper lip, a black, finely-shapen line marking his wide mouth. It rather repelled her. It reminded her of the thin, fine fur of his hair. She was aware of something strange in him.

His voice had rather high upper notes, and very resonant middle notes. It was queer. She wondered why he did it. But he sat very naturally in the Marsh living-room. He had some uncouthness, some natural self-possession of the Brangwens, that made him at home there.

Anna was rather troubled by the intimate, affectionate way her father had towards this young man. He seemed gentle towards him, he put himself aside in order to fill out the young man. This irritated Anna.

"Father," she said abruptly, "give me some collection."

"What collection?" asked Brangwen.

"Don't be ridiculous," she cried, flushing.

"Nay," he said, "what collection's this?"

"You know it's the first Sunday of the month."

Anna stood confused. Why was he doing this, why was he making her conspicuous before this stranger!

"I want some collection," she re-asserted.

"So tha says," he replied indifferently, looking at her then turning again to his nephew.

She went forward, and thrust her hand into his breeches pocket. He smoked stolidly, making no resistance, talking to his nephew. Her hand groped about in his pocket, and then drew out his leathern purse. Her colour was bright in her clear cheeks, her eyes shone. Brangwen's eyes were twinkling. The nephew sat sheepishly. Anna, in her finery, sat down and slid all the money into her lap. There was silver and gold. The youth could not help watching her. She was bent over the heap of money, fingering the different coins.

"I've a good mind to take half a sovereign," she said, and she looked up with glowing dark eyes. She met the light-brown eyes of her cousin, close and intent upon her. She was startled. She laughed quickly, and turned to her father.

"I've a good mind to take half a sovereign, our Dad," she said.

"Yes, nimble fingers," said her father. "You take what's your own."

"Are you coming, our Anna?" asked her brother from the door.

She suddenly chilled to normal, forgetting both her father and her cousin.

"Yes, I'm ready," she said, taking sixpence from the heap of money and sliding the rest back into the purse, which she laid on the table.

"Give it here," said her father.

Hastily she thrust the purse into his pocket and was going out.

"You'd better go wi' 'em, lad, hadn't you?" said the father to the nephew.

Will Brangwen rose uncertainly. He had golden-brown, quick, steady eyes, like a bird's, like a hawk's, which cannot look afraid.

"Your Cousin Will 'll come with you," said the father.

Anna glanced at the strange youth again. She felt him waiting there for her to notice him. He was hovering on the edge of her consciousness, ready to come in. She did not want to look at him: she was antagonistic to him.

She waited without speaking. Her cousin took his hat and joined her. It was summer outside. Her brother Fred was plucking a sprig of flowering currant to put in his coat, from the bush at the angle of the house. She took no notice. Her cousin followed just behind her.

They were on the high-road. She was aware of a strangeness in her being. It made her uncertain. She caught sight of the flowering currant in her brother's buttonhole.

"Oh, our Fred," she cried. "Don't wear that stuff to go to church."

Fred looked down protectively at the pink adornment on his breast.

"Why, I like it," he said.

"Then you're the only one who does, I'm sure," she said. And she turned to her cousin.

"Do *you* like the smell of it?" she asked.

He was there beside her, tall and uncouth and yet self-possessed. It excited her.

"I can't say whether I do or not," he replied.

"Give it here, Fred, don't have it smelling in church," she said to the little boy, her page.

Her fair, small brother handed her the flower dutifully. She sniffed it and gave it without a word to her cousin, for his judgment. He smelled the dangling flower curiously.

"It's a funny smell," he said.

And suddenly she laughed, and a quick light came on all their faces, there was a blithe trip in the small boy's walk.

The bells were ringing, they were going up the summery hill in their Sunday clothes. Anna was very fine in a silk frock of brown and white stripes, tight along the arms and the body, bunched up very elegantly behind the skirt. There was something of the cavalier about Will Brangwen, and he was well dressed.

He walked along with the sprig of currant-blossom dangling between his fingers, and none of them spoke. The sun shone brightly on little showers of buttercup down the bank, in the fields the fool's-parsley was foamy, held very high and proud above a number of flowers that flitted in the greenish twilight of the mowing-grass below.

They reached the church. Fred led the way to the pew, followed by the cousin, then Anna. She felt very conspicuous and important. Somehow, this young man gave her away to the other people. He stood aside and let her pass to her place, then sat next to her. It was a curious sensation, to sit next to him.

The colour came streaming from the painted window above her. It lit on the dark wood of the pew, on the stone, worn aisle, on the pillar behind her cousin, and on her cousin's hands, as they lay on his knees. She sat amid illumination, illumination and luminous shadow all around her, her soul very bright. She sat, without knowing it, conscious of the hands and motionless knees of her cousin. Something strange had entered into her world, something entirely strange and unlike what she knew.

She was curiously elated. She sat in a glowing world of unreality, very delightful. A brooding light, like laughter, was in her eyes. She was aware of a strange influence entering in to her, which she enjoyed. It was a dark, enrichening influence she had not known before. She did not think of her cousin. But she was startled when his hands moved.

She *wished* he would not say the responses so plainly. It diverted her from her vague enjoyment. Why would he obtrude, and draw notice to himself? It was bad taste. But she went on all right till the hymn came. He stood up beside her to sing, and that pleased her. Then suddenly, at the very first word, his voice came strong and over-riding, filling the church. He was singing the tenor. Her soul opened in amazement. His voice filled the church! It rang out like a trumpet, and rang out again. She started to giggle over her hymn-book. But he went on, perfectly steady. Up and down rang his voice, going its own way. She was helplessly shocked into laughter. Between moments of dead silence in herself she shook with laughter. On came the laughter, seized her and shook her till the tears were into her eyes. She was amazed, and rather enjoyed it. And still the hymn rolled on, and still she laughed. She bent over her hymn-book crimson with confusion, but still her sides shook with laughter. She pretended to cough, she pretended to have a crumb in her throat. Fred was gazing up at her with clear blue eyes. She was recovering herself. And then a slur in the strong, blind voice at her side brought it all on again, in a gust of mad laughter.

She bent down to prayer in cold reproof of herself. And yet, as she knelt, little eddies of giggling went over her. The very sight of his knees on the praying cushion sent the little shock of laughter over her.

She gathered herself together and sat with prim, pure face, white and pink and cold as a christmas rose, her hands in her silk gloves folded on her lap, her dark eyes all vague, abstracted in a sort of dream, oblivious of everything.

The sermon rolled on vaguely, in a tide of pregnant peace. Her cousin too out his pocket handkerchief. He seemed to be drifted absorbed into the sermon. He put his handkerchief to his face. Then something dropped on to his knee. There lay the bit of flowering currant! He was looking down at it in real astonishment. A wild snirt of laughter came from Anna. Everybody heard: it was torture. He had shut the crumpled flower in his hand and was looking up again with the same absorbed attention to the sermon. Another snirt of laughter from Anna. Fred nudged her remindingly. Her cousin sat motionless. Somehow she was aware that his face was red. She could feel him. His hand, closed over the flower, remained quite still, pretending to be normal. Another wild struggle in Anna's breast, and the snirt of laughter. She bent forward shaking with laughter. It was now no joke. Fred was nudge-nudging at her. She nudged him back fiercely. Then another vicious spasm of laughter seized her. She tried to ward it off in a little cough. The cough ended in a suppressed whoop. The whole church heard it. She wanted to die. And the closed hand crept away to the pocket. Whilst she sat in taut suspense, the laughter rushed back at her, knowing he was fumbling in his pocket to shove the flower away.

In the end, she felt weak, exhausted, and thoroughly depressed. A blankness of wincing depression came over her. She hated the presence of the other people. Her face became quite haughty. She was unaware of her cousin any more.

When the collection arrived, with the last hymn, her cousin was again singing resoundingly. And still it amused her. In spite of the shameful exhibition she had made of herself, it amused her still. She listened to it in a spell of amusement. And the bag was thrust in front of her, and her sixpence was mingled in the folds of her glove. In her haste to get it out, it flipped away and went tinkling in the next pew. She stood and giggled. She could not help it: she laughed outright, a figure of shame.

"What were you laughing about, our Anna?" asked Fred, the moment they were out of the church.

"Oh, I couldn't help it," she said, in her careless, half mocking fashion. "I don't know *why* Cousin Will's singing set me off."

"What was there in my singing to make you laugh?" he asked.

"It was so loud," she said.

They did not look at each other, but they both laughed again, both reddening.

"What were you snorting o'laughing for, our Anna?" asked Tom, the elder brother, at the dinner table, his hazel eyes bright with joy. "Everybody stopped to look at you." Tom was in the choir.

She was aware of Will's eyes shining steadily upon her, waiting for her to speak.

"It was Cousin Will's singing," she said.

At which her cousin burst into a suppressed, chuckling laugh, suddenly showing all his small, regular, rather sharp teeth, and just as quickly closing his mouth again.

"Has he got such a remarkable voice on him then?" asked Brangwen.

"No, it's not that," said Anna. "Only it tickled me—I couldn't tell you why."

And again a ripple of laughter went down the table. Will Brangwen thrust forward his dark face, his eyes dancing, and said:

"I'm in the choir of St Nicholas'."

"Oh, you go to church then?" said Brangwen.

"Mother does—father doesn't," replied the youth.

It was the little things, his movement, the funny tones of his voice, that showed up big to Anna. The matter-of-fact things he said were absurd in contrast. The things her father said seemed meaningless and neutral.

During the afternoon they sat in the parlour, that smelled of geranium, and they ate cherries, and talked. Will Brangwen was called on to give himself forth. And soon he was drawn out.

He was interested in churches, in church architecture. The influence of Ruskin had stimulated him to a pleasure in the mediæval forms. His talk was fragmentary, he was only half articulate. But listening to him, as he spoke of church after church, of nave and chancel and transept, of rood-screen and font, of hatchet-carving and moulding and tracery, speaking always with close passion of particular things, particular places, there gathered in her heart a pregnant hush of churches, a mystery, a ponderous significance of bowed stone, a dim coloured light through which something took place obscurely, passing into darkness: a high, delighted framework of the mystic screen, and beyond, in the furthest beyond, the altar. It was a very real experience. She was carried away. And the land seemed to be covered with a vast, mystic church, reserved in gloom, thrilled with an unknown Presence.

Almost it hurt her, to look out of the window and see the lilacs towering in the vivid sunshine. Or was this the jewelled glass?

He talked of Gothic and Renaissance and Perpendicular, and Early English and Norman. The words thrilled her.

"Have you been to Southwell?" he said. "I was there at twelve o'clock, at midday, eating my lunch in the churchyard. And the bells played a hymn.

"Ay, it's a fine Minster, Southwell, heavy. It's got heavy, round arches, rather low, on thick pillars. It's grand, the way those arches travel forward.

"There's a sedilia as well—pretty. But I like the main body of the church—and that north porch—"

He was very much excited and filled with himself that afternoon. A flame kindled round him, making his experience passionate and glowing, burningly real.

His uncle listened with twinkling eyes, half moved. His aunt bent forward her dark face, half moved, but held by other knowledge. Anna went with him.

He returned to his lodgings at night treading quick, his eyes glittering and his face shining darkly as if he came from some passionate, vital tryst.

The glow remained in him, the fire burned, his heart was fierce like a sun. He enjoyed his unknown life and his own self. And he was ready to go back to the Marsh.

Without knowing it, Anna was wanting him to come. In him she had escaped. In him the bounds of her experience were transgressed: he was a hole in the wall, beyond which the sunshine blazed on an outside world.

He came. Sometimes, not often, but sometimes, talking again, there recurred the strange, remote reality which carried everything before it. Sometimes he talked of his father, whom he hated with a hatred that was burningly close to love, of his mother, whom he loved with a love that was keenly close to hatred, or to revolt. His sentences were clumsy, he was only half articulate. But he had the wonderful voice, that could ring its vibration through the girl's soul, transport her into his feeling. Sometimes his voice was hot and declamatory, sometimes it had a strange, twanging, almost cat-like sound, sometimes it hesitated, puzzled, sometimes there was the break of a little laugh. Anna was taken by him. She loved the running flame that coursed through her as she listened to him. And his mother and his father became to her two separate people in her life.

For some weeks the youth came frequently, and was received gladly by them all. He sat amongst them, his dark face glowing, an eagerness and a touch of derisiveness on his wide mouth, something grinning and twisted, his eyes always shining like a bird's, utterly without depth. There was no getting hold of the fellow, Brangwen irritably thought. He was like a grinning young tom-cat, that came when he thought he would, and without cognisance of the other person.

At first the youth had looked towards Tom Brangwen when he talked; and then he looked towards his aunt, for her appreciation, valuing it more than his uncle's; and then he turned to Anna, because from her he got what he wanted, which was not in the older people.

So that the two young people, from being always attendant on the elder, began to draw apart and establish a separate kingdom. Sometimes Tom Brangwen was irritated. His nephew irritated him. The lad seemed to him too special, self-contained. His nature was fierce enough, but too much abstracted, like a separate thing, like a cat's nature. A cat could lie perfectly peacefully, on the hearthrug whilst its master or mistress writhed in agony a yard away. It had nothing to do with other people's affairs. What did the lad really care about anything, save his own instinctive affairs.

Brangwen was irritated. Nevertheless he liked and respected his nephew. Mrs Brangwen was irritated by Anna, who was suddenly changed, under the influence of the youth. The mother liked the boy: he was not quite an outsider. But she did not like her daughter to be so much under the spell.

So that gradually the two young people drew apart, escaped from the elders, to create a new thing by themselves. He worked in the garden to propitiate his uncle. He talked churches to propitiate his aunt. He followed Anna like a shadow: like a long, persistent, unswerving black shadow he went after the girl. It irritated Brangwen exceedingly. It exasperated him beyond bearing, to see the lit-up grin, the cat-grin as he called it, on his nephew's face.

And Anna had a new reserve, a new independence. Suddenly she began to act independently of her parents, to live beyond them. Her mother had flashes of anger.

But the courtship went on. Anna would find occasion to go shopping in Ilkeston at evening. She always returned with her cousin, he walking with his head over her shoulder, a little bit behind her, like the Devil looking over Lincoln, as Brangwen noted angrily and yet with satisfaction.

To his own wonder, Will Brangwen found himself in an electric state of passion. To his wonder, he had stopped her at the gate as they came home from Ilkeston one night, and had kissed her, blocking her way and kissing her whilst he felt as if some blow were struck at him in the dark. And when they went indoors, he was acutely angry that her parents looked up scrutinisingly at him and her. What right had they there: why should they look up! Let them remove themselves, or look elsewhere.

And the youth went home with the stars in heaven whirling fiercely about the blackness of his head, and his heart fierce, insistent, but fierce as if he felt something balking him. He wanted to smash through something.

A spell was cast over her. And how uneasy her parents were, as she went about the house unnoticing, not noticing them, moving in a spell as if she were invisible to them. She *was* invisible to them. It made them angry. Yet they had to submit. She went about absorbed, obscured for a while.

Over him too the darkness of obscurity settled. He seemed to be hidden in a tense, electric darkness, in which his soul, his life was intensely active, but without his aid or attention. His mind was obscured. He worked swiftly and mechanically, and he produced some beautiful things.

His favorite work was wood-carving. The first thing he made for her was a butter stamper. In it he carved a mythological bird, a phœnix, something like an eagle, rising on symmetrical wings, from a circle of very beautiful flickering flames that rose upwards from the rim of the cup.

Anna thought nothing of the gift on the evening when he gave it to her. In the morning, however, when the butter was made, she fetched his seal in place of the old wooden stamper of oak-leaves and acorns. She was curiously excited to see how it would turn out. Strange, the uncouth bird moulded there, in the cup-like hollow, with curious, thick waverings running inwards from a smooth rim. She pressed another mould. Strange, to lift the stamp and see that eagle-beaked bird raising its breast to her. She loved creating it over and over again. And every time she looked, it seemed a new thing come to life. Every piece of butter became this strange, vital emblem.

She showed it to her mother and father.

"That is beautiful," said her mother, a little light coming on to her face.

"Beautiful!" exclaimed the father, puzzled, fretted. "Why what sort of a bird does he call it?"

And this was the question put by the customers during the next weeks.

"What sort of a bird do you call *that*, as you've got on th' butter?"

When he came in the evening, she took him into the dairy to show him.

"Do you like it?" he asked, in his loud, vibrating voice that always sounded strange, re-echoing in the dark places of her being.

They very rarely touched each other. They liked to be alone together, near to each other, but there was still a distance between them.

In the cool dairy the candle-light lit on the large, white surfaces of the cream pans. He turned his head sharply. It was so cool and remote in there, so remote. His mouth was open in a little, strained laugh. She stood with her head bent, turned aside. He wanted to go near to her. He had kissed her once. Again his eye rested on the round blocks of butter, where the emblematic bird lifted its breast from the shadow cast by the candle flame. What was restraining him? Her breast was near him; his head lifted like an eagle's. She did not move. Suddenly, with an incredibly quick, delicate movement, he put his arms round her and drew her to him. It was quick, cleanly done, like a bird that swoops and sinks close, closer.

He was kissing her throat. She turned and looked at him. Her eyes were dark and flowing with fire. His eyes were hard and bright with a fierce purpose and gladness, like a hawk's. She felt him flying into the dark space of her flames, like a brand, like a gleaming hawk.

They had looked at each other, and seen each other strange, yet near, very near, like a hawk stooping, swooping, dropping into a flame of darkness. So she took the candle and they went back to the kitchen.

They went on in this way for some time, always coming together, but rarely touching, very seldom did they kiss. And then, often, it was merely a touch of the lips, a sign. But her eyes began to waken with a constant fire, she paused often in the midst of her transit, as if to recollect something, or to discover something.

And his face became sombre, intent, he did not readily hear what was said to him.

One evening in August he came when it was raining. He came in with his jacket collar turned up, his jacket buttoned close, his face wet. And he looked so slim and definite, coming out of the chill rain, she was suddenly blinded with love for him. Yet he sat and talked with her father and mother, meaninglessly, whilst her blood seethed to anguish in her. She wanted to touch him now, only to touch him.

There was the queer, abstract look on her silvery radiant face that maddened her father, her dark eyes were hidden. But she raised them to the youth. And they were dark with a flare that made him quail for a moment.

She went into the second kitchen and took a lantern. Her father watched her as she returned.

"Come with me, Will," she said to her cousin. "I want to see if I put the brick over where that rat comes in."

"You've no need to do that," retorted her father.

She took no notice. The youth was between the two wills. The colour mounted into the father's face, his blue eyes stared. The girl stood near the door, her head held slightly back, like an indication that the youth must come. He rose, in his silent, intent way, and was gone with her. The blood swelled in Brangwen's forehead veins.

It was raining. The light of the lantern flashed on the cobbled path and the bottom of the wall. She came to a small ladder, and climbed up. He reached her the lantern, and followed. Up there in the fowl-loft, the birds sat in fat bunches on the perches, the red combs shining like fire. Bright, sharp eyes opened. There was a sharp crawk of expostulation as one of the hens shifted over. The cock sat watching, his yellow neck-feathers bright as glass. Anna went across the dirty floor. Brangwen crouched in the loft, watching. The light was soft under the red, naked tiles. The girl crouched in a corner.

There was another explosive bustle of a hen springing from her perch.

Anna came back, stooping under the perches. He was waiting for her near the door. Suddenly she had her arms round him, was clinging close to him, cleaving her body against his, and crying, in a whispering, whimpering sound:

"Will, I love you, I love you, Will, I love you."

It sounded as if it were tearing her.

He was not even very much surprised. He held her in his arms, and his bones melted. He leaned back against the wall. The door of the loft was open. Outside, the rain slanted by in fine, steely, mysterious haste, emerging out of the gulf of darkness. He held her in his arms, and he and she together seemed to be swinging in big, swooping oscillations, the two of them clasped together up in the darkness. Outside the open door of the loft in which they stood, beyond them and below them, was darkness, with a travelling veil of rain.

"I love you, Will, I love you," she moaned, "I love you, Will."

He held her as though they were one, and was silent.

In the house, Tom Brangwen waited a while. Then he got up and went out. He went down the yard. He saw the curious misty shaft coming from the loft door. He scarcely knew it was the light in the rain. He went on till the illumination fell on him dimly. Then looking up, through the blur he saw the youth and the girl together, the youth with his back against the wall, his head sunk over the head of the girl. The elder man saw them blurred through the rain, but lit up. They thought themselves so buried in the night. He even saw the lighted dryness of the loft behind, and shadows and bunches of roosting fowl, up in the night, strange shadows cast from the lantern on the floor.

And a black gloom of anger, and a tenderness of self-effacement, fought in his heart. She did not understand what she was doing. She betrayed herself. She was a child, a mere child. She did not know how much of herself she was squandering. And he was blackly and furiously miserable. Was he then an old man, that he should be giving her away in marriage? Was he old? He was not old. He was younger than that young thoughtless fellow in whose arms she lay. Who knew her—he or that blind-headed youth? To whom did she belong, if not to himself?

He thought again of the child he had carried out at night into the barn, whilst his wife was in labour with the young Tom. He remembered the soft, warm weight of the little girl on his arm, round his neck. Now she would say he was finished. She was going away, to deny him, to leave an unendurable emptiness in him, a void that he could not bear. Almost he hated her. How dared she say he was old. He walked on in the rain, sweating with pain, with the horror of being old, with the agony of having to relinquish what was life to him.

Will Brangwen went home without having seen his uncle. He held his hot face to the rain, and walked on in a trance. "I love you, Will, I love you." The words repeated themselves endlessly. The veils had ripped and issued him naked into endless space, and he shuddered. The walls had thrust him out, and given him a vast space to walk in. Whither, through this darkness of infinite space, was he walking blindly? Where, at the end of all the darkness, was God the Almighty still darkly seated, thrusting him on? "I love you, Will, I love you." He trembled with fear as the words beat in his heart again. And he dared not think of her face, of her eyes which shone, and of her strange, transfigured face. The hand of the Hidden Almighty, burning bright, had thrust out of the darkness and gripped him. He went on subject, and in fear, his heart gripped and burning from the touch.

The days went by, they ran on dark-padded feet in silence. He went to see Anna, but again there had come a reserve between them. Tom Brangwen was gloomy, his blue eyes sombre. Anna was strange and delivered up. Her face in its delicate colouring was mute, touched dumb and poignant. The mother bowed her head and moved in her own dark world, that was pregnant again with fulfilment.

Will Brangwen worked at his wood-carving. It was a passion, a passion for him to have the chisel under his grip. Verily the passion of his heart lifted the fine bite of steel. He was carving, as he had always wanted, the Creation of Eve. It was a panel in low relief, for a church. Adam lay asleep as if suffering, and God, a dim, large figure, stooped towards him, stretching forward His unveiled hand; an Eve, a small, vivid, naked female shape, was issuing like a flame towards the hand of God, from the torn side of Adam.

Now, Will Brangwen was working at the Eve. She was thin, a keen, unripe thing. With trembling passion, fine as a breath of air, he sent the chisel over her belly, her hard, unripe, small belly. She was a stiff little figure, with sharp lines, in the throes and torture and ecstasy of her creation. But he trembled as he touched her. He had not finished any of his figures. There was a bird on a bough overhead, lifting its wings for flight, and a serpent wreathing up to it. It was not finished yet. He trembled with passion, at last able to create the new, sharp body of his Eve.

At the sides, at the far sides, at either end, were two angels covering their faces with their wings. They were like trees. As he went to the Marsh, in the twilight, he felt that the angels with covered faces were standing back as he went by. The darkness was of their shadows and the covering of their faces. When he went through the canal bridge, the evening glowed in its last deep colours, the sky was dark blue, the stars glittered from afar, very remote and approaching above the darkening cluster of the farm, above the puther of crystal along the edge of the heavens.

She waited for him like the glow of light, and as if his face were covered. And he dared not lift his face to look at her.

Corn-harvest came on. One evening they walked out through the farm-buildings at nightfall. A large gold moon hung heavily to the grey horizon, trees hovered tall, standing back in the dusk, waiting. Anna and the young man went on noiselessly by the hedge, along where the farm-carts had made dark ruts in the grass. They came through a gate into a wide open field where still much light seemed to spread against their faces. In the under-shadow the sheaves lay on the ground where the reapers had left them, many sheaves like bodies prostrate in shadowy bulk; others were riding hazily in shocks, like ships in the haze of moonlight and of dusk, further off.

They did not want to turn back, yet whither they were to go, towards the moon? For they were separate, single.

"We will put up some sheaves," said Anna.

So they could remain there in the broad, open place.

They went across the stubble to where the long rows of upreared shocks ended. Curiously populous that part of the field looked, where the shocks rode erect; the rest was open and prostrate.

The air was all hoary silver. She looked around her. Trees stood vaguely at their distance, as if waiting, like heralds, for the signal to approach. In this space of vague crystal her heart seemed like a bell ringing. She was afraid lest the sound should be heard.

"You take this row," she said to the youth, and passing on, she stooped in the next row of lying sheaves, grasping her hands in the tresses of the oats, lifting the heavy corn in either hand, carrying it, as it hung heavily against her, to the cleared space, where she set the two sheaves sharply down, bringing them together with a faint, keen clash. Her two bulks stood leaning together. He was coming, walking shadowily with the gossamer dusk, carrying his two sheaves. She waited near by. He set his sheaves with a keen, faint clash, next to her sheaves. They rode unsteadily. He tangled the tresses of corn. It hissed like a fountain. He looked up and laughed.

Then she turned away towards the moon, which seemed glowingly to uncover her bosom every time she faced it. He went to the vague emptiness of the field opposite, dutifully.

They stooped, grasped the wet, soft hair of the corn, lifted the heavy bundles, and returned. She was always first. She set down her sheaves, making a pent-house with those others. He was coming shadowy across the stubble, carrying his bundles. She turned away, hearing only the sharp hiss of his mingling corn. She walked between the moon and his shadowy figure.

She took her new two sheaves and walked towards him, as he rose from stooping over the earth. He was coming out of the near distance. She set down her sheaves to make a new stook. They were unsure. Her hands fluttered. Yet she broke away, and turned to the moon, which laid bare her bosom, so she felt as if her bosom were heaving and panting with moonlight.—And he had to put up her two sheaves, which had fallen down. He worked in silence. The rhythm of the work carried him away again, as she was coming near.

They worked together, coming and going, in a rhythm, which carried their feet and their bodies in tune. She stooped, she lifted the burden of sheaves, she turned her face to the dimness where he was, and went with her burden over the stubble. She hesitated, set down her sheaves, there was a swish and hiss of mingling oats, he was drawing near, and she must turn, again. And there was the flaring moon laying bare her bosom again, making her drift and ebb like a wave.

He worked steadily, engrossed, threading backwards and forwards like a shuttle across the strip of cleared stubble, weaving the long line of riding shocks, nearer and nearer to the shadowy trees, threading his sheaves with hers.

And always she was gone before he came. As he came, she drew away, as he drew away, she came. Were they never to meet? Gradually a low, deep-sounding will in him vibrated to her, tried to set her in accord, tried to bring her gradually to him, to a meeting, till they should be together, till they should meet as the sheaves that swished together.

And the work went on. The moon grew brighter, clearer, the corn glistened. He bent over the prostrate bundles, there was a hiss as the sheaves left the ground, a trailing of heavy bodies against him, a dazzle of moonlight on his eyes. And then he was setting the corn together at the stook. And she was coming near.

He waited for her, he fumbled at the stook. She came. But she stood back till he drew away. He saw her in shadow, a dark column, and spoke to her, and she answered. She saw the moonlight flash question on his face. But there was a space between them, and he went away, the work carried them, rhythmic.

Why was there always a space between them, why were they apart? Why, as she came up from under the moon, would she halt and stand off from him? Why was he held away from her? His will drummed persistently, darkly, it drowned everything else.

Into the rhythm of his work there came a pulse and a steadied purpose. He stooped, he lifted the weight, he heaved it towards her, setting it as in her, under the moonlit space. And he went back for more. Ever with increasing closeness he lifted the sheaves and swung striding to the centre with them, ever he drove her more nearly to the meeting, ever he did his share, and drew towards her, overtaking her. There was only the moving to and fro in the moonlight, engrossed, the swinging in the silence, that was marked only by the splash of sheaves, and silence, and a splash of sheaves. And ever the splash of his sheaves broke swifter, beating up to hers, and ever the splash of her sheaves recurred monotonously, unchanging, and ever the splash of his sheaves beat nearer.

Till at last, they met at the shock, facing each other, sheaves in hand. And he was silvery with moonlight, with a moonlit, shadowy face that frightened her. She waited for him.

"Put yours down," she said.

"No, it's your turn."

His voice was twanging and insistent.

She set her sheaves against the shock. He saw her hands glisten among the spray of grain. And he dropped his sheaves and he trembled as he took her in his arms. He had overtaken her, and it was his privilege, to kiss her. She was sweet and fresh with the night air, and sweet with the scent of grain. And the whole rhythm of him beat into his kisses, and still he pursued her, in his kisses, and still she was not quite overcome. He wondered over the moonlight on her nose! All the moonlight upon her, all the darkness within her! All the night in his arms, darkness and shine, he possessed of it all! All the night for him now, to unfold, to venture within, all the mystery to be entered, all the discovery to be made.

Trembling with keen triumph, his heart was white as a star as he drove his kisses nearer.

"My love!" she called, in a low voice, from afar.

The low sound seemed to call to him from far off, under the moon, to him who was unaware. He stopped, quivered, and listened.

"My love," came again the low, plaintive call, like a bird unseen in the night.

He was afraid. His heart quivered and broke. He was stopped.

"Anna," he said, as if he answered her from a distance, unsure. "My love."

And he drew near, and she drew near.

"Anna," he said, in wonder and birthpain of love.

"My love," she said, her voice growing rapturous.

And they kissed on the mouth, in rapture and surprise, long, real kisses. The kiss lasted, there among the moonlight. He kissed her again, and she kissed him. And again they were kissing together. Till something happened in him, he was strange. He wanted her. He wanted her exceedingly. She was something new. They stood there folded, suspended in the night. And his whole being quivered with surprise, as from a blow. He wanted her, and he wanted to tell her so. But the shock was too great to him. He had never realised before. He trembled with initiation and unusedness, he did not know what to do. He held her more gently, gently, much more gently. The conflict was gone by. And he was glad, and breathless, and almost in tears. But he knew he wanted her. Something fixed in him for ever. He was hers. And he was very glad, and afraid. He did not know what to do, as they stood there in the open, moonlit fields. He looked through her hair at the moon, which seemed to swim liquid-bright.

She sighed, and seemed to wake up. Then she kissed him again. Then she loosened herself away from him and took his hand. It hurt him when she drew away from his breast. It hurt him with a chagrin. Why did she draw away from him? But she held his hand.

"I want to go home," she said, looking at him in a way he could not understand.

He held close to her hand. He was dazed and he could not move, he did not know how to move. She drew him away.

He walked helplessly beside her, holding her hand. She went with bent head. Suddenly he said, as the simple solution stated itself to him:

"We'll get married, Anna."

She was silent.

"We'll get married, Anna, shall we?"

She stopped in the field again and kissed him, clinging to him passionately, in a way he could not understand. He could not understand. But he left it all now, to marriage. That was the solution now, fixed ahead. He wanted her, he wanted to be married to her, he wanted to have her altogether, as his own for ever. And he waited, intent, for the accomplishment. But there was all the while a slight tension of irritation.

He spoke to his uncle and aunt that night.

"Uncle," he said, "Anna and me think of getting married."

"Oh ay!" said Brangwen.

"But how, you have no money," said the mother.

The youth went pale. He hated these words. But he was like a gleaming, bright pebble, something bright and inalterable. He did not think. He sat there in his hard brightness, and did not speak.

"Have you mentioned it to your own mother?" asked Brangwen.

"No—I s'll tell her on Saturday."

"You'll go and see her?"

"Yes."

There was a long pause.

"And what are you going to marry on—your pound a week?"

Again the youth went pale, as if the spirit were being injured in him.

"I don't know," he said, looking at his uncle with his bright, inhuman eyes, like a hawk's.

Brangwen stirred in hatred.

"It needs knowing," he said.

"I shall have money later on," said the nephew. "I will raise some now, and pay it back then."

"Oh ay!—And why this desperate hurry? She's a child of eighteen, and you're a boy of twenty. You're neither of you of age to do as you like yet."

Will Brangwen ducked his head and looked at his uncle with swift, bright, mistrustful eyes, like a caged hawk.

"What does it matter how old she is, and how old I am," he said. "What's the difference between me now and when I'm thirty?"

"A big difference, let us hope."

"But you have no experience—you have no experience, and no money. Why do you want to marry, without experience or money?" asked the aunt.

"What experience do I want, Aunt?" asked the boy.

And if Brangwen's heart had not been hard and intact with anger, like a precious stone, he would have agreed.

Will Brangwen went home strange and untouched. He felt he could not alter from what he was fixed upon, his will was set. To alter it he must be destroyed. And he would not be destroyed. He had no money. But he would get some from somewhere, it did not matter. He lay awake for many hours, hard and clear and unthinking, his soul crystallising more inalterably. Then he went fast asleep.

It was as if his soul had turned into a hard crystal. He might tremble and quiver and suffer, *it* did not alter.

The next morning Tom Brangwen, inhuman with anger, spoke to Anna.

"What's this about wanting to get married?" he said.

She stood, paling a little, her dark eyes springing to the hostile, startled look of a savage thing that will defend itself, but trembles with sensitiveness.

"I do," she said, out of her unconsciousness.

His anger rose, and he would have liked to break her.

"You do—you do—and what for?" he sneered with contempt.

The old, childish agony, the blindness that could recognise nobody, the palpitating antagonism as of a raw, helpless, undefended thing came back on her.

"I do because I do," she cried, in the shrill, hysterical way of her childhood. "*You* are not my father—my father is dead—*you* are not my father."

She was still a stranger. She did not recognise him. The cold blade cut down, deep into Brangwen's soul. It cut him off from her.

"And what if I'm not?" he said.

But he could not bear it. It had been so passionately dear to him, her "Father—Daddie."

He went about for some days as if stunned. His wife was bemused.

She did not understand. She only thought the marriage was impeded for want of money and position.

There was a horrible silence in the house. Anna kept out of sight as much as possible. She could be for hours alone.

Will Brangwen came back, after stupid scenes at Nottingham. He too was pale and blank, but unchanging. His uncle hated him. He hated this youth, who was so inhuman and obstinate. Nevertheless, it was to Will Brangwen that the uncle, one evening, handed over the shares which he had had transferred to Anna Lensky. They were for two thousand five hundred pounds. Will Brangwen looked at his uncle. It was a great deal of the Marsh capital here given away. The youth, however, was only colder and more fixed. He was abstract, purely a fixed will. He gave the shares to Anna.

After which she cried for a whole day, sobbing her eyes out. And at night, when she had heard her mother go to bed, she slipped down and hung in the doorway. Her father sat in his heavy silence, like a monument. He turned his head slowly.

"Daddy," she cried from the doorway, and she ran to him sobbing as if her heart would break. "Daddy—daddy—daddy—"

She crouched on the hearthrug with her arms round him and her face against him. His body was so big and comfortable. But something hurt her heart intolerably. She sobbed almost with hysteria.

He was silent, with his hand on her shoulder. His heart was bleak. He was not her father. That beloved image she had broken. Who was he then? A man put apart with those whose life has no more developments. He was isolated from her. There was a generation between them, he was old, he had died out from hot life. A great deal of ash was in his fire, cold ash. He felt the inevitable coldness, and in bitterness forgot the fire. He sat in his coldness of age and isolation. He had his own wife. And he blamed himself, he sneered at himself, for this clinging to the young, wanting the young to belong to him.

The child who clung to him wanted her child-husband, as was natural. And from him, Brangwen, she wanted help, so that her life might be properly fitted out. But love she did not want. Why should there be love between them, between the stout, middle-aged man and this child. How could there be anything between them, but mere human willingness to help each other? He was her guardian, no more. His heart was like ice, his face cold and expressionless. She could not move him any more than a statue.

She crept to bed, and cried. But she was going to be married to Will Brangwen, and then she need not bother any more. Brangwen went to bed with a hard, cold heart, and cursed himself. He looked at his wife. She was still his wife. Her dark hair was threaded with grey, her face was beautiful in its gathering age. She was just fifty. How poignantly he saw her! And he wanted to cut out some of his own heart, which was incontinent, and demanded still to share the rapid life of youth. How he hated himself.

His wife was so poignant and timely. She was still young and naïve, with some girl's freshness. But she did not want any more the fight, the battle, the control, as he, in his incontinence, still did. She was so natural, and he was ugly, unnatural, in his inability to yield place. How hideous, this greedy middle-age, which must stand in the way of life, like a large demon.

What was missing in his life, that, in his ravening soul, he was not satisfied? He had had that friend at school, his mother, his wife, and Anna. What had he done? He had failed with his friend, he had been a poor son; but he had known satisfaction with his wife, let it be enough; he loathed himself for the state he was in over Anna. Yet he was *not* satisfied. It was agony to know it.

Was his life nothing? Had he nothing to show, no work? He did not count his work, anybody could have done it. What had he known, but the long, marital embrace with his wife? Curious, that this was what his life amounted to! At any rate, it was something, it was eternal. He would say so to anybody, and be proud of it. He lay with his wife in his arms, and she was still his fulfilment, just the same as ever. And that was the be-all and the end-all. Yes, and he was proud of it.

But the bitterness, underneath, that there still remained an unsatisfied Tom Brangwen, who suffered agony because a girl cared nothing for him. He loved his sons—he had them also. But it was the further, the creative life with the girl, he wanted as well. Oh, and he was ashamed. He trampled himself, to extinguish himself.

What weariness! There was no peace, however old one grew! One was never right, never decent, never master of oneself. It was as if his hope had been in the girl.

Anna quickly lapsed again into her love for the youth. Will Brangwen had fixed his marriage for the Saturday before Christmas. And he waited for her, in his bright, unquestioning fashion, until then. He wanted her, she was his, he suspended his being till the day should come. The wedding day, December the twenty third, had come into being for him as an absolute thing. He lived in it.

He did not count the days. But like a man who journeys in a ship, he was suspended till the coming to port.

He worked at his carving, he worked in his office, he came to see her: all was but a form of waiting, without thought or question.

She was much more alive. She wanted to enjoy courtship. He seemed to come and go like the wind, without asking why or whither. But she wanted to enjoy his presence. For her, he was the kernel of life, to touch him alone was bliss. But for him, she was the essence of life: she existed as much when he was at his carving in his lodging in Ilkeston, as when she sat looking at him in the Marsh kitchen. In himself, he knew her. But his outward faculties seemed suspended. He did not see her with his eyes, nor hear her with his voice.

And yet he trembled, sometimes into a kind of swoon, holding her in his arms. They would stand sometimes folded together in the barn, in silence. Then to her, as she felt his young, tense figure with her hands, the bliss was intolerable, intolerable the sense that she possessed him. For his body was so keen and wonderful, it was the only reality in her world. In her world, there was this one tense, vivid body of a man, and then many other shadowy men, all unreal. In him she touched the centre of reality. And they were together, he and she, at the heart of the secret. How she clutched him to her, his body the central body of all life. Out of the rock of his form the very fountain of life flowed.

But to him, she was a flame that consumed him. The flame flowed up his limbs, flowed through him, till he was consumed, till he existed only as an unconscious, dark transit of flame, deriving from her.

Sometimes, in the darkness, a cow coughed. There was, in the darkness, a slow sound of cud chewing. And it all seemed to flow round them and upon them as the hot blood flows through the womb, laving the unborn young.

Sometimes, when it was cold, they stood to be lovers in the stables, where the air was warm and sharp with ammonia. And during these dark vigils, he learned to know her, her body against his, they drew nearer and nearer together, the kisses came more subtly close and fitting. So when in the thick darkness, a horse suddenly scrambled to its feet, with a dull, thunderous sound, they listened as one person listening, they knew as one person, they were conscious of the horse.

Tom Brangwen had taken them a cottage at Cossethay, on a twenty one years lease. Will Brangwen's eyes lit up as he saw it. It was the cottage next the church, with dark yew-trees, very black old trees, along the side of the house and the grassy front garden; a red, squarish cottage with a low slate roof, and low windows. It had a long dairy-scullery, a big flagged kitchen, and a low parlour, that went up one step from the kitchen. There were whitewashed beams across the ceilings, and odd corners with cupboards. Looking out through the windows, there was the grassy garden, the procession of black yew-trees down one side, and along the other sides, a red wall with ivy separating the place from the high-road and the churchyard. The old, little church, with its small spire on a square tower, seemed to be looking back at the cottage windows.

"There'll be no need to have a clock," said Will Brangwen, peeping out at the white clock-face on the tower, his neighbour.

At the back of the house was a garden adjoining the paddock, a cowshed with standing for two cows, pig-cotes and fowl-houses. Will Brangwen was very happy. Anna was glad to think of being mistress of her own place.

Tom Brangwen was now the fairy god-father. He was never happy unless he was buying something. Will Brangwen, with his interest in all wood-work, was getting the furniture. He was left to buy tables and round-staved chairs and dressers, quite ordinary stuff, but such as was identified with his cottage.

Tom Brangwen, with more particular thought, spied out what he called handy little things for her. He appeared with a set of new-fangled cooking-pans, with a special sort of hanging lamp, though the rooms were so low, with canny little machines for grinding meat or mashing potatoes or whisking eggs.

Anna took a sharp interest in what he bought, though she was not always pleased. Some of the little contrivances, which he thought so canny, left her doubtful. Nevertheless she was always expectant, on market days there was always a long thrill of anticipation. He arrived with the first darkness, the copper lamps of his cart glowing. And she ran to the gate, as he, a dark, burly figure up in the cart, was bending over his parcels.

"It's cupboard love as brings you out so sharp," he said, his voice resounding in the cold darkness. Nevertheless he was excited. And she, taking one of the cart lamps, poked and peered among the jumble of things he had brought, pushing aside the oil or implements he had got for himself.

She dragged out a pair of small, strong bellows, registered them in her mind, and then pulled uncertainly at something else. It had a long handle, and a piece of brown paper round the middle of it, like a waistcoat.

"What's this?" she said, poking.

He stopped to look at her. She went to the lamp-light by the horse, and stood there bent over the new thing, while her hair was like bronze, her apron white and cheerful. Her fingers plucked busily at the paper. She dragged forth a little wringer, with clean indiarubber rollers. She examined it critically, not knowing quite how it worked.

She looked up at him. He stood a shadowy presence beyond the light.

"How does it go?" she asked.

"Why, it's for pulpin' turnips," he replied.

She looked at him. His voice disturbed her.

"Don't be silly. It's a little mangle," she said. "How do you stand it though?"

"You screw it on th' side o' your wash-tub."

He came and held it out to her.

"Oh yes!" she cried, with one of her little skipping movements, which still came when she was suddenly glad.

And without another thought she ran off into the house, leaving him to untackle the horse. And when he came in to the scullery, he found her there, with the little wringer fixed on the dolly-tub, turning blissfully at the handle, and Tilly beside her, exclaiming:

"My word, that's a natty little thing! That'll save you luggin' your inside out. That's the latest contraption, that is."

And Anna turned away at the handle, with great gusto of possession. Then she let Tilly have a turn.

"It fair runs by itself," said Tilly, turning on and on. "Your clothes'll nip out onto th' line."

CHAPTER V

Wedding at the Marsh

It was a beautiful sunny day for the wedding, a muddy earth but a bright sky. They had three cabs and two big closed-in vehicles. Everybody crowded in the parlour in excitement. Anna was still upstairs. Her father kept taking a nip of brandy. He was handsome in his black coat and grey trousers. His voice was hearty but troubled. His wife came down in dark grey silk with lace, and a touch of peacock blue in her bonnet. Her little body was very sure and definite. Brangwen was thankful she was there, to sustain him among all these people.

The carriages! The Nottingham Mrs Brangwen, in silk brocade, stands in the doorway saying who must go with whom. There is a great bustle. The front door is opened, and the wedding guests are walking down the garden path, whilst those still waiting peer through the window, and the little crowd at the gate gorps and stretches. How funny such dressed-up people look in the winter sunshine!

They are gone—another lot! There begins to be more room. Anna comes down, blushing and very shy, to be viewed in her white silk and her veil. Her mother-in-law surveys her objectively, twitches the white train, arranges the folds of the veil, and asserts herself.

Loud exclamations from the window that the bridegroom's carriage has just passed.

"Where's your hat, father, and your gloves?" cries the bride, stamping her white slipper, her eyes flashing through her veil. He hunts round—his hair is ruffled. Everybody has gone but the bride and her father. He is ready—his face very red and daunted. Tilly dithers in the little porch, waiting to open the door. A waiting woman walks round Anna, who asks:

"Am I all right?"

She is ready. She bridles herself and looks queenly. She waves her hand sharply to her father:

"Come here!"

He goes. She puts her hand very lightly on his arm, and holding her bouquet like a shower, stepping oh very graciously, just a little impatient with her father for being so red in the face, she sweeps slowly past the fluttering Tilly, and down the path. There are hoarse shouts at the gate, and all her floating, foamy whiteness passes slowly into the cab.

Her father notices her slim ankle and foot as she steps up: a child's foot. His heart is hard with tenderness. But she is in ecstasies with herself for making such a lovely spectacle. All the way she sat flamboyant with bliss because it was all so lovely. She looked down solicitously at her bouquet: white roses and lilies of the valley and tuberoses and maiden-hair fern—very rich and cascade-like.

Her father sat bewildered with all this strangeness, his heart was so full it felt hard, and he couldn't think of anything.

The church was decorated for Christmas, dark with evergreens, cold and snowy with white flowers. He went vaguely down to the altar. How long was it since he had gone to be married himself? He was not sure whether he was going to be married now, or what he had come for. He had a troubled notion that he had to do something or other. He saw his wife's bonnet, and wondered why *she* wasn't there with him.

They stood before the altar. He was staring up at the east window, that glowed intensely, a sort of blue purple: it was deep blue glowing, and some crimson, and little yellow flowers, held fast in veins of shadow, in a heavy web of darkness. How it burned alive in radiance among its black web.

"Who giveth this woman to be married to this man?"

He felt somebody touch him. He started. The words still re-echoed in his memory, but were drawing off.

"Me," he said hastily.

Anna bent her head and smiled in her veil. How absurd he was!

Brangwen was staring away at the burning blue window at the back of the altar, and wondering vaguely, with pain, if he ever *should* get old, if he ever should feel arrived and established. He was here at Anna's wedding. Well, what right had he to feel responsible, like a father? He was still as unsure and unfixed as when he had married himself. His wife and he! With a pang of anguish he realised what uncertainties they both were. He was a man of forty five. Forty five! In five more years, fifty. Then, sixty—then seventy—then it was finished. My God—and one still was so unestablished!

How did one grow old—how could one become confident? He

wished he felt older. Why, what difference was there, as far as he felt matured or completed, between him now and him at his own wedding? He might be getting married over again—he and his wife. He felt himself tiny, a little, upright figure on a plain circled round with the immense, roaring sky: he and his wife, two little, upright figures walking across this plain, whilst the heavens shimmered and roared about them. When did one come to an end? In which direction was it finished? There was no end, no finish, only this roaring vast space. Did one never get old, never die? That was the clue. He exulted strangely, with torture. He would go on with his wife, he and she like two children camping in the plains. What was sure but the endless sky? But that was so sure, so boundless.

Still the royal blue colour burned and blazed and sported itself in the web of darkness before him, unwearyingly rich and splendid. How rich and splendid his own life was, red and burning and blazing and sporting itself in the dark meshes of his body: and his wife, how she glowed and burned dark within her meshes! Always it was so unfinished and unformed!

There was a loud noise of the organ. The whole party was trooping to the vestry. There was a blotted, scrawled book—and that young girl putting back her veil in her vanity, and laying her hand with the wedding-ring self-consciously conspicuous, and signing her name proudly because of the vain spectacle she made.

"Anna Theresa Lensky."

"Anna Theresa Lensky"—what a vain, independent minx she was! The bridegroom, slender in his black swallow-tail and grey trousers, solemn as a young solemn cat, was writing seriously:

"William Brangwen."

That looked more like it.

"Come and sign father," cried the imperious young hussy.

"'Thomas Brangwen'—clumsy-fist," he said to himself as he signed.

Then his brother, a big, sallow fellow with black side-whiskers wrote:

"Alfred Brangwen."

"How many more Brangwens?" said Tom Brangwen, ashamed of the too-frequent recurrence of his family name.

When they were out again in the sunshine, and he saw the frost hoary and blue among the long grass under the tombstones, the holly-berries overhead twinkling scarlet as the bells rang, the yew-trees hanging their black, motionless, ragged boughs, everything seemed like a vision.

The marriage party went across the graveyard to the wall, mounted it by the little steps, and descended. Oh a vain white peacock of a bride perching herself on the top of the wall and giving her hand to the bridegroom on the other side, to be helped down! The vanity of her white, slim, daintily-stepping feet, and her arched neck. And the regal impudence with which she seemed to dismiss them all, the others, parents and wedding guests, as she went with her young husband.

In the cottage big fires were burning, there were dozens of glasses on the table, and holly and mistletoe hanging up. The wedding party crowded in, and Tom Brangwen, becoming roisterous, poured out drinks. Everybody must drink. The bells were ringing away against the windows.

"Lift your glasses up," shouted Tom Brangwen from the parlour, "lift your glasses up, an' drink to the hearth an' home—hearth an' home, an' may they enjoy it."

"Night an' day, an' may they enjoy it," shouted Frank Brangwen, in addition.

"Hammer an' tongs, and may they enjoy it," shouted Alfred Brangwen, the saturnine.

"Fill your glasses up, an' let's have it all over again," shouted Tom Brangwen.

"Hearth and home, an' may ye enjoy it."

There was a ragged shout of the company in response.

"Bed an' blessin', an' may ye enjoy it," shouted Frank Brangwen.

There was a swelling chorus in answer.

"Comin' and goin', an' may ye enjoy it," shouted the saturnine Alfred Brangwen, and the men roared by now boldly, and the women said "Just hark, now!"

There was a touch of scandal in the air.

Then the party rolled off in the carriages, full speed back to the Marsh, to a large meal of the high-tea order, which lasted for an hour and a half. The bride and bridegroom sat at the head of the table, very prim and shining both of them, wordless, whilst the company raged down the table.

The Brangwen men had brandy in their tea, and were becoming unmanageable. The saturnine Alfred had glittering, unseeing eyes, and a strange, fierce way of laughing that showed his teeth. His wife glowered at him and jerked her head at him like a snake. He was oblivious. Frank Brangwen, the butcher, flushed and florid and handsome, roared echoes to his two brothers. Tom Brangwen, in his solid fashion, was letting himself go at last.

These three brothers dominated the whole company. Tom Brangwen wanted to make a speech. For the first time in his life, he must spread himself wordily.

"Marriage," he began, his eyes twinkling and yet quite profound, for he was deeply serious and hugely amused at the same time; "Marriage," he said, speaking in the slow, full-mouthed way of the Brangwens, "is what we're made for—"

"Let him talk," said Alfred Brangwen, slowly and inscrutably, "let him talk." Mrs Alfred darted indignant eyes at her husband.

"A man," continued Tom Brangwen, "enjoys being a man: for what purpose was he made a man, if not to enjoy it?"

"That's a true word," said Frank, floridly.

"And likewise," continued Tom Brangwen, "a woman enjoys being a woman: at least we surmise she does—"

"Oh, don't you bother—" called a farmer's wife.

"You may back your life they'd be summisin'," said Frank's wife.

"Now," continued Tom Brangwen, "for a man to be a man, it takes a woman—"

"It does that," said a woman grimly.

"And for a woman to be a woman, it takes a *man*—" continued Tom Brangwen.

"All speak up, men," chimed in a feminine voice.

"Therefore we have marriage," continued Tom Brangwen.

"Hold, hold," said Alfred Brangwen. "Don't run us off our legs."

And in dead silence the glasses were filled. The bride and bridegroom, two children, sat with intent, shining faces at the head of the table, abstracted.

"There's no marriage in heaven," went on Tom Brangwen; "but on earth there *is* marriage."

"That's the difference between 'em," said Alfred Brangwen, mocking.

"Alfred," said Tom Brangwen, "keep your remarks till afterwards, and then we'll thank you for them.—There's very little else, on earth, but marriage. You can talk about making money, or saving souls. You can save your soul seven times over, and you may have a mint of money, but your soul goes gnawin', gnawin', gnawin', and it says there's something it must have. In heaven there is no marriage. But on earth there *is* marriage, else heaven drops out, and there's no bottom to it."

"Just hark you now," said Frank's wife.

"Go on, Thomas," said Alfred sardonically.

"*If* we've got to be angels," went on Tom Brangwen, haranguing the company at large, "and if there is no such thing as a man nor a woman amongst them, then it seems to me as a married couple makes *one* angel."

"It's the brandy," said Alfred Brangwen wearily.

"For," said Tom Brangwen, and the company was listening to the conundrum, "an angel can't be *less* than a human being. And if it was only the soul of a man *minus* the man, then it would be *less* than a human being—"

"Decidedly," said Alfred.

And a laugh went round the table. But Tom Brangwen was inspired.

"An angel's *got* to be more than a human being," he continued. "So I say, an angel is the soul of man and woman in one: they rise united at the Judgment Day, as one angel—"

"Praising the Lord," said Frank.

"Praising the Lord," repeated Tom.

"And what about the women left over?" asked Alfred, jeering. The company was getting uneasy.

"That I can't tell. How do I know as there *is* anybody left over at the Judgment Day? Let that be. What I say is, that when a man's soul and a woman's soul unites together—that makes one angel."

"I dunno about souls. I know as one plus one makes three, sometimes," said Frank. But he had the laugh to himself.

"Bodies and souls, it's the same," said Tom.

"And what about your Missis, who was married afore you knew her?" asked Alfred, set on edge by this discourse.

"That I can't tell you. If I am to become an angel, it'll be my married soul, and not my single soul. It'll not be the soul of me when I was a lad: for I hadn't a soul as would *make* an angel then."

"I can always remember," said Frank's wife, "when our Harold was bad, he did nothink but see an angel at th' back o' th' lookin' glass. 'Look mother,' 'e said, 'at that angel.' 'Theer isn't no angel, my duck,' I said, but he wouldn't have it. I took th' lookin' glass off'n th' dressin' table, but it made no difference. He kep' on sayin' it was there. My word, it did give me a turn. I thought for sure as I'd lost him."

"I can remember," said another man, Tom's sister's husband, "my mother gave me a good hidin' once, for sayin' I'd got an angel up my nose. She seed me pokin', an' she said: 'What are you pokin' at your nose for—give over.' 'There's an angel up it,' I said, an' she fetched me such a wipe. But there was. We used to call them thistle things 'angels,' as wafts about. An' I'd pushed one o' these up my nose, for some reason or other."

"It's wonderful what children will get up their noses," said Frank's wife. "I c'n remember our Hemmie, she shoved one o' them bluebell things out o' th' middle of a bluebell, what they call 'candles,' up her nose, and oh we had some work! I'd seen her stickin' 'em on the end of her nose, like, but I never thought she'd be so soft as to shove it right up. She was a gel of eight or more. Oh my word, we got a crochet-hook an' I don't know what— — —"

Tom Brangwen's mood of inspiration began to pass away. He forgot all about it, and was soon roaring and shouting with the rest. Outside the wake came, singing the carols. They were invited into the bursting house. They had two fiddles and a piccolo. There in the parlour they played carols, and the whole company sang them at the top of its voice. Only the bride and bridegroom sat with shining eyes and strange, bright faces, and scarcely sang, or only with just moving lips.

The wake departed, and the guysers came. There was loud applause, and shouting and excitement as the old mystery play of St George, in which every man present had acted as a boy, proceeded, with banging and thumping of club and dripping pan.

"By Jove, I got a crack once, when I was playin' Beelzebub," said Tom Brangwen, his eyes full of water with laughing. "It knocked all th' sense out of me as you'd crack an egg. But I tell you, when I come to, I played Old Johnny Roger with St George, I did that."

He was shaking with laughter. Another knock came at the door. There was a hush.

"It's th' cab," said somebody from the door.

"Walk in," shouted Tom Brangwen, and a red-faced, grinning man entered.

"Now you two, get yourselves ready an' off to blanket fair," shouted Tom Brangwen. "Strike a daisy, but if you're not off like a blink o' lightnin', you shanna go, you s'll sleep separate."

Anna rose silently and went to change her dress. Will Brangwen would have gone out, but Tilly came with his hat and coat. The youth was helped on.

"Well, here's luck, my boy," shouted his father.

"When th' fat's in th' fire, let it frizzle," admonished his uncle Frank.

"Fair and *softly* does it, fair an' *softly* does it," cried his aunt, Frank's wife, contrary.

"You don't want to fall over yourself," said his uncle by marriage. "You're not a bull at a gate."

"Let a man have his own road," said Tom Brangwen testily. "Don't be so free of your advice—it's his wedding this time, not yours."

" 'E won't want many sign-posts," said his father. "There's some roads a man has to be led, an' there's some roads a boz-eyed man can only follow wi' one eye shut. But this road can't be lost by a blind man nor a boz-eyed man nor a cripple—And he's neither, thank God."

"Don't you be so sure o' your walkin' powers," cried Frank's wife. "There's many a man gets no further than half way, nor can't to save his life, let him live for ever."

"Why how do you know?" said Alfred.

"It's plain enough in th' looks o' some," retorted Lizzie, his sister-in-law.

The youth stood with a faint, half-hearing smile on his face. He was tense and abstracted. These things, or anything, scarcely touched him.

Anna came down, in her day dress, very elusive. She kissed everybody, men and women, Will Brangwen shook hands with everybody, kissed his mother, who began to cry, and the whole party went surging out to the cab.

The young couple were shut up, last injunctions shouted at them.

"Drive on," shouted Tom Brangwen.

The cab rolled off. They saw the lights diminish under the ash-trees. Then the whole party, quietened, went indoors.

"They'll have three good fires burning," said Tom Brangwen, looking at his watch. "I told Emma to make 'em up at nine, an' then leave the door on th' latch. It's only half past. They'll have three fires burning, an' lamps lighted, an' Emma will ha' warmed th' bed wi' th' warmin' pan. So I s'd think they'll be all right."

The party was much quieter. They talked of the young couple.

"She said she didn't want a servant in," said Tom Brangwen. "The house isn't big enough, she'd always have the creature under her nose. Emma'll do what is wanted of her, an' they'll be to themselves."

"It's best," said Lizzie, "you're more free."

The party talked on slowly. Brangwen looked at his watch.

"Let's go an' give 'em a carol," he said. "We s'll find th' fiddles at the 'Cock an' Robin.'"

"Ay, come on," said Frank.

Alfred rose in silence. The brother-in-law and one of Will's brothers rose also.

The five men went out. The night was flashing with stars. Sirius blazed like a signal at the side of the hill, Orion, stately and magnificent, was sloping along.

Tom walked with his brother Alfred. The men's heels rang on the ground.

"It's a fine night," said Tom.

"Ay," said Alfred.

"Nice to get out."

"Ay."

The brothers walked close together, the bond of blood strong between them. Tom always felt very much the junior to Alfred.

"It's a long while since *you* left home," he said.

"Ay," said Alfred. "I thought I was getting a bit oldish—but I'm not. It's the things you've got as gets worn out, it's not you yourself."

"Why, what's worn out?"

"Most folks as I've anything to do with—as has anything to do with me. They all break down. You've got to go on by yourself, if it's only to perdition. There's nobody going alongside even there."

Tom Brangwen meditated this.

"Maybe you was never broken in," he said.

"No, I never was," said Alfred proudly.

And Tom felt his elder brother despised him a little. He winced under it.

"Everybody's got a way of their own," he said, stubbornly. "It's only a dog as hasn't. An' them as can't take what they give an' give what they take, they must go by themselves, or get a dog as'll follow 'em."

"They can do without the dog," said his brother.

And again Tom Brangwen was humble, thinking his brother was bigger than himself. But if he was, he was. And if it were finer to go alone, it was: he did not want to, for all that.

They went over the field, where a thin, keen wind blew round the ball of the hill; in the starlight. They came to the stile, and to the side of Anna's house. The lights were out, only on the blinds of the rooms downstairs, and of a bedroom upstairs, firelight flickered.

"We'd better leave 'em alone," said Alfred Brangwen.

"Nay nay," said Tom. "We'll carol 'em, for th' last time."

And in a quarter of an hour's time, eleven silent, rather tipsy men scrambled over the wall, and into the garden by the yew-trees, outside the windows where faint firelight glowed on the blinds. There came a shrill sound, two violins and a piccolo shrilling on the frosty air.

"In the fields with their flocks abiding." A commotion of men's voices broke out singing in ragged unison.

Anna Brangwen had started up, listening, when the music began. She was afraid.

"It's the wake," he whispered.

She remained tense, her heart beating heavily, possessed with strange, strong fear. Then there came the burst of men's singing, rather uneven. She strained still, listening.

"It's Dad," she said, in a low voice.

They were silent, listening.

"And my father," he said.

She listened still. But she was sure. She sank down again into bed, into his arms. He held her very close, kissing her. The hymn rambled on outside, all the men singing their best, having forgotten everything else under the spell of the fiddles and the tune. The firelight glowed against the darkness in the room. Anna could hear her father singing with gusto.

"Aren't they silly?" she whispered.

And they crept closer, closer together, hearts beating to one another. And even as the hymn rolled on, they ceased to hear it.

CHAPTER VI

Anna Victrix

Will Brangwen had some weeks of holiday after his marriage, so the two took their honeymoon in full hands, alone in their cottage together.

And to him, as the days went by, it was as if the heavens had fallen, and he were sitting with her among the ruins, in a new world, everybody else buried, themselves two blissful survivors, with everything to squander as they would. At first, he could not get rid of a culpable sense of licence on his part. Wasn't there some duty outside, calling him and he did not come?

It was all very well at night, when the doors were locked and the darkness drawn round the two of them. Then they *were* the only inhabitants of the visible earth, the rest were under the flood. And being alone in the world, they were a law unto themselves, they could enjoy and squander and waste like conscienceless gods.

But in the morning, as the carts clanked by, and children shouted down the lane: as the hucksters came calling their wares, and the church clock struck eleven, and he and she had not got up yet, even to breakfast: he could not help feeling guilty, as if he were committing a breach of the law—ashamed that he was not up and doing.

"Doing what?" she asked. "What is there to do? You will only lounge about."

Still, even lounging about was respectable. One was at least in connection with the world, then. Whereas now, lying so still and peacefully while the daylight came obscurely through the drawn blind, one was severed from the world, one shut oneself off in tacit denial of the world. And he was troubled.

But it was so sweet and satisfying lying there talking desultorily with her. It was sweeter than sunshine, and not so evanescent. It was even irritating the way the church clock kept on chiming: there seemed no space between the hours, just a moment, golden and still, whilst she traced his features with her finger-tips, utterly careless and happy, and he loved her to do it.

But he was strange and unused. So suddenly, everything that had been before was shed away and gone. One day, he was a bachelor, living with the world. The next day, he was with her, as remote from the world as if the two of them were buried like a seed in darkness. Suddenly, like a chestnut falling out of a burr, he was shed naked and glistening on to a soft, fecund earth, leaving behind him the hard rind of worldly knowledge and experience. There it lay, cast off, the worldly experience. He heard it in the hucksters' cries, the noise of carts, the calling of children. And it was like the hard shed rind, discarded. Inside, in the softness and stillness of the room, was the naked kernel, that palpitated in silent activity, absorbed in reality.

Inside the room was a great steadiness, a core of living eternity. Only far outside, at the rim, went on the noise and the distraction. Here at the centre the great wheel was motionless, centred upon itself. Here was a poised, unflawed stillness that was beyond time, because it remained the same, inexhaustible, unchanging, unexhausted.

As they lay close together, complete and beyond the touch of time or change, it was as if they were at the very centre of all the slow wheeling of space and the rapid agitation of life, deep, deep inside them all, at the centre where there is utter radiance, and eternal being, and the silence absorbed in praise: the steady core of all movements, the unawakened sleep of all wakefulness. They found themselves there, and they lay still, in each other's arms; for their moment they were at the heart of eternity, whilst time roared far off, forever far off, towards the rim.

Then gradually they were passed away from the supreme centre, down the circles of praise and joy and gladness, further and further out, towards the noise and the friction. But their hearts had burned and were tempered by the inner reality, they were unalterably glad.

Gradually they began to wake up, the noises outside became more real. They understood and answered the call outside. They counted the strokes of the bell. And when they counted midday, they understood that it was midday, in the world, and for themselves also.

It dawned upon her that she was hungry. She had been getting hungrier for a lifetime. But even yet it was not sufficiently real to rouse her. A long way off she could hear the words "I am dying of hunger." Yet she lay still, separate, at peace, and the words were unuttered. There was still another lapse.

And then, quite calmly, even a little surprised, she was in the present, and was saying:

"I am dying with hunger."

"So am I," he said calmly, as if it were of not the slightest significance. And they relapsed into the warm, golden stillness. And the minutes flowed unheeded past the window outside.

Then suddenly she stirred against him.

"My dear, I am dying of hunger," she said.

It was a slight pain to him to be brought to.

"We'll get up," he said, unmoving.

And she sank her head on to him again, and they lay still, lapsing. Half consciously, he heard the clock chime the hour. She did not hear.

"Do get up," she murmured at length, "and give me something to eat."

"Yes," he said, and he put his arms round her, and she lay with her face on him. They were faintly astonished that they did not move. The minutes rustled louder at the window.

"Let me go then," he said.

She lifted her head from him, relinquishingly. With a little breaking away, he moved out of bed, and was taking his clothes. She stretched out her hand to him.

"You are so nice," she said, and he went back for a moment or two.

Then actually he did slip into some clothes, and, looking round quickly at her, was gone out of the room. She lay translated again into a pale, clearer peace. As if she were a spirit, she listened to the noise of him downstairs, as if she were no longer of the material world.

It was half past one. He looked at the silent kitchen, untouched from last night, dim with the drawn blind. And he hastened to draw up the blind, so people should know they were not in bed any later. Well, it was his own house, it did not matter. Hastily he put wood in the grate and made a fire. He exulted in himself, like an adventurer on an undiscovered island. The fire blazed up, he put on the kettle. How happy he felt! How still and secluded the house was! There were only he and she in the world.

But when he unbolted the door, and, half dressed, looked out, he felt furtive and guilty. The world *was* there, after all. And he had felt so secure, as though this house were the Ark in the flood, and all the rest was drowned. The world was there: and it was afternoon. The morning had vanished and gone by, the day was growing old. Where was the bright, fresh morning? He was accused. Was the morning gone, and he had lain with blinds drawn, let it pass by unnoticed?

He looked again round the chill, grey afternoon. And he himself so soft and warm and glowing! There were two sprigs of yellow jasmine in the saucer that covered the milk-jug. He wondered who had been and left the sign. Taking the jug, he hastily shut the door. Let the day and the daylight drop out, let it go by unseen. He did not care. What did one day more or less matter to him. It could fall into oblivion unspent, if it liked, this one course of daylight.

"Somebody has been and found the door locked," he said when he went upstairs with the tray. He gave her the two sprigs of jasmine. She laughed as she sat up in bed, childishly threading the flowers in the breast of her nightdress. Her brown hair stuck out like a nimbus, all fierce, round her softly glowing face. Her dark eyes watched the tray eagerly.

"How good!" she cried, sniffing the cold air. "I'm glad you did a lot." And she held out her hands eagerly for her plate.—"Come back to bed, quick—it's cold." She rubbed her hands together sharply.

He put off what little clothing he had on, and sat beside her in the bed.

"You look like a lion, with your mane sticking out, and your nose pushed over your food," he said.

She tinkled with laughter, and gladly ate her breakfast.

The morning was sunk away unseen, the afternoon was steadily going too, and he was letting it go. One bright transit of daylight gone by unacknowledged! There was something unmanly, recusant in it. He could not quite reconcile himself to the fact. He felt he ought to get up, go out quickly into the daylight, and work or spend himself energetically in the open air of the afternoon, retrieving what was left to him of the day.

But he did not go. Well, one might as well be hung for a sheep as for a lamb. If he had lost this day of his life, he had lost it. He gave it up. He was not going to count his losses. *She* didn't care. *She* didn't care in the least. Then why should he? Should he be behind her in recklessness and independence? She was superb in her indifference. He wanted to be like her.

She took her responsibilities lightly. When she spilled her tea on the pillow, she rubbed it carelessly with a handkerchief, and turned over the pillow. He would have felt guilty. She did not. And it pleased him. It pleased him very much to see how these things did not matter to her.

When the meal was over, she wiped her mouth on her handkerchief quickly, satisfied and happy, and settled down on the pillows again, with her fingers in his close, strange, fur-like hair.

The evening began to fall, the light was half alive, livid. He hid his face against her.

"I don't like the twilight," he said.

"I love it," she answered.

He hid his face against her, who was warm and like sunlight. She seemed to have sunlight inside her. Her heart beating seemed like sunlight upon him. In her was a more real day than the day could give: so warm and steady and restoring. He hid his face against her whilst the twilight fell, whilst she lay staring out with her unseeing dark eyes, as if she wandered forth untrammelled in the vagueness. The vagueness gave her scope and set her free.

To him, turned towards her heart-pulse, all was very still and very warm and very close, like noon-tide. He was glad to know this warm, full noon. It ripened him and took away his responsibility, some of his conscience.

They got up when it was quite dark. She hastily twisted her hair into a knot, and was dressed in a twinkling. Then they went downstairs, drew to the fire, and sat in silence, saying a few words now and then.

Her father was coming. She bundled the dishes away, flew round and tidied the room, assumed another character, and again seated herself. He sat thinking of his carving of Eve. He loved to go over his carving in his mind, dwelling on every stroke, every line. How he loved it now! When he went back to his Creation-panel again, he would finish his Eve, tender and sparkling. It did not satisfy him yet. The Lord should labour over her in a silent passion of Creation, and Adam should be tense as if in a dream of immortality, and Eve should take form glimmeringly, shadowily, as if the Lord must wrestle with His own soul for her, yet she was a radiance.

"What are you thinking about?" she asked.

He found it difficult to say. His soul became shy when he tried to communicate it.

"I was thinking my Eve was too hard and lively."

"Why?"

"I don't know. She should be more—," he made a gesture of infinite tenderness.

There was a stillness with a little joy. He could not tell her any more. Why could he not tell her any more? She felt a pang of disconsolate sadness. But it was nothing. She went to him.

Her father came, and found them both very glowing, like an open flower. He loved to sit with them. Where there was a perfume of love, anyone who came must breathe it. They were both very quick and alive, lit up from the other-world, so that it was quite an experience for them, that anyone else could exist.

But still it troubled Will Brangwen a little, in his orderly, conventional mind, that the established rule of things had gone so utterly. One ought to get up in the morning and wash oneself and be a decent social being. Instead, the two of them stayed in bed till nightfall, then got up; she never washed her face, but sat there talking to her father as bright and shameless as a daisy opened out of the dew. Or she got up at ten o'clock, and quite blithely went to bed again at three, or at half past four, stripping him naked in the daylight, and all so gladly and perfectly, oblivious quite of his qualms. He let her do as she liked with him, and shone with strange pleasure. She was to dispose of him as she would. He was translated with gladness to be in her hands. And down went his qualms, his maxims, his rules, his smaller beliefs, she scattered them like an expert skittle-player. He was very much astonished and delighted to see them scatter.

He stood and gazed and grinned with wonder whilst his Tablets of Stone went bounding and bumping and splintering down the hill, dislodged for ever. Indeed, it was true as they said, that a man wasn't born before he was married. What a change indeed!

He surveyed the rind of the world: houses, factories, trams, the discarded rind; people scurrying about, work going on, all on the discarded surface. An earthquake had burst it all from inside. It was as if the surface of the world had been broken away entire: Ilkeston, streets, church, people, work, rule-of-the-day, all intact; and yet peeled away into unreality, leaving here exposed the inside, the reality: one's own being, strange feelings and passions and yearnings and beliefs and aspirations, suddenly become present, revealed, the permanent bedrock, knitted one rock with the woman one loved. It was confounding. Things are not what they seem! When he was a child, he had thought a woman was a woman merely by virtue of her skirts and petticoats. And now, lo, the whole world could be divested of its garment, the garment could lie there shed away intact, and one could stand in a new world, a new earth, naked in a new, naked universe. It was too astounding and miraculous.

This then was marriage! The old things didn't matter any more. One got up at four o'clock, and had broth at tea-time and made toffee in the middle of the night. One didn't put on one's clothes or one did put on one's clothes. He still was not quite sure it was not criminal. But it was a discovery to find one might be so supremely absolved. All that mattered was that he should love her and she should love him and they should live kindled to one another, like the Lord in two burning bushes that were not consumed. And so they lived for the time.

She was less hampered than he, so she came more quickly to her fulness, and was sooner ready to enjoy again a return to the outside world. She was going to give a tea-party. His heart sank. He wanted to go on, to go on as they were. He wanted to have done with the outside world, to declare it finished for ever. He was anxious with a deep desire and anxiety that she should stay with him where they were in the timeless universe of free, perfect limbs and immortal breast, affirming that the old, outward order was finished. The new order was begun to last for ever, the living life, palpitating from the gleaming core, to action, without crust or cover or outward lie. But no, he could not keep her. She wanted the dead world again—she wanted to walk on the outside once more. She was going to give a tea-party. It made him frightened and furious and miserable. He was afraid all would be lost that he had so newly come unto: like the youth in the fairy tale, who was king for one day in the year, and for the rest a beaten herd: like Cinderella also, at the feast. He was sullen. But she blithely began to make preparations for her tea-party. His fear was too strong, he was troubled, he hated her shallow anticipation and joy. Was she not forfeiting the reality, the one reality, for all that was shallow and worthless? Wasn't she carelessly taking off her crown to be an artificial figure having other artificial women to tea: when she might have been perfect with him, and kept him perfect, in the land of intimate connection? Now he must be deposed, his joy must be destroyed, he must put on the vulgar, shallow death of an outward existence.

He ground his soul in uneasiness and fear. But she rose to a real outburst of housework, turning him away as she shoved the furniture aside to her broom. He stood hanging miserably near. He wanted her back. Dread and desire for her to stay with him and shame at his own dependence on her drove him to anger. He began to lose his head. The wonder was going to pass away again. All the love, the magnificent new order was going to be lost, she would forfeit it all for the outside things. She would admit the outside world again, she would throw away the living fruit for the ostensible rind. He began to hate this in her. Driven by fear of her departure into a state of helplessness, almost of imbecility, he wandered about the house.

And she, with her skirts kilted up, flew round at her work, absorbed.

"Shake the rug then, if you must hang round," she said.

And fretting with resentment, he went to shake the rug. She was blithely unconscious of him. He came back, hanging near to her.

"Can't you do anything?" she said, as if to a child, impatiently. "Can't you do your wood-work?"

"Where shall I do it?" he asked, harsh with pain.

"Anywhere."

How furious that made him.

"Or go for a walk," she continued. "Go down to the Marsh. Don't hang about as if you were only half there."

He winced and hated it. He went away to read. Never had his soul felt so flayed and uncreated.

And soon he must come down again to her. His hovering near her, wanting her to be with him, the futility of him, the way his hands hung, irritated her beyond bearing. She turned on him blindly and destructively, he became a mad creature, black and electric with fury. The dark storms rose in him, his eyes glowed black and evil, he was fiendish in his thwarted soul.

There followed two black and ghastly days, when she was set in anguish against him, and he felt as if he were in a black, violent underworld, and his wrists quivered murderously. And she resisted him. He seemed a dark, almost evil thing pursuing her, hanging on to her, burdening her. She would give anything to have him removed.

"You need some work to do," she said. "You ought to be at work. Can't you *do* something?"

His soul only grew the blacker. His condition now became complete, the darkness of his soul was thorough. Everything had gone: he remained complete in his own tense, black will. He was now unaware of her. She did not exist. His dark, passionate soul had recoiled upon itself, and now, clinched and coiled round a centre of hatred, existed in its own power. There was a curiously ugly pallor, an expressionlessness in his face. She shuddered from him. She was afraid of him. His will seemed grappled upon her.

She retreated before him. She went down to the Marsh, she entered again the immunity of her parents' love for her. He remained at Yew Cottage, black and clinched, his mind dead. He was unable to work at his wood-carving. He went on working monotonously at the garden, blindly, like a mole.

As she came home, up the hill, looking away at the town dim and blue on the hill, her heart relaxed and became yearning. She did not want to fight him any more. She wanted love—oh, love. Her feet began to hurry. She wanted to get back to him. Her heart became tight with yearning for him.

He had been making the garden in order, cutting the edges of the turf, laying the path with stones. He was a good, capable workman.

"How nice you've made it," she said, approaching tentatively down the path.

But he did not heed, he did not hear. His brain was solid and dead.

"Haven't you made it nice?" she repeated, rather plaintively.

He looked up at her, with that fixed, expressionless face and unseeing eyes which shocked her, made her go dazed and blind. Then he turned away. She saw his slender, stooping figure groping. A revulsion came over her. She went indoors.

As she took off her hat in the bedroom, she found herself weeping bitterly, with some of the old, anguished, childish desolation. She sat still and cried on. She did not want him to know. She was afraid of his hard, evil movements, the head dropped a little, rigidly, in a crouching, cruel way. She was afraid of him. He seemed to lacerate her sensitive femaleness. He seemed to hurt her womb, to take pleasure in torturing her.

He came in to the house. The sound of his footsteps in his heavy boots filled her with horror: a hard, cruel, malignant sound. She was afraid he would come upstairs. But he did not. She waited apprehensively. He went out.

Where she was most vulnerable, he hurt her. Oh, where she was delivered over to him, in her very soft femaleness, he seemed to lacerate her and desecrate her. She pressed her hands over her womb in anguish, whilst the tears ran down her face. And why, and why? Why was he like this?

Suddenly she dried her tears. She must get the tea ready. She went downstairs and set the table. When the meal was ready, she called to him.

"I've mashed the tea, Will, are you coming?"

She herself could hear the sound of tears in her own voice, and she began to cry again. He did not answer, but went on with his work. She waited a few minutes, in anguish. Fear came over her, she was panic-stricken with terror, like a child; and she could not go home again to her father; she was held by the power in this man who had taken her.

She turned indoors so that he should not see her tears. She sat down to table. Presently he came in to the scullery. His movements jarred on her, as she heard them. How horrible was the way he pumped, exacerbating, so cruel! How she hated to hear him! How he hated her! How his hatred was like blows upon her! The tears were coming again.

He came in, his face wooden and lifeless, fixed, persistent. He sat down to tea, his head dropped over his cup, uglily. His hands were red from the cold water, and there were rims of earth in his nails. He went on with his tea.

It was negative insensitiveness to her that she could not bear, something clayey and ugly. His intelligence was self-absorbed. How unnatural it was to sit with a self-absorbed creature, like something negative ensconced opposite one. Nothing could touch him—he could only absorb things into his own self.

The tears were running down her face. Something startled him, and he was looking up at her with his hateful, hard, bright eyes, hard and unchanging as a bird of prey.

"What are you crying for?" came the grating voice.

She winced through her womb. She could not stop crying.

"What are you crying for?" came the question again, in just the same tone. And still there was silence, with only the sniff of her tears.

His eyes glittered evilly, and as if with malignant desire. She shrank and became blind. She was like a bird being beaten down. A sort of swoon of helplessness came over her. She was of another order than he, she had no defence against him. Against such an influence, she was only vulnerable, she was given up.

He rose and went out of the house, possessed by the evil spirit. It tortured him and wracked him, and fought in him. And whilst he worked, in the deepening twilight, it left him. Suddenly he saw that she was hurt. He had only seen her triumphant before. Suddenly his heart was torn with compassion for her. He became alive again, in an anguish of compassion. He could not bear to think of her tears—he could not bear it. He wanted to go to her and pour out his heart's blood to her. He wanted to give everything to her, all his blood, his life, to the last dregs, pour everything away to her. He yearned with passionate desire to offer himself to her, utterly.

The evening star came, and the night. She had not lighted the lamp. His heart burned with pain and with grief. He trembled to go to her.

And at last he went, hesitating, burdened with a great offering. The hardness had gone out of him, his body was sensitive, slightly trembling. His hand was curiously sensitive, shrinking, as he shut the door. He fixed the latch almost tenderly.

In the kitchen was only the fireglow, he could not see her. He quivered with dread lest she had gone—he knew not where. In shrinking dread, he went through to the parlour, to the foot of the stairs.

"Anna," he called.

There was no answer. He went up the stairs, in dread of the empty house—the horrible emptiness that made his heart ring with insanity. He opened the bedroom door, and his heart flashed with certainty that she had gone, that he was alone.

But he saw her on the bed, lying very still and scarcely noticeable, with her back to him. He went and put his hand on her shoulder, very gently, hesitating, in a great fear and self-offering. She did not move. He waited. The hand that touched her shoulder hurt him, as if she were sending it away. He stood dim with pain.

"Anna," he said.

But still she was motionless, like a curled up, oblivious creature. His heart beat with strange throes of pain. Then, by a motion under his hand, he knew she was crying, holding herself hard so that her tears should not be known. He waited. The tension continued—perhaps she was not crying—then suddenly relaxed with a sharp catch of a sob. His heart flamed with love and suffering for her. Kneeling carefully on the bed, so that his earthy boots should not touch it, he took her in his arms to comfort her. The sobs gathered in her, she was sobbing bitterly. But not to him. She was still away from him.

He held her against his breast, whilst she sobbed, withheld from him, and all his body vibrated against her.

"Don't cry—don't cry," he said, with an odd simplicity. His heart was calm and numb with a sort of innocence of love, now.

She still sobbed, ignoring him, ignoring that he held her. His lips were dry.

"Don't cry, my love," he said, in the same abstract way. In his breast his heart burned like a torch, with suffering. He could not bear the desolateness of her crying. He would have soothed her with his blood. He heard the church clock chime, as if it touched him, and he waited in suspense for it to have gone by. It was quiet again.

"My love," he said to her, bending to touch her wet face with his mouth. He was afraid to touch her. How wet her face was! His body trembled as he held her. He loved her till he felt his heart and all his veins would burst and flood her with his hot, healing blood. He knew his blood would heal and restore her.

She was becoming quieter. He thanked the God of mercy that at last she was becoming quieter. His head felt so strange and blazed. Still he held her close, with trembling arms. His blood seemed very strong, enveloping her.

And at last she began to draw near him, she nestled to him. His limbs, his body, took fire and beat up in flames. She clung to him, she cleaved to his body. The flames swept him, he held her in sinews of fire. If she would kiss him! He bent his mouth down. And her mouth, soft and moist, received him. He felt his veins would burst with anguish of thankfulness, his heart was mad with gratefulness, he could pour himself out upon her for ever.

When they came to themselves, the night was very dark. Two hours had gone by. They lay still and warm and weak, like the new-born, together. And there was a silence almost of the unborn. Only his heart was weeping happily, after the pain. He did not understand, he had yielded, given way. There *was* no understanding. There could be only acquiescence and submission, and tremulous wonder of consummation.

The next morning, when they woke up, it had snowed. He wondered what was the strange pallor in the air, and the unusual tang. Snow was on the grass and the window-sill, it weighed down the black, ragged branches of the yews, and smoothed the graves in the churchyard.

Soon, it began to snow again, and they were shut in. He was glad, for then they were immune in a shadowy silence, there was no world, no time.

The snow lasted for some days. On the Sunday they went to church. They made a line of foot-prints across the garden, he left a flat snow-print of his hand on the wall as he vaulted over, they traced the snow across the churchyard. For three days they had been immune in a perfect love.

There were very few people in church, and she was glad. She did not care much for church. She had never questioned any beliefs, and she was, from habit and custom, a regular attendant at morning service. But she had ceased to come with any anticipation. Today, however, in the strangeness of snow, after such consummation of love, she felt expectant again, and delighted. She was still in the eternal world.

She used, after she went to the High School and wanted to be a lady, wanted to fulfil some mysterious ideal, always to listen to the sermon and to try to gather suggestions. That was all very well for a while. The vicar told her to be good in this way and in that. She went away feeling it was her highest aim to fulfil these injunctions.

But quickly this palled. After a short time, she was not very much interested in being good. Her soul was in quest of something, which was not just being good, and doing one's best. No, she wanted something else: something that was not her ready-made duty. Everything seemed to be merely a matter of social duty, and never of her *self*. They talked about her soul, but somehow never managed to rouse or to implicate her soul. As yet her soul was not brought in at all.

So that whilst she had an affection for Mr Loverseed, the vicar, and a protective sort of feeling for Cossethay church, wanting always to help it and defend it, it counted very small in her life.

Not but that she was conscious of some unsatisfaction. When her husband was roused by the thought of the churches, then she became hostile to the ostensible Church, she hated it for not fulfilling anything in her. The Church told her to be good: very well, she had no idea of contradicting what it said. The Church talked about her soul, and about the welfare of mankind, as if the saving of her soul lay in her performing certain acts conducive to the welfare of mankind. Very good, she heard it all and was sure it was true. The salvation of her soul lay in her contributing to the welfare of mankind. Well and good—it was so, then.

Nevertheless, as she sat in church her face had a pathos and poignancy. Was this what she had come to hear: how, by doing this thing and by not doing that, she could save her soul? She did not contradict it. But the pathos of her face gave the lie. There was something else she wanted to hear, it was something else she asked for from the Church.

But who was *she* to affirm it? And what was *she* doing with unsatisfied desires? She was ashamed. She ignored them and left them out of count as much as possible, her underneath yearnings. They angered her. She wanted to be like other people, decently satisfied.

He angered her more than ever. Church had an irresistible attraction for him. And he paid no more attention to that part of the service which was Church to her, than if he had been an angel or a fabulous beast sitting there. He simply paid no heed to the sermon or to the meaning of the service. There was something thick, dark, dense, powerful about him that irritated her too deeply for her to speak of it. The Church teaching in itself meant nothing to him. "And forgive us our trespasses as we forgive them that trespass against us—" it simply did not touch him. It might have been mere sounds, and it would have acted upon him in the same way. He did not want things to be intelligible. And he did not care about his trespasses, neither about the trespasses of his neighbour, when he was in church. Leave that care for week-days. When he was in church, he took no more notice of his daily life. It was week-day stuff. As for the welfare of mankind,—he merely did not realise that there was any such thing: except on week-days, when he was good natured enough. In church, he wanted a dark, nameless emotion, the emotion of all the great mysteries of passion.

He was not interested in the *thought* of himself or of her: oh, and how that irritated her! He ignored the sermon, he ignored the greatness of mankind, he did not admit the immediate importance of mankind. He did not care about himself as a human being. He did not attach any vital importance to his life in the drafting office, or his life among men. That was just merely the margin to the text. The verity was his connection with Anna and his connection with the Church, his real being lay in his dark emotional experience of the Infinite, of the Absolute. And the great, mysterious, illuminated capitals to the text, were his feelings with the Church.

It exasperated her beyond measure. She could not get out of the

Church the satisfaction he got. The thought of her soul was intimately mixed up with the thought of her own self. Indeed, her soul and her own self were one and the same in her. Whereas he seemed simply to ignore the fact of his own self, almost to refute it. He had a soul—a dark, inhuman thing caring nothing for humanity. So she conceived it. And in the gloom and the mystery of the Church his soul lived and ran free, like some strange, underground thing, abstract.

He was very strange to her, and, in this Church spirit, in conceiving himself as a soul, he seemed to escape and run free of her. In a way, she envied it him, this dark freedom and jubilation of the soul, some strange entity in him. It fascinated her. Again she hated it. And again, she despised him, wanted to destroy it in him.

This snowy morning, he sat with a dark-bright face beside her, not aware of her, and somehow, she felt he was conveying to strange, secret places the love that sprang in him for her. He sat with a dark-rapt, half-delighted face, looking at a little stained window. She saw the ruby-coloured glass, with the shadow heaped along the bottom from the snow outside, and the familiar yellow figure of the lamb holding the banner, a little darkened now, but in the murky interior, strangely luminous, pregnant.

She had always liked this little red and yellow window. The lamb, looking very silly and self-conscious, was holding up a fore-paw, in the cleft of which was dangerously perched a little flag with a red cross. Very pale yellow, the lamb, with greenish shadows. Since she was a child she had liked this creature, with the same feeling she felt for the little woolly lambs on green legs that the children carried home from the fair every year. She had always liked those toys, and she had the same amused, childish liking for this church lamb. Yet she had always been uneasy about it. She was never sure that this Lamb with a flag did not want to be more than it appeared. So she half mistrusted it, there was a mixture of dislike in her attitude to it.

Now, by a curious gathering, knitting of his eyes, the faintest tension of ecstasy on his face, he gave her the uncomfortable feeling that he was in correspondence with the creature, the lamb in the window. A cold wonder came over her—her soul was perplexed. There he sat, motionless, timeless, with the faint bright tension on his face. What was he doing? What connection was there between him and the lamb in the glass?

Suddenly it gleamed to her dominant, this lamb with the flag.

Suddenly she had a powerful mystic experience, the power of the tradition seized on her, she was transported to another world. And she hated it, resisted it.

Instantly, it was only a silly lamb in the glass again. And dark, violent hatred of her husband swept up in her. What was he doing, sitting there gleaming, carried away, soulful?

She shifted sharply, she knocked him as she pretended to pick up her glove, she groped among his feet.

He came to, rather bewildered, exposed. Anybody but her would have pitied him. She wanted to rend him. He did not know what was amiss, what he had been doing.

As they sat at dinner, in their cottage, he was dazed by the chill of antagonism from her. She did not know why she was so angry. But she was incensed.

"Why do you never listen to the sermon?" she asked, seething with hostility and violation.

"I do," he said.

"You don't—you don't hear a single word."

He retired into himself, to enjoy his own sensation. There was something subterranean about him, as if he had an underworld refuge. The young girl hated to be in the house with him when he was like this.

After dinner, he retired into the parlour, continuing in the same state of abstraction, which was a burden intolerable to her. Then he went to the book-shelf and took down books to look at, that she had scarcely glanced over.

He sat absorbed over a book on the illuminations in old missals, and then over a book on paintings in churches; Italian, English, French and German. He had, when he was sixteen, discovered a Roman Catholic bookshop where he could find such things.

He turned the leaves in absorption, absorbed in looking, not thinking. He was like a man whose eyes were in his chest, she said of him later.

She came to look at the things with him. Half they fascinated her. She was puzzled, interested, and antagonistic.

It was when she came to pictures of the Pietà that she burst out.

"I do think they're loathsome," she cried.

"What?" he said, surprised, abstracted.

"Those bodies with slits in them, posing to be worshipped."

"You see, it means the Sacraments, the Bread," he said, slowly.

"Does it!" she cried. "Then it's worse. *I* don't want to see your chest slit, nor to eat your dead body, even if you offer it me. Can't you see it's horrible?"

"It isn't me, it's Christ."

"What if it is, it's you! And it's horrible, you wallowing in your own dead body, and thinking of eating it in the Sacrament."

"You've to take it for what it means."

"It means your human body put up to be slit and killed and then worshipped—what else?"

They lapsed into silence. His soul grew angry and aloof.

"And I think that Lamb in Church," she said, "is the biggest joke in the parish—"

She burst into a 'Pouf' of ridiculing laughter.

"It might be, to those that see nothing in it," he said. "You know it's the symbol of Christ, of His innocence and sacrifice."

"Whatever it means, it's a *lamb*," she said. "And I like lambs too much to treat them as if they had to mean something. As for the Christmas-tree flag—no—"

And again she poufed with mockery.

"It's because you don't know anything," he said violently, harshly. "Laugh at what you know, not at what you don't know."

"What don't I know?"

"What things mean."

"And what does it mean?"

He was reluctant to answer her. He found it difficult.

"*What* does it mean?" she insisted.

"It means the triumph of the Resurrection."

She hesitated, baffled. A fear came upon her. What were these things? Something dark and powerful seemed to extend before her. Was it wonderful after all?

But no—she refused it.

"Whatever it may pretend to mean, what it *is* is a silly absurd toy-lamb with a Christmas-tree flag ledged on its paw—and if it wants to mean anything else, it must look different from that."

He was in a state of violent irritation against her. Partly he was ashamed of his love for these things; he hid his passion for them. He was ashamed of the ecstasy into which he could throw himself with these symbols. And for a few moments he hated the Lamb and the mystic pictures of the Eucharist, with a violent, ashy hatred. His fire was put out, she had thrown cold water on it. The whole thing was distasteful to him, his mouth was full of ashes. He went out cold with corpse-like anger, leaving her alone. He hated her. He walked through the white snow, under a sky of lead.

And she wept again, in bitter recurrence of the previous gloom. But her heart was easy—oh, much more easy.

She was quite willing to make it up with him when he came home again. He was black and surly, but abated. She had broken a little of something in him. And at length he was glad to forfeit from his soul all his symbols, to have her making love to him. He loved it when she put her head on his knee, and he had not asked her to or wanted her to, he loved her when she put her arms round him and made bold love to him, and he did not make love to her. He felt a strong blood in his limbs again.

And she loved the intent, far look of his eyes when they rested on her: intent, yet far, not near, not with her. And she wanted to bring them near. She wanted his eyes to come to hers, to know her. And they would not. They remained intent, and far, and proud, like a hawk's, naïve and inhuman as a hawk's. So she loved him and caressed him and roused him like a hawk, till he was keen and instant, but without tenderness. He came to her fierce and hard, like a hawk striking and taking her. He was no mystic any more, she was his aim and object, his prey. And she was carried off, and he was satisfied, or satiated at last.

Then immediately she began to retaliate on him. She too was a hawk. If she imitated the pathetic plover running plaintive to him, that was part of the game. When he, satisfied, moved with a proud, insolent slouch of the body and a half-contemptuous drop of the head, unaware of her, ignoring her very existence after taking his fill of her and getting his satisfaction of her, her soul roused, its pinions became like steel, and she struck at him. When he sat on his perch glancing sharply round with solitary pride, pride eminent and fierce, she dashed at him and threw him from his station savagely, she goaded him from his keen dignity of a male, she harassed him from his unperturbed pride, till he was mad with rage, his light brown eyes burned with fury, they saw her now, like flames of anger they flared at her and recognised her as the enemy.

Very good, she was the enemy, very good. As he prowled round her, she watched him. As he struck at her, she struck back.

He was angry because she had carelessly pushed away his tools so that they got rusty.

"Don't leave them littering in my way, then," she said.

"I shall leave them where I like," he cried.

"Then I shall throw them where I like."

They glowered at each other, he with rage in his hands, she with her soul fierce with victory. They were very well matched. They would fight it out.

She turned to her sewing. Immediately the tea-things were cleared away, she fetched out the stuff, and his soul rose in rage. He hated beyond measure to hear the shriek of calico as she tore the web sharply, as if with pleasure. And the run of the sewing-machine gathered a frenzy in him at last.

"Aren't you going to stop that row." he shouted. "Can't you do it in the daytime?"

She looked up sharply, hostile from her work.

"No, I can't do it in the daytime, I have other things to do. Besides, I like sewing, and you're not going to stop me doing it."

Whereupon she turned back to her arranging, fixing, stitching, his nerves jumped with anger as the sewing-machine started and stuttered and buzzed.

But she was enjoying herself, she was triumphant and happy as the darting needle danced ecstatically down a hem, drawing the stuff along under its vivid stabbing, irresistibly. She made the machine hum. She stopped it imperiously, her fingers were deft and swift and mistress.

If he sat behind her stiff with impotent rage—it only made a trembling vividness come into her energy. On she worked. At last he went to bed in a rage, and lay stiff, away from her. And she turned her back on him. And in the morning they did not speak, except in mere cold civilities.

And when he came home at night, his heart relenting and growing hot for love of her, when he was just ready to feel he had been wrong, and when he was expecting her to feel the same, there she sat at the sewing-machine, the whole house was covered with clipped calico, the kettle was not even on the fire.

She started up, affecting concern.

"Is it so late?" she cried.

But his face had gone stiff with rage. He walked through to the parlour, then he walked back and out of the house again. Her heart sank. Very swiftly she began to make his tea.

He went black-hearted down the road to Ilkeston. When he was in this state he never thought. A bolt shot across the doors of his mind and shut him in, a prisoner. He went back to Ilkeston, and drank a glass of beer. What was he going to do? He did not want to see anybody.

He would go to Nottingham, to his own town. He went to the station and took a train. When he got to Nottingham, still he had nowhere to go. However, it was more agreeable to walk familiar streets. He paced them with a mad restlessness, as if he were running amok. Then he turned to a bookshop and found a book on Bamberg Cathedral. Here was a discovery! here was something for him! He went into a quiet restaurant to look at his treasure. He lit up with thrills of bliss as he turned from picture to picture. He had found something at last, in these carvings. His soul had great satisfaction. Had he not come out to seek, and had he not found! He was in a passion of fulfilment. These were the finest carvings, statues, he had ever seen. The book lay in his hands like a doorway. The world around was only an inclosure, a room. But he was going away. He lingered over the lovely statues of women. A marvellous, finely wrought universe crystallised out around him as he looked again, at the crowns, the twining hair, the woman-faces.

He liked all the better the unintelligible text of the German. He preferred things he could not understand with the mind. He loved the undiscovered and the undiscoverable. He pored over the pictures intensely. And these were wooden statues! "Holz"—he believed that meant wood. Wooden statues so shapen to his soul! He was a million times gladdened. How undiscovered the world was, how it revealed itself to his soul! What a fine, exciting thing his life was, at his hand! Did not Bamberg Cathedral make the world his own? He celebrated his triumphant strength and life and verity, and embraced the vast riches he was inheriting.

But it was about time to go home. He had better catch a train. All the time there was a steady bruise at the bottom of his soul, but so steady as to be forgettable. He caught a train for Ilkeston.

It was ten o'clock as he was mounting the hill to Cossethay, carrying his limp book on Bamberg Cathedral. He had not yet thought of Anna, not definitely. The dark finger pressing a bruise controlled him thoughtlessly.

Anna had started guiltily when he left the house. She had hastened preparing the tea, hoping he would come back. She had made some toast, and got all ready. Then he didn't come. She cried with vexation and disappointment. Why had he gone? Why couldn't he come back now? Why was it such a battle between them? She loved him—she did love him—why couldn't he be kinder to her, nicer to her?

She waited in distress—then her mood grew harder. He passed out of her thoughts. She had considered, indignantly, what right he had to interfere with her sewing? She had indignantly refused his right to interfere with her at all. She was not to be interfered with. Was she not herself, and he the outsider?

Yet a quiver of fear went through her. If he should leave her? That would destroy her. She never quite knew what he would do next. She disliked him that he was so unsure, so unfixed. What if he did leave her? She sat conjuring fears and sufferings, till she wept with very self-pity. She did not know what she would do if he left her, or if he turned against her. The thought of it chilled her, made her desolate and hard. And against him, the stranger, the outside being who wanted to arrogate authority, she remained steadily fortified. Was she not herself? How could one who was not of her own kind presume with authority? She knew she was immutable, unchangeable, she was not afraid for her own being. She was only afraid of all that was not herself. It pressed round her, it came to her and took part in her, in form of her man, this vast, resounding, alien world which was not herself. And he had so many weapons, he might strike from so many sides.

When he came in at the door, his heart was blazed with pity and tenderness, she looked so lost and forlorn and young. She glanced up, afraid. And she was surprised to see him, shining-faced, clear and beautiful in his movements, as if he were clarified. And a startled pang of fear, and shame of herself went through her.

They waited for each other to speak.

"Do you want to eat anything?" she said.

"I'll get it myself," he answered, not wanting her to serve him.

But she brought out food. And it pleased him she did it for him. He was again a bright lord.

"I went to Nottingham," he said mildly.

"To your mother?" she asked, in a flash of contempt.

"No—I didn't go home."

"Who did you go to see?"

"I went to see nobody."

"Then why did you go to Nottingham?"

"I went because I wanted to go."

He was getting angry that she again rebuffed him when he was so clear and shining.

"And who did you see?"

"I saw nobody."

"Nobody?"

"No—who should I see?"

"You saw nobody you knew?"

"No, I didn't," he replied irritably.

She believed him, and her mood became cold.

"I bought a book," he said, handing her the propitiatory volume.

She idly looked at the pictures. Beautiful, the pure women with their clear-dropping gowns. Her heart became colder. What did they mean to *him*.

He sat and waited for her. She bent over the book.

"Aren't they nice?" he said, his voice roused and glad.

Her blood flushed, but she did not lift her head.

"Yes," she said. In spite of herself, she was compelled by him. He was strange, attractive, exerting some power over her.

He came over to her, and touched her delicately. Her heart beat with wild passion, wild raging passion. But she resisted as yet. It was always the unknown, always the unknown, and she clung fiercely to her known self. But the rising flood carried her away.

They loved each other to transport again, passionately and fully.

"Isn't it more wonderful than ever?" she asked him, radiant like a newly-opened flower, with tears like dew.

He held her closer. He was strange and abstracted.

"It is always more wonderful," she asseverated, in a glad, child's voice, remembering her fear, and not quite cleared of it yet.

So it went on continually, the recurrence of love and conflict between them. One day it seemed as if everything was shattered, all life spoiled, ruined, desolated and laid waste. The next day it was all marvellous again, just marvellous. One day she thought she would go mad from his very presence, the sound of his drinking was detestable to her. The next day she loved and rejoiced in the way he crossed the floor, he was sun, moon and stars in one.

She fretted, however, at last, over the lack of stability. When the perfect hours came back, her heart did not forget that they would pass away again. She was uneasy. The surety, the surety, the inner surety, the confidence in the abidingness of love: that was what she wanted. And that she did not get. She knew also that he had not got it.

Nevertheless it was a marvellous world, she was for the most part lost in the marvellousness of it. Even her great woes were marvellous to her.

She could be very happy. And she wanted to be happy. She resented it when he made her unhappy. Then she could kill him, cast him out. Many days, she waited for the hour when he would be gone to work. Then the flow of her life, which he seemed to dam up, was let loose, and she was free. She was free, she was full of delight. Everything delighted her. She took up the rug and went to shake it in the garden. Patches of snow were on the fields, the air was light. She heard the ducks shouting on the pond, she saw them charge and sail across the water as if they were setting off on an invasion of the world. She watched the rough horses, one of which was clipped smooth on the belly, so that he wore a jacket and long stockings of brown fur, stand kissing each other in the wintry morning by the churchyard wall. Everything delighted her, now he was gone, the insulator, the obstruction removed, the world all hers, in connection with her.

She was joyfully active. Nothing pleased her more than to hang out the washing in a high wind that came full-butt over the round of the hill, tearing the wet garments out of her hands, making flap-flap-flap of the waving stuff. She laughed and struggled and grew angry. But she loved her solitary days.

Then he came home at night, and she knitted her brows because of some endless contest between them. As he stood in the doorway, her heart changed. It steeled itself. The laughter and zest of the day disappeared from her. She was stiffened.

They fought an unknown battle, unconsciously. Still they were in love with each other, the passion was there. But the passion was consumed in a battle. And the deep, fierce, unnamed battle went on. Everything glowed intensely about them, the world had put off its clothes and was awful, with new, primal nakedness.

Sunday came, when the strange spell was cast over her by him. Half she loved it. She was becoming more like him. All the week-days, there was a glint of sky and fields, the little church seemed to babble away to the cottages the morning through. But on Sundays, when he stayed at home, a deeply-coloured, tense gloom seemed to gather on the face of the earth, the church seemed to fill itself with shadow, to become big, a universe to her, there was a burning of blue and ruby, a sound of worship about her. And when the doors were opened, and she came out into the world, it was a world new-created, she stepped into the resurrection of the world, her heart beating to the memory of the darkness and the Passion.

If, as very often, they went to the Marsh for tea on Sundays, then she regained another, lighter world, that had never known the gloom and the stained glass and the ecstasy of chanting. Her husband was obliterated, she was with her father again, who was so fresh and free and all daylight. Her husband, with his intensity and his darkness, was obliterated. She left him, she forgot him, she accepted her father.

Yet, as she went home again with the young man, she put her hand on his arm tentatively, a little bit ashamed, her hand pleaded that he would not hold it against her, her recusancy. But he was obscured. He seemed to become blind, as if he were not there with her.

Then she was afraid. She wanted him. When he was oblivious of her, she almost went mad with fear. For she had become so vulnerable, so exposed. She was in touch so intimately. All things about her had become intimate, she had known them near and lovely, like presences hovering upon her. What if they should all go hard and separate again, standing back from her terrible and distinct, and she, having known them, should be at their mercy.

This frightened her. Always, her husband was to her the unknown to which she was delivered up. She was a flower that has been tempted forth into blossom, and has no retreat. He had her nakedness in his power. And who was he, what was he? A blind thing, a dark force, without knowledge. She wanted to preserve herself.

Then she gathered him to herself again and was satisfied for a moment. But as time went on, she began to realise more and more that he did not alter, that he was something dark, alien to herself. She had thought him just the bright reflex of herself. As the weeks and months went by she realised that he was a dark opposite to her, that they were opposites, not complements.

He did not alter, he remained separately himself, and he seemed to expect her to be part of himself, the extension of his will. She felt him trying to gain power over her, without knowing her. What did he want? Was he going to bully her?

What did she want herself? She answered herself, that she wanted to be happy, to be natural, like the sunlight and the busy daytime.

And, at the bottom of her soul, she felt he wanted her to be dark, unnatural. Sometimes, when he seemed like the darkness covering and smothering her, she revolted almost in horror, and struck at him. She struck at him, and made him bleed, and he became wicked. Because she dreaded him and held him in horror, he became wicked, he wanted to destroy. And then the fight between them was cruel.

She began to tremble. He wanted to impose himself on her. And he began to shudder. She wanted to desert him, to leave him a prey to the open, with the unclean dogs of the darkness setting on to devour him. He must beat her, and make her stay with him. Whereas she fought to keep herself free of him.

They went their ways now shadowed and stained with blood, feeling the world far off, unable to give help. Till she began to get tired. After a certain point, she became impassive, detached utterly from him. He was always ready to burst out murderously against her. Her soul got up and left him, she went her way. Nevertheless in her apparent blitheness, that made his soul black with opposition, she trembled as if she bled.

And ever and again, the pure love came in sunbeams between them, when she was like a flower in the sun to him, so beautiful, so shining, so intensely dear that he could scarcely bear it. Then as if his soul had six wings of bliss he stood absorbed in praise, feeling the radiance from the Almighty beat through him like a pulse, as he stood in the upright flame of praise, transmitting the pulse of Creation.

And ever and again he appeared to her as the dread flame of power. Sometimes, when he stood in the doorway, his face lit up, he seemed like an Annunciation to her, her heart beat fast. And she watched him, suspended. He had a dark, burning being that she dreaded and resisted. She was subject to him as to the Angel of the Presence. She waited upon him and heard his will, and she trembled in his service.

Then all this passed away. Then he loved her for her childishness and for her strangeness to him, for the wonder of her soul which was different from his soul, and which made him genuine when he would be false. And she loved him for the way he sat loosely in a chair, or for the way he came through a door with his face open and eager. She loved his ringing, eager voice, and the touch of the unknown about him, his absolute simplicity.

Yet neither of them was quite satisfied. He felt, somewhere, that she did not respect him. She only respected him as far as he was related to herself. For what he was, beyond her, she had no care. She did not care for what he represented in himself. It is true, he did not know himself what he represented. But whatever it was, she did not really honor it. She did no service to his work as a lace-designer, nor to himself as bread-winner. Because he went down to the office and worked every day—that entitled him to no respect or regard from her, he knew. Rather she despised him for it. And he almost loved her for this, though at first it maddened him like an insult.

What was much deeper, she soon came to combat his deepest feelings. What he thought about life and about society and mankind did not matter very much to her: he was right enough to be insignificant. This was again galling to him. She would judge beyond him on these things. But at length he came to accept her judgments, discovering them as if they were his own. It was not here the deep trouble lay. The deep root of his enmity lay in the fact that she jeered at his soul. He was inarticulate and stupid in thought. But to some things he clung passionately. He loved the Church. If she tried to get out of him, what he *believed*, then they were both soon in a white rage.

Did he believe the water turned to wine at Cana? She would drive him to the thing as a historical fact: so much rain-water—look at it—can it become grape-juice, wine? For an instant, he saw with the clear eyes of the mind and said no, his clear mind, answering her for a moment, rejected the idea. And immediately his whole soul was crying in a mad, inchoate hatred against this violation of himself. It *was* true for him. His mind was extinguished again at once, his blood was up. In his blood and bones, he wanted the scene, the wedding, the water brought forward from the firkins as red wine: and Christ saying to His mother:

"Woman, what have I to do with thee?—mine hour is not yet come."

And then:

"His mother saith unto the servants, 'Whatsoever he saith unto you, do it.'"

Brangwen loved it, with his bones and blood he loved it, he could not let it go. Yet she forced him to let it go. She hated his blind attachments.

Water, natural water, could it suddenly and unnaturally turn into wine, depart from its being and at hap-hazard take on another being? Ah no, he knew it was wrong.

She became again the palpitating, hostile child, hateful, putting things to destruction. He became mute and dead. His own being gave him the lie. He knew it was so: wine was wine, water was water, for ever: the water had not become wine. The miracle was not a real fact. She seemed to be destroying him. He went out, dark and destroyed, his soul running its blood. And he tasted of death. Because his life was formed in these unquestioned concepts.

She, desolate again as she had been when she was a child, went away and sobbed. She did not care, she did not care whether the water had turned to wine or not. Let him believe it if he wanted to. But she knew she had won. And an ashy desolation came over her.

They were ashenly miserable for some time. Then the life began to come back. He was nothing if not dogged. He thought again of the chapter of St John. There was a great biting pang. "But thou hast kept the good wine until now." "The best wine!" The young man's heart responded in a craving, in a triumph, although the knowledge that it was not true in fact bit at him like a weasel in his heart. Which was stronger, the pain of the denial or the desire for affirmation? He was stubborn in spirit, and abode by his desire. But he would not any more affirm the miracles as true.

Very well, it was not true, the water had not turned into wine. The water had not turned into wine. But for all that he would live in his soul as if the water *had* turned into wine. For truth of fact, it had not. But for his soul, it had.

"Whether it turned into wine or whether it didn't," he said, "it doesn't bother me. I take it for what it is."

"And *what* is it?" she asked, quickly, hopefully.

"It's the Bible," he said.

That answer enraged her, and she despised him. She did not actively question the Bible herself. But he drove her to contempt.

And yet he did not care about the Bible, the written letter. Although he could not satisfy her, yet she knew of herself that he had something real. He was not a dogmatist. He did not believe in *fact* that the water turned into wine. He did not want to make a fact out of it. Indeed, his attitude was without criticism. It was purely individual. He took that which was of value to him from the Written Word, he added to his spirit. His mind he let sleep.

And she was bitter against him, that he let his mind sleep. That which was human, belonged to mankind, he would not exert. He cared only for himself. He was no Christian. Above all, Christ had asserted the brotherhood of man.

She, almost against herself, clung to the worship of the human knowledge. Man must die in the body, but in his knowledge he was immortal. Such, somewhere, was her belief, quite obscure and unformulated. She believed in the omnipotence of the human mind.

He, on the other hand, blind as a subterranean thing, just ignored the human mind and ran after his own dark-souled desires, following his own tunnelling nose. She felt often she must suffocate. And she fought him off.

Then he, knowing he was blind, fought madly back again, frantic in sensual fear. He did foolish things. He asserted himself on his rights, he arrogated the old position of master of the house.

"You've a right to do as I want," he cried.

"Fool!" she answered. "Fool!"

"I'll let you know who's master," he cried.

"Fool!" she answered. "Fool! I've known my own father, who could put a dozen of you in his pipe and push them down with his finger-end. Don't I know what a fool you are."

He knew himself what a fool he was, and was flayed by the knowledge. Yet he went on trying to steer the ship of their dual life. He asserted his position as the captain of the ship. And captain and ship bored her. He wanted to loom important as master of one of the innumerable domestic craft that make up the great fleet of society. It seemed to her a ridiculous armada of tubs jostling in futility. She felt no belief in it. She jeered at him as master of the house, master of their dual life. And he was black with shame and rage. He knew, with shame, how her father had been a man without arrogating any authority.

He had gone on the wrong tack, and he felt it hard to give up the expedition. There was great surging and shame. Then he yielded. He had given up the master-of-the-house idea.

There was something he wanted, nevertheless, some form of mastery. Ever and anon, after his collapses into the petty and the shameful, he rose up again, and, stubborn in spirit, strong in his power to start afresh, set out once more in his male pride of being to fulfil the hidden passion of his spirit.

It began well, but it ended always in war between them, till they were both driven almost to madness. He said, she did not respect him. She laughed in hollow scorn of this. For her it was enough that she loved him.

"Respect what?" she asked.

But he always answered the wrong thing. And though she cudgelled her brains, she could not come at it.

"Why don't you go on with your wood-carving?" she said. "Why don't you finish your Adam and Eve?"

But she did not care for the Adam and Eve, and he never put another stroke to it. She jeered at the Eve, saying:

"She is like a little marionette. Why is she so small? You've made Adam as big as God, and Eve like a doll.

"It is impudence to say that Woman was made out of Man's body," she continued, "when every man is born of woman. What impudence men have, what arrogance!"

In a rage one day, after trying to work on the board, and failing, so that his belly was a flame of nausea, he chopped up the whole panel and put it on the fire. She did not know. He went about for some days very quiet and subdued after it.

"Where is the Adam and Eve board?" she asked him.

"Burnt."

She looked at him.

"But your carving."

"I burned it."

"When?"

She did not believe him.

"On Friday night."

"When I was at the Marsh?"

"Yes."

She said no more.

Then, when he had gone to work, she wept for a whole day, and was much chastened in spirit. So that a new, fragile flame of love came out of the ashes of this last pain.

Directly, it occurred to her that she was with child. There was a great trembling of wonder and anticipation through her soul. She wanted a child. Not that she loved babies so much, though she was touched by all young things. But she wanted to bear children. And a certain hunger in her heart wanted to unite her husband with herself, in a child.

She wanted a son. She felt, a son would be everything. She wanted to tell her husband. But it was such a trembling, intimate thing to tell him, and he was at this time hard and unresponsive. So that she went away and wept. It was such a waste of a beautiful opportunity, such a frost that nipped in the bud one of the beautiful moments of her life.

She went about heavy and tremulous with her secret, wanting to touch him, oh, most delicately, and see his face, dark and sensitive, attend to her news. She waited and waited for him to become gentle and still towards her. But he was always harsh and he bullied her.

So that the buds shrivelled from her confidence, she was chilled. She went down to the Marsh.

"Well," said her father, looking at her and seeing her at the first glance; "what's amiss wi' you now?"

The tears came at the touch of his careful love.

"Nothing," she said.

"Can't you hit it off, you two?" he said.

"He's so obstinate," she quivered; but her soul was obdurate itself.

"Ay, an' I know another who's all that," said her father.

She was silent.

"You don't want to make yourselves miserable," said her father: "all about nowt."

"*He* isn't miserable," she said.

"I'll back my life, if you can do nowt else, you can make him as miserable as a dog. You'd be a dab hand at that, my lass."

"*I* do nothing to make him miserable," she retorted.

"Oh no—oh no! A packet o' butterscotch, you are."

She laughed a little.

"You mustn't think I *want* to be miserable," she cried. "I don't."

"We quite readily believe it," retorted Brangwen. "Neither do you intend him to be hopping for joy like a fish in a pond."

This made her think. She was rather surprised to find that she did *not* intend her husband to be hopping for joy like a fish in a pond.

Her mother came, and they all sat down to tea, talking casually.

"Remember, child," said her mother, "that everything is not waiting for *your* hand just to take or leave. You mustn't expect it. Between two people, the love itself is the important thing, and that is neither you nor him. It is a third thing you must create. You mustn't expect it to be just your way."

"Ha—nor do I. If I did, I should soon find my mistake out. If *I* put my hand out to take anything, my hand is very soon bitten, I can tell you."

"Then you must mind where you put your hand," said her father.

Anna was rather indignant that they took the tragedy of her young married life with such equanimity.

"You love the man right enough," said her father, wrinkling his forehead in distress. "That's all as counts."

"I *do* love him, more shame to him," she cried. "I want to tell him—I've been waiting for four days now to tell him—" her face began to quiver, the tears came. Her parents watched her in silence. She did not go on.

"Tell him what?" said her father.

"That we're going to have an infant," she sobbed, "and he's never, never let me, not once, every time I've come to him, he's been horrid to me, and I wanted to tell him, I did. And he won't let me—he's cruel to me."

She sobbed as if her heart would break. Her mother went and comforted her, put her arms round her, and held her close. Her father sat with a queer, wrinkled brow, and was rather paler than usual. His heart went tense with hatred of his son-in-law.

So that, when the tale was sobbed out, and comfort administered, and tea sipped, and something like calm restored to the little circle, the thought of Will Brangwen's entry was not pleasantly entertained.

Tilly was set to watch out for him as he passed by on his way home. The little party at table heard the woman-servant's shrill call:

"You've got to come in, Will. Anna's here."

After a few moments, the youth entered.

"Are you stopping?" he asked in his hard, harsh voice.

He seemed like a blade of destruction standing there. She quivered to tears.

"Sit you down," said Tom Brangwen, "an' take a bit off your length."

Will Brangwen sat down. He felt something strange in the atmosphere. He was dark browed, but his eyes had the keen, intent, sharp look, as if he could only see in the distance; which was a beauty in him, and which made Anna so angry.

"Why does he always deny me?" she said to herself. "Why is it nothing to him, what I am?"

And Tom Brangwen, blue-eyed and warm, sat in opposition to the youth.

"How long are you stopping?" the young husband asked his wife.

"Not very long," she said.

"Get your tea, lad," said Tom Brangwen. "Are you itchin' to be off the moment you enter?"

They talked of trivial things. Through the open door the level rays of sunset poured in, shining on the floor. A grey hen appeared stepping swiftly in the doorway, pecking, and the light through her comb and her wattles made an oriflamme tossed here and there, as she went, her grey body was like a ghost.

Anna, watching, threw scraps of bread, and she felt the child flame within her. She seemed to remember again forgotten, burning, far-off things.

"Where was I born, mother?" she asked.

"In London."

"And was my father—" she spoke of him as if he were merely a strange name: she could never connect herself with him—"was he dark?"

"He had dark-brown hair and dark eyes and a fresh colouring. He went bald, rather bald, when he was quite young," replied the mother, also as if telling a tale which was just old imagination.

"Was he good-looking?"

"Yes—he was very good-looking—rather small. I have never seen an Englishman who looked like him."

"Why?"

"He was—" the mother made a quick, running movement with her hands—"his figure was alive and changing—it was never fixed. He was not in the least steady—like a running stream."

It flashed over the youth—Anna too was like a running stream. Instantly he was in love with her again.

Tom Brangwen was frightened. His heart always filled with fear, fear of the unknown, when he heard his women speak of their bygone men as of strangers they had known in passing and had taken leave of again.

In the room, there came a silence and a singleness over all their hearts. They were separate people with separate destinies. Why should they seek each to lay violent hands of claim on the other?

The young people went home as a sharp little moon was setting in a dusk of spring. Tufts of trees hovered in the upper air, the little church pricked up shadowily at the top of the hill, the earth was a dark blue shadow.

She put her hand lightly on his arm, out of her far distance. And out of the distance, he felt her touch him. They walked on, hand in hand, along opposite horizons, touching across the dusk. There was a sound of thrushes calling in the dark-blue twilight.

"I think we are going to have an infant, Bill," she said, from far off.

He trembled, and his fingers tightened on hers.

"Why?" he asked, his heart beating. "You don't know?"

"I do," she said.

They continued without saying any more, walking along opposite horizons, hand in hand across the intervening space, two separate people. And he trembled as if a wind blew on to him in strong gusts, out of the unseen. He was afraid. He was afraid to know he was alone. For she seemed fulfilled and separate and sufficient in her half of the world. He could not bear to know that he was cut off. Why could he not be always one with her? It was he who had given her the child. Why could she not be with him, one with him? Why must he be set in this separateness, why could she not be with him, close, close, as one with him? She must be one with him.

He held her fingers tightly in his own. She did not know what he was thinking. The blaze of light on her heart was too beautiful and dazzling, from the conception in her womb. She walked glorified, and the sound of the thrushes, of the trains in the valley, of the far-off faint noises of the town, were her "Magnificat."

But he was struggling in silence. It seemed as though there were before him a solid wall of darkness that impeded him and suffocated him and made him mad. He wanted her to come to him, to complete him, to stand before him so that his eyes did not, should not meet the naked darkness. Nothing mattered to him but that she should come and complete him. For he was ridden by the awful sense of his own limitation. It was as if he ended uncompleted, as yet uncreated on the darkness, and he wanted her to come and liberate him into the whole.

But she was complete in herself, and he was ashamed of his need, his helpless need of her. His need, and his shame of need, weighed on him like a madness. Yet still he was quiet and gentle, in reverence of her conception, and because she was with child by him.

And she was happy in showers of sunshine. She loved her husband, as a presence, as a grateful condition. But for the moment her need was fulfilled, and now she wanted only to hold her husband by the hand in sheer happiness, without taking thought, only being glad.

He had various folios of reproductions, and among them a cheap print from Fra Angelico's "Entry of the Blessed into Paradise." This filled Anna with bliss. The beautiful, innocent way in which the Blessed held each other by the hand as they moved towards the radiance, the real, real, angelic melody, made her weep with happiness. The floweriness, the beams of light, the linking of hands, was almost too much for her, too innocent.

Day after day came shining through the door of Paradise, day after day she entered into the brightness. The child in her shone till she herself was a beam of sunshine; and how lovely was the sunshine that loitered and wandered out of doors, where the catkins on the big hazel bushes at the end of the garden hung in their shaken, floating aureole, where little fumes like fire burst out from the black yew-trees as a bird settled clinging to the branches. One day bluebells were along the hedge-bottoms, then cowslips twinkled like manna, golden and evanescent on the meadows. She was full of a rich drowsiness and loveliness. How happy she was, how gorgeous it was to live: to have known herself, her husband, the passion of love and begetting; and to know that all this lived and waited and burned on around her, a terrible purifying fire, through which she had passed for once to come to this peace of golden radiance, when she was with child, and innocent, and in love with her husband and with all the many angels hand in hand. She lifted her throat to the breeze that came across the fields, and she felt it handling her like sisters fondling her, she drank it in perfume of cowslips and of apple-blossoms.

And in all the happiness a black shadow, shy, wild, a beast of prey, roamed and vanished from sight, and like strands of gossamer blown across her eyes, there was a dread for her.

She was afraid when he came home at night. As yet, her fear never spoke, the shadow never rushed upon her. He was gentle, humble, he kept himself withheld. His hands were delicate upon her, and she loved them. But there ran through her the thrill, crisp as pain, for she felt the darkness and other-world still in his soft, sheathed hands.

But the summer drifted in with the silence of a miracle, she was almost always alone. All the while, went on the long, lovely drowsiness, the maidenblush roses in the garden were all shed, washed away in a pouring rain, summer drifted into autumn, and the long, vague, golden day began to close. Crimson clouds fumed about the west, and as night came on, all the sky was fuming and steaming, and the moon, far above the swiftness of vapours, was white, bleared, the night was uneasy. Suddenly the moon would appear at a clear window in the sky, looking down from far above, like a captive. And

Anna did not sleep. There was a strange, dark tension about her husband.

She became aware that he was trying to force his will upon her, there was something he wanted, as he lay there dark and tense. And her soul sighed in weariness.

Everything was so vague and lovely, and he wanted to wake her up to the hard, hostile reality. She drew back in resistance. Still he said nothing. But she felt his power persisting on her, till she became aware of the strain, she cried out against the exhaustion. He was forcing her, he was forcing her. And she wanted so much the joy and the vagueness and the innocence of her pregnancy. She did not want his bitter-corrosive love, she did not want it poured into her, to burn her. Why must she have it? Why, oh why was he not content, contained?

She sat many hours by the window, in those days when he drove her most with the black constraint of his will, and she watched the rain falling on the yew-trees. She was not sad, only wistful, blanched. The child under her heart was a perpetual warmth. And she was sure. The pressure was only upon her from the outside, her soul had no stripes.

Yet in her heart itself was always this same strain, tense, anxious. She was not safe, she was always exposed, she was always attacked. There was a yearning in her for a fulness of peace and blessedness. What a heavy yearning it was—so heavy.

She knew, vaguely, that all the time he was not satisfied, all the time he was trying to force something from her. Ah, how she wished she could succeed with him, in her own way! He was there, so inevitable. She lived in him also. And how she wanted to be at peace with him, at peace. She loved him. She would give him love, pure love. With a strange, rapt look on her face, she awaited his homecoming that night.

Then, when he came, she rose with her hands full of love, as of flowers, radiant, innocent. A dark spasm crossed his face. As she watched, her face shining and flower-like with innocent love, his face grew dark and tense, the cruelty gathered in his brows, his eyes turned aside, she saw the whites of his eyes as he looked aside from her. She waited, touching him with her hands. But from his body through her hands came the bitter-corrosive shock of his passion upon her, destroying her in blossom. She shrank. She rose from her knees and went away from him, to preserve herself. And it was great pain to her.

To him also it was agony. He saw the glistening, flower-like love in her face, and his heart was black because he did not want it. Not this—not this. He did not want flowery innocence. He was unsatisfied. The rage and storm of unsatisfaction tormented him ceaselessly. Why had she not satisfied him? He had satisfied her. She was satisfied, at peace, innocent round the doors of her own paradise.

And he was unsatisfied, unfulfilled, he raged in torment, wanting, wanting. It was for her to satisfy him: then let her do it. Let her not come with flowery handfuls of innocent love. He would throw these aside and trample the flowers to nothing. He would destroy her flowery, innocent bliss. Was he not entitled to satisfaction from her, and was not his heart all raging desire, his soul a black torment of unfulfilment. Let it be fulfilled in him, then, as it was fulfilled in her. He had given her her fulfilment. Let her rise up and do her part.

He was cruel to her. But all the time he was ashamed. And being ashamed, he was more cruel. For he was ashamed that he could not come to fulfilment without her. And he could not. And she would not heed him. He was shackled and in darkness of torment.

She beseeched him to work again, to do his wood-carving. But his soul was too black. He had destroyed his panel of Adam and Eve. He could not begin again, least of all now, whilst he was in this condition.

For her there was no final release, since he could not be liberated from himself. Strange and amorphous, she must go yearning on through the trouble, like a warm, glowing cloud blown in the middle of a storm. She felt so rich, in her warm vagueness, that her soul cried out on him, because he harried her and wanted to destroy her.

She had her moments of exaltation still, re-births of old exaltations. As she sat by her bedroom window, watching the steady rain, her spirit was somewhere far off.

She sat in pride and curious pleasure. Where there was no-one to exult with, and the unsatisfied soul must dance and play, then one danced before the Unknown.

Suddenly she realised that this was what she wanted to do. Big with child as she was, she danced there in the bedroom by herself, lifting her hands and her body to the Unseen, to the unseen Creator who had chosen her, to Whom she belonged.

She would not have had anyone know. She danced in secret, and her soul rose in bliss. She danced in secret before the Creator, she took off her clothes and danced in the pride of her bigness.

It surprised her, when it was over. She was shrinking and afraid. To what was she now exposed? She half wanted to tell her husband. Yet she shrank from him.

All the time she ran on by herself. She liked the story of David, who danced before the Lord, and uncovered himself exultingly. Why should he uncover himself to Michal, a common woman? He uncovered himself to the Lord.

"Thou comest to me with a sword and a spear and a shield, but I come to thee in the name of the Lord:—for the battle is the Lord's, and he will give you into our hands."

Her heart rang to the words. She walked in her pride. And her battle was her own Lord's, her husband was delivered over.

In these days she was oblivious of him. Who was he, to come against her? No, he was not even the Philistine, the Giant. He was like Saul proclaiming his own kingship. She laughed in her heart. Who was he, proclaiming his kingship? She laughed in her heart with pride.

And she had to dance in exultation beyond him. Because he was in the house, she had to dance before her Creator in exemption from the man. On a Saturday afternoon, when she had a fire in her bedroom, again she took off her things and danced, lifting her knees and her hands in a slow, rhythmic exulting. He was in the house, so her pride was fiercer. She would dance his nullification, she would dance to her unseen Lord. She was exalted over him, before the Lord.

She heard him coming up the stairs, and she flinched. She stood with the firelight on her ankles and feet, naked in the shadowy, late afternoon, fastening up her hair. He was startled. He stood in the doorway, his brows black and lowering.

"What are you doing?" he said, gratingly. "You'll catch a cold."

And she lifted her hands and danced again, to annul him, the light glanced on her knees as she made her slow, fine movements down the far side of the room, across the firelight. He stood away near the door in blackness of shadow, watching, transfixed. And with slow, heavy movements, she swayed backwards and forwards, like a full ear of corn, pale in the dusky afternoon, threading before the firelight, dancing his non-existence, dancing herself to the Lord, to exultation.

He watched, and his soul burned in him. He turned aside, he could not look, it hurt his eyes. Her fine limbs lifted and lifted, her hair was sticking out all fierce, and her belly, big, strange, terrifying, uplifted to the Lord. Her face was rapt and beautiful, she danced exulting before her Lord, and knew no man.

It hurt him as he watched as if he were at the stake. He felt he was being burned alive. The strangeness, the power of her in her dancing consumed him, he was burned, he could not grasp, he could not understand. He waited obliterated. Then his eyes became blind to her, he saw her no more. And through the unseeing veil between them he called to her, in his jarring voice:

"What are you doing that for?"

"Go away," she said. "Let me dance by myself." .

"That isn't dancing," he said harshly. "What do you want to do that for?"

"I don't do it for you," she said, "you go away."

Her strange, lifted belly, big with his child! Had he no right to be there? He felt his presence a violation. Yet he had his right to be there. He went and sat on the bed.

She stopped dancing, and confronted him, again lifting her slim arms and twisting at her hair. Her nakedness hurt her, opposed to him.

"I can do as I like in my bedroom," she cried. "Why do you interfere with me?"

And she slipped on a dressing-gown and crouched before the fire. He was more at ease now she was covered up. The vision of her tormented him all the days of his life, as she had been then, a strange, exalted thing having no relation to himself.

After this day, the door seemed to shut on his mind. His brow shut and became impervious. His eyes ceased to see, his hands were suspended. Within himself his will was coiled like a beast, hidden under the darkness, but always potent, working.

At first she went on blithely enough with him shut down beside her. But then his spell began to take hold of her. The dark, seething potency of him, the power of a creature that lies hidden and exerts its will to the destruction of the free-running creature, as the tiger lying in the darkness of the leaves steadily enforces the fall and the death of the light creatures that drink by the waterside in the morning, gradually began to take effect on her. Though he lay there in his darkness and did not move, yet she knew he lay waiting for her. She felt his will fastening on her and pulling her down, even whilst he was silent and obscure.

She found that, in all her outgoings and her incomings, he prevented her. Gradually she realised that she was being borne down by him, borne down by the clinging, heavy weight of him, that he was pulling her down as a leopard clings to a wild cow and exhausts her and pulls her down.

Gradually she realised that her life, her freedom, was sinking under the silent grip of his physical will. He wanted her in his power. He wanted to devour her at leisure, to have her. At length she realised that her sleep was a long ache and a weariness and exhaustion, because of his will fastened upon her, as he lay there beside her, during the night.

She realised it all, and there came a momentous pause, a pause in her swift running, a moment's suspension in her life, when she was lost.

Then she turned fiercely on him, and fought him. He was not to do this to her, it was monstrous. What horrible hold did he want to have over her body? Why did he want to drag her down, and kill her spirit? Why did he want to deny her spirit? Why did he deny her spirituality, hold her for a body only? And was he to claim her carcase?

Some vast, hideous darkness he seemed to represent to her.

"What do you do to me?" she cried. "What beastly thing do you do to me? You put a horrible pressure on my head, you don't let me sleep, you don't let me *live*. Every moment of your life you are doing something to me, something horrible, that destroys me. There is something horrible in you, something dark and beastly in your will. What do you want of me? What do you want to do to me?"

All the blood in his body went black and powerful and corrosive as he heard her. Black and blind with hatred of her he was. He was in a very black hell, and could not escape.

He hated her for what she said. Did he not give her everything, was she not everything to him? And the shame was a bitter fire in him, that she was everything to him, that he had nothing but her. And then that she should taunt him with it, that he could not escape! The fire went black in his veins. For try as he might, he could not escape. She was everything to him, she was his life and his derivation. He depended on her. If she were taken away, he would collapse as a house from which the central pillar is removed.

And she hated him, because he depended on her so utterly. He was horrible to her. She wanted to thrust him off, to set him apart. It was horrible that he should cleave to her, so close, so close, like a leopard that had leapt on her, and fastened.

He went on from day to day in a blackness of rage and shame and frustration. How he tortured himself, to be able to get away from her. But he could not. She was as the rock on which he stood, with deep, heaving water all round, and he unable to swim. He *must* take his stand on her, he must depend on her.

What had he in life, save her? Nothing. The rest was a great, heaving flood. The terror of the night of heaving, overwhelming flood, which was his vision of life without her, was too much for him. He clung to her fiercely and abjectly.

And she beat him off, she beat him off. Where could he turn, like a swimmer in a dark sea beaten off from his hold, whither could he turn? He wanted to leave her, he wanted to be able to leave her. For his soul's sake, for his manhood's sake, he must be able to leave her.

But for what? She was the ark, and the rest of the world was flood. The only tangible, secure thing was the woman. He could leave her only for another woman. And where was the other woman, and who was the other woman? Besides, he would be just in the same state. Another woman would be woman, the case would be the same.

Why was she the all, the everything, why must he live only through her, why must he sink if he were detached from her? Why must he cleave to her in a frenzy as for his very life?

The only other way to leave her was to die. The only straight way to leave her was to die. His dark, raging soul knew that. But he had no desire for death.

Why could he not leave her? Why could he not throw himself into the hidden water to live or die, as might be? He could not, he could not. But supposing he went away, right away, and found work, and had a lodging again. He could be again as he had been before.

But he knew he could not. A woman, he must have a woman. And having a woman, he must be free of her. It would be the same position. For he could not be free of her.

For how can a man stand, unless he have something sure u̶

his feet. Can a man tread the unstable water all his life, and call that standing? Better give in and drown at once.

And upon what could he stand, save upon a woman? Was he then like the old man of the seas, impotent to move save upon the back of another life? Was he impotent, or a cripple, or a defective, or a fragment?

It was black, mad, shameful torture, the frenzy of fear, the frenzy of desire, and the horrible, grasping back-wash of shame.

What was he afraid of? Why did life, without Anna, seem to him just a horrible welter, everything jostling in a meaningless, dark, fathomless flood? Why, if Anna left him even for a week, did he seem to be clinging like a madman to the edge of reality, and slipping surely, surely into the flood of unreality that would drown him. This horrible slipping into unreality drove him mad, his soul screamed with fear and agony.

Yet she was pushing him off from her, pushing him away, breaking his fingers from their hold on her, persistently, ruthlessly. He wanted her to have pity. And sometimes for a moment she had pity. But she always began again, thrusting him off, into the deep water, into the frenzy and agony of uncertainty.

She became like a fury to him, without any sense of him. Her eyes were bright with a cold, unmoving hatred. Then his heart seemed to die in its last fear. She might push him off into the deeps.

She would not sleep with him any more. She said he destroyed her sleep. Up started all his frenzy and madness of fear and suffering. She drove him away. Like a cowed, lurking devil he was driven off, his mind working cunningly against her, devising evil for her. But she drove him off. In his moments of intensest suffering, she seemed to him inconceivable, a monster, the principle of cruelty.

However her pity might give way for moments, she was hard and cold as a jewel. He must be put off from her, she must sleep alone. She made him a bed in the small room.

And he lay there whipped, his soul whipped almost to death, yet unchanged. He lay in agony of suffering, thrown back into unreality, ′ke a man thrown overboard into a sea, to swim till he sinks, because ′e is no hold, only a wide, weltering sea.

did not sleep, save for the white sleep when a thin veil is drawn mind. It was not sleep. He was awake, and he was not awake. not be alone. He needed to be able to put his arms round 'd not bear the empty space against his breast and belly, where she used to be. He could not bear it. He felt as if he were suspended in space, held there by the grip of his will. If he relaxed his will he would fall, fall through endless space, into the bottomless pit, always falling, will-less, helpless, non-existent, just dropping to extinction, falling till the fire of friction had burned out, like a falling star, then nothing, nothing, complete nothing.

He rose in the morning grey and unreal. And she seemed fond of him again, she seemed to make up to him a little.

"I slept well," she said, with her slightly false brightness. "Did you?"

"All right," he answered.

He would never tell her.

For three or four nights he lay alone through the white sleep, his will unchanged, unchanged, still tense, fixed in its grip. Then, as if she were revived and free to be fond of him again, deluded by his silence and seeming acquiescence, moved also by pity, she took him back again.

Each night, in spite of all the shame, he had waited with agony for bed-time, to see if she would shut him out. And each night, as, in her false brightness, she said Goodnight, he felt he must kill her or himself. But she asked for her kiss, so pathetically, so prettily. So he kissed her, whilst his heart was ice.

And sometimes he went out. Once he sat for a long time in the church porch, before going in to bed. It was dark with a wind blowing. He sat in the church porch and felt some shelter, some security. But it grew cold, and he must go in to bed.

Then came the night when she said, putting her arms round him and kissing him fondly:

"Stay with me tonight, will you?"

And he had stayed without demur. But his will had not altered. He would have her fixed to him.

So that soon she told him again she must be alone.

"I don't *want* to send you away. I *want* to sleep with you. But I can't sleep, you don't let me sleep."

His blood turned black in his veins.

"What do you mean by such a thing? It's an arrant lie. *I* don't let you sleep—!"

"But you don't. I sleep so well when I'm alone. And I can't sleep when you're there. You do something to me, you put a pressure on my head. And I *must* sleep now, now the child is coming."

"It's something in yourself," he replied, "something wrong in you."

Horrible in the extreme were these nocturnal combats, when all the world was asleep, and they two were alone, alone in the world, and repelling each other. It was hardly to be borne.

He went and lay down alone. And at length, after a grey and livid and ghastly period, he relaxed, something gave way in him. He let go, he did not care what became of him. Strange and dim he became to himself, to her, to everybody. A vagueness had come over everything, like a drowning. And it was an infinite relief to drown, a relief, a great, great relief.

He would insist no more, he would force her no more. He would force himself upon her no more. He would let go, relax, lapse, and what would be, should be.

Yet he wanted her still, he always, always wanted her. In his soul, he was desolate as a child, he was so helpless. Like a child on its mother, he depended on her for his living. He knew it, and he knew he could hardly help it.

Yet he must be able to be alone. He must be able to lie down alongside the empty space, and let be. He must be able to leave himself to the flood, to sink or live as might be. For he recognised at length his own limitation, and the limitation of his power. He had to give in.

There was a stillness, a wanness between them. Half at least of the battle was over. Sometimes she wept as she went about, her heart was very heavy. But the child was always warm in her womb.

They were friends again, new, subdued friends. But there was a wanness between them. They slept together once more, very quietly, and distinct, not one together as before. And she was intimate with him as at first. But he was very quiet, and not intimate. He was glad in his soul, but for the time being he was not alive.

He could sleep with her, and let her be. He could be alone now. He had just learned what it was to be able to be alone. It was right and peaceful. She had given him a new, deeper freedom. The world might be a welter of uncertainty, but he was himself now. He had come into his own existence. He was born for a second time, born at last unto himself, out of the vast body of humanity. Now at last he had a separate identity, he existed alone, even if he were not quite alone. Before, he had only existed in so far as he had relations with another being. Now he had an absolute self, as well as a relative self.

But it was a very dumb, weak, helpless self, a crawling nursling. He went about very quiet and in a way, submissive. He had an unalterable self at last, free, separate, independent.

She was relieved, she was free of him. She had given him to himself. She wept sometimes with tiredness and helplessness. But he was a husband. And she seemed, in the child that was coming, to forget. It seemed to make her warm and drowsy. She lapsed into a long muse, indistinct, warm, vague, unwilling to be taken out of her vagueness. And she rested on him also.

Sometimes she came to him with a strange light in her eyes, poignant, pathetic, as if she were asking for something. He looked, and he could not understand. She was so beautiful, so visionary, the rays seemed to go out of his breast to her, like a shining. He was there for her, all for her. And she would hold his breast, and kiss it, and kiss it, kneeling beside him [almost dev]otionally, she who was waiting for the hour of her delivery. And he would lie looking down at his breast, till it seemed that his breast was not himself, that he had left it lying there. Yet it was himself also, and beautiful and bright with her kisses. He was glad with a strange, radiant pain. Whilst she kneeled beside him, and kissed his breast with a slow, rapt, half devotional movement.

He knew she wanted something, his heart yearned to give it her. His heart yearned over her. And as she lifted her face, that was radiant and rosy as a little cloud, his heart still yearned over her, and, now from the distance, adored her. She had a flower-like presence which he adored as he stood far off, a stranger.

The weeks passed on, the time drew near, they were very gentle, and delicately happy. The insistent, passionate, dark soul, the powerful unsatisfaction in him seemed stilled and tamed, the lion lay down with the lamb in him.

She loved him very much indeed, and he waited near her. She was a precious, remote thing to him at this time, as she waited for her child. Her soul was glad with an ecstasy because of the coming infant. She wanted a boy: oh very much she wanted a boy.

But she seemed so young and so frail. She was indeed only a girl. As she stood by the fire washing herself—she was proud to wash herself at this time—and he looked at her, his heart was full of extreme tenderness for her. Such fine, fine limbs, her slim, round arms like chasing lights, and her legs so simple and childish, yet so very proud. Oh, she stood on proud legs, with a lovely reckless balance of her full belly, and the adorable little roundnesses, and the breasts becoming important. Above it all, her face was like a rosy cloud shining.

How proud she was, what a lovely proud thing her young body! And she loved him to put his hand on her ripe fulness, so that he should thrill also with the stir and the quickening there. He was afraid and silent, but she flung her arms round his neck with proud, impudent joy.

The pains came on, and OO—how she cried! She would have him stay with her. And after her long cries she would look at him, with tears in her eyes and a sobbing laugh on her face, saying:

"I don't mind it really."

It was bad enough. But to her it was never deathly. Even the fierce, tearing pain was exhilarating. She screamed and suffered, but was all the time curiously alive and vital. She felt so powerfully alive and in the hands of such a masterly force of life, that her bottommost feeling was one of exhilaration. She knew she was winning, winning, she was always winning, with each onset of pain she was nearer to victory.

Probably he suffered more than she did. He was not shocked or horrified. But he was screwed very tight in the vise of suffering.

It was a girl. The second of silence on her face when they said so showed him she was disappointed. And a great, blazing passion of resentment and protest sprang up in his heart. In that moment he claimed the child.

But when the milk came, and the infant sucked her breast, she seemed to be leaping with extravagant bliss.

"It sucks me, it sucks me, it likes me—oh, it loves it!" she cried, holding the child to her breast with her two hands covering it, passionately.

And in a few moments, as she became used to her bliss, she looked at the youth with glowing, unseeing eyes, and said:

"Anna Victrix."

He went away, trembling, and slept. To her, her pains were the wound-smart of a victor, she was the prouder.

When she was well again she was very happy. She called the baby Ursula. Both Anna and her husband felt they must have a name that gave them private satisfaction. The baby was tawny skinned, it had a curious downy skin, and wisps of bronze hair, and the yellow grey eyes that wavered, and then became golden-brown like the father's. So they called her Ursula because of the picture of the saint.

It was a rather delicate baby at first, but soon it became stronger, and was restless as a young eel. Anna was worn out with the day-long wrestling with its young vigour.

As a little animal, she loved and adored it and was happy. She loved her husband, she kissed his eyes and nose and mouth, and made much of him, she said his limbs were beautiful, she was fascinated by the physical form of him.

And she was indeed Anna Victrix. He could not combat her any more. He was out in the wilderness, alone with her. Having occasion to go to London, he marvelled, as he returned, thinking of naked, lurking savages on an island, how these had built up and created the great mass of Oxford Street or Piccadilly. How had helpless savages, running with their spears on the river-side, after fish, how had they come to rear up this great London, the ponderous, massive, ugly superstructure of a world of man upon a world of nature? It frightened and awed him. Man was terrible, awful in his works. The works of man were more terrible than man himself, almost monstrous.

And yet, for his own part, for his private being, Brangwen felt that the whole of the man's world was exterior and extraneous to his own real life with Anna. Sweep away the whole monstrous superstructure of the world of today, cities and industries and civilisation, leave only the bare earth with plants growing and waters running, and he would not mind, so long as he were whole, had Anna and the child and the new, strange certainty in his soul. Then, if he were naked, he would find clothing somewhere, he would make a shelter and bring food to his wife.

And what more? What more would be necessary? The great mass of activity in which mankind was engaged meant nothing to him. By nature, he had no part in it. What did he live for, then? For Anna only, and for the sake of living? What did he want on this earth? Anna only, and his children, and his life with his children and her? Was there no more?

He was attended by a sense of something more, something further, which gave him absolute being. It was as if now he existed in Eternity, let Time be what it might. What was there outside? The fabricated world, that he did not believe in? What should he bring to her, from outside? Nothing? Was it enough, as it was? He was troubled in his acquiescence. She was not with him. Yet he scarcely believed in himself, apart from her, though the whole Infinite was with him. Let the whole world slide down and over the edge of oblivion, he would stand alone. But he was unsure of her. And he existed also in her. So he was unsure.

He hovered near to her, never quite able to forget the vague, haunting uncertainty, that seemed to challenge him, and which he would not hear. A pang of dread, almost guilt, as of insufficiency, would go over him as he heard her talking to the baby. She stood before the window, with the month-old child in her arms, talking in a musical, young singsong that he had not heard before, and which rang on his heart like a claim from the distance, or the voice of another world sounding its claim on him. He stood near, listening, and his heart surged, surged to rise and submit. Then it shrank back, and stayed aloof. He could not move, a denial was upon him, as if he could not deny himself. He must, he must be himself.

"Look at the silly blue-caps, my beauty," she crooned, holding up the infant to the window, where shone the white garden, and the blue-tits scuffling in the snow: "look at the silly blue-caps, my darling, having a fight in the snow! Look at them, my bird;—beating the snow about with their wings, and shaking their heads. Oh, aren't they wicked things, wicked things! Look at their yellow feathers on the snow there! They'll miss them, won't they, when they're cold later on.

"Must we tell them to stop, must we say 'stop it' to them, my bird? But they are naughty, naughty! Look at them!"

Suddenly her voice broke loud and fierce, she rapped the pane sharply:

"Stop it," she cried, "stop it, you little nuisances. Stop it!"

She called louder, and rapped the pane more sharply. Her voice was fierce and imperative.

"Have more sense," she cried.

"There, now they've gone. Where have they gone, the silly things? What will they say to each other? What will they say, my lambkin? They'll forget, won't they, they'll forget all about it, out of their silly little heads, and their blue caps."

After a moment, she turned her bright face to her husband.

"They were *really* fighting, they were really fierce with each other!" she said, her voice keen with excitement and wonder, as if she belonged to the birds' world, were identified with the race of birds.

"Ay, they'll fight, will blue-caps," he said, glad when she turned to him with her glow from elsewhere. He came and stood beside her and looked out at the marks on the snow where the birds had scuffled, and at the yew-trees' burdened, white and black branches. What was the appeal it made to him, what was the question of her bright face, what was the challenge he was called to answer? He did not know. But as he stood there he felt some responsibility which made him glad, but uneasy, as if he must put out his own light. And he could not move as yet.

Anna loved the child very much, oh very much. Yet still she was not quite fulfilled. She had a slight expectant feeling, as of a door half opened. Here she was, safe and still in Cossethay. But she felt as if she were not in Cossethay at all. She was straining her eyes to something beyond. And from her Pisgah mount, which she had attained, what could she see? A faint, gleaming horizon, a long way off, and a rainbow like an archway, a shadow-door with faintly coloured coping above it. Must she be moving thither?

Something she had not, something she did not grasp, could not arrive at. There was something beyond her. But why must she start on the journey? She stood so safely on this Pisgah mountain.

In the winter, when she rose with the sunrise, and out of the back windows saw the east flaming yellow and orange above the green, glowing grass, while the great pear-tree in between stood dark and magnificent as an idol, and under the dark pear-tree, the little sheet of water spread smooth in burnished, yellow light, she said, "It is here." And when, at evening, the sunset came in a red glare through the big opening in the clouds, she said again, "It is beyond."

Dawn and sunset were the feet of the rainbow that spanned the day, and she saw the hope, the promise. Why should she travel any further?

Yet she always asked the question. As the sun went down in his fiery winter haste, she faced the blazing close of the affair, in which she had not played her fullest part, and she made her demand still: "What are you doing, making this big shining commotion? What is it that you keep so busy about, that you will not let us alone?"

She did not turn to her husband, for him to lead her. He was apart from her, with her, according to her different conceptions of him. The child she might hold up, she might toss the child forward into the furnace, the child might walk there, amid the burning coals and the incandescent roar of heat, as the three witnesses walked with the angel in the fire.

Soon, she felt sure of her husband. She knew his dark face and the extent of its passion. She knew his slim, vigorous body, she said it was hers. Then there was no denying her. She was a rich woman enjoying her riches.

And soon again she was with child. Which made her satisfied and took away her discontent. She forgot that she had watched the sun climb up and pass his way, a magnificent traveller surging forward. She forgot that the moon had looked through a window of the high, dark night, and nodded like a magic recognition, signalled to her to follow. Sun and moon travelled on, and left her, passed her by, a rich woman enjoying her riches. She should go also. But she could not go, when they called, because she must stay at home now. With satisfaction she relinquished the adventure to the unknown. She was bearing her children.

There was another child coming, and Anna lapsed into vague content. If she were not the wayfarer to the unknown, if she were arrived now, settled in her builded house, a rich woman, still her doors opened under the arch of the rainbow, her threshold reflected the passing of the sun and moon, the great travellers, her house was full of the echo of journeying.

She was a door and a threshold, she herself. Through her another soul was coming, to stand upon her as upon the threshold, looking out, shading its eyes for the direction to take.

CHAPTER VII

The Cathedral

During the first year of her marriage, before Ursula was born, Anna Brangwen and her husband went to visit her mother's friend, the Baron Skrebensky. The latter had kept a slight connection with Anna's mother, and had always preserved some officious interest in the young girl, because she was a pure Pole.

When Baron Skrebensky was about forty years old, his wife died, and left him raving disconsolate. Lydia had visited him then, taking Anna with her. It was when the girl was fourteen years old. Since then she had not seen him. She remembered him as a small, sharp clergyman who cried and talked and terrified her, whilst her mother was most strangely consoling, in a foreign language.

The little Baron never quite approved of Anna, because she spoke no Polish. Still, he considered himself in some way her guardian, on Lensky's behalf, and he presented her with some old, heavy, Russian jewellery, the least valuable of his wife's relics. Then he lapsed out of the Brangwen life again, though he lived only about thirty miles away.

Three years later came the startling news that he had married a young English girl of good family. Everybody marvelled. Then came a copy of "The History of the Parish of Briswell—by Rudolph, Baron Skrebensky, Vicar of Briswell." It was a curious book, incoherent, full of interesting exhumations. It was dedicated: "To my wife, Millicent Maud Pearse, in whom I embrace the generous spirit of England."

"If he embraces no more than the spirit of England," said Tom Brangwen, "it's a bad look-out for him."

But paying a formal visit with his wife, he found the new Baroness a little, creamy-skinned, insidious thing with red-brown hair and a mouth that one must always watch, because it curved back continually in an incomprehensible, strange laugh that exposed her rather prominent teeth. She was not beautiful, yet Tom Brangwen was immediately under her spell. She seemed to snuggle like a kitten within his warmth, whilst she was at the same time elusive and ironical, suggesting the fine steel of her claws.

The Baron was almost dotingly courteous and attentive to her. She, almost mockingly, yet quite happy, let him dote. Curious little thing she was, she had the soft, creamy, elusive beauty of a ferret. Tom Brangwen was quite at a loss, at her mercy, and she laughed, a little breathlessly, as if tempted to cruelty. She did put fine torments on the elderly Baron.

When some months later she bore a son, the Baron Skrebensky was loud with delight.

Gradually she gathered a circle of acquaintances in the country. For she was of good family, half Venetian, educated in Dresden. The little foreign vicar attained to a social status which almost satisfied his maddened pride.

Therefore the Brangwens were surprised when the invitation came for Anna and her young husband to pay a visit to Briswell vicarage. For the Skrebenskys were now moderately well off, Millicent Skrebensky having some fortune of her own.

Anna took her best clothes, recovered her best high-school manner, and arrived with her husband. Will Brangwen, ruddy, bright, with long limbs and a small head, like some uncouth bird, was not changed in the least. The little Baroness was smiling, showing her teeth. She had a real charm, a kind of joyous coldness, laughing, delighted, like some weasel. Anna at once respected her, and was on her guard before her, instinctively attracted by the strange, child-like surety of the Baroness, yet mistrusting it, fascinated. The little Baron was now quite white-haired, very brittle. He was wizened and wrinkled, yet fiery, unsubdued. Anna looked at his lean body, at his small, fine, lean legs and lean hands as he sat talking, and she flushed. She recognised the quality of the male in him, his lean, concentrated age, his informed fire, his faculty for sharp, deliberate response. He was so detached, so purely objective. A woman was thoroughly outside him. There was no confusion. So he could give that fine, deliberate response.

He was something separate and interesting; his hard, intrinsic being, whittled down by age to an essentiality and a directness almost death-like, cruel, was yet so unswervingly sure in its action, so distinct in its surety, that she was attracted to him. She watched his cool, hard, separate fire, fascinated by it. Would she rather have it than her husband's diffuse heat, than his blind, hot youth?

She seemed to be breathing high, sharp air, as if she had just come out of a hot room. These strange Skrebenskys made her aware of another, freer element, in which each person was detached and isolated. Was not this her natural element? Was not the close Brangwen life stifling to her?

Meanwhile the little Baroness, with always a subtle light stirring in her full, lustrous, hazel eyes, was playing with Will Brangwen. He was not quick enough to see all her movements. Yet he watched her steadily, with unchanging, lit-up eyes. She was a strange creature to him. But she had no power over him. She flushed, and was irritated. Yet she glanced again and again at his dark, living face, curiously, as if she despised him. She despised his uncritical, unironical nature, it had nothing for her. Yet it angered her as if she were jealous. He watched her with deferential interest as he would watch a stoat playing. But he himself was not implicated. He was different in kind. She was all lambent, biting flames, he was a red fire glowing steadily. She could get nothing out of him. So she made him flush darkly by assuming a biting, subtle class-superiority. He flushed, but still he did not object. He was too different.

Her little boy came in with the nurse. He was a quick, slight child, with fine perceptiveness, and a cool transitoriness in his interest. At once he treated Will Brangwen as an outsider. He stayed by Anna for a moment, acknowledged her, then was gone again, quick, observant, restless, with a glance of interest at everything.

The father adored him, and spoke to him in Polish. It was queer, the stiff, aristocratic manner of the father with the child, the distance in their relationship, the classic fatherhood on the one hand, the filial subordination on the other. They played together, in their different degrees very separate, two different beings, differing as it were in rank rather than in relationship. And the Baroness smiled, smiled, smiled, always smiled, showing her rather protruding teeth, having always a mysterious attraction and charm.

Anna realised how different her own lot might have been, how different her own being. Her soul stirred, she became as another person. Her intimacy with her husband passed away, the curious enveloping Brangwen intimacy, so warm, so close, so stifling, when one seemed always to be in contact with the other person, like a blood-relation, was annulled. She denied it, this close relationship with her young husband. He and she were not one. His heat was not always to suffuse her, suffuse her, through her mind and her individuality, till she was of one heat with him, till she had not her own self apart. She wanted her own life. He seemed to lap her and suffuse her with his being, his hot life, till she did not know whether she were herself, or whether she were another creature, united with him in a world of close blood-intimacy that closed over her and excluded her from all the cool outside.

She wanted her own, old, sharp self, detached, detached, active but not absorbed, active for her own part, taking and giving, but never absorbed. Whereas he wanted this strange absorption with her, which still she resisted. But she was partly helpless against it. She had lived so long in Tom Brangwen's love, beforehand.

From the Skrebenskys' they went to Will Brangwen's beloved Lincoln Cathedral, because it was not far off. He had promised her, that one by one, they should visit all the cathedrals of England. They began with Lincoln, which he knew well.

He began to get excited as the time drew near to set off. What was it that changed him so much? She was almost angry, coming as she did from the Skrebenskys. But now he ran on alone. His very breast seemed to open its doors to watch for the great church brooding over the town. His soul ran ahead.

When he saw the cathedral in the distance, dark blue lifted watchful in the sky, his heart leapt. It was the sign in heaven, it was the Spirit hovering like a dove, like an eagle over the earth. He turned his glowing, ecstatic face to her, his mouth opened with a strange, ecstatic grin.

"There she is," he said.

The "she" irritated her. Why "she"? It was "it." What was the cathedral, a big building, a thing of the past, obsolete, to excite him to such a pitch? She began to stir herself to readiness.

They pressed up the steep hill, he eager as a pilgrim arriving at the shrine. As they came near the precincts, with castle on one side and cathedral on the other, his veins seemed to break into fiery blossom, he was transported.

They had passed through the gate, and the great west front was before them, with all its breadth and ornament.

"It is a false front," he said, looking at the golden stone and the twin towers, and loving them just the same. In a little ecstasy he found himself in the porch, on the brink of the unrevealed. He looked up to the lovely unfolding of the stone. He was to pass within to the perfect womb.

Then he pushed open the door, and the great, pillared gloom was before him, in which his soul shuddered and rose from her nest. His soul leapt, soared up into the great church. His body stood still, absorbed by the height. His soul leapt up into the gloom, into possession, it reeled, it swooned with a great escape, it quivered in the womb, in the hush and the gloom of fecundity, like seed of procreation in ecstasy.

She too was overcome with wonder and awe. She followed him in his progress. Here, the twilight was the very essence of life, the coloured darkness was the embryo of all light, and the day. Here, the very first dawn was breaking, the very last sunset sinking, and the immemorial darkness, whereof life's day would blossom and fall away again, re-echoed peace and profound, immemorial silence.

Away from time, always outside of time! Between east and west, between dawn and sunset, the church lay like a seed in silence, dark before germination, silenced after death. Containing birth and death, potential with all the noise and transitation of life, the cathedral remained hushed, a great, involved seed whereof the flower would be radiant life inconceivable, but whose beginning and whose end were the circle of silence. Spanned round with the rainbow, the jewelled gloom folded music upon silence, light upon darkness, fecundity upon death, as a seed folds leaf upon leaf and silence upon the root and the flower, hushing up the secret of all between its parts, the death out of which it fell, the life into which it has dropped, the immortality it involves, and the death it will embrace again.

Here in the church, "before" and "after" were folded together, all was contained in oneness. Brangwen came to his consummation. Out of the doors of the womb he had come, putting aside the wings of the womb and proceeding into the light. Through daylight and day-after-day he had come, knowledge after knowledge and experience after experience, remembering the darkness of the womb, having prescience of the darkness after death. Then betweenwhiles he had pushed open the doors of the cathedral, and entered the twilight of both darknesses, the hush of the two-fold silence, where dawn was sunset, and the beginning and the end were one.

Here the stone leapt up from the plain of earth, leapt up in a manifold, clustered desire each time, up, away from the horizontal earth, through twilight and dusk and the whole range of desire, through the swerving, the declination, ah, to the ecstasy, the touch, to the meeting and the consummation, the meeting, the clasp, the close embrace, the neutrality, the perfect, swooning consummation, the timeless ecstasy. There his soul remained, at the apex of the arch, clinched in the timeless ecstasy, consummated.

And there was no time nor life nor death, but only this, this timeless consummation, where the thrust from earth met the thrust from earth and the arch was locked on the keystone of ecstasy. This was all, this was everything. Till he came to himself in the world below. Then again he gathered himself together, in transit, every jet of him strained and leaped, leaped clear in to the darkness above, to the fecundity and the unique mystery, to the touch, the clasp, the consummation, the climax of eternity, the apex of the arch.

She too was overcome, but silenced rather than tuned to the place. She loved it as a world not quite her own, she resented his transports and ecstasies. His passion in the cathedral at first awed her, then made her angry. After all, there was the sky outside, and in here, in this mysterious half-night, when his soul leapt with the pillars upwards, it was not to the stars and the crystalline dark space, but to meet and clasp with the answering impulse of leaping stone, there in the dusk and secrecy of the roof. The far-off clinching and mating of arches, the leap and thrust of the stone, carrying a great roof overhead, awed and silenced her.

But yet—yet she remembered that the open sky was no blue vault, no dark dome hung with many twinkling lamps, but a space where stars were wheeling in freedom, with freedom above them always higher.

The cathedral roused her too. But she would never consent to the knitting of all the leaping stone in a great roof that closed her in, and beyond which was nothing, nothing, it was the ultimate confine. His soul would have liked it to be so: here, here is all, complete, eternal: motion, meeting, ecstasy, and no illusion of time, of night and day passing by, but only perfectly proportioned space and movement clinching and renewing, and passion surging its way in great waves to the altar, recurrence of ecstasy.

Her soul too was carried forward to the altar, to the threshold of Eternity, in reverence and fear and joy. But ever she hung back in the transit, mistrusting the culmination of the altar. She was not to be flung forward on the lift and lift of passionate flights, to be cast at last upon the altar steps as upon the shore of the unknown. There was a great joy and a verity in it. But even in the dazed swoon of the cathedral, she claimed another right. The altar was barren, its lights gone out. God burned no more in that bush. It was dead matter lying there. She claimed the right to freedom above her, higher than the roof. She had always a sense of being roofed in.

So that she caught at little things, which saved her from being swept forward headlong in the tide of passion that leaps on into the Infinite in a great mass, triumphant and flinging its own course. She wanted to get out of this fixed, leaping, forward-travelling movement, to rise from it as a bird rises with wet, limp feet from the sea, to lift herself as a bird lifts its breast and thrusts its body from the pulse and heave of a sea that bears it forward to an unwilling conclusion, tear herself away like a bird on wings, and in the open space where there is clarity, rise up above the fixed, surcharged motion, a separate speck that hangs suspended, moves this way and that, seeing and answering before it sinks again, having chosen or found the direction in which it shall be carried forward.

And it was as if she must grasp at something, as if her wings were too weak to lift her straight off the heaving motion. So she caught sight of the wicked, odd little faces carved in stone, and she stood before them arrested.

These sly little faces peeped out of the grand tide of the cathedral like something that knew better. They knew quite well, these little imps that retorted on man's own illusion, that the cathedral was not absolute. They winked and leered, giving suggestion of the many things that had been left out of the great concept of the church. "However much there is inside here, there's a good deal they haven't got in," the little faces mocked.

Apart from the lift and spring of the great impulse towards the altar, these little faces had separate wills, separate motions, separate knowledge, which rippled back in defiance of the tide, and laughed in triumph of their own very littleness.

"Oh look!" cried Anna, "Oh look, how adorable, the faces! Look at her."

Brangwen looked unwillingly. This was the voice of the serpent in his Eden. She pointed him to a plump, sly, malicious little face carved in stone.

"He knew her, the man who carved her," said Anna. "I'm sure she was his wife."

"It isn't a woman at all, it's a man," said Brangwen curtly.

"Do you think so?—No! That isn't a man. That is no man's face."

Her voice sounded rather jeering. He laughed shortly, and went on. But she would not go forward with him. She loitered about the carvings. And he could not go forward without her. He waited, impatient of this counteraction. She was spoiling his passionate intercourse with the cathedral. His brows began to gather.

"Oh, this is good!" she cried again. "Here is the same woman—look!—only he's made her cross! Isn't it lovely! Hasn't he made her hideous to a degree?" She laughed with pleasure. "Didn't he hate her? He must have been a nice man! Look at her—isn't it awfully good—just like a shrewish woman. He must have enjoyed putting her in like that. He got his own back on her, didn't he."

"It's a man's face, no woman's at all—a monk's—clean shaven." he said.

She laughed with a Pouf! of laughter.

"You hate to think he put his wife in your cathedral, don't you?" she mocked, with a tinkle of profane laughter. And she laughed with malicious triumph.

She had got free from the cathedral, she had even destroyed the passion he had. She was glad. He was bitterly angry. Strive as he would, he could not keep the cathedral wonderful to him. He was disillusioned. That which had been his absolute, containing all heaven and earth, was become to him as to her, a shapely heap of dead matter—but dead, dead.

His mouth was full of ash, his soul was furious. He hated her for having destroyed another of his vital illusions. Soon he would be stark, stark, without one place wherein to stand, without one belief in which to rest.

Yet somewhere in him he responded more deeply to the sly little face that knew better, than he had done before to the perfect surge of his cathedral.

Nevertheless for the time being his soul was wretched and homeless, and he could not bear to think of Anna's ousting him from his beloved realities. He wanted his cathedral, he wanted to satisfy his blind passion. And he could not any more. Something intervened.

They went home again, both of them altered. She had some new reverence for that which he wanted, he felt that his cathedrals would never again be to him as they had been. Before, he had thought them absolute. But now he saw them crouching under the sky, with still the dark, mysterious world of reality inside, but as a world within a world, a sort of side show, whereas before they had been as a world to him within a chaos: a reality, an order, an absolute, within a meaningless confusion.

He had felt, before, that could he but go through the great door and look down the gloom towards the far-off, concluding wonder of the altar, that then, with the windows suspended around like tablets of jewel emanating their own glory, then he had arrived. Here the satisfaction he had yearned after came near, towards this, the porch of the great Unknown, all reality gathered, and there, the altar was the mystic door, through which all and everything must move on to eternity.

But now, somehow, sadly and disillusioned, he realised that the doorway was no doorway. It was too narrow, it was false. Outside the cathedral were many flying spirits that could never be sifted through the jewelled gloom. He had lost his absolute.

He listened to the thrushes in the garden, and heard a note which the cathedrals did not include: something free and careless and joyous. He crossed a field that was all yellow with dandelions, on his way to work, and the bath of yellow glowing was something at once so sumptuous and so fresh, that he was glad he was away from his shadowy cathedral.

There was life outside the church. There was much that the church did not include. He thought of God, and of the whole blue rotonda of the day. That was something great and free. He thought of the ruins of the Grecian worship, and it seemed, a temple was never perfectly a temple, till it was ruined and mixed up with the winds and the sky and the herbs.

Still he loved the church. As a symbol, he loved it. He tended it for what it tried to represent, rather than for that which it did represent. Still he loved it. The little church across his garden-wall drew him, he gave it loving attention. But he went to take charge of it, to preserve it. It was as an old, sacred thing to him. He looked after the stone and wood-work, mending the organ and restoring a piece of broken carving, repairing the church furniture. Later, he became choir-master also.

His life was shifting its centre, becoming more superficial. He had failed to become really articulate, failed to find real expression. He had to continue in the old form. But in spirit, he was uncreated.

Anna was absorbed in the child now, she left her husband to take his own way. She was willing now to postpone all adventure into unknown realities. She had the child, her palpable and immediate future was the child. If her soul had found no utterance, her womb had.

The church that neighboured with his house became very intimate and dear to him. He cherished it, he had it entirely in his charge. If he could find no new activity, he would be happy cherishing the old, dear form of worship. He knew this little, whitewashed church. In its shadowy atmosphere he sank back into being. He liked to sink himself in its hush as a stone sinks into water.

He went across his garden, mounted the wall by the little steps, and entered the hush and peace of the church. As the heavy door clanged to behind him, his feet re-echoed in the aisle, his heart re-echoed with a little passion of tenderness and mystic peace. He was also slightly ashamed, like a man who has failed, who lapses back for his fulfilment.

He loved to light the candles at the organ, and sitting there alone in the little glow, practise the hymns and chants for the service. The whitewashed arches retreated into darkness, the sound of the organ and the organ-pedals died away upon the unalterable stillness of the church, there were faint, ghostly noises in the tower, and then the music swelled out again, loudly, triumphantly.

He ceased to fret about his life. He relaxed his will, and let everything go. What was between him and his wife was a great thing, if it was not everything. She had conquered, really. Let him wait, and abide, wait and abide. She and the baby and himself, they were one. The organ rang out his protestation. His soul lay in the darkness, as he pressed the keys of the organ.

To Anna, the baby was a complete bliss and fulfilment. Her desires sank into abeyance, her soul was in bliss over the baby. It was rather a delicate child, she had trouble to rear it. She never for a moment thought it would die. It was a delicate infant, therefore it behoved her to make it strong. She threw herself into the labour, the child was everything. Her imagination was all occupied here. She was a mother. It was enough to handle the new little limbs, the new little body, hear the new little voice crying in the stillness. All the future rang to her out of the sound of the baby's crying and cooing, she balanced the coming years of life in her hands, as she nursed the child. The passionate sense of fulfilment, of the future germinated in her, made her vivid and powerful. All the future was in her hands, in the hands of the woman. And before this baby was ten months old, she was again with child. She seemed to be in the fecund storm of life, every moment was full and busy with productiveness to her. She felt like the earth, the mother of everything.

Brangwen occupied himself with the church, he played the organ, he trained the choir-boys, he taught a Sunday School class of youths. He was happy enough. There was an eager, yearning kind of happiness in him as he taught the boys on Sundays. He was all the time exciting himself with the proximity of some secret that he had not yet fathomed.

In the house, he served his wife and the little matriarchy. She loved him because he was the father of her children. And she always had a physical passion for him. So he gave up trying to have the spiritual superiority and control, or even her respect for his conscious or public life. He lived simply by her physical love for him. And he served the little matriarchy, nursing the child and helping with the housework, indifferent any more of his own dignity and importance. But his abandoning of claims, his living isolated upon his own interest, made him seem unreal, unimportant.

Anna was not publicly proud of him. But very soon she learned to be indifferent to public life. He was not what is called a manly man: he did not drink or smoke or arrogate importance. But he was her man, and his very indifference to all claims of manliness set her supreme in her own world with him. Physically, she loved him and he satisfied her. He went alone and subsidiary always. At first it had irritated her, the outer world existed so little to him. Looking at him with outside eyes, she was inclined to sneer at him. But her sneer changed to a sort of respect. She respected him, that he could serve her so simply and completely. Above all, she loved to bear his children. She loved to be the source of children.

She could not understand him, his strange, dark rages and his devotion to the church. It was the church *building* he cared for; and yet his soul was passionate for something. He laboured cleaning the stonework, repairing the wood-work, restoring the organ, and making the singing as perfect as possible. To keep the church fabric and the church-ritual intact was his business; to have the intimate, sacred building utterly in his own hands, and to make the form of service complete. There was a little bright anguish and tension on his face, and in his intent movements. He was like a lover who knows he is betrayed, but who still loves, whose love is only the more tense. The Church was false, but he served it the more attentively.

During the day, at his work in the office, he kept himself

suspended. He did not exist. He worked automatically till it was time to go home.

He loved with a hot heart the dark-haired little Ursula, and he waited for the child to come to consciousness. Now the mother monopolised the baby. But his heart waited in its darkness. His hour would come.

In the long run, he learned to submit to Anna. She forced him to the spirit of her laws, whilst leaving him the letter of his own. She combated in him his devils. She suffered very much from his inexplicable and incalculable dark rages, when a blackness filled him, and a black wind seemed to sweep out of existence everything that had to do with him. She could feel herself, everything, being annihilated by him.

At first she fought him. At night, in this state, he would kneel down to say his prayers. She looked at his crouching figure.

"Why are you kneeling there, pretending to pray?" she said harshly. "Do you think anybody can pray, when they are in the vile temper you are in?"

He remained crouching by the bedside, motionless.

"It's horrible," she continued, "and such a pretence! What do you pretend you are saying? Who do you pretend you are praying to?"

He still remained motionless, seething with inchoate rage, when his whole nature seemed to disintegrate. He seemed to live with a strain upon himself, and occasionally came these dark, chaotic rages, the lust for destruction. She then fought with him, and their fights were horrible, murderous. And then the passion between them came just as black and awful.

But little by little, as she learned to love him better, she would put herself aside, and when she felt one of his fits upon him, would ignore him, successfully leave him in his world, whilst she remained in her own. He had a black struggle with himself, to come back to her. For at last he learned that he would be in hell until he came back to her. So he struggled to submit to her, and she was afraid of the ugly strain in his eyes. She made love to him, and took him. Then he was grateful to her love, humble.

He made himself a wood-work shed, in which to restore things which were destroyed in the church. So he had plenty to do: his wife, his child, the church, the wood-work, and his wage-earning, all occupying him. If only there were not some limit to him, some darkness across his eyes! He had to give in to it at last himself. He must submit to his own inadequacy, the limitation of his being. He even had to know of his own black, violent temper, and to reckon with it. But as she was more gentle with him, it became quieter.

As he sat sometimes very still, with a bright, vacant face, Anna could see the suffering among the brightness. He was aware of some limit to himself, of something unformed in his very being, of some buds which were not ripe in him, some folded centres of darkness which would never develop and unfold whilst he was alive in the body. He was unready for fulfilment. Something undeveloped in him limited him, there was a darkness in him which he *could* not unfold, which would never unfold in him.

CHAPTER VIII

The Child

From the first, the baby stirred in the young father a deep, strong emotion he dared scarcely acknowledge, it was so strong and came out of the dark of him. When he heard the child cry, a terror possessed him, because of the answering echo from the unfathomed distances in himself. Must he know in himself such distances, perilous and imminent?

He had the infant in his arms, he walked backwards and forwards troubled by the crying of his own flesh and blood. This was his own flesh and blood crying! His soul rose against the voice suddenly breaking out from him, from the distances in him.

Sometimes, in the night, the child cried and cried, when the night was heavy and sleep oppressed him. And half asleep, he stretched out his hand to put it over the baby's face, to stop the crying. But something arrested his hand: the very inhumanness of the intolerable, continuous crying arrested him. It was so impersonal, without human cause or object. Yet he echoed to it directly, his soul answered its madness. It filled him with terror, almost with frenzy.

He learned to acquiesce to this, to submit to the awful, obliterated sources which were the origin of his living tissue. He was not what he conceived himself to be! Then he was what he was, unknown, potent, dark.

He became accustomed to the child, he knew how to lift and balance the little body. The baby had a beautiful, rounded head that moved him passionately. He would have fought to the last drop to defend that exquisite, perfect round head.

He learned to know the little hands and feet, the strange, unseeing, golden-brown eyes, the mouth that opened only to cry, or to suck, or to show a queer, toothless laugh. He could almost understand even the dangling legs, which at first had created in him a feeling of aversion. They could kick in their queer little way, they had their own softness.

One evening, suddenly, he saw the tiny living thing rolling naked in the mother's lap, and he was sick, it was so utterly helpless and vulnerable and extraneous; in a world of hard surfaces and varying altitudes, it lay vulnerable and naked at every point. Yet it was quite blithe. And yet, in its blind, awful crying, was there not the blind, far-off terror of its own vulnerable nakedness, the terror of being so utterly delivered over, helpless at every point. He could not bear to hear it crying. His heart strained and stood on guard against the whole universe.

But he waited for the dread of these days to pass; he saw the joy coming. He saw the lovely, creamy, cool little ear of the baby, a bit of dark hair rubbed to a bronze floss, like bronze-dust. And he waited, for the child to become his, to look at him and answer him.

It had a separate being, but it was his own child. His flesh and blood vibrated to it. He caught the baby to his breast with his passionate, clapping laugh. And the infant knew him.

As the newly opened, newly dawned eyes looked at him, he wanted them to perceive him, to recognise him. Then he was verified. The child knew him, a queer contortion of laughter came on its face for him. He caught it to his breast, clapping with a triumphant laugh.

The golden-brown eyes of the child gradually lit up and dilated at the sight of the dark-glowing face of the youth. It knew its mother better, it wanted its mother more. But the brightest, sharpest little ecstasy was for the father.

It began to be strong, to move vigorously and freely, to make sounds like words. It was a baby girl now. Already it knew his strong hands, it exulted in his strong clasp, it laughed and crowed when he played with it.

And his heart grew red hot with passionate feeling for the child. She was not much more than a year old when the second baby was born. Then he took Ursula for his own. She his first little girl. He had set his heart on her.

The second had dark blue eyes and a fair skin: it was more a Brangwen, people said. The hair was fair. But they forgot Anna's stiff blond fleece of childhood. They called the newcomer Gudrun.

This time, Anna was stronger, and not so eager. She did not mind that the baby was not a boy. It was enough that she had milk and could suckle her child: Oh, Oh, the bliss of the little life sucking the milk of her body! Oh, Oh, Oh the bliss, as the infant grew stronger, of the two tiny hands clutching, catching blindly yet passionately at her breast, of the tiny mouth seeking her in blind, sure, vital knowledge, of the sudden consummate peace as the little body sank, the mouth and throat sucking, sucking, sucking, drinking life from her to make a new life, almost sobbing with passionate joy of receiving its own existence, the tiny hands clutching frantically as the nipple was drawn back, not to be gainsaid. This was enough for Anna. She seemed to pass off into a kind of rapture of motherhood, her rapture of motherhood was everything.

So that the father had the elder baby, the weaned child; the golden-brown, wondering, vivid eyes of the little Ursula were for him, who had waited behind the mother till the need was for him. The mother felt a sharp stab of jealousy. But she was still more absorbed in the tiny baby. It was entirely hers, its need was direct upon her.

So Ursula became the child of her father's heart. She was the little blossom, he was the sun. He was patient, energetic, inventive for her. He taught her all the funny little things, he filled her and roused her to her fullest tiny measure. She answered him with her extravagant infant's laughter and her call of delight.

Now there were two babies, a woman came in to do the house-work, Anna was wholly nurse. Two babies were not too much work for her. But she hated any form of work, now her children had come, except the charge of them.

When Ursula toddled about, she was an absorbed, busy child, always amusing herself, needing not much attention from other people. At evening, towards six o'clock, Anna very often went across the lane to the stile, lifted Ursula over into the field, with a: "Go and meet Daddy." Then Brangwen, coming up the steep round of the hill would see before him on the brow of the path a tiny, tottering, wind-blown little mite with a dark head, who, as soon as she saw him, would come running in tiny, wild, windmill fashion, lifting her arms up and down to him, down the steep hill. His heart leapt up, he ran his fastest to her, to catch her, because he knew she would fall. She came fluttering on, wildly, with her little limbs flying. And he was glad when he caught her up in his arms. Once she fell as she came flying to him, he saw her pitch forward suddenly as she was running with her hands lifted to him; and when he picked her up, her mouth was bleeding. He could never bear to think of it, he always wanted to cry, even when he was an old man and she had become a stranger to him. How he had loved that little Ursula!—his heart had been sharply seared for her, when he was a youth, first married.

When she was a little older, he would see her recklessly climbing over the bars of the stile, in her red pinafore, swinging in peril and tumbling over, picking herself up and flitting towards him. Sometimes she liked to ride on his shoulder, sometimes she preferred to walk with his hand, sometimes she would fling her arms round his legs for a moment, then race free again, whilst he went shouting and calling to her, a child along with her. He was still only a tall, thin, unsettled lad of twenty two.

It was he who had made her her cradle, her little chair, her little stool, her high chair. It was he who would swing her up to table or who would make for her a doll out of an old table-leg, whilst she watched him, saying:

"Make her eyes, Daddy, make her eyes!"

And he made her eyes with his knife.

She was very fond of adorning herself, so he would tie a piece of cotton round her ear, and hang a blue bead on it underneath for an ear-ring. The ear-rings varied with a red bead, and a golden bead, and a little pearl bead. And as he came home at night, seeing her bridling and looking very self-conscious, he took notice and said:

"So you're wearing your best golden and pearl ear-rings today?"

"Yes."

"I suppose you've been to see the queen?"

"Yes, I have."

"Oh, and what had she to say?"

"She said—she said—'You won't dirty your nice white frock.'"

He gave her the nicest bits from his plate, putting them into her red, moist mouth. And he would make on a piece of bread-and-butter a bird, out of jam: which she ate with extraordinary relish.

After the tea-things were washed up, the woman went away, leaving the family free. Usually Brangwen helped in the bathing of the children. He held long discussions with his child as she sat on his knee and he unfastened her clothes. And he seemed to be talking really of momentous things, deep moralities. Then suddenly she ceased to hear, having caught sight of a glassie rolled into a corner. She slipped away, and was in no hurry to return.

"Come back here," he said, waiting. She became absorbed, taking no notice.

"Come on," he repeated, with a touch of command.

An excited little chuckle came from her, but she pretended to be absorbed.

"Do you hear, Milady!"

She turned with a fleeting, exulting laugh. He rushed on her and swept her up.

"Who was it that didn't come!" he said, rolling her between his strong hands, tickling her. And she laughed heartily, heartily. She loved him that he compelled her with his strength and decision. He was all-powerful, the tower of strength which rose out of her sight.

When the children were in bed, sometimes Anna and he sat and talked, desultorily, both of them idle. He read very little. Anything he was drawn to read became a burning reality to him, another scene outside his window. Whereas Anna skimmed through a book to see what happened, then she had enough.

Therefore they would often sit together, talking desultorily. What was really between them they could not utter. Their words were only accidents in the mutual silence. When they talked, they gossiped. She did not care for sewing.

She had a beautiful way of sitting musing, gratefully, as if her heart were lit up. Sometimes she would turn to him, laughing, to tell him some little thing that had happened during the day. Then he would laugh, they would talk awhile, before the vital, physical silence was between them again.

She was thin but full of colour and life. She was perfectly happy to do just nothing, only to sit with a curious, languid dignity, so careless as to be almost regal, so utterly indifferent, so confident. The bond between them was undefinable, but very strong. It kept everyone else at a distance.

His face never changed whilst she knew him, it only became more intense. It was ruddy and dark in its abstraction, not very human, it had a strong, intent brightness. Sometimes, when his eyes met hers, a yellow flash from them caused a darkness to swoon over her consciousness, electric, and a slight, strange laugh came on his face. Her eyes would turn languidly, then close, as if hypnotised. And they lapsed into the same potent darkness. He had the quality of a young black cat, intent, unnoticeable, and yet his presence gradually made itself felt, stealthily and powerfully took hold of her. He called, not to her, but to something in her, which responded subtly, out of her unconscious darkness.

So they were together in a darkness, passionate, electric, forever haunting the back of the common day, never in the light. In the light, he seemed to sleep, unknowing. Only she knew him when the darkness set him free, and he could see with his gold-glowing eyes his intention and his desires in the dark. Then she was in a spell, then she answered his harsh, penetrating call with a soft leap of her soul, the darkness woke up, electric, bristling with an unknown, overwhelming insinuation.

By now they knew each other: she was the daytime, the daylight, he was the shadow, put aside, but in the darkness potent with an overwhelming voluptuousness.

She learned not to dread and to hate him, but to fill herself with him, to give herself to his black, sensual power, that was hidden all the daytime. And the curious rolling of the eyes, as if she were lapsing in a trance away from her ordinary consciousness became habitual with her, when something threatened and opposed her in life, the conscious life.

So they remained as separate in the light, and in the thick darkness, married. He supported her daytime authority, kept it inviolable at last. And she, in all the darkness, belonged to him, to his close, insinuating, hypnotic familiarity.

All his daytime activity, all his public life, was a kind of sleep. She wanted to be free, to belong to the day. And he ran avoiding the day in work. After tea, he went to the shed to his carpentry or his wood-carving. He was restoring the patched, degraded pulpit to its original form.

But he loved to have the child near him, playing by his feet. She was a piece of light that really belonged to him, that played within his darkness. He left the shed door on the latch. And when, with his second sense of another presence, he knew she was coming, he was satisfied, he was at rest. When he was alone with her, he did not want to take notice, to talk. He wanted to live unthinking, with her presence flickering upon him.

He always went in silence. The child would push open the shed door, and see him working by lamplight, his sleeves rolled back. His clothes hung about him, carelessly, like mere wrapping. Inside, his body was concentrated, with a flexible, charged power all of its own, isolated. From when she was a tiny child, Ursula could remember his fore-arm, with its fine black hairs and its electric flexibility, working at the bench through swift, unnoticeable movements, always ambushed in a sort of silence.

She hung a moment in the door of the shed, waiting for him to notice her. He turned, his black, curved eyebrows arching slightly.

"Hullo, Twittermiss!"

And he closed the door behind her. Then the child was happy, in the shed that smelled of sweet wood and resounded to the noise of the plane or the hammer or the saw, yet was charged with the silence of the worker. She played on, intent and absorbed, among the shavings and the little nogs of wood. She never touched him: his feet and legs were near, she did not approach them.

She liked to flit out after him when he was going to church at night. If he were going to be alone, he swung her over the wall, and let her come.

Again, she was transported when the door was shut behind them, and they two inherited the big, pale, void place. She would watch him as he lit the organ candles, wait whilst he began his practising, his tunes, then she ran foraging here and there, like a kitten playing by herself in the darkness, with eyes dilated. The ropes hung vaguely, twining on the floor, from the bells in the tower, and Ursula always wanted the fluffy, red-and-white, or blue-and-white rope-grips. But they were above her.

Sometimes her mother came to claim her. Then the child was seized with resentment. She passionately resented her mother's superficial authority. She wanted to assert her own detachment.

He, however, also gave her occasional cruel shocks. He let her play about in the church, she rifled foot-stools and hymn-books and cushions, like a bee among flowers, whilst the organ echoed away. This continued for some weeks. Then the char-woman worked herself up into a frenzy of rage, to dare to attack Brangwen, and one day descended on him like a harpy. He wilted away, and wanted to break the old beast's neck.

Instead he came glowering in fury to the house, and turned on Ursula:

"Why, you tiresome little monkey, can't you even come to church without pulling the place to bits?"

His voice was harsh and cat-like, he was blind to the child. She shrank away in childish anguish and dread. What was it, what awful thing was it?

The mother turned with her calm, almost superb manner.

"What has she done, then?"

"Done? She shall go in the church no more, pulling and littering and destroying."

The wife slowly rolled her eyes and lowered her eyelids.

"What has she destroyed, then?"

He did not know.

"I've just had Mrs Wilkinson at me," he cried, "with a list of things she's done."

Ursula withered under the contempt and anger of the "she," as he spoke of her.

"Send Mrs Wilkinson here to me with a list of the things she's done," said Anna. "*I* am the one to hear that.

"It's not the things the child has done," continued the mother, "that have put you out so much, it's because you can't bear being spoken to by that old woman. But you haven't the courage to turn on *her* when she attacks you, you bring your rage here."

He relapsed into silence. Ursula knew that he was wrong. In the outside, upper world, he was wrong. Already came over the child the cold sense of the impersonal world. There she knew her mother was right. But still her heart clamoured after her father, for him to be right, in his dark, sensuous underworld. But he was angry, and went his way in blackness and brutal silence again.

The child ran about absorbed in life, quiet, full of amusement. She did not notice things, not changes nor alterations. One day she would find daisies in the grass, another day apple-blossom would be sprinkled white on the ground, and she would run among it, for pleasure because it was there. Yet again birds would be pecking at the cherries, her father would throw cherries down from the tree all round her on the garden. Then the fields were full of hay.

She did not remember what had been nor what would be, the outside things were there each day. She was always herself, the world outside was accidental. Even her mother was accidental to her: a condition that happened to endure.

Only her father occupied any permanent position in the childish consciousness. When he came back, she remembered vaguely how he had gone away: when he went away, she knew vaguely that she must wait for his coming back. Whereas her mother, returning from an outing, merely became present, there was no reason for connecting her with some previous departure.

The return or the departure of the father was the one event which the child remembered. When he came, something woke up in her, some yearning. She knew when he was out of joint or irritable or tired: then she was uneasy, she could not rest.

When he was in the house, the child felt full and warm, rich like a creature in the sunshine. When he was gone, she was vague, forgetful. When he scolded her even, she was often more aware of him than of herself. He was her strength and her greater self.

Ursula was three years old when another baby girl was born. Then the two small sisters were much together, Gudrun and Ursula. Gudrun was a quiet child who played for hours alone, absorbed in her fancies. She was brown haired, fair skinned, strangely placid, almost passive. Yet her will was indomitable, once set. From the first she followed Ursula's lead. Yet she was a thing to herself, so that to watch the two together was strange. They were like two young animals playing together but not taking real notice of each other. Gudrun was the mother's favorite—except that Anna always lived in her latest baby.

The burden of so many lives depending on him wore the youth down. He had his work in the office, which was done purely by effort of will: he had his barren passion for the church; he had three young children. Also at this time his health was not good. So he was haggard and irritable, often a pest in the house. Then he was told to go to his wood-work, or to the church.

Between him and the little Ursula there came into being a strange alliance. They were aware of each other. He knew the child was always on his side. But in his consciousness he counted it for nothing. She was always for him. He took it for granted. Yet his life was based on her, even whilst she was a tiny child, on her support and her accord.

Anna continued in her violent trance of motherhood, always busy, often harassed, but always contained in her trance of motherhood. She seemed to exist in her own violent fruitfulness, and it was as if the sun shone tropically on her. Her colour was bright, her eyes full of a fecund gloom, her brown hair tumbled loosely over her ears. She had a look of richness. No responsibility, no sense of duty troubled her. The outside, public life was less than nothing to her, really.

Whereas when, at twenty six, he found himself father of four children, with a wife who lived intrinsically like the ruddiest lilies of the field, he let the weight of responsibility press on him and drag him. It was then that his child Ursula strove to be with him. She was with him, even as a baby of four, when he was irritable and shouted and made the household unhappy. She suffered from his shouting, but somehow it was not really him. She wanted it to be over, she wanted to resume her normal connection with him. When he was disagreeable, the child echoed to the crying of some need in him, and she responded blindly. Her heart followed him as if he had some tie with her, and some love which he could not deliver. Her heart followed him persistently, in its love.

But there was the dim, childish sense of her own smallness and inadequacy, a fatal sense of worthlessness. She could not do anything, she was not enough. She could not be important to him. This knowledge deadened her from the first.

Still she set towards him like a quivering needle. All her life was directed by her awareness of him, her wakefulness to his being. And she was against her mother.

Her father was the dawn wherein her consciousness woke up. But for him, she might have gone on like the other children, Gudrun and Theresa and Catherine, one with the flowers and insects and playthings, having no existence apart from the concrete object of her attention. But her father came too near to her. The clasp of his hands and the power of his breast woke her up almost in pain from the transient unconsciousness of childhood. Wide-eyed, unseeing, she was awake before she knew how to see. She was wakened too soon. Too soon the call had come to her, when she was a small baby, and her father held her close to his breast, her sleep-living heart was beaten into wakefulness by the striving of his bigger heart, by his clasping her to his body for love and for fulfilment, asking as a magnet must always ask. From her the response had struggled dimly, vaguely into being.

The children were dressed roughly for the country. When she was little, Ursula pattered about in little wooden clogs, a blue overall over her thick red dress, a red shawl crossed on her breast and tied behind again. So she ran with her father to the garden.

The household rose early. He was out digging by six o'clock in the morning, he went to his work at half past eight. And Ursula was usually in the garden with him, though not near at hand.

At Eastertime one year she helped him to set potatoes. It was the first time she had ever helped him. The occasion remained as a picture, one of her earliest memories. They had gone out soon after dawn. A cold wind was blowing. He had his old trousers tucked into his boots, he wore no coat nor waistcoat, his shirt-sleeves fluttered in the wind, his face was ruddy and intent, in a kind of sleep. When he was at work he neither heard nor saw. A long, thin man, looking still a youth, with a line of black moustache above his thick mouth, and his fine hair blown on his forehead, he worked away at the earth in the grey first light, alone. His solitariness drew the child like a spell.

The wind came chill over the dark-green fields. Ursula ran up and watched him push the setting-peg in at one side of his ready earth, stride across, and push it in the other side, pulling the line taut and clear upon the clods intervening. Then with a sharp, cutting noise the bright spade came towards her, cutting a grip into the new, soft earth.

He stuck his spade upright and straightened himself.

"Do you want to help me?" he said.

She looked up at him from out of her little woollen bonnet.

"Ay," he said, "you can put some taters in for me. Look—like that—these little sprits standing up—so much apart, you see."

And stooping down he quickly, surely placed the spritted potatoes in the soft grip, where they rested separate and pathetic on the heavy cold earth.

He gave her a little basket of potatoes, and strode himself to the other end of the line. She saw him stooping, working towards her. She was excited, and unused. She put in one potato, then rearranged it, to make it sit nicely. Some of the sprits were broken, and she was afraid. The responsibility excited her like a string tying her up. She could not help looking with dread at the string buried under the heaped-back soil. Her father was working nearer, stooping, working nearer. She was overcome by her responsibility. She put potatoes quickly into the cold earth.

He came near.

"Not so close," he said, stooping over her potatoes, taking some out and rearranging the others. She stood by with the painful terrified helplessness of childhood. He was so unseeing and confident, she wanted to do the thing and yet she could not. She stood by looking on, her little blue overall fluttering in the wind, the red woollen ends of her shawl blowing gustily. Then he went down the row, relentlessly, turning the potatoes in with his sharp spade cuts. He took no notice of her, only worked on. He had another world from hers.

She stood helplessly, stranded on his world. He continued his work. She knew she could not help him. A little bit forlorn, at last she turned away, and ran down the garden, away from him, as fast as she could go away from him, to forget him and his work.

He missed her presence, her face in her red woollen bonnet, her blue overall fluttering. She ran to where a little water ran trickling between grass and stones. That she loved.

When he came by he said to her:

"You didn't help me much."

The child looked at him dumbly. Already her heart was heavy because of her own disappointment. Her mouth was dumb and pathetic. But he did not notice, he went his way.

And she played on, because of her disappointment persisting even the more in her play. She dreaded work, because she could not do it as he did it. She was conscious of the great breach between them. She knew she had no power. The grown-up power to work deliberately was a mystery to her.

He would smash into her sensitive child's world destructively. Her mother was lenient, careless. The children played about as they would all day. Ursula was thoughtless—why should she remember things? If across the garden she saw the hedge had budded, and if she wanted these greeny-pink, tiny buds for bread-and-cheese, to play at tea-party with, over she went for them.

Then suddenly, perhaps the next day, her soul would almost start out of her body as her father turned on her, shouting:

"Who's been tramplin' an' dancin' across where I've just sowed seed. I know it's you, nuisance! Can you find nowhere else to walk, but just over my seed beds? But it's like you, that is—no heed but to follow your own greedy nose."

It had shocked him in his intent world to see the zig-zagging lines of deep little foot-prints across his work. The child was infinitely more shocked. Her vulnerable little soul was flayed and trampled. *Why* were the foot-prints there? She had not wanted to make them. She stood dazzled with pain and shame and unreality.

Her soul, her consciousness seemed to die away. She became shut off and senseless, a little fixed creature whose soul had gone hard and unresponsive. The sense of her own unreality hardened her like a frost. She cared no longer.

And the sight of her face, shut and superior with self-asserting indifference, made a flame of rage go over him. He wanted to break her.

"I'll break your obstinate little face," he said, through shut teeth, lifting his hand.

The child did not alter in the least. The look of indifference, complete glancing indifference, as if nothing but herself existed to her, remained fixed.

Yet far away in her, the sobs were tearing her soul. And when he had gone, she would go and creep under the parlour sofa, and lie clinched in the silent, hidden misery of childhood.

When she crawled out, after an hour or so, she went rather stiffly to play. She willed to forget. She cut off her childish soul from memory, so that the pain, and the insult should not be real. She asserted her self only. There was now nothing in the world but her own self. So very soon, she came to believe in the outward malevolence that was against her. And very early, she learned that even her adored father was part of this malevolence. And very early, she learned to harden her soul in resistance and denial of all that was outside her, harden herself upon her own being.

She never felt sorry for what she had done, she never forgave those who had made her guilty. If he had said to her "Why, Ursula, did you trample my carefully-made bed?" that would have hurt her to the quick, and she would have done anything for him. But she was always tormented by the unreality of outside things. The earth was to walk on. Why must she avoid a certain patch, just because it was called a seed bed. It was the earth to walk on. This was her instinctive assumption. And when he bullied her, she became hard, cut herself off from all connection, lived in the little separate world of her own violent will.

As she grew older, five, six, seven, the connection between her and her father was even stronger. Yet it was always straining to break. She was always relapsing on her own violent will into her own separate world of herself. This made him grind his teeth with bitterness, for he still wanted her. But she could harden herself into her own self's universe, impregnable.

He was very fond of swimming, and in warm weather would take her down to the canal, to a silent place, or to a big pond or reservoir, to bathe. He would take her on his back as he went swimming, and she clung close, feeling his strong movement under her, so strong, as if it would uphold all the world. Then he taught her to swim.

She was a fearless little thing, when he dared her. And he had a curious craving to frighten her, to see what she would do with him. He said, would she ride on his back whilst he jumped off the canal bridge down into the water beneath.

She would. He loved to feel the naked child clinging on to his shoulders. There was a curious fight between their two wills. He mounted the parapet of the canal bridge. The water was a long way down. But the child had a deliberate will set upon his. She held herself fixed to him.

He leapt, and down they went. The crash of the water as they went under struck through the child's small body, with a sort of unconsciousness. But she remained fixed. And when they came up again, and when they went to the bank, and when they sat on the grass side by side, he laughed, and said it was fine. And the dark-dilated eyes of the child looked at him wonderingly, darkly, wondering from the shock, yet reserved and unfathomable, so he laughed almost with a sob.

In a moment she was clinging safely on his back again, and he was swimming in deep water. She was used to his nakedness, and to her mother's nakedness, ever since she was born. They were clinging to each other, and making up to each other for the strange blow that had been struck at them. Yet still, on other days, he would leap again with her from the bridge, daringly, almost wickedly. Till at length, as he leapt, once, she dropped forward on to his head, and nearly broke his neck, so that they fell into the water in a heap, and fought for a few moments with death. He saved her, and sat on the bank, quivering. But his eyes were full of the blackness of death, it was as if death had cut between their two lives, and separated them.

Still they were not separate. There was this curious taunting intimacy between them. When the fair came, she wanted to go in the swingboats. He took her, and, standing up in the boat, holding on to the irons, began to drive higher, perilously higher. The child clung fast on her seat.

"Do you want to go any higher?" he said to her, and she laughed with her mouth, her eyes wide and dilated. They were rushing through the air.

"Yes," she said, feeling as if she would turn into vapour, lose hold of everything, and melt away. The boat swung far up, then down like a stone, only to be caught sickeningly up again.

"Any higher?" he called, looking at her over his shoulder, his face evil and beautiful to her.

She laughed with white lips.

He sent the swingboat sweeping through the air in a great semicircle, till it jerked and swayed at the high horizontal. The child clung on, pale, her eyes fixed on him. People below were calling. The jerk at the top had almost shaken them both out. He had done what he could—and he was attracting censure. He sat down, and let the swingboat swing itself out.

People in the crowd cried shame on him as he came out of the swingboat. He laughed. The child clung to his hand, pale and mute. In a while she was violently sick. He gave her lemonade, and she gulped a little.

"Don't tell your mother you've been sick," he said.

There was no need to ask that. When she got home, the child crept away under the parlour sofa, like a sick little animal, and was a long time before she crawled out.

But Anna got to know of this escapade, and was passionately angry and contemptuous of him. His golden-brown eyes glittered, he had a strange, cruel little smile. And as the child watched him, for the first time in her life a disillusion came over her, something cold and isolating. She went over to her mother. Her soul was dead towards him. It made her sick.

Still she forgot and continued to love him, but ever more coldly. He was at this time, when he was about twenty eight years old, strange and violent in his being, sensual. He acquired some power over Anna, over everybody he came into contact with.

After a long bout of hostility, Anna at last closed with him. She had now four children, all girls. For seven years she had been absorbed in wifehood and motherhood. For years he had gone on beside her, never really encroaching upon her. Then gradually another self seemed to assert its being within him. He was still silent and separate. But she could feel him all the while coming near upon her, as if his breast and his body were threatening her, and he was always coming closer. Gradually he became indifferent of responsibility. He would do what pleased him, and no more.

He began to go away from home. He went to Nottingham on Saturdays, always alone, to the football match and to the music-hall, and all the time he was watching, in readiness. He never cared to drink. But with his hard, golden-brown eyes, so keen seeing with their tiny black pupils, he watched all the people, everything that happened, and he waited.

In the Empire one evening he sat next to two girls. He was aware of the one beside him. She was rather small, common, with a fresh complexion and an upper lip that lifted from her teeth, so that, when she was not conscious, her mouth was slightly open and her lips pressed outwards in a kind of blind appeal. She was strongly aware of the man next to her, so that all her body was still, very still. Her face watched the stage. Her arms went down into her lap, very self-conscious and still.

A gleam lit up in him: should he begin with her? Should he begin with her to live the other, the unadmitted life of his desire? Why not? He had always been so good. Save for his wife, he was virgin. And why, when all women were different? Why, when he would only live once? He wanted the other life. His own life was barren, not enough. He wanted the other.

Her open mouth, showing the small, irregular, white teeth, appealed to him. It was open and ready. It was so vulnerable. Why should he not go in and enjoy what was there? The slim arm that went down so still and motionless to the lap, it was pretty. She would be small, he would be able almost to hold her in his two hands. She would be small, almost like a child, and pretty. Her childishness whetted him keenly. She would be helpless between his hands.

"That was the best turn we've had," he said to her, leaning over as he clapped his hands. He felt strong and unshakeable in himself, set over against all the world. His soul was keen and watchful, glittering with a kind of amusement. He was perfectly self-contained. He was himself, the absolute, the rest of the world was the object that should contribute to his being.

The girl started, turned round, her eyes lit up with an almost painful flash of a smile, the colour came deeply in her cheeks.

"Yes, it was," she said, quite meaninglessly, and she covered her rather prominent teeth with her lips. Then she sat looking straight before her, seeing nothing, only conscious of the colour burning in her cheek.

It pricked him with a pleasant sensation. His veins and his nerves attended to her, she was so young and palpitating.

"It's not such a good programme as last week's," he said.

Again she half turned her face to him, and her clear, bright eyes, bright like shallow water, filled with light, frightened, yet involuntarily lighting and shaking with response.

"Oh isn't it! I wasn't able to come last week."

He noted the common accent. It pleased him. He knew what class she came of. Probably she was a warehouse-lass. He was glad she was a common girl.

He proceeded to tell her about the last week's programme. She answered at random, very confusedly. The colour burned in her cheek. Yet she always answered him. The girl on the other side sat remotely, obviously silent. He ignored her. All his address was for his own girl, with her bright, shallow eyes and her vulnerably opened mouth.

The talk went on, meaningless and random on her part, quite deliberate and purposive on his. It was a pleasure to him to make this conversation, an activity pleasant as a fine game of chance and skill. He was very quiet and pleasant-humoured, but so full of strength. She fluttered beside his steady pressure of warmth and his surety.

He saw the performance drawing to a close. His senses were alert and wilful. He would press his advantages. He followed her and her plain friend down the stairs to the street. It was raining.

"It's a nasty night," he said. "Shall you come and have a drink of something—a cup of coffee—it's early yet."

"Oh, I don't think so," she said, looking away into the night.

"I wish you would," he said, putting himself as it were at her mercy.

There was a moment's pause.

"Come to Rollins," he said.

"No—not there."

"To Carson's then?"

There was a silence. The other girl hung on. The man was the centre of positive force.

"Will your friend come as well?"

There was another moment of silence, while the other girl felt her ground.

"No thanks," she said. "I've promised to meet a friend."

"Another time, then?" he said.

"Oh, thanks," she replied, very awkward.

"Goodnight," he said.

"See you later," said his girl to her friend.

"Where?" said the friend.

"You know, Gertie," replied his girl.

"All right, Jennie."

The friend was gone into the darkness. He turned with his girl to the tea-shop. They talked all the time. He made his sentences in sheer, almost muscular pleasure of exercising himself with her. He was looking at her all the time, perceiving her, appreciating her, finding her out, gratifying himself with her. He could see distinct attractions in her; her eyebrows, with their particular curve, gave him keen æsthetic pleasure. Later on he would see her bright, pellucid eyes, like shallow water, and know those. And there remained the opened, exposed mouth, red and vulnerable. That he reserved as yet. And all the while his eyes were on the girl, estimating and handling with pleasure her young softness. About the girl herself, who or what she was, he cared nothing, he was quite unaware that she was anybody. She was just the sensual object of his attention.

"Shall we go, then?" he said.

She rose in silence, as if acting without a mind, merely physically. He seemed to hold her in his will. Outside it was still raining.

"Let's have a walk," he said. "I don't mind the rain, do you?"

"No, I don't mind it," she said.

He was alert in every sense and fibre, and yet quite sure and steady, and lit up, as if transfused. He had a free sensation of walking in his own darkness, not in anybody else's world at all. He was purely a world to himself, he had nothing to do with any general consciousness. Just his own senses were supreme. All the rest was external, insignificant, leaving him alone with this girl whom he wanted to absorb, whose properties he wanted to absorb into his own senses. He did not care about her, except that he wanted to overcome her resistance, to have her in his power, fully and exhaustively to enjoy her.

They turned into the dark streets. He held her umbrella over her, and put his arm round her. She walked as if she were unaware. But gradually, as he walked, he drew her a little closer, into the movement of his side and hip. She fitted in there very well. It was a real good fit, to walk with her like this. It made him exquisitely aware of his own muscular self. And his hand that grasped her side felt one curve of her, and it seemed like a new creation to him, a reality, an absolute, an existing tangible beauty of the absolute. It was like a star. Everything in him was absorbed in the sensual delight of this one small, firm curve in her body, that his hand, and his whole being had lighted upon.

He led her into the Park, where it was almost dark. He noticed a corner between two walls, under a great overhanging bush of ivy.

"Let us stand here a minute," he said.

He put down the umbrella, and followed her into the corner, retreating out of the rain. He needed no eyes to see. All he wanted was to know through touch. She was like a piece of palpable darkness. He found her in the darkness, put his arms round her and his hands upon her. She was silent and inscrutable. But he did not want to know anything about her, he only wanted to discover her. And through her clothing, what absolute beauty he touched.

"Take your hat off," he said.

Silently, obediently, she took off her hat and gave herself to his arms again. He liked her—he liked the feel of her—he wanted to know her more closely. He let his fingers subtly seek out her cheek and neck. What amazing beauty and pleasure, in the dark! His fingers had often touched Anna on the face and neck like that. What matter! It was one man who touched Anna, another who now touched this girl. He liked best his new self. He was given over altogether to the sensuous knowledge of this woman, and every moment he seemed to be touching absolute beauty, something beyond knowledge.

Very close, marvelling and exceedingly joyful in their discoveries, his hands pressed upon her, so subtly, so seekingly, so finely and desirously searching her out, that she too was almost swooning in the absolute of sensual knowledge. In utter sensual delight she clenched her knees, her thighs, her loins together. It was an added beauty to him.

But he was patiently working for her relaxation, patiently, his whole being fixed in the smile of latent gratification, his whole body electric with subtle, powerful, reducing force upon her. So he came at length to kiss her, and she was almost betrayed by his insidious kiss. Her open mouth was too helpless and unguarded. He knew this, and his first kiss was very gentle, and soft, and assuring, so assuring. So that her soft, defenceless mouth became assured, even bold, seeking upon his mouth. And he answered her gradually, gradually, his soft kiss sinking in softly, softly, but every more heavily, more heavily yet, till it was too heavy for her to meet, and she began to sink under it. She was sinking, sinking, his smile of latent gratification was becoming more tense, he was sure of her. He let the whole force of his will sink upon her to sweep her away. But it was too great a shock for her.

With a sudden, horrible movement she ruptured the state that contained them both.

"Don't—don't!"

It was a rather horrible cry that seemed to come out of her, not to belong to her. It was some strange agony of terror crying out the words. There was something vibrating and beside herself in the noise. His nerves ripped like silk.

"What's the matter?" he said, as if calmly, "What's the matter?" She came back to him, but trembling, reservedly this time.

Her cry had given him gratification. But he knew he had been too sudden for her. He was now careful. For a while he merely sheltered her. Also there had broken a flaw into his perfect will. He wanted to persist, to begin again, to lead up to the point where he had let himself go on her, and then manage more carefully, successfully. So far she had won. And the battle was not over yet. But another voice woke in him and prompted him to let her go—let her go in contempt.

He sheltered her, and soothed her, and caressed her, and kissed her, and again began to come nearer, nearer. He gathered himself together. Even if he did not take her, he would make her relax, he would fuse away her resistance. So softly, softly, with infinite caressiveness he kissed her, and the whole of his being seemed to fondle her. Till, at the verge, swooning at the breaking point, there came from her a beaten, inarticulate, moaning cry:

"Don't—oh don't."

His veins fused with extreme voluptuousness. For a moment he almost lost control of himself, and continued automatically. But there was a moment of inaction, of cold suspension. He was not going to take her. He drew her to him and soothed her, and caressed her. But the pure zest had gone. She struggled to herself and realised he was not going to take her. And then, at the very last moment, when his fondling had come near again, his hot living desire despising her, against his cold sensual desire, she broke violently away from him.

"Don't," she cried, harsh now with hatred, and she flung her hand across and hit him violently. "Keep off of me."

His blood stood still for a moment. Then the smile came again within him, steady, cruel.

"Why, what's the matter?" he said, with suave irony. "Nobody's going to hurt you."

"I know what *you* want," she said.

"*I* know what I want," he said. "What's the odds?"

"Well you're not going to have it off *me*."

"Aren't I? Well then I'm not. It's no use crying about it, is it?"

"No, it isn't," said the girl, rather disconcerted by his irony.

"But there's no need to have a row about it. We can kiss goodnight just the same, can't we?"

She was silent in the darkness.

"Or do you want your hat and umbrella to go home this minute?"

Still she was silent. He watched her dark figure as she stood there on the edge of the faint darkness, and he waited.

"Come and say goodnight nicely, if we're going to say it," he said.

Still she did not stir. He put his hand out and drew her into the darkness again.

"It's warmer in here," he said; "a lot cosier."

His will yet had not relaxed from her. The moment of hatred exhilarated him.

"I'm going now," she muttered, as he closed his hand over her.

"See how well you fit your place," he said, as he drew her to her previous position, close upon him. "What do you want to leave it for?"

And gradually the intoxication invaded him again, the zest came back. After all, why should he not take her?

But she did not yield to him entirely.

"Are you a married man?" she asked at length,

"What if I am?" he said.

She did not answer.

"I don't ask you whether *you're* married or not," he said.

"You know jolly well I'm *not*," she answered hotly. Oh, if she could only break away from him, if only she need not yield to him.

At length her will became cold against him. She had escaped. But she hated him for her escape more than for her danger. Did he despise her so coldly. And she was in torture of adherence to him still.

"Shall I see you next week—next Saturday?" he said, as they returned to the town.

She did not answer.

"Come to the Empire with me—you and Gertie," he said.

"I should look well, going with a married man," she said.

"I'm no less of a man for being married, am I?" he said.

"Oh, it's a different matter altogether with a married man," she said, in a ready-made speech that showed her chagrin.

"How's that?" he asked.

But she would not enlighten him. Yet she promised, without promising, to be at the meeting-place next Saturday evening.

So he left her. He did not even know her name. He caught a train and went home.

It was the last train, he was very late. He was not home till midnight. But he was quite indifferent. He had no real relation with his home, not this man which he now was. Anna was sitting up for him. She saw the queer, absolved look on his face, a sort of latent, almost sinister smile, as if he were absolved from his "good" ties.

"Where have you been?" she asked, puzzled, interested.

"To the Empire."

"Who with?"

"By myself. I came home with Tom Cooper."

She looked at him, and wondered what he had been doing. She was indifferent as to whether he lied or not.

"You have come home very strange," she said. And there was an appreciative inflexion in the speech.

He was not affected. As for his humble, good self, he was absolved from it. He sat down and ate heartily. He was not tired. He seemed to take no notice of her.

For Anna the moment was critical. She kept herself aloof, and watched him. He talked to her, but with a little indifference, since he was scarcely aware of her. So, then she did not affect him? Here was a new turn of affairs! He was rather attractive, nevertheless. She liked him better than the ordinary mute, half-effaced, half-subdued man she usually knew him to be. So, he was blossoming out into his real self! It piqued her. Very good, let him blossom! She liked a new turn of affairs. He was a strange man come home to her. Glancing at him, she saw she could not reduce him to what he had been before. In an instant, she gave it up. Yet not without a pang of rage, which would insist on their old, beloved love, their old, accustomed intimacy and her old, established supremacy. She almost rose up to fight for them. But looking at him, and remembering his father, she was wary. This was the new turn of affairs!

Very good, if she could not influence him in the old way, she would be level with him in the new. Her old defiant hostility came up. Very good, she too was out on her own adventure. Her voice, her manner changed, she was ready for the game. Something was liberated in her. She liked him. She liked this strange man come home to her. He was very welcome, indeed. She was very glad to welcome a stranger. She had been bored by the old husband. To his latent, cruel smile she replied with brilliant challenge. He expected her to keep the moral fortress. Not she! It was much too dull a part. She challenged him back with a sort of radiance, very bright and free, opposite to him. He looked at her, and his eyes glinted. She too was out in the field.

His senses pricked up and keenly attended to her. She laughed, perfectly indifferent and loose as he was. He came towards her. She neither rejected him nor responded to him. In a kind of radiance, superb in her inscrutability, she laughed before him. She too could throw everything overboard, love, intimacy, responsibility. What were her four children to her now? What did it matter that this man was the father of her four children?

He was the sensual male seeking his pleasure, she was the female ready to take hers: but in her own way. A man could turn into a free lance: so then could a woman. She adhered as little as he to the moral world. All that had gone before was nothing to her. She was another woman, under the instance of a strange man. He was a stranger to her, seeking his own ends. Very good. She wanted to see what this stranger would do now, what he was.

She laughed, and kept him at arms' length, whilst apparently ignoring him. She watched him undress as if he were a stranger. Indeed he was a stranger to her.

And she roused him profoundly, violently, even before he touched her. The little creature in Nottingham had but been leading up to this. They abandoned in one motion the moral position, each was seeking gratification pure and simple.

Strange his wife was to him. It was as if he were a perfect stranger, as if she were infinitely and essentially strange to him, the other half of the world, the dark half of the moon. She waited for his touch as if he were a marauder who had come in, infinitely unknown and desirable to her. And he began to discover her. He had an inkling of the vastness of the unknown sensual store of delights she was. With a passion of voluptuousness that made him dwell on each tiny beauty in a kind of frenzy of enjoyment, he lit upon her: her beauty, the beauties, the separate, several beauties of her body.

He was quite ousted from himself, and sensually transported by that which he discovered in her. He was another man revelling over her. There was no tenderness, no love between them any more, only the maddening, sensuous lust for discovery and the insatiable, exorbitant gratification in the sensual beauties of her body. And she was a store, a store of absolute beauties that it drove him mad to contemplate. There was such a feast to enjoy, and he with only one man's capacity.

He lived in a passion of sensual discovery with her for some time—it was a duel: no love, no words, no kisses even, only the maddening perception of beauty consummate, absolute through touch. He wanted to touch her, to discover her, maddeningly he wanted to know her. Yet he must not hurry, or he missed everything. He must enjoy one beauty at a time. And the multitudinous beauties of her body, the many little rapturous places, sent him mad with delight, and with desire to be able to know more, to have strength to know more. For all was there.

He would say during the daytime:

"Tonight I shall know the little hollow under her ankle, where the blue vein crosses." And the thought of it, and the desire for it, made a thick darkness of anticipation.

He would go all the day waiting for the night to come, when he could give himself to the enjoyment of some luxurious absolute of beauty in her. The thought of the hidden resources of her, the undiscovered beauties and ecstatic place of delight in her body, waiting, only waiting for him to discover them, sent him slightly insane. He was obsessed. If he did not discover and make known to himself these delights, they might be lost for ever. He wished he had a hundred men's energies, with which to enjoy her. He wished he were a cat, to lick her with a rough, grating, lascivious tongue. He wanted to wallow in her, bury himself in her flesh, cover himself over with her flesh.

And she, separate, with a strange, dangerous, glistening look in her eyes received all his activities upon her as if they were expected by her, and provoked him when he was quiet to more, till sometimes he was ready to perish for sheer inability to be satisfied of her, inability to have had enough of her.

Their children became mere offspring to them, they lived in the darkness and death of their own sensual activities. Sometimes he felt he was going mad with a sense of Absolute Beauty, perceived by him in her through his senses. It was something too much for him. And in everything, was this same, almost sinister, terrifying beauty. But in the revelations of her body through contact with his body, was the ultimate beauty, to know which was almost death in itself, and yet for the knowledge of which he would have undergone endless torture. He would have forfeited anything, anything, rather than forego his right even to the instep of her foot, and the place from which the toes radiated out, the little, miraculous white plain from which ran the little hillocks of the toes and the folded, dimpling hollows between the toes. He felt he would have died rather than forfeit this.

This was what their love had become, a sensuality violent and extreme as death. They had no conscious intimacy, no tenderness of love. It was all the lust and the infinite, maddening intoxication of the senses, a passion of death.

He had always, all his life, had a secret dread of Absolute Beauty. It had always been like a fetish to him, something to fear, really. For it was immoral and against mankind. So he had turned to the Gothic form, which always asserted the broken desire of mankind in its pointed arches, escaping the rolling, absolute beauty of the round arch.

But now he had given way, and with infinite sensual violence gave himself to the realisation of this supreme, immoral, Absolute Beauty, in the body of woman. It seemed to him, that it came to being in the body of woman, under his touch. Under his touch, even under his sight, it was there. But when he neither saw nor touched the perfect place, it was not perfect, it was not there. And he must make it exist.

But still the thing terrified him. Awful and threatening it was, dangerous to a degree, even whilst he gave himself to it. It was pure darkness, also. All the shameful things of the body revealed themselves to him now with a sort of sinister, tropical beauty. All the shameful, natural and unnatural acts of sensual voluptuousness which he and the woman partook of together, created together, they had their heavy beauty and their delight. Shame, what was it? It was part of extreme delight. It was that part of delight of which man is usually afraid. Why afraid? The secret, shameful things are most terribly beautiful.

They accepted shame, and were one with it in their most unlicensed pleasures. It was incorporated. It was a bud that blossomed into beauty and heavy, fundamental gratification.

Their outward life went on much the same, but the inward life was revolutionised. The children became less important, the parents were absorbed in their own living.

And gradually, Brangwen began to find himself free to attend to the outside life as well. His intimate life was so violently active, that it set another man in him free. And this new man turned with interest to public life, to see what part he could take in it. This would give him scope for new activity, activity of a kind for which he was now created and released. He wanted to be unanimous with the whole of purposive mankind.

At this time Education was in the forefront as a subject of interest. There was talk of new Swedish methods, of handwork instruction, and so on. Brangwen embraced sincerely the idea of handwork in schools. For the first time, he began to take real interest in a public affair. He had at length, from his profound sensual activity, developed a real purposive self.

There was talk of night-schools, and of handicraft classes. He wanted to start a wood-work class in Cossethay, to teach carpentry and joinery and wood-carving to the village boys, two night a week. This seemed to him a supremely desirable thing to be doing. His pay would be very little—and when he had it, he spent it all on extra wood and tools. But he was very happy and keen in his new public spirit.

He started his night-classes in wood-work when he was thirty years old. By this time he had five children, the last a boy. But boy or girl mattered very little to him. He had a natural blood-affection for his children, and he liked them as they turned up: boys or girls. Only he was fondest of Ursula. Somehow, she seemed to be at the back of his new night-school venture.

The house by the yew-trees was in connection with the great human endeavour at last. It gained a new vigour thereby.

To Ursula, a child of eight, the increase in magic was considerable. She heard all the talk, she saw the parish room fitted up as a workshop. The parish room was a high, stone, barn-like, ecclesiastical building standing away by itself in the Brangwens' second garden, across the lane. She was always attracted by its age and its stranded obsoleteness. Now she watched preparations made, she sat on the flight of stone steps that came down from the porch to the garden, and heard her father and the vicar talking and planning and working. Then an inspector came, a very strange man, and stayed talking with her father all one evening. Everything was settled, and twelve boys enrolled their names. It was very exciting.

But to Ursula, everything her father did was magic. Whether he came from Ilkeston with news of the town, whether he went across to the church with his music or his tools on a sunny evening, whether he sat in his white surplice at the organ on Sundays, leading the singing with his strong tenor voice, or whether he were in the workshop with the boys, he was always a centre of magic and fascination to her, his voice, sounding out in command, cheerful, laconic, had always a twang in it that sent a thrill over her blood, and hypnotised her. She seemed to run in the shadow of some dark, potent secret of which she would not, of whose existence even she dared not become conscious, it cast such a spell over her, and so darkened her mind.

CHAPTER IX

The Marsh and the Flood

There was always regular connection between the Yew Cottage and the Marsh, yet the two households remained separate, distinct.

After Anna's marriage, the Marsh became the home of the two boys, Tom and Fred. Tom was a rather short, good-looking youth, with crisp black hair and long black eyelashes and soft, dark, possessed eyes. He had a quick intelligence. From the High School he went to London, to study. He had an instinct for attracting people of character and energy. He gave place entirely to the other person, and at the same time kept himself independent. He scarcely existed except through other people. When he was alone he was unresolved. When he was with another man, he seemed to add himself to the other, make the other bigger almost than life size. So that a few people loved him and attained a sort of fulfilment in him. He carefully chose these few.

He had a subtle, quick, critical intelligence, a mind that was like a scale or balance. There was something of a woman in all this.

In London he had been the favorite pupil of an engineer, a clever man, who became well-known at the time when Tom Brangwen had just finished his studies. Through this master the youth kept acquaintance with various individual, outstanding characters. He never asserted himself. He seemed to be there to estimate and establish the rest. He was like a presence that makes us aware of our own being. So that he was while still young connected with some of the most energetic scientific and mathematical people in London. They took him as an equal. Quiet and perceptive and impersonal as he was, he kept his place and learned how to value others in just degree. He was there like a judgment. Besides, he was very good-looking, of medium stature but beautifully proportioned, dark, with fine colouring, always perfectly healthy.

His father allowed him a liberal pocket-money, besides which he had a sort of post as assistant to his chief. Then from time to time the young man appeared at the Marsh, curiously attractive, well dressed, reserved, having by nature a subtle, refined manner. And he set the change in the farm.

Fred, the younger brother, was a Brangwen, large-boned, blue-eyed, English. He was his father's very son, the two men, father and son, were supremely at ease with one another. Fred was succeeding to the farm.

Between the elder brother and the younger existed an almost passionate love. Tom watched over Fred with a woman's poignant attention and self-less care. Fred looked up to Tom as to something miraculous, that which he himself would aspire to be, were he great also.

So that after Anna's departure, the Marsh began to take on a new tone. The boys were gentlemen; Tom had a rare nature, and had risen high, Fred was sensitive and fond of reading, he pondered Ruskin and then the Agnostic writings. Like all the Brangwens, he was very much a thing to himself, though fond of people, and indulgent to them, having an exaggerated respect for them.

There was a rather uneasy friendship between him and one of the young Hardys at the Hall. The two households were different, yet the young men met on shy terms of equality.

It was young Tom Brangwen, with his dark lashes and beautiful colouring, his soft, inscrutable nature, his strange repose and his informed air, added to his position in London, who seemed to emphasize the superior, foreign element in the Marsh. When he appeared, perfectly dressed, as if soft and affable and yet quite removed from everybody, he created an uneasiness in people, he was reserved in the minds of the Cossethay and Ilkeston acquaintances to a different, remote world.

He and his mother had a kind of affinity. The affection between them was of a mute, distant character, but radical. His father was always uneasy and slightly deferential to his eldest son. Tom also formed the link that kept the Marsh in real connection with the Skrebenskys, now quite important people in their own district.

So a change in tone came over the Marsh. Tom Brangwen, the father, as he grew older seemed to mature into a gentleman-farmer. His figure lent itself: burly and handsome. His face remained fresh and his blue eyes as full of light, his thick hair and beard had turned gradually to a silky whiteness. It was his custom to laugh a great deal, in his acquiescent, wilful manner. Things had puzzled him very much, so he had taken the line of easy, good-humoured acceptance.

He was not responsible for the frame of things. Yet he was afraid of the unknown in life.

He was fairly well-off. His wife was there with him, a different being from himself, yet somewhere vitally connected with him:—who was he to understand where and how? His two sons were gentlemen. They were men distinct from himself, they had separate beings of their own, yet they were connected with himself. It was all adventurous and puzzling. Yet one remained vital within one's own existence, whatever the off-shoots.

So, handsome and puzzled, he laughed and stuck to himself, as the only thing he could stick to. His youngness and the wonder remained almost the same in him. He became indolent, he developed a luxuriant ease. Fred did most of the farm-work, the father saw to the more important transactions. He drove a good mare, and sometimes he rode his cob. He drank in the hôtels and the inns with better-class farmers and proprietors, he had well-to-do acquaintances among men. But one class suited him no better than another.

His wife, as ever, had no acquaintances. Her hair was threaded now with grey, her face grew older in form without changing in expression. She seemed the same as when she had come to the Marsh twenty five years ago, save that her health was more fragile. She seemed always to haunt the Marsh rather than to live there. She was never part of the life. Something she represented was alien there, she remained a stranger within the gates, in some ways fixed and impervious, in some ways curiously refining. She caused the separateness and individuality of all the Marsh inmates, the friability of the household.

When young Tom Brangwen was twenty three years old there was some breach between him and his chief which was never explained, and he went away to Italy, then to America. He came home for a while, then went to Germany; always the same good-looking, carefully-dressed, attractive young man, in perfect health, yet somehow outside of everything. In his dark eyes was a deep misery which he wore with the same ease and pleasantness as he wore his close-sitting clothes.

To Ursula he was a romantic, alluring figure. He had a grace of bringing beautiful presents: a box of expensive sweets such as Cossethay had never seen; or he gave her a hair-brush and a long, slim mirror of mother-of-pearl, all pale and glimmering and exquisite; or he sent her a little necklace of rough stones, amethyst and opal and brilliants and garnet. He spoke other languages easily and fluently, his nature was curiously gracious and insinuating. With all that, he was undefinably an outsider. He belonged to nowhere, to no society.

Anna Brangwen had left her intimacy with her father undeveloped since the time of her marriage. At her marriage it had been abandoned. He and she had drawn a reserve between them. Anna went more to her mother.

Then suddenly the father died.

It happened one spring-time when Ursula was about eight years old, he, Tom Brangwen, drove off on a Saturday morning to the market in Nottingham, saying he might not be back till late, as there was a special show and then a meeting he had to attend. His family understood that he would enjoy himself.

The season had been rainy and dreary. In the evening it was pouring with rain. Fred Brangwen, unsettled, uneasy, did not go out, as was his wont. He smoked and read and fidgeted, hearing always the trickling of water outside. This wet, black night seemed to cut him off and make him unsettled, aware of himself, aware that he wanted something else, aware that he was scarcely living. There seemed to him to be no root to his life, no place for him to get satisfied in. He dreamed of going abroad. But his instinct knew that change of place would not solve his problem. He wanted change, deep, vital change of living. And he did not know how to get it.

Tilly, an old woman now, came in saying that the laborers who had been suppering up said the yard and everywhere was just a slew of water. He heard in indifference. But he hated a desolate, raw wetness in the world. He would leave the Marsh.

His mother was in bed. At last he shut his book, his mind was blank, he walked upstairs intoxicated with depression and anger, and, intoxicated with depression and anger, locked himself into sleep.

Tilly set slippers before the kitchen fire, and she also went to bed, leaving the door unlocked. Then the farm was in darkness, in the rain.

At eleven o'clock it was still raining. Tom Brangwen stood in the yard of the "Angel," in Nottingham, and buttoned his coat.

"Oh well," he said cheerfully, "it's rained on me before. Put 'er in, Jack my lad, put her in—Tha'rt a rare old cock, Jacky-boy, wi' a belly on thee as does credit to thy drink, if not to thy corn. Co' up, lass, let's get off ter th' old homestead. Oh my heart, what a wetness in the night! There'll be no volcanoes after this. Hey, Jack, my beautiful young slender feller, which of us is Noah? It seems as though the water-works is bursted. Ducks and ayquatic fowl 'll be king o' the castle at this rate—dove an' olive branch an' all. Stand up then, gel, stand up, we're not stoppin' here all night, even if you thought we was. I'm dashed if the jumping rain wouldn't make anybody think they was drunk. Hey Jack—does rain-water wash the sense in, or does it wash it out?"

And he laughed to himself at the joke.

He was always ashamed when he had to drive after he had been drinking, always apologetic to the horse. His apologetic frame made him facetious. He was aware of his inability to walk quite straight. Nevertheless his will kept stiff and attentive, in all his fuddledness.

He mounted and bowled off through the gates of the inn-yard. The mare went well, he sat fixed, the rain beating on his face. His heavy body rode motionless in a kind of sleep, one centre of attention was kept fitfully burning, the rest was dark. He concentrated his last attention on the fact of driving along the road he knew so well. He knew it so well, he watched for it attentively, with an effort of will.

He talked aloud to himself, sententious in his anxiety, as if he were perfectly sober, whilst the mare bowled along and the rain beat on him. He watched the rain before the gig-lamps, the faint gleaming of the shadowy horse's body, the passing of the dark hedges.

"It's not a fit night to turn a dog out," he said to himself, aloud. "It's high time as it did a bit of clearing up, I'll be damned if it isn't. It was a lot of use putting those ten loads of cinders on th' road. They'll be washed to kingdom-come if it doesn't alter. Well, it's our Fred's look-out, if they are. He's top-sawyer as far as those things go. I don't see why I should concern myself. They can wash to kingdom-come and back again for what I care. I suppose they *would* be washed back again some day. That's how things are. Th' rain tumbles down just to mount up in clouds again. So they say. There's no more water on the earth than there was in the year naught. That's the story, my boy, if you understand it. There's no more today than there was a thousand years ago—nor no less either. You can't wear water out. No, my boy: it'll give you the go-by. Try to wear it out, and it takes its hook into vapour, it has its fingers at its nose to you. It turns into cloud and falleth as rain on the just and unjust. I wonder if I'm the just or the unjust."

He started awake as the trap lurched deep into a rut. And he wakened to the point in his journey. He had travelled some distance since he was last conscious.

But at length he reached the gate, and stumbled heavily down, reeling, gripping fast to the trap. He descended into several inches of water.

"Be damned!" he said angrily. "Be damned to the miserable slop."

And he led the horse washing through the gate. He was quite drunk now, moving blindly, in habit. Everywhere there was water underfoot.

The raised causeway of the house and the farm-stead was dry, however. But there was a curious roar in the night which seemed to be made in the darkness of his own intoxication. Reeling, blinded, almost without consciousness, he carried his parcels and the rug and cushions into the house, dropped them, and went out to put up the horse.

Now he was at home, he was a sleep-walker, waiting only for the moment of activity to stop. Very deliberately and carefully, he led the horse down the slope to the cart-shed. She shied and backed.

"Why wha's amiss?" he hiccupped, plodding steadily on. And he was again in a wash of water, the horse splashed up water as she went. It was thickly dark, save for the gig-lamps, and they lit on a rippling surface of water.

"Well that's a knock-out," he said, as he came to the cart-shed, and was wading in six inches of water. But everything seemed to him amusing. He laughed to think of six inches of water being in the cart-shed.

He backed in the mare. She was restive. He laughed at the fun of untackling the mare with a lot of water washing round his feet. He laughed because it upset her. "What's amiss, what's amiss, a drop o' water won't hurt you!" As soon as he had undone the traces, she walked quickly away.

He hung up the shafts and took the gig-lamp. As he came out of the familiar jumble of shafts and wheels in the shed, the water, in little waves, came washing strongly against his legs. He staggered and almost fell.

"Well what the deuce!" he said, staring round at the running water in the black, watery night.

He went to meet the running flood, sinking deeper and deeper.

His soul was full of great astonishment. He *had* to go and look where it came from, though the ground was going from under his feet. He went on, down towards the pond, shakily. He rather enjoyed it. He was now knee deep, and the water was pulling heavily. He stumbled, reeled sickeningly.

Fear took hold of him. Gripping tightly to the lamp, he reeled, and looked round. The water was carrying his feet away, he was dizzy. He did not know which way to turn. The water was whirling, whirling, the whole black night was swooping in rings. He swayed uncertainly at the centre of all the attack, reeling in dismay. In his soul, he knew he would fall.

As he staggered, something in the water struck his legs, and he fell. Instantly he was in the turmoil of suffocation. He fought in a black horror of suffocation, fighting, wrestling, but always borne down, borne inevitably down. Still he wrestled and fought to get himself free, in the unutterable struggle of suffocation, but he always fell again deeper. Something struck his head, a great wonder of anguish went over him, then the blackness covered him entirely.

In the utter darkness, the unconscious, drowning body was rolled along, the waters pouring, washing, filling in the place. The cattle woke up and rose to their feet, the dog began to yelp. And the unconscious, drowning body was washed along in the black, swirling darkness, passively.

Mrs Brangwen woke up and listened. With preternaturally sharp senses she heard the movement of all the darkness that swirled outside. For a moment she lay still. Then she went to the window. She heard the sharp rain, and the deep running of water. She knew her husband was outside.

"Fred," she called, "Fred!"

Away in the night was a hoarse, brutal roar of a mass of water rushing downwards.

She went downstairs. She could not understand the multiplied running of water. Stepping down the step into the kitchen, she put her foot into water. The kitchen was flooded. Where did it come from? She could not understand.

Water was running in out of the scullery. She paddled through barefoot, to see. Water was bubbling fiercely under the outer door. She was afraid. Then something washed against her, something twined under her foot. It was the riding whip. On the table were the rug and the cushions and the parcels from the gig.

He had come home.

"Tom!" she called, afraid of her own voice.

She opened the door. Water ran in with a horrid sound. Everywhere was moving water, a sound of waters.

"Tom!" she cried, standing in her nightdress with the candle, calling into the darkness and the flood out of the doorway.

"Tom! Tom!"

And she listened. Fred appeared behind her, in trousers and shirt.

"Where is he?" he asked.

He looked at the flood, then at his mother. She seemed small and uncanny, elvish, in her nightdress.

"Go upstairs," he said. "He'll be in th' stable."

"To—om! To—om!" cried the elderly woman, with a long, unnatural, penetrating call that chilled her son to the marrow. He quickly pulled on his boots and his coat.

"Go upstairs, mother," he said, "I'll go an' see where he is."

"To—om! To—o—om!" rang out the shrill, unearthly cry of the small woman. There was only the noise of water and the mooing of uneasy cattle, and the long yelping of the dog, clamouring in the darkness.

Fred Brangwen splashed out into the flood with a lantern. His mother stood on a chair in the doorway, watching him go. It was all water, water, running, flashing under the lantern.

"Tom! Tom! To—o—om!" came her long, unnatural cry, ringing over the night. It made her son feel cold in his soul.

And the unconscious, drowning body of the father rolled on below the house, driven by the black water towards the high-road.

Tilly appeared, a skirt over her nightdress. She saw her mistress clinging on the top of a chair in the open doorway, a candle burning on the table.

"God's sake!" cried the old serving-woman. "The cut's burst. That embankment's broke down. Whativer are we goin' to do!"

Mrs Brangwen watched her son, and the lantern, go along the upper causeway to the stable. Then she saw the dark figure of a horse: then her son hung the lamp in the stable, and the light shone out faintly on him as he untackled the mare. The mother saw the soft blazed face of the horse thrust forward into the stable-door. The stables were still above the flood. But the water flowed strongly into the house.

"It's getting higher," said Tilly. "Hasn't master come in?"

Mrs Brangwen did not hear.

"Isn't he the—ere?" she called, in her far-reaching, terrifying voice.

"No," came the short answer out of the night.

"Go and loo—ok for him."

His mother's voice nearly drove the youth mad.

He put the halter on the horse and shut the stable door. He came splashing back through the water, the lantern swinging.

The unconscious, drowning body was pushed past the house in the deepest current. Fred Brangwen came to his mother.

"I'll go to th' cart-shed," he said.

"To—om—To—o—om!" rang out the strong, inhuman cry. Fred Brangwen's blood froze, his heart was very angry. He gripped his veins in a frenzy. Why was she yelling like this? He could not bear the sight of her, perched on a chair in her white nightdress in the doorway, elvish and horrible.

"He's taken the mare out of the trap, so he's all right," he said, growling, pretending to be normal.

But as he descended to the cart-shed, he sank into a foot of water. He heard the rushing in the distance, he knew the canal had broken down. The water was running deeper.

The trap was there all right, but no signs of his father. The young man waded down to the pond. The water rose above his knees, it swirled and forced him. He drew back.

"Is he the—e—ere?" came the maddening cry of the mother.

"No," was the sharp answer.

"To—om—To—o—om!" came the piercing, free, unearthly call. It seemed high and supernatural, almost pure. Fred Brangwen hated it. It nearly drove him mad. So awfully it sang out, almost like a song.

The water was flowing fuller into the house.

"You'd better go up to Beeby's, and bring him and Arthur down, and tell Mrs Beeby to fetch Wilkinson," said Fred to Tilly.

He forced his mother to go upstairs.

"I know your father is drowned," she said, in a curious dismay.

The flood rose through the night, till it washed the kettle off the hob in the kitchen. Mrs Brangwen sat alone at a window upstairs. She called no more. The men were busy with the pigs and the cattle. They were coming with a boat for her.

Towards morning the rain ceased, the stars came out over the noise and the terrifying clucking and trickling of the water. Then there was a pallor in the east, the light began to come. In the ruddy light of the dawn she saw the waters spreading out, moving sluggishly, the buildings rising out of a waste of water. Birds began to sing, drowsily, and as if slightly hoarse with the dawn. It grew brighter. Up the second field was the great, raw gap in the canal embankment.

Mrs Brangwen went from window to window, watching the flood. Somebody had brought a little boat. The light grew stronger, the red gleam was gone off the flood-waters, day took place. Mrs Brangwen went from the front of the house to the back, looking out, intent and unrelaxing, on the pallid morning of spring.

She saw a glimpse of her husband's buff coat in the floods, as the water rolled the body against the garden hedge. She called to the men in the boat. She was glad he was found. They dragged him out of the hedge. They could not lift him into the boat. Fred Brangwen jumped into the water, up to his waist, and half carried the body of his father through the flood to the road. Hay and twigs and dirt were in the beard and hair. The youth pushed through the water crying loudly without tears, like a stricken animal. The mother at the window cried, making no trouble.

The doctor came. But the body was dead. They carried it up to Cossethay, to Anna's house.

When Anna Brangwen heard the news, she pressed back her head and rolled her eyes, as if something were reaching forward to bite at her throat. She pressed back her head, her mind was driven back, to sleep. Since she had married and become a mother, the girl she had been was forgotten. Now, the shock threatened to break in upon her and sweep away all her intervening life, make her as a girl of eighteen again, loving her father. So she pressed back, away from the shock, she clung to her present life.

It was when they brought him to her house dead and in his wet clothes, his wet, sodden clothes, fully dressed as he came from market, yet all sodden and inert, that the shock really broke into her, and she was terrified. A big, soaked, inert heap, he was, who had been to her the image of power and strong life.

Almost in horror, she began to take the wet things from him, to pull off him the incongruous market-clothes of a well-to-do farmer. The children were sent away to the vicarage, the dead body lay on the parlour floor, Anna quickly began to undress him, laid his fob and seals in a wet heap on the table. Her husband and the woman helped her. They cleared and washed the body, and laid it on the bed.

There, it looked still and grand. He was perfectly calm in death, and, now he was laid in line, inviolable, unapproachable. To Anna, he was the majesty of the inaccessible male, the majesty of death. It made her still and awe-stricken, almost glad.

Lydia Brangwen, the mother, also came and saw the impressive, inviolable body of the dead man. She went pale, seeing death. He was beyond change or knowledge, absolute, laid in line with the infinite. What had she to do with him? He was a majestic Abstraction, made visible now for a moment, inviolate, absolute. And who could lay claim to him, who could speak of him, of the him who was revealed in the stripped moment of transit from life into death? Neither the living nor the dead could claim him, he was both the one and the other, inviolable, inaccessibly himself.

"I shared life with you, I belong in my own way to eternity," said Lydia Brangwen, her heart cold, knowing her own singleness.

"I did not know you in life. You are beyond me, supreme now in death," said Anna Brangwen, awe-stricken, almost glad.

It was the sons who could not bear it. Fred Brangwen went about with a set, blanched face and shut hands, his heart full of hatred and rage for what had been done to his father, bleeding also with desire to have his father again, to see him, to hear him again. He could not bear it.

Tom Brangwen only arrived on the day of the funeral. He was quiet and controlled as ever. He kissed his mother, who was still, dark-faced, inscrutable, he shook hands with his brother without looking at him, he saw the great coffin with its black handles. He even read the name-plate "Tom Brangwen, of the Marsh Farm. Born— Died—."

The good-looking, still face of the young man crinkled up for a moment in a terrible grimace, then resumed its stillness. The coffin was carried round to the church, the funeral bell tanged at intervals, the mourners carried their wreaths of white flowers. The mother, the Polish woman, went with dark, abstract face, on her son's arm. He was good-looking as ever, his face perfectly motionless and somehow pleasant. Fred walked with Anna, she strange and winsome, he with a face like wood, stiff, unyielding.

Only afterwards Ursula, flitting between the currant bushes down the garden, saw her uncle Tom standing in his black clothes, erect and fashionable, but his fists lifted, and his face distorted, his lips curled back from his teeth in a horrible grin, like an animal which grimaces with torment, whilst his body panted quick, like a panting dog's. He was facing the open distance, panting, and holding still, then panting rapidly again, but his face never changing from its almost bestial look of torture, the teeth all showing, the nose wrinkled up, the eyes unseeing, fixed.

Terrified, Ursula slipped away. And when her uncle Tom was in the house again, grave and very quiet, so that he seemed almost to affect gravity, to pretend grief, she watched his still, handsome face, imagining it again in its distortion. And she saw the nose was rather thick, rather Russian, under its transparent skin, she remembered the teeth under the carefully cut moustache were small and sharp and spaced. She could see him, in all his elegant demeanour, bestial, almost corrupt. And she was frightened. She never forgot to look for the bestial, frightening side of him, after this.

He said "good-bye" to his mother and went away at once. Ursula almost shrank from his kiss, now. She wanted it, nevertheless, and the little revulsion as well.

At the funeral, and after the funeral, Will Brangwen was madly in love with his wife. The death had shaken him. But death and all seemed to gather in him into a mad, overwhelming passion for his wife. She seemed so strange and winsome. He was almost beside himself with desire for her.

And she took him, she seemed ready for him, she wanted him.

The grandmother stayed a while at the Yew Cottage, till the Marsh was restored. Then she returned to her own rooms, quiet, and it seemed, wanting nothing. Fred threw himself into the work of restoring the farm. That his father was killed there seemed to make it only the more intimate and the more inevitably his own place.

There was a saying that the Brangwens always died a violent death. To them all, except perhaps Tom, it seemed almost natural. Yet Fred went about obstinate, his heart fixed. He could never forgive the Unknown this murder of his father.

After the death of the father, the Marsh was very quiet. Mrs Brangwen was unsettled. She could not sit all the evening peacefully, as she could before, and during the day, she was always rising to her feet and hesitating, as if she must go somewhere, and were not quite sure whither.

She was seen loitering about the garden, in her little woollen jacket. She was often driven out in the gig, sitting beside her son and watching the countryside or the streets of the town, with a childish, candid, uncanny face, as if it all were strange to her.

The children, Ursula and Gudrun and Theresa went by the garden gate on their way to school. The grandmother would have them call in each time they passed, she would have them come to the Marsh for dinner. She wanted children about her.

Of her sons, she was almost afraid. She could see the sombre passion and desire and dissatisfaction in them, and she wanted not to see it any more. Even Fred, with his blue eyes and his heavy jaw, troubled her. There was no peace. He wanted something, he wanted love, passion, and he could not find them. But why must he trouble her? Why must he come to her with his seething and suffering and dissatisfactions? She was too old.

Tom was more restrained, reserved. He kept his body very still. But he troubled her even more. She could not but see the black depths of disintegration in his eyes, the sudden glance upon her, as if she could save him, as if he would reveal himself.

And how could age save youth? Youth must go to youth. Always the storm! Could she not lie in peace, these years, in the quiet, apart from life? No, always the swell must heave upon her and break her against the barriers. Always she must be embroiled in the seethe and rage and passion, endless, endless, going on forever. And she wanted to draw away. She wanted at last her own innocence and peace. She did not want her sons to force upon her any more the old, brutal story, of desire and offerings and deep, deep-hidden rage of unsatisfied men against women. She wanted to be beyond it all, to know the peace and innocence of age.

She had never been a woman to work much. So that now she would stand often at the garden gate, watching the scant world go by. And the sight of children pleased her, made her happy. She had usually an apple or a few sweets in her pocket. She liked children to smile at her.

She never went to her husband's grave. She spoke of him simply, as if he were alive. Sometimes the tears would run down her face, in helpless sadness. Then she recovered, and was herself again, happy.

On wet days, she stayed in bed. Her bedroom was her city of refuge, where she could lie and muse and muse. Sometimes Fred would read to her. But that did not mean much. She had so many dreams to dream over, such an unsifted store. She wanted time.

Her chief friend at this period was Ursula. The little girl and the musing, fragile woman of sixty seemed to understand the same language. At Cossethay all was activity and passion, everything moved upon poles of passion. Then there were four children younger than Ursula, a throng of babies, all the time many lives beating against each other.

So that for the eldest child, the peace of the grandmother's bedroom was exquisite. Here Ursula came as to a hushed, paradisal land, here her own existence became simple and exquisite to her as if she were a flower.

Always on Saturdays she came down to the Marsh, and always clutching a little offering, either a little mat made of strips of coloured, woven paper, or a tiny basket made in the kindergarten lesson, or a little crayon drawing of a bird.

When she appeared in the doorway, Tilly, ancient but still in authority, would crane her skinny neck to see who it was.

"Oh, it's you, is it?" she said. "I thought we should be seein' you. My word, that's a bobby-dazzlin' posy you've brought!"

It was curious how Tilly preserved the spirit of Tom Brangwen, who was dead, in the Marsh. Ursula always connected her with her grandfather.

This day the child had brought a tight little nosegay of pinks, white ones, with a rim of pink ones. She was very proud of it, and very shy because of her pride.

"Your gran'mother's in her bed. Wipe your shoes well if you're goin' up, and don't go burstin' in on her like a sky-rocket. My word, but that's a fine posy! Did you do it all by yourself, an' all?"

Tilly stealthily ushered her into the bedroom. The child entered with a strange, dragging hesitation characteristic of her when she was moved. Her grandmother was sitting up in bed, wearing a little grey woollen jacket.

The child hesitated in silence near the bed, clutching the nosegay in front of her. Her childish eyes were shining. The grandmother's grey eyes shone with a similar light.

"How pretty!" she said. "How pretty you have made them! What a darling little bunch."

Ursula, glowing, thrust them into her grandmother's hand, saying: "I made them you."

"That is how the peasants tied them at home," said the grandmother, pushing the pinks with her finger, and smelling them. "Just

236

such tight little bunches! And they make wreaths for their hair—they weave the stalks. Then they go round with wreaths in their hair, and wearing their best aprons."

Ursula immediately imagined herself in this story-land.

"Did you used to have a wreath in your hair, grandmother?"

"When I was a little girl, I had golden hair, something like Katie's. Then I used to have a wreath of little blue flowers, oh, so blue, that come when the snow is gone. Andrey, the coachman, used to bring me the very first."

They talked, and then Tilly brought the tea-tray, set for two. Ursula had a special green and gold cup kept for herself at the Marsh. There was thin bread and butter, and cress for tea. It was all special and wonderful. She ate very daintily, with little, fastidious bites.

"Why do you have two wedding-rings, grandmother?—must you?" asked the child, noticing her grandmother's ivory coloured hand with blue veins, above the tray.

"If I had two husbands, child."

Ursula pondered a moment.

"Then must you wear both the rings together?"

"Yes."

"Which was my grandfather's ring?"

The woman hesitated.

"This grandfather whom you knew? This was his ring, the red one. The yellow one was your other grandfather's, whom you never knew."

Ursula looked interestedly at the two rings on the proffered finger.

"Where did he buy it you?" she asked.

"This one? In Warsaw, I think."

"You didn't know my own grandfather then?"

"Not this grandfather."

Ursula pondered this fascinating intelligence.

"Did he have white whiskers, as well?"

"No, his beard was dark. You have his brows, I think."

Ursula flushed and became self-conscious. She wanted to go and look at her brows in the mirror. She at once identified herself with her Polish grandfather.

"And did he have brown eyes?"

"Yes, dark eyes. He was a clever man, as quick as a lion. He was never still."

Lydia still resented Lensky. When she thought of him, she was always younger than he, she was always twenty, or twenty five, and under his domination. He incorporated her in his ideas as if she were not a person herself, as if she were just his aide-de-camp, or part of his baggage, or one among his surgical appliances. She still resented it. And he was always only thirty: he had died when he was thirty four. She did not feel sorry for him. He was older than she. Yet she still ached in the thought of those days.

"Did you like my first grandfather best?" asked Ursula.

"I liked them both," said her grandmother.

And, thinking, she became again Lensky's girl-bride. He was of good family, of better family even than her own, for she was half German. She was a young girl in a house of insecure fortune. And he, an intellectual, a clever surgeon and physician, had loved her. How she had looked up to him! She remembered her first transports when he talked to her, the important young man with the severe black beard. He had seemed so wonderful, such an authority. After her own lax household, his gravity and confident, hard authority seemed almost God-like to her. For she had never known it in her life, all her surroundings had been loose, lax, disordered, a welter.

"Miss Lydia, will you marry me?" he had said to her in German, in his grave, yet tremulous voice. She had been afraid of his dark eyes upon her. They did not see her, they were fixed upon her. And he was hard, confident. She thrilled with the excitement of it, and accepted. During the courtship, his kisses were a wonder to her. She always thought about them, and wondered over them. She never wanted to kiss him back. In her idea, the man kissed, and the woman examined in her soul the kisses she had received.

She had never quite recovered from her prostration of the first days, or nights, of marriage. He had taken her to Vienna, and she was utterly alone with him, utterly alone in another world, everything, everything foreign, even he foreign to her. Then came the real marriage, passion came to her, and she became his slave, he was her lord, her lord. She was the girl-bride, the slave, she kissed his feet, she had thought it an honor to touch his body, to unfasten his boots. For two years, she had gone on as his slave, crouching at his feet, embracing his knees.

Children had come, he had followed his ideas. She was there for him just to keep him in condition. She was to him one of the baser or material conditions necessary for his welfare in prosecuting his ideas, of nationalism, of liberty, of science.

But gradually, at twenty three, twenty four, she began to realise that she too might consider these ideas. By his acceptance of her self-subordination, he exhausted the feeling in her. There were those of his associates who would discuss the ideas with her, though he did not wish to do so himself. She adventured into the minds of other men. His, then, was not the only male mind! She did not exist, then, just as his attribute! She began to perceive the attentions of other men. An excitement came over her. She remembered now the men who had paid her court, when she was married, in Warsaw.

Then the rebellion broke out, and she was inspired too. She would go as nurse at her husband's side. He worked like a lion, he wore his life out. And she followed him helplessly. But she disbelieved in him. He was so separate, he ignored so much. He counted too much on himself. His work, his ideas—did nothing else matter?

Then the children were dead, and for her, everything became remote. He became remote. She saw him, she saw him go white when he heard the news, then frown, as if he thought "*Why* have they died now, when I have no time to grieve?"

"He has no time to grieve," she had said, in her remote, awful soul. "He has no time. It is so important, what he does! He is then so self-important, this half-frenzied man! Nothing matters, but this work of rebellion! He has not time to grieve, nor to think of his children! He had not time even to beget them, really."

She had let him go on alone. But, in the chaos, she had worked by his side again. And out of the chaos, she had fled with him to London.

He was a broken, cold man. He had no affection for her nor for anyone. He had failed in *his* work, so everything had failed. He stiffened himself, and died.

She could not subscribe. He had failed, everything had failed, yet behind the failure was the unyielding passion of life. The individual effort might fail, but not the human joy. She belonged to the human joy.

He died, and went his way, but not before there was another child. And this little Ursula was his grandchild. She was glad of it. For she still honored him, though he had been mistaken.

She, Lydia Brangwen, was sorry for him now. He was dead—he had scarcely lived. He had never known her. He had lain with her, but he had never known her. He had never received what she could give him. He had gone away from her empty. So, he had never lived. So, he had died and passed away. Yet there had been strength and power in him.

She could scarcely forgive him that he had never lived. If it were not for Anna, and for this little Ursula, who had his brows, there would be no more left of him than of a broken vessel thrown away, and just remembered.

Tom Brangwen had served her. He had come to her, and taken from her. He had died and gone his way into death. But he had made himself immortal in his knowledge with her. So she had her place here, in life, and in immortality. For he had taken his knowledge of her into death, so that she had her place in death. 'In my father's house are many mansions.'

She loved both her husbands. To one she had been a naked little girl-bride, running to serve him. The other she loved out of fulfilment, because he was good and had given her being, because he had served her honorably, and become her man, one with her.

She was established in this stretch of life, she had come to herself. During her first marriage, she had not existed, except through him, he was the substance and she the shadow running at his feet. She was very glad she had come to her own self. She was grateful to Brangwen. She reached out to him in gratitude, into death.

In her heart, she felt a vague tenderness and pity for her first husband, who had been her lord. He was so wrong when he died. She could not bear it, that he had never lived, never really become himself. And he had been her lord! Strange, it all had been! Why had he been her lord? He seemed now so far off, so without bearing on her.

"Which did you, grandmother?"

"What?"

"Like best."

"I liked them both. I married the first when I was quite a girl. Then I loved your grandfather when I was a woman. There is a difference."

They were silent for a time.

"Did you cry when my first grandfather died?" the girl asked.

Lydia Brangwen rocked herself on the bed, thinking aloud.

"When we came to England, he hardly ever spoke, he was too much concerned to take any notice of anybody. He grew thinner and thinner, till his cheeks were hollow and his mouth stuck out. He wasn't handsome any more. I knew he couldn't bear being beaten, I thought everything was lost in the world. Only I had your mother a baby, it was no use my dying.

"He looked at me with his black eyes, almost as if he hated me, when he was ill, and said 'It only wanted this. It only wanted that I should leave you and a young child to starve in this London.' I told him we should not starve. But I was young, and foolish, and frightened, which he knew.

"He was bitter, and he never gave way. He lay beating his brains, to see what he could do. 'I don't know what you will do,' he said. 'I am no good, I am a failure from beginning to end. I cannot even provide for my wife and child.'

"But you see, it was not for him to provide for us. My life went on, though his stopped, and I married your grandfather.

"I ought to have known, I ought to have been able to say to him: 'Don't be so bitter, don't die because this has failed. You are not the beginning and the end.' But I was too young, he had never let me become myself, I thought he was truly the beginning and the end. So I let him take all upon himself. Yet all did not depend on him. Life must go on, and I must marry your grandfather, and have your uncle Tom, and your uncle Fred. We cannot take so much upon our-selves—"

The child's heart beat fast as she listened to these things. She could not understand, but she seemed to feel far-off things. It gave her a deep, joyous thrill, to know she hailed from far off, from Poland, and that dark-bearded impressive man. Strange, her ante-cedents were, and she felt fate on either side of her terrible.

Almost every day, Ursula saw her grandmother, and every time, they talked together. Till the grandmother's sayings and stories, told in the complete hush of the Marsh bedroom, accumulated with mystic significance, and became a sort of Bible to the child.

And Ursula asked her deepest childish questions of her grand-mother.

"Will somebody love me, grandmother?"

"Many people love you, child. We all love you."

"But when I am grown up, will somebody love me?"

"Yes, some man will love you, child, because it's your nature. And I hope it will be somebody who will love you for what you are, and not for what he wants of you. But we have a right to what we want."

Ursula was frightened, hearing these things. Her heart sank, she felt she had no ground under her feet. She clung to her grandmother. Here was peace and security. Here, from her grandmother's peaceful room, the door opened on to the greater space, the past, which was so big, that all it contained seemed tiny, loves and births and deaths, tiny units and features within a vast horizon. That was a great relief, to know the tiny importance of the individual, within the great past.

CHAPTER X

The Widening Circle

It was very burdensome to Ursula, that she was the eldest of the family. By the time she was eleven, she had to take to school Gudrun and Theresa and Catherine. The boy, William, always called Billy, so that he should not be confused with his father, was a lovable, rather delicate child of three, so he stayed at home as yet. There was another baby girl, called Cassandra.

The children went for a time to the little church school just near the Marsh. It was the only place within reach, and being so small, Mrs Brangwen felt safe in sending her children there, though the village boys did nickname Ursula "Urtler," and Gudrun "Good-runner," and Theresa "Tea-pot."

Gudrun and Ursula were co-mates. The second child, with her long, sleepy body and her endless chain of fancies, would have nothing to do with realities. She was not for them, she was for her own fancies. Ursula was the one for realities. So Gudrun left all such to her elder sister, and trusted in her implicitly, indifferently. Ursula had a great tenderness for her co-mate sister.

It was no good trying to make Gudrun responsible. She floated along like a fish in the sea, perfect within the medium of her own difference and being. Other existences did not trouble her. Only she believed in Ursula, and trusted to Ursula.

The eldest child was very much fretted by her responsibility for the other young ones. Especially Theresa, a sturdy, bold-eyed thing, had a faculty for warfare.

"Our Ursula, Billy Pillins has lugged my hair."

"What did you say to him?"

"I said nothing."

Then the Brangwen girls were in for a feud with the Pillinses, or Phillipses.

"You won't pull my hair again, Billy Pillins," said Theresa, walking with her sisters, and looking superbly at the freckled, red-haired boy.

"Why shan't I?" retorted Billy Pillins.

"You won't because you dursn't," sang the tiresome Theresa.

"You come here then, Tea-pot, an' see if I dursna."

Up marched Tea-pot, and immediately Billy Pillins lugged her black, snaky locks. In a rage she flew at him. Immediately in rushed Ursula and Gudrun, and little Katie, in clashed the other Phillipses, Clem and Walter, and Eddie Anthony. Then there was a fray. The Brangwen girls were well-grown and stronger than many boys. But for pinafores and long hair, they would have carried easy victories. They went home, however, with hair lugged and pinafores torn. It was a joy to the Phillips boys to rip the pinafores of the Brangwen girls.

Then there was an outcry. Mrs Brangwen *would not* have it, no she would not. All her innate dignity and stand-offishness rose up. Then there was the vicar lecturing the school. "It was a sad thing that the boys of Cossethay could not behave more like gentlemen to the girls of Cossethay. Indeed, what kind of boy was it that should set upon a girl, and kick her, and beat her, and tear her pinafore. That boy deserved severe castigation, and the name of *coward*, for no boy who was not a *coward*—etc. etc."

Meanwhile much hang-dog fury in the Pillinses' hearts, much virtue in the Brangwen girls', particularly in Theresa's. And the feud continued, with periods of extraordinary amity, when Ursula was Clem Phillips's sweetheart, and Gudrun was Walter's, and Theresa was Billy's, and even the tiny Katie had to be Eddie Ant'ny's sweetheart. There was the closest union. At every possible moment, the little gang of Brangwens and Phillipses flew together. Yet neither Ursula nor Gudrun could have any real intimacy with the Phillips boys. It was a sort of fiction to them, this alliance and this dubbing of sweethearts.

Again Mrs Brangwen rose up.

"Ursula, I *will* not have you raking the roads with lads, so I tell you. Now stop it, and the rest will stop it."

How Ursula *hated* always to represent the little Brangwen club. She could never be herself, no, she was always Ursula-Gudrun-Theresa-Catherine—and later even Billy was added on to her. Moreover, she did not want the Phillipses either. She was out of taste with them.

However, the Brangwen-Pillins coalition readily broke down, owing to the unfair superiority of the Brangwens. The Brangwens were rich. They had free access to the Marsh Farm. The school teachers were almost respectful to the girls, the vicar spoke to them on equal terms. The Brangwen girls presumed, they tossed their heads.

"*You're* not ivrybody, Urtler Brangwin, ugly-mug," said Clem Phillips, his face going very red.

"I'm better than you, for all that," retorted Urtler.

"You *think* you are—wi' a face like that—Ugly-Mug,—Urtler Brangwin," he began to jeer, trying to set all the others in cry against her.

Then there was hostility again. How she *hated* their jeering. She became cold against the Phillipses. Ursula was very proud in her family. The Brangwen girls had all a curious blind dignity, even a kind of nobility in their bearing. By some result of breed and upbringing, they seemed to rush along their own lives without caring that they existed to other people. Never from the start did it occur to Ursula that other people might hold a low opinion of her. She thought that whosoever knew her, knew she was enough and accepted her as such. She thought it was a world of people like herself. She suffered bitterly if she were forced to have a low opinion of any person, and she never forgave that person.

This was maddening to many little people. All their lives, the Brangwens were meeting folk who tried to pull them down, to make them seem little. Curiously, the mother was aware of what would happen, and was always ready to give her children the advantage of the move.

When Ursula was twelve, and the common school and the companionship of the village children, niggardly and begrudging, was beginning to affect her, Anna sent her with Gudrun to the Grammar School in Nottingham. This was a great release for Ursula. She had a passionate craving to escape from the belittling circumstances of life, the little jealousies, the little differences, the little meannesses. It was a torture to her that the Phillipses were poorer and meaner than herself, that they used mean little reservations, took petty little advantages. She wanted to be with her equals: but not by diminishing herself. She *did* want Clem Phillips to be her equal. But by some puzzling, painful fate or other, when he was really there with her, he produced in her a tight feeling in the head. She wanted to beat her forehead, to escape.

Then she found, that the way to escape was easy. One departed from the whole circumstance. One went away to the Grammar

School, and left the little school, the meagre teachers, the Phillipses whom she had tried to love but who had made her fail, and whom she could not forgive. She had an instinctive fear of petty people, as a deer is afraid of dogs. Because she was blind, she could not calculate nor estimate people. She must think that everybody was just like herself.

She measured by the standard of her own people: her father and mother, her grandmother, her uncles. Her beloved father, so utterly simple in his demeanour, yet with his strong, dark soul fixed like a root in unexpressed depths that fascinated and terrified her: her mother, so strangely free of all money and convention and fear, entirely indifferent to the world, standing by herself, without connection: her grandmother, who had come from so far and was centred in so wide an horizon: people must come up to these standards before they could be Ursula's people.

So even as a girl of twelve she was glad to burst the narrow boundary of Cossethay, where only limited people lived. Outside, was all vastness, and a throng of real, proud people whom she would love.

Going to school by train, she must leave home at a quarter to eight in the morning, and she did not arrive again till half past five at evening. Of this she was glad, for the house was small and overfull. It was a storm of movement, whence there had been no escape. She hated so much being in charge.

The house was a storm of movement. The children were healthy and turbulent, the mother only wanted their animal well-being. To Ursula, as she grew a little older, it became a nightmare. When she saw, later, a Rubens picture with storms of naked babies, and found this was called "Fecundity," she shuddered, and the word became abhorrent to her. She knew as a child what it was to live amidst storms of babies, in the heat and welter of fecundity. And as a child, she was against her mother, passionately against her mother; she craved for some spirituality and stateliness.

In bad weather, home was a bedlam. Children dashed in and out of the rain, to the puddles under the dismal yew-trees, across the wet flagstones of the kitchen, whilst the cleaning-woman grumbled and scolded; children were swarming on the sofa, children were kicking the piano in the parlour, to make it sound like a bee-hive, children were rolling on the hearthrug, legs in air, pulling a book in two between them, children, fiendish, ubiquitous, were stealing upstairs to find out where our Ursula was, whispering at bedroom doors, hanging on the latch, calling mysteriously "Ursula!" "Ursula!" to the girl who had locked herself in to read. And it was hopeless. The locked door excited their sense of mystery, she had to open to dispel the lure. Then children hung on to her with round-eyed, excited questions.

The mother flourished amid all this.

"Better have them noisy than ill," she said.

But the growing girls, in turn, suffered bitterly. Ursula was just coming to the stage when Andersen and Grimm were being left behind for the "Idylls of the King" and romantic love-stories.

> "Elaine the fair, Elaine the lovable,
> Elaine the lily maid of Astolat,
> High in her chamber in a tower to the east
> Guarded the sacred shield of Launcelot."

How she loved it! How she leaned in her bedroom window with her black, rough hair on her shoulders, and her warm face all rapt, and gazed across at the churchyard and the little church, which was a turretted castell, whence Launcelot would ride just now, would wave to her as he rode by, his scarlet cloak passing behind the dark yew-trees and between the open space: whilst she, Ah she, would remain the lonely maid high up and isolated in the tower, polishing the terrible shield, weaving it a covering with a true device, and waiting, waiting, always remote and high.

At which point there would be a faint scuffle on the stairs, a high-pitched whispering outside the door, and a creaking of the latch: then Billy, excited, whispering:

"It's locked—it's locked."

Then the knocking, kicking at the door with childish knees, and the urgent, childish:

"Ursula—our Ursula? Ursula? Eh, our Ursula?"

No reply.

"Ursula! Eh—our Ursula?" the name was shouted now.

Still no answer.

"Mother, she won't answer," came the yell. "She's dead."

"Go away—I'm not dead. What do you want?" came the angry voice of the girl.

"Open the door, our Ursula," came the complaining cry.

It was all over. She must open the door. She heard the screech of the bucket downstairs dragged across the flagstones as the woman washed the kitchen floor. And the children were prowling in the bedroom, asking:

"What were you doing? What had you locked the door for?"

Then she discovered the key of the parish room, and betook herself there, and sat on some sacks with her books. There began another dream.

She was the only daughter of the old lord, she was gifted with magic. Day followed day of rapt silence, whilst she wandered ghostlike in the hushed, ancient mansion, or flitted along the sleeping terraces.

Here a grave grief attacked her: that her hair was dark. She *must* have fair hair and a white skin. She was rather bitter about her black mane.

Never mind, she would dye it when she grew up, or bleach it in the sun, till it was bleached fair. Meanwhile she wore a fair white coif of pure Venetian lace.

She flitted silently along the terraces, where jewelled lizards basked upon the stone, and did not move when her shadow fell upon them. In the utter stillness she heard the tinkle of the fountain, and smelled the roses whose blossoms hung rich and motionless. So she drifted, drifted on the wistful feet of beauty, past the water and the swans, to the noble park, where, underneath a great oak, a doe all dappled lay with four fine feet together, her fawn nestling sun-coloured beside her.

Oh, and this doe was her familiar. It would talk to her, because she was a magician, it would tell her stories as if the sunshine spoke.

Then one day, she left the door of the parish room unlocked, careless and unheeding as she always was; the children found their way in, Katie cut her finger and howled, Billy hacked notches in the fine chisels, and did much damage. There was a great commotion.

The crossness of the mother was soon finished. Ursula locked up the room again, and considered all was over. Then her father came in with the notched tools, his forehead knitted.

"Who the deuce opened the door?" he cried in anger.

"It was Ursula who opened the door," said the mother.

He had a duster in his hand. He turned and flapped the cloth hard across the girl's face. The cloth stung, for a moment the girl was as if stunned. Then she remained motionless, her face closed and stubborn. But her heart was blazing. In spite of herself the tears surged higher, in spite of her they surged higher.

In spite of her, her face broke, she made a curious gulping grimace, and the tears were falling. So she went away, desolate. But her blazing heart was fierce and unyielding. He watched her go, and a pleasurable pain filled him, a sense of triumph and easy power, followed immediately by acute pity.

"I'm sure that was unnecessary—to hit the girl across the face," said the mother coldly.

"A flip with a duster won't hurt her," he said.

"Nor will it do her any good."

For days, for weeks, Ursula's heart burned from this rebuff. She felt so cruelly vulnerable. Did he not know how vulnerable she was, how exposed and wincing? He, of all people, knew. And he wanted to do this to her. He wanted to hurt her right through her closest sensitiveness, he wanted to treat her with shame, to maim her with insult.

Her heart burnt in isolation, like a watchfire lighted. She did not forget, she did not forget, she never forgot. When she returned to her love for her father, the seed of mistrust and defiance burned unquenched, though covered up far from sight. She no longer belonged to him unquestioned. Slowly, slowly, the fire of mistrust and defiance burned in her, burned away her connection with him.

She ran a good deal alone, having a passion for all moving, active things. She loved the little brooks. Wherever she found a little running water, she was happy. It seemed to make her run and sing in spirit along with it. She could sit for hours by a brook or stream, on the roots of the alders, and watch the water hasten dancing over the stones, or among the twigs of a fallen branch. Sometimes, little fish vanished before they had become real, like hallucinations, sometimes wagtails ran by the water's brink, sometimes other little birds came to drink. She saw a kingfisher darting blue—and then she was very happy. The kingfisher was the key to the magic world: he was witness of the order of enchantment.

But she must move out of the intricately woven illusion of her life: the illusion of a father whose life was an Odyssey in an outer world; the illusion of her grandmother, of realities so shadowy and far-off that they became as mystic symbols:—peasant-girls with wreaths of blue flowers in their hair, the sledges and the depth of winter; the dark-bearded young grandfather, marriage and war and death; then the multitude of illusions concerning herself, how she was truly a princess of Poland, how in England she was under a spell, she was not really this Ursula Brangwen; then the mirage of her reading: out of the multicoloured illusion of this her life, she must move on, to the Grammar School in Nottingham.

She was shy, and she suffered. For one thing, she bit her nails, and had a cruel consciousness in her finger-tips, a shame, an exposure. Out of all proportion, this shame haunted her. She spent hours of torture, conjuring how she might keep her gloves on: if she might say her hands were scalded, if she might seem to forget to take off her gloves.

For she was going to inherit her own estate, when she went to the High School. There, each girl was a lady. There, she was going to walk amongst free souls, her co-mates and her equals, and all petty things would be put away. Ah, if only she did not bite her nails! If only she had not this blemish! She wanted so much to be perfect—without spot or blemish, living the high, noble life.

It was a grief to her that her father made such a poor introduction. He was brief as ever, like a boy saying his errand, and his clothes looked ill-fitting and casual. Whereas Ursula would have liked robes and a ceremonial of introduction to this her new estate.

She made a new illusion of school. Miss Grey, the head-mistress, had a certain silvery, school-mistressy beauty of character. The school itself had been a gentleman's house. Dark, sombre lawns separated it from the dark, select avenue. But its rooms were large and of good appearance, and from the back, one looked over lawns and shrubbery, over the trees and the grassy slope of the Arboretum, to the town which heaped the hollow with its roofs and cupolas and its shadows.

So Ursula seated herself upon the hill of learning, looking down on the smoke and confusion and the manufacturing, engrossed activity of the town. She was happy. Up here, in the Grammar School, she fancied the air was finer, beyond the factory smoke. She wanted to learn Latin and Greek and French and mathematics. She trembled like a postulant when she wrote the Greek alphabet for the first time.

She was upon another hill-slope, whose summit she had not scaled. There was always the marvellous eagerness in her heart, to climb and to see beyond. A Latin verb was virgin soil to her: she sniffed a new odour in it; it meant something, though she did not know what it meant. But she gathered it up: it was significant. When she knew that:

$$x^2 - y^2 = (x + y)(x - y)$$

then she felt that she had grasped something, that she was liberated into an intoxicating air, rare and unconditioned. And she was very glad as she wrote her French exercise:

"J'ai donné le pain à mon petit frère."

In all these things there was the sound of a bugle to her heart, exhilarating, summoning her to perfect places. She never forgot her brown "Longman's First French Grammar," nor her "Via Latina" with its red edges, nor her little grey Algebra book. There was always a magic in them.

At learning, she was quick, intelligent, instinctive, but she was not "thorough." If a thing did not come to her intuitively, she could not learn it. And then, her mad rage of loathing for all lessons, her bitter contempt of all teachers and school-mistresses, her recoil to a fierce, animal arrogance made her detestable.

She was a free, unabateable animal, she declared in her revolts: there was no law for her, nor any rule. She existed for herself alone. Then ensued a long struggle with everybody, in which she broke down at last, when she had run the full length of her resistance, and sobbed her heart out, desolate; and afterwards, in a chastened, washed-out, bodiless state, she received the understanding that would not come before, and went her way sadder and wiser.

Ursula and Gudrun went to school together. Gudrun was a shy, quiet, wild creature, a thin slip of a thing hanging back from notice or twisting past to disappear into her own world again. She seemed to avoid all contact, instinctively, and pursued her own intent way, pursuing half formed fancies that had no relation to anyone else.

She was not clever at all. She thought Ursula clever enough for two. Ursula understood, so why should she, Gudrun, bother herself? The younger girl lived her religious, responsible life in her sister, by proxy. For herself, she was indifferent and intent as a wild animal, and as irresponsible.

When she found herself at the bottom of the class, she laughed, lazily, and was content, saying she was safe now. She did not mind her father's chagrin nor her mother's twinge of mortification.

"What do I pay for you to go to Nottingham for?" her father asked, exasperated.

"Well Dad, you know you needn't pay for me," she replied, nonchalant. "I'm ready to stop at home."

She was happy at home, Ursula was not. Slim and unwilling abroad, Gudrun was easy in her own house as a wild thing in its lair. Whereas Ursula, attentive and keen abroad, at home was reluctant, uneasy, unwilling to be herself, or unable.

Nevertheless Sunday remained the maximum day of the week for both. Ursula turned passionately to it, to the sense of eternal security it gave. She suffered anguish of fears during the week-days, for she felt strong powers that would not recognise her. There was upon her always a fear and a dislike of authority. She felt she could always do as she wanted if she managed to avoid a battle with Authority and the authorised Powers. But if she gave herself away, she would be lost, destroyed. There was always the menace against her.

This strange sense of cruelty and ugliness always imminent, ready to seize hold upon her, this feeling of the grudging power of the mob lying in wait for her, who was the exception, formed one of the deepest influences of her life. Wherever she was, at school, among friends, in the street, in the train, she instinctively abated herself, made herself smaller, feigned to be less than she was, for fear that her undiscovered self should be seen, pounced upon, attacked by brutish resentment of the commonplace, the average Self.

She was fairly safe at school, now. She knew how to take her place there, and how much of herself to reserve. But she was free only on Sundays. When she was but a girl of fourteen, she began to feel a resentment growing against her in her own home. She knew she was the disturbing influence there. But as yet, on Sundays, she was free, really free, free to be herself, without fear or misgiving.

Even at its stormiest, Sunday was a blessed day. Ursula woke to it with a feeling of immense relief. She wondered why her heart was so light. Then she remembered:—it was Sunday. A gladness seemed to burst out around her, a feeling of great freedom. The whole world was for twenty four hours revoked, put back. Only the Sunday world existed.

She loved the very confusion of the household. It was lucky if the children slept till seven o'clock. Usually, soon after six, a chirp was heard, a voice, an excited chirrup began, announcing the creation of a new day, there was a thudding of quick little feet, and the children were up and about, scampering in their shirts, with pink legs and glistening, flossy hair all clean from the Saturday night's bathing, their souls excited by their bodies' cleanliness.

As the house began to teem with rushing, half naked clean children, one of the parents rose, either the mother, easy and slatternly, with her thick, dark hair loosely coiled and slipping over one ear, or the father, warm and comfortable, with ruffled black hair and shirt unbuttoned at the neck.

Then the girls upstairs heard the continual:

"Now then Billy, what are you up to?" in the father's strong, vibrating voice; or the mother's dignified:

"I have said, Cassie, I will not have it."

It was amazing how the father's voice could ring out like a gong, without his being in the least moved, and how the mother could speak like a queen holding an audience, though her blouse was sticking out all round and her hair was not fastened up and the children were yelling a pandemonium.

Gradually breakfast was produced, and the elder girls came down into the babel, whilst half naked children flitted round like the wrong ends of cherubs, as Gudrun said, watching the bare little legs and the chubby tails appearing and disappearing.

Gradually the young ones were captured, and nightdresses finally removed, ready for the clean Sunday shirt. But before the Sunday shirt was slipped over the fleecy head, away darted the naked body, to wallow in the sheep-skin which formed the parlour rug, whilst the mother walked after, protesting sharply, holding the shirt like a noose, and the father's bronze voice rang out, and the naked child wallowing on its back in the deep sheep-skin announced gleefully:

"I'm bading in the sea, mother."

"Why should I walk after you with your shirt?" said the mother. "Get up now."

"I'm bading in the sea, mother," repeated the wallowing, naked figure.

"We say bathing, not bading," said the mother, with her strange, indifferent dignity. "I am waiting here with your shirt."

At length shirts were on, and stockings were paired, and little trousers buttoned and little petticoats tied behind. The besetting cowardice of the family was its shirking of the garter question.

"Where are your garters, Cassie?"

"I don't know."

"Well look for them."

But not one of the elder Brangwens would really face the situation. After Cassie had grovelled under all the furniture and blacked up all her Sunday cleanliness, to the infinite grief of everybody, the garter was forgotten in the new washing of the young face and hands.

Later, Ursula would be indignant to see Miss Cassie marching into church from Sunday school with her stocking sluthered down to her ankle, and a grubby knee showing.

"It's disgraceful!" cried Ursula at dinner. "People will think we're pigs, and the children are *never* washed."

"Never mind what people think," said the mother superbly. "*I* see that the child is bathed properly, and if I satisfy myself I satisfy everybody. She can't keep her stocking up and no garter, and it isn't the child's fault she was let to go without one."

The garter trouble continued in varying degrees, but till each child wore long skirts or long trousers, it was not removed.

On this day of decorum, the Brangwen family went to church by the high-road, making a detour outside all the garden-hedge, rather than climb the wall into the churchyard. There was no law of this, from the parents. The children themselves were the wardens of the Sabbath decency, very jealous and instant with each other.

It came to be, gradually, that after church on Sundays the house was really something of a sanctuary, with peace breathing like a strange bird alighted in the rooms. Indoors, only reading and tale-telling and quiet pursuits, such as drawing, were allowed. Out of doors, all playing was to be carried on unobtrusively. If there were noise, yelling and shouting, then some fierce spirit woke up in the father and the elder children, so that the younger were subdued, afraid of being excommunicated.

The children themselves preserved the Sabbath. If Ursula in her vanity sang:

> "Il était un' bergère
> Et ron-ron-ron petit patapon,"

Theresa was sure to cry:

"*That's* not a Sunday song, our Ursula."

"You don't know," replied Ursula, superior. Nevertheless, she wavered. And her song faded down before she came to the end.

Because, though she did not know it, her Sunday was very precious to her. She found herself in a strange, undefined place, where her spirit could wander in dreams, unassailed.

The white-robed spirit of Christ passed between olive trees. It was a vision, not a reality. And she herself partook of the visionary being. There was a voice in the night calling "Samuel, Samuel!" And still the voice called in the night. But not this night, nor last night, but in the unfathomed night of Sunday, of the Sabbath silence.

There was Sin, the serpent, in whom was also wisdom. There was Judas with the money and the kiss.

But there was no *actual* Sin. If Ursula slapped Theresa across the face, even on a Sunday, that was not Sin, the everlasting. It was misbehaviour. If Billy played truant from Sunday school, he was bad, he was wicked, but he was not a Sinner.

Sin was absolute and everlasting: wickedness and badness were temporary and relative. When Billy, catching up the local jargon, called Cassie a "sinner," everybody detested him. Yet when there came to the Marsh a flippetty-floppetty fox-hound puppy, he was mischievously christened "Sinner."

The Brangwens shrank from applying their religion to their own immediate actions. They wanted the sense of the eternal and immortal, not a list of rules for everyday conduct. Therefore they were badly-behaved children, head-strong and arrogant, though their feelings were generous. They had moreover—intolerable to their ordinary neighbours—a proud gesture, that did not fit with the jealous idea of the democratic Christian. So that they were always extraordinary, outside of the ordinary.

How bitterly Ursula resented her first acquaintance with evangelical teachings. She got a peculiar thrill from the application of salvation to her own personal case. "Jesus died for *me*, He suffered for me." There was a pride and a thrill in it, followed almost immediately by a sense of dreariness. Jesus with holes in His hands and feet: it was distasteful to her. The shadowy Jesus with the Stigmata: that was her own vision. But Jesus the actual man, talking with teeth and lips, telling one to put one's finger into His wounds, like a villager gloating in his sores, repelled her. She was enemy of those who insisted on the humanity of Christ. If He were just a man, living in ordinary human life, then she was indifferent.

But it was the jealousy of vulgar people which must insist on the humanity of Christ. It was the vulgar mind which would allow nothing extra-human, nothing beyond itself to exist. It was the dirty, desecrating hands of the revivalists which wanted to drag Jesus into this everyday life, to dress Jesus up in trousers and frock coat, to compel Him to a vulgar equality of footing. It was the impudent suburban soul which would ask, "What would Jesus do, if He were in my shoes?"

Against all this, the Brangwens stood at bay. If anyone, it was the mother who was caught by, or who was most careless of the vulgar clamour. She would have nothing extra-human. She never really subscribed, all her life, to Brangwen's mystical passion.

But Ursula was with her father. As she became adolescent, thirteen, fourteen, she set more and more against her mother's practical indifference. To Ursula, there was something callous, almost wicked in her mother's attitude. What did Anna Brangwen, in these years, care for God or Jesus or Angels? She was the immediate life of today. Children were still being born to her, she was throng with all the little activities of her family. And almost instinctively she resented her husband's slavish service to the Church, his dark, subject hankering to worship an unseen God. What did the unrevealed God matter, when a man had a young family that needed fettling for? Let him attend to the immediate concerns of his life, not go projecting himself towards the ultimate.

But Ursula was all for the ultimate. She was always in revolt against babies and muddled domesticity. To her, Jesus was another world, He was not of this world. He did not thrust His hands under her face and, pointing to the wounds, say:

"Look, Ursula Brangwen, I got these for your sake. Now do as you're told."

To her, Jesus was beautifully remote, shining in the distance, like a white moon at sunset, a crescent moon beckoning as it follows the sun, out of our ken. Sometimes dark clouds standing very far off, pricking up into a clear yellow band of sunset, of a winter evening, reminded her of Calvary, sometimes the full moon rising blood-red upon the hill terrified her with the knowledge that Christ was now dead, hanging heavy and dead on the Cross.

On Sundays, this visionary world came to pass. She heard the long hush, she knew the marriage of dark and light was taking place. In church, the Voice sounded re-echoing not from this world, as if the church itself were a shell that still spoke the language of creation.

"The Sons of God saw the daughters of men that they were fair; and they took them wives of all which they chose.

"And the Lord said, My spirit shall not always strive with Man, for that he also is flesh; yet his days shall be an hundred and twenty years.

"There were giants in the earth in those days; and also after that, when the Sons of God came in unto the daughters of men, and they bare children unto them, the same became mighty men which were of old, men of renown."

Over this Ursula was stirred as by a call from far off. In those days, would not the Sons of God have found her fair, would she not have been taken to wife by one of the Sons of God? It was a dream that frightened her, for she could not understand it.

Who were the sons of God? Was not Jesus the only begotten Son? Was not Adam the only man created from God? Yet there were men not begotten by Adam. Who were these, and whence did they come? They too must derive from God. Had God many offspring, besides Adam and besides Jesus, children whose origin the children of Adam cannot recognise? And perhaps these children, these sons of God, had known no expulsion, no ignominy of the fall.

These came on free feet to the daughters of men, and saw they were fair, and took them to wife, so that the women conceived and brought forth men of renown. This was a genuine fate. She moved about in the essential days, when the Sons of God came in unto the daughters of men.

Nor would any comparison of myths destroy her passion in the knowledge. Jove had become a bull, or a man, in order to love a mortal woman. He had begotten in her a giant, a hero.

Very good, so he had, in Greece. For herself, she was no Grecian woman. Not Jove nor Pan nor any of those gods, not even Bacchus nor Apollo, could come to her. But the Sons of God who took to wife the daughters of men, these were such as should take her to wife.

She clung to the secret hope, the aspiration. She lived a dual life, one where the facts of daily life encompassed everything, being legion, and the other wherein the facts of daily life were superseded by the eternal truth. So utterly did she desire the Sons of God should come to the daughters of men; and she believed more in her desire and its fulfilment than in the obvious facts of life. The fact that a man was a man, did not state his descent from Adam, did not exclude that he was also one of the unhistoried, unaccountable Sons of God. As yet, she was confused, but not denied.

Again she heard the Voice:

"It is easier for a camel to go through the eye of a needle, than for a rich man to enter into heaven."

But it was explained, the needle's eye was a little gateway for foot-passengers, through which the great, humped camel with his load could not possibly squeeze himself: or perhaps, at a great risk, if he were a little camel, he might get through. For one could not absolutely exclude the rich man from heaven, said the Sunday School teacher.

It pleased her also to know, that in the East one must use hyperbole, or else remain unheard; because the Eastern man must see a thing swelling to fill all heaven, or dwindled to a mere nothing, before he is suitably impressed. She immediately sympathised with this Eastern mind.

Yet the words continued to have a meaning that was untouched either by the knowledge of gateways or hyperboles. The historical, or local, or psychological interest in the words was another thing. There remained unaltered the inexplicable value of the saying. What was this relation between a needle's eye, a rich man, and heaven? What sort of a needle's eye, what sort of a rich man, what sort of heaven? Who knows? It means the Absolute World, and can never be more than half interpreted in terms of the relative world.

But must one apply the speech literally? Was her father a rich man? Couldn't he get to heaven? Or was he only a half-rich man? Or was he nearly a poor man? At any rate, unless he gave everything away to the poor, he would find it much harder to get to heaven. The needle's eye would be tight for him. She almost wished he were penniless poor. If one were coming to the base of it, any man was rich who was not as poor as the poorest.

She had her qualms, when in imagination she saw her father giving away their piano and the two cows, and the capital at the bank, to the laborers of the district, so that they, the Brangwens, should be as poor as the Wherrys. And she did not want it. She was impatient.

"Very well," she thought, "we'll forego that heaven, that's all—at any rate the needle's eye sort." And she dismissed the problem. She was *not* going to be as poor as the Wherrys, not for all the sayings on earth—the miserable squalid Wherrys.

So she reverted to the non-literal application of the scriptures.

Her father very rarely read, but he had collected many books of reproductions, and he would sit and look at these, curiously intent, like a child, yet with a passion that was not childish. He loved the early Italian painters, but particularly Giotto and Fra Angelico and Filippo Lippi. The great compositions cast a spell over him. How many times had he turned to Raphael's "Dispute of the Sacrament" or Fra Angelico's "Last Judgment" or the beautiful, complicated renderings of the Adoration of the Magi, and always, each time, he received the same gradual fulfilment of delight. It had to do with the establishment of a whole mystical, architectural conception which used the human figure as a unit. Sometimes he had to hurry home, and go to the Fra Angelico "Last Judgment." The pathway of open graves, the huddled earth on either side, the seemly heaven arrayed above, the singing progress to paradise on the one hand, the stuttering descent to hell on the other, completed and satisfied him. He did not care whether or not he believed in devils or angels. The whole conception gave him the deepest satisfaction, and he wanted nothing more.

Ursula, accustomed to these pictures from her childhood, hunted out their detail. She adored Fra Angelico's flowers and light and angels, she liked the demons and enjoyed the hell. But the representation of the encircled God, surrounded by all the angels on high, suddenly bored her. The figure of the Most High bored her, and roused her resentment. Was this the culmination and the meaning of it all, this draped, null figure? The angels were so lovely, and the light so beautiful. And only for this, to surround such a banality for God!

She was dissatisfied, but not fit as yet to criticise. There was yet so much to wonder over. Winter came, pine branches were torn down in the snow, the green pine needles looked rich upon the ground. There was the wonderful, starry, straight track of a pheasant's foot-steps across the snow, imprinted so clear; there was the lobbing mark of the rabbit, two holes abreast, two holes following behind; the hare shoved deeper shafts, slanting, and his two hind feet came down together and made one large pit; the cat podded little holes, and birds made a lacy pattern.

Gradually there gathered the feeling of expectation. Christmas was coming. In the shed, at nights, a secret candle was burning, a sound of veiled voices was heard. The boys were learning the old mystery play of St George and Beelzebub. Twice a week, by lamplight, there was choir practice in the church, for the learning of old carols Brangwen wanted to hear. The girls went to these practices. Everywhere was a sense of mystery and rousedness. Everybody was preparing for something.

The time came near, the girls were decorating the church, with cold fingers binding holly and fir and yew about the pillars, till a new spirit was in the church, the stone broke out into dark, rich leaf, the arches put forth their buds, and cold flowers rose to blossom in the dim, mystic atmosphere. Ursula must weave mistletoe over the door, and over the screen, and hang a silver dove from a sprig of yew, till dusk came down, and the church was like a grove.

In the cow-shed the boys were blacking their faces for a dress-rehearsal; the turkey hung dead, with opened, speckled wings, in the dairy. The time was come to make pies, in readiness.

The expectation grew more tense. The star was risen into the sky, the songs, the carols were ready to hail it. The star was the sign in the sky. Earth too should give a sign. As evening drew on, hearts beat fast with anticipation, hands were full of ready gifts. There were the tremulously expectant words of the church service, the night was past and the morning was come, the gifts were given and received, joy and peace made a flapping of wings in each heart, there was a great burst of carols, the Peace of the World had dawned, strife had passed away, every hand was linked in hand, every heart was singing.

It was bitter, though, that Christmas day, as it drew on to evening, and night, became a sort of bank holiday, flat and stale. The morning was so wonderful, but in the afternoon and evening the ecstasy perished like a nipped thing, like a bud in a false spring. Alas, that Christmas was only a domestic feast, a feast of sweetmeats and toys! Why did not the grown-ups also change their everyday hearts, and give way to ecstasy? Where was the ecstasy?

How passionately the Brangwens craved for it, the ecstasy. The father was troubled, dark-faced and disconsolate, on Christmas night, because the passion was not there, because the day was become as every day, and hearts were not aflame. Upon the mother was a kind of absentness, as ever, as if she were exiled for all her life. Where was the fiery heart of joy, now the coming was fulfilled; where was the star, the Magis' transport, the thrill of new being that shook the earth?

Still it was there, even if it were faint and inadequate. The cycle of creation still wheeled in the Church year. After Christmas, the ecstasy slowly sank and changed. Sunday followed Sunday, trailing a fine movement, a finely developed transformation over the heart of the family. The heart that was big with joy, that had seen the star and had followed to the inner walls of the Nativity, that there had swooned in the great light, must now feel the light slowly withdrawing, a shadow falling, darkening. The chill crept in, silence came over the earth, and then all was darkness. The veil of the temple was rent, each heart gave up the ghost, and sank dead.

They moved quietly, a little wanness on the lips of the children, at Good Friday, feeling the shadow upon their hearts. Then, pale with a deathly scent, came the lilies of resurrection, that shone coldly till the Comforter was given.

But why the memory of the wounds and the death? Surely Christ rose with healed hands and feet, sound and strong and glad? Surely the passage of the cross and the tomb was forgotten? But no—always the memory of the wounds, always the smell of grave-cloths? A small thing was Resurrection, compared with the Cross and the death, in this cycle.

So the children lived the year of Christianity, the epic of the soul of mankind. Year by year the inner, unknown drama went on in them, their hearts were born and came to fulness, suffered on the cross, gave up the ghost, and rose again to unnumbered days, untired, having at least this rhythm of eternity in a ragged, inconsequential life.

But it was becoming a mechanical action now, this drama: birth at Christmas for death at Good Friday. On Easter Sunday the life-drama was as good as finished. For the Resurrection was shadowy and overcome by the shadow of death, the Ascension was scarce noticed, a mere confirmation of death.

What was the hope and the fulfilment? Nay, was it all only a useless after-death, a wan, bodiless after-death? Alas, and alas for the passion of the human heart, that must die so long before the body was dead.

For from the grave, after the passion and the trial of anguish, the body rose torn and chill and colourless. Did not Christ say 'Mary!' and when she turned with outstretched hands to Him, did He not hasten to add 'Touch me not; for I am not yet ascended to my father.'

Then how could the hands rejoice, or the heart be glad, seeing themselves repulsed. Alas, for the resurrection of the dead body! Alas, for the wavering, glimmering appearance of the risen Christ. Alas, for the Ascension into heaven, which is a shadow within death, a complete passing away.

Alas, that so soon the drama is over; that life is ended at thirty three; that the half of the year of the soul is cold and historiless! Alas that a risen Christ has no place with us! Alas, that the memory of the passion of Sorrow and Death and the Grave holds triumph over the pale fact of Resurrection!

But why? Why shall I not rise with my body whole and perfect, shining with strong life? Why, when Mary says: Rabboni, shall I not take her in my arms and kiss her and hold her to my breast? Why is the risen body deadly, and abhorrent with wounds?

The Resurrection is to life, not to death. Shall I not see those who have risen again walk here among men perfect in body and spirit, whole and glad in the flesh, living in the flesh, loving in the flesh, begetting children in the flesh, arrived at last to wholeness, perfect without scar or blemish, healthy without fear of ill-health? Is this not the period of manhood and of joy and fulfilment, after the Resurrection? Who shall be shadowed by Death and the Cross, being risen, and who shall fear the mystic, perfect flesh that belongs to heaven?

Can I not, then, walk this earth in gladness, being risen from sorrow? Can I not eat with my brother happily, and with joy kiss my beloved, after my resurrection, celebrate my marriage in the flesh with feastings, go about my business eagerly, in the joy of my fellows? Is heaven impatient for me, and bitter against this earth, that I should hurry off, or that I should linger pale and untouched? Is the flesh which was crucified become as poison to the crowds in the street, or is it as a strong gladness and hope to them, as the first flower blossoming out of the earth's humus?

CHAPTER XI

First Love

As Ursula passed from girlhood towards womanhood, gradually the cloud of self-responsibility gathered upon her. She became aware of herself, that she was a separate entity in the midst of an unseparated obscurity, that she must go somewhere, she must become something. And she was afraid, troubled. Why, oh why must one grow up, why must one inherit this heavy, numbing responsibility of living an undiscovered life? Out of the nothingness and the undifferentiated mass, to make something of oneself! But what? In the obscurity and pathlessness, to take a direction! But whither? How take even one step? And yet, how stand still? This was torment indeed, to inherit the responsibility of one's own life.

The religion which had been another world for her, a glorious sort of play-world, where she lived, climbing the tree with the short-statured man, walking shakily on the sea like the disciple, breaking the bread into five thousand portions, like the Lord, giving a great picnic to five thousand people, now fell away from reality, and became a tale, a myth, an illusion, which, however much one might assert it to be true in historical fact, one knew was not true—at least, for this present-day life of ours. There could, within the limits of this life we know, be no Feeding of Five Thousand. And the girl had come to the point where she held that that which one cannot experience in daily life is not true for oneself.

So, the old duality of life, wherein there had been a week-day world of people and trains and duties and reports, and besides that a Sunday world of absolute truth and living mystery, of walking upon the waters and being blinded by the face of the Lord, of following the pillar of cloud across the desert and watching the bush that crackled yet did not burn away, this old, unquestioned duality suddenly was found to be broken apart. The week-day world had triumphed over the Sunday world. The Sunday world was not real, or at least, not actual. And one lived by action.

Only the week-day world mattered. She herself, Ursula Brangwen, must know how to take the week-day life. Her body must be a week-day body, held in the world's estimate. Her soul must have a week-day value, known according to the world's knowledge.

Well then, there was a week-day life to live, of action and deeds. And so there was a necessity to choose one's action and one's deeds. One was responsible to the world for what one did.

Nay, one was more than responsible to the world. One was responsible to oneself. There was some puzzling, tormenting residue of the Sunday world within her, some persistent Sunday self, which insisted upon a relationship with the now shed-away vision world. How could one keep up a relationship with that which one denied? Her task was now to learn the week-day life.

How to act, that was the question? Whither to go, how to become oneself? One was not oneself, one was merely a half-stated question. How to become oneself, how to know the question and the answer of oneself, when one was merely an unfixed something-nothing, blowing about like the winds of heaven, undefined, unstated.

She turned to the visions, which had spoken far-off words that ran along the blood like ripples of an unseen wind, she heard the words again, she denied the vision, for she must be a week-day person, to whom visions were not true, and she demanded only the week-day meaning of the words.

There *were* words spoken by the vision: and words must have a week-day meaning, since words were week-day stuff. Let them speak now: let them bespeak themselves in week-day terms. The vision should translate itself into week-day terms.

"Sell all thou hast, and give to the poor," she heard on Sunday morning. That was plain enough, plain enough for Monday morning too. As she went down the hill to the station, going to school, she took the saying with her.

"Sell all thou hast, and give to the poor."

Did she want to do that? Did she want to sell her pearl-backed brush and mirror, her silver candlestick, her pendant, her lovely little necklace, and go dressed in drab like the Wherrys: the unlovely, uncombed Wherrys, who were "the poor" to her? She did not.

She walked this Monday morning on the verge of misery. For she *did* want to do what was right. And she *didn't* want to do what the gospels said. She didn't want to be poor—really poor. The thought was a horror to her: to live like the Wherrys, so ugly, to be at the mercy of everybody!

"Sell that thou hast, and give to the poor."

One could not do it, in real life. How dreary and hopeless it made her!

Nor could one turn the other cheek. Theresa slapped Ursula on the face. Ursula, in a mood of Christian humility, silently presented the other side of her face. Which Theresa, in exasperation at the challenge, also hit. Whereupon Ursula, with boiling heart, went meekly away.

But anger and deep, writhing shame tortured her, so she was not easy till she had again quarrelled with Theresa and had almost shaken her sister's head off.

"That'll teach *you*," she said grimly.

And she went away, unChristian but clean.

There was something unclean and degrading about this humble side of Christianity. Ursula suddenly revolted to the other extreme.

"I hate the Wherrys, and I wish they were dead. Why does my father leave us in the lurch like this, making us be poor and insignificant? Why is he not more? If we had a father as he ought to be, he would be Earl William Brangwen, and I should be the Lady Ursula. What right have *I* to be poor, crawling along the lane like vermin? If I had my rights, I should be seated on horseback in a green riding-habit, and my groom would be behind me. And I should stop at the gates of the cottages, and inquire of the cottage woman who came out with a child in her arms, how did her husband, who had hurt his foot. And I would pat the flaxen head of the child, stooping from my horse, and I would give her a shilling from my purse, and order nourishing food to be sent from the hall to the cottage."

So she rode in her pride. And sometimes, she dashed into flames to rescue a forgotten child; or she dived into the canal locks, and supported a boy who was seized with cramp; or she swept up a toddling infant from the feet of a runaway horse: always imaginatively, of course.

But in the end there returned the poignant yearning from the Sunday world. As she went down in the morning from Cossethay, and saw Ilkeston smoking blue and tender upon its hill, then her heart surged with far-off words:

"Oh Jerusalem Jerusalem—how often would I have gathered thy children together as a hen gathereth her chickens under her wings, and ye would not—"

The passion rose in her, for Christ, for the gathering under the wings of security and warmth. But how did it apply to the week-day world? What could it mean, but that Christ should clasp her to his breast, as a mother clasps her child? And Oh, for Christ, for him who could hold her to his breast and lose her there. Oh, for the breast of Man, where she should have refuge and bliss for ever! All her senses quivered with passionate yearning.

Vaguely, she knew that Christ meant something else: that in the vision world, He spoke of Jerusalem, something that did not exist in the everyday world. It was not houses and factories He would hold in His bosom: nor householders nor factory-workers nor poor people: but something that had no part in the week-day world, not seen nor touched with week-day hands and eyes.

Yet she *must* have it in week-day terms—she must. For all her life was a week-day life, now, this was the whole. So he must gather her body to his breast, that was strong with a broad bone, and which sounded with the beating of the heart, and which was warm with this life of which she partook, the life of the running blood.

So she craved for the breast of the Son of Man, to lie there. And she was ashamed in her soul, ashamed. For whereas Christ spoke for the Vision to answer, she answered from the week-day fact. It was a betrayal, a transference of meaning, from the vision world, to the matter-of-fact world. So she was ashamed of her religious ecstasy, and dreaded lest anyone should see it.

Early in the year, when the lambs came, and shelters were built of straw, and on her uncle's farm the men sat at night with a lantern and a dog, then again there swept over her this passionate confusion between the vision world and the week-day world. Again she felt Jesus in the countryside. Ah, he would lift up the lambs in his arms! Ah, and she was the lamb. Again, in the morning, going down the lane, she heard the ewe call, and the lambs came running, shaking and twinkling with new-born bliss. And she saw them stooping, nuzzling, groping to the udder, to find the teats, whilst the mother turned her head gravely and sniffed her own. And they were sucking, vibrating with bliss on their little, long legs, their throats stretched up, their new bodies quivering to the stream of blood-warm, loving milk.

Oh, and the bliss, the bliss! She could scarcely tear herself away to go to school. The little noses nuzzling at the udder, the little bodies so glad and sure, the little black legs crooked, the mother standing still, yielding herself to their quivering attraction—then the mother walked calmly away.

Jesus—the vision world—the everyday world—all mixed inextric-
ably in a confusion of pain and bliss. It was almost agony, the
confusion, the inextricability. Jesus, the vision, speaking to her, who
was non-visionary! And she would take His words of the spirit and
make them to pander to her own carnality.

This was a shame to her. The confusing of the spirit world with
the material world, in her own soul, degraded her. She answered the
call of the spirit in terms of immediate, everyday desire.

"Come unto me, all ye that labour and are heavy laden, and I will
give you rest."

It was the temporal answer she gave. She leapt with sensuous
yearning, to respond to Christ. If she could go to him really, and lay
her head on his breast, to have comfort, to be made much of,
caressed like a child!

All the time she walked in a confused heat of religious yearning.
She wanted Jesus to love her deliciously, to take her sensuous
offering, to give her sensuous response. For weeks she went in a
muse of enjoyment.

And all the time she knew underneath that she was playing false,
accepting the passion of Jesus for her own physical satisfaction. But
she was in such a daze, such a tangle. How could she get free?

She hated herself, she wanted to trample on herself, destroy
herself. How could one become free? She hated religion, because it
lent itself to her confusion. She abused everything. She wanted to
become hard, indifferent, brutally callous to everything but just the
immediate need, the immediate satisfaction. To have a yearning
towards Jesus, only that she might use him to pander to her own soft
sensation, use him as a means of re-acting upon herself, maddened
her in the end. There was then no Jesus, no sentimentality. With all
the bitter hatred of helplessness she hated sentimentality.

At this period came the young Skrebensky. She was nearly sixteen
years old, a slim, smouldering girl, deeply reticent, yet lapsing into
unreserved expansiveness now and then, when she seemed to give
away her whole soul, but when in fact she only made another
counterfeit of her soul for outward presentation. She was sensitive in
the extreme, always tortured, always affecting a callous indifference
to screen herself.

She was at this time a nuisance on the face of the earth, with her
spasmodic passion and her slumberous torment. She seemed to go
with all her soul in her hands, yearning, to the other person. Yet all

the while, deep at the bottom of her, was a childish antagonism of mistrust. She thought she loved everybody and believed in everybody. But because she could not love herself nor believe in herself, she mistrusted everybody with the mistrust of a serpent or a captured bird. Her starts of revulsion and hatred were more inevitable than her impulses to love.

So she wrestled through her dark days of confusion, soulless, uncreated, unformed.

One evening, as she was studying in the parlour, her head buried in her hands, she heard new voices in the kitchen speaking. At once, from its apathy, her excitable spirit started and strained to listen. It seemed to crouch, to lurk under cover, tense, glaring forth unwilling to be seen.

There were two strange men's voices, one soft and candid, veiled with soft candour, the other veiled with easy mobility, running quickly. Ursula sat quite tense, shocked out of her studies, lost. She listened all the time to the sound of the voices, scarcely heeding the words.

The first speaker was her uncle Tom. She knew the naïve candour covering the girding and savage misery of his soul. Who was the other speaker, whose voice ran on so easy, yet with an inflamed pulse? It seemed to hasten and urge her forward, that other voice.

"I remember you," the young man's voice was saying. "I remember you from the first time I saw you, because of your dark eyes and fair face."

Mrs Brangwen laughed, shy and pleased.

"You were a curly-headed little lad," she said.

"Was I? Yes, I know. They were very proud of my curls."

And a laugh ran to silence.

"You were a very well-mannered lad, I remember," said her father.

"Oh! Did I ask you to stay the night? I always used to ask people to stay the night. I believe it was rather trying for my mother."

There was a general laugh. Ursula rose. She had to go.

At the click of the latch everybody looked round. The girl hung in the doorway, seized with a moment's fierce confusion. She was going to be good-looking. Now, she had an attractive gawkiness, as she hung a moment, not knowing how to carry her shoulders. Her dark hair was tied behind, her yellow-brown eyes shone without direction.

Behind her, in the parlour, was the soft light of a lamp upon open books.

A superficial readiness took her to her uncle Tom, who kissed her, greeting her with warmth, making a show of intimate possession of her, and at the same time leaving evident his own complete detachment.

But she wanted to turn to the stranger. He was standing back a little, waiting. He was a young man with very clear greyish eyes that waited until they were called upon, before they took expression.

Something in his self-possessed waiting moved her, and she broke into a confused, rather beautiful laugh as she gave him her hand, catching her breath like an excited child. His hand closed over hers very close, very near, he bowed, and his eyes were watching her with some attention. She felt proud, her spirit leapt to life.

"You don't know Mr Skrebensky, Ursula," came her uncle Tom's intimate voice. She lifted her face with an impulsive flash to the stranger, as if to declare a knowledge, laughing her palpitating, excited laugh.

His eyes became confused with roused lights, his detached attention changed to a readiness for her. He was a young man of twenty one, with a slender figure and soft brown hair brushed up in the German fashion straight from his brow.

"Are you staying long?" she asked.

"I've got a month's leave," he said, glancing at Tom Brangwen. "But I've various places I must go to—put in some time here and there."

He brought her a strong sense of the outer world. It was as if she were set on a hill and could feel, vaguely, the whole world lying spread before her.

"What have you a month's leave from?" she asked.

"I'm in the Engineers—in the army."

"Oh!" she exclaimed, glad.

"We're taking *you* away from your studies," said her uncle Tom.

"Oh no," she replied quickly.

Skrebensky laughed, young and inflammable.

"She won't wait to be taken away," said her father.

But that seemed clumsy. She wished he would leave her to say her own things.

"Don't you like study?" asked Skrebensky, turning to her, putting the question from his own case.

"I like some things," said Ursula. "I like Latin and French—and grammar."

He watched her, and all his being seemed attentive to her, then he shook his head.

"I don't," he said. "They say all the brains of the army are in the Engineers. I think that's why I joined them—to get the credit of other people's brains."

He said this quizzically and with chagrin. And she became alert to him. It interested her. Whether he had brains or not, he was interesting. His directness attracted her, his independent motion. She was aware of the movement of his life over against her.

"I don't think brains matter," she said.

"What does matter then?" came her uncle Tom's intimate, caressing, half-jeering voice.

She turned to him.

"It matters whether people have courage or not," she said.

"Courage for what?" asked her uncle.

"For everything."

Tom Brangwen gave a sharp little laugh. The mother and father sat silent, with listening faces. Skrebensky waited. She was speaking for him.

"Everything's nothing," laughed her uncle.

She disliked him at that moment.

"She doesn't practise what she preaches," said her father, stirring in his chair and crossing one leg over the other. "She has courage for mighty little."

But she would not answer. Skrebensky sat still, waiting. His face was irregular, almost ugly, flattish, with a rather thick nose. But his eyes were pellucid, strangely clear, his brown hair was soft and thick as silk, he had a slight moustache. His skin was fine, his figure slight, beautiful. Beside him, her uncle Tom looked full-blown, her father seemed uncouth. Yet he reminded her of her father, only he was finer, and he seemed to be shining. And his face was almost ugly.

He seemed simply acquiescent in the fact of his own being, as if he were beyond any change or question. He was himself. There was a sense of fatality about him that fascinated her. He made no effort to prove himself to other people. Let it be accepted for what it was, his own being. In its isolation it made no excuse or explanation for itself.

So he seemed perfectly, even fatally established, he did not ask to be rendered before he could exist, before he could have relationship with another person.

This attracted Ursula very much. She was so used to unsure people who took on a new being with every new influence. Her uncle Tom was always more or less what the other person would have him. In consequence, one never knew the real uncle Tom, only a fluid, unsatisfactory flux with a more or less consistent appearance.

But, let Skrebensky do what he would, betray himself entirely, he betrayed himself always upon his own responsibility. He permitted no question about himself. He was irrevocable in his isolation.

So Ursula thought him wonderful, he was so finely constituted, and so distinct, self-contained, self-supporting. This, she said to herself, was a gentleman, he had a nature like fate, the nature of an aristocrat.

She laid hold on him at once for her dreams. Here was one such as those Sons of God who saw the daughters of men, that they were fair. He was no son of Adam. Adam was servile. Had not Adam been driven cringing out of his native place, had not the human race been a beggar ever since, seeking its own being. But Anton Skrebensky could not beg. He was in possession of himself, of that, and no more. Other people could not really give him anything nor take anything from him. His soul stood alone.

She knew that her mother and father acknowledged him. The house was changed. There had been a Visit paid to the house. Once three angels stood in Abraham's doorway, and greeted him, and stayed and ate with him, leaving his household enriched for ever when they went.

The next day she went down to the Marsh according to invitation. The two men were not come home. Then, looking through the window, she saw the dog-cart drive up and Skrebensky leapt down. She saw him draw himself together, jump, laugh to her uncle, who was driving, then come towards her, to the house. He was so spontaneous and revealed in his movements. He was isolated within his own clear, fine atmosphere, and as still as if fated.

His resting in his own fate gave him an appearance of indolence, almost of languor: he made no exuberant movement. When he sat down, he seemed to go loose, languid.

"We are a little late," he said.

"Where have you been?"

"We went to Derby to see a friend of my father's."

"Who?"

It was an adventure to her to put direct questions and get plain answers. She knew she might do it with this man.

"Why, he is a clergyman too—he is my guardian—one of them."

Ursula knew that Skrebensky was an orphan.

"Where is really your home, now?" she asked.

"My home?—I wonder. I am very fond of my colonel—Colonel Hepburn: then there are my aunts: but my real home, I suppose, is the army."

"Do you like being on your own?"

His clear, greenish grey eyes rested on her a moment, and, as he considered, he did not see her.

"I suppose so," he said. "You see my father—well, he was never acclimatised here. He wanted—I don't know what he wanted, but it was a strain. And my mother—I always knew she was too good to me. I could feel her being too good to me—my mother! Then I went away to school so early. And I must say, the outside world was always more naturally a home to me than the vicarage—I don't know why."

"Do you feel like a bird blown out of its own latitude?" she asked, using a phrase she had met.

"No—no. I find everything very much as I like it."

He seemed more and more to give her a sense of the vast world, a sense of distances and large masses of humanity. It drew her as a scent draws a bee from afar. But also it hurt her.

It was summer, and she wore cotton frocks. The third time he saw her she had on a dress with fine blue and white stripes, with a white collar, and a large white hat. It suited her golden, warm complexion.

"I like you best in that dress," he said, standing with his head slightly on one side, and appreciating her in a perceiving, critical fashion.

She was thrilled with a new life. For the first time, she was in love with a vision of herself: she saw as it were a fine little reflection of herself in his eyes. And she must act up to this: she must be beautiful. Her thoughts turned swiftly to clothes, her passion was to make a beautiful appearance. Her family looked on in amazement at the sudden transformation of Ursula. She became elegant, really elegant, in figured cotton frocks she made for herself, and hats she bent to her fancy. An inspiration was upon her.

He sat with a sort of languor in her grandmother's rocking chair, rocking slowly, languidly backward and forward, as Ursula talked to him.

"You are not poor, are you?" she said.

"Poor in money? I have about a hundred and fifty a year of my own—so I am poor or rich, as you like. I am poor enough, in fact."

"But you will earn money?"

"I shall have my pay—I have my pay now. I've got my commission. That is another hundred and fifty."

"You will have more though."

"I shan't have more than £200 a year for ten years to come. I shall always be poor, if I have to live on my pay."

"Do you mind?"

"Being poor? Not now—not very much. I may later. People—the officers, are good to me. Colonel Hepburn has a sort of fancy for me—he is a rich man, I suppose."

A chill went over Ursula. Was he going to sell himself, in some way?

"Is Colonel Hepburn married?"

"Yes—with two daughters."

But she was too proud at once to care whether Colonel Hepburn's daughter wanted to marry him or not.

There came a silence. Gudrun entered, and Skrebensky still rocked languidly in the chair.

"You look very lazy," said Gudrun.

"I am lazy," he answered.

"You look really floppy," she said.

"I am floppy," he answered.

"Can't you stop?" asked Gudrun.

"No—it's the *perpetuum mobile*."

"You look as if you hadn't a bone in your body."

"That's how I like to feel."

"I don't admire your taste."

"That's my misfortune."

And he rocked on.

Gudrun seated herself behind him, and as he rocked back, she caught his hair between her finger and thumb, so that it tugged him as he swung forward again. He took no notice. There was only the sound of the rockers on the floor. In silence, like a crab, Gudrun caught a strand of his hair each time he rocked back. Ursula flushed, and sat in some pain. She saw the irritation gathering on his brow.

At last he leapt up, suddenly, like a steel spring going off, and stood on the hearthrug.

"Damn it, *why* can't I rock?" he asked petulantly, fiercely.

Ursula loved him for his sudden, steel-like start out of the languor. He stood on the hearthrug fuming, his eyes gleaming with anger.

Gudrun laughed in her deep, mellow fashion.

"Men don't rock themselves," she said.

"Girls don't pull men's hair," he said.

Gudrun laughed again.

Ursula sat amused, but waiting. And he knew Ursula was waiting for him. It roused his blood. He had to go to her, to follow her call.

Once he drove her to Derby in the dog-cart. He belonged to the horsey set of the sappers. They had lunch in an inn, and went through the market, pleased with everything. He bought her a copy of "Wuthering Heights" from a book-stall. Then they found a little fair in progress, and she said:

"My father used to take me in the swingboats."

"Did you like it?" he asked.

"Oh, it was fine!" she said.

"Would you like to go now?"

"Love it," she said, though she was afraid. But the prospect of doing an unusual, exciting thing was too attractive for her.

He went straight to the stand, paid the money, and helped her to mount. He seemed to ignore everything but just what he was doing. Other people were mere objects of indifference to him. She would have liked to hang back, but she was more ashamed to retreat from him than to expose herself to the crowd or to dare the swingboat. His eyes laughed, and standing before her with his sharp, sudden figure, he set the boat swinging. She was not afraid, she was thrilled. His colour flushed, his eyes shone with a roused light, and she looked up at him, her face like a flower in the sun, so bright and attractive. So they rushed through the bright air, up at the sky as if flung from a catapult, then falling terribly back. She loved it. The motion seemed to fan their blood to fire, they laughed, feeling like flames.

After the swingboats, they went on the roundabouts to calm down, he twisting astride on his jerky wooden steed, towards her, and always seeming at his ease, enjoying himself. A zest of antagonism to the convention made him fully himself. As they sat on the whirling carousel, with the music grinding out, she was aware of the people on the earth outside, and it seemed that he and she were riding carelessly over the faces of the crowd, riding forever buoyantly, proudly, gallantly over the upturned faces of the crowd, moving on a higher level, spurning the common mass.

When they must descend and walk away, she was unhappy, feeling like a giant suddenly cut down to ordinary level, at the mercy of the mob.

They left the fair, to return for the dog-cart. Passing the large church, Ursula must look in. But the whole interior was filled with scaffolding, fallen stone and rubbish were heaped on the floor, bits of plaster crunched underfoot, and the place re-echoed to the calling of secular voices and to blows of the hammer.

She had come to plunge in the utter gloom and peace for a moment, bringing all her yearning, that had returned on her uncontrolled after the reckless riding over the face of the crowd, in the fair. After pride, she wanted comfort, solace, for pride and scorn seemed to hurt her most of all.

And she found the immemorial gloom full of bits of falling plaster and dust of floating plaster, smelling of old lime, having scaffolding and rubbish heaped about, dust cloths over the altar.

"Let us sit down a minute," she said.

They sat unnoticed in the back pew, in the gloom, and she watched the dirty, disorderly work of bricklayers and plasterers. Workmen in heavy boots walked grinding down the aisles, calling out in a vulgar accent:

"Hi, mate, has them corner mouldin's come?"

There were shouts of coarse answer from the roof of the church. The place echoed desolate.

Skrebensky sat close to her. Everything seemed wonderful, if dreadful, to her, the world tumbling into ruins, and she and he clambering unhurt, lawless over the face of it all. He sat close to her, touching her, and she was aware of his influence upon her. But she was glad. It excited her to feel the press of him upon her, as if his being were urging her to something.

As they drove home, he sat near to her. And when he swayed to the cart, he swayed in a voluptuous, lingering way, against her, lingering as he swung away to recover balance. Without speaking, he took her hand across, under the wrap, and with his unseeing face lifted to the road, his soul intent, he began with his one hand to unfasten the buttons of her glove, to push back her glove from her hand, carefully, laying bare her hand. And the close-working, instinctive subtlety of his fingers upon her hand sent the young girl mad with voluptuous delight. His hand was so wonderful, intent as a living creature skilfully pushing and manipulating in the dark underworld, removing her glove and laying bare her palm, her fingers. Then his hand closed over hers, so firm, so close, as if the flesh knitted to one thing, his hand and hers. Meanwhile his face watched the road and the ears of the horse, he drove with steady attention through the villages, and she sat beside him, rapt, glowing, blinded with a new light. Neither of them spoke. In outward attention they were entirely separate. But between them was the compact of his flesh with hers, in the hand-clasp.

Then, in a strange voice, affecting nonchalance and superficiality, he said to her:

"Sitting in the church there reminded me of Ingram."

"Who is Ingram?" she asked.

She also affected calm superficiality. But she knew that something forbidden was coming.

"He is one of the other men with me down at Chatham—a subaltern—but a year older than I am."

"And why did the church remind you of him?"

"Well—he had a girl in Rochester, and they always sat in a particular corner in the cathedral for their love-making."

"How nice!" she cried impulsively.

They misunderstood each other.

"It had its disadvantages, though. The verger made a row about it."

"What a shame! Why shouldn't they sit in a cathedral?"

"I suppose they all think it a profanity—except you and Ingram and the girl."

"I don't think it a profanity—I think it's right, to make love in a cathedral."

She said this almost defiantly, in despite of her own soul.

He was silent.

"And was she nice?"

"Who, Emily? Yes, she was rather nice. She was a milliner, and she wouldn't be seen in the streets with Ingram. It was rather sad, really, because the verger spied on them, and got to know their names, and then made a regular row. It was a common tale afterwards."

"What did she do?"

"She went to London, into a big shop. Ingram still goes up to see her."

"Does he love her?"

"It's a year and a half he's been with her now."

"What was she like?"

"Emily? Little, shy-violet sort of girl with nice eyebrows."

Ursula meditated this. It seemed like real romance of the outer world.

"Do all the men have lovers?" she asked, amazed at her own temerity. But her hand was still fastened with his, and his face still had the same unchanging fixity of outward calm.

"They're always mentioning some amazing fine woman or other, and getting drunk to talk about her. Most of them dash up to London the moment they are free."

"What for?"

"To some amazing fine woman or other."

"What sort of women?"

"Various. Her name changes pretty frequently, as a rule. One of the fellows is a perfect maniac. He keeps a suit-case always ready, and the instant he is at liberty, he bolts with it to the station, and changes in the train. No matter who is in the carriage, off he whips his tunic, and performs at least the top half of his toilet."

Ursula quivered, and wondered.

"Why is he in such a hurry?" she asked.

Her throat was becoming hard and difficult.

"He's got a woman in his mind, I suppose."

She was chilled, hardened. And yet this world of passions and lawlessness was fascinating to her. It seemed to her a splendid recklessness. Her adventure in life was beginning. It seemed very splendid.

That evening she stayed at the Marsh till after dark, and Skrebensky escorted her home. For she could not go away from him. And she was waiting, waiting for something more.

In the warm of the early night, with the shadows new about them, she felt in another, harder, more beautiful, less personal world. Now a new state should come to pass.

He walked near to her, and with the same silent, intent approach, put his arm round her waist, and softly, very softly, insidiously, drew her to him, till his arm was hard and pressed in upon her; she seemed to be carried along, floating, her feet scarce touching the ground, borne upon the firm, moving surface of his body, upon whose side she seemed to lie, in a delicious swoon of motion. And whilst she swooned, his face bent nearer to her, her head was leaned on his shoulder, she felt his warm breath on her face. Then softly, oh softly, so softly that she seemed to faint away, his lips touched her cheek, and she drifted through strands of heat and darkness.

Still, she waited, in her swoon and her drifting, waited, like the Sleeping Beauty in the story. She waited, and again his face was bent to hers, his lips came warm on her face, their footsteps lingered and ceased, they stood still under the trees, whilst his lips waited on her face, waited like a butterfly that does not move on a flower. She pressed her breast a little nearer to him, he moved, put both his arms round her, and drew her close.

And then, in the darkness, he bent to her mouth, softly, and touched her mouth with his mouth. She was afraid, she lay still on his arms, feeling his lips on her lips. She kept still, helpless. Then his mouth drew near, pressing open her mouth, a hot, drenching surge rose within her, she opened her lips to him, in pained, poignant eddies she drew him nearer, she let him come further, his lips came and surging, surging, soft, oh soft, yet oh, like the powerful surge of water, irresistible, till with a little blind cry, she broke away.

She heard him breathing heavily, strangely, beside her. A terrible and magnificent sense of his strangeness possessed her. But she shrank a little now, within herself. Hesitating, they continued to walk on, quivering like shadows under the ash-trees of the hill, where her grandfather had walked with his daffodils to make his proposal, and where her mother had gone with her young husband, walking close upon him as Ursula was now walking upon Skrebensky.

Ursula was aware of the dark limbs of the trees stretching overhead, clothed with leaves, and of fine ash-leaves tressing the summer night.

They walked with their bodies moving in complex unity, close together. He held her hard, and they went the long way round by the road, to be further. Always she felt as if she were supported off her feet, as if her feet were light as little breezes in motion.

He would kiss her again—but not again that night with the same, deep-reaching kiss. She was aware now, aware of what a kiss might be. And so, it was more difficult to come to him.

She went to bed feeling all warm with electric warmth, as if the gush of dawn were within her, upholding her. And she slept deeply, sweetly, oh, so sweetly. In the morning she felt sound as an ear of wheat, fragrant and firm and full.

They continued to be lovers, in the first, wondering state of unrealisation. Ursula told nobody: she was entirely lost in her own world.

Yet some strange affectation made her seek for a spurious confidence. She had at school a quiet, meditative, serious-souled friend called Ethel, and to Ethel must Ursula confide the story. Ethel listened absorbedly, with bowed, unbetraying head, whilst Ursula told her secret. Oh, it was so lovely, his gentle, delicate way of making love! Ursula talked like a practised lover.

"Do you think," asked Ursula, "it is wicked to let a man kiss you—*real* kisses, not flirting?"

"I should think," said Ethel, "it depends."

"He kissed me under the ash-trees on Cossethay hill—do you think it was wrong?"

"When?"

"On Thursday night when he was seeing me home—but real kisses—real—. He is an officer in the army."

"What time was it?" asked the deliberate Ethel.

"I don't know—about half past nine."

There was a pause.

"*I* think it's wrong," said Ethel, lifting her head with impatience. "You don't *know* him."

She spoke with some contempt.

"Yes I do. He is half a Pole, and a Baron too. In England he is equivalent to a Lord. My grandmother was his father's friend."

But the two friends were hostile. It was as if Ursula *wanted* to divide herself from her acquaintances, in asserting her connection with Anton, as she now called him.

He came a good deal to Cossethay, because her mother was fond of him. Anna Brangwen became something of a *grande dame* with Skrebensky, very calm, taking things for granted.

"Aren't the children in bed?" cried Ursula petulantly as she came in with the young man.

"They will be in bed in half an hour," said her mother.

"There is *no* peace," cried Ursula.

"The children must *live*, Ursula," said her mother.

And Skrebensky was against Ursula in this. Why should she be so insistent?

But then, as Ursula knew, he did not have the perpetual tyranny of young children about him. He treated her mother with great courtliness, to which Mrs Brangwen returned an easy, friendly hospitality. Something pleased the girl in her mother's calm assumption of state. It seemed impossible to abate Mrs Brangwen's position. She could never be beneath anyone in public relation. Between Brangwen and Skrebensky there was an unbridgeable silence. Sometimes the two men made a slight conversation, but there was no interchange. Ursula rejoiced to see her father retreating into himself against the young man.

She was proud of Skrebensky in the house. His lounging, languorous indifference irritated her and yet cast a spell over her. She knew it was the outcome of a spirit of *laisser-aller* combined with profound young vitality. Yet it irritated her deeply.

Notwithstanding, she was proud of him as he lounged in his lambent fashion in her home, he was so attentive and courteous to her mother and to herself all the time. It was wonderful to have his awareness in the room. She felt rich and augmented by it, as if she were the positive attraction and he the flow towards her. And his courtesy and his agreement might be all her mother's, but the lambent flicker of his body was for herself. She held it.

She must even prove her power.

"I meant to show you my little wood-carving," she said.

"I'm sure it's not worth showing, that," said her father.

"Would you like to see it?" she asked, leaning towards the door.

And his body had risen from the chair, though his face seemed to want to agree with her parents.

"It is in the shed," she said.

And he followed her out of the door, whatever his feelings might be.

In the shed they played at kisses, really played at kisses. It was a delicious, exciting game. She turned to him, her face all laughing, like a challenge. And he accepted the challenge at once. He twined his hand full of her hair, and gently, with his hand wrapped round with hair behind her head, gradually brought her face nearer to his, whilst she laughed breathless with challenge, and his eyes gleamed with answer, with enjoyment of the game. And he kissed her, asserting his will over her, and she kissed him back, asserting her deliberate enjoyment of him. Daring and reckless and dangerous they knew it was, their game, each playing with fire, not with love. A sort of defiance of all the world possessed her in it—she would kiss him just because she wanted to. And a dare-devilry in him, like a cynicism, a cut at everything he pretended to serve, retaliated in him.

She was very beautiful then, so wide opened, so radiant, so palpitating, exquisitely vulnerable and poignantly, wrongly throwing herself to risk. It roused a sort of madness in him. Like a flower shaking and wide opened in the sun, she tempted him and challenged him, and he accepted her challenge, something went fixed in him. And under all her laughing, poignant, reckless, was the quiver of tears. That almost sent him mad, mad with desire, with pain, whose only issue was through possession of her body.

So, shaken, afraid, they went back to her parents in the kitchen, and dissimulated. But something was roused in both of them that they could not now allay. It intensified and heightened their senses, they were more vivid and powerful in their being. But under it all, was a poignant sense of transience. It was a magnificent self-assertion on the part of both of them, he asserted himself before her, he felt himself infinitely male and infinitely irresistible, she asserted herself before him, she knew herself infinitely desirable and hence infinitely strong. And after all, what could either of them get from such a passion but a sense of his or of her own maximum self, in contradistinction to all the rest of life? Wherein was something finite and sad, for the human soul at its maximum wants a sense of the infinite.

Nevertheless, it was begun, now, this passion, and must go on, the passion of Ursula to know her own maximum self, limited and so defined against him. She could limit and define herself against him, the male, she could be her maximum self, female, oh female, triumphant for one moment in exquisite assertion against the male, in supreme contradistinction to the male.

The next afternoon, when he came, prowling, she went with him across to the church. Her father was gradually gathering in anger against him, her mother was hardening in anger against her. But the parents were naturally tolerant in action.

They went together across the churchyard, Ursula and Skrebensky, and ran to hiding in the church. It was dimmer in there than the sunny afternoon outside, but the mellow glow among the bowed stone was very sweet. The windows burned in ruby and in blue, they made magnificent arras to their bower of secret stone.

"What a perfect place for a *rendez-vous*," he said, in a hushed voice, glancing round.

She too glanced round the familiar interior. The dimness and stillness chilled her. But her eyes lit up with daring. Here, here she would assert her indomitable, gorgeous female self, here. Here she would open her female flower like a flame, in this dimness that was more passionate than light.

They hung apart a moment, then wilfully turned to each other for the desired contact. She put her arms round him, she cleaved her body to his, and with her hands pressed upon his shoulders, on his back, she seemed to feel right through him, to know his young, tense body right through. And it was so fine, so hard, yet so exquisitely subject and under her control. She reached him her mouth and drank his full kiss, drank it fuller and fuller.

And it was good, it was very, very good. She seemed to be filled with his kiss, filled as if she had drunk strong, glowing sunshine. She glowed all inside, the sunshine seemed to beat upon her heart underneath, she had drunk so beautifully.

She drew away, and looked at him radiant, exquisitely, glowingly beautiful, and satisfied, but radiant as an illumined cloud.

To him this was bitter, that she was so radiant and satisfied. She laughed upon him, blind to him, so full of her own bliss, never doubting but that he was the same as she was. And radiant as an angel she went with him out of the church, as if her feet were beams of light that walked on flowers for footsteps.

He went beside her, his soul clenched, his body unsatisfied. Was she going to make this easy triumph over him? For him, there was now no self-bliss, only pain and confused anger.

It was high summer, and the hay-harvest was almost over. It would be finished on Saturday. On Saturday however Skrebensky was going away. He could not stay any longer.

Having decided to go, he became very tender and loving to her, kissing her gently, with such soft, sweet, insidious closeness that they were both of them intoxicated.

The very last Friday of his stay, he met her coming out of school and took her to tea in the town. Then he had a motor-car to drive her home.

Her excitement at riding in a motor-car was greatest of all. He too was very proud of this last *coup*. He saw Ursula kindle and flare up to the romance of the situation, she raised her head like a young horse snuffing with wild delight.

The car swerved round a corner, and Ursula was swung against Skrebensky. The contact made her aware of him. With a swift, foraging impulse she sought for his hand and clasped it in her own, so close, so combined, as if they were two children. But they were more than two children.

The wind blew in on Ursula's face, the mud flew in a soft, wild rush from the wheels, the country was blackish green, with the silver of new hay here and there, and masses of trees under a silver-gleaming sky.

Her hand tightened on his with a new consciousness, troubled. They did not speak for some time but sat, handfast, with averted, shining faces.

And every now and then the car swung her against him. And they waited for the motion to bring them together. Yet they stared out of the windows, mute.

She saw the familiar country racing by. But now, it was no familiar country, it was wonderland. There was the Hemlock Stone standing on its grassy hill. Strange, it looked, on this wet, early summer evening, remote, in a magic land. Some rooks were flying out of the trees.

Ah, if only she and Skrebensky could get out, dismount into this enchanted land where nobody had ever been before! Then they would be enchanted people, they would put off the dull, customary self. If she were wandering there, on that hill-slope under a silvery, changing sky, in which many rooks melted like hurrying showers of blots! If they could walk past the wetted hay-swaths, smelling the early evening, and pass in to the wood where the honeysuckle scent was sweet on the cold tang of the air, and showers of drops fell when one brushed a bough, cold and lovely on the face!

But she was here with him in the car, close to him, and the wind was rushing on her lifted, eager face, blowing back the hair. He turned and looked at her, at her face clean as a chiselled thing, her hair chiselled back by the wind, her fine nose keen and lifted.

It was agony to him, seeing her swift and clean-cut and virgin. He wanted to kill himself, and throw his detested carcase at her feet. His desire to turn round on himself and rend himself was an agony to him.

Suddenly she glanced at him. He seemed to be crouching towards her, reaching, he seemed to wince between the brows. But instantly, seeing her lighted eyes and radiant face, his expression changed, his old, reckless laugh shone to her. She pressed his hand in utter delight, and he abided. And suddenly she stooped and kissed his hand, bent her head and caught it to her mouth, in generous homage. And the blood burned in him. Yet he remained still, he made no move.

She started. They were swinging into Cossethay. Skrebensky was going to leave her. But it was all so magic, her cup was so full of bright wine, her eyes could only shine.

He tapped, and spoke to the man. The car swung up by the yew-trees. She gave him her hand and said goodbye, naïve and brief as a school-girl. And she stood watching him go, her face shining. The fact of his driving on meant nothing to her, she was so filled by her own bright ecstasy. She did not see him go, for she was filled with light, which was of him. Bright with an amazing light as she was, how could she miss him?

In her bedroom she threw her arms in the air in clear pain of magnificence. Oh, it was her transfiguration, she was beyond herself. She wanted to fling herself into all the hidden brightness of the air. It was there, it was there! If she could but meet it.

But the next day, she knew he had gone. Her glory had partly died down—but never from her memory. It was too real. Yet it was gone by, leaving a wistfulness. A deeper yearning came into her soul, a new reserve.

She shrank from touch and question. She was very proud, but very new, and very sensitive. Oh, that no-one should lay hands on her!

She was happiest running on by herself. Oh, it was a joy to run along the lanes without seeing things, yet being with them. It was such a joy to be alone with all one's riches.

The holidays came, when she was free. She spent most of her time running on by herself, curled up in a squirrel-place in the garden, lying in a hammock in the coppice, while the birds came near—near,—so near. Or, in rainy weather, she flitted to the Marsh, and lay hidden with her book in a hay-loft.

All the time, she dreamed of him, sometimes definitely, but when she was happiest, only vaguely. He was the warm colouring to her dreams, he was the hot blood beating within them.

When she was less happy, out of sorts, she pondered over his appearance, his clothes, the button with his regimental badge, which he had given her. Or she tried to imagine his life in barracks. Or she conjured up a vision of herself as she appeared in his eyes.

His birthday was in August, and she spent some pains on making him a cake. She felt that it would not be in good taste for her to give him a present.

Their correspondence was brief, mostly an exchange of post-cards, not at all frequent. But with her cake she must send him a letter.

"Dear Anton—The sunshine has come back specially for your birthday, I think.

I made the cake myself, and wish you many happy returns of the day. Don't eat it if it isn't good. Mother hopes you will come and see us when you are near enough,

I am

Your sincere friend

Ursula Brangwen."

It bored her to write a letter even to him. After all, writing words on paper had nothing to do with him and her.

The fine weather had set in, the cutting machine went on from dawn till sunset, chattering round the fields. She heard from Skrebensky; he too was on duty in the country, on Salisbury Plain. He was now a second lieutenant in a Field Troop. He would have a few days off shortly, and would come to the Marsh for the wedding.

Fred Brangwen was going to marry a school-mistress out of Ilkeston, as soon as corn-harvest was at an end.

The dim, blue-and-gold of a hot, sweet autumn saw the close of the corn-harvest. To Ursula, it was as if the world had opened its softest, purest flower, its chicory flower, its meadow saffron. The sky was blue and sweet, the yellow leaves down the lane seemed like free, wandering flowers as they chittered round the feet, making a keen, poignant, almost unbearable music to her heart. And the scents of autumn were like a summer madness to her. She fled away from the little, purple-red button-chrysanthemums like a frightened dryad, the bright yellow little chrysanthemums smelled so strong her feet seemed to dither in a drunken dance.

Then her uncle Tom appeared, always like the cynical Bacchus in the picture. He would have a jolly wedding, a harvest supper and a wedding feast in one: a tent in the home close, and a band for dancing, and a great feast out of doors.

Fred demurred, but Tom must be satisfied. Also Laura, a handsome, clever girl, the bride, she also must have a great and jolly feast. It appealed to her educated sense. She had been to Salisbury Training College, knew folk-songs and morris-dancing.

So the preparations were begun, directed by Tom Brangwen. A marquee was set up on the home close, two large bon-fires were prepared. Musicians were hired, a feast made ready.

Skrebensky was to come, arriving in the morning. Ursula had a new white dress of soft crape, and a white hat. She liked to wear white. With her black hair and clear, golden skin, she looked southern, or rather tropical, like a Creole. She wore no colour whatsoever.

She trembled that day as she prepared to go down to the wedding. She was to be a bridesmaid. Skrebensky would not arrive till afternoon. The wedding was at two o'clock.

As the wedding party returned home, Skrebensky stood in the parlour at the Marsh. Through the window he saw Tom Brangwen, who was best man, coming up the garden path most elegant in cut-away coat and white slip and spats, with Ursula laughing on his arm. Tom Brangwen was handsome, with his womanish colouring and dark eyes and black, close-cut moustache. But there was something subtly coarse and suggestive about him, for all his beauty: his strange, bestial nostrils, opened so hard and wide, and his well-shaped head almost disquieting in its nakedness, rather bald from the front, and all its soft fulness betrayed.

Skrebensky saw the man rather than the woman. She was brilliant with a curious, wordless, distracted animation which she always felt when with her uncle Tom, always confused in herself.

But when she met Skrebensky everything vanished. She saw only the slender, unchangeable youth waiting there inscrutable, like her fate. He was beyond her, with his loose, slightly horsey appearance, that made him seem very manly and foreign. Yet his face was smooth and soft and impressionable. She shook hands with him, and her voice was like the rousing of a bird startled by the dawn.

"Isn't it nice," she cried, "to have a wedding!"

There were bits of coloured confetti lodged in her dark hair.

Again the confusion came over him, as if he were losing himself and becoming all vague, undefined, inchoate. Yet he wanted to be hard, manly, horsey. And he followed her.

There was a light tea, and the guests scattered. The real feast was for the evening. Ursula walked out with Skrebensky through the stackyard to the fields, and up the embankment to the canal-side.

The new corn-stacks were big and golden as they went by, an army of white geese marched aside in braggart protest. Ursula was light as a white ball of down, Skrebensky drifted beside her, indefinite, his old form loosened, and another self, grey, vague, drifting out, as from a bud. They talked lightly, of nothing.

The blue way of the canal wound softly between the autumn hedges, on towards the greenness of a small hill. On the left was the whole black agitation of colliery and railway and the town which rose on its hill, the church-tower topping all. The round white dot of the clock on the tower was distinct in the evening light.

That way, Ursula felt, was the way to London, through the grim, alluring seethe of the town. On the other hand was the evening, mellow over the green water-meadows and the winding alder trees beside the river, and the pale stretches of stubble beyond. There the evening glowed softly, and even a pee-wit was flapping in solitude and peace.

Ursula and Anton Skrebensky walked along the ridge of the canal between. The berries on the hedges were crimson and bright red, above the leaves. The glow of evening and the wheeling of the solitary pee-wit and the faint cry of the birds came to meet the shuffling noise of the pits, the dark, fuming stress of the town opposite, and they two walked the blue strip of water-way, the ribbon of sky between.

He was looking, Ursula thought, very beautiful, because of a flush of sunburn on his hands and face. He was telling her how he had learned to shoe horses and select cattle fit for killing.

"Do you like to be a soldier?" she asked.

"I am not exactly a soldier," he replied.

"But you only do things for wars," she said.

"Yes."

"Would you like to go to war?"

"I? Well, it would be exciting. If there were a war, I would want to go."

A strange, distracted feeling came over her, a sense of potent unrealities.

"Why would you want to go?"

"I should be doing something, it would be genuine. It's a sort of toy-life, as it is."

"But what would you be doing if you went to war?"

"I would be making railways or bridges, working like a nigger."

"But you'd only make them to be pulled down again when the armies had done with them. It seems just as much a game."

"If you call war a game."

"What is it?"

"It's about the most serious business there is, fighting."

A sense of hard separateness came over her.

"Why is fighting more serious than anything else?" she asked.

"You either kill or get killed—and I suppose it is serious enough, killing."

"But when you're dead, you don't matter any more," she said.

He was silenced for a moment.

"But the result matters," he said. "It matters whether we settle the Mahdi or not."

"Not to you—nor me—we don't care about Khartoum."

"You want to have room to live in: and somebody has to make room."

"But I don't want to live in the desert of Sahara—do you?" she replied, laughing with antagonism.

"*I* don't—but we've got to back up those who do."

"Why have we?"

"Where is the nation, if we don't?"

"But we aren't the nation. There are heaps of other people who are the nation."

"They might say *they* weren't, either."

"Well, if everybody said it, there wouldn't be a nation. But I should still be myself," she asserted, brilliantly.

"You wouldn't be yourself, if there were no nation."

"Why not?"

"Because you'd just be a prey to everybody or anybody."

"How a prey?"

"They'd come and take everything you've got."

"Well, they couldn't take much even then. I don't care what they take. I'd rather have a robber who carried me off than a millionaire who gave me everything you can buy."

"That's because you are a romanticist."

"Yes I am. I want to be romantic. I hate houses that never go away, and people just living in the houses. It's all so stiff and stupid. I hate soldiers, they are stiff and wooden. What do you fight for, really?"

"I would fight for the nation."

"For all that, you aren't the nation. What would you do for yourself?"

"I belong to the nation and must do my duty by the nation."

"But when it didn't need your services in particular—when there *is* no fighting? What would you do then?"

He was irritated.

"I would do what everybody else does."

"What?"

"Nothing. I would be in readiness for when I was needed."

The answer came in exasperation.

"It seems to me," she answered, "as if you weren't anybody—as if there weren't anybody there, where you are. Are you anybody, really? You seem like nothing to me."

They had walked till they reached a wharf, just above a lock. There an empty barge, painted with a red and yellow cabin hood, but with a long, coal-black hold, was lying moored. A man, lean and grimy, was sitting on a box against the cabin-side by the door, smoking, and nursing a baby that was wrapped in a drab shawl, and looking into the glow of evening. A woman bustled out, sent a pail dashing into the canal, drew her water and bustled in again. Children's voices were heard. A thin blue smoke ascended from the cabin chimney, there was a smell of cooking.

Ursula, white as a moth, lingered to look. Skrebensky lingered by her. The man glanced up.

"Good-evening," he called, half impudent, half attracted.

He had blue eyes which glanced impudently from his grimy face.

"Good-evening," said Ursula, delighted. "*Isn't* it nice now!"

"Ay," said the man, "very nice."

His mouth was red under his ragged, sandy moustache, his teeth were white as he laughed.

"Oh but—" stammered Ursula, laughing. "it *is*. Why do you say it as if it weren't?"

"'Appen for them as is childt-nursin' it's none so rosy."

"May I look inside your barge?" asked Ursula.

"There's nobody'll stop you; you come if you like."

The barge lay at the opposite bank, at the wharf. It was the "Annabel," belonging to J. Ruth of Loughborough. The man watched Ursula closely from his keen, twinkling eyes. His fair hair was wispy on his grimed forehead. Two dirty children appeared, to see who was talking.

Ursula glanced at the great lock gates. They were shut, and the water was sounding, spurting and trickling down in the gloom beyond. On this side the bright water was almost to the top of the gate. She went boldly across, and round to the wharf.

Stooping from the bank, she peeped into the cabin, where was a red glow of fire and the shadowy figure of a woman. She *did* want to go down.

"You'll mess your frock," said the man, warningly.

"I'll be careful," she answered. "May I come?"

"Ay, come if you like."

She gathered her skirts, lowered her foot to the side of the boat, and leapt down, laughing. Coal-dust flew up.

The woman came to the door. She was plump and sandy haired, young, with an odd, stubby nose.

"Oh you *will* make a mess of yourself," she cried, surprised and laughing with a little wonder.

"I did want to see. Isn't it lovely living on a barge?" asked Ursula.

"I don't live on one altogether," said the woman cheerfully.

"She's got her parlour an' her plush suite in Loughborough," said her husband, with just pride.

Ursula peeped into the cabin, where saucepans were boiling and some dishes were on the table. It was very hot. Then she came out again. The man was talking to the baby. It was a blue-eyed, fresh-faced thing with floss of red-gold hair.

"Is it a boy or a girl?" she asked.

"It's a girl—aren't you a girl, eh?" he shouted at the infant, shaking his head. Its little face wrinkled up into the oddest, funniest smile.

"Oh!" cried Ursula, "Oh, the dear! Oh, how nice, when she laughs!"

"She'll laugh hard enough," said the father.

"What is her name?" asked Ursula.

"She hasn't got a name, she's not worth one," said the man. "Are you, you fag-end o' nothing," he shouted to the baby.

The baby laughed.

"No, we've been that busy, we've never took her to th' registry office," came the woman's voice. "She was born on th' boat here."

"But you know what you're going to call her?" asked Ursula.

"We did think of Gladys Em'ly," said her mother.

"We thought of nowt o' th' sort," said the father.

"Hark at him! What *do* you want?" cried the mother in exasperation.

"She'll be called Annabel, after th' boat she was born on."

"She's not, so there," said the mother, viciously defiant.

The father sat in humorous malice, grinning.

"Well, you'll see," he said.

And Ursula could tell, by the woman's vibrating exasperation, that he would never give way.

"They're all nice names," she said. "Call her Gladys Annabel Emily."

"Nay, that's heavy-laden if you like," he answered.

"You see!" cried the woman. "He's that *pig-headed*!"

"And she's so nice, and she laughs, and she hasn't even got a name," crooned Ursula to the child.

"Let me hold her," she added.

He yielded her the child, that smelt of babies. But it had such blue, wide, china eyes, and it laughed so oddly, with such a taking grimace, Ursula loved it. She cooed and talked to it. It was such an odd, exciting child.

"What's *your* name?" the man suddenly asked of her.

"My name is Ursula—Ursula Brangwen," she replied.

"Ursula!" he exclaimed, dumb-founded.

"There was a Saint Ursula. It's a very old name," she added hastily, in justification.

"Hey, mother!" he called.

There was no answer.

"Pem!" he called, "can't y' hear?"

"What?" came the short answer.

"What about 'Ursula'?" he grinned.

"What about *what*?" came the answer, and the woman appeared in the doorway, ready for combat.

"Ursula—it's the lass's name there," he said gently.

The woman looked the young girl up and down. Evidently she was attracted by her slim, graceful, new beauty, her effect of white elegance, and her tender way of holding the child.

"Why, how do you write it?" the mother asked, awkward now she was touched.

Ursula spelled out her name. The man looked at the woman. A bright, confused flush came over the mother's face, a sort of luminous shyness.

"It's not a *common* name, is it!" she exclaimed, excited as by an adventure.

"Are you goin' to have it then?" he asked.

"I'd rather have it than Annabel," she said, decisively.

"An' I'd rather have it than Gladys Em'ler," he replied.

There was a silence. Ursula looked up.

"Will you really call her Ursula?" she asked.

"Ursula Ruth," replied the man, laughing vainly, as pleased as if he had found something.

It was now Ursula's turn to be confused.

"It *does* sound *awfully* nice," she said. "I *must* give her something. And I haven't got anything at all."

She stood in her white dress, wondering, down there in the barge. The lean man sitting near to her watched her as if she were a strange being, as if she lit up his face. His eyes smiled on her, boldly and yet with exceeding admiration underneath.

"Could I give her my necklace?" she said.

It was the little necklace made of pieces of amethyst and topaz and pearl and crystal, strung at intervals on a little golden chain, which her uncle Tom had given her. She was very fond of it. She looked at it lovingly, when she had taken it from her neck.

"Is it valuable?" the man asked her, curiously.

"I think so," she replied.

"The stones and pearl are real: it is worth three or four pounds," said Skrebensky from the wharf above. Ursula could tell he disapproved of her.

"I *must* give it to your baby—may I?" she said to the bargee.

He flushed, and looked away into the evening.

"Nay," he said, "it's not for me to say."

"What would your father and mother say?" cried the woman curiously, from the door.

"It is my own," said Ursula, and she dangled the little glittering string before the baby. The infant spread its little fingers. But it could not grasp. Ursula closed the tiny hand over the jewel. The baby waved the bright ends of the string. Ursula had given her necklace away. She felt sad. But she did not want it back.

The jewel swung from the baby's hand and fell in a little heap on the coal-dusty bottom of the barge. The man groped for it, with a kind of careful reverence. Ursula noticed the coarsened, blunted fingers groping at the little jewelled heap. The skin was red on the back of the hand, the fair hairs glistened stiffly. It was a thin, sinewy, capable hand nevertheless, and Ursula liked it. He took up the necklace, carefully, and blew the coal-dust from it, as it lay in the hollow of his hand. He seemed still and attentive. He held out his hand with the necklace shining small in its hard, black hollow.

"Take it back," he said.

Ursula hardened with a kind of radiance.

"No," she said, "It belongs to little Ursula."

And she went to the infant and fastened the necklace round its warm, soft, weak little neck.

There was a moment of confusion, then the father bent over his child:

"What do you say?" he said. "Do you say thank you? Do you say thank you, Ursula?"

"Her name's Ursula *now*," said the mother, smiling a little bit ingratiatingly from the door. And she came out to examine the jewel on the child's neck.

"It *is* Ursula, isn't it?" said Ursula Brangwen.

The father looked up at her, with an intimate, half gallant, half impudent, but wistful look. His captive soul loved her: but his soul was captive, he knew, always.

She wanted to go. He set a little ladder for her to climb up to the wharf. She kissed the child, which was in its mother's arms, and then she turned away. The mother was effusive. The man stood silent by the ladder. Ursula joined Skrebensky. The two young figures crossed the lock above the shining yellow water. The barge-man watched them go.

"I *loved* them," she was saying. "He was so gentle—oh, so gentle! And the baby was such a dear!"

"Was he gentle?" said Skrebensky. "The woman had been a servant, I'm sure of that."

Ursula winced.

"But I loved his impudence—it was so gentle underneath."

She went hastening on, gladdened by having met the grimy, lean man with the ragged moustache. He gave her a pleasant, warm feeling. He made her feel the richness of her own life. Skrebensky, somehow, had created a deadness round her, a sterility, as if the world were ashes.

They said very little as they hastened home to the big supper. He was envying the lean father of three children, for his impudent directness and his worship of the woman in Ursula, a worship of body and soul together, the man's body and soul wistful and worshipping the body and spirit of the girl, with a desire that knew the inaccessibility of its object, but was only glad to know that the perfect thing existed, glad to have had a moment of communion.

Why could not he himself desire a woman so? Why did he never really want a woman, not with the whole of him: never loved, never worshipped, only just physically wanted her.

But he would want her with his body, let his soul do as it would. A kind of flame of physical desire was gradually beating up in the Marsh, kindled by Tom Brangwen, and by the fact of the wedding of Fred, the shy, fair, stiff-set farmer with the handsome, half-educated girl. Tom Brangwen, with all his secret power, seemed to fan the flame that was rising. The bride was strongly attracted by him, and he was exerting his influence on another beautiful, fair girl, chill and burning as the sea, who said witty things which he appreciated, making her glint with more, like phosphorescence. And her greenish eyes seemed to rock a secret, and her hands like mother-of-pearl seemed luminous, transparent, as if the secret were burning visible in them.

At the end of supper, during dessert, the music began to play, violins and flutes. Everybody's face was lit up. A glow of excitement prevailed. When the little speeches were over, and the port remained unreached-for any more, those who wished were invited out to the open for coffee. The night was warm.

Bright stars were shining, the moon was not yet up. And under the stars burned two great, red, flameless fires, and round these, lights and lanterns hung, the marquee stood open before a fire, with its lights inside.

The young people flocked out into the mysterious night. There was sound of laughter and voices, and a scent of coffee. The farm-buildings loomed dark in the background. Figures, pale and dark, flitted about, intermingling. The red fire glinted on a white or a silken skirt, the lanterns gleamed on the transient heads of the wedding guests.

To Ursula, it was wonderful. She felt she was a new being. The darkness seemed to breathe like the sides of some great beast, the hay-stacks loomed half-revealed, a crowd of them, a dark, fecund lair just behind. Waves of delirious darkness ran through her soul. She wanted to let go. She wanted to reach and be amongst the flashing stars, she wanted to race with her feet and be beyond the confines of this earth. She was mad to be gone. It was as if a hound were straining on the leash, ready to hurl itself after a nameless quarry, into the dark. And she was the quarry, and she was also the hound. The darkness was passionate and breathing with immense, unperceived heaving. It was waiting to receive her in her flight. And how could she start—and how could she let go? She must leap from the known into the unknown. Her hands and feet beat like a madness, her breast strained as if in bonds.

The music began, and the bonds began to slip. Tom Brangwen was dancing with the bride, quick and fluid and as if in another element, inaccessible as the creatures that move in the water. Fred Brangwen went in with another partner. The music came in waves. One couple after another was washed and absorbed into the deep underwater of the dance.

"Come," said Ursula to Skrebensky, laying her hand on his arm.

At the touch of her hand on his arm, his consciousness melted away from him. He took her into his arms, as if into the sure, subtle power of his will, and they became one movement, one dual movement, dancing on the slippery grass. It would be endless, this movement, it would continue for ever. It was his will and her will locked in a trance of motion, two wills locked in one motion, yet never fusing, never yielding one to the other. It was a glaucous, intertwining, delicious flux and contest in flux.

They were both absorbed into a profound silence, into a deep, fluid, underwater energy that gave them unlimited strength. All the dancers were waving intertwined in the flux of music. Shadowy couples passed and re-passed before the fire, the dancing feet danced silently by into the darkness, it was a vision of the depths of the underworld, under the great flood.

There was a wonderful rocking of the darkness, slowly, a great, slow swinging of the whole night, with the music playing lightly on the surface, making the strange, ecstatic rippling on the surface of the dance, but underneath only one great flood heaving slowly backwards to the verge of oblivion, slowly forward to the other verge, the heart sweeping along each time, and tightening with anguish as the limit was reached, and the movement, at crisis, turned and swept back.

As the dance surged heavily on, Ursula was aware of some influence looking-in upon her. Something was looking at her. Some powerful, glowing sight was looking right into her, not upon her, but right at her. Out of the great distance, and yet imminent, the powerful, overwhelming watch was kept upon her. And she danced on and on with Skrebensky, while the great, white watching continued, balancing all in its revelation.

"The moon has risen," said Anton, as the music ceased and they found themselves suddenly stranded, like bits of jetsam on a shore. She turned, and saw a great white moon looking at her over the hill. And her breast opened to it, she was cleaved like a transparent jewel to its light. She stood filled with the full moon, offering herself. Her two breasts opened to make way for it, her body opened wide like a quivering anemone, a soft, dilated invitation touched by the moon. She wanted the moon to fill in to her, she wanted more, more communion with the moon, consummation. But Skrebensky put his arm round her and led her away. He put a big, dark cloak round her, and sat holding her hand, whilst the moonlight streamed above the glowing fires.

She was not there. Patiently she sat, under the cloak, with Skrebensky holding her hand. But her naked self was away there beating upon the moonlight, dashing the moonlight with her breasts and her belly and her thighs and her knees, in meeting, in communion. She half started, to go in actuality, to fling away her clothing and flee away, away from this dark confusion and chaos of people to the hill and the moon. But the people stood round her like stones, like magnetic stones, and she could not go, in actuality. Skrebensky, like a loadstone weighed on her, the weight of his presence detained her. She felt the burden of him, the blind, persistent, inert burden. He was inert, and he weighed upon her. She sighed in pain. Oh for the coolness and entire liberty and brightness of the moon. Oh for the cold liberty to be herself, to do entirely as she liked. She wanted to get right away. She felt like bright metal weighted down by dark, impure magnetism. He was the dross, people were the dross. If she could but get away to the clean free moonlight.

"Don't you like me tonight?" said his low voice, the voice of the shadow over her shoulder. She clenched her hands in the dewy brilliance of the moon, as if she were mad.

"Don't you like me tonight?" repeated the soft voice.

And she knew that, if she turned, she would die. A strange rage filled her, a rage to tear things asunder. Her hands felt destructive, like metal blades of destruction.

"Let me alone," she said.

A darkness, an obstinacy settled on him too, in a kind of inertia. He sat inert beside her. She threw off her cloak and walked towards the moon, silver white herself. He followed her closely.

The music began again, and the dance. He appropriated her. There was a fierce, white, cold passion in her heart. But he held her close, and danced with her. Always present, like a soft weight upon her, bearing her down, was his body against her as they danced. He held her very close, so that she could feel his body, the weight of him sinking, settling upon her, overcoming her life and energy, making her inert along with him, she felt his hands pressing behind her, upon her. But still in her body was the subdued, cold, indomitable passion. She liked the dance: it eased her, put her into a sort of trance. But it was only a kind of waiting, of using up the time that intervened between her and her pure being. She left herself against him, she let him exert all his power over her, as if he would gain power over her, to bear her down. She received all the force of his power. She even wished he might overcome her. She was cold and unmoved as a pillar of salt.

His will was set and straining with all its tension to encompass her and compel her. If he could only compel her. He seemed to be annihilated. She was cold and hard and compact of brilliance as the moon itself, and beyond him as the moonlight was beyond him, never to be grasped or known. If he could only set a bond round her and compel her!

So they danced four or five dances, always together, always his will becoming more tense, his body more subtle, playing upon her. And still he had not got her, she was hard and bright as ever, intact. But he must weave himself round her, enclose her, enclose her in a net of shadow, of darkness, so she would be like a bright creature gleaming in a net of shadows, caught. Then he would have her, he would enjoy her. How he would enjoy her, when she was caught.

At last, when the dance was over, she would not sit down, she walked away. He came with his arm round her, keeping her upon the movement of his walking. And she seemed to agree. She was bright as a piece of moonlight, as bright as a steel blade, he seemed to be clasping a blade that hurt him. Yet he would clasp her, if it killed him.

They went towards the stackyard. There he saw, with something like terror, the great new stacks of corn glistening and gleaming transfigured, silvery and present under the night-blue sky, throwing dark, substantial shadows, but themselves majestic and dimly present. She, like glimmering gossamer, seemed to burn among them, as they rose like cold fires to the silvery-bluish air. All was intangible, a burning of cold, glimmering, whitish-steely fires. He was afraid of the great moon-conflagration of the corn-stacks rising above him. His heart grew smaller, it began to fuse like a bead. He knew he would die.

She stood for some moments out in the overwhelming luminosity of the moon. She seemed a beam of gleaming power. She was afraid of what she was. Looking at him, at his shadowy, unreal, wavering presence a sudden lust seized her, to lay hold of him and tear him and make him into nothing. Her hands and wrists felt immeasurably hard and strong, like blades. He waited there beside her like a shadow which she wanted to dissipate, destroy as the moonlight destroys a darkness, annihilate, have done with. She looked at him and her face gleamed bright and inspired. She tempted him.

And an obstinacy in him made him put his arm round her and draw her to the shadow. She submitted: let him try what he could do. Let him try what he could do. He leaned against the side of the stack, holding her. The stack stung him keenly with a thousand cold, sharp flames. Still obstinately he held her.

And temerously, his hands went over her, over the salt, compact brilliance of her body. If he could but have her, how he would enjoy her! If he could but net her brilliant, cold, salt-burning body in the soft iron of his own hands, net her, capture her, hold her down, how madly he would enjoy her. He strove subtly, but with all his energy, to enclose her, to have her. And always she was burning and brilliant and hard as salt, and deadly. Yet obstinately, all his flesh burning and corroding, as if he were invaded by some consuming, scathing poison, still he persisted, thinking at last he might overcome her. Even, in his frenzy, he sought for her mouth with his mouth, though it was like putting his face into some awful death. She yielded to him, and he pressed himself upon her in extremity, his soul groaning over and over:

"Let me come—let me come."

She took him in the kiss, hard her kiss seized upon him, hard and fierce and burning corrosive as the moonlight. She seemed to be destroying him. He was reeling, summoning all his strength to keep his kiss upon her, to keep himself in the kiss.

But hard and fierce she had fastened upon him, cold as the moon and burning as a fierce salt. Till gradually his warm, soft iron yielded, yielded, and she was there fierce, corrosive, seething with his destruction, seething like some cruel, corrosive salt around the last substance of his being, destroying him, destroying him in the kiss. And her soul crystallised with triumph, and his soul was dissolved with agony and annihilation. So she held him there, the victim, consumed, annihilated. She had triumphed: he was not any more.

Gradually she began to come to herself. Gradually a sort of daytime consciousness came back to her. Suddenly the night was struck back into its old, accustomed, mild reality. Gradually she realised that the night was common and ordinary, that the great, blistering, transcendent night did not really exist. She was overcome with slow horror. Where was she? What was this nothingness she felt? The nothingness was Skrebensky. Was he really there?—who was he? He was silent, he was not there. What had happened? Had she been mad. What horrible thing had possessed her? She was filled with overpowering fear of herself, overpowering desire that it should not be, that other burning, corrosive self. She was seized with a frenzied desire that what had been should never be remembered, never be thought of, never be for one moment allowed possible. She denied it with all her might. With all her might she turned away from it. She was good, she was loving. Her heart was warm, her blood was dark and warm and soft. She laid her hand caressively on Anton's shoulder.

"Isn't it lovely?" she said, softly, coaxingly, caressingly.

And she began to caress him to life again. For he was dead. And she intended that he should never know, never become aware of what had been. She would bring him back from the dead without leaving him one trace of fact to remember his annihilation by.

She exerted all her ordinary, warm self, she touched him, she did him homage of loving awareness. And gradually he came back to her, another man. She was soft and winning and caressing. She was his servant, his adoring slave. And she restored the whole shell of him. She restored the whole form and figure of him. But the core was gone. His pride was bolstered up, his blood ran once more in pride. But there was no core to him: as a distinct male he had no core. His triumphant, flaming, overweening heart of the intrinsic male would never beat again. He would be subject now, reciprocal, never the indomitable thing with a core of overweening, unabateable fire. She had abated that fire, she had broken him.

But she caressed him. She would not have him remember what had been. She would not remember herself.

"Kiss me, Anton, kiss me," she pleaded.

He kissed her, but she knew he could not touch her. His arms were round her, but they had not got her. She could feel his mouth upon her, but she was not at all compelled by it.

"Kiss me," she whispered, in acute distress, "kiss me."

And he kissed her as she bade him, but his heart was hollow. She took his kisses, outwardly. But her soul was empty and finished.

Looking away, she saw the delicate glint of oats dangling from the side of the stack, in the moonlight, something proud and royal, and quite impersonal. She had been proud with them, where they were, she had been also. But in this temporary warm world of the common-place, she was a kind, good girl. She reached out yearningly for goodness and affection. She wanted to be kind and good.

They went home through the night that was all pale and glowing around, with shadows and glimmerings and presences. Distinctly, she saw the flowers in the hedge-bottoms, she saw the thin, raked sheaves flung white upon the thorny hedge.

How beautiful, how beautiful it was! She thought with anguish how wildly happy she was tonight, since he had kissed her. But as he walked with his arm round her waist, she turned with a great offering of herself to the night that glistened tremendous, a magnificent godly moon white and candid as a bridegroom, flowers silvery and transformed filling up the shadows.

He kissed her again, under the yew-trees at home, and she left him. She ran from the intrusion of her parents at home, to her bedroom, where, looking out on the moonlit country, she stretched up her arms, hard, hard, in bliss, agony, offering herself to the blond, debonair presence of the night.

But there was a wound of sorrow, she had hurt herself, as if she had bruised herself, in annihilating him. She covered up her two young breasts with her hands, covering them to herself; and covering herself with herself, she crouched in bed, to sleep.

In the morning the sun shone, she got up strong and dancing. Skrebensky was still at the Marsh. He was coming to church. How lovely, how amazing life was! On the fresh Sunday morning she went out to the garden, among the yellows and the deep-vibrating reds of autumn, she smelled the earth and felt the gossamer, the cornfields across the country were pale and unreal, everywhere was the intense silence of the Sunday morning, filled with unacquainted noises. She smelled the body of the earth, it seemed to stir its powerful flank beneath her as she stood. Into the bluish air came the powerful exudation, the peace was the peace of strong, exhausted breathing, the reds and yellows and the white gleam of stubble were the quivers and motion of the last subsiding transports and clear bliss of fulfilment.

The church bells were ringing when he came. She looked up in keen anticipation at his entry. But he was troubled and his pride was hurt. He seemed very much clothed, she was conscious of his tailored suit.

"Wasn't it lovely, last night?" she whispered to him.

"Yes," he said. But his face did not open nor become free.

The service and the singing in church that morning passed unnoticed by her. She saw the coloured glow of the windows, the forms of the worshippers. Only she glanced at the book of Genesis, which was her favorite book in the Bible.

"And God blessed Noah and his sons, and said unto them, Be fruitful and multiply and replenish the earth.

"And the fear of you and the dread of you shall be upon every beast of the earth, and upon every fowl of the air, upon all that moveth upon the earth, and upon all the fishes in the sea; into your hand are they delivered.

"Every moving thing that liveth shall be meat for you; even as the green herb have I given you all things."

But Ursula was not moved by the history this morning, Multiplying and replenishing the earth bored her. Altogether it seemed merely a vulgar and stock-raising sort of business. She was left quite cold by man's stock-breeding lordship over beast and fishes.

"And you, be ye fruitful and multiply: bring forth abundantly in the earth, and multiply therein."

In her soul she mocked at this multiplication, every cow becoming two cows, every turnip ten turnips.

"And God said: This is the token of the covenant which I make between me and you and every living creature that is with you, for perpetual generations:

"I do set my bow in the cloud, and it shall be a token of a covenant between me and the earth.

"And it shall come to pass, when I bring a cloud over the earth, that a bow shall be seen in the cloud:

"And I will remember my covenant, which is between me and you and every living creature of all flesh; and the waters shall no more become a flood to destroy all flesh."

"Destroy all flesh," why "flesh" in particular? Who was this lord of flesh? After all, how big was the Flood? Perhaps a few dryads and fauns had just run into the hills and the further valleys and woods, frightened, but most had gone on blithely unaware of any flood at all, unless the nymphs should tell them. It pleased Ursula to think of the naiads in Asia Minor meeting the nereids at the mouth of the streams, where the sea washed against the fresh, sweet tide, and calling to their sisters the news of Noah's Flood. They would tell amusing accounts of Noah in his ark. Some nymphs would relate how they had hung on the side of the ark, peeped in, and heard Noah and Shem and Ham and Japheth, sitting in their place under the rain, saying, how they four were the only men on earth now, because the Lord had drowned all the rest, so that they four would have everything to themselves and be masters of every thing, sub-tenants under the great Proprietor.

Ursula wished she had been a nymph. She would have laughed through the window of the ark, and flicked drops of the flood at Noah, before she drifted away to people who were less important in their Proprietor and their Flood.

What was God, after all? If maggots in a dead dog be but God kissing carrion, what then is not God? She was surfeited of this God. She was weary of the Ursula Brangwen who felt troubled about God. Whatever God was, He was, and there was no need for her to trouble about Him. She felt she had now all licence.

Skrebensky sat beside her, listening to the sermon, to the voice of law and order. "The very hairs of your head are all numbered." He did not believe it. He believed his own things were quite at his own disposal. You could do as you liked with your own things, so long as you left other people's alone.

Ursula caressed him and made love to him. Nevertheless he knew she wanted to react upon him and to destroy his being. She was not with him, she was against him. But her making love to him, her complete admiration of him, in open life, gratified him.

She caught him out of himself, and they were lovers, in a young, romantic, almost fantastic way. He gave her a little ring. They put it in Rhine wine, in their glass, and she drank, then he drank. They drank till the ring lay exposed in the bottom of the glass. Then she took the simple jewel, and tied it on a thread round her neck, where she wore it.

He asked her for a photograph, when he was going away. She went in great excitement to the photographer, with five shillings. The result was an ugly little picture of herself with her mouth on one side. She wondered over it and admired it.

He saw only the live face of the girl. The picture hurt him. He kept it, he always remembered it, but he could scarcely bear to see it. There was a hurt to his soul in the clear, fearless face that was touched with abstraction. Its abstraction was certainly away from him.

Then war was declared with the Boers in South Africa, and everywhere was a fizz of excitement. He wrote that he might have to go. And he sent her a box of sweets.

She was slightly dazed at the idea of his going to the war, not knowing how to feel. It was a sort of romantic situation that she knew so well in fiction she hardly understood it in fact. Underneath a top elation was a sort of dreariness, deep, ashy disappointment.

However she secreted the sweets under her bed, and ate them all herself, when she went to bed and when she woke in the morning. All the time she felt very guilty and ashamed, but she simply did not want to share them.

That box of sweets remained stuck in her mind afterwards. Why had she secreted them and eaten them every one? Why? She did not feel guilty—she only knew she ought to feel guilty. And she could not make up her mind. Curiously monumental that box of sweets stood up, now it was empty. It was a crux for her. What was she to think of it?

The idea of war altogether made her feel uneasy, uneasy. When men began organised fighting with each other it seemed to her as if the poles of the universe were cracking, and the whole might go tumbling into the bottomless pit. A horrible bottomless feeling she had. Yet of course there was the minted superscription of romance and honor and even religion about war. She was very confused.

Skrebensky was busy, he could not come to see her. She asked for no assurance, no security. What was between them, was, and could not be altered by avowals. She knew that by instinct, she trusted to the intrinsic reality.

But she felt an agony of helplessness. She could do nothing. Vaguely she knew the huge powers of the world rolling and crashing together, darkly, clumsily, stupidly, yet colossal, so that one was brushed along almost as dust. Helpless, helpless, swirling like dust! Yet she wanted so hard to rebel, to rage, to fight. But with what?

Could she with her hands fight the face of the earth, beat the hills in their places? Yet her breast wanted to fight, to fight the whole world. And these two small hands were all she had to do it with.

The months went by, and it was Christmas—the snowdrops came. There was a little hollow in the wood near Cossethay, where snowdrops grew wild. She sent him some in a box, and he wrote her a quick little note of thanks—very grateful and wistful he seemed. Her eyes grew childlike and puzzled. Puzzled, from day to day she went on, helpless, carried along by all that must happen.

He went about at his duties, giving himself up to them. At the bottom of his heart his self, the soul that aspired and had true hope of self-effectuation lay as dead, still-born, a dead weight in his womb. Who was he, to hold important his personal connections? What did a man matter, personally? He was just a brick in the whole great social fabric, the nation, the modern humanity. His personal movements were small, and entirely subsidiary. The whole form must be ensured, not ruptured, for any personal reason whatsoever, since no personal reason could justify such a breaking. What did personal intimacy matter? One had to fill one's place in the whole, the great scheme of man's elaborate civilisation, that was all. The Whole mattered—but the unit, the person, had no importance, except as he represented the Whole.

So Skrebensky left the girl out and went his way, serving what he had to serve, and enduring what he had to endure, without remark. To his own intrinsic life, he was dead. And he could not rise again from the dead. His soul lay in the tomb. His life lay in the established order of things. He had his five senses too. They were to be gratified. Apart from this, he represented the great, established, extant Idea of life, and as this he was important and beyond question.

The good of the greatest number was all that mattered. That which was the greatest good for them all, collectively, was the greatest good for the individual. And so, every man must give himself to support the State, and so labour for the greatest good of all. One might make improvements in the State, perhaps, but always with a view to preserving it intact.

No highest good of the community would, however, give him the vital fulfilment of his soul. He knew this. But he did not consider the soul of the individual sufficiently important. He believed a man was important in so far as he represented all humanity.

He could not see, it was not born in him to see, that the highest good of the community as it stands is no longer the highest good of even the average individual. He thought that, because the community represents millions of people, therefore it must be millions of times more important than any individual, forgetting that the community is an abstraction from the many, and is not the many themselves. Now when the statement of the abstract good for the community has become a formula lacking in all inspiration or value to the average intelligence, then the "common good" becomes a general nuisance, representing the vulgar, conservative materialism at a low level.

And by the highest good of the greatest number is chiefly meant the material prosperity of all classes. Skrebensky did not really care about his own material prosperity. If he had been penniless—well, he would have taken his chances. Therefore how could he find his highest good in giving up his life for the material prosperity of everybody else? What he considered an unimportant thing for himself he could not think worthy of every sacrifice on behalf of other people. And that which he would consider of the deepest importance to himself as an individual—oh, he said, you mustn't consider the community from that standpoint. No—no—we know what the community wants; it wants something solid, it wants good wages, equal opportunities, good conditions of living, that's what the community wants. It doesn't want anything subtle or difficult. Duty is very plain—keep in mind the material, the immediate welfare of every man, that's all.

So there came over Skrebensky a sort of nullity, which more and more terrified Ursula. She felt there was something hopeless which she had to submit to. She felt a great sense of disaster impending. Day after day was made inert with a sense of disaster. She became morbidly sensitive, depressed, apprehensive. It was anguish to her when she saw one rook slowly flapping in the sky. That was a sign of ill-omen. And the foreboding became so black and so powerful in her, that she was almost extinguished.

Yet what was the matter? At the worst he was only going away. Why did she mind, what was it she feared? She did not know. Only she had a black dread possessing her. When she went at night and saw the big, flashing stars they seemed terrible, by day she was always expecting some charge to be made against her.

He wrote in March to say that he was going to South Africa in a short time, but before he went, he would snatch a day at the Marsh.

As if in a painful dream, she waited suspended, unresolved. She did not know, she could not understand. Only she felt that all the threads of her fate were being held taut, in suspense. She only wept sometimes as she went about, saying blindly:

"I am so fond of him, I am so fond of him."

He came. But why did he come? She looked at him for a sign. He gave no sign. He did not even kiss her. He behaved as if he were an affable, usual acquaintance. This was superficial, but what did it hide? She waited for him, she wanted him to make some sign.

So the whole of the day they wavered and avoided contact, until evening. Then, laughing, saying he would be back in six months' time and would tell them all about it, he shook hands with her mother and took his leave.

Ursula accompanied him into the lane. The night was windy, the yew-trees seethed and hissed and vibrated. The wind seemed to rush about among the chimneys and the church-tower. It was dark.

The wind blew Ursula's face, and her clothes cleaved to her limbs. But it was a surging, turgid wind, instinct with compressed vigour of life. And she seemed to have lost Skrebensky. Out there in the strong, urgent night she could not find him.

"Where are you?" she asked.

"Here!" came his bodiless voice.

And groping, she touched him. A fire like lightning drenched them.

"Anton?" she said.

"What?" he answered.

She held him with her hands in the darkness, she felt his body again with hers.

"Don't leave me—come back to me," she said.

"Yes," he said, holding her in his arms.

But the male in him was scotched by the knowledge that she was

306

not under his spell nor his influence. He wanted to go away from her. He rested in the knowledge that tomorrow he was going away, his life was really elsewhere. His life was elsewhere—his life was elsewhere—the centre of his life was not what she would have. She was different—there was a breach between them. They were hostile worlds.

"You will come back to me?" she reiterated.

"Yes," he said. And he meant it. But as one keeps an appointment, not as a man returning to his fulfilment.

So she kissed him, and went indoors, lost. He walked down to the Marsh abstracted. The contact with her hurt him and threatened him. He shrank, he had to be free of her spirit. For she would stand before him, like the angel before Balaam, and drive him back with a sword from the way he was going, into a wilderness.

The next day she went to the station to see him go. She looked at him, she turned to him, but he was always so strange and null—so null. He was so collected. She thought it was that which made him null. Strangely nothing he was.

Ursula stood near to him with a mute, pale face which he would rather not see. There seemed some shame at the very root of life, cold, dead shame for her.

The three made a noticeable group on the station: the girl in her fur cap and tippet and her olive green costume, pale, tense with youth, isolated, unyielding; the soldierly young man in a crush hat and a heavy over-coat, his face rather pale and reserved above his purple scarf, his whole figure neutral; then the elder man, a fashionable bowler hat pressed low over his dark brows, his face warm-coloured and calm, his whole figure curiously suggestive of full-blooded indifference; he was the eternal audience, the chorus, the spectator at the drama; in his own life he would have no drama.

The train was rushing up. Ursula's heart heaved, but the ice was frozen too strong upon it.

"Good-bye," she said, lifting her hand, her face laughing with her peculiar blind, almost dazzling laugh. She wondered what he was doing, when he stooped and kissed her. He should be shaking hands and going.

"Goodbye," she said again.

He picked up his little bag and turned his back on her. There was a hurry along the train. Ah, here was his carriage. He took his seat.

Tom Brangwen shut the door, and the two men shook hands as the whistle went.

"Good-bye—and good luck," said Brangwen.

"Thank you—good-bye."

The train moved off. Skrebensky stood at the carriage window, waving, but not really looking to the two figures, the girl and the warm-coloured, almost effeminately-dressed man. Ursula waved her handkerchief. The train gathered speed, it grew smaller and smaller. Still it ran in a straight line. The speck of white vanished. The rear of the train was small in the distance. Still she stood on the platform, feeling a great emptiness about her. In spite of herself her mouth was quivering: she did not want to cry: her heart was dead cold.

Her uncle Tom had gone to an automatic machine, and was getting matches.

"Would you like some sweets," he said, turning round.

Her face was covered with tears, she made curious, downward grimaces with her mouth, to get control. Yet her heart was not crying—it was cold and earthy.

"What kind would you like—any?" persisted her uncle.

"I should love some peppermint drops," she said, in a strange, normal voice, from her distorted face. But in a few moments she had gained control of herself, and was still, detached.

"Let us go into the town," he said, and he rushed her into a train moving to the town station. They went to a café to drink coffee, she sat looking at the people in the street, and a great wound was in her breast, a cold imperturbability in her soul.

This cold imperturbability of spirit continued in her now. It was as if some disillusion had frozen upon her, a hard disbelief. Part of her had gone cold, apathetic. She was too young, too baffled to understand, or even to know that she suffered much. And she was too deeply hurt to submit.

She had her blind agonies, when she wanted him, she wanted him. But from the moment of his departure, he had become a visionary thing of her own. All her roused torment and passion and yearning she turned to him.

She kept a diary, in which she wrote impulsive thoughts. Seeing the moon in the sky, her own heart surcharged, she went and wrote:

"If I were the moon, I know where I would fall down."

It meant so much to her, that sentence—she put into it all the anguish of her youth and her young passion and yearning. She called to him from her heart wherever she went, her limbs vibrated with anguish towards him wherever she was, radiating force of her soul seemed to travel to him, endlessly, endlessly, and in her soul's own creation, find him.

But who was he, and where did he exist? In her own desire only.

She received a post-card from him, and she put it in her bosom. It did not mean much to her, really. The second day, she lost it, and never even remembered she had had it, till some days afterwards.

The long weeks went by. There came the constant bad news of the war. And she felt as if all, outside there in the world, were a hurt, a hurt, a hurt against her. And something in her soul remained cold, apathetic, unchanging.

Her life was always only partial at this time, never did she live completely. There was the cold, unliving part of her. Yet she was madly sensitive. She could not bear herself. When a dirty, red-eyed old woman came begging of her in the street, she started away as from an unclean thing. And then, when the old woman shouted acrid insults after her, she winced, her limbs palpitated with insane torment, she could not bear herself. Whenever she thought of the red-eyed old woman, a sort of madness ran in inflammation over her flesh and her brain, she almost wanted to kill herself.

And in this state, her sexual life flamed into a kind of disease within her. She was so overwrought and sensitive, that the mere touch of coarse wool seemed to tear her nerves.

CHAPTER XII

Shame

Ursula had only two more terms at school. She was studying for her matriculation examination. It was dreary work, for she had very little intelligence when she was disjointed from happiness. Stubbornness and a consciousness of impending fate kept her half-heartedly pinned to it. She knew that soon she would want to become a self-responsible person, and her dread was, that she would be prevented. An all-containing will in her for complete independence, complete social independence, complete independence from any personal authority, kept her dullishly at her studies. For she knew that she had always her price of ransom—her femaleness. She was always a woman, and what she could not get because she was a human being, fellow to the rest of mankind, she would get because she was a female, other than the man. In her femaleness she felt a secret riches, a reserve, she had always the price of freedom.

However, she was sufficiently reserved about this last resource. The other things should be tried first. There was the mysterious man's world to be adventured upon, the world of daily work and duty and existence as a working member of the community. Against this she had a subtle grudge. She wanted to make her conquest also of this man's world.

So she ground away at her work, never giving herself, never giving it up. Some things she liked. Her subjects were English, Latin, French, mathematics and history. Once she knew how to read French and Latin, the syntax bored her. Most tedious was the close study of English literature. Why should one remember the things one read? Something in mathematics, their cold absoluteness, fascinated her, but the actual practice was tedious. Some people in history puzzled her and made her ponder, but the political parts angered her, and she hated ministers. Only in odd streaks did she get a poignant sense of acquisition and enrichment and enlarging, from her studies: one afternoon, reading "As You Like It"; once when, with her blood, she heard a passage of Latin, and she knew how the blood beat in a Roman's body, so that ever after she felt she knew the

Romans, by contact; she enjoyed the vagaries of English Grammar, because it gave her pleasure to detect the live movements of words and sentences; and mathematics, the very sight of the letters in Algebra, had a real lure for her.

She felt so much and so confusedly at this time, that her face got a queer, wondering, half-scared look, as if she were not sure what might seize upon her at any moment out of the unknown.

Odd little bits of information stirred unfathomable passion in her. When she knew that in the tiny brown buds of autumn were folded, minute and complete, the finished flowers of the summer nine months hence, tiny, folded up, and left there waiting, a flash of triumph and love went over her.

"I could never die while there was a tree," she said passionately, sententiously, standing before a great ash, in worship.

It was the people who, somehow, walked as an upright menace to her. Her life at this time was unformed, palpitating, essentially shrinking from all touch. She gave something to other people, but she was never herself, since she *had* no self. She was not afraid nor ashamed before trees and birds and the sky. But she shrank violently from people, ashamed she was not as they were, fixed, emphatic, but a wavering, undefined sensibility only, without form or being.

Gudrun was at this time a great comfort and shield to her. The younger girl was a lithe, farouche animal who mistrusted all approach, and would have none of the petty secrecies and jealousies of school-girl intimacy. She would have no truck with the tame cats, nice or not, because she believed that they were all only untamed cats with a nasty, untrustworthy habit of tameness.

This was a great stand-back to Ursula, who suffered agonies when she thought a person disliked her, no matter now much she despised that person. How could anyone *dislike her*, Ursula Brangwen? The question terrified her and was unanswerable. She sought refuge in Gudrun's natural, proud indifference.

It had been discovered that Gudrun had a talent for drawing. This solved the problem of the girl's indifference to all study. It was said of her "She can draw marvellously."

Suddenly Ursula found a queer awareness existed between herself and her class-mistress, Miss Inger. The latter was a rather beautiful woman of twenty eight, a fearless-seeming, clean type of modern girl whose very independence betrays her to sorrow. She was clever, and expert in what she did, accurate, quick, commanding.

To Ursula she had always given pleasure, because of her clear, decided, yet graceful appearance. She carried her head high, a little thrown back, and, Ursula thought, there was a look of nobility in the way she twisted her smooth brown hair upon her head. She always wore clean, attractive, well-fitting blouses, and a well-made skirt. Everything about her was so well-ordered, betraying a fine, clear spirit, that it was a pleasure to sit in her class.

Her voice was just as ringing and clear, and with unwavering, finely-touched modulation. Her eyes were blue, clear, proud, she gave one altogether the sense of a fine-mettled, scrupulously groomed person and of an unyielding mind. Yet there was an infinite poignancy about her, a great pathos in her lonely, proudly closed mouth.

It was after Skrebensky had gone that there sprang up between the mistress and the girl that strange awareness, then the unspoken intimacy that sometimes connects two people who may never even make each other's acquaintance. Before, they had always been good friends, in the undistinguished way of the classroom, with the professional relationship of mistress and scholar always present. Now, however, another thing came to pass. When they were in the room together, they were aware of each other, almost to the exclusion of everything else. Winifred Inger felt a hot delight in the lessons when Ursula was present, Ursula felt her whole life begin when Miss Inger came into the room. Then, with the beloved, subtly-intimate teacher present, the girl sat as within the rays of some enriching sun, whose intoxicating heat poured straight into her veins.

The state of bliss, when Miss Inger was present, was supreme in the girl, but always eager, eager. As she went home, Ursula dreamed of the school-mistress, made infinite dreams of things she could give her, of how she might make the elder woman adore her.

Miss Inger was a Bachelor of Arts who had studied at Newnham. She was a clergyman's daughter, of good family. But what Ursula adored so much was her fine, upright, athletic bearing and her indomitably proud nature. She was proud and free as a man, yet exquisite as a woman.

The girl's heart burned in her breast as she set off for school in the morning. So eager was her breast, so glad her feet, to travel towards the beloved. Ah, Miss Inger, how straight and fine was her back, how strong her loins, how clean and free her limbs!

Ursula craved ceaselessly to know if Miss Inger cared for her. As yet no definite signs had been passed between the two. Yet surely, surely Miss Inger loved her too, was fond of her, liked her at least more than the rest of the scholars in the class. Yet she was never certain. It might be that Miss Inger cared nothing for her. And yet, and yet, with blazing heart, Ursula felt that if only she could speak to her, touch her, she would know.

The summer term came, and with it the swimming class. Miss Inger was to take the swimming class. Then Ursula trembled and was dazed with passion. Her hopes were soon to be realised. She would see Miss Inger in her bathing dress.

The day came. In the great bath the water was glimmering pale emerald-green, a lovely, glimmering mass of colour within the whitish, marble-like confines. Overhead the light fell softly and the great green body of pure water moved under it as someone dived from the side.

Ursula, trembling, hardly able to contain herself, pulled off her clothes, put on her tight bathing suit, and opened the door of her cabin. Two girls were in the water. The mistress had not appeared. She waited. A door opened, Miss Inger came out, dressed in a rust-red tunic like a Greek girl's, tied round the waist, and a red silk handkerchief round her head. How lovely she looked. Her knees were so white and strong and proud, she was firm-bodied as Diana. She walked simply to the side of the bath, and with a negligent movement, flung herself in. For a moment Ursula watched the white, smooth, strong shoulders and the easy arms swimming. Then she too dived into the water.

Now, ah now she was swimming in the same water with her dear mistress. The girl moved her limbs voluptuously, and swam by herself, deliciously, yet with a craving of unsatisfaction. She wanted to touch the other, to touch her, to feel her.

"I will race you, Ursula," came the well-modulated voice.

Ursula started violently. She turned to see the warm, unfolded face of her mistress looking at her, to her. She was acknowledged. Laughing her own beautiful, startled laugh, she began to swim. The mistress was just ahead, swimming with easy strokes. Ursula could see the head put back, the water flickering upon the white shoulders, the strong legs kicking shadowily. And she swam blinded with passion. Ah, the beauty of the firm, white, cool flesh! Ah, the wonderful firm limbs. If she could but hold them, hug them, press them between her own small breasts! Ah, if she did not so despise her own thin, dusky fragment of a body, if only she too were fearless and capable.

She swam on, eagerly, not wanting to win, only wanting to be near her mistress, to swim in a race with her. They neared the end of the bath—the deep end. Miss Inger touched the pipe, swung herself round, and caught Ursula round the waist, in the water, and held her for a moment against herself. The bodies of the two women touched, heaved against each other for a moment, then were separate.

"I won," said Miss Inger, laughing.

There was a moment of suspense. Ursula's heart was beating so fast, she clung to the rail, and could not move. Her dilated, warm, unfolded, glowing face turned to the mistress, as if to her very sun.

"Goodbye," said Miss Inger, and she swam away to the other pupils, taking professional interest in them.

Ursula was dazed. She could still feel the touch of the mistress's body against her own—only this, only this. The rest of the swimming time passed like a trance. When the call was given to leave the water, Miss Inger walked down the bath towards Ursula. Her rust-red, thin tunic was clinging to her, the whole body was defined, firm and magnificent, as it seemed to the girl.

"I enjoyed our race, Ursula," said Miss Inger. "Did you?"

The girl could only laugh with revealed, open, glowing face.

The love was now tacitly confessed. But it was some time before any further progress was made. Ursula continued in suspense, in inflamed bliss.

Then one day, when she was alone, the mistress came near to her, and touching her cheek with her fingers, said, with some difficulty:

"Would you like to come to tea with me on Saturday, Ursula?"

The girl flushed all gratitude.

"We'll go to a lovely little bungalow on the Soar, shall we. I stay the week-ends there sometimes."

Ursula was beside herself. She could not endure till the Saturday came, her thoughts burned up like a fire. If only it were Saturday, if only it were Saturday.

Then Saturday came, and she set out. Miss Inger met her in Sawley, and they walked about three miles to the bungalow. It was a moist, warm, cloudy day.

The bungalow was a tiny, two-roomed shanty set on a steep bank.

Everything in it was exquisite. In delicious privacy, the two girls made tea, and then they talked. Ursula need not be home till about ten o'clock.

The talk was led, by a kind of spell, to love. Miss Inger was telling Ursula of a friend, how she had died in childbirth, and what she had suffered: then she told of a prostitute, and of some of her experiences with men.

As they talked thus, on the little verandah of the bungalow, the night fell, there was a little warm rain.

"It is really stifling," said Miss Inger.

They watched a train, whose lights were pale in the lingering twilight, rushing across the distance.

"It will thunder," said Ursula.

The electric suspense continued, the darkness sank, they were eclipsed.

"I think I shall go and bathe," said Miss Inger, out of the cloud-black darkness.

"At night?" said Ursula.

"It is best at night. Will you come?"

"I should like to"

"It is quite safe—the grounds are private. We had better undress in the bungalow, for fear of the rain, then run down."

Shyly, stiffly, Ursula went into the bungalow and began to remove her clothes. The lamp was turned low, she stood in the shadow. By another chair Winifred Inger was undressing.

Soon the naked, shadowy figure of the elder girl came to the younger.

"Are you ready?" she said.

"One moment."

Ursula could hardly speak. The other naked woman stood by, stood near, silent. Ursula was ready.

They ventured out into the darkness, feeling the soft air of night upon their skins.

"I can't see the path," said Ursula.

"It is here," said the voice, and the wavering, pallid figure was beside her, a hand grasping her arm. And the elder held the younger close against her, close, as they went down, and by the side of the water, she put her arms round her, and kissed her. And she lifted her in her arms, close, saying softly:

"I shall carry you into the water."

Ursula lay still in her mistress's arms, her forehead against the beloved, maddening breast.

"I shall put you in," said Winifred.

But Ursula twined her body about her mistress.

After a while the rain came down on their flushed, hot limbs, startling, delicious. A sudden, ice-cold shower burst in a great weight upon them. They stood up to it with pleasure. Ursula received the stream of it upon her breasts and her belly and her limbs. It made her cold, and a deep, bottomless silence welled up in her, as if bottomless darkness were returning upon her.

So the heat vanished away, she was chilled, as if from a waking up. She ran indoors, a chill, non-existent thing, wanting to get away. She wanted the light, the presence of other people, the external connection with the many. Above all she wanted to lose herself among natural surroundings.

She took her leave of her mistress and returned home. She was glad to be on the station with a crowd of Saturday-night people, glad to sit in the lighted, crowded railway carriage. Only she did not want to meet anybody she knew. She did not want to talk. She was alone, immune.

All this stir and seethe of lights and people was but the rim, the shores of a great inner darkness and void. She wanted very much to be on the seething, partially illuminated shore, for within her was the void reality of dark space.

For a time, Miss Inger, her mistress, was gone; she was only a dark void, and Ursula was free as a shade walking in an underworld of extinction, of oblivion. Ursula was glad, with a kind of motionless, lifeless gladness, that her mistress was extinct, gone out of her.

In the morning, however, the love was there again, burning, burning. She remembered yesterday, and she wanted more, always more. She wanted to be with her mistress. All separation from her mistress was a restriction from living. Why could she not go to her today, today? Why must she pace about revoked at Cossethay, whilst her mistress was elsewhere? She sat down and wrote a burning, passionate love-letter: she could not help it.

The two women became intimate. Their lives suddenly seemed to fuse into one, inseparable. Ursula went to Winifred's lodging, she spent there her only living hours. Winifred was very fond of water—of swimming, or rowing. She belonged to various athletic clubs. Many delicious afternoons the two girls spent in a light boat on the river, Winifred always rowing. Indeed, Winifred seemed to delight in having Ursula in her charge, in giving things to the girl, in filling and enrichening her life.

So that Ursula developed rapidly during the few months of her intimacy with her mistress. Winifred had had a scientific education. She had known many clever people. She wanted to bring Ursula to her own position of thought.

They took religion and rid it of its dogmas, its falsehoods. Winifred humanised it all. Gradually it dawned upon Ursula that all the religion she knew was but a particular clothing to a human aspiration. The aspiration was the real thing—the clothing was a matter almost of national taste or need. The Greeks had a naked Apollo, the Christians a white-robed Christ, the Buddhists a royal prince, the Egyptians their Osiris. Religions were local and religion was universal. Christianity was a local branch. There was as yet no assimilation of local religions into universal religion.

In religion, there were the two great motives of fear and love. The motive of fear was as great as the motive of love. Christianity accepted crucifixion to escape from fear: "do your worst to me, that I may have no more fear of the worst." But that which was feared was not necessarily all evil, and that which was loved not necessarily all good. Fear shall become reverence, and reverence is submission in identification; love shall become triumph, and triumph is delight in identification.

So much she talked of religion, getting the gist of many writings. In philosophy she was brought to the conclusion that the human desire is the criterion of all truth and all good. Truth does not lie beyond humanity, but is one of the products of the human mind and feeling. There is really nothing to fear. The motive of fear in religion is base, and must be left to the ancient worshippers of power, worship of Moloch. We do not worship power, in our enlightened souls. Power is degenerated to money and Napoleonic stupidity.

Ursula could not help dreaming of Moloch. Her God was not mild and gentle, neither Lamb nor Dove. He was the lion and the eagle. Not because the lion and the eagle had power, but because they were proud and strong; they were themselves, they were not passive subjects of some shepherd, or pets of some loving woman, or sacrifices of some priest. She was weary to death of mild, passive lambs and monotonous doves. If the lamb might lie down with the lion, it would be a great honor to the lamb, but the lion's powerful heart would suffer no diminishing. She loved the dignity and self-possession of lions.

She did not see how lambs could love. Lambs could only be loved. They could only be afraid, and tremblingly submit to fear, and become sacrificial; or they submit to love, and become beloveds. In both they were passive. Raging, destructive lovers, seeking the moment when fear is greatest and triumph is greatest, the fear not greater than the triumph, the triumph not greater than the fear, these were no lambs nor doves. She stretched her own limbs like a lion or a wild horse, her heart was relentless in its desires. It would suffer a thousand deaths, but it would still be a lion's heart when it rose from death, a fiercer lion she would be, a surer, knowing herself different from and separate from the great, conflicting universe that was not herself.

Winifed Inger was also interested in the Women's Movement.

"The men will do no more—they have lost the capacity for doing," said the elder girl. "They fuss, and talk, but they are really inane. They make everything fit into an old, inert idea. Love is a dead idea to them. They don't come to one and love one, they come to an idea, and they say 'You are my idea,' so they embrace themselves. As if I were any man's idea! As if I exist because a man has an idea of me! As if I will be betrayed by him, lend him my body as an instrument for his idea, to be a mere apparatus of his dead theory. But they are too fussy to be able to act: they are all impotent, they can't *take* a woman. They come to their own idea every time, and take that. They are like serpents trying to swallow themselves because they are hungry."

Ursula was introduced by her friend to various women and men, educated, unsatisfied people, who still moved within the smug provincial society as if they were nearly as tame as their outward behaviour showed, but who were inwardly raging and mad.

It was a strange world the girl was swept into, like a chaos, like the end of the world. She was too young to understand it all. Yet the inoculation passed into her, through her love for her mistress.

The examination came, and then school was over. It was the long vacation. Winifred Inger went away to London. Ursula was left alone in Cossethay. A terrible outcast, almost poisonous despair possessed her. It was no use doing anything or being anything. She had no connection with other people. Her lot was isolated and deadly. There was nothing for her anywhere, but this black disintegration. Yet, within all the great attack of disintegration upon her, she remained herself. It was the terrible core of all her suffering, that she was always herself. Never could she escape that: she could not put off being herself.

She still adhered to Winifred Inger. But a sort of nausea was coming over her. She loved her mistress. But a heavy, clogged sense of deadness began to gather upon her, from the other woman's contact. And sometimes she thought Winifred was ugly, clayey. Her female hips seemed big and earthy, her ankles and her arms were too thick. She wanted some fine intensity, instead of this heavy cleaving of moist clay, that cleaves because it has no life of its own.

Winifred still loved Ursula. She had a passion for the fine flame of the girl, she served her endlessly, would have done anything for her.

"Come with me to London," she pleaded to the girl. "I will make it nice for you—you shall do lots of things you will enjoy."

"No," said Ursula stubbornly and dully. "No, I don't want to go to London, I want to be by myself."

Winifred knew what this meant. She knew that Ursula was beginning to reject her. The fine, unquenchable flame of the younger girl would consent no more to mingle with the perverted life of the elder woman. Winifred knew it would come. But she was too proud. At the bottom of her was a black pit of despair. She knew perfectly well that Ursula would cast her off.

And that seemed like the end of her life. But she was too hopeless to rage. Wisely, economising what was left of Ursula's love, she went away to London, leaving the beloved girl alone.

And after a fortnight, Ursula's letters became tender again, loving. Her uncle Tom had invited her to go and stay with him. He was managing a big new colliery in Yorkshire. Would Winifred come too?

For now Ursula was imagining marriage for Winifred. She wanted her to marry her uncle Tom. Winifred knew this. She said she would come to Wiggiston. She would now let fate do as it liked with her, since there was nothing remaining to be done. Tom Brangwen also saw Ursula's intention. He too was at the end of his desires. He had done the things he had wanted to. They had all ended in a disintegrated lifelessness of soul, which he hid under an utterly tolerant good-humour. He no longer cared about anything on earth, neither man nor woman nor God nor humanity. He had come to a stability of nullification. He did not care any more, neither about his body nor about his soul. Only he would preserve intact his own life.

Only, the simple, superficial fact of living persisted. He was still healthy. He lived. Therefore he would fill each moment. That had always been his creed. It was not instinctive easiness: it was the inevitable outcome of his nature. When he was in the absolute privacy of his own life, he did as he pleased, unscrupulous, without any ulterior thought. He believed neither in good nor evil. Each moment was like a separate little island, isolated from time, and blank, unconditioned by time.

He lived in a large new house of red-brick standing outside a mass of homogeneous red-brick dwellings called Wiggiston. Wiggiston was only seven years old. It had been a hamlet of eleven houses on the edge of healthy, half-agricultural country. Then the great seam of coal had been opened. In a year Wiggiston appeared, a great mass of pinkish rows of thin, unreal dwellings of five rooms each. The streets were like visions of pure ugliness: a grey-black, macadamised road, asphalt causeways, held in between a flat succession of wall, window and door, a new-brick channel that began nowhere and ended nowhere. Everything was amorphous, yet everything repeated itself endlessly. Only now and then, in one of the house-windows, vegetables or small groceries were displayed for sale.

In the middle of the town was a large, open, shapeless space, or market-place of black, trodden earth, surrounded by the same flat material of dwellings, new red-brick becoming grimy, small oblong windows and oblong doors repeated endlessly, with just, at one corner, a great and gaudy public-house, and somewhere lost on one of the sides of the square, a large window opaque and darkish green, which was the post-office.

The place had the strange desolation of a ruin. Colliers hanging about in gangs and groups, or passing along the asphalt pavements heavily to work, seemed not like living people, but like spectres. The rigidity of the blank streets, the homogeneous amorphous sterility of the whole suggested death rather than life. There was no meeting place, no centre, no artery, no organic formation. There it lay, like the new foundations of a red-brick confusion rapidly spreading, like a skin-disease.

Just outside of this, on a little hill, was Tom Brangwen's big, red-brick house. It looked from the front upon the edge of the place, a meaningless squalor of ash-pits and closets and irregular rows of the backs of houses, each with its small activity made sordid by barren cohesion with the rest of the small activities. Further off was the great colliery that went night and day. And all around was the country, green with two winding streams, ragged with gorse, and heath, the darker woods in the distance.

The whole place was just unreal, just unreal. Even now, when he had been there for two years, Tom Brangwen did not believe in the actuality of the place. It was like some gruesome dream, some ugly, dead, amorphous mood become concrete.

Ursula and Winifred were met by the motor-car at the raw little station, and drove through what seemed to them like the horrible raw beginnings of something. The place was a moment of chaos perpetuated, persisting, chaos fixed and rigid. Ursula was fascinated by the many men who were there—groups of men standing in the streets, four or five men walking in a gang together, their dogs running behind or before. They were all decently dressed, and most of them rather gaunt. The terrible gaunt repose of their bearing fascinated her. Like creatures with no more hope, but which still live and have passionate being, within some utterly unliving shell, they passed meaninglessly along, with strange, isolated dignity. It was as if a hard, horny shell enclosed them all.

Shocked and startled, Ursula was carried to her uncle Tom's house. He was not yet at home. His house was simply but well furnished. He had taken out a dividing wall, and made the whole front of the house into a large library, with one end devoted to his science. It was a handsome room, appointed as a laboratory and reading room, but giving the same sense of hard, mechanical activity, activity mechanical yet inchoate, and looking out on the hideous abstraction of the town, and at the green meadows and rough country beyond, and at the great, mathematical colliery on the other side.

They saw Tom Brangwen walking up the curved drive. He was getting stouter, but, with his bowler hat worn well set down on his brows, he looked manly, handsome, curiously like any other man of action. His colour was as fresh, his health as perfect as ever, he walked like a man rather absorbed.

Winifred Inger was startled when he entered the library, his coat fastened close and correct, his head bald to the crown, but not shiny, rather like something naked that one is accustomed to see covered, and his dark eyes liquid and formless. He seemed to stand in the shadow, like a thing ashamed. And the clasp of his hand was so soft and yet so forceful, that it chilled the heart. She was afraid of him, repelled by him, and yet attracted.

He looked at the athletic, seemingly fearless girl, and he detected in her a kinship with his own dark corruption. Immediately, he knew they were akin.

His manner was polite, almost foreign, and rather cold. He still laughed in his curious, animal fashion, suddenly wrinkling up his wide nose and showing his sharp teeth. The fine beauty of his skin and his complexion, some almost waxen quality, hid the strange, repellent grossness of him, the slight sense of putrescence, the commonness which revealed itself in his rather fat thighs and loins.

Winifred saw at once the deferential, slightly servile, slightly cunning regard he had for Ursula, which made the girl at once so proud and so perplexed.

"But is this place as awful as it looks?" the young girl asked, a strain in her eyes.

"It is just what it looks," he said. "It hides nothing."

"Why are the men so sad?"

"Are they sad?" he replied.

"They seem unutterably, unutterably sad," said Ursula, out of a passionate throat.

"I don't think they are that. They just take it for granted."

"What do they take for granted?"

"This—the pits and the place altogether."

"Why don't they alter it?" she passionately protested.

"They believe they must alter themselves to fit the pits and the place, rather than alter the pits and the place to fit themselves. It is easier," he said.

"And you agree with them," burst out his niece, unable to bear it. "You think like they do—that living human beings must be taken and adapted to all kinds of horrors. We could easily do without the pits."

He smiled, uncomfortably, cynically. Ursula felt again the revolt of hatred from him.

"I suppose their lives are not really so bad," said Winifred Inger, superior to the Zolaesque tragedy.

He turned with his polite, distant attention.

"Yes, they are pretty bad. The pits are very deep, and hot, and in some places wet. The men die of consumption fairly often. But they earn good wages."

"How gruesome!" said Winifred Inger.

"Yes," he replied, gravely. It was his grave, solid, self-contained manner which made him so much respected as a colliery-manager.

The servant came in to ask where they would have tea.

"Put it in the summer house, Mrs Smith," he said.

The fair-haired, good-looking young woman went out.

"Is she married and in service?" asked Ursula.

"She is a widow. Her husband died of consumption a little while ago." Brangwen gave a sinister little laugh. "He lay there in the house-place at her mother's, and five or six other people in the house, and died very gradually. I asked her if his death wasn't a great trouble to her. 'Well,' she said, 'he was very fretful towards the last, never satisfied, never easy, always fret-fretting, an' never knowing what would satisfy him. So in one way it was a relief when it was over—for him and for everybody.'—They had only been married two years, and she has one boy. I asked her if she hadn't been very happy. 'Oh, yes Sir, we was very comfortable at first, till he took bad—oh, we was very comfortable—oh yes—! But you see—you get used to it. I've had my father an' two brothers go off just the same. You get used to it.'"

"It's a horrible thing to get used to," said Winifred Inger, with a shudder.

"Yes," he said, still smiling. "But that's how they are. She'll be getting married again directly. One man or another—it doesn't matter very much. They're all colliers."

"What do you mean?" asked Ursula, "—'they're all colliers'?"

"It is with the women as with us," he replied. "Her husband was John Smith, loader. We reckoned him as a loader, he reckoned himself as a loader, and so she knew he represented his job. Marriage and home is a little side-show. The women know it right enough, and take it for what it's worth. One man or another, it doesn't matter all the world. The pit matters. Round the pit there will always be the side-shows, plenty of 'em."—He looked round at the red chaos, the rigid, amorphous confusion of Wiggiston.—"Every man his own little side-show, his home, but the pit owns every man. The women have what is left. What's left of this man, or what is left of that—it doesn't matter altogether. The pit takes all that really matters."

"It is the same everywhere," burst out Winifred. "It is the office, or the shop or the business that gets the man, the woman gets the bit the shop can't digest. What is he, at home, a man? He

323

is a meaningless lump—a standing machine, a machine out of work."

"They know they are sold," said Tom Brangwen. "That's where it is. They know they are sold to their job. If a woman talks her throat out, what difference can it make? The man is sold to his job. So the women don't bother. They take what they can catch—and *vogue la galère*."

"Aren't they very strict here?" asked Miss Inger.

"Oh no. Mrs Smith has two sisters who have changed husbands. They're not very particular—neither are they very interested. They go dragging along what is left from the pits. They're not interested enough to be very immoral—it all amounts to the same thing, moral or immoral—just a question of pit-wages. The most moral duke in England makes two hundred thousand a year out of these pits. He keeps the morality end up."

Ursula sat black-souled and very bitter, hearing the two of them talk. There seemed something ghoulish even in their very deploring of the state of things. They seemed to take a ghoulish satisfaction in it. The pit was the great mistress. Ursula looked out the window and saw the proud, demon-like colliery with her wheels twinkling in the heavens, the formless, squalid mass of the town lying aside. It was the squalid heap of side-shows. The pit was the main show, the *raison d'être* of all.

How terrible it was! There *was* a horrible fascination in it—human bodies and lives subjected in slavery to that symmetric monster of the colliery. There was a swooning, perverse satisfaction in it. For a moment she was dizzy.

Then she recovered, felt herself in a great loneliness, wherein she was sad but free. She had departed. No more would she subscribe to the great colliery, to the great machine which has taken us all captives. In her soul, she was against it, she disowned even its power. It had only to be forsaken to be inane, meaningless. And she knew it was meaningless. But it needed a great, passionate effort of will on her part, seeing the colliery, still to maintain her knowledge that it was meaningless.

But her uncle Tom and her mistress remained there among the horde, cynically reviling the monstrous state and yet adhering to it, like a man who reviles his mistress yet who is in love with her. She knew her uncle Tom perceived what was going on. But she knew moreover that in spite of his criticism and condemnation, he still wanted the great machine. His only happy moments, his only moments of pure freedom, were when he was serving the machine. Then, and then only, when the machine caught him up, was he free from the hatred of himself, could he act wholely, without cynicism and unreality.

His real mistress was the machine, and the real mistress of Winifred was the machine. She too, Winifred, worshipped the impure abstraction, the mechanisms of matter. There, there, in the machine, in service of the machine, was she free from the clog and degradation of human feeling. There, in the monstrous mechanism that held all matter, living or dead, in its service, did she achieve her consummation and her perfect unison, her immortality.

Hatred sprung up in Ursula's heart. If she could she would smash the machine. Her soul's action should be the smashing of the great machine. If she could destroy the colliery, and make all the men of Wiggiston out of work, she would do it. Let them starve and grub in the earth for roots, rather than serve such a Moloch as this.

She hated her uncle Tom, she hated Winifred Inger. They went down to the summer house for tea. It was a pleasant place among a few trees, at the end of a tidy garden, on the edge of a field. Her uncle Tom and Winifred seemed to jeer at her, to cheapen her. She was miserable and desolate. But she would never give way.

Her coldness for Winifred should never cease. She knew it was over between them. She saw gross, ugly movements in her mistress, she saw a clayey, inert, unquickened flesh, that reminded her of the great prehistoric lizards. One day her uncle Tom came in out of the broiling sunshine, heated from walking. Then the perspiration stood out upon his head and brow, his hand was wet and hot and suffocating in its clasp. He too had something marshy about him—the succulent moistness and turgidity, and the same brackish, nauseating effect of a marsh, where life and decaying are one.

He was repellent to her, who was so dry and fine in her fire. Her very bones seemed to bid him keep his distance from her.

It was in these weeks that Ursula grew up. She stayed two weeks at Wiggiston, and she hated it. All was grey, dry ash, cold and dead and ugly. But she stayed. She stayed also to get rid of Winifred. The girl's hatred and her sense of repulsiveness in her mistress and in her uncle seemed to throw the other two together. They drew together as if against her.

In hardness and bitterness of soul, Ursula knew that Winifred was become her uncle's lover. She was glad. She had loved them both. Now she wanted to be rid of them both. Their marshy, bitter-sweet corruption came sick and unwholesome in her nostrils. Anything, to get out of the fœtid air. She would leave them both for ever, leave for ever their strange, soft, half corrupt element. Anything to get away.

One night Winifred came all burning into Ursula's bed, and put her arms round the girl, holding her to herself in spite of unwillingness, and said:

"Dear, my dear—shall I marry Mr Brangwen—shall I?"

The clinging, heavy, muddy question weighed on Ursula intolerably.

"Has he asked you?" she said, using all her might of hard resistance.

"He's asked me," said Winifred. "Do you want me to marry him, Ursula?"

"Yes," said Ursula.

The arms tightened more on her.

"I knew you did, my sweet—and I will marry him. You're *fond* of him, aren't you?"

"I've been *awfully* fond of him—ever since I was a child."

"I know—I know. I can see what you like in him. He *is* a man by himself, he has something apart from the rest."

"Yes," said Ursula.

"But he's not like you, my dear—ha, he's not as good as you. There's something even objectionable in him—his thick thighs—"

Ursula was silent.

"But I'll marry him, my dear—it will be best. Now say you love me."

A sort of profession was extorted out of the girl. Nevertheless her mistress went away sighing, to weep in her own chamber.

In two days' time Ursula left Wiggiston. Miss Inger went to Nottingham. There was an engagement between her and Tom Brangwen, which the uncle seemed to vaunt as if it were an assurance of his validity.

Brangwen and Winifred Inger continued engaged for another term. Then they married. Brangwen had reached the age when he wanted children. He wanted children. Neither marriage nor the domestic establishment meant anything to him. He wanted to propagate himself. He knew what he was doing. He had the instinct of a growing inertia, of a thing that chooses its place of rest in which to lapse into apathy, complete, profound indifference. He would let the machinery carry him: husband, father, pit-manager, warm clay lifted through the recurrent action of day after day by the great machine from which it derived its motion. As for Winifred, she was an educated woman, and of the same sort as himself. She would make a good companion. She was his mate.

CHAPTER XIII

The Man's World

Ursula came back to Cossethay to fight with her mother. Her school-days were over. She had passed the matriculation examination. Now she came home to face that empty period between school and possible marriage.

At first she thought it would be just like holidays all the time, she would feel just free. Her soul was in chaos, blinded, suffering, maimed. She had no will left to think about herself. For a time she must just lapse.

But very shortly, she found herself up against her mother. Her mother had, at this time, the power to irritate and madden the girl continuously. There were already seven children, yet Mrs Brangwen was again with child, the ninth she had borne. One had died of diphtheria in infancy.

Even this fact of her mother's pregnancy enraged the eldest girl. Mrs Brangwen was so complacent, so utterly fulfilled in her breeding. She would not have the existence at all of anything but the immediate, physical, common things. Ursula, inflamed in soul, was suffering all the anguish of youth's reaching for some unknown ideal, that it can't grasp, can't even distinguish or conceive. Maddened, she was fighting all the darkness she was up against. And part of this darkness was her mother. To limit, as her mother did, everything to the ring of physical considerations, and complacently to reject the reality of anything else, was horrible. Not a thing did Mrs Brangwen care about, but the children, the house, and a little local gossip. And she *would not* be touched, she would let nothing else live near her. She went about, big with child, slovenly, easy, having a certain lax dignity, taking her own time, pleasing herself, always, always doing things for the children, and feeling that thereby she fulfilled the whole of womanhood.

This long trance of complacent child-bearing had kept her young and undeveloped. She was scarcely a day older than when Gudrun was born. All these years, nothing had happened save the coming of the children, nothing had mattered but the bodies of her babies. As her children came into consciousness, as they began to suffer their own fulfilment, she cast them off. But she remained dominant in the house. Brangwen continued in a kind of rich drowse of physical heat, in connection with his wife. They were neither of them quite personal, quite defined as individuals, so much were they pervaded by the physical heat of breeding and rearing their young.

How Ursula resented it, how she fought against the close, physical, limited life of herded domesticity. Calm, placid, unshakeable as ever, Mrs Brangwen went about in her dominance of physical maternity.

There were battles. Ursula would fight for things that mattered to her. She would have the children less rude and tyrannical, she *would* have a place in the house. But her mother pulled her down, pulled her down. With all the cunning instinct of a breeding animal, Mrs Brangwen ridiculed and held cheap Ursula's passions, her ideas, her pronunciations. Ursula would try to insist, in her own home, on the right of women to take equal place with men in the field of action and work.

"Ay," said the mother, "there's a good crop of stockings lying ripe for mending. Let that be your field of action."

Ursula disliked mending stockings, and this retort maddened her. She hated her mother bitterly. After a few weeks of enforced domestic life, she had had enough of her home. The commonness, the triviality, the immediate meaninglessness of it all drove her to frenzy. She talked and stormed ideas, she corrected and nagged at the children, she turned her back in silent contempt on her breeding mother, who treated her with supercilious indifference, as if she were a pretentious child not to be taken seriously.

Brangwen was sometimes dragged into the trouble. He loved Ursula, therefore he always had a sense of shame, almost of betrayal, when he turned on her. So he turned fiercely and scathingly and with a wholesale brutality that made Ursula go white, mute, and numb. Her feelings seemed to be becoming deadened in her, her temper hard and cold.

Brangwen himself was in one of his states of flux. After all these years, he began to see a loop-hole of freedom. For twenty years he had gone on at his office as a draughtsman, doing work in which he had no interest, because it seemed his allotted work. The growing up of his daughters, their developing rejection of old forms set him also free.

He was a man of ceaseless activity. Blindly, like a mole, he pushed his way out of the earth that covered him, working always away from the physical element in which his life was captured. Slowly, blindly, gropingly, with what initiative was left to him, he made his way towards individual expression and individual form.

At last, after twenty years, he came back to his wood-carving, almost to the point where he had left off his Adam and Eve panel when he was courting. But now he had knowledge and skill without vision. He saw the puerility of his young conceptions, he saw the unreal world in which they had been conceived. He now had a new strength in his sense of reality. He felt as if he were real, as if he handled real things. He had worked for many years at Cossethay, building the organ for the church, restoring the wood-work, gradually coming to a knowledge of beauty in the plain labours. Now he wanted again to carve things that were utterances of himself.

But he could not quite hitch on—always he was too busy, too uncertain, confused. Wavering, he began to study modelling. To his surprise he found he could do it. Modelling in clay, in plaster, he produced beautiful reproductions, really beautiful. Then he set-to to make a head of Ursula, in high relief, in the Donatello manner. In his first passion, he got a beautiful suggestion of his desire. But the pitch of concentration would not come. With a little ash in his mouth, he gave up. He continued to copy, or to make designs by selecting motives from classic stuff. He loved the Della Robbia and Donatello as he had loved Fra Angelico when he was a young man. His work had some of the freshness, the naïve alertness of the early Italians. But it was only reproduction.

Having reached his limit in modelling, he turned to painting. But he tried water-colour painting after the manner of any other amateur. He got his results but was not much interested. After one or two drawings of his beloved church, which had the same alertness as his modelling, but seemed to be incongruous with the modern atmospheric way of painting, so that his church-tower stood up, really stood and asserted its standing, but was ashamed of its own lack of meaning, he turned away again.

He took up jewellery, read Benvenuto Cellini, pored over reproductions of ornament, and began to make pendants in silver and pearl and matrix. The first things he did, in his start of discovery, were really beautiful. Those later were more imitative. But, starting with his wife, he made a pendant each for all his women folk. Then he made rings and bracelets.

Then he took up beaten and chiselled metal work. When Ursula left school, he was making a silver bowl of lovely shape. How he delighted in it, almost lusted after it.

All this time, his only connection with the real outer world was through his winter evening classes, which brought him into contact with state education. So that he did read papers in education, he did actually watch the politics of education. About all the rest, he was oblivious and entirely indifferent—even about the war. The nation did not exist to him. He was in a private retreat of his own, that had neither nationality nor any great adherent.

Ursula watched the newspapers, vaguely, concerning the war in South Africa. They made her miserable, and she tried to have as little to do with them as possible. But Skrebensky was out there. He sent her an occasional post-card. But it was as if she were a blank wall in his direction, without windows or out-going. She adhered to the Skrebensky of her memory.

Her love for Winifred Inger had wrenched her life as it seemed from the roots and native soil where Skrebensky had belonged to it, and she was aridly transplanted. He was really only a memory. She revived his memory with strange passion, after the departure of Winifred. He was to her almost the symbol of her real life. It was as if, through him, in him, she might return to her own self, which she was before she had loved Winifred, before this deadness had come upon her, this pitiless transplanting. But even her memories were the work of her imagination.

She dreamed of him and her as they had been together. She could not dream of him progressively, of what he was doing now, of what relation he would have to her now. Only sometimes she wept to think how cruelly she had suffered when he left her—ah, *how* she had suffered! She remembered what she had written in her diary:

"If I were the moon, I know where I would fall down."

Ah, it was a dull agony to her to remember what she had been then. For it was remembering a dead self. All that was dead after Winifred. She knew the corpse of her young, loving self, she knew its grave. And the young loving self she mourned for had scarcely existed, it was the creature of her imagination.

Deep within her a cold despair remained unchanging and

unchanged. No-one would ever love her now—she would love no-one. The body of love was killed in her after Winifred, there was something of the corpse in her. She would live, she would go on, but she would have no lovers, no lover would want her any more. She herself would want no lover. The vividest little flame of desire was extinct in her for ever. The tiny, vivid germ that contained the bud of her real self, her real love, was killed, she would go on growing as a plant, she would do her best to produce her minor flowers, but her leading flower was dead before it was born, all her growth was the conveying of a corpse of hope.

The miserable weeks went on, in the poky house crammed with children. What was her life—a sordid, formless, disintegrated nothing: Ursula Brangwen, a person without worth or importance, living in the mean village of Cossethay, within the sordid scope of Ilkeston. Ursula Brangwen, at seventeen worthless and unvalued, neither wanted nor needed by anybody, and conscious herself of her own dead value. It would not bear thinking of.

But still her dogged pride held its own. She might be defiled, she might be a corpse that should never be loved, she might be a core-rotten stalk living upon the food that others provided: yet she would give in to nobody.

Gradually she became conscious that she could not go on living at home as she was doing, without place or meaning or worth. The very children that went to school held her uselessness in contempt. She must do something.

Her father said she had plenty to do to help her mother. From her parents she would never get more than a hit in the face. She was not a practical person. She thought of wild things, of running away and becoming a domestic servant, of asking some man to take her.

She wrote to the mistress of the High School for advice.

"I cannot see very clearly what you should do, Ursula," came the reply, "unless you are willing to become an elementary school-teacher. You have matriculated, and that qualifies you to take a post as uncertificated teacher in any school, at a salary of about fifty pounds a year.

"I cannot tell you how deeply I sympathise with you in your desire to do something. You will learn that mankind is a great body of which you are one useful member, you will take your own place at the great task which humanity is trying to fulfil. That will give you a satisfaction and a self-respect which nothing else could give."

Ursula's heart sank. It was a cold, dreary satisfaction to think of. Yet her cold will acquiesced. This was what she wanted.

"You have an emotional nature," the letter went on, "a quick, natural response. If only you could learn patience and self-discipline, I do not see why you should not make a good teacher. The least you could do is to try. You need only serve a year, or perhaps two years, as uncertificated teacher. Then you would go to one of the training colleges, where I hope you would take your degree. I most strongly urge and advise you to keep up your studies always with the intention of taking a degree. That will give you a qualification and a position in the world, and will give you more scope to choose your own way.

"I shall be proud to see one of my girls win her own economical independence, which means so much more than it seems. I shall be glad indeed to know that one more of my girls has provided for herself the means of freedom to choose for herself."

It all sounded grim and desperate. Ursula rather hated it. But her mother's contempt and her father's harshness had made her raw at the quick, she knew the ignominy of being a hanger-on, she felt the festering thorn of her mother's animal estimation.

At length she had to speak. Hard and shut down and silent within herself, she slipped out one evening to the work-shed. She heard the tap-tap-tap of the hammer upon the metal. Her father lifted his head as the door opened. His face was ruddy and bright with instinct, as when he was a youth, his black moustache was cut close over his wide mouth, his black hair was fine and close as ever. But there was about him an abstraction, a sort of instrumental detachment from human things. He was a worker. He watched his daughter's hard, expressionless face. A hot anger came over his breast and belly.

"What now?" he said.

"Can't I," she answered, looking aside, not looking at him, "can't I go out to work?"

"Go out to work, what for?"

His voice was so strong and ready and vibrant. It irritated her.

"I want some other life than this."

A flash of strong rage arrested all his blood for a moment.

"Some other life!" he repeated. "Why what other life do you want?"

She hesitated.

"Something else besides housework and hanging about. And I want to earn something."

Her curious, brutal hardness of speech, and the fierce invincibility of her youth, which ignored him, made him also harden with anger.

"And how do you think *you're* going to earn anything?" he asked.

"I can become a teacher—I'm qualified by my matric."

He wished her matric. in hell.

"And how much are you qualified to earn, by your matric?" he asked, jeering.

"Fifty pounds a year," she said.

He was silent, his power taken out of his hand.

He had always hugged a secret pride in the fact that his daughters need not go out to work. With his wife's money and his own, they had four hundred a year. They could draw on the capital if need be, later on. He was not afraid for his old age. His daughters might be ladies.

Fifty pounds a year was a pound a week—which was enough for her to live on independently.

"And what sort of a teacher do you think *you'd* make? You haven't the patience of a Jack-gnat with your own brothers and sisters, let alone with a class of children. And I thought you didn't like 'dirty, board-school brats.'"

"They're not all dirty."

"You'd find they're not all clean."

There was silence in the work-shop. The lamp-light fell on the burned silver bowl that lay before him, on mallet and furnace and chisels. Brangwen stood with a queer, cat-like light on his face, almost like a smile. But it was no smile.

"Can I try?" she said.

"You can do what the deuce you like, and go where you like."

Her face was fixed and expressionless and indifferent. It always sent him to a pitch of frenzy to see it like that. He kept perfectly still.

Cold, without any betrayal of feeling, she turned and left the shed. He worked on, with all his nerves jangled. Then he had to put down his tools and go into the house.

In a bitter tone of anger and contempt, he told his wife. Ursula was present. There was a brief altercation, closed by Mrs Brangwen's saying, in a tone of biting superiority and indifference:

"Let her find out what it's like. She'll soon have had enough."

The matter was left there. But Ursula considered herself free to act. For some days she made no move. She was reluctant to take the cruel step of finding work, for she shrank with extreme sensitiveness and shyness from new contact, new situations. Then at length a sort of doggedness drove her. Her belly was full of bitterness.

She went to the Free Library in Ilkeston, copied out addresses from the "Schoolmistress," and wrote for application forms. After two days she rose early to meet the postman. As she expected, there were three long envelopes.

Her heart beat painfully as she went up with them to her bedroom. Her fingers trembled, she could hardly force herself to look at the long, official forms she had to fill in. The whole thing was so cruel, so impersonal. Yet it must be done.

"Name (surname first): _____."
In a trembling hand she wrote "Brangwen—Ursula."
"Age and Date of Birth: _____."
After a long time considering, she filled in that line.
"Qualifications, with Dates of Examinations: _____."
With a little pride she wrote:
"London Matriculation Examination. June 1900."
"Previous Experience and Where Obtained: _____."
Her heart sank as she wrote:
"None."

Still there was much to answer. It took her two hours to fill in the three forms. Then she had to copy her testimonials from her head-mistress and from the clergyman.

At last, however, it was finished. She had sealed the three long envelopes. In the afternoon she went down to Ilkeston to post them. She said nothing of it all to her parents. As she stamped her long letters, and put them into the box at the main post-office, she felt as if already she was out of the reach of her father and mother, as if she had connected herself with the outer, greater world of activity, the man-made world.

As she returned home, she dreamed again in her own fashion her old, gorgeous dreams. One of her applications was to Gillingham, in Kent, one to Kingston-on-Thames, and one to Swanwick in Derbyshire.

"Gillingham" was such a lovely name, and Kent was the Garden of England. So that, in Gillingham, an old, old village by the hop-fields, where the sun shone softly, she came out of school in the afternoon into the shadow of the plane-trees by the gate, and turned down the sleepy road towards the cottage where corn-flowers poked their blue heads through the old wooden fence, and phlox stood built up of blossom, beside the path.

A delicate, silver-haired lady rose with delicate, ivory hands uplifted as Ursula entered the room, and:

"Oh my dear, what do you think!"

"What is it, Mrs Wetherall?"

Frederick had come home. Nay, his manly step was heard on the stair, she saw his strong boots, his blue trousers, his uniformed figure, and then his face, clean and keen as an eagle's, and his eyes lit up with the glamour of strange seas, ah, strange seas that had woven through his soul, as he descended into the kitchen.

This dream, with its amplifications, lasted her a mile of walking. Then she went to Kingston-on-Thames.

Kingston-on-Thames was an old, historic place just south of London. There lived the well-born, dignified souls who belonged to the metropolis but who loved peace. There she met a wonderful family of girls, living in a large, old, Queen-Anne house whose lawns sloped to the river, and, in an atmosphere of stately peace, she found herself among her soul's intimates. They loved her as sisters, they shared with her all noble thoughts.

She was happy again. In her musings she spread her poor, clipped wings, and flew into the pure empyrean.

Day followed day. She did not speak to her parents. There came the return of her testimonials from Gillingham. She was not wanted—neither at Swanwick. The bitterness of rejection followed the sweets of hope. Her bright feathers were in the dust again.

Then, suddenly, after a fortnight, came an intimation from Kingston-on-Thames. She was to appear at the Education Office of that town on the following Thursday, for an interview with the Committee. Her heart stood still. She knew she would make the Committee accept her. Now, she was afraid, now that her removal was imminent. Her heart quivered with fear and reluctance. But underneath, her purpose was fixed.

She passed shadowily through this day, unwilling to tell her news to her mother, waiting for her father. Suspense and fear were strong upon her. She dreaded going to Kingston. Her easy dreams disappeared from the grasp of reality.

And yet, as the afternoon wore away, the sweetness of the dream returned again. Kingston-on-Thames—there was such sound of dignity to her. The shadow of history and the glamour of stately progress enveloped her. The palaces would be old and darkened, the place of kings obscured. Yet it was a place of kings for her—Richard and Henry and Wolsey and Queen Elizabeth. She divined great lawns with noble trees, and terraces whose steps the water washed softly, where the swans sometimes came to earth. Still she must see the stately, gorgeous barge of the Queen float down, the crimson carpet put upon the landing stairs, the gentlemen in their purple-velvet cloaks bare-headed, standing in the sunshine grouped on either side, waiting.

"Sweet Thames run softly till I end my song—."

Evening came, her father returned home, sanguine and alert and detached as ever. He was less real than her fancies. She waited whilst he ate his tea. He took big mouthfuls, big bites, and ate unconsciously, with the same abandon an animal gives to its food.

Immediately after tea he went over to the church. It was choir-practice, and he wanted to try the tunes, on his organ.

The latch of the big door clicked loudly as she came after him, but the organ rolled more loudly still, he was unaware. He was practising the anthem. She saw his small, jet-black head and alert face between the candle-flames, his slim body sagged on the music stool. His face was so luminous and fixed, the movement of his limbs seemed strange, apart from him. The sound of the organ seemed to belong to the very stone of the pillars, like sap running in them.

Then there was a close of music, and silence.

"Father!" she said.

He looked round as if at an apparition. Ursula stood shadowily within the candle-light.

"What now?" he said, not coming to earth.

It was difficult to speak to him.

"I've got a situation," she said, forcing herself to speak.

"You've got what?" he answered, unwilling to come out of his mood of organ-playing. He closed the music before him.

"I've got a situation to go to."

Then he turned to her, still abstracted, unwilling.

"Oh, where's that?" he said.

"At Kingston-on-Thames. I must go on Thursday for an inter-view with the Committee."

"You must go on Thursday?"

"Yes."

And she handed him the letter. He read it by the light of the candles:

"Ursula Brangwen, Yew Tree Cottage, Cossethay, Derbyshire.

"Dear Madam, You are requested to call at the above offices on Thursday next, the 10th., at 11.30 a.m., for an interview with the committee, referring to your application for the post of assistant mistress at the Wellingborough Green School."

It was very difficult for Brangwen to take in this remote and official information, glowing as he was within the quiet of his church and his anthem music.

"Well you needn't bother me with it now, need you?" he said impatiently, giving her back the letter.

"I've got to go on Thursday," she said.

He sat motionless. Then he reached more music, and there was a rushing sound of air, then a long, emphatic, trumpet-note of the organ as he laid his hands on the keys. Ursula turned and went away.

He tried to give himself again to the organ. But he could not. He could not get back. All the time a sort of string was tugging, tugging him elsewhere, miserably.

So that when he came into the house after choir-practice his face was dark and his heart black. He said nothing, however, until all the younger children were in bed. Ursula, however, knew what was brewing.

At length he asked:

"Where's that letter?"

She gave it to him. He sat looking at it. "You are requested to call at the above offices on Thursday next—" It was a cold, official notice to Ursula herself, and had nothing to do with him. So! She existed now as a separate social individual. It was for her to answer this note without regard to him. He had even no right to interfere. His heart was hard and angry.

"You had to do it behind our backs, had you?" he said with a sneer. And her heart leapt with hot pain. She knew she was free—she had broken away from him. He was beaten.

"You said 'let her try,'" she retorted, almost apologising to him. He did not hear. He sat looking at the letter.

"Education Office, Kingston-on-Thames"—and then the type-written "Miss Ursula Brangwen—Yew Tree Cottage—Cossethay." It was all so complete and so final. He could not but feel the new position Ursula held, as recipient of that letter. It was an iron in his soul.

"Well," he said at length, "you're not going."

Ursula started and could find no words to clamour her revolt.

"If you think you're going dancing off to th' other side of London, you're mistaken."

"Why not?" she cried, at once hard fixed in her will to go.

"That's why not," he said.

And there was silence till Mrs Brangwen came downstairs.

"Look here, Anna," he said, handing her the letter.

She put back her head, seeing a type-written letter, anticipating trouble from the outside world. There was the curious sliding motion of her eyes, as if she shut off her sentient, maternal self, and a kind of hard trance, meaningless, took its place. Thus, meaningless, she glanced over the letter, careful not to take it in. She apprehended the contents with her callous, superficial mind. Her feeling self was shut down.

"What post is it?" she asked.

"She wants to go and be a teacher in Kingston-on-Thames, at fifty pounds a year."

"Oh indeed."

The mother spoke as if it were a hostile fact concerning some stranger. She would have let her go, out of callousness. Mrs Brangwen would begin to grow up again only with her youngest child. Her eldest girl was in the way now.

"She's not going all that distance," said the father.

"I have to go where they want me," cried Ursula. "And it's a *good* place to go to."

"What do *you* know about the place?" said her father harshly.

"And it doesn't matter whether they want you or not, if your father says you are not to go," said the mother calmly.

How Ursula hated her!

"You said I was to try," the girl cried. "Now I've got a place, and I'm going to go."

"You're not going all that distance," said her father.

"Why don't you get a place at Ilkeston, where you can live at home?" asked Gudrun, who hated conflicts, who could not understand Ursula's uneasy way, yet who must stand by her sister.

"There aren't any places in Ilkeston," cried Ursula. "And I'd rather go right away."

"If you'd asked about it, a place could have been got for you in Ilkeston. But you had to play Miss High-an'-mighty, and go your own way," said her father.

"I've no doubt you'd rather go right away," said her mother, very caustic. "And I've no doubt you'd find other people didn't put up with you for very long, either. You've too much opinion of yourself, for your good."

Between the girl and her mother was a feeling of pure hatred. There came a stubborn silence. Ursula knew she must break it.

"Well, they've written to me, and I s'll have to go," she said.

"Where will you get the money from?" asked her father.

"Uncle Tom will give it me," she said.

Again there was silence. This time she was triumphant.

Then at length her father lifted his head. His face was abstracted, he seemed to be abstracting himself, to make a pure statement.

"Well, you're not going all that distance away," he said. "I'll ask Mr Burt about a place here. I'm not going to have you by yourself at the other side of London."

"But I've *got* to go to Kingston," said Ursula. "They've sent for me."

"They'll do without you," he said.

There was a trembling silence, when she was on the point of tears.

"Well," she said, low and tense, "you can put me off this, but I'm *going* to have a place. I'm *not* going to stop at home."

"Nobody wants you to stop at home," he suddenly shouted, going livid with rage.

She said no more. Her nature had gone hard and smiling in its own arrogance, in its own antagonistic indifference to the rest of them. This was the state in which he wanted to kill her. She went singing into the parlour:

> "C'est la mère Michel qui a perdu son chat
> Qui cri par la fenêtre qu'est-ce qui le lui rendra—"

During the next days Ursula went about bright and hard, singing to herself, making love to the children, but her soul hard and cold with regard to her parents. Nothing more was said.

The hardness and brightness lasted for four days. Then it began to break up. So at evening she said to her father:

"Have you spoken about a place for me?"

"I spoke to Mr Burt."

"What did he say?"

"There's a committee meeting tomorrow. He'll tell me on Friday."

So she waited till Friday. Kingston-on-Thames had been an exciting dream. Here she could feel the hard, raw reality. So she knew that this would come to pass. Because nothing was ever fulfilled, she found, except in the hard, limited reality. She did not want to be a teacher in Ilkeston, because she knew Ilkeston, and hated it. But she wanted to be free, so she must take her freedom where she could.

On Friday her father said there was a place vacant in Brinsley Street school. This could most probably be secured for her at once, without the trouble of application.

Her heart halted. Brinsley Street was a school in a poor quarter, and she had had a taste of the common children of Ilkeston. They had shouted after her and thrown stones. Still, as a teacher, she would be in authority. And it was all unknown. She was excited. The very forest of dry, sterile brick had some fascination for her. It was so hard and ugly, so relentlessly ugly, it would purge her of some of her floating sentimentality.

She dreamed how she would make the little, ugly children love her. She would be so *personal*. Teachers were always so hard and impersonal. There was no vivid relationship. She would make everything personal and vivid, she would give herself, she would give, give, give all her great stores of wealth to her children, she would make them *so* happy, and they would prefer her to any teacher on the face of the earth.

At Christmas she would choose such fascinating Christmas cards for them, and she would give them such a happy party in one of the classrooms.

The head-master, Mr Harby, was a short, thick-set, rather common man, she thought. But she would hold before him the light of grace and refinement, he would have her in such high esteem, before long; she would be the gleaming sun of the school, the children would blossom like little weeds, the teachers like tall, hard plants would burst into rare flower.

The Monday morning came. It was the end of September, and a drizzle of fine rain like veils round her, making her seem intimate, a world to herself. She walked forward to the new land. The old was blotted out. The veil would be rent that hid the new world. She was gripped hard with suspense as she went down the hill in the rain, carrying her dinner bag.

Through the thin rain she saw the town, a black, extensive mount. She must enter in upon it. She felt at once a feeling of repugnance and of excited fulfilment. But she shrank.

She waited at the terminus for the tram. Here it was beginning. Behind her was the station to Nottingham, whence Theresa had gone to school half an hour before: behind her was the little church school she had attended when she was a child, when her grandmother was alive. Her grandmother had been dead two years now. There was a strange woman at the Marsh, with her uncle Fred, and a small baby. Behind her was Cossethay, and blackberries were ripe on the hedges.

As she waited at the tram-terminus she reverted swiftly to her childhood: her teasing grandfather with his fair beard and blue eyes and his big, monumental body; he had got drowned: her grandmother, whom Ursula would sometimes say she had loved more than anyone else in the world: the little church school, the Phillips boys; one was a soldier in the Life Guards now, one was a collier. With a passion she clung to the past.

But as she dreamed of it, she heard the tram-car grinding round a bend, rumbling dully, she saw it draw into sight, and hum nearer. It sidled round the loop at the terminus, and came to a standstill, looming above her. Some shadowy grey people stepped from the far end, the conductor was walking in the puddles, swinging round the pole.

She mounted into the wet, comfortless tram, whose floor was dark with wet, whose windows were all steamed, and she sat in suspense. It had begun, her new existence.

One other passenger mounted—a sort of char-woman with a drab, wet coat. Ursula could not bear the waiting of the tram. The bell clanged, there was a lurch forward. The car moved cautiously down the wet street. She was being carried forward, into her new existence. He heart burned with pain and suspense, as if something were cutting her living tissue.

Often, oh often the tram seemed to stop, and wet, cloaked people mounted and sat mute and grey, in stiff rows opposite her, their umbrellas between their knees. The windows of the tram grew more steamy, opaque. She was shut in with those unliving, spectral people. Even yet it did not occur to her that she was one of them. The conductor came down issuing tickets. Each little ring of his clipper sent a pang of dread through her. But her ticket surely was different from the rest.

They were all going to work; she also was going to work. Her ticket was the same. She sat trying to fit in with them. But fear was at her bowels, she felt an unknown, terrible grip upon her.

At Bath Street she must dismount and change trams. She looked uphill. It seemed to lead to freedom. She remembered the many Saturday afternoons she had walked up to the shops. How free and careless she had been.

Ah, her tram was sliding gingerly downhill. She dreaded every yard of her conveyance. The car halted, she mounted hastily.

She kept turning her head as the car ran on, because she was uncertain of the street. At last, her heart a flame of suspense, trembling, she rose. The conductor rang the bell brusquely.

She was walking down a small, mean, wet street, empty of people. The school squatted low within its railed, asphalt yard, that shone black with rain. The building was grimy, and horrible, dry plants were shadowily looking through the windows.

She entered the arched doorway of the porch. The whole place seemed to have a threatening expression, imitating the church's architecture for the purpose of domineering, like a gesture of vulgar authority. She saw that one pair of feet had paddled across the flagstone floor of the porch. The place was silent, deserted, like an empty prison, waiting the return of tramping feet.

Ursula went forward, to the teachers' room that burrowed in a gloomy hole. She knocked timidly.

"Come in!" called a surprised man's voice, as from a prison cell. She entered the dark little room, that never got any sun. The gas was lighted naked and raw. At the table, a thin man in shirt-sleeves was rubbing a paper on a jelly-tray. He looked up at Ursula with his narrow, sharp face, said "Good morning," then turned away again, and stripped the paper off the tray, glancing at the violet-coloured writing transferred, before he dropped the curled sheet aside, among a heap.

Ursula watched him fascinated. In the gas-light and gloom and the narrowness of the room, all seemed unreal.

"Isn't it a nasty morning?" she said.

"Yes," he said. "It's not much of weather."

But in here, it seemed that neither morning nor weather really existed. This place was timeless. He spoke in an occupied voice, like an echo. Ursula did not know what to say. She took off her waterproof.

"Am I early?" she asked.

The man looked first at a little clock, then at her. His eyes seemed to be sharpened to needle-points of vision.

"Twenty five past," he said. "You're the second to come. I'm first this morning."

Ursula sat down gingerly on the edge of a chair, and watched his thin red hands rubbing away on the white surface of the paper, then pausing, pulling up a corner of the sheet, peering, and rubbing away again. There was a great heap of curled, white and scribbled sheets on the table.

"Must you do so many?" asked Ursula.

Again the man glanced up sharply. He was about thirty or thirty three years old, thin, greenish, with a long nose and a sharp face. His eyes were blue, and sharp as points of steel, rather beautiful, the girl thought.

"Sixty three," he answered.

"So many!" she said, gently. Then she remembered.

"But they're not all for your class, are they?" she added.

"Why aren't they?" he replied, a fierceness in his voice. Ursula was rather frightened by his mechanical ignoring of her and his directness of statement. It was something new to her. She had never been treated like this before, as if she did not count, as if she were addressing a machine.

"It is too many," she said sympathetically.

"You'll get about the same," he said.

That was all she received. She sat rather blank, not knowing how to feel. Still she liked him. He seemed so cross. There was a queer, sharp, keen-edge feeling about him that attracted her and frightened her at the same time. It was so cold, and against his nature.

The door opened, and a short, neutral-tinted young woman of about twenty eight appeared.

"Oh Ursula!" the newcomer exclaimed. "You *are* here early! My word, I'll warrant you don't keep it up.—That's Mr Williamson's peg—*This* is yours. Standard Five Teacher always has this. Aren't you going to take your hat off?"

Miss Violet Harby removed Ursula's waterproof from the peg on which it was hung, to one a little further down the row. She had already snatched the pins from her own stuff hat, and jammed them through her coat. She turned to Ursula, as she pushed up her frizzed, flat, dun-coloured hair.

"Isn't it a beastly morning!" she exclaimed, "beastly! And if there's one thing I hate above another, it's a wet Monday morning; —pack of kids trailing in anyhow-nohow, and no holding 'em—"

She had taken a black pinafore from a newspaper package, and was tying it round her waist.

"You've brought an apron, haven't you?" she said jerkily, glancing at Ursula. "Oh—you'll want one. You've no idea what a sight you'll look before half past four, what with chalk and ink and kids' dirty feet.—Well I can send a boy down to Mamma's for one."

"Oh, it doesn't matter," said Ursula.

"Oh, yes—I can send, easily," cried Miss Harby.

Ursula's heart sank. Everybody seemed so cock-sure, and so bossy. How was she going to get on with such jolty, jerky, bossy people. And Miss Harby had not spoken a word to the man at the table. She simply ignored him. Ursula felt the callous, crude rudeness between the two teachers.

The two girls went out into the passage. A few children were already clattering in the porch.

"Jim Richards," called Miss Harby, hard and authoritative. A boy came sheepishly forward.

"Shall you go down to our house for me, eh?" said Miss Harby, in a commanding, condescending, coaxing voice. She did not wait for an answer. "Go down and ask Mamma to send me one of my school pinas, for Miss Brangwen—shall you?"

The boy muttered a sheepish "Yes, Miss," and was moving away.

"Hey!" called Miss Harby. "Come here—Now what are you going for:—what shall you say to Mamma?"

"A school pina—" muttered the boy.

"'Please, Mrs Harby, Miss Harby says will you send her another school pinafore for Miss Brangwen, because she's come without one.'"

"Yes Miss," muttered the boy, head ducked, and was moving off. Miss Harby caught him back, holding him by the shoulder.

"What are you going to say?"

"Please Mrs Harby, Miss Harby wants a pinny for Miss Brang-win," muttered the boy very sheepishly.

"Miss *Brangwen*!" laughed Miss Harby, pushing him away. "Here, you'd better have my umbrella—wait a minute."

The unwilling boy was rigged up with Miss Harby's umbrella, and set off.

"Don't take long over it," called Miss Harby after him. Then she turned to Ursula, and said brightly:

"Oh, he's a caution, that lad—but not bad you know."

"No," Ursula agreed, weakly.

The latch of the door clicked, and they entered the big room. Ursula glanced down the place. Its rigid, long silence was official and chilling. Halfway down was a glass partition, the doors of which were open. A clock ticked re-echoing, and Miss Harby's voice sounded double as she said:

"This is the big room—Standard Five-Six-and-Seven.—Here's your place—Five—"

She stood in the near end of the great room. There was a small high teacher's desk facing a squadron of long benches, two high windows in the wall opposite.

It was fascinating and horrible to Ursula. The curious, unliving light in the room changed her character. She thought it was the rainy morning. Then she looked up again, because of the horrid feeling of being shut in a rigid, inflexible air, away from all feeling of the ordinary day; and she noticed that the windows were of ribbed, suffused glass.

The prison was round her now! She looked at the walls, colour washed, pale green and chocolate, at the large windows with frowsy geraniums against the pale glass, at the long rows of desks, arranged in a squadron, and dread filled her. This was a new world, a new life, with which she was threatened. But still excited, she climbed into her chair at her teacher's desk. It was high, and her feet could not reach the ground, but must rest on the step. Lifted up there, off the ground, she was in office. How queer, how queer it all was! How different it was from the mist of rain blowing over Cossethay. As she thought of her own village, a spasm of yearning crossed her, it seemed so far off, so lost to her.

She was here in this hard, stark reality—*reality*. It was queer that she should call this the reality, which she had never known till today, and which now so filled her with dread, that she wished she might go away. This was the reality—and Cossethay, her beloved, beautiful, well-known Cossethay, which was as herself unto her, that was minor reality. This prison of a school was reality. Here, then, she would sit in state, the queen of scholars! Here she would realise her dream of being the beloved teacher bringing light and joy to her children! But the desks before her had an abstract angularity that bruised her sentiment and made her shrink. She winced, feeling she had been a fool in her anticipations. She had brought her feelings and her generosity to where neither generosity nor emotion were wanted. And already she felt rebuffed, troubled by the new atmosphere, out of place.

She slid down, and they returned to the teachers' room. It was queer to feel that one ought to alter one's personality. She was nobody, there was no reality in herself, the reality was all outside of her, and she must apply herself to it.

Mr Harby was in the teachers' room, standing before a big, open cupboard, in which Ursula could see piles of pink blotting paper, heaps of shiny new books, boxes of chalk and bottles of coloured inks. It looked a treasure store.

The school-master was a short, sturdy man, with a fine head, and a heavy jowl. Nevertheless he was good-looking, with his shapely brows and nose, and his great, hanging moustache. He seemed absorbed in his work, and took no notice of Ursula's entry. There was something insulting in the way he could be so actively unaware of another person, so occupied.

When he had a moment of absence, he looked up from the table and said good-morning to Ursula. There was a pleasant light in his brown eyes. He seemed very manly and incontrovertible, like something she wanted to push over.

"You had a wet walk," he said to Ursula.

"Oh, I don't mind, I'm used to it," she replied, with a nervous little laugh.

But already he was not listening. Her words sounded ridiculous and babbling. He was taking no notice of her.

"You will sign your name here," he said to her, as if she were some child—"and the time when you come and go."

Ursula signed her name in the time book and stood back. No-one took any further notice of her. She beat her brains for something to say, but in vain.

"I'd let them in now," said Mr Harby to the thin man, who was very hastily arranging his papers.

The assistant teacher made no sign of acquiescence, and went on with what he was doing. The atmosphere in the room grew tense. At the last moment, Mr Brunt slipped into his coat.

"You will go to the girls' lobby," said the school-master to Ursula, with a fascinating, insulting geniality, purely official and domineering.

She went out and found Miss Harby, and another girl teacher, in the porch. On the asphalt yard the rain was failling. A toneless bell tang-tang-tanged drearily overhead, monotonously, insistently. It came to an end. Then Mr Brunt was seen, bare-headed, standing at the other gate of the school yard, blowing shrill blasts on a whistle and looking down the rainy, dreary street.

Boys in gangs and streams came trotting up, running past the master and with a loud clatter of feet and voices, over the yard to the boys' porch. Girls were running and walking through the other entrance.

In the porch where Ursula stood there was a great noise of girls who were tearing off their coats and hats, and hanging them on the racks bristling with pegs. There was a smell of wet clothing, a tossing out of wet, draggled hair, a noise of voices and feet.

The mass of girls grew greater, the rage around the pegs grew steadier, the scholars tended to fall into little noisy gangs in the porch. Then Violet Harby clapped her hands, clapped them louder, with a shrill "Quiet girls, quiet!"

There was a pause. The hubbub died down, but did not cease.

"What did I say?" cried Miss Harby shrilly.

There was almost complete silence. Sometimes a girl, rather late, whirled into the porch and flung off her things.

"Leaders—in place," commanded Miss Harby shrilly.

Pairs of girls in pinafores and long hair stood separate in the porch.

"Standard Four, Five and Six—fall in," cried Miss Harby.

There was a hubbub, which gradually resolved itself into three columns of girls, two and two, standing smirking in the passage. In among the peg-racks, other teachers were putting the lower classes into ranks.

Ursula stood by her own Standard Five. They were jerking their shoulders, tossing their hair, nudging, writhing, staring, grinning, whispering and twisting.

A sharp whistle was heard, and Standard Six, the biggest girls, set off, led by Miss Harby. Ursula, with her Standard Five, followed after. She stood beside a smirking, grinning row of girls, waiting in a narrow passage. What she was herself, she did not know.

Suddenly the sound of a piano was heard, and Standard Six set off hollowly down the big room. The boys had entered by another door. The piano played on, a march tune. Standard Five followed to the door of the big room. Mr Harby was seen away beyond at his desk. Mr Brunt guarded the other door of the room. Ursula's class pushed up. She stood near them. They glanced and smirked and shoved.

"Go on," said Ursula.

They tittered.

"Go on," said Ursula, for the piano continued.

The girls broke loosely into the room. Mr Harby, who had seemed immersed in some occupation, away at his desk, lifted his head and thundered,

"Halt!"

There was a halt, the piano stopped. The boys who were just starting through the other door, pushed back. The harsh, subdued voice of Mr Brunt was heard, then the booming shout of Mr Harby, from far down the room:

"Who told Standard Five girls to come in like that?"

Ursula crimsoned. Her girls were glancing up at her, smirking their accusation.

"I sent them in, Mr Harby," she said, in a clear, struggling voice. There was a moment of silence. Then Mr Harby roared from the distance:

"Go *back* to your places, Standard Five girls."

The girls glanced up at Ursula, accusing, rather jeering, furtive. They pushed back. Ursula's heart hardened with ignominious pain.

"Forward—march," came Mr Brunt's voice, and the girls set off, keeping time with the ranks of boys.

Ursula faced her class, some fifty five boys and girls who stood filling the ranks of the desks. She felt utterly non-existent. She had no place nor being there. She faced the block of children.

Down the room she heard the rapid firing of questions. She stood before her class not knowing what to to. She waited painfully. Her block of children, fifty unknown faces, watched her, hostile, ready to jeer. She felt as if she were in torture over a fire of faces. And on every side she was naked to them. Of unutterable length and torture the seconds went by.

Then she gathered courage. She heard Mr Brunt asking questions in mental arithmetic. She stood near to her class, so that her voice need not be raised too much, and faltering, uncertain, she said:

"Seven hats at two-pence ha'penny each?"

A grin went over the face of the class, seeing her commence. She was red and suffering. Then some hands shot up like blades, and she asked for the answer.

The day passed incredibly slowly. She never knew what to do, there came horrible gaps, when she was merely exposed to the children; and when, relying on some pert little girl for information, she had started a lesson, she did not know how to go on with it properly. The children were her masters. She deferred to them. She could always hear Mr Brunt. Like a machine, always in the same hard, high, inhuman voice he went on with his teaching, oblivious of everything. And before this inhuman number of children she was always at bay. She could not get away from it. There it was, this class of fifty collective children, depending on her for command, for command it hated and resented. It made her feel she could not breathe: she must suffocate, it was so inhuman. They were so many, that they were not children. They were a squadron. She could not speak as she would to a child, because they were not individual children, they were a collective inhuman thing.

Dinner-time came, and stunned, bewildered, solitary, she went into the teachers' room for dinner. Never had she felt such a stranger to life before. It seemed to her she had just disembarked from some strange horrible state where everything was as in hell, a condition of hard, malevolent system. And she was not really free. The afternoon ahead drew at her like some bondage.

The first week passed in a blind confusion. She did not know how to teach, and she felt she never would know. Mr Harby came down every now and again to her class, to see what she was doing. She felt so incompetent as he stood by, bullying and threatening, so unreal, that she wavered, became neutral and non-existent. But he stood there watching with that listening-genial smile of the eyes, that was really threatening; he said nothing, he made her go on teaching, she felt she had no soul in her body. Then he went away, and his going was like a derision. The class was his class. She was a wavering substitute. He thrashed and bullied, he was hated. But he was master. Though she was gentle and always considerate of her class, yet they belonged to Mr Harby, and they did not belong to her. Like some invincible source of the mechanism he kept all power to himself. And the class owned his power. And in school, it was power and power alone that mattered.

Soon Ursula came to dread him, and at the bottom of her dread was a seed of hate, for she despised him, yet he was master of her. Then she began to get on. All the other teachers hated him, and fanned their hatred among themselves. For he was master of them and the children, he stood like a bull to make absolute his authority over the herd. That seemed to be his one reason in life, to hold blind authority over the school. His teachers were his subjects as much as the pupils. Only, because they had some authority, his instinct was to detest them.

Ursula could not make herself a favorite with him. From the first moment she set hard against him. She set against Violet Harby also, even though she did not dislike her. Mr Harby was, however, too much for her, he was something she could not come to grips with, something too strong for her. She tried to approach him as a young bright girl usually approaches a man, expecting a little chivalrous courtesy. But the fact that she was a girl, a woman, was ignored or used as a matter for contempt against her. She did not know what she was, nor what she must be. She wanted to remain her own responsive, personal self.

So she taught on. She made friends with the Standard Three teacher, Maggie Schofield. Miss Schofield was about twenty years old, a subdued girl who held aloof from the other teachers. She was rather beautiful, meditative, and seemed to live in another, lovelier world.

Ursula took her dinner to school, and during the second week ate it in Miss Schofield's room. Standard Three classroom stood by itself and had windows on two sides, looking on to the playground. It was a passionate relief to find such a retreat in the jarring school. For there were pots of chrysanthemums and coloured leaves, and a big jar of berries: there were pretty little pictures on the wall, photogravure reproductions from Greuze and Reynolds's "Age of Innocence," giving an air of intimacy; so that the room, with its window space, its smaller, tidier desks, its touch of pictures and flowers, made Ursula at once glad. Here at last was a little personal touch, to which she could respond.

It was Monday. She had been at school a week and was getting used to the surroundings, though she was still an entire foreigner in herself. She looked forward to having dinner with Maggie. That was the bright spot in the day. Maggie was so strong and remote, walking with slow, sure steps down a hard road, carrying the dream within her. Ursula went through the class-teaching as through a meaningless daze.

Her class tumbled out at midday in haphazard fashion. She did not yet realise what host she was gathering against herself by her superior tolerance, her kindness and her *laisser-aller*. They were gone, and she was rid of them, and that was all. She hurried away to the teachers' room.

Mr Brunt was crouching at the small stove, putting a little rice-pudding into the oven. He rose then, and attentively poked in a small saucepan on the hob with a fork. Then he replaced the saucepan lid.

"Aren't they done?" asked Ursula gaily, breaking in on his tense absorption.

She always kept a bright, blithe manner and was pleasant to all the teachers. For she felt like the swan among the geese, of superior heritage and belonging. And her pride at being the swan in this ugly school was not yet abated.

"Not yet," replied Mr Brunt, laconic.

"I wonder if my dish is hot," she said, bending down at the oven. She half expected him to look for her, but he took no notice. She was hungry, and she poked her finger eagerly in the pot, to see if her brussels sprouts and potatoes and meat were ready. They were not.

"Don't you think it's rather jolly, bringing dinner?" she said to Mr Brunt.

"I don't know as I do," he said, spreading a serviette on a corner of a table, and not looking at her.

"I suppose it is too far for you to go home?"

"Yes," he said. Then he rose and looked at her. He had the bluest, fiercest, most pointed eyes that she had ever met. He stared at her with growing fierceness.

"If I were you, Miss Brangwen," he said, menacingly, "I should get a bit tighter hand over my class."

Ursula shrank.

"Would you?" she asked, sweetly, yet in terror. "Aren't I strict enough?"

"Because!" he repeated, taking no notice of her, "they'll get you down if you don't tackle 'em pretty quick. They'll pull you down, and worry you, till Harby gets you shifted—that's how it'll be ... you won't be here another six weeks—" and he filled his mouth with food—"if you don't tackle 'em, and tackle 'em quick."

"Oh but—" Ursula said, resentfully, ruefully. The terror was deep in her.

"Harby'll not help you. This is what he'll do—he'll let you go on, getting worse and worse, till either you clear out or he clears you out.—It doesn't matter to me, except that you'll leave a class behind you as I hope *I* shan't have to cope with—"

She heard the accusation in the man's voice, and felt condemned. But still, school had not yet become a definite reality to her. She was shirking it. It was reality, but it was all outside her. And she fought against Mr Brunt's representation. She did not want to realise.

"Will it be so terrible?" she said, quivering, rather beautiful, but with a slight touch of condescension, because she would not betray her own trepidation.

"Terrible?" said the man, turning to his potatoes again. "I dunno about terrible."

"I *do* feel frightened," said Ursula. "The children seem so—."

"What?" said Miss Harby, entering at that moment.

"Why," said Ursula, "Mr Brunt says I ought to tackle my class," and she laughed uneasily.

"Oh, you have to keep order if you want to teach," said Miss Harby, hard, superior, trite.

Ursula did not answer. She felt non valid before them.

"If you want to be let to *live*, you have," said Mr Brunt.

"Well if you can't keep order, what good *are* you?" said Miss Harby.

"An' you've got to do it by yourself,"—his voice rose like the bitter cry of the prophets. "You'll get no *help* from anybody."

"Oh indeed!" said Miss Harby. "Some people can't be helped." And she departed.

The air of hostility and disintegration, of wills working in antagonistic subordination, was hideous. Mr Brunt, subordinate, afraid, acid with shame, frightened her. Ursula wanted to run. She only wanted to clear out, not to understand.

Then Miss Schofield came in, and with her another, more restful note. Ursula at once turned for confirmation to the newcomer. Maggie remained personal within all this unclean system of authority.

"Is the big Anderson here?" she asked of Mr Brunt. And they spoke of some affair about two scholars, coldly, officially.

Miss Schofield took her brown dish, and Ursula followed with her own. The cloth was laid in the pleasant Standard Three room, there was a jar with two or three monthly roses on the table.

"It is so nice in here, you *have* made it different," said Ursula, gaily. But she was afraid. The atmosphere of the school was upon her.

"The big room," said Miss Schofield; "ha, it's misery to be in it!"

She too spoke with bitterness. She too lived in the ignominious position of an upper servant hated by the master above and the class beneath. She was, she knew, liable to attack from either side at any minute, or from both at once, for the authorities would listen to the complaints of parents, and both would turn round on the mongrel authority, the teacher.

So there was a hard, bitter withholding in Maggie Schofield even as she poured out her savoury mess of big, golden beans and brown gravy.

"It is a vegetarian hot-pot," said Miss Schofield. "Would you like to try it?"

"I should love to," said Ursula.

Her own dinner seemed coarse and ugly beside this savoury, clean dish.

"I've never eaten vegetarian things," she said. "But I should think they can be good."

"I'm not really a vegetarian," said Maggie, "I don't like to bring meat to school."

"No," said Ursula, "I don't think I do either."

And again her soul rang an answer to a new refinement, a new liberty. If all vegetarian things were as nice as this, she would be glad to escape the slight uncleanness of meat.

"How good!" she cried.

"Yes," said Miss Schofield, and she proceeded to tell her the receipt. The two girls passed on to talk about themselves. Ursula told all about the High School and about her matriculation, bragging a little. She felt so poor, here, in this ugly place. Miss Schofield listened with brooding, handsome face, rather gloomy.

"Couldn't you have got to some better place than this?" she asked at length.

"I didn't know what it was like," said Ursula, doubtfully.

"Ah!" said Miss Schofield, and she turned aside her head with a bitter motion.

"Is it as horrid as it seems?" asked Ursula, frowning lightly, in fear.

"It *is*," said Miss Schofield bitterly. "Ha!—it is *hateful!*"

Ursula's heart sank, seeing even Miss Schofield in the deadly bondage.

"It is Mr Harby," said Maggie Schofield, breaking forth. "I don't think I *could* live again in the big room.—Mr Brunt's voice and Mr Harby—ah—"

She turned aside her head with a deep hurt. Some things she could not bear.

"Is Mr Harby really horrid?" asked Ursula, venturing into her own dread.

"He!—why, he's just a bully," said Miss Schofield, raising her shamed dark eyes, that flamed with tortured contempt. "He's not bad as long as you keep in with him, and refer to him, and do everything in his way—but—it's all so *mean*! It's just a question of fighting on both sides—and those great *louts*—"

She spoke with difficulty, and with increased bitterness. She had evidently suffered. Her soul was raw with ignominy. Ursula suffered in response.

"But why is it so horrid?" she asked, helplessly.

"You can't do *anything*," said Miss Schofield. "*He's* against you on one side, and he sets the children against you on the other. The children are simply awful. You've got to *make* them do everything. Everything, everything has got to come out of you. Whatever they learn, you've got to force it into them—and that's how it is."

Ursula felt her heart faint inside her. Why must she grasp all this, why must she force learning on fifty five reluctant children, having all the time an ugly, rude jealousy behind her, ready to throw her to the mercy of the herd of children, who would like to rend her as a weaker representative of authority. A great dread of her task possessed her. She saw Mr Brunt, Miss Harby, Miss Schofield, all the school-teachers, drudging unwillingly at the graceless task of compelling many children into one disciplined, mechanical set, reducing the whole set to an automatic state of obedience and attention, and then of commanding their acceptance of various pieces of knowledge. The first great task was to reduce sixty children to one state of mind, or being. This state must be produced automatically, through the will of the teacher and the will of the whole school authority, imposed upon the will of the children. The point was that the head-master and the teachers should have one will in authority, which should bring the will of the children into accord. But the head-master was narrow and exclusive. The will of the teachers could not agree with his, their separate wills refused to be so subordinated. So there was a state of anarchy, leaving the final judgment to the children themselves, which authority should exist.

So there existed a set of separate wills, each straining itself to the utmost to exert its own authority. Children will never naturally acquiesce to sitting in a class and submitting to knowledge. They must be compelled by a stronger, wiser will. Against which will they must always strain to revolt. So that the first great effort of every teacher of a large class must be to bring the will of the children into accordance with his own will. And this he can only do through an abnegation of his personal self, and an application of a system of laws, for the purpose of achieving a certain calculable result, the imparting of certain knowledge. Whereas Ursula thought she was going to become the first wise teacher, by making the whole business personal, and using no compulsion. She believed entirely in her own personality.

So that she was in a very deep mess. In the first place she was offering to a class a relationship which only one or two of the children were sensitive enough to appreciate, so that the mass were left outsiders, therefore against her. Secondly she was placing herself in passive antagonism to the one fixed authority of Mr Harby, so that the scholars could more safely harry her. She did not know, but her instinct gradually warned her. She was tortured by the voice of Mr Brunt. On it went, jarring, harsh, full of hate, but so monotonous, it nearly drove her mad: always the same set, harsh monotony. The man was become a mechanism working on and on and on. But the personal man was in subdued friction all the time. It was horrible—all hate! Must she be like this? She could feel the ghastly necessity. She must become the same—put away her personal self, become an instrument, an abstraction, working upon a certain material, the class, to achieve a set purpose of making them know so much each day. And she could not submit. Yet gradually she felt the invincible iron closing upon her. The sky was being blocked out. Often, when she went out at playtime and saw a luminous blue sky with changing clouds, it seemed just a fantasy, like a piece of painted scenery. Her heart was so black and tangled in the teaching, her personal self was shut in prison, abolished, she was subjugate to a bad, destructive will. How then could the sky be shining? There was no sky, there was no luminous atmosphere of out-of-doors. Only the inside of the school was real—hard, concrete, real and vicious.

She would not yet, however, let school quite overcome her. She always said "It is not a permanency, it will come to an end." She could always see beyond the place, see the time when she had left it. On Sundays, and on holidays, when she was away at Cossethay or in the woods where the beech-leaves were fallen, she could think of St Philips Church School, and by an effort of will put it in the picture as a dirty little low-squatting building that made a very tiny mound under the sky, while the great beech woods spread immense about her, and the afternoon was spacious and wonderful. Moreover the children, the scholars, they were insignificant little objects far away, oh far away. And what power had they over her free soul? A fleeting thought of them, as she kicked her way through the beech-leaves, and they were gone! But her will was tense against them all the time.

All the while, they pursued her. She had never had such a passionate love of the beautiful things about her. Sitting on top of the tram-car, at evening, sometimes school was swept away as she saw a magnificent sky settling down. And her breast, her very hands clamoured for the lovely flare of sunset. It was poignant almost to agony, her reaching for it. She almost cried aloud, seeing the sundown so lovely.

For she was held away. It was no matter how she said to herself that school existed no more once she had left it. It existed. It was within her like a dark weight, controlling her movement. It was in vain the high-spirited, proud young girl flung off the school and its association with her. She was Miss Brangwen, she was Standard Five Teacher, she had her most important being in her work now.

Constantly haunting her, like a darkness hovering over her heart and threatening to swoop down on it at every moment, was the sense that somehow, somehow she was brought down. Bitterly she denied unto herself that she was really a school-teacher. Leave that to the Violet Harbys. She herself would stand clear of the accusation.—It was in vain she denied it.

Within herself some recording hand seemed to point mechanically to a negation. She was incapable of fulfilling her task. She could never for a moment escape from the fatal weight of the knowledge.

And so she felt inferior to Violet Harby. Miss Harby was a splendid teacher. She could keep order and inflict knowledge on a class with remarkable efficiency. It was no good Ursula's protesting to herself that she was infinitely, infinitely the superior of Violet Harby. She knew that Violet Harby succeeded where she failed, and this in a task which was almost a test of her. She felt something all the time wearing upon her, wearing her down. She went about in these first weeks trying to deny it, to say she was free as ever. She tried not to feel at a disadvantage before Miss Harby, tried to keep up the effect of her own superiority. But a great weight was on her, which Violet Harby could bear, and she herself could not.

Though she did not give in, she never succeeded. Her class was getting in worse condition, she knew herself less and less secure in teaching it. Ought she to withdraw and go home again? Ought she to say she had come to the wrong place, and so retire? Her very life was at test.

She went on rather doggedly, blindly, waiting for a crisis. Mr Harby had now begun to persecute her. Her dread and hatred of him grew and loomed larger and larger. She was afraid he was going to bully her and destroy her. He began to persecute her because she could not keep her class in proper condition, because her class was the weak link in the chain which made up the school.

One of the offences was that her class was noisy and disturbed Mr Harby, as he took Standard Seven at the other end of the room. She was taking composition on a certain morning, walking in among the scholars. Some of the boys had dirty ears and necks, their clothing smelled unpleasantly, but she could ignore it. She corrected the writing as she went.

"When you say 'their fur is brown,' how do you write 'their'?" she asked.

There was a little pause: the boys were always jeeringly backward in answering. They had begun to jeer at her authority altogether.

"Please Miss, t-h-e-i-r," spelled a lad, loudly, with a note of mockery.

At that moment Mr Harby was passing.

"Stand up Hill!" he called, in a big voice.

Everybody started. Ursula watched the boy. He was evidently poor, and rather cunning. A stiff bit of hair stood straight off his forehead, the rest fitted close to his meagre head. He was pale and colourless.

"Who told you to call out?" thundered Mr Harby.

The boy looked up and down, with a guilty air, and a cunning, cynical reserve.

"Please Sir, I was answering," he replied, with the same humble insolence.

"Go to my desk."

The boy set off down the room, the big black jacket hanging in dejected folds about him, his thin legs, rather knocked at the knees, going already with the pauper's crawl, his feet in their big boots scarcely lifted. Ursula watched him in his crawling, slinking progress down the room. He was one of *her* boys! When he got to the desk, he looked round, half furtively, with a sort of cunning grin and pathetic leer, at the big boys of Standard VII. Then, pitiable, pale, in his dejected garments, he lounged under the menace of the head-master's desk, with one thin leg crooked at the knee and the foot stuck out sideways, his hands in the low-hanging pockets of his man's jacket.

Ursula tried to get her attention back to the class. The boy gave her a little horror, and she was at the same time hot with pity for him. She felt she wanted to scream. She was responsible for the boy's punishment. Mr Harby was looking at her handwriting on the board. He turned to the class.

"Pens down."

The children put down their pens and looked up.

"Fold arms."

They pushed back their books and folded arms.

Ursula, stuck among the back forms, could not extricate herself.

"*What* is your composition about?" asked the head-master. Every hand shot up. "The—" stuttered some voice in its eagerness to answer.

"I wouldn't advise you to call out," said Mr Harby. He would have a pleasant voice, full and musical, but for the detestable menace that always tailed in it. He stood unmoved, his eyes twinkling under his bushy black brows, watching the class. There was something fascinating in him, as he stood, and again she wanted to scream. She was all jarred, she did not know what she felt.

"Well, Alice?" he said.

"The rabbit," piped a girl's voice.

"A very easy subject for Standard Five."

Ursula felt a slight shame of incompetence. She was exposed

before the class. And she was tormented by the contradictoriness of everything. Mr Harby stood so strong, and so male, with his black brows and clear forehead, the heavy jaw, the big, overhanging moustache: such a man, with strength and male power, and a certain blind, native beauty. She might have liked him as a man. And here he stood in some other capacity, bullying over such a trifle as a boy's speaking out without permission. Yet he was not a little, fussy man. He seemed to have some cruel, stubborn, evil spirit, he was imprisoned in a task too small and petty for him, which yet, in a servile acquiescence, he would fulfil, because he had to earn his living. He had no finer control over himself, only this blind, dogged, wholesale will. He would keep the job going, since he must. And his job was to make the children spell the word "caution" correctly, and put a capital letter after a full-stop. So at this he hammered with his suppressed hatred, always suppressing himself, till he was beside himself. Ursula suffered bitterly as he stood, short and handsome and powerful, teaching her class. It seemed such a miserable thing for him to be doing. He had a decent, powerful, rude soul. What did he care about the composition on "The Rabbit"? Yet his will kept him there before the class, threshing the trivial subject. It was habit with him now, to be so little and vulgar, out of place. She saw the shamefulness of his position, felt the fettered wickedness in him which would blaze out into evil rage in the long run, so that he was like a persistent, strong creature tethered. It was really intolerable. The jarring was torture to her. She looked over the silent, attentive class that seemed to have crystallised into order and rigid, neutral form. This he had it in his power to do, to crystallise the children into hard, mute fragments, fixed under his will: his brute will, which fixed them by sheer force. She too must learn to subdue them to her will: she must. For it was her duty, since the school was such. He had crystallised the class into order. But to see him, a strong, powerful man, using all his power for such a purpose, seemed almost horrible. There was something hideous about it. The strange, genial light in his eye was really vicious, and ugly, his smile was one of torture. He could not be impersonal. He could not have a clear, pure purpose, he could only exercise his own brute will. He did not believe in the least in the education he kept inflicting year after year upon the children. So he must bully, only bully, even while it tortured his strong, wholesome nature with shame like a spur always galling. He was so blind and ugly and out of place. Ursula could not bear it as he stood there. The whole situation was wrong and ugly.

The lesson was finished, Mr Harby went away. At the far end of the room, she heard the whistle and thud of the cane. Her heart stood still within her. She could not bear it, no, she could not bear it when the boy was beaten. It made her sick. She felt that she must go out of his school, this torture-place. And she hated the schoolmaster, thoroughly and finally. The brute, had he no shame? He should never be allowed to continue the atrocity of this bullying cruelty. Then Hill came crawling back, blubbering piteously. There was something desolate about his blubbering that nearly broke her heart. For after all, if she had kept her class in proper discipline, this would never have happened, Hill would never have called out, and been caned.

She began the arithmetic lesson. But she was distracted. The boy Hill sat away on the back desk, huddled up, blubbering and sucking his hand. It was a long time. She dared not go near, nor speak to him. She felt ashamed before him. And she felt she could not forgive the boy for being the huddled, blubbering object, all wet and snivelled, which he was.

She went on correcting the sums. But there were too many children. She could not get round the class. And Hill was on her conscience. At last he had stopped crying, and sat bunched over his hands, playing quietly. Then he looked up at her. His face was dirty with tears, his eyes had a curious washed look, like the sky after rain, a sort of wanness. He bore no malice. He had already forgotten, and was waiting to be restored to the normal position.

"Go on with your work Hill," she said.

The children were playing over their arithmetic, and, she knew, cheating thoroughly. She wrote another sum on the blackboard. She could not get round the class. She went again to the front to watch. Some were ready. Some were not. What was she to do?

At last it was time for recreation. She gave the order to cease working, and in some way or other got her class out of the room. Then she faced the disorderly litter of blotted, uncorrected books, of broken rulers and chewed pens. And her heart sank in sickness. The misery was getting deeper.

The trouble went on and on, day after day. She had always piles of books to mark, myriads of errors to correct, a heart-wearying task that she loathed. And the work got worse and worse. When she tried to flatter herself that the composition grew more alive, more interesting, she had to see that the handwriting grew more and more slovenly, the books more filthy and disgraceful. She tried what she could, but it was of no use. But she was not going to take it seriously. Why should she? Why should she say to herself, that it mattered, if she failed to teach a class to write perfectly neatly? Why should she take the blame unto herself?

Pay day came, and she received four pounds two shillings and one penny. She was very proud that day. She had never had so much money before. And she had earned it all herself. She sat on the top of the tram-car fingering the gold and fearing she might lose it. She felt so established and strong, because of it. And when she got home, she said to her mother:

"It is pay day today, mother."

"Ay," said her her mother coolly.

Then Ursula put down fifty shillings on the table.

"That is my board," she said.

"Ay," said her mother, letting it lie.

Ursula was hurt. Yet she had paid her scot. She was free. She paid for what she had. There remained moreover thirty two shillings of her own. She would not spend any, she who was naturally a spendthrift, because she could not bear to damage her fine gold.

She had a standing ground now apart from her parents. She was something else besides the mere daughter of William and Anna Brangwen. She was independent. She earned her own living. She was an important member of the working community. She was sure that fifty shillings a month quite paid for her keep. If her mother received fifty shillings a month for each of the children, she would have twenty pounds a month and no clothes to provide. Very well then.

Ursula was independent of her parents. She now adhered elsewhere. Now, the "Board of Education" was a phrase that rang significant to her, and she felt Whitehall far beyond her as her ultimate home. In the government, she knew which minister had supreme control over Education, and it seemed to her that, in some way, he was connected with her, as her father was connected with her.

She had another self, another responsibility. She was no longer only Ursula Brangwen, daughter of William Brangwen. She was also

Standard Five Teacher in St Philips School. And it was a case now of being Standard Five Teacher, and nothing else. For she could not escape.

Neither could she succeed. That was her horror. As the weeks passed on, there was no Ursula Brangwen, free and jolly. There was only a girl of that name obsessed by the fact that she could not manage her class of children. At week-ends there came days of passionate reaction, when she went mad with the taste of liberty, when merely to be free in the morning, to sit down at her embroidery and stitch the coloured silks was a passion of delight. For the prison house was always awaiting her!—this was only a respite. As her chained heart knew well. So that she seized hold of the swift hours of the week-end, and wrung the last drop of sweetness out of them, in a little, cruel frenzy.

She did not tell anybody how this state was a torture to her. She did not confide, either to Gudrun or to her parents, how horrible she found it, to be a school-teacher. But when Sunday night came, and she felt the Monday morning at hand, she was strung up tight with dreadful anticipation, because the strain and the torture was near again.

She did not believe she could ever teach that great, brutish class, in that brutal school: ever, ever. And yet, if she failed, she must in some way go under. She must admit that the man's world was too strong for her, she could not take her place in it; she must go down before Mr Harby. And all her life henceforth, she must go on, never having freed herself of the man's world, never having achieved the freedom of the great world of responsible work. Maggie had taken her place there, she had even stood level with Mr Harby, and got free of him; and her soul was always wandering in far-off alleys and glades of poetry. Maggie was free. Yet there was something like subjection in Maggie's very freedom. Mr Harby, the man, disliked the reserved woman, Maggie. Mr Harby, the school-master, respected his teacher, Miss Schofield.

For the present, however, Ursula only envied and admired Maggie. She herself had still to get where Maggie had got. She had still to make her footing. She had taken up a position on Mr Harby's ground, and she must keep it. For now he was beginning a regular attack on her, to drive her away out of his school. She could not keep order. Her class was a turbulent crowd, and the weak spot in the school's work. Therefore she must go, and someone more useful must come in her place, someone who could keep discipline.

The head-master had worked himself into an obsession of fury against her. He only wanted her gone. She had come, she had got worse as the weeks went on, she was absolutely no good. His system, which was his very life in school, the outcome of his bodily movement, was attacked and threatened at the point where Ursula was included. She was the danger that threatened his body with a blow, a fall. And blindly, thoroughly, moving from strong instinct of opposition, he set to work to expel her.

When he punished one of her children as he had punished the boy Hill, for an offence against *himself*, he made the punishment extra heavy with the significance that the extra stroke came in because of the weak teacher who allowed all these things to be. When he punished for an offence against *her*, he punished lightly, as if offences against her were not significant. Which all the children knew, and they behaved accordingly.

Every now and again Mr Harby would swoop down to examine exercise books. For a whole hour, he would be going round the class, taking book after book, comparing page after page, whilst Ursula stood aside for all the remarks and fault-finding to be pointed at her through the scholars. It was true, since she had come, the composition books had grown more and more untidy, disorderly, filthy. Mr Harby pointed to the pages done before her régime, and to those done after, and fell into a passion of rage. Many children he sent out to the front with their books. And after he had thoroughly gone through the silent and quivering class, he caned the worst offenders well, in front of the others, thundering in real passion of anger and chagrin:

"Such a condition in a class, I can't believe it! It is simply disgraceful! I can't think how you have been let to get like this! Every Monday morning I shall come down and examine these books. So don't think that because there is nobody paying any attention to you, that you are free to unlearn everything you ever learnt and go back till you are not fit for Standard Three. I shall examine all books every Monday—"

Then in a rage, he went away with his cane, leaving Ursula to confront a pale, quivering class, whose childish faces were shut in blank resentment, fear, and bitterness, whose souls were full of anger and contempt of *her* rather than of the master, whose eyes looked at her with the cold, inhuman accusation of children. And she could hardly make mechanical words to speak to them. When she gave an order, they obeyed with an insolent off-handedness, as if to say: "As for you, do you think we would obey *you*, but for the master?" She sent the blubbering, caned boys to their seats, knowing that they too jeered at her and her authority, holding her weakness responsible for what punishment had overtaken them. And she knew the whole position, so that even her horror of physical beating and suffering sank to a deeper pain, and became a moral judgment upon her, worse than any hurt.

She must, during the next week, watch over her books, and punish any fault. Her soul decided it coldly. Her personal desire was dead for that day at least. She must have nothing more of herself in school. She was to be Standard Five Teacher only. That was her duty. In school, she was nothing but Standard Five Teacher. Ursula Brangwen must be excluded.

So that, pale, shut, at last distant and impersonal, she saw no longer the child, how his eyes danced, or how he had a queer little soul that could not be bothered with shaping handwriting so long as he dashed down what he thought. She saw no children, only the task that was to be done. And keeping her eyes there, on the task and not on the child, she was impersonal enough to punish where she could otherwise only have sympathised, understood, and condoned, to approve where she would have been merely uninterested before. But her interest had no place any more.

It was agony to the impulsive, bright girl of seventeen to become distant and official, having no personal relationship with the children. For a few days, after the agony of the Monday, she succeeded, and had some success with her class. But it was a state not natural to her, and she began to relax.

Then came another infliction. There were not enough pens to go round the class. She sent to Mr Harby for more. He came in person.

"Not enough pens, Miss Brangwen?" he said, with the smile and calm of exceeding rage against her.

"No, we are six short," she said, quaking.

"Oh, how is that?" he said, menacingly. Then, looking over the class, he asked:

"How many are there here today?"

"Fifty two," said Ursula, but he did not take any notice, counting for himself.

"Fifty two," he said. "And how many pens are there, Staples?"

Ursula was now silent. He would not heed her if she answered, since he had addressed the monitor.

"That's a very curious thing," said Mr Harby, looking over the silent class with a slight grin of fury. All the childish faces looked up at him blank and exposed.

"A few days ago," the master went on, "there were sixty pens for this class—now there are forty eight. What is forty eight from sixty, Williams?" There was a sinister suspense in the question. A thin, ferret-faced boy in a sailor suit started up exaggeratedly.

"Please Sir!" he said. Then a slow, sly grin came over his face. He did not know. There was a tense silence. The boy dropped his head. Then he looked up again, a little cunning triumph in his eyes. "Twelve," he said.

"I would advise you to attend," said the head-master dangerously. The boy sat down.

"Forty eight from sixty is twelve: so there are twelve pens to account for. Have you looked for them, Staples?"

"Yes Sir."

"Then look again."

The scene dragged on. Two pens were found: ten were missing. Then the storm burst.

"Am I to have you thieving, besides your dirt and bad work and bad behaviour?" the head-master began. "Not content with being the worst-behaved and dirtiest class in the school, you are thieves into the bargain, are you? It is a very funny thing! Pens don't melt into the air: pens are not in the habit of mizzling away into nothing. What has become of them? For they must be found, and found by Standard Five. They were lost by Standard Five, and they must be found."

Ursula stood and listened, her heart hard and cold. She was so much upset, that she felt almost mad. Something in her tempted her to turn on the head-master and tell him to stop, about the miserable pens. But she did not. She could not.

After every session, morning and evening, she had the pens counted. Still they were missing. And pencils and indiarubbers disappeared. She kept the class staying behind, till the things were found. But as soon as Mr Harby had gone out of the room, the boys began to jump about and shout, and at last they bolted in a body from the school.

This was drawing near a crisis. She could not tell Mr Harby because, while he would punish the class, he would make her the cause of the punishment, and her class would pay her back with disobedience and derision. Already there was a deadly hostility grown up between her and the children. After keeping in the class, at evening, to finish some work, she would find boys dodging behind her, calling after her:

"Brangwen, Brangwen—Proud-arse."

When she went into Ilkeston of a Saturday morning with Gudrun she heard again the voices yelling after her:

"Brangwen, Brangwen."

She pretended to take no notice, but she coloured with shame at being held up to derision in the public street. She, Ursula Brangwen of Cossethay, could not escape from the Standard Five Teacher which she was. In vain she went out to buy ribbon for her hat. They called after her, the boys she tried to teach.

And one evening, as she went from the edge of the town into the country, stones came flying at her. Then the passion of shame and anger surpassed her. She walked on unheeding, beside herself. Because of the darkness, she could not see who were those that threw. But she did not want to know.

Only in her soul a change took place. Never more, and never more would she give herself as individual to her class. Never more would she, Ursula Brangwen, the girl she was, the person she was, come into contact with those boys. She would be Standard Five Teacher, as far away personally from her class as if she had never set foot in St Philips School. She would just obliterate them all, and keep herself apart, take them as scholars only.

So her face grew more and more shut, and over her flayed, exposed soul of a young girl who had gone open and warm to give herself to the children, there set a hard, insentient thing, that worked mechanically according to a system imposed.

It seemed she scarcely saw her class the next day. She could only feel her will, and what she would have of this class which she must grasp into subjection. It was no good, any more, to appeal, to play upon the better feelings of the class. Her swift-working soul realised this.

She, as teacher, must bring them all, as scholars, into subjection. And this she was going to do. All else she would forsake. She had become hard and impersonal, almost avengeful on herself as well as

The Rainbow

on them, since the stone-throwing. She did not want to be a person, to be herself any more, after such humiliation. She would assert herself for mastery, be only teacher. She was set now. She was going to fight and subdue.

She knew by now her enemies in the class. The one she hated most was Williams. He was a sort of defective, not bad enough to be so classed. He could read with fluency, and had plenty of cunning intelligence. But he could not keep still. And he had a kind of sickness very repulsive to a sensitive girl, something cunning and etiolated and degenerate. Once he had thrown an inkwell at her, in one of his mad little rages. Twice he had run home out of class. He was a well-known character.

And he grinned up his sleeve at this girl-teacher, sometimes hanging round her to fawn on her. But this made her dislike him the more. He had a kind of leech-like power.

From one of the children she took a supple cane, and this she determined to use when real occasion came. One morning, at composition, she said to the boy Williams:

"Why have you made this blot?"

"Please Miss, it fell off my pen," he whined out, in the mocking voice that he was so clever in using. The boys near snorted with laughter. For Williams was an actor. He could tickle the feelings of his hearers subtly. Particularly he could tickle the children with him into ridiculing his teacher, or indeed, any authority of which he was not afraid. He had that peculiar gaol instinct.

"Then you must stay in and finish another page of composition," said the teacher.

This was against her usual sense of justice, and the boy resented it derisively. At twelve o'clock, she caught him slinking out.

"Williams, sit down," she said.

And there she sat, and there he sat, alone, opposite to her, on the back desk, looking up at her with his furtive eyes every minute.

"Please Miss, I've got to go an errand," he called out insolently.

"Bring me your book," said Ursula.

The boy came out, flapping his book along the desks. He had not written a line.

"Go back and do the writing you have to do," said Ursula.

And she sat at her desk trying to correct books. She was trembling and upset. And for an hour the miserable boy writhed and grinned in his seat. At the end of that time he had done five lines.

368

"As it is so late now," said Ursula, "you will finish the rest this evening."

The boy kicked his way insolently down the passage.

The afternoon came again. Williams was there, glancing at her, and her heart beat thick for she knew it was a fight between them. She watched him.

During the geography lesson, as she was pointing to the map with her cane, the boy continually ducked his whitish head under the desk, and attracted the attention of other boys.

"Williams," she said, gathering her courage, for it was critical now to speak to him, "what are you doing?"

He lifted his face, the sore-rimmed eyes half smiling. There was something intrinsically indecent about him. Ursula shrank away.

"Nothing," he replied, feeling a triumph.

"What are you doing?" she repeated, her heart-beat suffocating her.

"Nothing," replied the boy, insolently, aggrieved, comic.

"If I speak to you again, you must go down to Mr Harby," she said.

But this boy was a match even for Mr Harby. He was so persistent, so cringing and flexible, he howled so when he was hurt, that the master hated more the teacher who sent him than he hated the boy himself. For of the boy he was sick of the sight. Which Williams knew. He grinned visibly.

Ursula turned to the map again, to go on with the geography lesson. But there was a little ferment in the class. Williams' spirit infected them all. She heard a scuffle, and then she trembled inwardly. If they all turned on her this time, she was beaten.

"Please Miss—" called a voice in distress.

She turned round. One of the boys she liked was ruefully holding out a torn celluloid collar. She heard the complaint, feeling futile.

"Go in front, Wright," she said.

She was trembling in every fibre. A big, sullen boy, not bad but very difficult, slouched out to the front. She went on with the lesson, aware that Williams was making faces at Wright, and that Wright was grinning behind her. She was afraid. She turned to the map again. And she was afraid.

"Please Miss, Williams—" came a sharp cry, and a boy on the back row was standing up, with drawn, pained brows, half a mocking grin on his pain, half real resentment against Williams—"Please Miss, he's nipped me,"—and he rubbed his leg ruefully.

"Come in front, Williams," she said.

The rat-like boy sat with his pale smile and did not move.

"Come in front," she repeated, definite now.

"I shan't," he cried, snarling, rat-like, grinning.

Something went click in Ursula's soul. Her face and eyes set, she went through the class, straight. The boy cowered before her glowering, fixed eyes. But she advanced on him, seized him by the arm, and dragged him from his seat. He clung to the form. It was the battle between him and her. Her instinct had suddenly become calm and quick. She jerked him from his grip, and dragged him, struggling and kicking, to the front. He kicked her several times, and clung to the forms as he passed, but she went on. The class was on its feet in excitement. She saw it, but made no move.

She knew if she let go the boy he would dash to the door. Already he had run home once out of her class. So she snatched her cane from the desk, and brought it down on him. He was writhing and kicking. She saw his face beneath her, white, with eyes like the eyes of a fish, stony, yet full of hate and horrible fear. And she loathed him, the hideous writhing thing that was nearly too much for her. In horror lest he should overcome her, and yet at the heart quite calm, she brought down the cane again and again, whilst he struggled making inarticulate noises, and lunging vicious kicks at her. With one hand she managed to hold him, and now and then, the cane came down on him. He writhed, like a mad thing. But the pain of the strokes cut through his writhing, vicious, coward's courage, bit deeper, till at last, with a long whimper that became a yell, he went limp. She let him go, and he rushed at her, his teeth and eyes glinting. There was a second of agonised terror in her heart: he was a beast thing. Then she caught him, and the cane came down on him. A few times, madly, in a frenzy, he lunged and writhed, to kick her. But again the cane broke him, he sank with a howling yell on the floor, and like a beaten beast lay there yelling.

Mr Harby had rushed up towards the end of this performance.

"What's the matter?" he roared.

Ursula felt as if something were going to break in her.

"I've thrashed him," she said, her breast heaving, forcing out the words on the last breath. The head-master stood choked with rage, helpless. She look at the writhing, howling figure on the floor.

"Get up," she said. The thing writhed away from her. She took a step forward. She had realised the presence of the head-master for one second, and then she was oblivious of it again.

"Get up," she said. And with a little dart, the boy was on his feet. His yelling dropped to a mad blubber. He had been in a frenzy.

"Go and stand by the radiator," she said.

As if mechanically, blubbering, he went.

The head-master stood robbed of movement or speech. His face was yellow, his hands twitched convulsively. But Ursula stood stiff not far from him. Nothing could touch her now: she was beyond Mr Harby. She was as if violated to death.

The head-master muttered something, turned, and went down the room, whence, from the far end, he was heard roaring in mad rage at his own class.

The boy blubbered wildly by the radiator. Ursula looked at the class. There were fifty pale, still faces watching her, a hundred round eyes fixed on her in an attentive, expressionless stare.

"Give out history readers," she said to the monitors.

There was dead silence. As she stood there, she could hear again the ticking of the clock, and the chock of piles of books taken out of the low cupboard. Then came the faint flap of books on the desks. The children passed in silence, their hands working in unison. They were no longer a pack, but each one separated into a silent, closed thing.

"Take page 125, and read that chapter," said Ursula.

There was a click of many books opened. The children found the page, and bent their heads obediently to read. And they read, mechanically.

Ursula, who was trembling violently, went and sat in her high chair. The blubbering of the boy continued. The strident voice of Mr Brunt, the roar of Mr Harby, came muffled through the glass partition. And now and then a pair of eyes rose from the reading book, rested on her a moment, watchful, as if calculating impersonally, then sank again.

She sat still without moving, her eyes watching the class, unseeing. She was quite still, and weak. She felt she could not raise her hand from the desk. If she sat there forever, she felt she could not move again, nor utter a command. It was a quarter past four. She almost dreaded the closing of the school, when she would be alone.

The class began to recover its ease, the tension relaxed. Williams was still crying. Mr Brunt was giving orders for the closing of the lesson. Ursula got down.

"Take your place, Williams," she said.

He dragged his feet across the room, wiping his face on his sleeve. As he sat down, he glanced at her furtively, his eyes still redder. Now he looked like some beaten rat.

At last the children were gone. Mr Harby trod by heavily, without looking her way, or speaking. Mr Brunt hesitated as she was locking her cupboard.

"If you settle Clarke and Letts in the same way, Miss Brangwen, you'll be all right," he said, his blue eyes glancing down in strange fellowship, his long nose pointing at her.

"Shall I?" she laughed nervously. She did not want anybody to talk to her.

As she went along the street, clattering on the granite pavement, she was aware of boys dodging behind her. Something struck her hand that was carrying her bag, bruising her. As it rolled away she saw it was a potato. Her hand was hurt, but she gave no sign. Soon she would take the tram.

She was afraid, and strange. It was to her quite strange and ugly, like some dream where she was degraded. She would have died rather than admit it to anybody. She could not look at her swollen hand. Something had broken in her; she had passed a crisis. Williams was beaten, but at a cost.

Feeling much too upset to go home, she rode a little further into the town, and got down from the tram at a small tea-shop. There, in the dark little place behind the shop, she drank her tea and ate the bread and butter. She did not taste anything. The taking tea was just a mechanical action, to cover over her existence. There she sat in the dark, obscure little place, without knowing. Only unconsciously she nursed the back of her hand, which was bruised.

When finally she took her way home, it was sunset red across the west. She did not know why she was going home. There was nothing for her there. She had, true, only to pretend to be normal. There was nobody she could speak to, nowhere to go for escape. But she must keep on, under this red sunset, alone, knowing the horror in humanity, that would destroy her, and with which she was at war. Yet it had to be so.

In the morning again she must go to school. She got up and went without murmuring even to herself. She was in the hands of some bigger, stronger, coarser will.

School was fairly quiet. But she could feel the class watching her, ready to spring on her. Her instinct was aware of the class instinct, to catch her if she were weak. But she kept cold and was guarded.

Williams was absent from school. In the middle of the morning, there was a knock at the door: someone wanted the head-master. Mr Harby went out, heavily, angrily, nervously. He was afraid of irate parents. After a moment in the passage, he came again into school.

"Sturgess," he called to one of his larger boys.—"Stand in front of the class and write down the name of anyone who speaks. Will you come this way, Miss Brangwen."

He seemed vindictively to seize upon her.

Ursula followed him, and found in the lobby a thin woman with a whitish skin, not ill dressed in a grey costume and a purple hat.

"I called about Vernon," said the woman, speaking in a refined accent. There was about the woman altogether an appearance of refinement and of cleanliness, curiously contradicted by her half beggar's deportment, and a sense of her being unpleasant to touch, like something going bad inside. She was neither a lady nor an ordinary working man's wife, but a creature separate from society. By her dress, she was not poor.

Ursula knew at once that she was Williams' mother, and that he was Vernon. She remembered that he was always clean, and well dressed, in a sailor suit. And he had this same peculiar, half transparent unwholesomeness, rather like a corpse.

"I wasn't able to send him to school today," continued the woman, with a false grace of manner. "He came home last night *so* ill—he was violently sick—I thought I should have to send for the doctor. —You know he has a weak heart."

The woman looked at Ursula with her pale, dead eyes.

"No," replied the girl, "I did not know."

She stood still with repulsion and uncertainty. Mr Harby, large and male, with his overhanging moustache, stood by with a slight, ugly smile at the corner of his eyes. The woman went on insidiously, not quite human:

"Oh yes. He has had heart-disease ever since he was a child. That is why he isn't very regular at school. And it is very bad to beat him.

He was awfully ill this morning—I shall call on the doctor as I go back."

"Who is staying with him now, then?" put in the deep voice of the school-master, cunningly.

"Oh I left him with a woman who comes in to help me—and who understands him. But I shall call in the doctor on my way home."

Ursula stood still. She felt vague threats in all this. But the woman was so utterly strange to her, that she did not understand.

"He told me he had been beaten," continued the woman, "and when I undressed him to put him to bed, his body was covered with marks—I could show them to any doctor."

Mr Harby looked at Ursula to answer. She began to understand. The woman was threatening to take out a charge of assault on her son, against her. Perhaps she wanted money.

"I caned him," she said. "He was so much trouble."

"I'm sorry if he was troublesome," said the woman, "but he must have been shamefully beaten. I could show the marks to any doctor. I'm sure it isn't allowed, if it was known."

"I caned him while he kept kicking me," said Ursula, getting angry because she was half excusing herself, Mr Harby standing there with the twinkle at the side of his eyes, enjoying the dilemma of the two women.

"I'm sure I'm sorry if he behaved badly," said the woman. "But I can't think he deserved treating as he has been. I can't send him to school, and really can't afford to pay the doctor—Is it allowed for the teachers to beat the children like that, Mr Harby?"

The head-master refused to answer. Ursula loathed herself, and loathed Mr Harby with his twinkling cunning and malice on the occasion. The other miserable woman watched her chance.

"It is an expense to me, and I have a great struggle to keep my boy decent."

Ursula still would not answer. She looked out on the asphalt yard, where a dirty rag of paper was blowing.

"And it isn't allowed to beat a child like that, I am sure, especially when he is delicate."

Ursula stared with a set face on the yard, as if she did not hear. She loathed all this, and had ceased to feel or to exist.

"Though I know he is troublesome sometimes—but I think it was too much. His body is covered with marks."

Mr Harby stood sturdy and unmoved, waiting now to have done,

374

with the twinkling, tiny wrinkles of an ironical smile at the corners of his eyes. He felt himself master of the situation.

"And he was violently sick. I couldn't possibly send him to school today. He couldn't keep his head up."

Yet she had no answer.

"You will understand, Sir, why he is absent," she said, turning to Mr Harby.

"Oh yes," he said, rough and off-hand. Ursula detested him, for his male triumph. And she loathed the woman. She loathed everything.

"You will try to have it remembered, Sir, that he has a weak heart. He *is* so sick after these things."

"Yes," said the head-master, "I'll see about it."

"I know he is troublesome,"—the woman only addressed herself to the male now—"but if you could have him punished without beating—he is really delicate."

Ursula was beginning to feel upset. Harby stood in rather superb mastery, the woman cringing to him tickled him as one tickles trout.

"I had to come to explain why he was away this morning, Sir. You will understand."

She held out her hand. Harby took it and let it go, surprised and angry.

"Good morning," she said, and she gave her gloved, seedy hand to Ursula. She was not ill looking, and had a curious insinuating way, very distasteful yet effective.

"Good morning, Mr Harby, and thank you."

The figure in the grey costume and the purple hat was going across the school yard with a curious lingering walk. Ursula felt a strange pity for her, and revulsion from her. She shuddered. She went into the school again.

The next morning Williams turned up, looking paler than ever, very neat and nicely dressed in his sailor blouse. He glanced at Ursula with a half-smile: cunning, subdued, ready to do as she told him. There was something about him that made her shiver. She loathed the idea of having laid hands on him. His elder brother was standing outside the gate at playtime, a youth of about fifteen, tall and thin and pale. He raised his hat, almost like a gentleman. But there was something subdued, insidious about him too.

"Who is it?" said Ursula.

"It's the big Williams," said Violet Harby roughly. "*She* was here yesterday, wasn't she?"

"Yes."

"It's no good her coming—her character's not good enough for her to make any trouble.—"

Ursula shrank from the scandal and the brutality. But it had some vague, horrid fascination. How sordid everything seemed! She felt sorry for the queer woman with the lingering walk, and those queer, insidious boys. The Williams in her class was wrong somewhere. How nasty is was altogether.

So the battle went on till her heart was sick. She had several more boys to subjugate before she could establish herself. And Mr Harby hated her almost as if she were a man. She knew now that nothing but a thrashing would settle some of the big louts who wanted to play cat and mouse with her. Mr Harby would not give them the thrashing if he could help it. For he hated the teacher, the stuck-up, insolent high-school miss with her independence.

"Now Wright, what have you done this time?" he would say genially to the boy who was sent to him from Standard Five for punishment. And he left the lad standing, lounging, wasting his time.

So that Ursula would appeal no more to the head-master, but, when she was driven wild, she seized her cane, and with fixed, desperate eyes gleaming almost cold with anger, she slashed the boy who was insolent to her, over head and ears and hands. And at length they were afraid of her, she had them in order.

But she had paid a great price out of her own soul to do this. It seemed as if a great flame had gone through her and burnt her sensitive tissue. She, who shrank from the thought of physical suffering in any form, had been forced to fight and beat with a cane and rouse all her instincts to hurt. And afterwards she had been forced to endure the sound of their blubbering and desolation, when she had broken them to order.

Oh, and sometimes she felt as if she would go mad. What did it matter, what did it matter if their books were dirty and they did not obey? She would rather, in reality, that they disobeyed the whole rules of the school, than that they should be beaten, broken, reduced to this crying, hopeless state. She would rather bear all their insults and insolences a thousand times than reduce herself and them to this. Bitterly she repented having got beside herself, and having tackled the boy she had beaten.

Yet it had to be so. She did not want to do it. Yet she had to. Oh why, why had she leagued herself to this evil system where she must brutalise herself to live? Why had she become a school-teacher, why, why?

The children had forced her to the beatings. No, she did not pity them. She had come to them full of kindness and love, and they would have torn her to pieces. They chose Mr Harby. Well then, they must know her as well as Mr Harby, they must first be subjugate to her. For she was not going to be made nought, no, neither by them, nor by Mr Harby, nor by all the system around her. She was not going to be put down, prevented from standing free. It was not to be said of her, she could not take her place and carry out her task. She would fight and hold her place in this state also, in the world of work and of man's convention.

She was isolated now from the life of her childhood, a foreigner in a new life, of work and mechanical consideration. She and Maggie, in their dinner hours and their occasional teas at the little restaurant, discussed life and ideas. Maggie was a great suffragette, trusting in the vote. To Ursula the vote was never a reality. She had within her the strange, passionate knowledge of religion and living far transcending the limits of the automatic system that contained the vote. But her fundamental, organic-knowledge had as yet to take form and rise to utterance.

For her, as for Maggie, the liberty of woman meant something real and deep. She felt that somewhere, in something, she was not free. And she wanted to be. She was in revolt. For once she were free she could get somewhere. Ah, the wonderful, real somewhere that was beyond her, the somewhere that she felt deep, deep inside her.

In coming out and earning her own living she had made a strong, cruel move towards freeing herself. But having more freedom, she only became more profoundly aware of the big want. She wanted so many things. She wanted to read great, beautiful books, and be rich with them; she wanted to see beautiful things, and have the joy of them for ever; she wanted to know big, free people; and there remained always the want she could put no name to.

It was so difficult! There were so many things, so much to meet and surpass. And one never knew where one was going. It was a blind fight. She had suffered bitterly in this school of St Philips. She was like a young filly that has been broken in to the shafts, and has lost its freedom. And now she was suffering bitterly from the agony of the shafts. The agony, the galling, the ignominy of her breaking in. This wore into her soul. But she would never submit. To shafts like these, she would never submit for long. But she would know them. She would serve them, that she might destroy them.

She and Maggie went to all kinds of places together, to big suffrage meetings in Nottingham, to concerts, to theatres, to exhibitions of pictures. Ursula saved her money and bought a bicycle, and the two girls rode to Lincoln, to Southwell, and into Derbyshire. They had an endless wealth of things to talk about. And it was a great joy, finding, discovering.

But Ursula never told about Winifred Inger. That was a sort of secret side-show to her life, never to be opened. She did not even think of it. It was the closed door she had not strength to open.

Once she was broken in to her teaching, Ursula began gradually to have a new life of her own again. She was going to college in eighteen months' time. Then she would take her degree, and she would—ah, she would perhaps be a big woman, and lead a movement. Who knows?—At any rate, she would go to college in eighteen months' time. All that mattered now was work, work.

And till college, she must go on with this teaching in St Philips School, which was always destroying her, but which she could now manage, without spilling all her life. She would submit to it for a time, since the time had a definite limit.

The class-teaching itself at last became almost mechanical. It was a strain on her, an exhausting wearying strain, always unnatural. But there was a certain amount of pleasure in the sheer oblivion of teaching, so much work to do, so many children to see after, so much to be done, that one's self was forgotten. When the work had become like habit to her, and her individual soul was left out, had its growth elsewhere, then she could be almost happy.

Her real, individual self drew together and became more coherent during these two years of teaching, during the struggle against the odds of class-teaching. It was always a prison to her, the school. But it was a prison where her wild, chaotic soul became hard and independent. When she was well enough, and not tired, then she did not hate the teaching. She enjoyed getting into the swing of work of a morning, putting forth all her strength, making the thing go. It was for her a strenuous form of exercise. And her soul was left to rest, it had the time of torpor in which to gather itself together in strength again. But the teaching hours were too long, the tasks too heavy, and the disciplinary condition of the school too unnatural for her. She was worn very thin and quivering.

She came to school in the morning seeing the hawthorn flowers wet, the little, rosy grains swimming in a bowl of dew. The larks quivered their song up into the new sunshine, and the country was so glad. It was a violation to plunge into the dust and greyness of the town.

So that she stood before her class unwilling to give herself up to the activity of teaching, to turn her energy, that longed for the country and for joy of early summer, into the dominating of fifty children and the transferring to them some morsels of arithmetic. There was a little absentness about her. She could not force herself into forgetfulness. A jar of buttercups and fool's-parsley in the window-bottom kept her away in the meadows, where in the lush grass the moon-daisies were half submerged, and a spray of pink ragged robin. Yet before her were faces of fifty children. They were almost like big daisies in a dimness of the grass.

A brightness was on her face, a little unreality in her teaching. She could not quite see her children. She was struggling between two worlds, her own world of young summer and flowers, and this other world of work. And the glimmer of her own sunlight was between her and her class.

Then the morning passed with a strange far-awayness and quietness. Dinner-time came, when she and Maggie ate joyously, with all the windows open. And then they went out into St Philips churchyard, where was a shadowy corner under red hawthorn trees. And there they talked and read Shelley or Browning or some work about "Woman and Labour."

And when she went back to school, Ursula lived still in the shadowy corner of the graveyard, where pink-red petals lay scattered from the hawthorn tree, like myriad tiny shells on a beach, and a church bell sometimes rang sonorously, and sometimes a bird called out, whilst Maggie's voice went on low and sweet.

These days she was happy in her soul: oh, she was so happy, that she wished she could take her joy and scatter it in armfuls broadcast. She made her children happy too, with a little tingling of delight. But to her, the children were not a school class this afternoon. They were flowers, birds, little bright animals, children, anything. They only were not Standard Five. She felt no responsibility for them. It was for once a game, this teaching. And if they got their sums wrong—what matter? And she would take a pleasant bit of reading. And instead of history with dates, she would tell a lovely tale. And for grammar, they could have a bit of written analysis that was not difficult, because they had done it before:

> "She shall be sportive as a fawn
> That wild with glee across the lawn
> Or up the mountain springs."

She wrote that, from memory, because it pleased her.

So the golden afternoon passed away, and she went home happy. She had finished her day of school, and was free to plunge into the glowing evening of Cossethay. And she loved walking home. But it had not been school. It had been playing at school beneath red hawthorn blossom.

She could not go on like this. The quarterly examination was coming, and her class was not ready. It irritated her that she must drag herself away from her happy self, and exert herself with all her strength to force, to compel this heavy class of children to work hard at arithmetic. They did not want to work, she did not want to compel them. And yet, some second conscience gnawed at her, telling her the work was not properly done. It irritated her almost to madness, and she let loose all the irritation in the class. Then followed a day of battle and hate and violence, when she went home raw, feeling the golden evening taken away from her, herself incarcerated in some dark, heavy place, and chained there with a consciousness of having done badly at work.

What good was it that it was summer, that right till evening, when the corncrakes called, the larks would mount up into the light, to sing once more before nightfall. What good was it all, when she was out of tune, when she must only remember the burden and shame of school that day.

And still, she hated school. Still she cried, she did not believe in it. Why should the children learn, and why should she teach them? It was all so much milling the wind. What folly was it, that made life into this, the fulfilling of some stupid, factitious duty? It was all so made up, so unnatural. The school, the sums, the grammar, the quarterly examinations, the register—it was all a barren nothing.

Why should she give her allegiance to this world, and let it so dominate her, that her own world of warm sun and growing, sap-filled life was turned into nothing? She was not going to do it. She was not going to be prisoner in the dry, tyrannical man-world. She was not going to care about it. What did it matter if her class did ever so badly in the quarterly examination. Let it—what did it matter?

Nevertheless, when the time came, and the report on her class was bad, she was miserable, and the joy of the summer was taken away from her, she was shut up in gloom. She could not really escape from this world of system and work, out into her fields where she was happy. She must have her place in the working world, be a recognised member with full rights there. It was more important to her than fields and sun and poetry, at this time. But she was only the more its enemy.

It was a very difficult thing, she thought, during the long hours of intermission in the summer holidays, to be herself, her happy self that enjoyed so much to lie in the sun, to play and swim and be content, and also to be a school-teacher getting results out of a class of children. She dreamed fondly of the time when she need not be a teacher any more. But vaguely, she knew that responsibility had taken place in her for ever. And as yet, her prime business was to work.

The autumn passed away, the winter was at hand. And Ursula became more and more an inhabitant of the world of work, and of what is called life. She could not see her future, but a little way off was college, and to the thought of this she clung fixedly. She would go to college, and get her two or three years training, free of cost. Already she had applied, and had her place appointed for the coming year.

So she continued to study for her degree. She would take French, Latin, English, Mathematics and Botany. She went to classes in Ilkeston, she studied at evening. For there was this world to conquer, this knowledge to acquire, this qualification to attain. And she worked with intensity, because of a want inside her that drove her on. Almost everything was subordinated now to this one desire to take her place in the world. What kind of place it was to be she did not ask herself. The blind desire drove her on. She must take her place.

She knew she would never be much of a success as an elementary school-teacher. But neither had she failed. She hated it, but she had managed it.

Maggie had left St Philips School, and had found a more congenial post. The two girls remained friends. They met at evening classes, they studied and somehow encouraged a firm hope each in the other. They did not know whither they were making, nor what they ultimately wanted. But they knew they wanted now to learn, to know, and to do.

They talked of love and marriage, and the position of woman in marriage. Maggie said that love was the flower of life, and blossomed unexpectedly and without law, and must be plucked where it was found, and enjoyed for the brief hour of its duration.

To Ursula this was unsatisfactory. She thought she still loved Anton Skrebensky. But she did not forgive him that he had not been strong enough to acknowledge her. He had denied her. How then could she love him? How then was love so absolute? She did not believe it. She believed that love was a way, a means, not an end in itself, as Maggie seemed to think. And always the way of love would be found. But whither did it lead?

"I believe there are many men in the world one might love—there is not only one man," said Ursula.

She was thinking of Skrebensky. Her heart was hollow with the knowledge of Winifred Inger.

"But you must distinguish between love and passion," said Maggie, adding, with a touch of contempt: "Men will easily have a passion for you, but they won't love you."

"Yes," said Ursula, vehemently, the look of suffering, almost of fanaticism, on her face. "Passion is only part of love. And it seems so much because it knows it can't last. That is why passion is never happy."

She was staunch for joy, for happiness, and permanency, in contrast with Maggie, who was for sadness, and the inevitable passing-away of things. Ursula suffered bitterly at the hands of life, Maggie was always single, always withheld, so she went in a heavy, brooding sadness that was almost meat to her. In Ursula's last winter at St Philips the friendship of the two girls came to its climax. It was during this winter that Ursula suffered and enjoyed most keenly Maggie's fundamental sadness of enclosure. Maggie enjoyed and suffered Ursula's struggles against the confines of her life. And then the two girls began to drift apart, as Ursula broke from that form of life wherein Maggie must remain enclosed.

CHAPTER XIV

The Widening Circle

Maggie's people, the Schofields, lived in the large gardener's cottage, that was half a farm, behind Belcote Hall. The hall was too damp to live in, so the Schofields were caretakers, gamekeepers, gardeners, farmers, all in one. The father was gamekeeper and stock-breeder, the eldest son was market-gardener, using the big hall gardens, the second son was farmer and gardener. There was a large family, as at Cossethay.

Ursula loved to stay at Belcote, to be treated as a grand lady by Maggie's brothers. They were good-looking men. The eldest was twenty six years old. He was the gardener, a man not very tall but strong and well-made, with brown, sunny, easy eyes and a face handsomely hewn, brown, with a long, fair moustache which he pulled as he talked to Ursula.

The girl was excited because these men attended to her when she came near. She could make their eyes light up and quiver, she could make Anthony, the eldest, twist and twist his moustache. She knew she could move them almost at will with her light laughter and chatter. They loved her ideas, watched her as she talked vehemently about politics or economics. And she, while she talked, saw the golden-brown eyes of Anthony gleam like the eyes of a satyr as they watched her. He did not listen to her words, he listened to her. It excited her.

He was like a faun, pleased, when she would go with him over his hot-houses, to look at the green and pretty plants, at the pink primulas nodding among their leaves, and cinerarias flaunting purple and crimson and white. She asked about everything, and he told her very exactly and minutely, in a queer, pedantic way that made her want to laugh. Yet she was really interested in what he did. And he had the curious light in his face, like the light in the eyes of the goat that was tethered by the farm-yard gate.

She went down with him into the warmish cellar, where already, in the darkness, the little yellow knobs of rhubarb were coming. He held the lantern down to the dark earth. She saw the shiny knob-end of the rhubarb thrusting upwards, upon the thick red stem, thrusting itself like a knob of flame through the soft soil. His face was turned up to her, the light glittered on his eyes and his teeth as he laughed, with a faint, musical neigh. He looked handsome. And she heard a new sound in her ears, the faintly-musical, neighing laugh of Anthony, whose moustache twisted up and whose eyes were luminous with a cold, steady, arrogant-laughing glare. There seemed a little prance of triumph in his movement, she could not rid herself of a movement of acquiescence, a touch of acceptance. Yet he was so humble, his voice was so caressing. He held his hand for her to step on when she must climb a wall. And she stepped on the living firmness of him, that quivered firmly under her weight.

She was aware of him as if in a mesmeric state. In her ordinary sense, she had nothing to do with him. But the peculiar ease and unnoticeableness of his entering the house, the power of his cold, gleaming light on her when he looked at her, was like a bewitchment. In his eyes, as in the pale grey eyes of a goat, there seemed some of that steady, hard fire of moonlight which has nothing to do with the day. It made her alert, and yet her mind went out like an extinguished thing. She was all senses, all her senses were alive.

Then she saw him on Sunday, dressed up in Sunday clothes, trying to impress her. And he looked ridiculous. She clung to the ridiculous effect of his stiff Sunday clothes.

She was always conscious of some unfaithfulness to Maggie, on Anthony's score. Poor Maggie stood apart as if betrayed. Maggie and Anthony were enemies by instinct. Ursula had to go back to her friend brimming with affection and a poignancy of pity. Which Maggie received with a little stiffness. Then poetry and books and learning took the place of Anthony, with his goats' movements and his cold, gleaming humour.

While Ursula was at Belcote, the snow fell. In the morning, a covering of snow weighed on the rhododendron bushes.

"Shall we go out?" said Maggie.

She had lost some of her leader's sureness, and was now tentative, a little in reserve from her friend.

They took the key of the gate and wandered into the park. It was a white world on which dark trees and tree masses stood under a sky keen with frost. The two girls went past the hall, that was shuttered and silent, their foot-prints marking the snow on the drive. Down the park, a long way off, a man was carrying armfuls of hay across the snow. He was a small, dark figure, like an animal moving in its un-awareness.

Ursula and Maggie went exploring, down to a tinkling, chilly brook that had worn the snow away in little scoops, and ran dark between. They saw a robin glance its bright eyes and burst scarlet and grey into the hedge, then some pertly-marked blue-tits scuffled. Meanwhile the brook slid on coldly, chuckling to itself.

The girls wandered across the snowy grass to where the artificial fish-ponds lay under thin ice. There was a big tree with a thick trunk twisted with ivy, that hung almost horizontal over the ponds. Ursula climbed joyfully into this, and sat amid bosses of bright ivy and dull berries. Some ivy leaves were like green spears held out, and tipped with snow. The ice was seen beneath them.

Maggie took out a book, and, sitting lower down the trunk, began to read Coleridge's "Christabel." Ursula half listened. She was wildly thrilled. Then she saw Anthony coming across the snow, with his confident, slightly strutting stride. His face looked brown and hard against the snow, smiling with a sort of tense confidence.

"Hello!" she called to him.

A response went over his face, his head was lifted in an answering, jerking gesture.

"Hello!" he said. "You're like a bird in there!"

And Ursula's laugh rang out. She answered to the peculiar reedy twang in his penetrating voice.

She did not think of Anthony, yet she lived in a sort of connection with him, in his world. One evening she met him as she was coming down the lane, and they walked side by side.

"I think it's so *lovely* here," she cried.

"Do you?" he said. "I'm glad you like it."

There was a curious confidence in his voice.

"Oh I love it. What more does one want than to live in this beautiful place, and make things grow in your garden. It is like the Garden of Eden."

"Is it?" he said, with a little laugh. "Yes—well, it's not so bad—" he was hesitating. The pale gleam was strong in his eyes, he was looking at her steadily, watching her, as an animal might. Something leaped in her soul. She knew he was going to suggest to her that she should be as he was.

"Would you like to stay here with me?" he asked, tentatively.

She blenched with fear and with the intense sensation of proffered licence suggested to her.

They had come to the gate.

"How?" she asked. "You aren't alone here."

"We could marry," he answered, in the strange, coldly-gleaming, insinuating tone that chilled the sunshine into moonlight. All substantial things seemed transformed. Shadows and dancing moonlight were real, and all cold, inhuman, gleaming sensations. She realised with something like terror that she was going to accept this. She was going inevitably to accept him. His hand was reaching out to the gate before them. She stood still. His flesh was brown and hard and final. She seemed to be in the grip of some insult.

"I couldn't," she answered involuntarily.

He gave the same brief, neighing little laugh, very sad and bitter now, and slotted back the bar of the gate. Yet he did not open. For a moment they both stood looking at the fire of sunset that quivered among the purple twigs of the trees. She saw his brown, hard, well-hewn face gleaming with anger and humiliation and sub-mission. He was an animal that knows that it is subdued. Her heart flamed with sensation of him, of the fascinating thing he offered her, and with sorrow, and with an inconsolable sense of loneliness. Her soul was an infant crying in the night. He had no soul. Oh, and why had she? He was the cleaner.

She turned away, she turned round from him, and saw the east flushed strangely rose, the moon coming yellow and lovely upon a rosy sky, above the darkening, bluish snow. All this so beautiful, all this so lovely! He did not see it. He was one with it. But she saw it, and was one with it. Her seeing separated them infinitely.

They went on in silence down the path, following their different fates. The trees grew darker and darker, the snow made only a dimness in an unreal world. And like a shadow, the day had gone into a faintly luminous, snowy evening, while she was talking aimlessly to him, to keep him at a distance, yet to keep him near her, and he walked heavily. He opened the garden gate for her quietly, and she felt she was entering into her own pleasaunces, leaving him outside the gate.

Then even whilst she was escaping, or trying to escape, this feeling of pain, came Maggie the next day, saying:

"I wouldn't make Anthony love you, Ursula, if you don't want him.—It is not nice."

"But Maggie, I never made him love me," cried Ursula, dismayed and suffering, and feeling as if she had done something base.

She liked Anthony, though. All her life, at intervals, she returned to the thought of him and of that which he offered. But she was a traveller, she was a traveller on the face of the earth, and he was an isolated creature living in the fulfilment of his own senses.

She could not help it, that she was a traveller. She knew Anthony, that he was not one. But oh, ultimately and finally, she must go on and on, seeking the goal that she knew she did draw nearer to.

She was wearing away her second and last cycle at St Philips. As the months went, she ticked them off, first October, then November, December, January. She was careful always to subtract a month from the remainder, for the summer holidays. She saw herself travelling round a circle, only an arc of which remained to complete. Then, she was in the open, like a bird tossed into mid-air, a bird that had learned in some measure to fly.

There was college ahead; that was her mid-air, unknown, spacious. Come college, and she would have broken from the confines of all the life she had known. For her father also was going to move. They were all going to leave Cossethay.

Brangwen had kept his carelessness about his circumstances. He knew his work in the lace designing meant little to him personally, he just earned his wage by it. He did not know what meant much to him. Living close to Anna Brangwen, his mind was always suffused through with physical heat, he moved from instinct to instinct, groping, always groping on.

When it was suggested to him that he might apply for one of the posts as handwork instructor, posts about to be created by the Nottingham Education Committee, it was as if a space had been given to him, into which he could remove from his hot, dusky enclosure. He sent in his application, confidently, expectantly. He had a sort of belief in his supernatural fate. The inevitable weariness of his daily work had stiffened some of his muscles, and made a slight deadness in his ruddy, alert face. Now he might escape.

He was full of the new possibilities, and his wife was acquiescent. She was willing now to have a change. She too was tired of Cossethay. The house was too small for the growing children. And since she was nearly forty years old, she began to come awake from her sleep of motherhood, her energy moved more outwards. The din of growing lives roused her from her apathy. She too must have her hand in making life. She was quite ready to move, taking all her brood. It would be better now if she transplanted them. For she had borne her last child, it would be growing up.

So that in her easy, unused fashion, she talked plans and arrangements with her husband, indifferent really as to the method of the change, since a change was coming; even if it did not come in this way, it would come in another.

The house was full of ferment. Ursula was wild with excitement. At last her father was going to be something, socially. So long, he had been a social cypher, without form or standing. Now he was going to be Art and Handwork Instructor for the County of Nottingham. That was really a status. It was a position. He would be a specialist in his way. And he was an uncommon man. Ursula felt they were all getting foothold at last. He was coming to his own. Who else that she knew could turn out from his own fingers the beautiful things her father could produce? She felt he was certain of this new job.

They would move. They would leave this cottage at Cossethay which had grown too small for them; they would leave Cossethay, where the children had all been born, and where they were always kept to the same measure. For the people who had known them as children along with the other village boys and girls would never, could never understand that they should grow up different. They had held "Urtler Brangwen" one of themselves, and had given her her place in her native village, as in a family. And the bond was strong. But now, when she was growing to something beyond what Cossethay would allow or understand, the bond between her and her old associates was becoming a bondage.

"'Ello Urs'ler, 'ow are yer goin' on?" they said when they met her. And it demanded of her in the old voice the old response. And something in her must respond and belong to people who knew her. But something else denied bitterly. What was true of her ten years ago was not true now. And something else which she was, and must be, they could neither see nor allow. They felt it there nevertheless, something beyond them, and they were injured. They said she was proud and conceited, that she was too big for her shoes nowadays. They said, she needn't pretend, because they knew what she was. They had known her since she was born. They quoted this and that about her. And she was ashamed because she really did feel different from the people she had lived amongst. It hurt her that she could not be at her ease with them any more. And yet—and yet—one's kite will rise on the wind as far as ever one has string to let it go. It tugs and tugs and will go, and one is glad the further it goes, even if everybody else is nasty about it. So Cossethay hampered her, and she wanted to go away, to be free to fly her kite as high as she liked. She wanted to go away, to be free to stand straight up to her own height.

So that when she knew that her father had the new post, and that the family would move, she felt like skipping on the face of the earth and making psalms of joy. The old, bound shell of Cossethay was to be cast off, and she was to dance away into the blue air. She wanted to dance and sing.

She made dreams of the new place she would live in, where stately cultured people of high feeling would be friends with her, and she would live with the noble in the land, moving to a large freedom of feeling. She dreamed of a rich, proud, simple girl-friend, who had never known Mr Harby and his like, nor ever had a note in her voice, of bondaged contempt and fear, as Maggie had.

And she gave herself to all that she loved in Cossethay, passionately, because she was going away now. She wandered about to her favorite spots. There was a place where she went trespassing to find the snowdrops that grew wild. It was evening and the winter-darkened meadows were full of mystery. When she came to the woods, an oak-tree had been newly chopped down in the dell. Pale drops of flowers glimmered many under the hazels, and by the sharp, golden splinters of wood that were splashed about, the grey-green blades of snowdrop leaves pricked unheeding, the drooping still little flowers were without heed.

Ursula picked some lovingly, in an ecstasy. The golden chips of wood shone yellow like sunlight, the snowdrops in the twilight were like the first stars of night. And she, alone amongst them, was wildly happy to have found her way into such a glimmering dusk, to the intimate little flowers and the splash of wood chips like sunshine over the twilight of the ground. She sat down on the felled tree and remained awhile remote.

Going home, she left the purplish dusk of the trees for the open lane, where the puddles shone long and jewel-like in the ruts, the land about her was darkened, and the sky a jewel overhead. Oh, how amazing it was to her! It was almost too much. She wanted to run, and sing, and cry out for very wildness and poignancy, but she could not run and sing and cry out in such a way as to cry out the deep things in her heart, so she was still, and almost sad with loneliness.

At Easter she went again to Maggie's home, for a few days. She was, however, shy and fugitive. She saw Anthony, how suggestive he was to look on, and how his eyes had a sort of supplicating light, that was rather beautiful. She looked at him, and she looked again, for him to become real to her. But it was her own self that was occupied elsewhere. She seemed to have some other being.

And she turned to spring and the opening buds. There was a large pear-tree by a wall, and it was full, thronged with tiny, grey-green buds, myriads. She stood before it arrested with delight, and a realisation went deep into her heart. There was so great a host in array behind the cloud of pale, dim green, so much to come forth—so much sunshine to pour down.

So the weeks passed on, trance-like and pregnant. The pear-tree at Cossethay burst into bloom against the cottage-end, like a wave burst into foam. Then gradually the bluebells came, blue as water standing thin in the level places under the trees and bushes, flowing in more and more, till there was a flood of azure, and pale green leaves burning, and tiny birds with fiery little song and flight. Then swiftly, the flood sank and was gone, and it was summer.

There was to be no going to the seaside this year for a holiday. The holiday was the removal from Cossethay.

They were going to live near Willey Green, which place was most central for Brangwen. It was an old, quiet village on the edge of the thronged colliery-district. So that it served, in its quaintness of odd, old cottages lingering in their sunny gardens, as a sort of bower or pleasaunce to the sprawling colliery-townlet of Beldover, a pleasant walk-round for the colliers on Sunday morning, before the public-houses opened.

In Willey Green stood the Grammar School where Brangwen was occupied for two days during the week, and where experiments in education were being carried on.

Ursula wanted to live in Willey Green, on the remoter side, towards Southwell, and Sherwood Forest. There it was so lovely and romantic. But out into the world meant out into the world. Will Brangwen must become modern.

He bought, with his wife's money, a fairly large house in the new, red-brick part of Beldover. It was a villa built by the widow of the late colliery-manager, and stood in a quiet, new little side-street near the large church.

Ursula was rather sad. Instead of having arrived at distinction, they had come to new red-brick suburbia in a grimy, small town.

Mrs Brangwen was happy. The rooms were splendidly large—a splendid dining-room, drawing room, and kitchen, besides a very pleasant study, downstairs. Everything was admirably appointed. The widow had settled herself in lavishly. She was a native of Beldover, and had intended to reign almost queen. Her bath-room was white and silver, her stairs were of oak, her chimney-pieces were massive and oaken, with bulging, columnar supports.

"Good and substantial," was the keynote. But Ursula resented the stout, inflated prosperity implied everywhere. She made her father promise to chisel down the bulging oaken chimney-pieces, chisel them flat. That sort of important paunch was very distasteful to her. Her father was himself long and loosely built. What had he to do with so much "good and substantial" importance?

They bought a fair amount, also, of the widow's furniture. It was in common good taste—the great Wilton carpet, the large round table, the chesterfield covered with glossy chintz in roses and birds. It was all really very sunny and nice, with large windows, and a view right across the shallow valley.

After all, they would be, as one of their acquaintances said, among the *élite* of Beldover. They would represent culture. And as there was no-one of higher social importance than the doctors, the colliery-managers, and the chemists, they would shine, with their Della Robbia, beautiful Madonna, their lovely reliefs from Donatello, their reproductions from Botticelli. Nay, the large photographs of the Primavera and the Aphrodite and the Nativity in the dining-room, the ordinary reception room, would make dumb the mouth of Beldover.

And after all, it is better to be princess in Beldover than a vulgar nobody in the country.

There was great preparation made for the removal of the whole Brangwen family, ten in all. The house in Beldover was prepared, the house in Cossethay was dismantled. Come the end of school-term, the removal would begin.

Ursula left school at the end of July, when the summer holiday commenced. The morning outside was bright and sunny, and the freedom got inside the school-room this last day. It was as if the walls of the school were going to melt away. Already they seemed shadowy and unreal. It was breaking-up morning. Soon, scholars and teachers would be outside, each going his own way. The irons were struck off, the sentence was expired, the prison was a momentary shadow halting about them. The children were carrying away books and inkwells, and rolling up maps. All their faces were bright with gladness and goodwill. There was a bustle of cleaning and clearing away all marks of this last term of imprisonment. They were all breaking free. Busily, eagerly, Ursula made up her totals of attendances in the register. With pride, she wrote down the thousands: to so many thousands of children had she given another session's lesson. It looked tremendous. The excited hours passed slowly in suspense. Then at last it was over. For the last time, she stood before her children whilst they said their prayers and sang a hymn. Then it was all over.

"Goodbye, children," she said. "I shall not forget you, and you must not forget me."

"No Miss," cried the children in chorus, with shining faces.

She stood smiling on them, moved, as they filed out. Then she gave her monitors their term sixpences, and they too departed. Cupboards were locked, blackboards washed, inkwells and dusters removed. The place stood bare and vacated. She had triumphed over it. It was a shell now. She had fought a good fight here, and it had not been altogether unenjoyable. She owed some gratitude even to this harsh, vacant place, that stood like a memorial or a trophy. So much of her life had been fought for and won and lost here. Something of this school would always belong to her, something of her to it. She acknowledged it. And now came the leave-taking.

In the teachers' room the teachers were chatting and loitering, talking excitedly of where they were going: to the Isle of Man, to Llandudno, to Yarmouth. They were eager, and attached to each other, like comrades leaving a ship.

Then it was Mr Harby's turn to make a speech to Ursula. He looked handsome, with his silver-grey temples and black brows, and his imperturbable, male solidity.

"Well," he said, "we must say goodbye to Miss Brangwen and wish her all good fortune for the future. I suppose we shall see her again some time, and hear how she is getting on."

"Oh yes," said Ursula, stammering, blushing, laughing. "Oh yes, I shall come and see you."

Then she realised that this sounded too personal, and she felt foolish.

"Miss Schofield suggested these two books," he said, putting a couple of volumes on the table: "I hope you will like them."

Ursula, feeling very shy, picked up the books. There was a volume of Swinburne's poetry, and a volume of Meredith's.

"Oh I shall love them," she said. "Thank you very much—thank you all so much—it is so—"

She stuttered to an end, and very red, turned the leaves of the books nervously, pretending to be taking the first pleasure, but really seeing nothing.

Mr Harby's eyes were twinkling. He alone was at his ease, master of the situation. It was pleasing to him to make Ursula the gift, and for once extend good feeling to his teachers. As a rule, it was so difficult, each one was so strained in resentment under his rule.

"Yes," he said, "we hoped you would like the choice—"

He looked with his peculiar challenging smile, for a moment, then returned to his cupboards.

Ursula felt very confused. She hugged her books, loving them. And she felt she loved all the teachers, and Mr Harby. It was very confusing.

At last she was out. She cast one hasty glance over the school buildings squatting on the asphalt yard in the hot, glistening sun, one look down the well-known road, and turned her back on it all. Something strained in her heart. She was going away.

"Well, good luck," said the last of the teachers, as she shook hands at the end of the road. "We'll expect you back some day."

He spoke in irony. She laughed, and broke away. She was free. As she sat on the top of the tram in the sunlight, she looked round her with tremulous delight. She had left something which had meant much to her. She would not go to school any more, and do the familar things. Queer! There was a little pang amid her exultation, of fear, not of regret. Yet how she exulted this morning!

She was tremulous with pride and joy. She loved the two books. They were tokens to her, representing the fruit and trophies of her two years which, thank God, were over.

"To Ursula Brangwen, with best wishes for her future and in warm memory of the time she spent in St Philips School," was written in the head-master's neat, scrupulous handwriting. She could see the careful hand holding the pen, the thick fingers with tufts of black hair on the back of each one.

He had signed, all the teachers had signed. She liked having all their signatures. She felt she loved them all, they were her fellow-workers. She carried away from the school a pride she could never lose. She had her place as comrade and sharer in the work of school, her fellow teachers had signed to her, as one of them. And she was one of all workers, she had put in her tiny brick to the fabric man was building, she had qualified herself as co-builder.

Then the day for the home removal came. Ursula rose early, to pack up the remaining goods. The carts arrived, lent by her uncle at the Marsh, in the lull between hay and corn harvest. The goods roped in the cart, Ursula mounted her bicycle and sped away to Beldover.

The house was hers. She entered its clean-scrubbed silence. The dining-room had been covered with a thick rush matting, hard and of the beautiful, luminous, clean colour of sun-dried reeds. The walls were pale grey, the doors were darker grey. Ursula admired it very much, as the sun came through the large windows, streaming in.

She flung open doors and windows to the sunshine. Flowers were bright and shining round the small lawn, which stood above the road looking over the raw field opposite, which would later be built upon. No-one came. So she wandered down the garden at the back, to the wall. The eight bells of the church rang the hour. She could hear the many sounds of the town about her.

At last, the cart was seen coming round the corner, familiar furniture piled undignified on top, Tom, her brother, and Theresa, marching on foot beside the mass, proud of having walked ten miles or more, from the tram terminus. Ursula poured out beer, and the man drank thirstily, by the door. A second cart was coming. Her father appeared on his motor bicycle. There was the staggering transport of furniture up the steps to the little lawn, where it was deposited all pell-mell in the sunshine, very queer and discomforting.

Brangwen was a pleasant man to work with, cheerful and easy. Ursula loved deciding him where the heavy things should stand. She watched anxiously the struggle up the steps and through the doorways. Then the big things were in, the carts set off again. Ursula and her father worked away carrying in all the light things that remained upon the lawn, and putting them in place. Dinner-time came. They ate bread and cheese in the kitchen.

"Well, we're getting on," said Brangwen cheerfully.

Two more loads arrived. The afternoon passed away in a struggle with the furniture, upstairs. Towards five o'clock, appeared the last loads, consisting also of Mrs Brangwen and the younger children, driven by uncle Fred in the trap. Gudrun had walked with Margaret from the station. The whole family had come.

"There!" said Brangwen, as his wife got down from the cart: "Now we're all here."

"Ay," said his wife pleasantly.

And the very brevity, the silence of intimacy between the two made a home in the hearts of the children, who clustered round feeling strange in the new place.

Everything was at sixes and sevens. But a fire was made in the kitchen, the hearthrug put down, the kettle set on the hob, and Mrs Brangwen began towards sunset to prepare the first meal. Ursula and Gudrun were slaving in the bedrooms, candles were rushing about. Then from the kitchen came the smell of ham and eggs and coffee, and in the gaslight, the scrambled meal began. The family seemed to huddle together like a little camp in a strange place. Ursula felt a load of responsibility upon her, caring for the half-little ones. The smallest kept near the mother.

It was dark, and the children went sleepy but excited to bed. It was a long time before the sound of voices died out. There was a tremendous sense of adventure.

In the morning, everybody was awake soon after dawn, the children crying:

"When I wakened up, I didn't know where I was."

There were the strange sounds of the town, and the repeated chiming of the big church bells, so much harsher and more insistent than the little bells of Cossethay. They looked through the windows, past the other new red houses, to the wooded hill across the valley. They had all a delightful sense of space and liberation, space, and light and air.

But gradually all set to work. They were a careless, untidy family. Yet when once they set about to get the house in order, the thing went with felicity and quickness. By evening, the place was roughly established.

They would not have a servant to live in the house, only a woman who could go home at night. And they would not even have the woman yet. They wanted to do as they liked in their own home, with no stranger in the midst.

CHAPTER XV

The Bitterness of Ecstasy

A storm of industry raged on in the house. Ursula did not go to college till October. So, with a distinct feeling of responsibility, as if she must express herself in this house, she laboured arranging, re-arranging, selecting, contriving.

She could use her father's ordinary tools, both for wood-work and metal work, so she hammered and tinkered. Her mother was quite content to have the thing done. Brangwen was interested. He had a ready belief in his daughter. He himself was at work putting up his work-shed in the garden.

At last she had finished for the time being. The drawing room was big and empty. It had the good Wilton carpet, of which the family was so proud, and the large couch and large chairs covered with shiny chintz, and the piano, a little sculpture in plaster that Brangwen had done, and not very much more. It was too large and empty-feeling for the family to occupy very much. Yet they liked to know it was there, large and empty.

The home was the dining-room. There the hard rush floor-covering made the ground light, reflecting light upon the bottom of their hearts; in the window-bay was a broad, sunny seat, the table was so solid one could not jostle it, and the chairs so strong one could knock them over without hurting them. The familiar organ that Brangwen had made stood on one side, looking peculiarly small, the sideboard was comfortably reduced to normal proportion. This was the family living-room.

Ursula had a bedroom to herself. It was really a servant's bedroom, small and plain. Its window looked over the back garden at other back gardens, some of them old and very nice, some of them littered with packing-cases, then at the backs of the houses whose fronts were the shops in High Street, or the genteel homes of the under-manager or the chief cashier, facing the chapel.

She had six weeks still before going to college. In this time she nervously read over some Latin and some Botany, and fitfully worked at some mathematics. She was going into college as a teacher, for her training. But, having already taken her matriculation examination, she was entered for a university course. At the end of a year she would sit for the Intermediate Arts, then two years after for her B.A. So her case was not that of the ordinary school-teacher. She would be working among the private students who came only for pure education, not for mere professional training. She would be of the elect.

For the next three years she would be more or less dependent on her parents again. Her training was free. All college fees were paid by the government, she had moreover a few pounds grant every year. This would just pay for her train-fares and her clothing. Her parents would only have to feed her. She did not want to cost them much. They would not be well-off. Her father would earn only two hundred a year, and a good deal of her mother's capital was spent in buying the house. Still, there was enough to get along with.

Gudrun was attending the Art School in Nottingham. She was working particularly at sculpture. She had a gift for this. She loved making little models in clay, of children or of animals. Already some of these had appeared in the Students' Exhibition in the Castle, and Gudrun was a distinguished person. She was chafing at the Art School, and wanted to go to London. But there was not enough money. Neither would her parents let her go so far.

Theresa had left the High School. She was a great, strapping, bold hussy, indifferent to all higher claims. She would stay at home. The others were at school, except the youngest. When term started, they would all be transferred to the Grammar School at Willey Green.

Ursula was excited at making acquaintances in Beldover. The excitement soon passed. She had tea at the clergyman's, at the Chemist's, at the other chemists', at the three doctors', at the under-manager's—then she knew practically everybody. She could not take people very seriously, though at the time she wanted to.

She wandered the country, on foot and on her bicycle, finding it very beautiful in the forest direction, between Mansfield and Southwell and Worksop. But she was here only skirmishing for amusement. Her real exploration would begin in college.

Term began. She went into town each day by train. The cloistered quiet of the college began to close around her.

She was not at first disappointed. The big college built of stone, standing in the quiet street, with a rim of grass and lime-trees all so peaceful: she felt it remote, a magic-land. Its architecture was foolish, she knew from her father. Still, it was different from that of all other buildings. Its rather pretty, plaything, Gothic form was almost a style, in the dirty industrial town.

She liked the hall, with its big stone chimney-piece and its Gothic arches supporting the balcony above. To be sure the arches were ugly, the chimney-piece of cardboard-like carved stone, with its armorial decoration, looked silly just opposite the bicycle stand and the radiator, whilst the great notice-board with its fluttering papers seemed to slam away all sense of retreat and mystery from the far wall. Nevertheless, amorphous as it might be, there was in it a reminiscence of the wondrous, cloistral origin of education. Her soul flew straight back to the mediæval times, when the monks of God held the learning of men and imparted it within the shadow of religion. In this spirit she entered college.

The harshness and vulgarity of the lobbies and cloak-rooms hurt her at first. Why was it not all beautiful? But she could not openly admit her criticism. She was on holy ground.

She wanted all the students to have a high, pure spirit, she wanted them to say only the real, genuine things, she wanted their faces to be still and luminous as the nuns' and the monks' faces.

Alas, the girls chattered and giggled and were nervous, they were dressed up and frizzed, the men looked mean and clownish.

Still, it was lovely to pass along the corridor with one's books in one's hand, to push the swinging, glass-panelled door, and enter the big room where the first lecture would be given. The windows were large and lofty, the myriad brown students' desks stood waiting, the great blackboard was smooth behind the rostrum.

Ursula sat beside her window, rather far back. Looking down, she saw the lime-trees turning yellow, the tradesman's boy passing silent down the still, autumn-sunny street. There was the world, remote, remote.

Here, within the great, whispering sea-shell, that whispered all the while with reminiscence of all the centuries, time faded away, and the echo of knowledge filled the timeless silence.

She listened, she scribbled her notes with joy, almost with ecstasy, never for a moment criticising what she heard. The lecturer was a mouth-piece, a priest. As he stood, black-gowned, on the rostrum, some strands of the whispering confusion of knowledge that filled the whole place seemed to be singled out and woven together by him, till they became a lecture.

At first, she preserved herself from criticism. She would not consider the professors as men, ordinary men who ate bacon and pulled on their boots before coming to college. They were the black-gowned priests of knowledge, serving forever in a remote, hushed temple. They were the initiated, and the beginning and end of the mystery was in their keeping.

Curious joy she had of the lectures. It was a joy to hear the theory of education, there was such freedom and pleasure in ranging over the very stuff of knowledge, and seeing how it moved and lived and had its being. How happy Racine made her! She did not know why. But as the big lines of the drama unfolded themselves, so steady, so measured, she felt a thrill as of being in the realm of the reality. Of Latin, she was doing Livy and Horace. The curious, intimate, gossiping tone of the Latin class suited Horace. Yet she never cared for him, nor even for Livy. There was an entire lack of sternness in the gossipy classroom. She tried hard to keep her old grasp of the Roman Spirit. But gradually the Latin became mere gossip-stuff and artificiality to her, a question of manners and verbosities.

Her terror was the mathematics class. The lecturer went so fast, her heart beat excitedly, she seemed to be straining every nerve. And she struggled hard, during private study, to get the stuff under control.

Then came the lovely, peaceful afternoons in the Botany laboratory. They were few students. How she loved to sit on her high stool before the bench, with her pith and her razor and her material, carefully mounting her slides, carefully bringing her microscope into focus, then turning with joy to record her observation, drawing joyfully in her book, if the slide were good.

She soon made a college-friend, a girl who had lived in Florence, a girl who wore a wonderful purple or figured scarf draped over a plain, dark dress. She was Dorothy Russell, daughter of a south-country advocate. Dorothy lived with a maiden aunt in Nottingham, and spent her spare moments slaving for the Women's Social and Political Union. She was quiet and intense, with an ivory face and dark hair looped plain over her ears. Ursula was very fond of her, but afraid of her. She seemed so old and so relentless towards herself. Yet she was only twenty two. Ursula always felt her to be a creature of fate, like Cassandra.

The two girls had a close, stern friendship. Dorothy worked at all things with the same passion, never sparing herself. She came closest to Ursula during the Botany hours. For she could not draw. Ursula made beautiful and wonderful drawings of the sections under the microscope, and Dorothy always came to learn the manner of the drawing.

So the first year went by, in magnificent seclusion and activity of learning. It was strenuous as a battle, her college life, yet remote as peace.

She came to Nottingham in the morning with Gudrun. The two sisters were distinguished wherever they went, slim, strong girls, eager and extremely sensitive. Gudrun was the more beautiful of the two, with her sleepy, half languid girlishness that looked so soft, and yet was balanced and inalterable underneath. She wore soft, easy clothing, and hats which fell by themselves into a careless grace.

Ursula was much more carefully dressed, but she was self-conscious, always falling into depths of admiration of somebody else, and modelling herself upon this other, and so producing a hopeless incongruity. When she dressed for practical purposes, she always looked well. In winter, wearing a tweed coat-and-skirt and a small hat of black fur pulled over her eager, palpitant face, she seemed to move down the street in a drifting motion of suspense and exceeding sensitive receptivity.

At the end of the first year Ursula got through her Intermediate Arts examination, and there came a lull in her eager activities. She slackened off, she relaxed altogether. Worn nervous and inflammable by the excitement of the preparation for the examination, and by the sort of exaltation which carried her through the crisis itself, she now fell into a quivering passivity, her will all loosened.

The family went to Scarborough for a month. Gudrun and the father were busy at the handicraft holiday school there, Ursula was left a good deal with the children. But when she could, she went off by herself.

She stood and looked out over the shining sea. It was very beautiful to her. The tears rose hot in her heart.

Out of the far, far space there drifted slowly in to her a passionate, unborn yearning. "There are so many dawns that have not yet risen." It seemed as if, from over the edge of the sea, all the unrisen dawns were appealing to her, all her unborn soul was crying for the unrisen dawns.

As she sat looking out at the tender sea, with its lovely, swift glimmer, the sob rose in her breast, till she caught her lip suddenly under her teeth, and the tears were forcing themselves from her. And in her very sob, she laughed. Why did she cry? She did not want to cry. It was so beautiful, that she laughed. It was so beautiful, that she cried.

She glanced apprehensively round, hoping no-one would see her in this state.

Then came a time when the sea was rough. She watched the water travelling in to the coast, she watched a big wave running unnoticed, to burst in a shock of foam against a rock, enveloping all in a great white beauty, to pour away again, leaving the rock emerged black and teeming. Oh, and if, when the wave burst into whiteness, it were only set free!

Sometimes she loitered along the harbour, looking at the sea-browned sailors, who, in their close blue jerseys, lounged on the harbour-wall and laughed at her with impudent, communicative eyes.

There was established a little relation between her and them. She would never speak to them or know any more of them. Yet as she walked by and they leaned on the sea-wall, there was something between her and them, something keen and delightful and painful. She liked best the young one whose fair, salty hair tumbled over his blue eyes. He was *so* new and fresh and salt and not of this world.

From Scarborough she went to her uncle Tom's. Winifred had a small baby, born at the end of the summer. She had become strange and alien to Ursula. There was an unmentionable reserve between the two women. Tom Brangwen was an attentive father, a very domestic husband. But there was something spurious about his domesticity, Ursula did not like him any more. Something ugly, blatant in his nature had come out now, making him shift everything over to a sentimental basis. A materialistic unbeliever, he carried it all off by becoming full of human feeling, a warm, attentive host, a generous husband, a model citizen. And he was clever enough to rouse admiration everywhere, and to take in his wife sufficiently. She did not love him. She was glad to live in a state of complacent self-deception with him, she worked according to him.

Ursula was relieved to go home. She had still two peaceful years before her. Her future was settled for two years. She returned to college to prepare for her final examination.

But during this year, the glamour began to depart from college. The professors were not priests initiated into the deep mysteries of life and knowledge. After all, they were only middle-men handling wares they had become so accustomed to that they were oblivious of them. What was Latin?—so much dry goods of knowledge. What was the Latin class altogether but a sort of second-hand curio shop, where one bought curios and learned the market value of curios: dull curios too, on the whole. She was as bored by the Latin curiosities as she was by Chinese and Japanese curiosities in the antique shops. "Antiques"—the very word made her soul fall flat and dead.

The life went out of her studies, why, she did not know. But the whole thing seemed sham, spurious: spurious Gothic arches, spurious peace, spurious Latinity, spurious dignity of France, spurious naïveté of Chaucer. It was a second-hand dealer's shop, and one bought an equipment for an examination. This was only a little side-show to the factories of the town. Gradually the perception stole into her. This was no religious retreat, no seclusion of pure learning. It was a little apprentice-shop where one was further equipped for making money. The college itself was a little, slovenly laboratory for the factory.

A harsh and ugly disillusion came over her again, the same darkness and bitter gloom from which she was never safe now, the realisation of the permanent substratum of ugliness under everything. As she came to the college in the afternoon, the lawns were frothed with daisies, the lime-trees hung tender and sunlit and green; and oh, the deep, white froth of the daisies was anguish to see.

For inside, inside the college, she knew she must enter the sham workshop. All the while, it was a sham store, a sham warehouse, with a single motive of material gain, and no productivity. It pretended to exist by the religious virtue of knowledge. But the religious virtue of knowledge was become a flunkey to the god of material success.

A sort of inertia came over her. Mechanically, from habit, she went on with her studies. But it was almost hopeless. She could scarcely attend to anything. At the Anglo-Saxon lecture, in the afternoon, she sat looking down, out of the window, hearing no word of Beowulf or of anything else. Down below, in the street, the sunny grey pavement went beside the palisade. A woman in a pink frock, with a scarlet sunshade, crossed the road, a little white dog running like a fleck of light about her. The woman with the scarlet sunshade came over the road, a lilt in her walk, a little shadow attending her. Ursula watched spell-bound. The woman with the scarlet sunshade and the flickering terrier was gone—and whither? Whither?

In what world of reality was the woman in the pink dress walking? To what warehouse of dead unreality was she herself confined?

What good was this place, this college? What good was Anglo-Saxon, when one only learned it in order to answer examination questions, in order that one should have a higher commercial value later on? She was sick with this long service at the inner commercial shrine. Yet what else was there? Was life all this, and this only? Everywhere, everything was debased to the same service. Everything went to produce vulgar things, to encumber material life.

Suddenly she threw over French. She would take honors in Botany. This was the one study that lived for her. She had entered into the life of the plants. She was fascinated by the strange laws of the vegetable world. She had here a glimpse of something working entirely apart from the purpose of the human world.

College was barren, cheap, a temple converted to the most vulgar, petty commerce. Had she not come to hear the echo of learning pulsing back to the source of the mystery?—The source of mystery! And barrenly, the professors in their gowns offered commercial commodity that could be turned to good account in the examination room; ready-made stuff, too, and not really worth the money it was intended to fetch;—which they all knew.

All the time in the college, now, save when she was labouring in her Botany laboratory, for there the mystery still glimmered, she felt she was degrading herself in a kind of trade of sham gewgaws.

Angry and stiff, she went through her last terms. She would rather be out again earning her own living. Even Brinsley Street and Mr Harby seemed real in comparison. Her violent hatred of the Ilkeston school was nothing compared with the sterile degradation of college. But she was not going back to Brinsley Street, either. She would take her B.A., and become a mistress in some Grammar School for a time.

The last year of her college career was wheeling slowly round. She could see ahead her examination and her departure. She had the ash of disillusion gritting under her teeth. Would the next move turn out the same? Always the shining doorway ahead: and then, upon approach, always the shining doorway was a gate into another ugly yard, dirty and active and dead. Always the crest of the hill gleaming ahead under heaven: and then, from the top of the hill, only another sordid valley full of amorphous, squalid activity.

No matter! Every hill-top was a little different, every valley was somehow new. Cossethay and her childhood with her father; the Marsh and the little church school near the Marsh, and her grand-mother and her uncles; the High School at Nottingham and Anton Skrebensky; Anton Skrebensky and the dance in the moonlight between the fires; then the time she could not think of without feeling blasted, Winifred Inger, and the months before becoming a school-teacher; then the horrors of Brinsley Street, lapsing into comparative peacefulness; Maggie, and Maggie's brother, whose influence she could still feel in her veins, when she conjured him up; then college, and Dorothy Russell, who was now in France; then the next move, into the world again!

Already it was a history. In every phase she was so different. Yet she was always Ursula Brangwen. But what did it mean, Ursula Brangwen? She did not know what she was. Only she was full of rejection, of refusal. Always, always she was spitting out of her mouth the ash and grit of disillusion, of falsity. She could only stiffen in rejection, in rejection. She seemed always negative in her action.

That which she was, positively, was dark and unrevealed, it could not come forth. It was like a seed buried in dry ash. This world in which she lived was like a circle lighted by a lamp. This lighted area, lit up by man's completest consciousness, she thought was all the world: that here all was disclosed for ever. Yet all the time, within the darkness she had been aware of points of light, like the eyes of wild beasts, gleaming, penetrating, vanishing. And her soul had acknowledged in a great heave of terror, only the outer darkness. This inner circle of light in which she lived and moved, wherein the trains rushed and the factories ground out their machine-produce and the plants and the animals worked by the light of science and knowledge, suddenly it seemed like the area under an arc-lamp, wherein the moths and children played in the security of blinding light, not even knowing there was any darkness, because they stayed in the light.

But she could see the glimmer of dark movement just out of range, she saw the eyes of the wild beast gleaming from the darkness, watching the vanity of the camp fire and the sleepers; she felt the strange, foolish vanity of the camp, which said "Beyond our light and our order there is nothing," turning their faces always inward towards the sinking fire of illuminating consciousness, which com-prised sun and stars, and the Creator, and the System of Righteousness, ignoring always the vast darkness that wheeled round about, with half-revealed shapes lurking on the edge.

Yea, and no man dared even throw a firebrand into the darkness. For if he did, he was jeered to death by the others, who cried "Fool, anti-social knave, why would you disturb us with bogeys? There *is* no darkness. We move and live and have our being within the light, and unto us is given the eternal light of knowledge, we comprise and comprehend the innermost core and issue of knowledge. Fool and knave, how dare you belittle us with the darkness?"

Nevertheless the darkness wheeled round about, with grey shadow-shapes of wild beasts, and also with dark shadow-shapes of the angels, whom the light fenced out, as it fenced out the more familiar beasts of darkness. And some, having for a moment seen the darkness, saw it bristling with the tufts of the hyena and wolf; and some, having given up their vanity of the light, having died in their own conceit, saw the gleam in the eyes of the wolf and the hyena, that it was the flash of the sword of angels, flashing at the door to come in, that the angels in the darkness were lordly and terrible and not to be denied, like the flash of fangs.

It was a little while before Easter, in her last year of college, when Ursula was twenty two years old, that she heard again from Skrebensky. He had written to her once or twice from South Africa, during the first months of his service out there in the war, and since had sent her a post-card every now and then, at ever longer intervals. He had become a first lieutenant, and had stayed out in Africa. She had not heard of him now for more than two years.

Often her thoughts returned to him. He seemed like the gleaming dawn, yellow, radiant, of a long, grey, ashy day. The memory of him was like the thought of the first radiant hours of morning. And here was the blank grey ashiness of later daytime. Ah, if he had only remained true to her, she might have known the sunshine, without all this toil and hurt and degradation of a spoiled day. He would have been her angel. He held the keys of the sunshine. Still he held them. He could open to her the gates of succeeding freedom and delight. Nay, if he had remained true to her, he would have been the doorway to her, into the boundless sky of happiness and plunging, inexhaustible freedom which was the paradise of her soul. Ah the great range he would have opened to her, the illimitable, endless space for self-realisation and delight for ever.

The one thing she believed in, was in the love she had held for him. It remained shining and complete, a thing to hark back to. And she said to herself, when present things seemed a failure:

"Ah, I *was* fond of him,"

as if with him the leading flower of her life had died.

Now she heard from him again. The chief effect was pain. The pleasure, the spontaneous joy was not there any longer. But her *will* rejoiced. Her will had fixed itself to him. And the old excitement of her dreams stirred and woke up. He was come, the man with the wondrous lips that could send the kiss wavering to the very end of all space. Was he come back to her? She did not believe.

"My dear Ursula, I am back in England again for a few months before going out again, this time to India. I wonder if you still keep the memory of our times together. I have still got the little photograph of you. You must have changed since then, for it is about six years ago. I am fully six years older, I have lived through another life since I knew you at Cossethay: I wonder if you would care to see me. I shall come up to Derby next week, and I would call in Nottingham, and we might have tea together. Will you let me know? I shall look for your answer—Anton Skrebensky."

Ursula had taken this letter from the rack in the hall at college, and torn it open as she crossed to the Women's room. The world seemed to dissolve away from around her, she stood alone in clear air.

Where could she go to, to be alone? She fled away, upstairs, and through the private way to the reference library. Seizing a book, she sat down and pondered the letter. Her heart beat, her limbs trembled. As in a dream, she heard one gong sound in the college, then strangely, another. The first lecture had gone by.

Hurriedly she took one of her note books and began to write.

"Dear Anton, Yes, I still have the ring. I should be very glad to see you again. You can come here to college for me, or I will meet you somewhere in the town. Will you let me know? Your sincere friend—"

Trembling, she asked the librarian, who was her friend, if he would give her an envelope. She sealed and addressed her letter, and went out, bare-headed, to post it. When it was dropped into the pillar-box, the world became a very still, pale place, without confines. She wandered back to college, to her pale dream, like a first wan light of dawn.

Skrebensky came one afternoon in the following week. Day after day, she had hurried swiftly to the letter-rack, on her arrival at college in the morning, and during the intervals between lectures. Several times, swiftly, with secretive fingers, she had plucked his letter down from its public prominence, and fled across the hall holding it fast and hidden. She read her letters in the Botany laboratory, where her corner was always reserved for her.

Several letters, and then, he was coming. It was Friday afternoon he appointed. She worked over her microscope with feverish activity, able to give only half her attention, yet working closely and rapidly. She had on her slide some special stuff come up from London that day, and the professor was fussy and excited about it. At the same time, as she focussed the light on her field, and saw the plant-animal lying shadowy in a boundless light, she was fretting over a conversation she had had a few days before, with Dr. Frankstone, who was a woman doctor of physics in the college.

"No really," Dr. Frankstone had said, "I don't see why we should attribute some special mystery to life—do you? We don't understand it as we understand electricity, even, but that doesn't warrant our saying it is something special, something different in kind and distinct from everything else in the universe—do you think it does? May it not be that life consists in a complexity of physical and chemical activities, of the same order as the activities we already know in science? I don't see, really, why we should imagine there is a special order for life, and life alone— — — —"

The conversation had ended on a note of uncertainty, indefinite, wistful. But the purpose, what was the purpose? Electricity had no soul, light and heat had no soul. Was she herself an impersonal force, or conjunction of forces, like one of these? She looked still at the unicellular shadow that lay within the field of light, under her microscope. It was alive. She saw it move—she saw the bright mist of its ciliary activity, she saw the gleam of its nucleus, as it slid across the plane of light. What then was its will? If it was a conjunction of forces, physical and chemical, what held these forces unified, and for what purpose were they unified?

For what purpose were the incalculable physical and chemical activities nodalised in this shadowy, moving speck under her microscope? What was the will which nodalised them and created the one thing she saw? What was its intention? To be itself? Was its purpose just mechanical and limited to itself?

It intended to be itself. But what self? Suddenly in her mind the world gleamed strangely, with an intense light, like the nucleus of the creature under the microscope. Suddenly she had passed away into an intensely-gleaming light of knowledge. She could not understand what it all was. She only knew that it was not limited mechanical energy, nor mere purpose of self-preservation and self-assertion. It was a consummation, a being infinite. Self was a oneness with the infinite. To be oneself was a supreme, gleaming triumph of infinity.

Ursula sat abstracted over her microscope, in suspense. Her soul was busy, infinitely busy, in the new world. In the new world, Skrebensky was waiting for her—he would be waiting for her. She could not go yet, because her soul was engaged. Soon she would go.

A stillness, like passing away, took hold of her. Far off, down the corridors, she heard the gong booming five o'clock. She must go. Yet she sat still.

The other students were pushing back their stools and putting their microscopes away. Everything broke into turmoil. She saw, through the window, students going down the steps, with books under their arms, talking, all talking.

A great craving to depart came upon her. She wanted also to be gone. She was in dread of the material world, and in dread of her own transfiguration. She wanted to run to meet Skrebensky—the new life, the reality.

Very rapidly she wiped her slides and put them back, cleared her place at the bench, active, active, active. She wanted to run to meet Skrebensky—hasten—hasten. She did not know what she was to meet. But it would be a new beginning. She must hurry.

She flitted down the corridor on swift feet, her razor and note books and pencil in one hand, her pinafore over her arm. Her face was lifted and tense with eagerness. He might not be there.

Issuing from the corridor, she saw him at once. She knew him at once. Yet he was so strange. He stood with the curious self-effacing diffidence which so frightened her in well-bred young men whom she knew. He stood as if he wished to be unseen. He was very well-dressed. She would not admit to herself the chill like a sunshine of frost that came over her. This was he, the key, the nucleus to the new world.

He saw her coming swiftly across the hall, a slim girl in a white flannel blouse and dark skirt, with some of the abstraction and gleam of the unknown upon her, and he started, excited. He was very nervous. Other students were loitering about the hall.

She laughed, with a blind, dazzled face, as she gave him her hand. He too could not perceive her.

In a moment, she was gone, to get her outdoor things. Then again, as when she had been at school, they walked out into the town to tea. And they went to the same tea-shop.

She knew a great difference in him. The kin-ship was there, the old kin-ship, but he had belonged to a different world from hers. It was as if they had cried a state of truce between him and her, and in this truce they had met. She knew, vaguely, in the first minute, that they were enemies come together in a truce. Every movement and word of his was alien to her being.

Yet still she loved the fine texture of his face, of his skin. He was rather browner, physically stronger. He was a man now. She thought his manliness made the strangeness in him. When he was only a youth, fluid, he was nearer to her. She thought a man must inevitably set into this strange separateness, cold otherness of being. He talked, but not to her. She tried to speak to him, but she could not reach him.

He seemed so balanced and sure, he made such a confident presence. He was a great rider, so there was about him some of a horseman's sureness and habitual definiteness of decision, also some of the horseman's animal darkness. Yet his soul was only the more wavering, vague. He seemed made up of a set of habitual actions and decisions. The vulnerable, variable quick of the man was inaccessible. She knew nothing of it. She could only feel the dark, heavy fixity of his animal desire.

This dumb desire on his part had brought him to her. She was puzzled, hurt by some hopeless fixity in him, that terrified her with a cold feeling of despair. What did he want? His desires were so underground. Why did he not admit himself? What did he want? He wanted something that should be nameless. She shrank in fear.

Yet she flashed with excitement. In his dark, subterranean, male soul, he was kneeling before her, darkly exposing himself. She quivered, the dark flame ran over her. He was waiting at her feet. He was helpless, at her mercy. She could take or reject. If she rejected him, something would die in him. For him it was life or death. And yet, all must be kept so dark, the consciousness must admit nothing.

"How long," she said, "are you staying in England?"

"I am not sure—but not later than July, I believe."

Then they were both silent. He was here, in England, for six months. They had a space of six months between them. He waited. The same iron rigidity, as if the world were made of steel, possessed her again. It was no use turning with flesh and blood to this arrangement of forged metal.

Quickly, her imagination adjusted itself to the situation.

"Have you an appointment in India?" she asked.

"Yes—I have just the six months leave."

"Will you like being out there?"

"I think so—There's a good deal of social life, and plenty going on—hunting, polo—and always a good horse—and plenty of work—any amount of work."

He was always side-tracking, always side-tracking his own soul. She could see him so well out there, in India—one of the governing class, superimposed upon an old civilisation, lord and master of a clumsier civilisation than his own. It was his choice. He would become again an aristocrat, invested with authority and responsibility, having a great helpless populace beneath him. One of the ruling class, his whole being would be given over to the fulfilling and the executing of the better idea of the state. And in India, there would be real work to do. The country did need the civilisation which he himself represented: it did need his roads and bridges, and the enlightenment of which he was part. He would go to India. But that was not her road.

Yet she loved him, the body of him, whatever his decisions might be. He seemed to want something of her. He was waiting for her to decide of him. It had been decided in her long ago, when he had kissed her first. He was her lover, though good and evil should cease. Her will never relaxed, though her heart and soul must be imprisoned and silenced. He waited upon her, and she accepted him. For he had come back to her.

A glow came into his face, into his fine, smooth skin, his eyes, gold grey, glowed intimately to her. He burned up, he caught fire and became splendid, royal, something like a tiger. She caught his brilliant, burnished glamour. Her heart and her soul were shut away fast down below, hidden. She was free of them. She was to have her satisfaction.

She became proud and erect, like a flower putting itself forth in its proper strength. His warmth invigorated her. His beauty of form, which seemed to glow out in contrast with the rest of people, made her proud. It was like deference to her, and made her feel as if she represented before him all the grace and flower of humanity. She was no mere Ursula Brangwen. She was Woman, she was the whole of Woman in the human order. All-containing, universal, how should she be limited to individuality?

She was exhilarated, she did not want to go away from him. She had her place by him. Who should take her away.

They came out of the café.

"Is there anything you would like to do?" he said. "Is there anything we *can* do?"

It was a dark, windy night in March.

"There is nothing to do," she said.

Which was the answer he wanted.

"Let us walk then—where shall we walk?" he asked.

"Shall we go to the river?" she suggested, timidly.

In a moment they were on the tram, going down to Trent Bridge. She was so glad. The thought of walking in the dark, far-reaching water-meadows, beside the full river, transported her. Dark water flowing in silence through the big, restless night made her feel wild.

They crossed the bridge, descended, and went away from the lights. In an instant, in the darkness, he took her hand and they went in silence, with subtle feet treading the darkness. The town fumed away on their left, there were strange lights and sounds, the wind rushed against the trees and under the bridge. They walked close together, powerful in unison. He drew her very close, held her with a subtle, stealthy, powerful passion, as if they had a secret agreement which held good in the profound darkness. The profound darkness was their universe.

"It is like it was before," she said.

Yet it was not in the least as it was before. Nevertheless his heart was perfectly in accord with her. They thought one thought.

"I knew I should come back," he said at length.

She quivered.

"Did you always love me?" she asked.

The directness of the question overcame him, submerged him for a moment. The darkness travelled massively along.

"I had to come back to you," he said, as if hypnotised. "You were always at the back of everything."

She was silent with triumph, like fate.

"I loved you," she said, "always."

The dark flame leaped up in him. He must give her himself. He must give her the very foundations of himself. He drew her very close, and they went on in silence.

She started violently, hearing voices. They were near a stile across the dark meadows.

"It's only lovers," he said to her, softly.

She looked to see the dark figures against the fence, wondering that the darkness was inhabited.

"Only lovers will walk here tonight," he said.

Then in a low, vibrating voice he told her about Africa, the strange darkness, the strange, blood fear.

"I am not afraid of the darkness in England," he said. "It is soft, and natural to me, it is my medium, especially when you are here. But in Africa it seems massive and fluid with terror—not fear of anything—just fear. One breathes it, like a smell of blood. The blacks know it. They worship it, really, the darkness. One almost likes it—the fear—something sensual."

She thrilled again to him. He was to her a voice out of the darkness. He talked to her all the while, in low tones, about Africa, conveying something strange and sensual to her: the negro, with his loose, soft passion that could envelop one like a bath. Gradually he transferred to her the hot, fecund darkness that possessed his own blood. He was strangely secret. The whole world must be abolished. He maddened her with his soft, cajoling, vibrating tones. He wanted her to answer, to understand. A turgid, teeming night, heavy with fecundity in which every molecule of matter grew big with increase, secretly urgent with fecund desire, seemed to come to pass. She quivered, taut and vibrating, almost pained. And gradually, he ceased telling her of Africa, there came a silence, whilst they walked the darkness beside the massive river. Her limbs were rich and tense, she felt they must be vibrating with a low, profound vibration. She could scarcely walk. The deep vibration of the darkness could only be felt, not heard.

Suddenly, as they walked, she turned to him and held him fast, as if she were turned to steel.

"*Do* you love me?" she cried in anguish.

"Yes," he said, in a curious, lapping voice, unlike himself. "Yes, I love you."

He seemed like the living darkness upon her, she was in the embrace of the strong darkness. He held her enclosed, soft, unutterably soft, and with the unrelaxing softness of fate, the relentless softness of fecundity. She quivered, and quivered, like a tense thing that is struck. But he held her all the time, soft, unending, like darkness closed upon her, omnipresent as the night. He kissed her, and she quivered as if she were being destroyed, shattered. The lighted vessel vibrated, and broke in her soul, the light fell, struggled, and went dark. She was all dark, will-less, having only the receptive will.

He kissed her, with his soft, enveloping kisses, and she responded to them completely, her mind, her soul gone out. Darkness cleaving to darkness, she hung close to him, pressed herself into soft flow of his kiss, pressed herself down, down to the source and core of his kiss, herself covered and enveloped in the warm, fecund flow of his kiss, that travelled over her, flowed over her, covered her, flowed over the last fibre of her, so they were one stream, one dark fecundity, and she clung at the core of him, with her lips holding open the very bottommost source of him.

So they stood in the utter, dark kiss, that triumphed over them both, subjected them, knitted them into one fecund nucleus of the fluid darkness.

It was bliss, it was the nucleolating of the fecund darkness. Once the vessel had vibrated till it was shattered, the light of consciousness gone, then the darkness reigned, and the unutterable satisfaction.

They stood enjoying the unmitigated kiss, taking it, given to it endlessly, and still it was not exhausted. Their veins fluttered, their blood ran together as one stream.

Till gradually a sleep, a heaviness settled on them, a drowse, and out of the drowse, a small light of consciousness woke up. Ursula became aware of the night around her, the water lapping and running full just near, the trees roaring and soughing in gusts of wind.

She kept near to him, in contact with him, but she became ever more and more herself. And she knew she must go to catch her train. But she did not want to draw away from contact with him.

At length they roused and set out. No longer they existed in the unblemished darkness. There was the glitter of a bridge, the twinkle of lights across the river, the big flare of the town in front and on their right.

But still, dark and soft and incontestable, their bodies walked untouched by the lights, darkness supreme and arrogant.

"The stupid lights," Ursula said to herself, in her dark, sensual arrogance. "The stupid, artificial, exaggerated town, fuming its lights. It does not exist really. It rests upon the unlimited darkness, like a gleam of coloured oil on dark water, but what is it?—nothing, nothing."

In the tram, in the train, she felt the same. The lights, the civic uniform was a trick played, the people as they moved or sat were only dummies exposed. She could see, beneath their pale, wooden pretence of composure and civic purposefulness, the dark stream that contained them all. They were like little paper ships in their motion. But in reality each one was a dark, blind, eager wave urging blindly forward, dark with the same homogeneous desire. And all their talk and all their behaviour was sham, they were dressed-up creatures. She was reminded of the Invisible Man, who was a piece of darkness made visible only by his clothes.

During the next weeks, all the time she went about in the same dark richness, her eyes dilated and shining like the eyes of a wild animal, a curious half-smile on her darkly lighted face, a half-smile which seemed to be gibing at the civic pretence of all the human life about her.

"What are you, you pale citizens?" her face seemed to say, gleaming. "You subdued beast in sheep's clothing, you primeval darkness falsified to a social mechanism."

She went about in the sensual subconsciousness all the time, mocking at the ready-made, artificial daylight of the rest.

"They assume selves as they assume suits of clothing," she said to herself, looking in mocking contempt at the stiffened, neutralised men. "They think it better to be clerks or professors than to be the dark, fertile beings that exist in the potential darkness.—What do you think you are?" her soul asked of the professor as she sat opposite him in class. "What do you think you are, as you sit there in your gown and your spectacles? You are a lurking, blood-sniffing creature with eyes peering out of the jungle darkness, snuffing for your desires. That is what you *are*, though nobody would believe it, and you would be the very last to allow it."

Her soul mocked at all this pretence. Herself, she kept on pretending. She dressed herself and made herself fine, she attended her lectures and scribbled her notes. But all in a mood of superficial, mocking facility. She understood well enough their two-and-two-make-four tricks. She was as clever as they were. But care!—did she care about their monkey tricks of knowledge or learning or civic deportment? She did not care in the least.

There was Skrebensky, there was her dark, vital self. Outside her college, the other darkness, Skrebensky, was waiting. On the edge of the night, he was attentive. Did he care?

She was free as a leopard that sends up its raucous cry in the night. She had the potent, dark stream of her own blood, she had the glimmering core of fecundity, she had her mate, her complement, her sharer in fruition. So, she had all, everything.

Skrebensky was staying in Nottingham all this time. He too was free. He knew no-one in this town, he had no civic self to maintain. He was free. Their trams and markets and theatres and public meetings were a shaken kaleidoscope to him, he watched as a lion or a tiger may lie with narrowed eyes watching the people pass before its cage, the kaleidoscopic unreality of people, or a leopard lie blinking, watching the incomprehensible feats of the keepers. He despised it all—it was all non-existent. Their good professors, their good clergymen, .their good political speakers, their good, earnest women—all the time he felt his soul was grinning, grinning at the sight of them. So many performing puppets, all wood and rag for the performance!

He watched the citizen, a pillar of society, a model, saw the stiff goat's legs, which have become almost stiffened to wood in the desire to make them puppet in their action, he saw the trousers formed to the puppet-action: man's legs, but man's legs become rigid and deformed, ugly, mechanical.

He was curiously happy, being alone, now. The glimmering grin was on his face. He had no longer any necessity to take part in the performing tricks of the rest. He had discovered the clue to himself, he had escaped from the show, like a wild beast escaped straight back into its jungle. Having a room in a quiet hôtel, he hired a horse and rode out into the country, staying sometimes for the night in some village, and returning the next day.

He felt rich and abundant in himself. Everything he did was a voluptuous pleasure to him—either to ride on horse-back, or to walk, or to lie in the sun, or to drink in a public-house. He had no use for people, nor for words. He had an amused pleasure in everything, a great sense of voluptuous richness in himself, and of the fecundity of the universal night he inhabited. The puppet-shapes of people, their wood-mechanical voices, he was remote from them.

For there were always his meetings with Ursula. Very often, she did not go to college in the afternoon, but walked with him instead.

Or he took a motor-car or a dog-cart and they drove into the country, leaving the car and going away by themselves into the woods. He had not taken her yet. With subtle, instinctive economy, they went to the end of each kiss, each embrace, each pleasure in intimate contact, knowing, subconsciously, that the last was coming. It was to be their final entry into the source of creation.

She took him home, and he stayed a week-end at Beldover with her family. She loved having him in the house. Strange, how he seemed to come into the atmosphere of her family, with his laughing, insidious grace. They all loved him, he was kin to them. His raillery, his warm, voluptuous mocking presence was meat and joy to the Brangwen household. For this house was always quivering with darkness, they put off their puppet-form when they came home, to lie and drowse in the sun.

There was a sense of freedom among them all, of the under-current of darkness among them all. Yet here, at home, Ursula resented it. It became distasteful to her. And she knew that, if they understood the real relationship between her and Skrebensky, her parents, her father in particular, would go mad with rage. So subtly, she seemed to be like any other girl who is more or less courted by a man. And she *was* like any other girl. But in her, the antagonism to the social imposition was for the time complete and final.

She waited, every moment of the day, for his next kiss. She admitted it to herself in shame and bliss. Almost consciously, she waited. He waited, but, until the time came, more unconsciously. When the time came that he should kiss her again, a prevention was an annihilation to him. He felt his flesh go grey, he was heavy with a corpse-like inanition, he did not exist, if the time passed unfulfilled.

He came to her finally in a superb consummation. It was very dark, and again a windy, heavy night. They had come down the lane towards Beldover, down to the valley. They were at the end of their kisses, and there was the silence between them. They stood as at the edge of a cliff, with a great darkness beneath.

Coming out of the lane along the darkness, with the dark space spreading down to the wind, and the twinkling lights of the station below, the far-off windy chuff of a shunting train, the tiny clink-clink-clink of the wagons blown between the wind, the lights of Beldover-edge twinkling upon the blackness of the hill opposite, the glow of the furnaces along the railway to the right, their steps began to falter. They would soon come out of the darkness into the lights. It was like turning back. It was unfulfilment. Two quivering, unwilling creatures, they lingered on the edge of the darkness, peering out at the lights and the machine glimmer beyond. They could not turn back to the world—they could not.

So lingering along, they came to a great oak-tree by the path. In all its budding mass it roared to the wind, and its trunk vibrated in every fibre, powerful, indomitable.

"We will sit down," he said.

And in the roaring circle under the tree, that was almost invisible yet whose powerful presence received them, they lay a moment looking at the twinkling lights on the darkness opposite, saw the sweeping brand of a train past the edge of their darkened field.

Then he turned and kissed her, and she waited for him. The pain to her was the pain she wanted, the agony was the agony she wanted. She was caught up, entangled in the powerful vibration of the night. The man, what was he?—a dark, powerful vibration that encompassed her. She passed away as on a dark wind, far, far away, into the pristine darkness of paradise, into the original immortality. She entered the dark fields of immortality.

When she rose, she felt strangely free, strong. She was not ashamed—why should she be? He was walking beside her, the man who had been with her. She had taken him, they had been together. Whither they had gone, she did not know. But it was as if she had received another nature. She belonged to the eternal, changeless place into which they had leapt together.

Her soul was sure and indifferent of the opinion of the world of artificial light. As they went up the steps of the foot-bridge over the railway, and met the train-passengers, she felt herself belonging to another world, she walked past them immune, a whole darkness dividing her from them. When she went into the lighted dining-room at home, she was impervious to the lights and the eyes of her parents. Her everyday self was just the same. She merely had another, stronger self that knew the darkness.

This curious separate strength, that existed in darkness and pride of night, never forsook her. She had never been more herself. It could not occur to her that anybody, not even the young man of the world, Skrebensky, should have anything at all to do with her permanent self. As for her temporal, social self, she let it look after itself.

Her whole soul was implicated with Skrebensky—not the young

man of the world, but the undifferentiated man he was. She was perfectly sure of herself, perfectly strong, stronger than all the world. The world was not strong—she was strong. The world existed only in a secondary sense:—she existed supremely.

She continued at college, in her ordinary routine, merely as a cover to her dark, powerful under-life. The fact of herself, and with her Skrebensky, was so powerful, that she took rest in the other. She went to college in the morning, and attended her classes, flowering, and remote.

She had lunch with him in his hotel; every evening she spent with him, either in town, at his rooms, or in the country. She made the excuse at home of evening study for her degree. But she paid not the slightest attention to her study.

They were both absolute and happy and calm. The fact of their own consummate being made everything else so entirely subordinate that they were free. The only thing they wanted, as the days went by, was more time to themselves. They wanted the time to be absolutely their own.

The Easter vacation was approaching. They agreed to go right away. It would not matter if they did not come back. They were indifferent to the actual facts.

"I suppose we ought to get married," he said, rather wistfully. It *was* so magnificently free and in a deeper world, as it was. To make public their connection would be to put it in range with all the things which nullified him, and from which he was for the moment entirely dissociated. If he married he would have to assume his social self. And the thought of assuming his social self made him at once diffident and abstract. If she were his social wife, if she were part of that complication of dead reality, then what had his under-life to do with her? One's social wife was almost a material symbol. Whereas now she was something more vivid to him than anything in conventional life could be, she gave the complete lie to all conventional life, he and she stood together, dark, fluid, infinitely potent, giving the living lie to the dead whole which contained them.

He watched her pensive, puzzled face.

"I don't think I want to marry you," she said, her brow clouded. It piqued him rather.

"Why not?" he asked.

"Let's think about it afterwards, shall we?" she said.

He was crossed, yet he loved her violently.

"You've got a *museau*, not a face," he said.

"Have I?" she cried, her face lighting up like a pure flame. She thought she had escaped. Yet he returned—he was not satisfied.

"Why?" he asked, "Why don't you want to marry me?"

"I don't want to be with other people," she said. "I want to be like this. I'll tell you if ever I want to marry you."

"All right," he said.

He would rather the thing was left indefinite, and that she took the responsibility.

They talked of the Easter vacation. She thought only of complete enjoyment.

They went to an hôtel in Piccadilly. She was supposed to be his wife. They bought a wedding-ring for a shilling, from a shop in a poor quarter.

They had revoked altogether the ordinary mortal world. Their confidence was like a possession upon them. They were possessed. Perfectly and supremely free they felt, proud beyond all question, and surpassing mortal conditions.

They were perfect, therefore nothing else existed. The world was a world of servants whom one civilly ignored. Wherever they went, they were the sensuous aristocrats, warm, bright, glancing with pure pride of the senses.

The effect upon other people was extraordinary. The glamour was cast from the young couple upon all they came into contact with, waiters or chance acquaintances.

"*Oui Monsieur le baron*," she would reply with a mocking curtsey to her husband.

So they came to be treated as titled people. He was an officer in the engineers. They were just married, going to India immediately.

Thus a tissue of romance was round them. She believed she was a young wife of a titled husband on the eve of departure for India. This, the social fact, was a delicious make-belief. The living fact was that he and she were man and woman, absolute and beyond all limitation.

The days went by—they were to have three weeks together—in perfect success. All the time, they themselves were reality, all outside was tribute to them. They were quite careless about money, but they did nothing very extravagant. He was rather surprised when he found that he had spent twenty pounds in a little under a week, but it was only the irritation of having to go to the bank. The machinery of the old system lasted for him, not the system. The money simply did not exist.

Neither did any of the old obligations. They came home from the theatre, had supper, undressed, then flitted about in their dressing-gowns. They had a large bedroom and a corner sitting-room high up, remote and very cosy. They ate all their meals in their own rooms, attended by a young German called Hans, who thought them both wonderful, and answered assiduously:

"Gewiss, Herr Baron—bitte sehr, Frau Baronin."

Often, they saw the pink of dawn away across the park. The tower of Westminster Cathedral was emerging, the lamps of Piccadilly, stringing away beside the trees of the park, were becoming pale and moth-like, the morning traffic was clock-clocking down the shadowy road, which had gleamed all night like metal, down below, running far ahead into the night, beneath the lamps, and which was now vague, as in a mist, because of the dawn.

Then, as the flush of dawn became stronger, they opened the glass doors and went out on to the giddy balcony, feeling triumphant as two angels in bliss, looking down at the still sleeping world, which would wake to a dutiful, rumbling, sluggish turmoil of unreality.

But the air was cold. They went into their bedroom, and bathed before going to bed, leaving the partition doors of the bath-room open, so that the vapour came into the bedroom and faintly dimmed the mirror. She was always in bed first. She watched him as he bathed, his quick, unconscious movements, the electric light glinting on his wet shoulders. He stood out of the bath, his hair all washed flat over his forehead, and pressed the water out of his eyes. He was slender and, to her, perfect, a clean, straight-cut youth, without a grain of superfluous body. The brown hair on his body was soft and fine and adorable, he was all beautifully flushed, as he stood in the white bath-apartment.

He saw her warm, dark, lit-up face watching him from the pillow—yet he did not see it—it was always present, and was to him as his own eyes. He was never aware of the separate being of her. She was like his own eyes and his own heart beating to him.

So he went across to her, to get his sleeping suit. It was always a passionate adventure to go near to her. She put her arms round him, round his loins, and snuffed his warm, softened skin.

"Scent," she said.

"Soap," he answered.

"Soap," she repeated, looking up with bright eyes. They were both laughing, always laughing.

Soon they were fast asleep, asleep till midday, close together, sleeping one sleep. Then they awoke to the ever-changing reality of their state. They alone inhabited the world of reality. All the rest lived on a lower sphere.

Whatever they wanted to do, they did. They saw a few people— Dorothy, whose guest she was supposed to be, and a couple of friends of Skrebensky, young Oxford men, who called her Mrs Skrebensky with entire simplicity. They treated her, indeed, with such respect, that she began to think she was really queen of the whole universe, of the old world as well as of the new. She forgot she was outside the pale of the old world. She thought she had brought it under the spell of her own, real world. And so she had.

In such ever-changing reality the weeks went by. All the time, they were an unknown world to each other. Every movement made by the one was a reality and an adventure to the other. They did not want outside excitements. They went to very few theatres, they were often in their sitting-room high up over Piccadilly, with windows open on two sides, and the door open on to the balcony, looking over the Green Park, or down upon the minute travelling of the traffic.

Then suddenly, looking at a sunset, she wanted to go. She must be gone. She must be gone at once. And in two hours' time, they were at Charing Cross taking train for Paris. Paris was his suggestion. She did not care where it was. The great joy was in setting out. And for a few days she was happy in the novelty of Paris.

Then, for some reason, she must call in Rouen on the way back to London. He had an instinctive mistrust of her desire for the place. But, perversely, she wanted to go there. It was as if she wanted to try its effect on her.

For the first time, in Rouen, he had a cold feeling of death: not afraid of any other man, but of her. She seemed to leave him. She followed after something that was not him. She did not want him. The old streets, the cathedral, the age and the monumental peace of the town took her away from him. She turned to it as if to something she had forgotten, and wanted. This was now the reality: this great stone cathedral slumbering there in its mass, which knew no transience nor heard any denial. It was majestic in its stability, its splendid absoluteness.

Her soul began to run by itself. He did not realise, nor did she. Yet in Rouen he had the first deadly anguish, the first sense of the death towards which they were wandering. And she felt the first heavy yearning, heavy, heavy hopeless warning, almost like a deep, uneasy sinking into apathy, hopelessness.

They returned to London. But still they had two days. He began to tremble, he grew feverish with the fear of her departure. She had in her some fatal prescience, that made her calm. What would be, would be.

He remained fairly easy, however, still in his state of heightened glamour, till she had gone, and he had turned away from St Pancras, and sat on the tram-car going up Pimlico to the Angel, to Moorgate Street on Sunday evening.

Then the cold horror gradually soaked into him. He saw the horror of the City Road, he realised the ghastly cold sordidness of the tram-car in which he sat. Cold, stark, ashen sterility had him surrounded. Where then was the luminous, wonderful world he belonged to by rights? How did he come to be thrown on this refuse-heap where he was?

He was as if mad. The horror of the brick buildings, of the tram-car, of the ashen-grey people in the street made him reeling and blind as if drunk. He went mad. He had lived with her in a close, living, pulsing world, where everything pulsed with rich being. Now he found himself struggling amid an ashen-dry, cold world of rigidity, dead walls and mechanical traffic, and creeping, spectre-like people. The life was extinct, only ash moved and stirred or stood rigid, there was a horrible, clattering activity, a rattle like the falling of dry slag, cold and sterile. It was as if the sunshine that fell were unnatural light exposing the ash of the town, as if the lights at night were the sinister gleam of decomposition.

Quite mad, beside himself, he went to his club and sat with a glass of whiskey, motionless, as if turned to clay. He felt like a corpse that is inhabited with just enough life to make it appear as any other of the spectral, unliving beings which we call people in our dead language. Her absence was worse than pain to him. It destroyed his being.

Dead, he went on from lunch to tea. His face was all the time fixed and stiff and colourless, his life was a dry, mechanical movement. Yet even he wondered slightly at the awful misery that had overcome him. How could he be so ash-like and extinct? He wrote her a letter.

"I have been thinking that we must get married before long. My pay will be more when I get out to India, we shall be able to get along.

Or if you don't want to go to India, I could very probably stay here in England. But I think you would like India. You could ride, and you would know just everybody out there. Perhaps if you stay on to take your degree, we might marry immediately after that. I will write to your father as soon as I hear from you— —"

He went on, disposing of her. If only he could be with her! All he wanted now was to marry her, to be sure of her. Yet all the time he was perfectly, perfectly hopeless, cold, extinct, without emotion or connection.

He felt as if his life were dead. His soul was extinct. The whole being of him had become sterile, he was a spectre, divorced from life. He had no fulness, he was just a flat shape. Day by day the madness accumulated in him. The horror of not-being possessed him.

He went here, there, and everywhere. But whatever he did, he knew that only the cypher of him was there, nothing was filled in. He went to the theatre: what he heard and saw fell upon a cold surface of consciousness, which was now all that he was, there was nothing behind it, he could have no experience of any sort. Mechanical registering took place in him, no more. He had no being, no contents. Neither had the people he came into contact with. They were mere permutations of known quantitites. There was no roundness or fulness in this world he now inhabited, everything was a dead shape mental arrangement, without life or being.

Much of the time, he was with friends and comrades. Then he forgot everything. Their activities made up for his own negation, they engaged his negative horror.

He only became happy when he drank, and he drank a good deal. Then he was just the opposite of what he had been. He became a warm, diffuse, glowing cloud, in a warm, diffuse, aërial world. He was one with everything, in a diffuse formless fashion. Everything melted down into a rosy glow, and he was the glow, and everything was the glow, everybody else was the glow, and it was very nice, very nice. He would sing songs, it was so nice.

Ursula went back to Beldover shut and firm. She loved Skrebensky, of that she was resolved. She would allow nothing else.

She read his long, obsessed letter about getting married and going to India, without any particular response. She seemed to ignore what he said about marriage. It did not come home to her. He seemed, throughout the greater part of his letter, to be talking without much meaning.

She replied to him pleasantly and easily. She rarely wrote long letters.

"India sounds lovely. I can just see myself on an elephant swaying between lanes of obsequious natives. But I don't know if father would let me go. We must see.

"I keep living over again the lovely times we have had. But I don't think you liked me quite so much towards the end, did you? You did not like me when we left Paris. Why didn't you?

"I love you very much. I love your body. It is so clear and fine. I am glad you do not go naked, or all the women would fall in love with you. I am very jealous of it, I love it so much."

He was more or less satisfied with this letter. But day after day he was walking about, dead, non-existent.

He could not come again to Nottingham until the end of April. Then he persuaded her to go with him for a week-end to a friend's house near Oxford. By this time they were engaged. He had written to her father, and the thing was settled. He brought her an emerald ring, of which she was very proud.

Her people treated her now with a little distance, as if she had already left them. They left her very much alone.

She went with him for the three days in the country house near Oxford. It was delicious, and she was very happy. But the thing she remembered most was when, getting up in the morning after he had gone back quietly to his own room, having spent the night with her, she found herself very rich in being alone; and enjoying to the full her solitary room, she drew up her blind and saw the plum-trees in the garden below all glittering and snowy and delighted with the sunshine, in full bloom under a blue sky. They threw out their blossom, they flung it about under the blue heavens, the whitest blossom! How excited it made her.

She had to hurry through her dressing to go and walk in the garden under the plum-trees, before anyone should come and talk to her. Out she slipped, and paced like a queen in fairy pleasaunces. The blossom was silver-shadowy when she looked up from under the tree at the blue sky. There was a faint scent, a faint noise of bees, a wonderful quickness of happy morning.

She heard the breakfast gong and went indoors.

"Where have you been?" asked the others.

"I had to go out under the plum-trees," she said, her face glowing like a flower. "It is so lovely."

A shadow of anger crossed Skrebensky's soul. She had not wanted him to be there. He hardened his will.

At night there was a moon, and the blossom glistened ghostly, they went together to look at it. She saw the moonlight on his face as he waited near her, and his features were like silver, and his eyes in shadow were unfathomable. She was in love with him. He was very quiet.

They went indoors and she pretended to be tired. So she went quickly to bed.

"Don't be long coming to me," she whispered as she was supposed to be kissing him goodnight.

And he waited, intent, obsessed, for the moment when he could come to her.

She enjoyed him, she made much of him. She liked to put her fingers on the soft skin of his sides, or on the softness of his back, when he made the muscles hard underneath, the muscles developed very strong through riding; and she had a great thrill of excitement and passion, because of the unimpressible hardness of his body, that was so soft and smooth under her fingers, that came to her with such absolute service.

She owned his body and enjoyed it with all the delight and carelessness of a possessor. But he had become gradually afraid of her body. He wanted her, he wanted her endlessly. But there had come a tension into his desire, a constraint which prevented his enjoying the delicious approach and the lovable close of the endless embrace. He was afraid. His will was always tense, fixed.

Her final examination was at midsummer. She insisted on sitting for it, although she had neglected her work during the past months. He also wanted her to go in for the degree. Then, he thought, she would be satisfied. Secretly he hoped she would fail, so that she would be more glad of him.

"Would you rather live in India or in England, when we are married?" he asked her.

"Oh in India, by far," she said, with a careless lack of consideration which annoyed him.

Once she said, with heat:

"I shall be glad to leave England. Everything is so meagre and paltry, it is so unspiritual—I hate democracy."

He became angry to hear her talk like this, he did not know why.

Somehow he could not bear it, when she attacked things. It was as if she were attacking him.

"What do you mean;" he asked her, hostile, "why do you hate democracy?"

"Only the greedy and ugly people come to the top in a democracy," she said, "because they're the only people who will push themselves there. Only degenerate races are democratic."

"What do you want then—an aristocracy?" he asked, secretly moved. He always felt that by rights, he belonged to the ruling aristocracy. Yet to hear her speak for his class pained him with a curious, painful pleasure. He felt he was acquiescing in something illegal, taking to himself some wrong, reprehensible advantage.

"I *do* want an aristocracy," she cried. "And I'd far rather have an aristocracy of birth than of money. Who are the aristocrats now—who are chosen as the best to rule? Those who have money and the brains for money. It doesn't matter what else they have: but they must have money-brains;—because they are ruling in the name of money."

"The people elect the government," he said.

"I know they do. But what are the people? Each one of them is a money-interest. I hate it, that anybody is my equal who has the same amount of money as I have. I *know* I am better than all of them. I hate them. They are not my equals. I hate equality on a money-basis. It is the equality of dirt."

Her eyes blazed at him, he felt as if she wanted to destroy him. She had gripped him and was trying to break him. His anger sprang up, against her. At least he would fight for his existence with her. A hard, blind resistance possessed him.

"*I* don't care about money," he said, "neither do I want to put my finger in the pie. I am too sensitive about my finger."

"What is your finger to me!" she cried, in a passion. "You with your dainty fingers, and your going to India because you will be one of the somebodies there! It's a mere dodge, your going to India."

"In what way a dodge?" he cried, white with anger and fear.

"You think the Indians are simpler than us, and so you'll enjoy being near them and being a lord over them," she said. "And you'll feel so righteous, governing them for their own good. Who are you, to feel righteous. What are you righteous about, in your governing.

Your governing stinks. What do you govern for, but to make things there as dead and mean as they are here?"

"I don't feel righteous in the least," he said.

"Then what *do* you feel. It's all such a nothingness, what you feel and what you don't feel."

"What do you feel yourself?" he asked. "Aren't you righteous in your own mind?"

"Yes I am, because I'm against you, and all your old, dead things," she cried.

She seemed, with the last words, uttered in hard knowledge, to strike down the flag that he kept flying. He felt cut off at the knees, a figure made worthless. A horrible sickness gripped him, as if his legs were really cut away, and he could not move, but remained a crippled trunk, dependent, worthless. The ghastly sense of helplessness, as if he were a mere figure that did not exist vitally, made him mad, beside himself.

Now, even whilst he was with her, this death of himself came over him, when he walked about like a body from which all individual life is gone. In this state he neither heard nor saw nor felt, only the mechanism of his life continued.

He hated her, as far as, in this state, he could hate. His cunning suggested to him all the ways of making her esteem him. For she did not esteem him. He left her and did not write to her. He flirted with other women, with Gudrun.

This last made her very fierce. She was still fiercely jealous of his body. In passionate anger she upbraided him because, not being man enough to satisfy one woman, he hung round others.

"Don't I satisfy you?" he asked of her, again going white to the throat.

"No," she said. "You've never satisfied me since the first weeks in London. You never satisfy me now. What does it mean to me, your having me—"

She lifted her shoulders and turned aside her face in a motion of cold, indifferent worthlessness. He felt he would kill her.

When she had roused him to a pitch of madness, when she saw his eyes all dark and mad with suffering, then a great suffering overcame her soul, a great, inconquerable suffering. And she loved him. For Oh, she wanted to love him. Stronger than life or death was her craving to be able to love him.

And at such moments, when he was mad with her destroying him, when all his complacency was destroyed, all his everyday self was broken, and only the stripped, rudimentary, primal man remained, demented with torture, her passion to love him became love, she took him again, they came together in an overwhelming passion, in which he knew he satisfied her.

But it all contained a developing germ of death. After each contact, her anguished desire for him or for that which she never had from him was stronger, her love was more hopeless. After each contact, his mad dependence on her was deepened, his hope of standing strong and taking her in his own strength was weakened. He felt himself a mere attribute of her.

Whitsuntide came, just before her examination. She was to have a few days of rest. Dorothy had inherited her patrimony, and had taken a cottage in Sussex. She invited them to stay with her.

They went down to Dorothy's neat, low cottage at the foot of the downs. Here they could do as they liked. Ursula was always yearning to go to the top of the downs. The white track wound up to the rounded summit. And she must go.

Up there, she could see the Channel a few miles away, the sea raised up and faintly glittering in the sky, the Isle of Wight a shadow lifted on the far distance, the river winding bright through the patterned plain to seaward, Arundel Castle a shadowy bulk, and then the rolling of the high, smooth downs, making a high, smooth land under heaven, acknowledging only the heavens in their great, sun-glowing strength, and suffering only a few bushes to trespass on the intercourse between their great, unabateable body and the changeful body of the sky.

Below she saw the villages and the woods of the weald, and the train running bravely, a gallant little thing, running with all the importance of the world over the water-meadows and into the gap of the downs, waving its white steam, yet all the while so little. So little, yet its courage carried it from end to end of the earth, till there was no place where it did not go. Yet the downs, in magnificent indifference, baring limbs and body to the sun, drinking sunshine and sea-wind and sea-wet cloud into its golden skin, with superb stillness and calm of being, was not the downs still more wonderful? The blind, pathetic, energetic courage of the train as it steamed tinily away through the patterned levels to the sea's dimness, so fast and so energetic, made her weep. Where was it going? It was going nowhere, it was just going. So blind, so without goal or aim, yet so hasty! She sat on an old prehistoric earth-work and cried, and the tears ran down her face. The train had tunnelled all the earth, blindly, and uglily. And she lay face downward on the downs, that were so strong, that cared only for their intercourse with the everlasting skies, and she wished she could become a strong mound smooth under the sky, bosom and limbs bared to all winds and clouds and bursts of sunshine.

But she must get up again and look down from her foothold of sunshine, down and away at the patterned, level earth, with its villages and its smoke and its energy. So shortsighted the train seemed, running to the distance, so terrifying in their littleness the villages, with such pettiness in their activity.

Skrebensky wandered dazed, not knowing where he was or what he was doing with her. All her passion seemed to be, to wander up there on the downs, and when she must descend, to earth, she was heavy. Up there she was exhilarated and free.

She would not love him in a house any more. She said she hated houses, and particularly she hated beds. There was something distasteful in his coming to her bed.

She would stay the night on the downs. Up there, he with her. It was midsummer, the days were glamorously long. At about half past ten, when the bluey-black darkness had at last fallen, they took rugs and climbed the steep track to the summit of the downs, he and she.

Up there, the stars were big, the earth below was gone into darkness. She was free up there with the stars. Far out they saw tiny yellow lights—but it was very far out, at sea, or on land. She was free up among the stars.

She took off all her clothes, and made him take off all his, and they ran over the smooth, moonless turf, a long way, more than a mile from where they had left their clothing, running in the dark, soft wind, utterly naked, as naked as the downs themselves. Her hair was loose and blew about her shoulders, she ran swiftly, wearing sandals when she set off on the long run to the dew-pond.

In the round dew-pond the stars were untroubled. She ventured softly into the water, grasping at the stars with her hands.

And then suddenly she started back, running swiftly. He was there, beside her, but only on sufferance. He was a screen for her fears. He served her. She took him, she clasped him, clenched him close, but her eyes were open looking at the stars, it was as if the stars were lying with her and entering the unfathomable darkness of her womb, fathoming her at last. It was not him.

The dawn came. They stood together on a high place, an earth-work of the stone-age men, watching for the light. It came over the land. But the land was dark. She watched a pale rim on the sky, away against the darkened land. The darkness became bluer. A little wind was running in from the sea behind. It seemed to be running to the pale rift of the dawn. And she and he darkly, on an outpost of the darkness, stood watching for the dawn.

The light grew stronger, gushing up against the dark sapphire of the transparent night. The light grew stronger, whiter, then over it hovered a flush of rose. A flush of rose, and then yellow, pale, new-created yellow, the whole quivering and poising momentarily over the fountain of the sky's rim.

The rose hovered and quivered, burned, fused to flame, to a transient red, whilst the yellow urged out in great waves, thrown from the ever-increasing fountain, great waves of yellow flinging into the sky, scattering its spray over the darkness, which became bluer and bluer, paler, till soon it would itself be a radiance, which had been darkness.

The sun was coming. There was a quivering, a powerful, terrifying swim of molten light. Then the molten source itself surged forth, revealing itself. The sun was in the sky, too powerful to look at.

And the ground beneath lay so still, so peaceful. Only now and again a cock crew. Otherwise, from the distant, yellow hills to the pine trees at the foot of the downs, everything was newly washed into being, in a flood of new, golden creation.

It was so unutterably still and perfect with promise, the golden-lighted, distinct land, that Ursula's soul rocked and wept. Suddenly he glanced at her. The tears were running over her cheeks, her mouth was working strangely.

"What is the matter?" he asked.

After a moment's struggle with her voice,

"It is so beautiful," she said, looking at the glowing, beautiful land. It was so beautiful, so perfect, and so unsullied.

He too realised what England would be in a few hours' time—a blind, sordid, strenuous activity, all for nothing, fuming with dirty smoke and running trains and groping in the bowels of the earth, all for nothing. A ghastliness came over him.

He looked at Ursula. Her face was wet with tears, very bright, like a transfiguration in the refulgent light. Nor was his the hand to wipe away the burning, bright tears. He stood apart, overcome by a cruel ineffectuality.

Gradually, a great, helpless sorrow was rising in him. But as yet, he was fighting it away, he was struggling for his own life. He became very quiet and unaware of the things about him, awaiting, as it were, her judgment on him.

They returned to Nottingham, the time of her examination came. She must go to London. But she would not stay with him in an hôtel. She would go to a quiet little pension near the British Museum.

Those quiet residential squares of London made a great impression on her mind. They were very complete. Her mind seemed imprisoned in their quietness. Who was going to liberate her?

In the evening, her practical examination being over, he went with her to dinner at one of the hôtels down the river, near Richmond. It was golden and beautiful, with yellow water and white and scarlet-striped boat-awnings, and blue shadows under the trees.

"When shall we be married?" he asked her, quietly, simply, as if it were a mere question of comfort.

She watched the changing pleasure-traffic of the river. He looked at her golden, puzzled *museau*. The knot gathered in his throat.

"I don't know," she said.

A hot grief gripped his throat.

"Why don't you know—don't you want to be married?" he asked her.

Her head turned slowly, her face, puzzled, like a boy's face, expressionless because she was trying to think, looked towards his face. She did not see him, because she was pre-occupied. She did not quite know what she was going to say.

"I don't think I want to be married," she said, and her naïve, troubled, puzzled eyes rested a moment on his, then travelled away, pre-occupied.

"Do you mean never, or not just yet?" he asked.

The knot in his throat grew harder, his face was drawn as if he were being strangled.

"I mean never," she said, out of some far self which spoke for once beyond her.

His drawn, strangled face watched her blankly for a few moments, then a strange sound took place in his throat. She started, came to herself, and, horrified, saw him. His head made a queer motion, the chin jerked back against the throat, the curious crowing, hiccupping sound came again, his face twisted like insanity, and he was crying, crying blind and twisted as if something were broken which kept him in control.

"Tony—don't," she cried, starting up.

It tore every one of her nerves, to see him. He made groping movements to get out of his chair. But he was crying uncontrollably, noiselessly, with his face twisted like a mask, contorted, and the tears running down the amazing grooves in his cheeks. Blindly, his face always this horrible working mask, he groped for his hat, for his way down from the terrace. It was eight o'clock, but still brightly light. The other people were staring. In great agitation, part of which was exasperation, she stayed behind, paid the waiter with a half sovereign, took her yellow silk coat, then followed Skrebensky.

She saw him walking with brittle, blind steps along the path by the river. She could tell by the strange stiffness and brittleness of his figure that he was still crying. Hurrying after him, running, she took his arm.

"Tony," she cried, "don't! Why are you like this? What are you doing this for? Don't! It's not necessary."

He heard, and his manhood was cruelly, coldly defaced. Yet it was no good. He could not gain control of his face. His face, his breast, were weeping violently, as if automatically. His will, his knowledge had nothing to do with it. He simply could not stop.

She walked holding his arm, silent with exasperation and perplexity and pain. He took the uncertain steps of a blind man, because his mind was blind with weeping.

"Shall we go home? Shall we have a taxi?" she said.

He could pay no attention. Very flustered, very agitated, she signalled indefinitely to a taxi-cab that was going slowly by. The driver saluted and drew up. She opened the door and pushed Skrebensky in, then took her own place. Her face was uplifted, the mouth closed down, she looked hard and cold and ashamed. She winced as the driver's dark, red face was thrust round upon her, a full-blooded, animal face with black eyebrows and a thick, short-cut moustache.

"Where to, lady?" he said, his white teeth showing.

Again for a moment she was flustered.

"Forty Rutland Square," she said.

433

He touched his cap and stolidly set the car in motion. He seemed to have a league with her to ignore Skrebensky.

The latter sat as if trapped within the taxi-cab, his face still working, whilst occasionally he made quick slight movements of the head, to shake away his tears. He never moved his hands. She could not bear to look at him. She sat with face uplifted and averted to the window.

At length, when she had regained some control over herself, she turned again to him. He was much quieter. His face was wet, and twitched occasionally, his hands still lay motionless. But his eyes were quite still, like a washed sky after rain, full of a wan light, and quite steady, almost ghost-like.

A pain flamed in her womb, for him.

"I didn't think I should hurt you," she said, laying her hand very lightly, tentatively, on his arm. "The words came without my knowing. They didn't mean anything, really."

He remained quite still, hearing, but washed all wan and without feeling. She waited, looking at him, as if he were some curious, not-understandable creature.

"You won't cry again, will you, Tony?"

Some shame and bitterness against her burned him in the question. She noticed how his moustache was soddened wet with tears. Taking her handkerchief, she wiped his face. The driver's heavy, stolid back remained always turned to them, as if conscious but indifferent. Skrebensky sat motionless whilst Ursula wiped his face, softly, carefully, and yet clumsily, not as well as he would have wiped it himself.

Her handkerchief was too small. It was soon wet through. She groped in his pocket for his own. Then, with its more ample capacity, she carefully dried his face. He remained motionless all the while. Then she drew his cheek to hers, and kissed him. His face was cold. Her heart was hurt. She saw the tears welling quickly to his eyes again. As if he were a child, she again wiped away his tears. By now she herself was on the point of weeping. Her underlip was caught between her teeth.

So she sat still, for fear of her own tears, sitting close by him, holding his hand warm and close and loving. Meanwhile the car ran on, and a soft, midsummer dusk began to gather. For a long while they sat motionless. Only now and again her hand closed more closely, lovingly, over his hand, then gradually relaxed.

The dusk began to fall. One or two lights appeared. The driver drew up to light his lamps. Skrebensky moved for the first time, leaning forward to watch the driver. His face had always the same still, clarified, almost childlike look, impersonal.

They saw the driver's strange, full, dark face peering into the lamps under drawn brows. Ursula shuddered. It was the face almost of an animal, yet of a quick, strong, wary animal that had them within its knowledge, almost within its power. She clung closer to Skrebensky.

"My love?" she said to him, questioningly, when the car was again running in full motion.

He made no movement or sound. He let her hold his hand, he let her reach forward, in the gathering darkness, and kiss his still cheek. The crying had gone by—he would not cry any more. He was whole and himself again.

"My love," she repeated, trying to make him notice her.

But as yet, he could not.

He watched the road. They were running by Kensington Gardens. For the first time, his lips opened.

"Shall we get out and go into the park?" he asked.

"Yes," she said, quietly, not sure what was coming.

After a moment he took the tube from its peg. She saw the stout, strong, self-contained driver lean his head.

"Stop at Hyde Park Corner."

The dark head nodded, the car ran on just the same.

Presently they pulled up. Skrebensky paid the man. Ursula stood back. She saw the driver salute as he received his tip, and then, before he set the car in motion, turn and look at her, with his quick, powerful, animal's look, his eyes very concentrated and the whites of his eyes flickering. Then he drove away into the crowd. He had let her go. She had been afraid.

Skrebensky turned with her into the park. A band was still playing and the place was thronged with people. They listened to the ebbing music, then went aside to a dark seat, where they sat closely, hand in hand.

Then at length, as out of the silence, she said to him, wondering:

"What hurt you so?"

She really did not know, at this moment.

"When you said you wanted never to marry me," he replied, with a childish simplicity.

"But why did that hurt you so?" she said. "You needn't mind everything I say, so particularly."

"I don't know—I didn't want to do it," he said, humbly, ashamed.

She pressed his hand warmly. They sat close together, watching the soldiers go by with their sweethearts, the lights trailing in myriads down the great thoroughfares that beat on the edge of the park.

"I didn't know you cared so much," she said, also humbly.

"I didn't," he said. "I was knocked over myself.—But I care—all the world."

His voice was so quiet and colourless, it made her heart go pale with fear.

"My love!" she said, drawing near to him. But she spoke out of fear, not out of love.

"I care all the world—I care for nothing else—neither in life nor death," he said, in the same steady, colourless voice of essential truth.

"Than for what?" she murmured duskly.

"Than for you—to be with me."

And again she was afraid. Was she to be conquered by this? She cowered close to him, very close to him. They sat perfectly still, listening to the great, heavy, beating sound of the town, the murmur of lovers going by, the footsteps of soldiers.

She shivered against him.

"You are cold?" he said.

"A little."

"We will go and have some supper."

He was now always quiet and decided and remote, very beautiful. He seemed to have some strange, cold power over her.

They went to a restaurant, and drank chianti. But his pale, wan look did not go away.

"Don't leave me tonight," he said at length, looking at her, pleading. He was so strange and impersonal, she was afraid.

"But the people of my place," she said, quivering.

"I will explain to them—they know we are engaged."

She sat pale and mute. He waited.

"Shall we go?" he said at length.

"Where?"

"To an hôtel."

Her heart was hardened. Without answering, she rose to acquiesce. But she was now cold and unreal. Yet she could not refuse him. It seemed like fate, a fate she did not want.

They went to an Italian hôtel somewhere, and had a sombre bedroom with a very large bed, clean, but sombre. The ceiling was painted with a bunch of flowers in a big medallion over the bed. She thought it was pretty.

He came to her, and cleaved to her very close, like steel cleaving and clinching on to her. Her passion was roused, it was fierce but cold. But it was fierce, and extreme, and good, their passion this night. He slept with her fast in his arms. All night long he held her fast against him. She was passive, acquiescent. But her sleep was not very deep nor very real.

She woke in the morning to a sound of water dashed on a courtyard, to sunlight streaming through a lattice. She thought she was in a foreign country. And Skrebensky was there an incubus upon her.

She lay still, thinking, whilst his arm was round her, his head against her shoulders, his body against hers, just behind her. He was still asleep.

She watched the sunshine coming in bars through the *persiennes*, and her immediate surroundings again melted away.

She was in some other land, some other world, where the old restraints had dissolved and vanished, where one moved freely, not afraid of one's fellow men, nor wary, nor on the defensive, but calm, indifferent, at one's ease. Vaguely, in a sort of silver light, she wandered at large and at ease. The bonds of the world were broken. This world of England had vanished away. She heard a voice in the yard below calling:

"O' Giovann'—O'-O'-O' Giovann'—!"

And she knew she was in a new country, in a new life. It was very delicious to lie thus still, with one's soul wandering freely and simply in the silver light of some other, simpler, more finely natural world.

But always there was a foreboding waiting to command her. She became more aware of Skrebensky. She knew he was waking up. She must modify her soul, depart from her further world, for him.

She knew he was awake. He lay still, with a concrete stillness, not as when he slept. Then his arm tightened almost convulsively upon her, and he said, half timidly:

"Did you sleep well?"

The Rainbow

"Very well."

"So did I."

There was a pause.

"And do you love me?" he asked.

She turned and looked at him, searchingly. He seemed outside her.

"I do," she said.

But she said it out of complacency and a desire not to be harried. There was a curious breach of silence between them, which frightened him.

They lay rather late, then he rang for breakfast. She wanted to be able to go straight downstairs and away from the place, when she got up. She was happy in this room, but the thought of the publicity of the hall downstairs rather troubled her.

A young Italian, a Sicilian, dark and slightly pock-marked, buttoned up in a sort of grey tunic, appeared with the tray. His face had an almost African imperturbability, impassive, incomprehensible.

"One might be in Italy," Skrebensky said to him, genially.

A vacant look, almost like fear, came on the fellow's face. He did not understand.

"This is like Italy," Skrebensky explained.

The face of the Italian flashed with a non-comprehending smile, he finished setting out the tray, and was gone. He did not understand: he would understand nothing: he disappeared from the door like a half-domesticated wild animal. It made Ursula shudder slightly, the quick, sharp-sighted, intent animality of the man.

Skrebensky was beautiful to her this morning, his face softened and transfused with suffering and with love, his movements very still and gentle. He was beautiful to her, but she was detached from him by a chill distance. Always she seemed to be bearing up against the distance that separated them. But he was unaware. This morning he was transfused and beautiful. She admired his movements, the way he spre̶ ̶ ̶y on his roll, or poured out the coffee.

̶ ̶ ̶ast was over she lay still again on the pillows, whilst ̶ ̶ ̶his toilet. She watched him, as he sponged himself ̶ ̶ ̶himself with the towel. His body was beautiful, his ̶ ̶ ̶and quick, she admired him and she appreciated ̶ ̶ ̶e. He seemed completed now. He roused no ̶ ̶ ̶her. He seemed added up, finished. She knew him all round, not on any side did he lead into the unknown. Poignant, almost passionate appreciation she felt for him, but none of the dreadful wonder, none of the rich fear, the connection with the unknown, or the reverence of love. He was, however, unaware this morning. His body was quiet and fulfilled, his veins complete with satisfaction, he was happy, finished.

Again she went home. But this time he went with her. He wanted to stay by her. He wanted her to marry him. It was already July. In early September he must sail for India. He could not bear to think of going alone. She must come with him. Nervously, he kept beside her.

Her examination was finished, her college career was over. There remained for her now to marry or to work again. She applied for no post. It was concluded she would marry. India tempted her—the strange, strange land. But with the thought of Calcutta, or Bombay, or of Simla, and of the European population, India was no more attractive to her than Nottingham.

She had failed in her examination: she had gone down: she had not taken her degree. It was a blow to her. It hardened her soul.

"It doesn't matter," he said. "What are the odds, whether you are a Bachelor of Arts or not, according to the London University? All you know, you know, and if you are Mrs Skrebensky, the B.A. is meaningless."

Instead of consoling her, this made her harder, more ruthless. She was now up against her own fate. It was for her to choose between being Mrs Skrebensky, even Baroness Skrebensky, wife of a lieutenant in the Royal Engineers, the Sappers, as he called them, living with the European population in India—or being Ursula Brangwen, spinster, school-mistress. She was qualified by her Intermediate Arts examination. She would probably even now get a post quite easily as assistant in one of the higher grade schools, or even in Willey Green Grammar School. Which was she to do?

She hated most of all entering the bondage of teaching once more. Very heartily she detested it. Yet at the thought of marriage and living with Skrebensky amid the European population in India, her soul was locked and would not budge. She had very little feeling about it: only there was a dead-lock.

Skrebensky waited, she waited, everybody waited for the decision. When Anton talked to her, and seemed insidiously to suggest himself as a husband to her, she knew how utterly locked out he was. On the other hand, when she saw Dorothy, and discussed the matter, she felt she would marry him promptly, at once, as a sharp disavowal of adherence with Dorothy's views.

The situation was almost ridiculous.

"But do you love him?" asked Dorothy.

"It isn't a question of loving him," said Ursula. "I love him well enough—certainly more than I love anybody else in the world. And I shall never love anybody else the same again. We have had the flower of each other. But I don't *care* about love. I don't value it. I don't care whether I love or whether I don't, whether I have love or whether I haven't. What is it to me?"

And she shrugged her shoulders in fierce, cruel contempt.

Dorothy pondered, rather angry and afraid.

"Then what *do* you care about?" she asked, exasperated.

"I don't know," said Ursula. "But something impersonal. Love —love—love—what does it mean—what does it amount to? So much personal gratification. It doesn't lead anywhere."

"It isn't supposed to lead anywhere, is it?" said Dorothy satirically. "I thought it was the one thing which is an end in itself."

"Then what does it matter to me?" cried Ursula. "As an end in itself, I could love a hundred men, one after the other. Why should I end with a Skrebensky? Why should I not go on, and love all the types I fancy, one after another, if love is an end in itself? There are plenty of men who aren't Anton, whom I could love—whom I would like to love."

"Then you don't love *him*," said Dorothy.

"I tell you I do;—quite as much, and perhaps more than I should love any of the others. Only there are plenty of things that aren't in Anton that I would love in the other men."

"What, for instance?"

"It doesn't matter. But a sort of strong understanding, in some men, and then a dignity, a directness, something unquestioned that there is in working men, and then a jolly, reckless passionateness that you see—a man who could really let go—"

Dorothy could feel that Ursula was already hankering after something else, something that this man did not give her.

"The question is, what *do* you want," propounded Dorothy. "Is it just other men?"

Ursula was silenced. This was her own dread. Was she just promiscuous?

"Because if it is," continued Dorothy, "you'd better marry Anton. The other can only end badly."

So out of fear of herself, Ursula was to marry Skrebensky.

He was very busy now, preparing to go to India. He must visit relatives and contract business. He was almost sure of Ursula now. She seemed to have given in. And he seemed to become again an important, self-assured man.

It was the first week in August, and he was one of a large party in a bungalow on the Lincolnshire coast. It was a tennis, golf, motor-car, motor-boat party, given by his great-aunt, a lady of social pretensions. Ursula was invited to spend the week with the party.

She went rather reluctantly. Her marriage was more or less fixed for the twenty eighth of the month. They were to sail for India on September the fifth. One thing she knew, in her subconsciousness, and that was, she would never sail for India.

She and Anton, being important guests on account of the coming marriage, had rooms in the large bungalow. It was a big place, with a great central hall, two smaller writing-rooms, and then two corridors from which opened eight or nine bedrooms. Skrebensky was put on one corridor, Ursula on the other. They felt very lost, in the crowd.

Being lovers, however, they were allowed to be out alone together as much as they liked. Yet she felt very strange, in this crowd of strange people, uneasy, as if she had no privacy. She was not used to these homogeneous crowds. She was afraid.

She felt different from the rest of them, with their hard, easy, shallow intimacy, that seemed to cost them so little. She felt she was not pronounced enough. It was a kind of hold-your-own unconventional atmosphere. She did not like it. In crowds, in assemblies of people, she liked formality. She felt she did not produce the right effect. She was not effective: she was not beautiful: she was nothing. Even before Skrebensky she felt unimportant, almost inferior. He could take his part very well with the rest.

He and she went out into the night. There was a moon behind clouds, shedding a diffused light, gleaming now and again in bits of smoky mother-of-pearl. So they walked together on the wet, ribbed sands near the sea, hearing the run of the long, heavy waves, that made a ghostly whiteness and a whisper.

He was sure of himself. As she walked, the soft silk of her dress—she wore a blue shantung, full-skirted—blew away from the sea and flapped and clung to his legs. She wished it would not.

Everything seemed to give her away, and she could not rouse herself to deny, she was so confused.

He would lead her away to a pocket in the sand-hills, secret amid the grey thorn-bushes and the grey, glassy grass. He held her close against him, felt all her firm, unutterably desirable mould of body through the fine fire of the silk that fell about her limbs. The silk, slipping fierily on the hidden, yet revealed roundness and firmness of her body, her loins, seemed to run in him like fire, make his brain burn like brimstone. She liked it, the electric fire of the silk under his hands upon her limbs, the fire flew over her, as he drew nearer and nearer to discovery. She vibrated like a jet of electric, firm fluid in response. Yet she did not feel beautiful. All the time, she felt she was not beautiful to him, only exciting. She let him take her, and he seemed mad, mad with excited passion. But she, as she lay after-wards on the cold, soft sand, looking up at the blotted, faintly luminous sky, felt that she was as cold now as she had been before. Yet he, breathing heavily, seemed almost savagely satisfied. He seemed revenged.

A little wind wafted the sea grass and passed over her face. Where was the supreme fulfilment she would never enjoy? Why was she so cold, so unroused, so indifferent?

As they went home, and she saw the many, hateful lights of the bungalow, of several bungalows in a group, he said softly:

"Don't lock your door."

"I'd rather, here," she said.

"No, don't. We belong to each other. Don't let us deny it."

She did not answer. He took her silence for consent.

He shared his room with another man.

"I suppose," he said, "it won't alarm the house if I go across to happier regions."

"So long as you don't make a great row going, and don't try the wrong door," said the other man, turning in to sleep.

Skrebensky went out in his wide-striped cotton sleeping suit. He crossed the big dining hall, whose low firelight smelled of cigars and whiskey and coffee, entered the other corridor and found Ursula's room. She was lying awake, wide-eyed and suffering. She was glad he had come, if only for consolation. It was consolation to be held in his arms, to feel his body against hers. Yet how foreign his arms and body were! Yet still, not so horribly foreign and hostile as the rest of the house felt to her.

She did not know how she suffered in this house. She was healthy and exorbitantly full of interest. So she played tennis and learned golf, she rowed out and swam in the deep sea, and enjoyed it very much indeed, full of zest. Yet all the time, among those others, she felt shocked and wincing, as if her violently-sensitive nakedness were exposed to the hard, brutal, material impact of the rest of the people.

The days went by unmarked, in a full, almost strenuous enjoyment of one's own physique. Skrebensky was one among the others, till evening came, and he took her for himself. She was allowed a great deal of freedom and was treated with a good deal of respect, as a girl on the eve of marriage, about to depart for another continent.

The trouble began at evening. Then a yearning for something unknown came over her, a passion for something she knew not what. She would walk the foreshore alone after dusk, expecting, expecting something, as if she had gone to a *rendez-vous*. The salt, bitter passion of the sea, its indifference to the earth, its swinging, definite motion, its strength, its attack, and its salt burning, seemed to provoke her to a pitch of madness, tantalising her with vast suggestions of fulfilment. And then, for personification, would come Skrebensky, Skrebensky, whom she knew, whom she was fond of, who was attractive, but whose soul could not contain her in its waves of strength, nor his breast compel her in burning, salty passion.

One evening they went out after dinner, across the low golf links to the dunes and the sea. The sky had small, faint stars, all was still and faintly dark. They walked together in silence, then ploughed, labouring, through the heavy loose sand of the gap between the dunes. They went in silence under the even, faint darkness, in the darker shadow of the sand-hills.

Suddenly, cresting the heavy, sandy pass, Ursula lifted her head and shrank back, momentarily frightened. There was a great whiteness confronting her, the moon was incandescent as a round furnace door, out of which came the high blast of moonlight, over the sea-ward half of the world, a dazzling, terrifying glare of white light. They shrank back for a moment into shadow, uttering a cry. He felt his chest laid bare, where the secret was heavily hidden. He felt himself fusing down to nothingness, like a bead that rapidly disappears in an incandescent flame.

"How wonderful!" cried Ursula, in low, calling tones. "How wonderful!"

And she went forward, plunging into it. He followed behind. She too seemed to melt into the white glare, towards the moon.

The sands were as ground silver, the sea moved in solid brightness, coming towards them, and she went to meet the advance of the flashing, buoyant water. She gave her breast to the moon, her belly to the flashing, heaving water. He stood behind, encompassed, a shadow ever dissolving.

She stood on the edge of the water, at the edge of the solid, flashing body of the sea, and the wave rushed over her feet.

"I want to go," she cried, in a strong, dominant voice. "I want to go."

He saw the moonlight on her face, so she was like metal, he heard her ringing, metallic voice, like the voice of a harpy to him.

She prowled, ranging on the edge of the water like a possessed creature, and he followed her. He saw the froth of the wave followed by the hard, bright water swirl over her feet and her ankles, she swung out her arms, to balance, he expected every moment to see her walk in to the sea, dressed as she was, and be carried swimming out.

But she turned, she walked to him.

"I want to go," she cried again, in the high, hard voice, like the scream of gulls.

"Where?" he asked.

"I don't know."

And she seized hold of his arm, held him fast, as if captive, and walked him a little way by the edge of the dazzling, dazing water.

Then there, in the great flare of light, she clinched hold of him, hard, as if suddenly she had the strength of destruction, she fastened her arms round him and tightened him in her grip, whilst her mouth sought his in a hard, rending, ever-increasing kiss, till his body was powerless in her grip, his heart melted in fear from the fierce, beaked, harpy's kiss. The water washed again over their feet, but she took no notice. She seemed unaware, she seemed to be pressing in her beaked mouth till she had the heart of him. Then, at last, she drew away and looked at him—looked at him. He knew what she wanted. He took her by the hand and led her across the foreshore back to the sand-hills. She went silently. He felt as if the ordeal of proof was upon him, for life or death. He led her to a dark hollow.

"No, here," she said, going out to the slope full under the moonshine. She lay motionless, with wide-open eyes looking at the moon. He came direct to her, without preliminaries. She held him pinned down at the chest, awful. The fight, the struggle for consummation was terrible. It lasted till it was agony to his soul, till he succumbed, till he gave way as if dead, and lay with his face buried partly in her hair partly in the sand, motionless, as if he would be motionless now for ever, hidden away in the dark, buried, only buried, he only wanted to be buried in the goodly darkness, only that, no more.

He seemed to swoon. It was a long time before he came to himself. He was aware of an unusual motion of her breast. He looked up. Her face lay like an image in the moonlight, the eyes wide open, rigid. But out of the eyes, slowly, there rolled a tear, that glittered in the moonlight as it ran down her cheek.

He felt as if the knife were being pushed into his already dead body. With head strained back, he watched, drawn tense, for some minutes, watched the unaltering, rigid face like metal in the moonlight, the fixed, unseeing eyes, in which slowly the water gathered, shook with glittering moonlight, then, surcharged, brimmed over and ran trickling, a tear with its burden of moonlight, into the darkness, to fall in the sand.

He drew gradually away as if afraid, drew away—she did not move. He glanced at her—she lay the same. Could he break away. He turned, saw the open foreshore, clear in front of him, and he plunged away, on and on, ever further from the horrible figure that lay stretched in the moonlight on the sands with the tears gathering and travelling on the motionless, eternal face.

He felt, if ever he must see her again, his bones must be broken, his body crushed, obliterated for ever. And as yet, he had the love of his own living body. He wandered on a long, long way, till his brain grew dark and he was unconscious with weariness. Then he curled in the deepest darkness he could find, under the sea grass, and lay there without consciousness.

She broke from her tense cramp of agony gradually, though each movement was a goad of heavy pain. Gradually, she lifted her dead body from the sands, and rose at last. There was now no moon for her, no sea. All had passed away. She trailed her dead body to the house, to her room, where she lay down, inert.

Morning brought her a new access of superficial life. But all within her was cold, dead, inert. Skrebensky appeared at breakfast. He was white and obliterated. They did not look at each other nor speak to each other. Apart from the ordinary, trivial talk of civil people, they were separate, they did not speak of what was between them during the remaining two days of their stay. They were like two dead people who dare not recognise, dare not see each other.

Then she packed her bags and put on her things. There were several guests leaving together, for the same train. He would have no opportunity to speak to her.

He tapped at her bedroom door, at the last minute. She stood with her umbrella in her hand. He closed the door. He did not know what to say.

"Have you done with me?" he asked her at length, lifting his head.

"It isn't me," she said. "You have done with me—we have done with each other."

He looked at her, at the closed face, which he thought so cruel. And he knew he could never touch her again. His will was broken, he was seared, but he clung to the life of his body.

"Well, what have I done?" he asked, in a rather querulous voice.

"I don't know," she said, in the same dull, feelingless voice. "It is finished. It has been a failure."

He was silent. The words still burned his bowels.

"Is it my fault?" he said, looking up at length, challenging the last stroke.

"You couldn't—" she began. But she broke down.

He turned away, afraid to hear more. She began to gather her bag, her handkerchief, her umbrella. She must be gone now. He was waiting for her to be gone.

At length the carriage came and she drove away with the rest. When she was out of sight, a great relief came over him, a pleasant banality. In an instant, everything was obliterated. He was childishly amiable and companionable all the day long. He was astonished that life could be so nice. It was better than it had been before. What a simple thing it was to be rid of her! How friendly and simple everything felt to him! What false thing had she been forcing on him?

But at night, he dared not be alone. His room-mate had gone, and the hours of darkness were an agony to him. He watched the window in suffering and terror. When would this horrible darkness be lifted off him? Setting all his nerves, he endured it. He went to sleep with the dawn.

He never thought of her. Only his terror of the hours of night grew on him, obsessed him like a mania. He slept fitfully, with constant wakings of anguish. The fear wore away the core of him.

His plan was, to sit up very late: to drink in company until one or half past one in the morning: then he would get three hours of sleep, of oblivion. It was light by five o'clock. But he was shocked almost to madness if he opened his eyes on the darkness.

In the daytime he was all right, always occupied with the thing of the moment, adhering to the trivial present, which seemed to him ample and satisfying. No matter how little and futile his occupations were, he gave himself to them entirely, and felt normal and fulfilled. He was always active, cheerful, gay, charming, trivial. Only he dreaded the darkness and silence of his own bedroom, when the darkness should challenge him upon his own soul. That he could not bear, as he could not bear to think about Ursula. He had no soul, no background. He never thought of Ursula, not once, he gave her no sign. She was the darkness, the challenge, the horror. He turned to immediate things. He wanted to marry, quickly, to screen himself from the darkness, the challenge for his own soul. He would marry his Colonel's daughter. Quickly, without hesitation, pursued by his obsession for activity, he wrote to this girl, telling her his engagement was broken—it had been a temporary infatuation which he less than anyone else could understand now it was over—and could he see his very dear friend soon. He would not be happy till he had an answer.

He received a rather surprised reply from the girl, but she would be glad to see him. She was living with her aunt. He went down to her at once, and proposed to her the first evening. He was accepted. The marriage took place quietly within fourteen days' time. Ursula was not notified of the event. In another week, Skrebensky sailed with his new wife to India.

CHAPTER XVI

The Rainbow

Ursula went home to Beldover faint, dim, closed up. She could scarcely speak or notice. It was as if her energy were frozen. Her people asked her what was the matter. She told them, she had broken off the engagement with Skrebensky. They looked blank and angry. But she could not feel any more.

The weeks crawled by in apathy. He would have sailed for India now. She was scarcely interested. She was inert, without strength or interest.

Suddenly a shock ran through her, so violent that she thought she was struck down. Was she with child? She had been so stricken under the pain of herself and of him, this had never occurred to her. Now like a flame it took hold of her limbs and body. Was she with child?

In the first flaming hours of wonder, she did not know what she felt. She was as if tied to the stake. The flames were licking her and devouring her. But the flames were also good. They seemed to wear her away to rest. She let the flames wrap her and destroy her to rest. What she felt in her heart and her womb she did not know. It was a kind of swoon.

Then gradually the heaviness of her heart pressed and pressed into consciousness. What was she doing? Was she bearing a child? Bearing a child? To what?

Her flesh thrilled, but her soul was sick. It seemed, this child, like the seal set on her own nullity. Yet she was glad in her flesh that she was with child. She began to think, that she would write to Skrebensky, that she would go out to him, and marry him, and live simply as a good wife to him. What did the self, the form of life, matter? Only the living from day to day mattered, the beloved existence in the body, rich, peaceful, complete, with no beyond, no further trouble, no further complication. She had been wrong, she had been arrogant and wicked, wanting that other thing, that fantastic freedom, that illusory, conceited fulfilment which she had imagined she could not have with Skrebensky. Who was she to be wanting some fantastic fulfilment in her life? Was it not enough that she had her man, her children, her place of shelter under the sun? Was it not enough for her, as it had been enough for her mother? She would marry and love her husband and fill her place simply. That was the ideal.

Suddenly she saw her mother in a just and true light. Her mother was simple and radically true. She had taken the life that was given. She had not, in her arrogant conceit, insisted on creating life to fit herself. Her mother was right, profoundly right, and she herself had been false, trashy, conceited.

A great mood of humility came over her, and in this humility a bondaged sort of peace. She gave her limbs to the bondage, she loved the bondage, she called it peace. In this state she sat down to write to Skrebensky.

"Since you left me I have suffered a great deal, and so have come to myself. I cannot tell you the remorse I feel for my wicked, perverse behaviour. It was given to me to love you, and to know your love for me. But instead of thankfully, on my knees, taking what God had given, I must have the moon in my keeping, I must insist on having the moon for my own. Because I could not have it, everything else must go.

"I do not know if you can ever forgive me. I could die with shame to think of my behaviour with you during our last times, and I don't know if I could ever bear to look you in the face again. Truly the best thing for me would be to die, and cover my fantasies for ever. But I find I am with child, so that cannot be.

"It is your child, and for that reason I must revere it and submit my body entirely to its welfare, entertaining no thought of death, which once more is largely conceit. Therefore, because you once loved me, and because this child is your child, I ask you to have me back. If you will cable me one word, I will come to you as soon as I can. I swear to you to be a dutiful wife, and to serve you in all things. For now I only hate myself and my own conceited foolishness. I love you—I love the thought of you—you were natural and decent all through, whilst I was so false. Once I am with you again, I shall ask no more than to rest in your shelter all my life—."

This letter she wrote, sentence by sentence, as if from her deepest, sincerest heart. She felt that now, now, she was at the depths of herself. This was her true self, for ever. With this document she would appear before God at the Judgment Day.

For what had a woman but to submit? What was her flesh but for childbearing, her strength for her children and her husband, the giver of life? At last she was a woman.

She posted her letter to his club, to be forwarded to him in Calcutta. He would receive it soon after his arrival in India—within three weeks of his arrival there. In a month's time she would receive word from him. Then she would go.

She was quite sure of him. She thought only of preparing her garments and of living quietly, peacefully, till the time when she should join him again and her history would be concluded for ever. The peace held like an unnatural calm for a long time. She was aware, however, of a gathering restiveness, a tumult impending within her. She tried to run away from it. She wished she could hear from Skrebensky, in answer to her letter, so that her course should be resolved, she should be engaged in fulfilling her fate. It was this inactivity which made her liable to the revulsion she dreaded.

It was curious how little she cared about his not having written to her before. It was enough that she had sent her letter. She would get the required answer, that was all.

One afternoon in early October, feeling the seething rising to madness within her, she slipped out in the rain, to walk abroad, lest the house should suffocate her. Everywhere was drenched wet and deserted, the grimed houses glowed dull red, the butt house burned scarlet in a gleam of light, under the glistening, blackish purple slates. Ursula went on towards Willey Green. She lifted her face and walked swiftly, seeing the passage of light across the shallow valley, seeing the colliery and its clouds of steam for a moment visionary in dim brilliance, away in the chaos of rain. Then the veils closed again. She was glad of the rain's privacy and intimacy.

Making on towards the wood, she saw the pale gleam of Willey Water through the cloud below, she walked the open space where hawthorn trees streamed like hair on the wind and round bushes were presences showing through the atmosphere. It was very splendid, free and chaotic.

Yet she hurried to the wood, for shelter. There, the vast booming overhead vibrated down and encircled her, tree-trunks spanned the circle of tremendous sound, myriads of tree-trunks, enormous and streaked black with water, thrust like stanchions upright between the roaring overhead and the sweeping of the circle underfoot. She glided between the tree-trunks, afraid of them. They might turn and shut her in as she went through their marshalled silence.

So she flitted along, keeping an illusion that she was unnoticed. She felt like a bird that has flown in through the window of a hall where vast warriors sit at the board. Between their grave, booming ranks she was hastening, assuming she was unnoticed, till she emerged, with beating heart, through the far window and out into the open, upon the vivid green, marshy meadow.

She turned under the shelter of the common, seeing the great veils of rain swinging with slow, floating waves across the landscape. She was very wet and a long way from home, far enveloped in the rain and the waving landscape. She must beat her way back through all this fluctuation, back to stability and security.

A solitary thing, she took the track straight across the wilderness, going back. The path was a narrow groove in the turf between high, sere, tussocky grass; it was scarcely more than a rabbit run. So she moved swiftly along, watching her footing, going like a bird on the wind, with no thought, contained in motion. But her heart had a small, living seed of fear, as she went through the wash of hollow space.

Suddenly she knew there was something else. Some horses were looming in the rain, not near yet. But they were going to be near. She continued her path, inevitably. They were horses in the lee of a clump of trees beyond, above her. She pursued her way with bent head. She did not want to lift her face to them. She did not want to know they were there. She went on in the wild track.

She knew the heaviness on her heart. It was the weight of the horses. But she would circumvent them. She would bear the weight steadily, and so escape. She would go straight on, and on, and be gone by.

Suddenly the weight deepened and her heart grew tense to bear it. Her breathing was laboured. But this weight also she could bear. She knew without looking that the horses were moving nearer. What were they? She felt the thud of their heavy hoofs on the ground. What was it that was drawing near her, what weight oppressing her heart? She did not know, she did not look.

Yet now her way was cut off. They were blocking her back. She knew they had gathered on a log bridge over the sedgy dike, a dark, heavy, powerfully heavy knot. Yet her feet went on and on. They would burst before her. They would burst before her. Her feet went on and on. And tense, and more tense became her nerves and her veins, they ran hot, they ran white hot, they must fuse and she must die.

But the horses had burst before her. In a sort of lightning of knowledge their movement travelled through her, the quiver and strain and thrust of their powerful flanks, as they burst before her and drew on, beyond.

She knew they had not gone, she knew they awaited her still. But she went on over the log bridge that their hoofs had churned and drummed, she went on, knowing things about them. She was aware of their breasts gripped, clenched narrow in a hold that never relaxed, she was aware of their red nostrils flaming with long endurance, and of their haunches, so rounded, so massive, pressing, pressing, pressing to burst the grip upon their breasts, pressing forever till they went mad, running against the walls of time, and never bursting free. Their great haunches were smoothed and darkened with rain. But the darkness and wetness of rain could not put out the hard, urgent, massive fire that was locked within these flanks, never, never.

She went on, drawing near. She was aware of the great flash of hoofs, a bluish, iridescent flash surrounding a hollow of darkness. Large, large seemed the bluish, incandescent flash of the hoof-iron, large as a halo of lightning round the knotted darkness of the flanks. Like circles of lightning came the flash of hoofs from out of the powerful flanks.

They were awaiting her again. They had gathered under an oak-tree, knotting their awful, blind, triumphing flanks together, and waiting, waiting. They were waiting for her approach. As if from a far distance she was drawing near, towards the line of twiggy oak-trees where they made their intense darkness, gathered on a slight bank.

She must draw near. But they broke away, they cantered round, making a wide circle to avoid noticing her, and cantered back into the open hillside behind her.

They were behind her. The way was open before her, to the gate in the high hedge in the near distance, so she could pass into the smaller, cultivated field, and so out to the high-road and the ordered world of man. Her way was clear. She lulled her heart. Yet her heart was couched with fear, couched with fear all along.

Suddenly she hesitated as if seized by lightning. She seemed to fall, yet found herself faltering forward with small steps. The thunder of horses galloping down the path behind her shook her, the weight came down upon her, down, to the moment of extinction. She could not look round, so the horses thundered upon her.

Cruelly, they swerved and crashed by her on her left hand. She saw the fierce flanks crinkled and as yet inadequate, the great hoofs flashing bright as yet only brandished about her, and one by one the horses crashed by, intent, working themselves up.

They had gone by, brandishing themselves thunderously about her, enclosing her. They slackened their burst transport, they slowed down, and cantered together into a knot once more, in the corner by the gate and the trees ahead of her. They stirred, they moved uneasily, they settled their uneasy flanks into one group, one purpose. They were up against her.

Her heart was gone, she had no more heart. She knew she dare not draw near. That concentrated, knitted flank of the horse-group had conquered. It stirred uneasily, awaiting her, knowing its triumph. It stirred uneasily, with the uneasiness of awaited triumph. Her heart was gone, her limbs were dissolved, she was dissolved like water. All the hardness and looming power was in the massive body of the horse-group.

Her feet faltered, she came to a standstill. It was the crisis. The horses stirred their flanks uneasily. She looked away, failing. On her left, two hundred yards down the slope, the thick hedge ran parallel. At one point there was an oak-tree. She might climb into the boughs of that oak-tree, and so round and drop on the other side of the hedge.

Shuddering, with limbs like water, dreading every moment to fall, she began to work her way as if making a wide detour round the horse-mass. The horses stirred their flanks in a knot against her. She trembled forward as if in a trance.

Then suddenly, in a flame of agony, she darted, seized the rugged knots of the oak-tree and began to climb. Her body was weak but her hands were as hard as steel. She knew she was strong. She struggled in a great effort till she hung on the bough. She knew the horses were aware. She gained her foot-hold on the bough. The horses were loosening their knot, stirring, trying to realise. She was working her way round to the other side of the tree. As they started to canter towards her, she fell in a heap on the other side of the hedge.

For some moments she could not move. Then she saw through

the rabbit-cleared bottom of the hedge the great, working hoofs of the horses as they cantered near. She could not bear it. She rose and walked swiftly, diagonally across the field. The horses galloped along the other side of the hedge to the corner, where they were held up. She could feel them there in their huddled group all the while she hastened across the bare field. They were almost pathetic, now. Her will alone carried her, till, trembling, she climbed the fence under a leaning thorn-tree that overhung the grass by the high-road. The use went from her, she sat on the fence leaning back against the trunk of the thorn-tree, motionless.

As she sat there, spent, time and the flux of change passed away from her, she lay as if unconscious upon the bed of the stream, like a stone, unconscious, unchanging, unchangeable, whilst everything rolled by in transience, leaving her there, a stone at rest on the bed of the stream, inalterable and passive, sunk to the bottom of all change.

She lay still a long time, with her back against the thorn-tree trunk in her final isolation. Some colliers passed, tramping heavily up the wet road, their voices sounding out, their shoulders up to their ears, their figures blotched and spectral in the rain. Some did not see her. She opened her eyes languidly as they passed by. Then one man going alone saw her. The whites of his eyes showed in his black face as he looked in wonderment at her. He hesitated in his walk, as if to speak to her, out of frightened concern for her. How she dreaded his speaking to her, dreaded his questioning her.

She slipped from her seat and went vaguely along the path— vaguely. It was a long way home. She had an idea that she must walk for the rest of her life, wearily, wearily. Step after step, step after step, and always along the wet, rainy road between the hedges. Step after step, step after step, the monotony produced a deep, cold sense of nausea in her. How profound was her cold nausea, how profound! That too plumbed the bottom. She seemed destined to find the bottom of all things today: the bottom of all things. Well, at any rate she was walking along the bottommost bed—she was quite safe: quite safe, if she had to go on and on for ever, seeing this was the very bottom, and there was nothing deeper. There was nothing deeper, you see, so one could not but feel certain, passive.

She arrived home at last. The climb up the hill to Beldover had been very trying. Why must one climb up the hill? Why must one climb? Why not stay below? Why force one's way up the slope? Why force one's way up and up, when one is at the bottom? Oh, it was very trying, very wearying, very burdensome! Always burdens, always, always burdens. Still, she must get to the top and go home to bed. She must go to bed.

She got in and went upstairs in the dusk without its being noticed she was in such a sodden condition. She was too tired to go downstairs again. She got into bed and lay shuddering with cold, yet too apathetic to get up or to call for relief. Then gradually she became more ill.

She was very ill for a fortnight, delirious, shaken and racked. But always, amid the ache of delirium, she had a dull firmness of being, a sense of permanency. She was in some way like the stone at the bottom of the river, inviolable and unalterable, no matter what storm raged in her body. He soul lay still and permanent, full of pain, but itself for ever. Under all her illness persisted a deep, inalterable knowledge.

She knew, and she cared no more. Throughout her illness, distorted into vague forms, persisted the question of herself and Skrebensky, like a gnawing ache that was still superficial, and did not touch her isolated, impregnable core of reality. But the corrosion of him burned in her till it burned itself out.

Must she belong to him, must she adhere to him? Something compelled her, and yet it was not real. Always the ache, the ache of unreality, of her belonging to Skrebensky. What bound her to him when she was not bound to him? Why did the falsity persist? Why did the falsity gnaw, gnaw, gnaw at her, why could she not wake up to clarity, to reality? If she could but wake up, if she could but wake up, the falsity of the dream, of her connection with Skrebensky, would be gone. But the sleep, the delirium pinned her down. Even when she was calm and sober she was in its spell.

Yet she was never in its spell. What extraneous thing bound her to him? There was some bond put upon her. Why could she not break it through? What was it? What was it?

In her delirium she beat and beat at the question. And at last her weariness gave her the answer—it was the child. The child bound her to him. The child was like a bond round her brain, tightened on her brain. It bound her to Skrebensky.

But why, why did it bind her to Skrebensky? Could she not have a child of herself? Was not the child her own affair, all her own affair? What had it to do with him? Why must she be bound, aching and cramped with the bondage, to Skrebensky and Skrebensky's world?

Anton's world: it became in her feverish brain a compression which enclosed her. If she could not get out of the compression she would go mad. The compression was Anton and Anton's world: not the Anton she possessed, but the Anton she did not possess, that which was owned by some other influence, by the world.

She fought and fought and fought all through her illness to be free of him and his world, to put it aside, to put it aside, into its place. Yet ever anew it gained ascendancy over her, it laid new hold on her. Oh the unutterable weariness of her flesh, which she could not cast off, nor yet extricate. If she could but extricate herself, if she could but disengage herself from feeling, from her body, from all the vast encumbrance of the world that was in contact with her, from her father, and her mother, and her lover, and all her acquaintance.

Repeatedly, in an ache of utter weariness she repeated: "I have no father nor mother nor lover, I have no allocated place in the world of things, I do not belong to Beldover nor to Nottingham nor to England nor to this world, they none of them exist, I am trammelled and entangled in them, but they are all unreal. I must break out of it, like a nut from its shell which is an unreality."

And again, to her feverish brain, came the vivid reality of acorns in February lying on the floor of a wood with their shells burst and discarded and the kernel issued naked, to put itself forth. She was the naked, clear kernel thrusting forth the clear, powerful shoot, and the world was a bygone winter, discarded, her mother and father and Anton, and college and all her friends, all cast off like a year that has gone by, whilst the kernel was free and naked and striving to take new root, to create a new knowledge of Eternity in the flux of Time. And the kernel was the only reality: the rest was cast off into oblivion.

This grew and grew upon her. When she opened her eyes in the afternoon and saw the window of her room and the faint, smoky landscape beyond, this was all husk and shell lying by, all husk and shell, she could see nothing else, she was enclosed still, but loosely enclosed. There was a space between her and the shell. It was burst, there was a rift in it. Soon she would have her root fixed in a new Day, her nakedness would take itself the bed of a new sky and a new air, this old, decaying, fibrous husk would be gone.

Gradually she began really to sleep. She slept in the confidence of her new reality. She slept breathing with her soul the new air of a new world. The peace was very deep and enrichening. She had her root in new ground, she was gradually absorbed into growth.

When she woke at last it seemed as if a new day had come on the earth. How long, how long had she fought through the dust and obscurity, for this new dawn? How frail and fine and clear she felt, like the most fragile flower that opens in the end of winter. But the pole of night was turned and the dawn was coming in.

Very far off was her old experience—Skrebensky, her parting with him—very far off. Some things were real: those first glamorous weeks. Before, these had seemed like hallucination. Now they seemed like common reality. The rest was unreal. She knew that Skrebensky had never become finally real. In the weeks of passionate ecstasy he had been with her in her desire, she had created him for the time being. But in the end he had failed and broken down.

Strange, what a void separated him and her. She liked him now, as she liked a memory, some bygone self. He was something of the past, finite. He was that which is known. She felt a poignant affection for him, as for that which is past. But, when she looked with her face forward, he was not. Nay, when she looked ahead, into the undiscovered land before her, what was there she could recognise but a fresh glow of light and inscrutable trees going up from the earth like smoke. It was the unknown, the unexplored, the undiscovered upon whose shore she had landed, alone, after crossing the void, the darkness which washed the New World and the Old.

There would be no child: she was glad. If there had been a child, it would have made little difference, however. She would have kept the child and herself, she would not have gone to Skrebensky. Anton belonged to the past.

There came the cablegram from Skrebensky: "I am married." An old pain and anger and contempt stirred in her. Did he belong so utterly to the cast-off past? She repudiated him. He was as he was. It was good that he was as he was. Who was she to have a man according to her own desire? It was not for her to create, but to recognise a man created by God. The man should come from the Infinite and she should hail him. She was glad she could not create her man. She was glad she had nothing to do with his creation. She was glad that this lay within the scope of that vaster power in which she rested at last. The man would come out of Eternity to which she herself belonged.

As she grew better, she sat to watch a new creation. As she sat at her window, she saw the people go by in the street below, colliers, women, children, walking each in the husk of an old fruition, but visible through the husk, the swelling and the heaving contour of the new germination. In the still, silenced forms of the colliers she saw a sort of suspense, a waiting in pain for the new liberation: she saw the same in the false hard confidence of the women. The confidence of the women was brittle. It would break quickly to reveal the strength and patient effort of the new germination.

In everything she saw she grasped and groped to find the creation of the living God, instead of the old, hard barren form of bygone living. Sometimes great terror possessed her. Sometimes she lost touch, she lost her feeling, she could only know the old horror of the husk which bound in her and all mankind. They were all in prison, they were all going mad.

She saw the stiffened bodies of the colliers, which seemed already enclosed in a coffin, she saw their unchanging eyes, the eyes of those who are buried alive: she saw the hard, cutting edges of the new houses, which seemed to spread over the hillside in their insentient triumph, the triumph of horrible, amorphous angles and straight lines, the expression of corruption triumphant and unopposed, corruption so pure that it is hard and brittle: she saw the dun atmosphere over the blackened hill opposite, the dark blotches of houses, slate roofed and amorphous, the old church-tower standing up in hideous obsoleteness above raw new houses on the crest of the hill, the amorphous, brittle, hard-edged new houses advancing from Beldover to meet the corrupt new houses from Lethley, the houses. of Lethley advancing to mix with the houses of Hainor, a dry, brittle, terrible corruption spreading over the face of the land, and she was sick with a nausea so deep that she perished as she sat. And then, in the blowing clouds, she saw a band of faint iridescence colouring in faint colours a portion of the hill. And forgetting, startled, she looked for the hovering colour and saw a rainbow forming itself. In one place it gleamed fiercely, and, her heart anguished with hope, she sought the shadow of iris where the bow should be. Steadily the colour gathered, mysteriously, from nowhere, it took presence upon itself, there was a faint, vast rainbow. The arc bended and strengthened itself till it arched indomitable, making great architecture of light and colour and the space of heaven, its pedestals luminous in the corruption of new houses on the low hill, its arch the top of heaven.

And the rainbow stood on the earth. She knew that the sordid people who crept hard-scaled and separate on the face of the world's corruption were living still, that the rainbow was arched in their blood and would quiver to life in their spirit, that they would cast off their horny covering of disintegration, that new, clean, naked bodies would issue to a new germination, to a new growth, rising to the light and the wind and the clean rain of heaven. She saw in the rainbow the earth's new architecture, the old, brittle corruption of houses and factories swept away, the world built up in a living fabric of Truth, fitting to the over-arching heaven.

Appendix I

Fragment of 'The Sisters II'

Note on the Text

This manuscript fragment (numbered pp. 373–80) is located at the University of Texas, and is numbered E441a in the catalogue in Warren Roberts's *A Bibliography of D. H. Lawrence*, 2nd edn (Cambridge University Press, 1982). It probably represents the ending of the uncompleted second draft of the novel, written August 1913–January 1914. 'The second "Sisters" was not, then, a rewriting of the first [the surviving fragment of which is printed as Appendix II to the Penguin edition of *Women in Love*], but rather an attempt to get back behind it, into the past of Ella, the prototype of Ursula, in order to discover how she came to be as she was through some deep bruise to her inner being, in an earlier love affair with Ben Templeman – mentioned at the close of the fragment' (Mark Kinkead-Weekes, Introduction to *The Rainbow*, Cambridge University Press, 1989, p. xxiv). DHL was sure that Ella/Ursula needed some kind of 'love episode, a significant one' (*Letters*, ii. 142) before she met Rupert Birkin (the partner she eventually meets in *Women in Love*). In the novel's second draft this love affair was with 'Ben Templeman', but the latter would be replaced by Anton Skrebensky in the version of the novel eventually written as *The Rainbow* between November 1914 and March 1915, when the *Women in Love* material had finally been excised.

trembling, flushed, ashamed. And he sat passive, but in opposition to her going. Every movement she made, every breath she took, seemed made or taken in spite of him. So that she trembled as she fastened her boots. It seemed to her cruel.

When she was ready, he rose politely to see her to the door.

"Don't come out of the room," she said. "Is there any commission I could take for you?—No?—sure?—Goodbye."

She had got away, leaving him silent, impassive, but inside himself raging, only denying it all, because he was a gentleman. She hurried through the wet afternoon, as if running away from something. She was as yet free of him.

August came, when the family, all but Ella and Gudrun, went away to Scarborough, as was usual. The eldest two girls preferred to stay at home. For them, it would be a great treat to have the house to themselves. Besides, neither of them wanted very much to go away from Willey Green at this time.

Ella enjoyed being alone, and doing little. She felt lethargic. A curious, rich lassitude kept her lying late in bed. She felt her life was going on inside her, she could not concern herself with outside things. Gudrun, on the other hand, was very active. So Ella lounged, dreamed, meditated, thinking, thinking about Mr Birkin. She did not know if she loved him. She did not want to kiss him. She did not want him to go away. What was it? She read absorbedly without quite taking in what she read. Then she caught herself up. She was reading Le Rouge et le Noir, and the hero fascinated her. She wanted to understand him: she wanted to understand men: she wanted to understand Rupert Birkin. She hunted everywhere for understanding of herself and him, quite happy to be alone doing little or nothing, because her soul was so busy, even if her body were indolent.

The second day after the family had gone, Gudrun went out to a tennis party. Ella refused the invitation. People were a strain upon her. Her soul was too deeply occupied in itself. She wanted to be alone. Gudrun would come back to supper. It was a golden afternoon. Ella sat in the sunshine, read, sewed, mused, and was happy.

With the twilight a restlessness and a yearning come over her. She went into the drawing-room, and there, in the half light, she sat singing to herself, singing the sentimental songs like "Ich weiss nicht was soll es bedeuten." Her idea of time was sketchy, but she had a strong, rather beautiful voice. And sitting alone in the house, with the twilight dying golden about her, the end of the hot summer day sinking down, she sang from a full heart, her voice going on wings of yearning and sadness.

She started at the end of one verse, hearing the bell tingling down in the kitchen. Resentfully, she got up and left the piano. People, whoever it was, must have heard her, and she did not wish to be heard. She did not wish to answer the door.

It was Birkin, standing rather hesitating on the threshold.

"I wondered if you would be at home," he said.

"I am alone," she said, half to keep him from coming in, half inviting him.

"Your people have gone away?" he answered, entering, "I did not know you sang so well—you have a beautiful voice."

"I didn't know anyone would hear," she replied.

"I like to hear you," he said, "Will you sing again?"

"No."

The house seemed very silent and ghostly about them, in the twilight, with doors and windows open.

"I am lucky in finding you in," he said.

He sat in the shadow near the door. He was wearing grey, and was almost invisible. She could see the shape of his finely modelled head faintly and yet distinctly, in the grey clair-obscur.

"I am glad you were not out," he said, unconsciously repeating himself.

Ella felt embarrassed. Her heart was beating fast.

"Where is your sister?" he asked.

"I am expecting her," she replied.

They spoke quietly, because of the still house.

"When do you go away?" she asked at length.

"In two days," he said.

"You will have a good time up there," she said, making conversation. "What will you do, shoot, golf—?"

"More or less," he replied.

There ensued an awkward silence. It was getting dark in the room. Suddenly, with a jerk, she got up, saying:

"I'll get some matches."

He rose also quickly, insidiously.

"I have some," he replied, shaking the box between his fingers. She was thwarted.

"Oh!" she said.

And hesitating, she held out her hand for the matches. Her fingers touched his, and she shrank away, quickly.

"Let me light it," he said quietly.

He went to the mantel-piece. The light leaped out, and fell on his upturned face. Ella was fascinated and half-terrified by it. It was intent, hard, without expression. The steady hardness of the eyes was dreadful to her. He threw the burnt match in the fireplace, adjusted the light, then turned to her.

"One lamp is enough?" he said.

His voice had a hard, vibrating quality, his eyes held hers with a hard look. She felt herself powerless against him, and yet not with him. She turned aside her face as she answered. Outside, on the lawn, she could see the bushes standing darkly. He stood near to her. Neither moved. Then he seemed to be coming to her. Summoning all her self-restraint, she put her hand on his arm and said, pleadingly, pathetically:

"No—no."

He stood still, silent. She felt his living arm beneath his sleeve. It was torture to her. Suddenly she caught him to her, and hid her face on his breast, crying, in a muffled, tortured voice:

"Do you love me?"

She clung to him. But his breast was strange to her. His arms were around her tight, hard, compressing her, he was quivering, rigid, holding her against him. But he was strange to her. He was strange to her, and it was almost agony. He was cold to her, however he held her hard in his power and quivered. She felt he was cold to her. And the quivering man stiffened with desire was strange and horrible to her. She got free again, and, with her hands to her temples, she slid away to the floor at his feet, unable to stand, unable to hold her body erect. She must double up, for she could not bear it. But she got up again to go away. And before she reached the door, she was crouching on the floor again, holding her temples in agony. Her womb, her belly, her heart were all in agony. She crouched together on the floor, crying like some wild animal in pain, with a kind of mooing noise, very dreadful to hear, a sound she was unaware of, that came from her unproduced, out of the depths of her body in torture. For some wild moments the paroxysms continued, when she crouched on the ground with her head down, mad, crying with an inarticulate, animal noise. Then suddenly it all stopped. It was gone. Her head was clear. And then she was confused with shame. She found herself crouching on the floor, her face running wet with tears, a sobbing going on involuntarily. A moment longer she crouched so, giving little, sniffing sobs.

Then, very quiet, almost too quiet, too far gone for shame, she dried her face on the end of her skirts, like an animal wiping its face, and she got up.

His power, her pain, nay, all her emotion, was gone. She was tremulous, but quiet and almost still in herself.

"I am sorry" she said, turning to him but not looking at him. "I'm sorry. It isn't fair for you.—But I couldn't help it."

She was sorry for him, that he had been subjected to this outburst. And her pride also rose against him—for his coldness.

He stood white to the gills, with wide, dark eyes staring blankly. His heart inside him felt red-hot, so that he panted as he breathed. His mind was blank. He knew she did not feel him any more. He knew he had no part in her, that he was out of place. And he had nothing to say.—But gradually he grew a little calmer, his eyes lost their wide, dark, hollow look. He was coming to himself.

"What did I do?" he asked.

"You—it was nothing you did—I couldn't help it—I'm sorry." Her simple, faltering answer, so devoid of any feeling for him, sent a wave like flame over his heart, so that his brain seemed to swoon. He stood in a curious, motionless position of recoil. For a long time neither spoke. She stood averted by the mantel-piece.

"Hadn't you better go?" she asked, cruelly.

But he still stood staring, wide-eyed, motionless.

"Do you really care for me?" he asked, in a strange, changed voice. It seemed to her even now, he only wanted to know, he did not care.

"I don't know," she said. "Don't ask me now. You'd better go and leave me."

But he stood motionless, staring with dark, wide eyes.

And suddenly she caught her lip between her teeth. The hurt, the grief was rising again. In spite of all her efforts, her tears rose, and fell over her dark lashes onto her cheeks. But she kept her face still, her lower lip clenched between her teeth, and let the tears fall. He watched, wide-eyed, for some moments. It was agony to him.

"Don't," he said, "don't—don't cry—don't cry—"

But the sound of his lost, helpless voice only made the tears come faster, as from a touched wound. And as they came, and as they fell, they seemed to him to come upon his breast bone eating into it like fire.

She took her handkerchief and wiped her face and blew her nose loudly. As she fumbled blindly for her handkerchief, it hurt him so much, he felt he would die for her.

"I," he stammered, blanched with the struggle to speak—"I love you."

Her tears came again. She felt no response, only the cruel, hurting, yet easing surge up of her tears. He had not moved. Still he stood with wide, unblinking eyes.

Again she was wiping her face, and blowing her nose, when they heard the gate.

"That's Gudrun," she said, dully.

And she went out of the room.

Birkin stood motionless. He heard Gudrun's quick footstep come freely up the path and through the open door. Another instant and her white, beautiful form started with surprise in the doorway.

"Oh!" she cried, and for a moment could not speak.

"Well," she said, "it did surprise me—"

She was hiding her eyes from the light. She was flushed and bright from the party.

"Did you have a good time?" he asked.

"Oh very," she replied, rather off-hand. "Where is Ella."

"She went upstairs," he said.

There was an awkward pause. Evidently Gudrun was not quite at ease with him.

"Are you still staying at Wamsley Mill?" she asked, stiffly.

They kept up a little desultory small talk, till Ella at last came down, showing traces of weeping.

"You're late, Prune, aren't you?" she said.

"It isn't eight yet," said Gudrun.

Ella did not look at Birkin, as she asked him:

"Will you stay to supper, Mr Birkin?"

"No thank you," he replied. "Perhaps you will come down to tea on the island again, à la Robinson Crusoe, tomorrow."

"Thanks," said Ella, looking at Gudrun. "I don't know—"

"Oh, thank you," said Gudrun, vaguely.

He walked away, feeling as if the heavens had fallen, and he were not himself, he were somebody else, walking in a different life. In one crash, the whole form of his life, the whole conception of himself, which he had, was gone: he did not know what he was, who he was: he did not know what he knew or what he did not know. Reduced to an elementary chaos, he drifted to his rooms, to sit till dawn by the fire, stunned, motionless.

"What is the matter, Ella?" Gudrun asked sharply.

"He proposed to me," said Ella.

"Proposed to you!" cried Gudrun in amazement.

Ella went to bed, very still after her outburst. She felt ashamed, but only superficially. Underneath she was not ashamed of having showed her deepest feelings to him. But it was a big responsibility, to have been quite so naked before another person. She felt a responsibility coming upon her, that almost silenced her. She must wait and go slowly. She did not yet know quite where she was. She only knew that her fate was bringing her closer and closer into connection with this man, that something was taking place, implicating her with him, which she could never revoke or escape. And blindly, almost shrinking, she lapsed forward.

The next day, she did not want to go to Wamsley Mill. It was too soon, she was too uncertain. Even the fact that he would be hurt did not influence her. She must stay away yet awhile.

Then there came a letter, the next morning, saying that the three little children were all ill, and that the eldest girls must come to look after them. Ella was angry, Gudrun was disgusted. There never was any illness in the family, so they did not believe in it. But they began to prepare immediately to depart. They would catch the ten oclock train to Nottingham.

In the train Ella wrote to Birkin.

"I am sorry I've had to go away," she said. "You mustn't mind the scene I made you the other evening. I don't know how it is. But I think it takes us a long time to get rid of the old things. It is like the man who foamed at the mouth when the devils were cast out of him. In a way I love you because I can make a fool of myself before you, and you don't mind. But you mustn't despise me. I am really not hysterical—not naturally. One gets so strained. And it is working the old strain off that makes one so upset. I am sorry I have to go away. Today I wanted to see you. It makes me miserable that the train threads out all this distance behind me. But you will write to me, won't you?"

3

The children were not very ill. In a few days' time they were running about. The third day after her arrival in Scarborough, Ella had a letter from Birkin.

"I don't know why you should think I despise you," he said. "I despise myself hard enough, that my own feelings are always so mixed, and I can never get them straight. I am a little afraid of you, and for you. I will do anything you want me to do. It seems that everything has come toppling down, like an earthquake, since I have known you, and here I am entangled in the ruins and fragments of my old life, and struggling to get out. You seem to me some land beyond—somewhere where I have never attained, a shore upon which I have never yet climbed out. As I say, I am a little afraid of you. Already so much has gone smash because of you. But I want to see more of you. I want you to come back soon. I shall go to Scotland immediately, but intend to stay only a few days. Perhaps I shall call in Scarborough on my way home. . ."

Ella puzzled over this letter. He always seemed so queer and abstract. It was as if he stated his love in algebraic terms.

When the children got better, she and Ella set out to walk to Filey. It was a bright day, but windy, and the sea was breaking over Filey Brigg. The two girls wandered out along the causeway of rock. Green water heaved and smote on either side, the spray was in their hair. All the open space was fretted with restless water. A little steamer was rolling along, pitching, labouring, by Flamborough Head, where the water was smoking white.

The two girls were exhilarated and laughing with the wind and motion. They clung to their hats, the refreshing, strong coldness of the sea penetrated their clothing. Soon it got too cold.

As they returned, and were almost at the shore, they noticed two other people, a man and a woman, coming, turning from the wind embarassed with their clothing.

"Ella," cried Gudrun. "There's Ben Templeman."

Ella felt the blood rush from her heart. For a second she seemed to lose consciousness. A wave of terror, deep, annihilating, went over her. She knew him without looking: his peculiar, straying walk, the odd, separate look about him which filled her with dread. He had still power over her: he was still Man to her. She knew he would not see her, because he was rather short-sighted.

[end of manuscript]

Appendix II

Chronology of *The Rainbow*

1823–36	New route for Nottingham canal, after Cossall Marsh embankment collapsed
1830	Paul Lensky born; died at 34 in 1864; 238:6
Late 1832	Lydia Lensky born ['just fifty' in late 1882, still 34 in Spring 1867; 120:5, 45:39]
Spring 1838	Tom Brangwen born [still 28 in Spring 1867, but 'a man of forty five' on 23 December 1882 (actually 44⅔); 45:40, 125:37]
'*About 1840*'	*Rainbow* begins
1840	London & Midland railway at foot of Ilkeston hill opened; Erewash spur, 1847
1850–?1855	Tom to Derby Grammar School [at 12, father's accident at hay-harvest when 17, Tom takes over farm completely at 18; 16:32, 19:20, 37]
?March 1862	Will Brangwen born [20 in Spring 1882, 22 in 1884; 99:40, 199:7]
January–Autumn 1863	INSURRECTION IN POLAND; the Lenskys possibly flee to London in the Autumn before the final suppression, since Anna is born in London and yet must be at least 3 when Lydia comes to the Marsh in Winter 1866 [see note at 49:14 and note 1 below]
October/November 1863	Anna Lensky born in London; 50:1–12, 239:27–36 ['nearly forty' in Summer 1902 though in a loose context, 18 when she meets Will in Spring 1882 and after corn-harvest; 388:1, 99:37, 117:38]
Late 1864	Paul Lensky dies, shortly after Anna's first birthday; 37:39, 50:13–32, 238:6–7
Spring 1865	Lydia to Yorkshire as housekeeper to dying vicar, who dies shortly after the end of the year; 51:8–52:26
February/March 1866	Lydia to vicarage in Cossethay, seen on the hill in the Spring by Tom (nearly 28), and for the season; 29:1ff., 52:37–54:1
March 1867	Betrothal of Tom (28) and Lydia (34); 40:32, 45:39–40
?May 1867	Tom marries Lydia

Appendix II

January 1868	Tom Brangwen, Jnr born; 70:10
?1869/70	Fred Brangwen born
1872	Anna Brangwen (9) to dame school in Cossethay; 92:3–4
?1873	Anna ('about ten') taken on first visit to Baron Skrebensky when his first wife alive; 93:1 (She has just died according to the MS version)
?late 1873/4	Anna and Lydia visit Baron Skrebensky; 183:8–10 [see note 2]
?1875/6	Anna to Nottingham High School for Girls, founded 1875 ['a tall, awkward girl' sounds post-puberty, perhaps 13, ?1876; 93:37, 40; enough time after the second visit to the Skrebenskys for the impression to be fading into memory]
?late 1876/7	Tom and Lydia visit 'Three years later' than the second visit, after the Baron has remarried in late 1876; 183:19–28
August 1877	Anton Skrebensky born [21 in July 1899; 184:7, 269:21–2, 285:5]
Autumn 1882	Betrothal of Will and Anna [she is 18 when they meet in Spring, he is 20; 99:37–40, 117:38–9]
Saturday 23 December 1882	Will marries Anna ['the Saturday before Christmas ... December the 'twenty third'; 120:38–121:1; Lydia is 50, Tom '45' but actually 44⅔; 120:5, 125:37]
October/November 1883	Anna and Will visit the Skrebenskys and Lincoln Cathedral; 183:3–4 [Anton a 'curly-headed little lad' and 'well-mannered'; 268:27, 30; old enough to remember Anna many years later]
November/December 1883	Ursula Brangwen born ['month-old' Ursula held up to see bluecaps in snow; 180:9–19, and Anna is pregnant early Spring; 165:33]
December 1884/January 1885	Gudrun Brangwen born [spoken of as just over a year younger than Ursula, Will still 22; 197:28, 199:7; but see note 3]
1886	Theresa Brangwen born [3 years younger than Ursula, leaves High School 1902, aged ?16; 204:3, 398:23]

474

Chronology of The Rainbow

by January 1888	Catherine ('Kate') Brangwen born [Will 26 after she is born, Ursula spoken of as a child of 4 so Catherine probably born between October 1887 and January 1888; 204:32–6]
Late 1891	William ('Billy') Brangwen born [8 years younger than Ursula, Will 'about' 28 when begins going to Nottingham in the football season of 1890–1, after 7 years of marriage and 4 girls; 243:4–7, 210:19; by early 1892, when Will about 30, Billy has been born; 221:17–18] Will starts carving class [Ursula 8, Will 30; 221:17, 25 – actually would be just short of these ages if classes began in Autumn]
1892–1901	Four more children: Cassandra, Tom, Margaret and one died in infancy; 243:7–8, 394:27, 395:7, 328:14–15 [all nine born before mid-1901, since Anna pregnant with the last when Ursula leaves school in mid-1900, Tom is old enough to walk 10 miles to Beldover in 1902; 328:4–14, 394:27–9]
Spring 1892	Tom Brangwen drowned (53 or 54) [Ursula 'about eight', Tom Jnr about 24 since 23 when he broke with his chief, 25 years after marriage with Lydia; 226:10, 225:28, 21. After Tom's death, Lydia spoken of as 60, i.e. late 1892/3, and 4 children younger than Ursula; 236:2, 4]
Autumn 1895/6	Ursula to Nottingham High School for Girls (12); 245:26–9 [she leaves in June 1900; if after 5 school-years would have gone in September 1895, aged not quite 12, Gudrun only $10\frac{2}{3}$; if 'was twelve' means 1896, Ursula would only have had 4 years at High School]
1898	Lydia Brangwen dies ['two years' before September 1900; 341:37, 342:10]
July 1899	Skrebensky comes to the Marsh [Ursula 'nearly sixteen', Anton 21; 267:31, 269:22; 'It was summer': must be July because he only has a month's leave and has gone before his birthday; 272:26, 269:25, 285:5]
Late Summer 1899	The wedding dance at the Marsh, talk about Khartoum, recaptured by Kitchener in 1898; 288:17–19

Appendix II

October 1899	WAR DECLARED AGAINST BOERS IN SOUTH AFRICA: 'He wrote that he might have to go', and the 'constant bad news' in 1900; 303:18–20, 309:10. Skrebensky leaves for South Africa; 396:8–9 [deleted sentence on MS p. 486 says he is 22: in fact, not quite]
June 1900	London Matriculation and Ursula leaves school; 335:18
September 1900–July 1902	Ursula teaches at St Philip's School, Brinsley Street, Ilkeston [she is 17 for most of the first year, teaches for 2 school years, ending in July; 341:37, 357:10–11, 365:26, 378:15–16, 391:38]
Summer 1902	Brangwens move from Cossethay to Beldover; 397:24–8 [Anna 'nearly' 40, Tom Jnr old enough to walk 'ten miles or more'; 394:10ff., 388:1, 394:28–9]
October 1902–June 1905	Ursula at University College, Nottingham
March 1905	Skrebensky returns from South Africa; 415:31 [Ursula is 22 (actually 21½; see note 4), 'about six years' from the dance ; 406:21, 407:14–15]
Easter 1905	Ursula and Skrebensky spend the vacation in a London hotel, and in Paris and Rouen
June 1905	Ursula fails her examinations [after weekend in Dorothy's cottage at Whitsun, news of failure in July; 429:12ff., 439:8, 18]
August 1905	Beach-party in Lincolnshire, 'first week in August', Ursula breaks with Skrebensky, and he marries in late August; 441:8, 447:27
Early October 1905	Ursula encounters the horses and miscarries; 450:20ff.

Italics indicate fixed dates mentioned in *The Rainbow*.

NOTES

1. Lydia gives Anna's age as 'four years' when she first visits Tom at the Marsh (37:37), but this must be wrong. Anna is 1 when Lensky dies in late 1864; Lydia goes to Yorkshire in the Spring of 1865 (51:8ff.), and the following February–March (1866) to Cossethay, and is seen by Tom on the road in the Spring (52:37–54:1). Her first visit to the Marsh occurs sometime between May 1866 and the Winter of that year, so that Anna could be just 3 when Lydia says she is 4; DHL has perhaps forgotten that Anna was not born in Poland but in London.

2. Anna's age is also wrong for the second visit to the Skrebenskys (183:8–10) since if she is 14 it must be late 1877. DHL has become muddled among the four visits paid by the Brangwens to the Skrebenskys. The first visit is when Anna is 'about ten' (93:1) and the visit is therefore probably in 1873, when the first Baroness is still alive. The second visit, after her death, comes three years before the Baron remarries, and the third visit when Tom and Lydia call on the new Baroness (?1876/7, 183:28). The fourth visit, by the newly-wed Anna and Will, is in 1883: Anton (born in August 1877) is a 'curly-headed little lad' (268:27). Working backwards from the date of Anton's birth, the Baron would have to have remarried no later than November 1876; and that suggests that his first wife must have died around December 1873 or January 1874. Anna would have been 11 at the time of the second visit. This would make the third visit December 1876 or January 1877; and *then* Anna would have been 13. DHL seems to have confused the date of the second visit with that of the third.

3. At one point, DHL says that Ursula is 'not much more than a year old' (197:28) when her sister Gudrun is born. A little earlier, however, he had implied that Ursula is 16–18 months older than her sister: Anna knows she is pregnant for the second time before Ursula is 'ten months old' (192:39–40). However, since Ursula was born around October 1883, and Will is still 22 when Gudrun is born (he becomes 23 around March 1885), Gudrun cannot be 16–18 months younger than her sister. It is perhaps a little precocious of Ursula to be climbing stiles while Will is still only 22 (198:40–199:7), though this anecdote may have been added a bit later in composition.

4. Since Ursula is born towards the end of October 1883, she cannot be 22 just 'before Easter' 1905 (406:20–1) – she is 21½. DHL has simply calculated from the *years* (1905 minus 1883 equals 22), forgetting that Ursula – like her mother – is born late in the year.

Explanatory Notes

5 **TO ELSE**   The novel is dedicated to DHL's sister-in-law Else Jaffe, née von Richthofen (1874–1973). Ursula's career seems in some ways to have been modelled on Else's (see Introduction, pp xx). DHL originally wanted the dedication to be in German and in Gothic script, but, not surprisingly in wartime, the publishers refused this. See *Letters*, ii. 349, 354.

9:4 **little country town**   Cossethay is modelled on the village of Cossall, near Ilkeston, Derbyshire.

9:28–10:5 **But heaven ... worth hiding**   Cf. Genesis viii. 22. The 'prologue' to the novel carries many echoes of Genesis. Its imagery seems to conflate the story of the Creation and the 'fall' from Eden (Genesis i–iii) with that of Noah and his sons (Genesis vi–ix) who live in abundance after the Flood and who are, like the Brangwens, 'inheritors' (see 9:13).

10:25 **The women were different**   Compare the rest of the prologue, in its emphasis on the women's desire for knowledge, with Genesis iii. See also *Study of Thomas Hardy*, pp. 40–45, on the relationship between being and knowing. The gender roles in the prologue are the reverse of those in the Hardy study, where the female symbolizes unity and stability and the male mobility and individuation (see *Study of Thomas Hardy*, chapters six and seven).

10:39 **beast**   The use of the collective singular is also reminiscent of Genesis. Cf. Genesis i. 24, 25.

12:35–6 **Odyssey ... endless web**   The Greek epic poem attributed to Homer describes the adventures of Odysseus (in Latin, Ulysses) in the course of his return from the siege of Troy to his home in Ithaca where his wife Penelope awaits him. Cherishing hopes that Odysseus is still alive, Penelope wards off her numerous suitors by insisting that she must finish weaving a shroud for Odysseus's father; but each night she secretly unravels her day's weaving. Odysseus's adventures on his long voyage home include being washed up on the island of Aeaea where the enchantress Circe turns his companions into swine.

15:30 **to pedgill**   To pick over (dialect); so here, to work with attention to minute detail.

16:11 **crew-yard**   Straw-yard, bedded fold for cattle (dialect).

17:34–5 **Tennyson's 'Ulysses' or Shelley's 'Ode to the West Wind.'**   These poems by Alfred, Lord Tennyson (1809–92) and Percy

Bysshe Shelley (1792–1822), published in 1842 and 1820 respectively, are both highly emotive, voicing the need to face life's challenges afresh after a period of intense suffering.

19:5 **David and Jonathan** 1 Samuel xviii. 1–4; xix. 1–7; xx. Cf. DHL's play *David* (1926).

19:25 **mardy** Spoiled, soft (dialect).

19:34 **Prometheus Bound** Greek tragedy attributed to Aeschylus (525–456 BC). Prometheus the Titan angers Zeus by giving fire and culture to mankind; he is nailed to a rock and subjected to various tortures including having his liver pecked at daily by Zeus's eagle. Cf. *Letters*, ii. 248, 283.

20:12 **Be my conscience-keeper, be the angel at the doorway** Cf. *The Angel in the House* (1854–63), a sequence of poems celebrating married love, by Coventry Patmore (1823–96): the title has become a stock expression for the Victorian ideal of chaste, virtuous femininity.

20:13 **my outgoing and my incoming** Cf. 2 Samuel iii. 25; 2 Kings xix. 27; Psalm cxxi. 8; Isaiah xxxvii. 28; Ezekiel xliii. 11.

24:1 **this road** In this way, like this (dialect).

27:3 **gorping** Staring, gaping (dialect).

29:12 **britching** From the 'breeching', that portion of the harness round the hind parts of a shaft-horse, enabling it to push backwards (dialect).

31:14 **menagerie confabulation** A menagerie is a collection of odds and ends, a confused state of things (dialect), so here perhaps a muddled or inaccurate story.

31:18 **summat** Something (dialect).

31:25 **fuzz-ball** Usually the puff-ball fungus (dialect), but here perhaps a dandelion clock.

31:31 **axed** Asked (dialect).

35:37 **Sluther up** Hurry up (dialect), since to sluther is to slip, slide.

39:7 **the wedding-ring** 'The Wedding Ring' was the title of the penultimate version of *The Rainbow*. See Introduction, p. xvi.

41:13–14 **clutterin'** Doing a job awkwardly and dirtily (dialect), so here, suckling messily.

49:1 **daughter of a Polish landowner** Although Lydia Lensky shares DHL's mother's first name, her background resembles that of Frieda's paternal grandmother, Amalia Louise von Laschowski, who was Polish and whose mother's maiden name was Skrebensky.

49:12 **the great rebellion** The Russians had controlled large parts of Poland since 1772. The 1863 rebellion, sparked off by the Russian government's introduction of conscription, was the last of a series of rebellions against Russian rule; it was brutally quelled.

50:15–16 **the dark, savage, mystic ride of dread, of death** Cf. Revelation vi. 8; cf. also the Valkyries of Germanic myth, warrior goddesses who rode over the battlefields of the world choosing those who must die.

53:16 **mezereon tree** Daphne mezereum is a small shrub with fragrant purple or pink flowers; DHL probably meant Crocus vernus, called 'the Mezerion tree' in 'Of Gardens' by Francis Bacon (1561–1626).

56:18 **his trial ... Gethsemane ... Triumphal Entry** [56:19] Cf. Christ's agony in the garden at Gethsemane and the trial before Pilate (Matthew xxvi. 36–75; xxvii. 1–26; Mark xiv. 32–72; xv. 1–15; Luke xxiii. 1–25; John xviii; xix. 1–16) and Christ's entry into Jerusalem (Matthew xxi. 1–11; Mark xi. 1–11; Luke xix. 29–38; John xii. 12–15).

59:11 *filles* Used here to mean 'prostitutes', not simply 'girls' (French).

61:2 **at the mill with slaves** *Samson Agonistes* (1671) by John Milton (1608–74), l. 41.

61:5 **outer darkness** Cf. Matthew viii. 12; xxii. 13; xxv. 30.

62:23–4 **the upper millstone** Cf. Deuteronomy xxiv. 6; Job xli. 24.

67:21 **thysen** Yourself (dialect).

68:5 **Topsy** The little slave girl in *Uncle Tom's Cabin* (1851–2) by Harriet Beecher Stowe (1811–52).

68:21 **Slippy** Quick, prompt, sharp (dialect).

69:8 **nobbut** Literally 'not but', i.e. nothing but, only (dialect).

69:15 **Can ter** Can't thou, the intimate form of 'Can't you' (dialect).

69:25 **pitted** Heaped up and covered with earth for storage (dialect).

71:33 **one flesh** Cf. Genesis ii. 24; Mark x. 8.

71:37–9 **and still ... life gushed** Cf. Numbers xx. 11; John xix. 34.

77:20 **What had she to do with him?** Cf. John ii. 4.

79:6 **kicking against the pricks** Struggling against overwhelming opposition. See Acts ix. 5 and xxvi. 14, where the reference is to an ox or ass kicking when goaded.

80:16–18 **When the pie ... a king?** Lines from the nursery rhyme 'Sing a song of sixpence'.

80:26–7 **Pocketful ... Ascha!** Anna at this point accidentally switches to a different nursery rhyme, 'Ring a ring o' roses'. 'Ash-a!', the imitation of a sneeze in the nineteenth-century version, is nowadays more commonly sung as 'A-tishoo'.

81:16 **You're off out a bit** You're doing some courting (dialect).

81:30 **fawce** Sharp-witted, cunning (dialect).

81:37 **sharp-shins** Sharp-witted person (dialect).

82:26 **stirks** Heifers, bullocks, or sometimes calves of either sex.

82:30 **met** Might (dialect).

85:4 **that road ... wambling** [85:5] In that way ... walking awkwardly or unsteadily (dialect).

86:7 **Spencer ... Browning** [86:8] Herbert Spencer (1820–1903), philosopher and evolutionary theorist ... Robert Browning (1812–89), poet. Spencer saw the whole universe in terms of a single, all-pervading evolutionary principle, for which DHL criticizes him in the *Study of Thomas Hardy*, 97:37–98:6.

90:34 **lost, and ... found** [90:35] Cf. Matthew x. 39; Luke ix. 24.

90:35–9 **The new world ... complete liberty** There may be an echo of John Donne's Elegie xix ('Going to Bed'), 27–31: 'O my America! my new-found-land ... To enter in these bonds, is to be free'. Cf. also 'whose service is perfect freedom' in the Collect for Peace in the Order for Morning Prayer of the *Book of Common Prayer*, and Psalm cxvi. 16.

91:3 **transfiguration ... glorification ... admission** Cf. Luke ix. 28–36.

91:23–4 **house was finished ... His abode** Cf. 1 Kings viii. 13; 2 Chronicles v. 1.

91:35–40 **She played ... beneath, between** Cf. the discussion of pillar and arch in *Study of Thomas Hardy*, 72:6–22, 74:35–75:17. For the pillars of fire and cloud, cf. Exodus xiii. 21–2.

92:30–31 **Baron Skrebensky** For the name Skrebensky, see note on 49:1. The Baron is modelled on Baron Rudolph von Hube (?1834–1910) who, having escaped the Russian authorities in Poland, became Vicar of Greasley, Nottinghamshire, in 1866. See also note on 183:20.

92:32 **Mr Gladstone** William Ewart Gladstone (1809–98), Liberal Prime Minister 1868–74, 1880–85, 1886, 1892–94.

93:28 **knight of Malta** A knight of the Order of St John, an order which originated with the Crusades but which from 1530 onwards was a charitable organization.

94:22 **bagatelle** A trifle (French); also a game in which small balls are struck into numbered holes on a board, hence Tom's pun.

95:19 **'As You Like It.'** Shakespearean comedy, written *c.* 1599. Cf. Ursula's response to the play at 310:31.

95:33 **Alexandra** Alexandra (1844–1925), the wife of the future King Edward VII, was a celebrated beauty.

96:20 **Goose Fair** The traditional Nottingham Fair, held annually in early autumn. Cf. DHL's short story 'Goose Fair', in *The Prussian Officer and Other Stories* (Penguin Books, 1995).

98:3 **Ave Maria ... Pater Noster** 'Hail Mary' (Latin), the Angel's greeting to Mary at the Annunciation in the Vulgate (cf. Luke i. 28), and subsequently a Roman Catholic devotional recitation ... 'Our Father' (Latin), opening words of the Lord's Prayer. Cf. Matthew vi. 9; Luke xi. 2.

98:4–7 **Ave Maria ... Amen** 'Hail Mary, full of grace, the Lord is with thee, blessed art thou among women and blessed is the fruit of thy womb, Jesus. Hail Mary, Holy Mary, pray for us sinners now, and in the hour of our death, Amen' (Latin). 'Ave Maria, Sancta Maria' (98:6) should be 'Sancta Maria, Mater Dei' ('Holy Mary, Mother of God').

99:31–2 **a certain Bishop of France** Bishop la Balue, imprisoned in 1469 in the Château of Loches where he remained for eleven years.

105:39–40 **Ruskin ... mediaeval forms** John Ruskin (1819–1900), influential art critic and social commentator. He was central to the Gothic

Revival. See his famous essay 'The Nature of Gothic' (1853) and Introduction, p. xxx.

106:22 **sedilia** (Latin, plural of sedile). A series of usually three stone seats in the south wall of the chancel for the use of the officiating clergy.

108:12 **like the Devil looking over Lincoln** The phrase occurs as early as 1562 and is thought to refer to a grotesque carving at Lincoln Cathedral.

112:10–11 **The veils had ripped** Cf. Matthew xxvii. 51; Mark xv. 38; Luke xxiii. 45.

112:32 **the Creation of Eve** Genesis ii. 21–3.

113:7 **covering their faces with their wings** Cf. Isaiah vi. 2.

113:13 **puther** A cloud, as of smoke or dust (dialect).

120:27 **the be-all and the end-all** *Macbeth* I. vii. 5; cf. also *Study of Thomas Hardy*, 10:19.

123:26 **dolly-tub** Wash-tub fitted with a shafted 'dolly', a wooden stick used to stir the clothes (dialect).

128:32 **no marriage in heaven** Cf. Matthew xxii. 30.

129:6–35 *If* we've got to be angels ... *make* an angel then Cf. DHL's argument in *Study of Thomas Hardy*, chapter six.

130:19 **the wake** Group of musicians and singers who went from house to house during a 'wake' (dialect), an annual religious or village festival (in this case, Christmas).

130:25 **guysers ... old mystery play of St George** [130:26–7] (Or 'guisers'), mummers; men and boys in disguise, with smeared faces ... The Mummers' Play or St George Play, a folk-play evolved from the sword-dance. Cf. 'A Prelude', in *Love Among the Haystacks and Other Stories*, ed. John Worthen (Cambridge, 1987), pp. 8–11. There is a celebrated description of mumming in Hardy's *The Return of the Native* (1878), Bk II, ch. 5.

130:28 **club and dripping pan** Objects wielded by Beelzebub (prince of the devils) in the St George Play. Beelzebub does not traditionally fight St George; he is one of the grotesque characters who enter after the main combat.

130:38 **blanket fair ... Strike a daisy** [130:39] Bedtime fun (dialect) ... a jocular imprecation, perhaps from 'daisy' meaning remarkable or extraordinary (dialect). Cf. 'Strike me blind, lucky, pink', etc.

131:15 **boz-eyed** Cross-eyed (dialect).

133:15 **'In the fields with their flocks abiding.'** A carol by Frederick William Farrar (1831–1904) ['. . . field . . .']. Cf. Luke ii. 8.

134 **Anna Victrix** Anna the (female) conqueror or victor (Latin).

134:12 **under the flood** Cf. Genesis vi–ix.

136:38 **the Ark in the flood** Cf. Genesis vi–ix.

139:26–7 **Tablets of Stone** Exodus xxxi. 18.

140:11–12 **the Lord ... not consumed** Exodus iii. 2.

Explanatory Notes

140:28–9 **king . . . herd** No such fairytale has been identified but cf. the medieval 'Feast of Fools' when 'Kings' were crowned for a single day.

147:19–20 **'And forgive . . . against us—'** From the Lord's Prayer in the *Book of Common Prayer*; cf. Matthew vi. 12; Luke xi. 4.

148:20 **lamb holding the banner** In Revelation v. 6–14, the lamb is the symbol of the risen Christ. The widely used icon of the lamb holding the flag or banner combines the idea of sacrificial victim with that of victorious Lord of Heaven.

149:36 **Pietà** Picture or sculpture of the Virgin Mary holding the dead body of Christ.

153:9–10 **Bamberg Cathedral** The Cathedral of St Peter and St George in Bamberg, Bavaria, founded in 1004. Its sculptures and carvings include sixteenth-century ones by Veit Stoss and Tilman Riemenschneider; Stoss's Queen of Sheba has braided hair and is crowned (cf. 153:20).

156:22 **full-butt** Charging head-on, like a butting animal.

157:5 **Passion** The sufferings of Christ on the cross.

157:34 **opposites, not complements** The idea of productive conflict, of opposing principles as the source of creativity, both in art and in human relationships, is central to the *Study of Thomas Hardy*. See especially chapters six to ten.

158:22 **six wings . . . absorbed in praise** Cf. Isaiah vi. 1–3; Revelation iv. 8; Milton's *Paradise Lost* (1667), v. 277–85. See also *Letters*, ii. 249.

158:28–30 **Annunciation . . . Angel of the Presence** Cf. Luke i. 26–38, 19.

159:19 **Cana** Cf. John ii. 1–11.

159:29–33 **'Woman, what . . . do it.'** John ii. 4, 5.

160:5 **tasted of death** Cf. Matthew xvi. 28.

160:13–14 **'But thou . . . until now.'** John ii. 10.

160:40 **the brotherhood of man** Cf. Mark xii. 31; John xiii. 34; xv. 12–13; Hebrews xiii. 1; 1 Peter ii. 17.

161:12 **You've a right** It is right for you (dialect).

162:9–10 **Woman was made out of Man's body** Cf. Genesis ii. 21–3. DHL had reversed the primogeniture of Genesis in his 'Foreword' to *Sons and Lovers*; Frieda Lawrence's former lover, Otto Gross, had also reversed it. See Introduction, p. xxiv.

162:10 **man is born of woman** Cf. Job xiv. 1.

166:18 **'Magnificat.'** A canticle in the Evensong service of the *Book of Common Prayer*, based on the Virgin Mary's words, Luke i. 46–55.

166:38 **Fra Angelico's 'Entry of the Blessed into Paradise.'** The left-hand portion of the 'Last Judgement' in the Museum of San Marco in Florence, painted in 1430–31 by Fra Angelico (*c*. 1387 or perhaps *c*. 1400–1455). Cf. *Study of Thomas Hardy*, 69:12–15, 28–30. Cf. also 259:4–24 below.

170:9–12 **David . . . uncovered himself to the Lord** Cf. 2 Samuel vi. 14–23.

Explanatory Notes

170:13–15 **'Thou comest ... our hands.'**   David's words to Goliath, 1 Samuel xvii. 45, 47 ['. . . sword, and with a spear, and with a shield; but . . . of the Lord . . . for . . .'].

170:20 **Saul proclaiming his own kingship**   Saul does not, strictly, proclaim his own kingship, though he disobeys the Lord's commands three times. On the first occasion, he arrogates to himself the priestly office, offering sacrifice at Gilgal. See 1 Samuel x. 8; xiii. 7–14.

173:21 **ark ... flood**   Cf. Genesis vi–ix.

174:4 **the old man of the seas**   In the story of Sindbad in the *Arabian Nights*, the Old Man of the Sea persuades Sindbad to carry him on his shoulders, and once mounted, refuses to let go.

174:21 **a fury**   In Greek myth, the Furies were avenging spirits.

176:36 **born for a second time**   Cf. John iii. 3–8.

177:16 **the hour of her delivery**   Cf. John xvi. 21.

177:29–30 **the lion lay down with the lamb**   A semi-proverbial expression adapted from Isaiah xi. 6–7.

179:2 **Ursula because of the picture of the saint**   St Ursula was a holy martyr who supposedly met a glorious death in Cologne defending her virginity from the Huns. The picture could be that by Memling, in Bruges, or that by Carpaccio, in Venice.

181:13 **Pisgah mount**   The mountain from which Moses views the Promised Land. Cf. Deuteronomy xxxiv. 1–5.

181:39–40 **the three witnesses ... in the fire**   Shadrach, Meshak and Abednego in Daniel iii. 23–8.

182:17 **builded house**   Cf. 1 Kings viii. 27, 43; 1 Chronicles xxii. 5, etc.

183:19–20 **'The History ... of Briswell'**   Baron Rodolph von Hube (see note on 92:30–31) wrote a history of Greasley, *Griseleia in Snotinghscire* (Nottingham, 1901).

186:19–191:20 **When he saw the cathedral ... shadowy cathedral**   Compare the cathedral scene as a whole with *Study of Thomas Hardy*, chapter seven.

189:19–29 **These sly little faces ... very littleness**   Cf. *Study of Thomas Hardy*, 66:1–5, and Introduction, p. xxx. The specific reference is probably to the 'Lincoln Imp' in the Angel Choir of Lincoln Cathedral.

191:23 **rotonda**   Variant of 'rotunda', a circular building, especially one with a dome.

196:9 **flesh and blood**   Cf. Matthew xvi. 17; 1 Corinthians xv. 50.

197:33 **Gudrun**   A figure from Norse mythology who features in the Nibelungen legend.

199:33 **glassie**   A glass marble (dialect).

204:33–4 **the ruddiest lilies of the field**   Cf. Matthew vi. 28–9; Luke xii. 27. Cf. also *Study of Thomas Hardy*, 8:6 ff., where DHL uses the poppy as the symbol of a spontaneous, creative impulse that has nothing to do with survival or the accumulation of wealth.

205:8 **quivering needle** I.e. the needle of a compass.

206:7 **grip** A furrow (dialect).

206:12 **taters . . . sprits** [206:13] Potatoes (dialect) . . . potatoes that have sprouted (dialect).

221:5 **new Swedish methods** The new system of manual instruction in elementary woodwork introduced from Sweden was called 'sloyd'. Woodwork was recognized by the Education Department as a proper subject for elementary schools in 1890.

223:6 **High School** Nottingham High School, a boys' grammar school dating back to the thirteenth century. DHL won a county scholarship there and attended the school from 1898 to 1901.

224:15 **Ruskin and then the Agnostic writings** For Ruskin, see note on 105:39–40. The 'Agnostic writings' were by T. H. Huxley (1825–95), who coined the term 'Agnosticism', in particular the *Lay Sermons* (1870), and Matthew Arnold (1822–88), such as *Literature and Dogma* (1872).

225:24 **a stranger within the gates** Cf. Exodus xx. 8–10.

226:26 **suppering up . . . slew** Feeding the animals (dialect) . . . in a general sense, an expanse or mass of water; but also a coal-mining term for a natural swamp in a coal seam.

227:3 **Noah . . . dove an' olive branch** [227:5] Cf. Genesis viii. 11.

227:37–8 **takes its hook** (Or 'slings its hook'), runs away, makes off (dialect).

227:39 **falleth as rain on the just and unjust** Cf. Matthew v. 45.

230:31 **The cut's** The canal's (dialect).

236:18 **bobby-dazzlin'** Striking, beautiful (dialect).

240:13–14 **In my . . . many mansions** John xiv. 2 ['. . . Father's . . .'].

241:17–18 **the beginning and the end** Cf. Revelation i. 8; xxi. 6; xxii. 13.

244:31 **raking** Roaming (dialect).

246:28–9 **a Rubens picture . . . called 'Fecundity,'** No such picture by Peter Paul Rubens, the Flemish painter (1577–1640) exists; see however 'Sacrifice to Venus' (1628), in the Stockholm National Museum, and 'The Feast of Venus' (1632), in the Kunsthistorisches Museum, Vienna.

247:10 **Andersen and Grimm . . . 'Idylls of the King'** [247:11] . . . **Launcelot** [247:15] Hans Christian Andersen (1805–75), the Danish writer and collector of fairytales; the German brothers Jacob Ludwig Grimm (1785–1863) and Wilhelm Karl Grimm (1786–1859), collectors of fairytales . . . A poem sequence (1859–85) based on Arthurian legend, by Alfred, Lord Tennyson (1809–92). The quotation is from the third Idyll, 'Elaine' (1859), ll. 1–4 ['. . . the loveable . . . Elaine, the lily . . . up a tower . . . Lancelot'].

249:36 **Odyssey** See note on 12:35–6.

250:17 **without spot or blemish** Cf. Numbers xix. 2.

251:7 **'J'ai donné . . . petit frère.'** 'I have given the bread to my little brother' (French).

254:31–2 'Il était ... petit patapon,' A French folksong: 'There was a little shepherdess/And purr, purr, purr, little pussypaw'.

255:1 **Christ passed between olive trees** I.e. in the garden of Gethsemane on the Mount of Olives. Cf. Matthew xxvi. 36–45; Mark xiv. 32–41, etc.

255:3 **'Samuel, Samuel!'** Cf. 1 Samuel iii. 3–10.

255:7 **Sin, the serpent ... Judas with the money and the kiss** [255:8] Genesis iii. 1–15 ... Matthew xxvi. 14–16, 47–9; Mark xiv. 10–11, 44–5.

255:24 **democratic Christian** Cf. *Letters*, ii. 364–8, 370–71. Cf. also Nietzsche's attack on Christianity and democracy in, for example, *Der Wille zur Macht* (*The Will to Power*) (2nd edn, 1906), Book II. See Introduction, pp. xxii–xxiv.

255:32 **Stigmata ... His wounds** [255:33] Marks left on Christ's body by the nails and spear at the Crucifixion ... Cf. John xx. 27.

256:14 **throng** Busy (dialect).

256:19 **fettling for** Looking after, providing for (dialect).

256:31 **Calvary** The place of the Crucifixion.

256:38–257:6 **Sons of God ... men of renown** Genesis vi. 2–4 ['... sons ... man ... flesh: ... sons ... children to them ...']. Cf. *Letters*, ii. 273.

257:11 **the only begotten Son** Cf. John i. 14, and the Nicene Creed ('the only-begotten Son of God').

257:24–5 **Jove had become a bull ... a giant, a hero** In the form of a bull, Zeus (Jupiter, Jove), the supreme god, wooed Europa who bore him three sons. None of these was actually a giant, though Zeus also fathered Heracles (Hercules) and numerous powerful gods.

257:27 **Pan ... Bacchus ... Apollo** [257:28] The Greek god of shepherds and flocks; he had the legs, ears and horns of a goat ... The Roman equivalent of the Greek god Dionysus, the god of wine and ecstasy ... The Greek sun-god and the epitome of male beauty and moral excellence.

258:1–2 **'It is ... enter into heaven.'** Matthew xix. 24 ['... into the kingdom of God']; cf. Luke xviii. 25.

258:24–5 **unless he ... the poor** Cf. Matthew xix. 16–21; Luke xviii. 18–23.

259:4 **Raphael's 'Dispute of the Sacrament' or Fra Angelico's 'Last Judgment'** The first (1509–11) by Raphael (1483–1520) is in the Vatican; for the second, see note on 166:38 and cf. *Letters*, ii. 263.

259:35–6 **old mystery play of St George and Beelzebub** See notes on 130:27, 28.

260:11 **The star was risen** Cf. Matthew ii. 1–10.

260:18 **Peace of the World** Cf. Luke ii. 13–14.

260:33 **the Magis' transport** Cf. Matthew ii. 1–11.

261:1 **the great light** Cf. Isaiah ix. 2; Matthew iv. 16.

261:3–4 **The veil of the temple ... the ghost** Cf. Matthew xxvii. 50–51; Mark xv. 37–8; Luke xxiii. 45–6; John xix. 30.

261:8 **the Comforter was given**   The Comforter was the Holy Spirit. Cf. John xiv. 16–18, 26; Acts ii.

261:24 **the Ascension**   Mark xvi. 19; Luke xxiv. 51; Acts i. 9–11.

261:33–4 **. . .'Touch me not . . . my father.'**   John xx. 17 ['. . . Father:'].

261:40–262:1 **thirty-three**   According to tradition, the age at which Christ died.

262:6 **Rabboni**   Master (Hebrew). John xx. 16.

262:9 **The Resurrection is to life, not to death**   Cf. *Letters*, ii. 248–50, 267–9, and DHL's late story 'The Escaped Cock' ('The Man Who Died').

262:17 **walk this earth in gladness**   A phrase from a poem by the artist and illustrator Ernest Collings (1882–1932) with whom DHL corresponded ['. . . the Earth . . .']. See *Letters*, i. 472.

263:13–15 **climbing the tree . . . like the Lord**   The story of Zacchaeus is in Luke xix. 1–10; for Peter walking on the waves see Matthew xiv. 22–32; for the feeding of the five thousand see Mark vi. 35–44; John vi. 5–14.

263:25–8 **walking upon . . . burn away**   For Christ walking on the waters see Matthew xiv. 25; Mark vi. 48; Saul is blinded by the face of the Lord in Acts ix. 3–9; for the pillar of cloud, see Exodus xiv. 21–2; and for the burning bush, see Exodus iii. 2.

264:26 **'Sell all . . . the poor,'**   A conflation of Luke xviii. 22 and Matthew xix. 21.

265:3 **turn the other cheek**   Matthew v. 39.

265:36–8 **'Oh Jerusalem . . . would not—'**   Matthew xxiii. 37 ['O Jerusalem, Jerusalem, . . . how . . . together, even as . . . not!'].

266:17 **the Son of Man**   Cf. Ezekiel ii. 1; Matthew viii. 20; Mark ii. 10.

266:27 **lift up the lambs in his arms**   Cf. Psalm xxiii; Luke xv. 4–5; John x. 1–16; xxi. 15–17.

267:9–10 **'Come unto . . . you rest.'**   Matthew xi. 28.

271:14–15 **the nature of an aristocrat**   Cf. *Study of Thomas Hardy*, 45–9, 95–100. DHL's concept of aristocracy is essentially Nietzschean. See, for example, *Der Wille zur Macht*, sections 53, 866, 933, 936. See also Introduction, p. xxii.

271:18–19 **Adam . . . driven cringing**   Genesis iii. 23–4.

271:26 **three angels . . . Abraham's doorway**   Genesis xviii. 1–2.

273:29 *perpetuum mobile*   Perpetual motion (Latin).

274:13 **sappers**   Soldiers of the Royal Engineers.

274:15 **'Wuthering Heights'**   Novel (1847) by Emily Brontë (1818–48).

278:8 **Sleeping Beauty**   The fairytale 'The Sleeping Beauty' is about a princess who is magically put to sleep for a hundred years until awakened by the kiss of the prince she will marry.

285:33 **chittered**   Shook, trembled (dialect).

285:39–286:1 **the cynical Bacchus in the picture**   There are numerous pictures of Bacchus, the god of wine, but the reference is probably to

'The Young Bacchus' (1593) by Caravaggio (1573–1610) in the Uffizi, Florence.

288:17–19 **settle the Mahdi . . . Khartoum** The followers of the Mahdi, Abdullah Sejjid Mohammed, having beseiged Khartoum and killed General Gordon, were defeated by General Kitchener at the battle of Omdurman in 1898.

288:27–289:18 **'But we aren't the nation . . . nothing to me.'** Cf. *Study of Thomas Hardy*, 38–9, and Introduction, p. xxii.

297:23 **a pillar of salt** Lot's wife was turned into a pillar of salt in Genesis xix. 26.

301:24–31 **'And God . . . all things.'** Genesis ix. 1–3 ['. . . fruitful, and multiply, . . . fishes of the . . .'].

301:36–7 **'And you . . . multiply therein.'** Genesis ix. 7 ['. . . fruitful, and multiply; . . .'].

301:40–302:9 **'And God . . . all flesh.'** Genesis ix. 12–15 ['. . . said, This . . . be for a token . . . that the bow . . .'].

302:19–20 **Noah and . . . Japheth** Genesis vii. 10ff.

302:29 **maggots in a dead dog** *Hamlet* II. ii. 181.

302:35 **'The very . . . all numbered.'** Matthew x. 30.

303:18 **war was declared . . . in South Africa** The Boer War (between Britain and the Boer republics of the Transvaal and the Orange Free State) broke out in October 1899 and ended in May 1902.

305:3–4 **always with a view to preserving it intact** Cf. *Study of Thomas Hardy*, chapters one, two and four, and *Letters*, ii. 282–6. See also Introduction, pp. xx–xxii.

305:20 **the highest good of the greatest number** 'The greatest happiness of the greatest number' was a phrase used by Jeremy Bentham (1748–1832), the founder of Utilitarianism, and became the slogan of the movement. Cf. *Study of Thomas Hardy*, chapter two.

307:13 **like the angel before Balaam** Numbers xxii. 22–35.

310 **Shame** A common term for homosexual love at this period. This chapter was singled out as particularly offensive in the 1915 Court Proceedings against *The Rainbow*.

310:2 **matriculation examination** An entrance-qualification to degree courses at the University of London. See 335:18.

312:32 **Newnham** One of the two pioneering colleges for women in Cambridge, founded in 1871 (the other was Girton).

313:23 **Diana** Roman goddess of the woodland (identified with the Greek goddess Artemis), virgin huntress and protector of women; also sometimes thought of as a moon-goddess.

317:13–14 **Buddhists a royal prince, the Egyptians their Osiris** Gautama Siddartha (563–479 BC), the North Indian noble who became the Buddha, 'the Enlightened One'; Osiris was the most widely worshipped of the Egyptian gods, the god of death, but also a symbol of male fertility.

317:31 **Moloch**   Usually Molech; a god worshipped by the Ammonites and associated with the sacrifice of children by fire. See Leviticus xviii. 21; xx. 2–5; 2 Kings xxiii. 10, etc.

317:34 **neither Lamb nor Dove**   Cf. John i. 29, 32.

318:15 **the Women's Movement**   Collective term for the numerous campaigns for women's rights, the earliest of which were launched at about the time of *The Rainbow*'s opening (*c.* 1840), and continued into the twentieth century. See note at 400:33–4, and Introduction, pp. xvii–xix.

318:26 **serpents trying to swallow themselves**   The snake swallowing its own tail is a traditional symbol of eternity, but for DHL it was, as here, a symbol of solipsism, or of barren, circular logic. Cf. DHL's essay 'Him With His Tail in His Mouth' in *Reflections on the Death of a Porcupine and Other Essays*, ed. Michael Herbert (Cambridge University Press, 1988), pp. 307–17, and Nietzsche's *Die Geburt der Tragödie* (*The Birth of Tragedy*) (1872), chapter fifteen, which uses the image of logic curling about itself and biting its own tail.

322:24 **alter themselves to fit the pits**   Cf. Thomas Carlyle in *Signs of the Times* (1829) and John Ruskin in 'The Nature of Gothic' (1853). See also Introduction, p. xxx.

322:34 **Zolaesque tragedy**   I.e. reminiscent of the French novel *Germinal* (1885) by Emile Zola (1840–1902), which explores the destructive effects of the coal-mining industry on the lives of its employees.

324:6–7 *vogue la galère*   Come what may (French); literally, 'let the galley sail where it will'.

330:20 **Donatello manner**   Donato di Niccolo di Betto Bardi (1386–1466), Florentine sculptor whose high reliefs include the 'Annunciation' in Santa Croce, Florence.

330:24 **Della Robbia**   The most famous of this family of Florentine sculptors are Luca (1400–1482) and his nephew Andrea (1435–1525).

330:36 **Benvenuto Cellini**   Florentine sculptor, metalsmith and jeweller (1500–1571), whose autobiography (1728) DHL had read by 1907.

334:18 **patience of a Jack-gnat**   Virtually no patience; the expression comes from either the minuscule size of the gnat, or its restlessness.

337:11 **'Sweet Thames ... my song—.'**   The refrain of 'Prothalamion' (1595) by Edmund Spenser (*c.* 1552–99) [... 'softly, till . . .'].

340:31–2 **'C'est la ... lui rendra—'**   French children's song: 'It's mother Michel who has lost her cat, and who cries from the window "Who'll give it back"'.

346:7 **a caution**   A curious or amusing person or thing (slang).

351:33 **Greuze ... Reynolds's "Age of Innocence,"** [351:33–4]   Jean Baptiste Greuze (1725–1805), French painter, known for family portraits and genre scenes ... Sir Joshua Reynolds (1723–92), English portrait painter whose 'Age of Innocence' (1788) is in the National Gallery, London.

366:27 **mizzling** Vanishing (dialect).

379:27 **Shelley or Browning ... 'Woman and Labour.'** [379:28] For Shelley and Browning, see notes on 17:35 and 86:8 ... There were numerous works on women and labour, but the reference here is almost certainly to Olive Schreiner's *Woman and Labour*, though it was not published until 1911. See *Letters*, i. 287–9 and Introduction, pp. xiii–xiv.

380:5–7 **'She shall ... mountain springs.'** Lines 13–15 of 'Three years she grew in sun and shower' (1800) by William Wordsworth (1770–1850) ['. . . the fawn . . .'].

385:16 **Coleridge's 'Christabel.'** Unfinished narrative ballad (1816) by Samuel Taylor Coleridge (1772–1834).

386:23 **an infant crying in the night** From Canto lv of *In Memoriam* (1850) by Alfred, Lord Tennyson (1809–92).

391:26–8 **their Della Robbia, beautiful Madonna ... reliefs from Donatello** Perhaps a reproduction of 'Madonna of the Cushion' by Andrea Della Robbia, of which there are several examples including one in the Bargello Museum, Florence. For the Della Robbia family and Donatello, see notes on 330:20, 24.

391:29 **the Primavera and the Aphrodite and the Nativity** 'La Primavera' (*c.* 1478) and 'Aphrodite' (also known as 'The Birth of Venus') (*c.* 1483–4), by Sandro Botticelli (1445–1510), Florentine artist, are in the Uffizi Gallery, Florence; he painted a number of Nativities, the best-known being 'The Mystic Nativity' (1500) in the National Gallery, London.

392:23 **fought a good fight** Cf. 1 Timothy vi. 12, and the hymn 'Fight the good fight with all thy might', which DHL mentions in 'Hymns in a Man's Life' (1928).

393:6 **Swinburne's ... Meredith's** Algernon Charles Swinburne (1837–1909), poet; George Meredith (1828–1909), poet and novelist. Cf. *Letters*, i. 241–2, ii. 180, and *Study of Thomas Hardy*, p. 91.

400:9–10 **moved and lived and had its being ... Racine** [400:10] Cf. Acts xviii. 28 ... Jean Racine (1639–99), French neo-classical dramatist.

400:13 **Livy and Horace** Livy (Titus Livius) was a Roman historian (59 BC–AD 17); Horace (Quintus Horatius Flaccus) a Roman poet (65–8 BC).

400:33–4 **Women's Social and Political Union** Society dedicated to achieving women's suffrage, founded by Emmeline Pankhurst in 1903; it was notorious for its militancy.

400:38 **Cassandra** In Greek myth, a beautiful prophetess, daughter of King Priam, who vainly foretold the fall of Troy. She was given the gift of prophecy by Apollo, but when she refused his love he condemned her to the fate of never being believed. Cf. *Study of Thomas Hardy*, p. 109.

401:35–6 **'There are ... yet risen.'** A line from the *Rigveda*, a sacred Hindu text, quoted by Nietzsche on the title-page of *Morgenröte* (*The Dawn*) (1881). See *Letters*, ii. 315, 317, and Introduction, p. xxii.

Explanatory Notes

405:30 **area under an arc-lamp** Cf. *Sons and Lovers*, ed. Helen and Carl Baron (Penguin Books, 1994), pp. 101–2.

415:12 **the Invisible Man** The eponymous hero of the novel (1897) by H. G. Wells (1866–1946).

420:1 *museau* muzzle (French).

421:9 **'Gewiss, Herr . . . Frau Baronin.'** 'Certainly, Baron – it's a pleasure, Baroness' (German).

421:11 **Westminster Cathedral** Roman Catholic cathedral in the Byzantine style, built 1895–1903.

443:33 **furnace door** Cf. Daniel iii. 23–8.

444:13 **a harpy** In Greek myth, the harpies were violent, predatory creatures, often represented as birds with the faces of women.

451:4–5 **She felt like a bird . . . the board** Cf. Bede's account of the conversion of Edwin in *History of the English Church* (p. 731).

457:19–20 **inscrutable trees . . . like smoke** Cf. Genesis ii. 6.

458:39 **the rainbow stood on the earth** Cf. Genesis ix. 11–17.

Further Reading

Bell, Michael, *D. H. Lawrence: Language and Being*, Cambridge University Press, 1992. (*Philosophically based analysis of* The Rainbow *as resistant to Cartesian dualism.*)

Bonds, Diane S., *Language and the Self in D. H. Lawrence*, UMI Research Press, 1987. (*Post-structuralist reading of the novel.*)

Draper. R. P., *D. H. Lawrence: The Critical Heritage*, Routledge and Kegan Paul, 1970. (*Contemporary reviews, reactions to the banning of the novel, etc.*)

Ebbatson, Roger, *The Evolutionary Self: Hardy, Forster, Lawrence*, Harvester Press, 1982. (*Includes a chapter showing the impact of evolutionary theory on the novel.*)

Green, Martin, *The von Richthofen Sisters: The Triumphant and the Tragic Modes of Love*, Weidenfeld and Nicolson, 1974. (*Account of the German cultural climate which DHL encountered on meeting Frieda; useful material on e.g. Nietzsche and Otto Gross.*)

Harris, Janice H., 'Lawrence and the Edwardian Feminists', in *The Challenge of D. H. Lawrence*, ed. Michael Squires and Keith Cushman, Wisconsin University Press, 1990, pp. 62–76. (*Reads* The Rainbow *as a 'Modern Girl novel' alongside those of Wells, Bennett, Forster, etc.*)

Holderness, Graham, *D. H. Lawrence: History, Ideology and Fiction*, Gill and Macmillan, 1982. (*Sees the novel as an escape from history into myth.*)

Ingram, Allan, *The Language of D. H. Lawrence*, Macmillan, 1990. (*Includes a chapter exploring the relationships between articulacy and inarticulacy in* The Rainbow.)

Kinkead-Weekes, Mark, 'The Marriage of Opposites in *The Rainbow*', in *D. H. Lawrence: Centenary Essays*, ed. Mara Kalnins, Bristol Classical Press, 1986, pp. 21–39. (*Explores the tension between the historical and the archetypal in the novel.*)

Kinkead-Weekes, Mark, 'The Sense of History in *The Rainbow*', in *D. H. Lawrence in the Modern World*, ed. Peter Preston and Peter Hoare, Macmillan, 1989, pp. 121–38.

Milton, Colin, *Lawrence and Nietzsche: A Study in Influence*, Aberdeen University Press, 1987.

Nixon, Cornelia, *Lawrence's Leadership Politics and the Turn Against Women*, University of California Press, 1986. (*Contrasts* The Rainbow *and* Women in Love *as novels written before and after the 'turn' towards the ideal of male leadership.*)

Further Reading

Pinkney, Tony, *D. H. Lawrence*, Harvester Wheatsheaf, 1990. (*Emphasizes socialist and feminist elements in* The Rainbow *and links the novel to German Expressionism.*)

Simpson, Hilary, *D. H. Lawrence and Feminism*, Croom Helm, 1982. (*Historicizes DHL's changing attitudes towards women and women's movements.*)

Widdowson, Peter (ed.), *D. H. Lawrence*, Longman, 1992. (*Critical reader charting recent developments in Lawrence criticism; includes extracts on* The Rainbow *from Holderness and Pinkney.*)

Worthen, John, *D. H. Lawrence and the Idea of the Novel*, Macmillan, 1979. (*Charts the novel's composition, drawing extensively on letters.*)

Worthen, John, *D. H. Lawrence*, Edward Arnold, 1991. (*Locates the novel chronologically in relation to DHL's work as a whole; useful biographical material.*)